W9-BQI-615

Twayne's Introductions to World Literature Series

**A PROGRAM DESIGNED TO INTRODUCE
FOREIGN WRITERS OF MERIT
TO READERS OF ENGLISH**

Jacob Steinberg, General Editor

Twayne's Introductions to World Literature Series

INTRODUCTION TO MODERN POLISH LITERATURE
(*Adam Gillon and Ludwik Krzyzanowski, Eds.*)

INTRODUCTION TO ROMANIAN LITERATURE
(*Jacob Steinberg, Ed.*)

INTRODUCTION TO SPANISH LITERATURE
(*Kessel Schwartz, Ed.*)

INTRODUCTION TO MODERN GREEK LITERATURE
(*Mary Gianos, Ed.*)

INTRODUCTION TO MODERN BULGARIAN LITERATURE
(*Nikolai Kirilov and Frank Kirk, Eds.*)

Introduction to Modern

BULGARIAN LITERATURE

An Anthology of

Short Stories

Edited by

NIKOLAI KIRILOV

and

FRANK KIRK

TWAYNE PUBLISHERS, INC.

New York

891.8
K58i

Copyright © 1969 by Twayne Publishers, Inc.

All Rights Reserved

Library of Congress Catalog Card Number: 72–91322

MANUFACTURED IN THE UNITED STATES OF AMERICA

Contents

5

68725

PART II

National Consciousness:
Rebellion—Hope—War

PART III

Modern Mentalities:
City, Factory, Town

8 Contents

Introduction

The thirty-six stories in this anthology were selected on the basis of quality from more than two hundred stories considered. They are grouped to represent some of the main lines of development of modern Bulgarian fiction and to indicate some of the major features of contemporary short story writing. The principal traditions, themes, and styles of the fiction are products of the Bulgarian way of life and of the Bulgarian experience of history—an extraordinary experience marked by deprivation and tenacity, resignation and hope lasting centuries—and illuminating in itself of the capabilities of the human spirit as well as for the light it casts on the imaginative prose writing to which it gave birth.

The first two parts of the collection are intended to serve as a means of focus on changes in the chief traditions since the 1890's; part III contains stories which are contemporary by virtue of time, subject matter, intellectual content, and sometimes stylistic treatment. The stories are organized in an order which, it is hoped, best reveals altering uses and views of story writing, within the traditions in parts I and II, and as they indicate significant contemporary strains and trends in part III.

The Bulgarian state was first established during the seventh century as a rival to the already existing Byzantine Empire. The Bulgars, a nomad people of uncertain origin, appeared in the Balkans in the year 660 and conquered the Slavic inhabitants of the region now known as Bulgaria, preventing their assimilation by the powerful Byzantines. The Bulgars intermarried with the Slavs, absorbing many of their customs, adopting their language, and taking up their settled agricultural way of life.

The ninth to the thirteenth centuries saw the rise and fall of two Bulgarian empires. During the height of power of the second empire (1218–41) the Kingdom of Bulgaria was the most powerful political state in the Balkans, ruling virtually all of the Balkan Peninsula except for Greece. The collapse of the first empire in the tenth century and of the second in the middle decades of the fourteenth century occurred largely because of the resurgence of Byzantine strength. Christianity was introduced in 865, and in 893 the Slavic Bulgarian language was made the official language of the Bulgarian Church, thus setting it in opposition to both the Byzantine and Roman churches. The Greeks, involved in political rivalry with the Bulgarians, tried for centuries to abolish the Bulgarian Church. But the pervasive influence of the national church, and the development in the ninth century of the language and literature now known as Old Slavonic (formed in part from the Cyrillic alphabet, the basis of modern Bulgarian), combined to create an enduring national consciousness, nascent in the struggles with the Byzantine Empire.

In 1330 the Bulgarian kingdom became a tributary nation to the Serbian state and, while its Byzantine foe shrank in the face of an aggressive Ottoman Empire, Bulgaria fell completely under Ottoman control after the Turks defeated the Western Crusaders at the Battle of Nikopol in 1396. Bulgaria was to remain a conquered land for five centuries.

During the first and second Bulgarian empires, written literature was largely religious, comprising lives of the saints, moral tales, didactic stories, and the like. Preceding the church literature, and continuing throughout the five hundred years of Ottoman domination, was an altogether separate tradition: the folk tale, the folk song, the proverbs, and other oral genres that were passed from generation to generation. Repeated in the vernacular, they provided a continuity to expressions of native life. Thus, though constantly changing by nature, the oral tradition was a vehicle of cultural stability and provided modern Bulgaria's educated writers with a rich feeling for the sound of the spoken word and the refrain as well as with vital themes and motifs. Tales of village life, of the peasant's crucial tasks and realities, of resistance to the ruling invaders, as well as of the great universal events in life—birth, courtship, marriage, parenthood, death—provided Bulgarian writers with limitless areas of exploration.

Bulgaria was subjected to oppressive rule by the Turks and to cultural domination by the Greek Exarchate until it was liberated in 1878. By cooperation with the sultanate, the Greek Orthodox Church was permitted to oversee the organization of Christians within the Turkish Empire. The motivating factor in the policies of the Turks, the Greeks, and their essential instrument, the *chorbadjis* (Bulgarian rich man; collaborator), was greed, and hence the exaction of money or its equivalent in various forms and under various pretexts—whether under civil or religious administration—was the major preoccupation of the ruling groups. During this period—while Western Europe was experiencing the Renaissance that was to transform and revitalize nations, the explorations of the globe that led to the discovery of the American continent, the Reformation that forever altered the direction of Christian thought, the beginning of the first industrial revolution—Bulgaria sank into a state of periodic chaos, internal and external strife, exploitation, endemic poverty, and nearly total illiteracy. The only schools were church schools and, during the seventeenth century, when the Greek Orthodox Church tightened its control over and exploitation of its own and other subject peoples of the Ottoman Empire, only Greek was taught in the schools, and much existing Bulgarian literature was destroyed. The Bulgarian language was kept alive among town and city artisans, among the peasantry, and in the remote monasteries of the rugged Carpathians. In 1762, during the darkest period of Bulgarian history, one monk, Father Paissi, by writing in his native tongue at the Mount Athos Monastery, gave impetus to a renewal of national consciousness. In his *History* of Bulgarian and Slavic peoples he challenged the Greeks and Turks and his countrymen as well by forcefully embracing Bulgarian nationality and worth. But at this time—there was not one printing press in Bulgaria when Paissi composed his work—his words were not to have an effect for half a century.

Paissi had an influence on another cleric, Sophronius of Vratsa, who was ordained a priest in 1762, the year Father Paissi began writing his *History*. Sophronius used the Bulgarian tongue, but this time to describe Bulgarian life as it was being lived. His autobiography, *The Life and Sufferings of the Sinful Sophronius*, composed between 1800 and 1813, may be quoted briefly for its picture of the Bulgarian dark age:

> . . . And some of the foremost *chorbadjis* heard this and they sent for me and said: "Do not go anywhere, stay here! Our bishop will be coming soon, and we shall ask him to make you a priest." On the third day the bishop did arrive, and they asked him and he at once agreed to ordain me as a priest on Sunday. And they gave him seventy grosha.
>
> This was on Wednesday, and I got everything necessary for the Sunday. But on Friday evening the bishop's steward came and brought me back the money and said: "Know that the bishop will not ordain you, because another has given him a hundred and fifty grosha and that is the man he will ordain." Oh, what sadness and sorrow laid hold of me, for I had made my confession to the priest and taken out a certificate and

prepared all that was necessary. To whom was I to tell my sorrow? I went to those men who had intervened on my behalf and given the money and they went and gave another thirty grosha. And he ordained me in the year 1762, on September 1.

But as I knew how to read a little, the other priests hated me, for at that time they were all simple plowmen. And being young and recklessly foolish, I did not obey them, because they were so simple and uneducated. And they slandered me before the bishop, and how many times he removed me from office and hated me! And the bishop had a coadjutor, an uneducated and illiterate Greek who hated me very much. For this is natural: an educated man likes him who is educated, a simple one him who is simple, and a drunkard him who is drunken. And thus, my life went on full of worry for several years.

In the summer of 1768 a war broke out between the Turks and the Muscovites. What can I tell you: When those hot-tempered and cruel heathen set out, what harm did they not do to the Christians! They did all except what entered not into their minds! How many people they killed! And as our village lies on four roads and my home was very far from the church, and according to our custom I had to be in the church for evensong and for matins, along how many side streets I had to pass on going to the church and then on coming back to my home! How many times they caught me and beat me and broke my head and wanted to kill me, but God preserved me. Then pashas began to pass and made me write certificates and file applications for billets, because I wrote rapidly. But they did not like the billets, and came back, and how many times they drew their pistols at me to kill me! Once one of them threw a spear at me, but missed me. . . .

The Bulgarian Revival began in the nineteenth century among the educated clergy and educated émigré merchants. Both the clergy and the merchants were influenced by the works of fathers Paissi and Sophronius and, ironically enough, by the activities of Greek émigrés. The Greeks, stimulated by the American and French revolutions, returned to their native land and organized rebellions against the occupying Turks. Many of the Bulgarian émigrés who witnessed the Greek uprisings in the 1820's were, however, content to work for social improvement within the framework of the empire. Some of these wealthy merchants returned to Bulgaria and, taking advantage of tottering Ottoman control, established schools throughout the country—schools in which Bulgarian would be taught; printing presses were established in the major cities; and many native-language newspapers were founded.

Desire for change took another form among many of Bulgaria's earliest writers and poets, however. Georgi Rakovski (1821–67), Lyuben Karavelov (1837–79), Hristo Botev (1848–76), and

Rachev Slaveykov (1827–95), among other notables, sought to undo the Turk-Greek stranglehold on their country and participated in revolutionary activities as both verbal and armed combatants. Botev, a tempestuous romantic poet and polemicist, was aroused by the cries of nationalism and freedom that swept across Europe during the "century of peace"—by Garibaldi and Byron, by Pushkin and Bakunin—and he savagely attacked Bulgarians who were content to be the pawns, as he saw it, of the great powers, East and West. In "Political Winter," a bitter summons to conscience, he wrote:

It is a pleasant thing for a man to have a warm room, a loaf of bread, a piece of bacon and several head of leeks, then to lie down and think, or fall asleep and dream. It's a pleasant thing, but he should have one of these two diseases: either a young wife or old rheumatism. You lie there and you lie there. . . . But what do you dream? You dream that the world is like a pub and that the hungry, ragged, and frozen peoples have gathered in it and are praising Bacchus on their knees. . . .*

Botev was killed in an abortive uprising on May 29, 1876, at the age of twenty-eight, less than two years before the Bulgarian liberation.

Karavelov (1837–79), a peasant leader and a revolutionary like his compatriot Botev, traveled to Russia, where he was attracted to the ideas of the Populist revolutionaries of the 1860's; he spread these ideas throughout the Balkans, joining in various revolutionary schemes with the bandit-patriots. He is generally considered to have produced the first Bulgarian fiction of literary merit. His stories and novels are realistic—the products of his own experience and observations of life in the cities, the villages, and the countryside. His nationalism is laced with no apologies, as the following passage, the opening paragraph of a story entitled "The Ill-Fated Family," well illustrates:

We have suffered a great deal, we have endured much at the hands of the hateful Turks. God grant we may not suffer any more! I shall tell you things that are already past, I shall tell you what befell our family in our own home. If the Bulgarians still have Bulgarian hearts and Bulgarian ears, let them hear my story. . . .†

Bulgaria was liberated from Turkish rule because of Russian intervention after Russian victories over Turkey in the wars of 1877–78. Although Turkey retained nominal suzerainty over Bulgaria, and although the Congress of Berlin (1878) altered the original territorial

* Translated by Marguerite Alexieva.
† Translated by M. Todorov.

settlement in favor of Turkey, which regained complete control over Macedonia, Bulgaria was, after half a millennium, essentially free of foreign domination and free to administer its own church.

After the liberation, Bulgaria was first ruled by Prince Alexander and then by Prince Ferdinand, both of German descent. Ferdinand ruled as prince from 1887 to 1908, when he proclaimed Bulgaria independent, and as tsar from 1908 to 1918. Liberation did not yield either automatic administrative reform or a united commitment to a new, enlightened order. Already conflicting social purposes divided the country politically. However, the nationalism that had been accumulating for decades among all groups and classes propelled the nation into the Balkan Wars of 1912–13, through which Bulgaria hoped to annex Macedonia, to which it felt legitimately entitled. In spite of some efforts to remain neutral at the outbreak of World War I—a difficult task, for Bulgaria's location makes it of crucial strategic importance to three continents—Bulgaria pitched its hopes with the central powers and entered the war in 1915. Instead of acquiring territory, however, the nation lost land as a result of both the Balkan and the world wars.

The internal political situation remained unstable, with Liberals, Agrarians, Communists, and military elements wrestling for control, and a series of factional governments and dictatorships appeared and disappeared until in 1935 Ferdinand's son, Boris III, established a firm royal dictatorship. A festering desire to regain lost territory and to gain new land was a precipitating factor in Bulgaria's entry into World War II on the side of the Axis Powers. However, after Bulgaria refused to declare war on Russia, Russia invaded Bulgaria, and the Communists quickly seized power.

The Soul of Bulgaria:
Peasants and Villages

Romanticism and realism, already philosophically mature modes of consciousness and literary expression throughout most of Europe, has characterized Bulgarian prose writing since the liberation period, with which parts I and II of the present collection begin. The peasant tradition, which had achieved literary significance in the writing of Lyuben Karavelov and other regionalists, achieved stature in the stories of Elin Pelin (1877–1949) and in the works of Ivan Vazov (1850–1922). Both writers pictured the peasant as being inextricably caught up in a web of social injustice. Pelin has been characterized as follows: "Elin Pelin found his chief literary character in the farm hand . . . with merciless force he pointed to the evil in village life: the chorbadji, the priest, the tax-collector, the mayor, the policeman." *

The first story in the collection, "Andreshko," illustrates Pelin's love of the peasant and hatred of injustice. It is a simple story of hope, humor, passion, and contempt and, by the way, it is a tale with a happy ending that develops out of the situation of the story. In the second story, "All Souls' Day," Pelin concentrates on specific aspects of peasant life without directly attacking particular causes of evil and without evaluating the peculiar kind of reasoning that characterizes the peasants' solution to their personal unhappiness: Will their solution work? We do not know, nor does Pelin provide a hint.

The other stories in this part resemble "All Souls' Day" in that they treat of peasant and village life for its own sake, without direct social protest. In these stories, the realist-romantic modes of viewing and telling vary considerably as does the stance of the author with respect to his subject.

The dispassionate stance taken by Elin Pelin in the last story becomes detachment in the next two stories. In "Shibil" Yordan Yovkov (1880–1937) depicts the tragic betrayal of a young *haidout* (guerrilla-bandit) who is trapped into re-entering his native village out of love for the daughter of the chief shepherd, the *kehaya*. The young man is slain on a signal by the *kehaya* despite the last-minute protest of the Turkish province governor who objects to the killing of the youth because of his remarkable good looks. Yovkov's view of the story, which is romantic in conception and execution, as well as his capacity to see the Turk in human terms, indicate the depth of his detachment. Authorial detachment also characterizes "The White Swallow," which, although symbolic in suggestiveness, is realistic in "slice-of-life" fashion even from the point of view of Peter Mokhanin, to whom the tale is told, and through whose mind we understand the story: the wandering peasant family stops, the father tells Peter the sad story of his daughter, and then moves on, leaving the reader with Peter to reflect for a moment on what he has heard, and then to resume, as Peter does, ordinary living.

"Groudka" by Iliya Volen (1905–   ) is less deliberately trained on the peasant qua peasant than are the foregoing stories; it concentrates on the farmhand and farmowner as human beings; their class and occupations are "accidents"; their "substance" is in their

* Introduction in *Elin Pelin—Short Stories*, ed. Mercia Macdermott (Sofia: Foreign Languages Press, 1965).

lusts, fears, and hatreds—in their capacities for compassion on the one hand and for selfish cruelty on the other. The banal, presented in matter-of-fact, literal, crude description, is wrenched into a broader perspective—as are the characters and events of the story—by means of enlarging representations of nature and emotion that superimpose a poetic quality over the whole.

A naturalistic detachment characterizes "The Begonia" by Svetoslav Minkov (1902–66), a detachment that has gone so far as to become a kind of involvement, if only by implication, in the senselessness it discovers in the life of the villager it delineates. The pre-existing unimportance of the character coupled with a near-complete externality of vision (which the author's intrusive questions only enhance), sharpens the intrinsic unimportance of the simple actions the character performs. The sense of futility—we have here an "early modern" villager—is reinforced by the unadorned, lineal prose.

In contrast to "The Begonia," "Reb Yossl" by Armand Barouh (1908–   ) is a morality tale told with a garrulous realism; its characterizations are textured by a rough humor. The humor, however, is employed as irony by means of which the author keeps his characters at arm's length while at the same time imparting to them a warm appeal. Thus the author is able to make his point—a moral point of the common wisdom variety about human folly, not about organized evil or ideological error—without making his characters into allegorical cardboard cutouts. In "The Stone Pigeons" by Serafim Severnyak (1930–   ), a sophisticated villager relates a story to two vacationers. This story is also a morality tale, but here the meaning emerges through the symbol of the stone pigeons. The mood is emotional and direct and reflects an intense local patriotism.

Emotion is the substance of "Spring Juice," an impressionistically rendered vignette by Diko Fouchedjiev (1928–   ). The story expresses a sentimental but nonetheless real feeling for nature and love of the simple life, a romantic strain which is transformed in Fouchedjiev's "The Woman Who Walked About the Sky" into a passionately mystical vision of the oneness of man and nature that reaches back not only into the primitive Christianity of the ancient Bulgarian mountain village but also into the primitive sources of man's deepest physical and spiritual yearnings.

"Blue," by Boris Aprilov (1921–   ), combines a mood of romantic buoyancy and receptivity to nature with a practical human problem, through which the psychology of the narrator is explored. A contemporary note—that of the alienation of the artist from the people—is sounded in this story, although reasons for this phenomenon are merely suggested.

"Day By Day" by Konstantin Konstantinov (1890–   ), the last story in part I, is detached in stance, realistic in style, and critical in tone of the society, of the forms of corruption that produce the animal, brainless, petty lives led by those such as Dinka, a village prostitute. Dinka, too, is a contemporary villager, but she is foremost a new kind of displaced person, a modern transplant whose rightful hopes—dashed though they are by a deus ex machina—would have been the exception to the rule had they been fulfilled. Dinka, through whose mind and emotions the reader experiences the story, is a contemporary victim, not of foreign oppression or ideological persecution, nor even so much of the individuals who use her, but of the swift advances demanded by modern industrial and backward states alike in the name of the common good.

National Consciousness:
Rebellion—Hope—War

Although a diversity of style and literary approach is also observable in the stories of part II, what is more notable is the changing shape of Bulgarian national consciousness during pre-liberation times and throughout the decades of the twentieth century. Anton Strashimirov's (1872–1937) darkly atmospheric "Soura Bir," the opening story, romantic in mood, setting, and story and symbolic in presentation, is powerful in its evocation of the near-insane emotionalism manifested in some forms of pre-liberation regional patriotism. "Heroes' Heads" by Yordan Yovkov (1880–1937) combines realism in dialogue and subject matter with symbolism in imagery to convey courage and cowardice and bewilderment among ordinary villagers in the face of Ottoman terrorism. Ivan Vazov's (1850–1922) "Old Yotso Is Watching" expresses this prose master's capacity to evoke a sense of gentle patriotic fervor while examining with detachment the ironies of the liberation: among his fellow villagers only blind Old Yotso truly sees "the Bulgarian thing."

The remaining stories in this part show the influence of Socialist Realism, which has had precise effects on the premises and values of contemporary prose artistry. Contrary to what might be assumed, however, these stories are by no means all of a piece; they exhibit a diversity of stance, reaction, style, and a capacity to touch the universal.

In "One Night, One Day," by Vesselin Andreyev (1918–

), national consciousness emerges in a new form: resistance to
native military dictatorship has replaced resistance to foreign rule;
insistence on rights has grown far beyond the earlier demand for the
minimal rights to language, to learning, and to relative economic
stability. It has reached the point of a people's demand for some control over its own future—for freedom in the truly modern sense of
that word. Another different note is added in "The Portrait" by
Georgi Karaslavov (1904–   ): the impersonality of the modern
state that demands the lives of its youth is set against the personal
needs and hopes of an old man and beckons to the idealism of his
son; both are smashed by the son's death. But the point of the story
is that the son and the state are right; the old man is sentimental and
morally bankrupt. This new, harsh note is eminently realistic in modern social and political terms, East and West.

In "Vanya and the Statuette" by Emil Manov (1918–   ),
"The Painlevé Case" by Peter Neznakomov (1920–   ), and
"Laughter in Ramonia" by Svetoslav Minkov (1902–66), national
consciousness has become completely transformed: it has become
synonymous with the social and ideological purposes of Communist
Bulgaria, though in entirely different senses. The last-mentioned
story is a comic, satiric, ideologically moralistic fable. "Vanya and
the Statuette" uses an event in the Communist takeover during
World War II as a touchstone to probe into the psychology of man
—into that part of man which is good or evil regardless of his
ideology. This story evidences a complete acceptance of the fusion
of Communist and national purpose; assuming this fusion to be a
fact, the author extends his examination to deeper, more universal
questions than those defined by political philosophies of whatever
variety.

"The Painlevé Case," which takes yet another, superficial
stance toward ideology, recounts with gusto a fantastic episode
among Royal Bulgarian army regulars of the post-liberation period
into which it projects the early rumblings of Communist feelings
among the ordinary troops. This overlay, however true to life it
may be, is far less convincingly presented than are the chief characters, who are remarkably believable in what is an improbable but
broadly funny story.

Modern Mentalities:
City, Factory, Town

The sixteen stories in part III represent modern themes, motifs, and
viewpoints bred of the transformation of Bulgarian life and society

since the 1930's. The most significant event of recent times was the establishment of Communist control in 1945, which was followed by collectivization of the farms and increased industrialization. Too, urbanization—actual and intellectual—has had an impact on the life and literature of this still largely agricultural nation. Finally, the influence of foreign thought and literatures has continued to be felt, as of course have the dictates of Socialist Realism.

The first four stories in part III illustrate the reach of the new mentalities. "Null with a Capital Letter" by Orlin Vassilev (1904–) depicts the inner world of an underground man *à la* Dostoevsky. It presumes an urbane audience and uses the first-person technique to voice new perceptions and recognitions. "The Boy with the Violin" by Pavel Vezhinov (1914–) focuses on the problem of juvenile delinquency among well-to-do inhabitants of a large city; the psychological motivation of the delinquent boy is explored both as it is experienced by the boy and as it is examined from the outside by the inspector. Vezhinov's "Spanish Cholera" presents an oblique, poignant sidelight on the problems—personal and societal—of male and female co-engineers on vacation at a state-run holiday hotel. "A New Attitude Toward Life" by Stoyan Daskalov (1909–) depicts the effect of success on the son of a village peasant, revealing the loss of humanity, the hardening, that has overwhelmed the son in his process of achievement. The father and the old village ways are thrust into dramatic relief by the son's arrival in his expensive automobile—a symbol about which the events of the story turn.

In "The Second-Hand Shop" by Maria Groubeshlieva (1900–), the city is the setting for a different contrast—between the old order that writhes in corruption and callousness and the new, idealistic generation of pure-minded Communist youth. Set against the Hungarian uprising of 1956, this well-told story is Socialist Realism par excellence. The city is more than the setting for "Rush Hour" by Bogomil Rainov (1919–); it is the experience of the life of the bus driver, Claude—an anti-hero of pathetic diminutiveness for whom we feel pity and contempt. He is modern man swallowed up in a frustrating meaninglessness of which he is conscious but about which he is unable to do anything. "A Strict Upbringing" by Dragomir Assenov (1926–) is a sympathetically told domestic vignette; that the characters are city dwellers is only incidental: the story is an expression of the psychology of the parents whose young son is going away to a camp-school for the first time —an experience common to middle-class parents the world over.

Psychological imbalance is the keynote of the next four

stories. "A Visitor" and "Youth" by Lyuben Stanev (1924–   ) are
character portraits of men of average achievement in professional
and governmental capacities who have in middle age arrived at life-
styles involving a crude escapism in Georgi Kalkanov, a financial
inspector, in the first story, and in a cruel bitterness in Ivan Palaveyev, a court chairman, in the second. Both men experience a series
of inner perceptions which, though producing anguish, yield the
promise of restored humanity. In "The Stranger" Lyuben Dilov
(1927–   ) contrasts a young, idealistic philosophy professor with
his wife and mother-in-law who are unlovely personifications of
middle-class greed and self-centeredness. The story is the growth of
self-perception of Peter Lechev, the professor, who is at first carica-
tured as a man so caught up in abstractions that he is a helpless fool
in the face of ordinary reality. Through the shock of recognition
of the hypocrisy of his acceptance of a maid in his apartment, Peter
comes to recognize the human realities with which his abstractions
ought to deal, and he takes action: he becomes a complete, if dis-
traught, man. "Radiant Skies" by Nikolai Kirilov (1922–   ) por-
trays a local "boss" named Mourgin whose obsessional envy of the
once powerful ruling classes leads him to go to extraordinary lengths
to degrade—through intimidation and rape—one of its members.
Unlike the characters in the last three stories, Mourgin is damned
and does not know it.

    The modern bureaucratic mentality—a mentality increasingly
pervasive in advanced and advancing states—is explored in "Boundless Time" by Nikolai Kirilov (1922–   ), "The Rabbit Census"
by Georgi Mishev (1935–   ), and "Paths" by Nikolai Haitov
(1919–   ). "Boundless Time" presents a conscientious, sensitive,
frustrated outpost bureaucrat, named Boudinsky, caught in the press
of official requirements, some of intrinsic but of seemingly distant
value, another of purely ceremonial, but immediate importance;
against these demands are the individual needs of the people whose
fate is at least partly contingent on his decisions. His decision leads
directly to a chance for personal advancement and indirectly to the
death of a village child. Boudinsky is tortured, but the bureaucracy
of which he is a part is unapproachable in human terms, although
it does express human irritation at his concern about the child. "The
Rabbit Census" pokes fun at the obvious lunacy of a state-ordered
futile mission which robs a village of some of its most needed members for a full day. In "Paths" the inherent capacity of bureaucracy
for perversity is translated into personal expression by a local department head who toys with and then lambastes the simple-minded but

individually creative Vlasho, a sixty-year-old cobbler whose chief joy in life is building mountain paths for the benefit of others—paths which, however, are unauthorized.

In "Let's Go Vacationing" by Vassil Tsonev (1925–   ), a light story that can be read purely for entertainment, the humor derives from the psychology of the narrator. Like "Null with a Capital Letter," the opening story of part III, this story assumes a readership of some sophistication, though of course the chords struck in the two stories are on totally different scales. Also like "Null with a Capital Letter" is the last story, "This Beautiful Mankind" by Vassil Popov (1930–   ), both of which dwell within the minds of atypical human beings. Unlike the first story, however, this last story does not portray the mind of a character shaped into a unique type by social or political or economic factors. The private world of a retarded or perhaps emotionally disturbed girl is projected by the writer as a subject worthy of esthetic consideration for its own sake. Although the story is interesting, too, as an indication of concern with mental disturbance as a social problem that requires humane responses, what is most notable is that, through the poetic exploration of the untypical, distorted perceptions and feelings of the girl, the writer presents us with a story of universal human import.

Bulgaria has produced a unique if comparatively recent literature of value not only to itself but to the Western world. Thus, in literary terms, the need for an anthology of modern Bulgarian fiction is obvious.

The present collection of stories is an attempt to provide the Western reader with a worthy and—as far as possible within the limits of form and availability of material—representative sample of the modern fiction. Although this anthology does not pretend to represent adequately every major strain in past and contemporary Bulgarian letters, the stories are presented in a way which, to this editor, seemed most likely to serve the end of introducing to the English-reading public a virtually unknown literature. The part divisions are not intended to be requisite forms of classification. Rather, it is hoped that they will function as guidelines to the major concerns of Bulgarian writers. Within these guidelines I have tried, in this introduction, to suggest areas of meaning, lines of evaluation, and possible directions in the literature.

A broader cultural need also exists, that of understanding be-

tween peoples, especially between peoples who are separated by the
formidable barrier of opposing ideologies. It is this editor's modest
hope that the anthology will contribute in some small measure to
such understanding, for it is one of the functions of literature to
reveal the humanity of people—to express those elements which
people have in common as well as those things that divide them. Not
all the stories written in Communist Bulgaria are molded by Socialist
Realism; indeed, the variety of theme and interpretation present in
the stories in this collection were startling to this reader. But even
those stories that bear most completely the stamp of Socialist Realism carry, by virtue of their existence, a message of importance, for
they mirror the social concerns and themes of their times.

The existence of this anthology is in itself an example of co-
operation among individuals of the two nations involved. It is the
result of personal meetings and discussion carried on by the pub-
lisher in several visits to Bulgaria. Selections were debated and dis-
cussed between this editor and Nikolai Kirilov, the Bulgarian editor,
through the mail. We have never met, but the long process of select-
ing the stories to be included was carried out in a spirit of cooperation and professional respect.

Acknowledgments are extended gratefully to the translators,
whose names appear at the end of each story, to S. Stephanova of
the Copyright Protection Agency in Sofia, through whose good
offices numerous exchanges were courteously and expeditiously
handled, and I especially want to thank Mr. Kirilov for the privilege
of working with him and also for the information he provided about
the history of Bulgarian literature. Responsibility for this introduction, however, is totally that of the undersigned.

FRANK KIRK

Glossary

The following Bulgarian and Turkish terms are to be found in the stories in this anthology:

aga, master
bashi-bazouks, Turkish irregulars, known for their cruelty
boya, a nonalcoholic drink made of millet
chorbadji, rich man, master
effendi, master, sir
haidout, usually, a man who has taken refuge from the Turks in the mountains; also, a robber
kehaya, chief shepherd
konak, headquarters of governors and police
koum, one who has been a sponsor at another's wedding; *koum* and *koumitsa* usually designate a married couple who are sponsors at another couple's wedding and are thereafter considered their spiritual parents
kurdesar, governor of a Turkish province
mahmudis, Turkish gold or silver coins
metoh, convent or branch of a monastery
nestinarka, firedancer
pop, priest
rubés, small gold coins
sapoundjia, soap maker
shoppe, shopi, a resident of the Sofia district
soubash, police chief
trepha, food forbidden by the Jewish faith
voivoda, a *haidout* chief
yamourlouk, heavy, homespun cape
Yourouk, tribe of nomad Turks
zaptieh, Turkish policeman
zourla, primitive oboe

The Soul of Bulgaria: Peasants and Villages

PART I

The Soul of Bulgaria:
Peasants and Villages

Elin Pelin

(1877–1949)

Elin Pelin, whose real name was Dimiter Ivanov, was born on July 18, 1877 in the village of Bailovo, Sofia district. His first short stories and poems were printed while he was still at school. In 1896/97 he contributed regularly to the *Voinishka Sbirka* magazine. He failed to finish secondary school and returned to his native village. Later he enrolled as an extramural student at the Faculty of Law, and at the end of 1899 he went to live in Sofia. During the autumn and winter of 1902/3 he edited the magazine *Selska Razgovorka*.

In 1910 Professor Ivan Shishmanov, Minister of Education, appointed Elin Pelin a teacher at the Third Sofia Elementary School and gave him a post at the University Library. In August 1905 he visited Italy with the artist A. Bozhinov, where they spent some twenty days in Venice and Florence. In September 1906 Shishmanov sent Elin Pelin and the poet Peyo Yavorov on a journey to France.

In January 1904 the humorous magazine *Bulgaran* started publication in Sofia, edited, at the outset, by A. Kiprol and H. Silyanov. Later the magazine was taken over by A. Bozhinov, A. Balabanov, and Elin Pelin. In *Bulgaran* the author began to publish short stories which criticized and exposed contemporary life.

During World War I he was mobilized and worked as a war correspondent for *Otechestvo* and *Voenni Izvestia* magazine. Later, in 1921, he was one of the founders and editors of *Razvigor*, a newspaper. For two decades (from May 1, 1926 to July 1, 1944) Elin Pelin was curator of the Ivan Vazov Museum. He was one of the first members of the Bulgarian Academy of Sciences.

After September 9, 1944 the author wrote a number of stories for children. He was also called to work at the editorial office of the *Septemvriiché* newspaper, where he did valuable work. Elin Pelin died on December 3, 1949 in Sofia.

The books he has published include: *Short Stories*, Volume I (1904); *Ashes from My Cigarette* (1905); *From the Window* (1906); *Short Stories*, Volume II (1911); *Land* (1928); *Black Roses* (1929); *I, You, He* (1936); *Under the Monastery Vine* (1936).

Andreshko

"We'll get there early, sir. While it's still light. There's the village—right there by the little forest. D'you see? When we cross that hill over there, the low one, we're almost there." And, cracking his whip over the horses, the young carter shouted to them loudly and encouragingly: "Gee-up, hey! . . . Gee-up, gentlemen!"

The four wheels of the cart splashed faster through the liquid mud of the village lane. Its rickety frame rattled dully through the mournful, deserted and rain-soaked plain. The peasant shouted again, settled himself more comfortably on the wooden case upon which he was sitting, tossed back the damp hood of his heavy cape and began to hum quietly and indifferently to himself.

"What's your name, boy?" the fat gentleman who was sitting in the cart asked from the depths of his enormous fur coat.

The youth went on humming.

"Hey, boy!" cried the gentleman loudly and hoarsely.

"Eh?"

"Your name, your name? What was your name?"

"Andreshko."

"A-ah, Andreshko . . . you're a sly one. That's what you've all become. You peasants are all cunning now. You only know how to lie and be sly. And how you pretend! I see you in the law courts—a very sheep, a fool, but in reality a veritable wolf! They just play with the judges."

"We're simple folk, sir, it's just that people slander us. It seems so to you, but it isn't so. Our villagers lie from simplicity. Simplicity and poverty."

"Ah, poverty, poverty, indeed! A thrashing is what they deserve. They complain of poverty and drink like swine."

"And why do you think they do? Because of their fine lives? No, no. They certainly drink, they all drink. To forget their troubles, not because they have none. A man like you should take good note of that."

"A-ah, you seem to have had a drop, too, friend! Yet you're still young, your mustaches have scarcely grown yet. Your peasants . . . write them off as a dead loss, and that's that!"

"You'd better write them, sir, we don't know how to write," said the youth and turning to his lean horses he called to them: "Gee-up, gee-up, gentlemen!" and fell athinking.

The horses jogged on quicker and also fell athinking. The gentleman raised the collar of his immense fur coat, sank into it and fell athinking, too. A raven with ruffled feathers perched on the lonely tree by the roadside, swung on its withered branch, cawed depressedly and also fell athinking. Across the ragged sky, damp and gloomy winter clouds crawled heavily and slowly and were sometimes torn asunder to show pieces of blue sky equally moody and cold. The earth had sunk into mud and dampness. The scattered landscapes of the villages, rivers, distant forests and mountains were dead and sorrowfully dark. Large pools shone in the plain, cold and fixed, like the eyes of the dead.

The little cart staggered through the deep, liquid mud, sank, emerged, and zigzagged along. A loose board at the side rattled constantly, monotonously, hollowly and senselessly; it persistently struck the nerves of the stout gentleman in the fur coat and made him lose patience. He undid his collar, thrust his fat face out, and demanded: "What is that dreadful rattling, devil take it? It gives me no peace."

"My cart has a screw loose, sir. It rattles away like a learned man—it doesn't understand itself, neither do others understand it."

"You're a sly one, Andreshko, a sly one! You must be one with the girls if you are not married. You people usually marry young and have pretty little wives."

The gentleman turned down the collar of his coat.

"Say what you like, sir, but they are nothing to the ladies . . . I know that very well! What are you, sir? What brings you to our village?"

"I'm a bailiff."

"So you've come to sell someone up, have you?"

"Yes, of course. One of your people has been leading me a dance, but this time I'll show him what's what. I've been after him several times, but he's always given me the slip. I got onto him, though; I found out he was tricking me, and tonight I'm going to catch him, and he'll have cause to remember me all right. I'll sequestrate his wheat! That'll teach him what's what and give you an example; you'll know better than to play tricks on us another time. You cheat the tradesmen, you cheat the townspeople, selling them bad eggs and rancid butter. But you just wait, you sly peasants—you can't cheat the authorities so easily! They have a tight grip—a good tight grip! A whip's what you need, that'll learn you! You've become drunkards, you're rotten, you'll be bad taxpayers and ruin the state. Ah, why haven't I more power! I would make angels of you!"

The bailiff undid his coat, and his body moved inside it like that of a chick about to leave its shell.

"Well, Mr. Bailiff, God made the world and decided that women don't need beards, so he didn't give them any. He decided that the donkey needed long ears and gave it some," answered Andreshko with pretended naïveté.

"Don't chatter so much, but drive on, because it's getting dark. You charged me a lot, you devil! So much money for twenty kilometers! You know how to stick it on. Drive on, then, drive on. Your jades have gone to sleep!"

"Gee-up, gee-up, gentlemen!" shouted Andreshko and twirled his whip.

"You call them gentlemen, eh? Better call them brothers," remarked the bailiff crossly.

"That would annoy them, Mr. Bailiff! I would offend their honor if I didn't call them gentlemen! Their service is like that of officials—it goes by the clock. They get up by the clock, go to bed by the clock, and are fed by the clock. After that we harness them, that is to say, they enter their offices, and that's that. And sometimes in their stalls they even read their papers."

"Just tell me where you drank, my friend, and don't chatter. Drive on, because we're late. You've sly eyes, very sly."

"There are no wolves, sir, don't be afraid," said the carter in such a tone that the respectable official glanced around in alarm.

"I'm not afraid of wolves, my friend, but it's getting cold. I haven't time to catch my death."

"Wrap yourself up in the sacking. My horses never complain of a cold. The sacking is very warm."

"What beastly weather!" thought the bailiff and said sternly: "Drive on, drive on, you swine!" And swelling with angry pride, he sank into his big coat and fell silent.

"A-ha, you've fallen into good hands, friend," thought Andreshko to himself. And turning around he asked in a serious tone: "So you're going to sell some one up, are you? And whose heart are you going to warm?"

The bailiff was silent for awhile, then answered crossly: "There's one . . . Stanoicho they call him—shortish—with a thick neck."

"I know him. So it's his wheat you're going to sequestrate, is it? He's a poor man, Mr. Bailiff, leave him alone."

"A poor man, indeed—a very devil!"

The bailiff fell silent again. It was getting dark already. The horses were barely crawling up the little hill behind which the village probably lay. Andreshko no longer called to them, neither did he twirl his whip over them. He stopped talking and humming and began to think.

When they were going down the other side of the hill into the plain beyond, night had come on, but the village was not yet visible. A cold, penetrating wind began to blow over the earth, which was sunk in dampness. The blue cupola of the cold, frozen sky cleared, widened, and soared higher. Soon stars began to twinkle in it, bright and icy stars. The air became very cold. The bailiff was in a state of constant irritation: "Drive on there, you *Shoppe!* We'll freeze to death!"

Andreshko shouted indifferently to the horses and lazily twirled his whip over their heads. They were pulling the cart along carelessly and moodily as if they heard nothing. Andreshko was thinking of poor Stanoia, whose wheat was going to be sequestrated the next day by the bailiff, whom he was driving.

"That man must be helped somehow, he must be helped," thought Andreshko. "He must be told to hide the wheat during the night and sweep the barn well, otherwise he'll have to tighten his belt all the year. I must help him—I must!"

It was dark and nothing could be distinguished on the earth except mud, deep thick mud. The road vanished in that mud and led nowhere except to more mud. At one spot Andreshko jerked the reins and stopped the horses: "Wait a bit. I seem to have missed the road!"

And the youth began to peer around in the darkness. The bailiff watched his stern face on which there was no trace of his former joking spirit, and said: "Have a care, boy, or I won't answer for the consequences. You'll get a drubbing!"

Andreshko jerked the reins, twirled his whip and shouted: "Hold tight, Mr. Bailiff!"

Far ahead in the darkness shone the lights of the village. Judging by the barking of the dogs, it was obviously near at hand. A few paces to the right, a large sheet of still water shone with a pearly gleam. The cart turned straight toward it.

"What's that?" asked the bailiff.

"A marsh, Mr. Bailiff. The road runs through it. It's quite shallow, don't be afraid. There are only a few holes here and there. How many times I've crossed it both on foot and in the cart and . . . gee-up, gee-up, gentlemen! Hold tight, Mr. Bailiff!"

The horses entered the cold water, in which the sky was mirrored, and cautiously splashed forward, going in deeper and deeper. The deadly still, shining, nearly green water of the marsh moved and came to life.

"Stop, you animal!" shouted the bailiff at one moment and stood up frightened in his coat. "You'll drown me, you *Shoppe!* Can't you see that the cart is full of water? Stop, stop!"

The bailiff, enraged, began to swear. Andreshko stopped the horses. The cart, up to its bottom in water, stood amid the marsh the end of which was lost in the impenetrable darkness.

"Gee-up . . . forward!" shouted Andreshko to the horses. His powerful and vigorous voice echoed loudly in the night and sank into that impenetrable void. Close at hand some wild duck flew up with a great noise and disappeared. "We, too, shall have to turn into ducks to get out," remarked Andreshko thoughtfully, "otherwise . . ."

"Oh, you swine! If we ever get out—I'll give you the thrashing of your life! We'll be drowned! You dolt!"

"No, no, Mr. Bailiff, don't be afraid. In this darkness anyone might make a mistake, just keep calm," Andreshko spoke up and busied himself about the straps. He undid them and did them up again, swore, and damned their eyes; finally he sat back again on the case, twirled his whip and shouted: "Gee-up! . . . Forward!"

The horses made an effort and started. One of them got loose from the traces and splashed off through the marsh free. The other stood there alone with the cart.

"Heavens! What has happened?" shouted the bailiff, standing in the cart trembling and frightened.

Just then Andreshko quickly mounted the other horse and started off after Dorcho, calling him incessantly: "Dorcho, Dorcho, Dorcho!"

"Where are you off to . . . hey! What are you doing, you swine? Dolt! Oh, you lousy peasant—I'll teach you!"

Malevolent laughter answered him from the darkness.

"Hey, you swine, you've left me here! . . . To perish! To be torn to pieces by wild beasts! Don't do it, boy, I beg you!" the bailiff now spoke in a piteous voice in which there was a hint of tears.

"Don't be frightened, don't be frightened, Mr. Bailiff," Andreshko's voice was heard. "The wild beasts won't go into the marsh. Wrap yourself up in the sacking so that you don't catch cold. Tomorrow morning bright and early, I'll come . . . there's some straw in the cart, spread it out . . . I shan't charge you anything!"

The bailiff could hear the malevolent voice coming from the darkness and was filled with horror. What? Stay here? In the middle of the marsh? Amid that cold, green, marshy water, the end of which could not be seen?

"Come here, Andreshko! I'll give you money, as much as you like! . . . Have you no heart, you dolt?" he shouted in desperation, but nobody answered.

Then, desperately and unreasoningly, the bailiff roared toward the village: "Hey dolt! . . . swine . . . cannibal . . . ox . . . fool! Come here! Save me! Have mercy! Animal . . . lout . . . *Shoppe!* Oh—oh! . . . Help, help!"

Then, sitting down in the cart, he sank into his fur coat and wept like a child.

But the darkness did not answer him.

Translated by MARGUERITE ALEXIEVA

All Souls' Day

A damp and misty autumn day enveloped the village. Fine rain fell steadily, bringing down the last yellow leaves of the now sparsely covered poplar trees, which stood around the little old church, as sad and sorrowful as widows. The old unfenced cemetery was full of women moving restlessly hither and thither, sad and serious. That day was set aside for the souls of the departed, and each and every one sank his own sorrow into the common sorrow for the dead. The old, crooked, moss-covered stone crosses were decorated with bunches of dried autumn flowers. On the oldest graves, now barely discernible under the weeds, which had grown over them, people had placed bread and plates of boiled wheat on the gaily colored table runners which they had spread there.

White-haired *Pop* Seraphim, censer in hand, hurried from

grave to grave, reading prayers and the names of the dead, and crossly scolding the women. After him came his twin sons, lugging a sack, which Uncle Todor, the verger, zealously filled with hunks of bread.

Under the low-hung porch of the church stood the school children in orderly rows. Their schoolmistress, a tall, thin, withered spinster, blue in the face with the cold, ceaselessly scolded the naughty ones.

The women served the wheat with painted spoons, brought from the Holy Sepulcher, crying: "There—and say 'God rest his soul!' "

The children sniffed, stretched out their hands one after the other, and cried: "God rest his soul! God rest his soul!"

Along the church walls, by the rainpipes, a row of poor orphans squatted on their bare heels, looking like antheaps in their old garments which were far too wide for them; they stretched out their hands and waited with pitiful eyes to be given something. Next to them mad Hristo stood guiltily, perpetually wrapping himself up in the torn skirts of his wide coat, through which his flesh showed, blue with the cold.

Further on, a blind beggar was singing pitifully.

And over this whole mournful picture, sunk in the damp and misty air, permeated with the penetrating smell of wax and incense, hovered an indistinct hubbub, amid which the priest's deep voice could be heard, clear and monotonous.

Amid this crowd of women, the tall figure of Stancho the Field Watchman appeared, carrying round wheat for his late wife, as if he were a woman. The general sad and serious air was stamped on his withered and sorrowful face with its long drooping mustache. He went from group to group, from child to child, handing around the wheat, thoughtful and reverent at the memory of the late Bozhana. He caught sight of his *koumitsa* in the distance and made his way through the crowd to her side.

"Help yourself, *koumitsa*, and say 'God rest Bozhana's soul.' "

"Oh-oh, *koum*, I didn't see you—may evil never see you, either! How are you, how goes it with you? How are the children? Why didn't you bring them to honor their mother's memory, God rest her soul?"

"Eh, they're not fit to be seen, *koumitsa*, and that's the truth of it!"

"God rest her soul, poor Bozhana," the *koumitsa* went on, full of sympathy, "she was cut off in her prime! And she left you alone, like a cuckoo, for people to make jokes about and to have the womenfolk fear you, as the saying is! But it's not so bad for you, *koum*—you'll sorrow and then you'll stop sorrowing; you'll find another woman, and you'll forget Bozhana, as the saying is, as if she had never been. But the children, the children, poor things! They'll never find a mother. They'll cry for her like chicks. God rest her soul and give her his kingdom, and put her at his right side, as the saying is, so that all will be well with her there at least."

And Aunt Divdena, the *koumitsa*, shook her head, and taking the brandy flask, shook it close to her ear, then took a long pull of its contents.

"There, *koum*, have a drink, too! Eh, dear Lord, I'm that busy, I can't come and see the children—dear little things. I'm sorry for them, that I am!"

"Eh, if Bozhana were living, things would be different," Stancho said sadly, and his eyes filled with tears, "now I have to look after them alone!"

"God's will, *koum*—there's nothing to be done about it!"

Stancho sniffed, then blew his nose with emotion.

"There, *koumitsa*, have another drink, have some more! Trouble is for us people. That's what we're born for, to have troubles—what else are poor folk for?"

"Never you mind that, *koum*, good and evil go hand in hand. The one comes and then the other. There, you have another drink! God rest the souls of the dead, say I, and give health and life to the living."

Stancho took the lead brandy flask and took a good pull at it. "God rest her soul!"

"God rest it, *koum*, and that's that. Don't worry and think about it so much, but try to find someone—anyone—to look after your house. You know, that's life. As for the dead, may the soil rest lightly over them, but live with the living." The *koumitsa*'s tongue was wagging fast now.

"God rest the dead souls, and give the living a full crop," Stancho answered, cheered by the brandy and his *koumitsa*'s comforting words. "To tell you the truth, *koumitsa*," he added, "I think so, too."

"That's right, *koum*. Good or bad, just you find somebody," the *koumitsa* answered.

His mother-in-law, the late Bozhana's mother, came up to them. "O-oh, Stancho, my lad! Poor fellow, I'm that upset when I see you. You've given yourself up to grieving, my lad! I see you shying away from people like a horse. You shouldn't, my boy; you should mix with people. Bozhana, God rest her soul, such was her fate!"

These words saddened Stancho again. His eyes, dark sufferer's eyes, filled with tears once more. "Well, granny," he said with a sigh, "it had better have been me, not her."

"Eh, so it had, lad, so it had, but that's the Lord's business. Children get on better without a father than without a mother," the old woman said, by way of comfort. Stancho fished a handkerchief out of his waistband and began to wipe his eyes and nose. "Don't you cry, my boy! Stop mourning for Bozhana and get yourself a wife—a wife, a housekeeper—you can't go on living like that."

"I can't find anybody like her," Stancho answered, raising the brandy flask to his lips.

"I know, my boy, I know; you're not much of a fellow, so it won't be easy to find somebody—women are hard to please. But when it comes to work, you're like an ox. Oh, my boy, what a state you're in!"

Stancho looked down at the ragged and dirty sleeves of his shirt and sighed deeply.

"We're all so sorry for you, *koum*," the *koumitsa* went on again after having been diverted into a conversation with Piomiya the nun. "We talked about you the other day again, your *koumets* Dimo and I. 'Tell him to get married again,' he says, 'and not to go about like that. He's too young,' he says."

"Eh, I'm young, says he," Stancho said shame-facedly, and wiped his drooping mustache. "I'm not young any more, but . . ." His eyes filled with tears again. He raised the brandy flask to his lips.

Other women claimed his *koumitsa*'s attention, his mother-in-law went off with the priest's wife; Stancho found himself standing alone again, like a pole, and wandered about aimlessly, dish in hand.

Everybody looked at him pityingly. A man—and there he was carrying wheat around—a lone man! He seemed to have taken pains with his appearance, having changed his clothes, and done his best to make himself neat and trim, but he looked funny just the same in his old trousers, which he had washed and mended himself, sticking the patches on the outside. Two or three mocking young married women glanced at him slyly, whispered something, giggled, and the next minute remembered that it was All Souls' Day, and looked sad again.

And the rain, as fine as dust, came down unceasingly, wetting people's clothes, and the cold damp penetrated everywhere.

People began to leave, some alone, some in groups, disappearing like shadows into the damp blue mist. The withered schoolmistress led her shivering charges away, scowling and, little by little, the cemetery began to grow deserted. Stancho looked this way and that, then sat down, quite tired out, on the stones under the eaves of the church, and began to eat some bread and cheese.

Stoïlka, the widow of the late Yanachko, the cowherd, came up to him then. A tall, bony pole of a woman, with a long face, fairish hair and gray eyes, with wide lips, which she kept closely pressed together timidly, as if to guard her big white teeth; but she was a good and careful housewife for all that.

"Stancho, I had almost forgotten you!" she cried in a singsong voice when she caught sight of him. "How are your children getting on, are they growing big?" she began to question him loudly and sharply, in the same way as she used to speak to her Yanachko, who was somewhat hard of hearing.

Stancho shyly drew in his long legs, muttered something through his full mouth, and handed the flask to Stoïlka. "Eh, we too live somehow, along with the others, Stoïlka. There, take it and drink to her rest!"

She took the flask and handed him hers. "So we do, and that's the truth. Drink to his rest, Stancho!"

"God rest the souls of the dead, Stoïlka, and give the living health and a long life! And how are you? Are you getting used to being alone?"

"God spare us all, Stancho!"

Stoïlka took two long pulls at Stancho's brandy.

"God spare us all, as you say, Stoïlka, but he hasn't spared us."

"Well, that's how it is; it's the Lord's will."

"We've been left lone and lorn, Stoïlka," sighed Stancho, and grew thoughtful.

The mist was growing dense, darker and damper. Stancho and Stoïlka sat on the stone, their eyes fixed on the mist, deep in thought.

"It's very hard like this, Stoïlka," Stancho said after a time, shaking his head sadly without looking at her.

"That it is, very hard," Stoïlka answered, her eyes firmly fixed on the ground, and she sighed again. "I sit there thinking and thinking the livelong night, and really don't know."

"I think a lot, too, and I wonder what to do. I can see it can't go on like this. I'll have to do something about it. Mostly because of the children. Someone's got to look after them. If a man's in it, he might just as well be up to his neck in it. Bozhana, poor woman, used to annoy me terribly. Eh, if you only knew how she used to nag me! But I was fond of her, and I never laid a hand on her, as the saying is. A man who beats his wife, beats his angel . . ."

"Come, Stancho, don't say that . . . if you only knew what some of them are like! They deserve the stick all right," Stoïlka said, swaying sadly, like a dried-up tree.

"I'm not that sort," Stancho answered. "Would you believe it, since she died, I'm not the same man! I'm miserable!"

"My Yanachko was a good chap, poor fellow, may the soil rest lightly on his grave. But I was in luck when he died. The way he was carrying on, if he had lived another year, he would have drunk up all he had," Stoïlka said, holding her hand over her mouth, to hide her big teeth. "We would have had nothing left, nothing, nothing at all. The children would have been crying for a bit of bread!"

Stoïlka took another pull at the brandy flask and handed it to Stancho. He took it from her without looking at her and grew more thoughtful.

The cemetery was already quite deserted. The old crosses stood there sad and lonely now with their faded flowers. The mist grew denser and denser. The eaves of the old church seemed to be weeping large tears. The rain drops pattered down sadly and made little runnels in the wet sand. That old, low building, crumbling under the weight of its years, seemed to be weeping disconsolately. Down through the cemetery passed Bogdan the Beggar, leaning on his big stick, and wrapped in his rags. In the tavern opposite a bagpipe skirled out sadly, then piped a few dancing notes and fell silent. After it came a short gay drunken cry, then silence reigned again. Stoïlka and Stancho looked at each other.

"Who can be having a good time?" Stoïlka asked, still deep in her sorrow.

"Poor people," Stancho answered. "They're drinking."

"What are you thinking about, Stancho?"

"What am I thinking of? Just nonsense. They're trying to persuade me to get married."

"Well, do get married."

"All very well, but how do I know how it'll turn out? First of all who would have me—me with four children? And I'm old already, and ugly, too." Stancho wiped his drooping mustaches, pulled their ends, and coughed.

"You're not all that old. And you're not all that ugly either;

though you *are* lean and black," Stoïlka comforted him. "You're a man, and it's easy for you. All you have to do is say the word, and there'll be at least ten willing to say yes; but we womenfolk . . ."

"You womenfolk are dreadful hard to please, if I may say so, and a man simply daren't . . ."

Stancho had another drink and handed the flask to Stoïlka. She took it and smiled. That's all her big teeth were waiting for to shine forth in all their splendor.

"D'you know what, Stancho, people have often spoken to me of you. Why should Stancho want me, I says to them. He's used to a handsome wife. Bozhana was that handsome, I says . . ."

"So she was. Bozhana was handsome. What eyes she had!"

A flock of memories came into his mind of his past youth, and choked his words. He sighed, bent his head, spat, and fell silent.

"They tell me: 'Stancho is a good man, you'll live like a queen with him,' " Stoïlka took up the attack again.

"Well, if you want to know, they've talked to me about you!"

"And you wouldn't hear a word about me," Stoïlka interrupted him, and wriggled her shoulders like a girl.

"Well, how was I to know what you would say to it? And then the mother-in-law started in with 'Stoïlka's this, and Stoïlka's that! Even if you dream of her,' she says, 'drive her away. She has a baby every year, and will saddle you with a pack of children. What'll you do with 'em?' she says."

"Oh, shame on her, Stancho!"

"You know what a cussed and evil old hag she is, don't you? Bozhana was just like her."

Stoïlka sighed. She was sitting on the stones, bent almost double, her hands thrust into her sheepskin jacket, shivering with the cold, and ashamed to look Stancho in the eye. She felt saddened by the old woman's words.

"D'you know what?" Stancho went on. "If I asked you, would you have me?"

Stoïlka wriggled her body, and said nothing.

"Let's put our troubles and our children together, and the Lord help us," Stancho plucked up courage to say. "There, I've been alone a year and a half. Why?—I ask myself, looking at the world wagging around me. Eh? What d'you say to that?"

"Eh, d'you know what I'd say to that?" Stoïlka answered, blushing. "What a one you are! Just making a mock of me." And she gave him a coy look.

"You leave that alone; we're not bachelor and maid to play about. Our day is over."

"Perhaps it isn't, after all," Stoïlka smiled, with her hand over her mouth.

"Just so! There, I give you my word, and if you're willing, all right!"

"Eh, I'm willing enough—why shouldn't I be? How can I manage alone? If I don't have you, it'll be another man."

"That's how it is! If you like, we'll go to the priest at once and tell him." Stancho got up. Stoïlka looked around with her gray eyes, picked up her dish, and rose to her feet.

The two set out together in silence. The rain was still falling, wetting their faces with its cold wet drops and bringing color into them. Stancho's head was swimming from the brandy, and his feet were unsteady. Stoïlka walked beside him, doubled with the cold, carrying the two brandy flasks and the two dishes, and cursing the weather.

More mist came down from the hills, dense and gray, crowding over the village.

Stancho was suddenly seized by a gay mood. He gazed into Stoïlka's eyes, as gray as the mist, like a boy, and kept repeating: "D'you know what I'll tell the priest? 'Father Priest,' I'll say, 'the Lord has taken Bozhana, but has sent me Stoïlka!' Eh?—that's what I'll say to him, just you wait."

And Stoïlka smiled happily at him, hiding her mouth with her hand.

Translated by MARGUERITE ALEXIEVA

Yordan Yovkov

(1880–1937)

Born on November 9, 1880 in the village of Zheravna, Sliven district, Yordan Yovkov spent part of his childhood in Çifutköy (now Yovkovo), Tolbukhin district. He received his elementary education in his native village and finished secondary school in Sofia in 1900. In the winter of 1902 he entered the school for second lieutenants of the reserve in Knyazhevo, where he served for two years. Then he enrolled as a law student at Sofia University but returned to Dobroudja without graduating. He worked as a teacher in the village of Chiflik Musobey (now Dolen Izvor), Saradja (now Rossitsa), and Karalyi (now Krassen). After the Balkan Wars he settled in Sofia as librarian for the Ministry of Home Affairs. During World War I he served in the 37th Pirin Regiment, in the 9th Frontier Battalion, the 85th Regiment, and on the editorial board of the periodical, *Voenni Izvestia*. From 1920 to 1927 he was employed at the Bulgarian legation in Bucharest, first as a press secretary, and then as secretary and translator. From 1927 to the end of his life he lived in Sofia and worked as a clerk at the Ministry of Foreign Affairs.

The first work of Yovkov's to see print was the poem "Fate," published in the *Probouda* magazine (Gabrovo, 1905). Later he published some more poems in the *Suznanié* newspaper, *Novo Obshtestvo* magazine (1907), and *Houdozhnik* magazine. His first published prose work was the short story "The Shepherd's Complaint" (*Prosveta* magazine, Vol. V, No. 6). Later he published in the *Nablyudatel* magazine and all major Bulgarian periodicals.

Yovkov died on October 15, 1937 in Plovdiv.

The following are his more important works: *Short Stories,* Volume I (1917), Volume II (1918); *The Harvester,* a novelette (1920); *The Last Joy,* short stories (1926); *Legends of Stara Planina* (1927); *Evenings at the Antimovo Inn,* short stories (1928); *Albena,* a drama (1930); *The Millionaire,* a comedy (1930); *Boryana,* a drama (1932); *Short Stories,* Volume III (1932); *The Farm by the Border,* a novel (1934); *A Woman's Heart,* short stories (1935); *An Ordinary Man,* a drama (1936); *The Adventures of Gorolomov,* a novel (1938).

Shibil

> *Radka stood at the gateway.*
> *From below came up Mustafa . . .*
> Folksong

Shibil, the terrible *haidout* whom *zaptiehs* and *kurserdars* were seeking under stone and tree, was coming down from the mountain to give himself up. Next day the news would spread like wildfire, and no one would believe it. Shibil cared little about that. He was hurrying, and his thoughts were elsewhere.

He was thinking how a month or two ago from the high peaks of the Blue Rocks where among the eagles' eyries was his own *haidout*'s lair, he had seen women passing along the road below. To fall upon women was not in the rules of the *haidouts*, nor was there room in a *haidout*'s heart for a woman. But Shibil had broken many laws, and he no longer knew nor wished to know what was sin and what was not. "Women here in Hell Gorge," he thought, "that's a fine booty, too!" And he rose, not caring in the least where his curiosity was taking him. The *haidouts* followed him laughing, and their teeth flashed like the fangs of hungry wolves.

They descended, cut across the wood which had not begun to sprout yet, and came out on the road through Hell Gorge. Here the road cut inward, into the gorge, forming two bends on either side, the jaws of a trap in which many a traveler had found his death. And, as they had done many times, the *haidouts* blocked the road, standing there, fearsome, bearded, wrapped in their black hooded Albanian cloaks, bristling with weapons. The women appeared at the bend and, catching sight of the waiting men, stopped, horror-stricken, then scattered and fled in all directions. But their legs gave way beneath them, and they only fluttered about on the same spot like stricken birds, falling on the ground and weeping, dissolved in fear.

The *haidouts* were unmoved; they did not even glance at them—their attention was elsewhere. One woman still stood in the road—young and beautiful. And her clothes, too! A dress of blue silk, a scarlet satin waistcoat, a striped apron from Jerusalem, silver clasps. Around her neck were heavy strings of coins, a row of large gold pieces, and a row of *rubés* and *mahmudis*. Was it a wedding she was going to decked out like that? Was her father mad to let her go unprotected into these mountains?

Shibil advanced. The girl watched him calmly, looking straight into his eyes. A perpendicular line flickered between the black arches of her eyebrows, and her red lips trembled.

"Heigh!" she called, and her clear voice echoed strangely among the wails of the women, "be off with you! What do you think you are? Aren't you ashamed, what do you want of women folk?"

At those words the *haidouts*, who could not take their eyes off the gold pieces, rushed forward, stretching out their sinewy arms. Shibil stopped them with a wave of his hand. Then he turned, stretching himself up to his full height and measuring the girl. How white her face was! And her slender waist and full skirts. Like a doll! And well-plucked, too! His eyes glinted merrily; he felt like laughing. But the girl had begun to laugh aloud before him. Her face brightened, became still prettier, and now he could see that her eyes were blue and her teeth white. Shibil stared at her in wonder. What sort of an imp was this?

How everything happened after that Shibil himself hardly knew. The women recovered, and though still as timid as does, came toward him. It was as though the whole mountain had brightened: from down below came the babble of the stream, and a bird called in the wood. Shibil himself was sitting on a stone, smiling, listening to the girl's chatter. What was she saying? Heaven only knew; words that meant nothing, words that one forgets. But how her eyes flashed, and how pleasant it was to look at her! On one side, tamed as though by a miracle, the *haidouts* squatted, smoking quietly.

"So you're Veliko the *kehaya*'s girl," Shibil said. "Your name's Rada. And how did your father let you go out like that? And with all those gold pieces and rows of *mahmudis*? I'm going to take them now."

"Bah! You'll take them! You'd better give me some more. These aren't enough for me. Look there," she cried, pointing to him, "look at your torn sleeve. Wait, I'll sew it up."

Shibil looked at his arm resting on the muzzle of his musket; the red cloth was actually torn. And before he could make out whether she was joking or not, there she was before him. He could see the down on her white face, her red lips, and when she looked at him her eyes bathed him in a soft, sweet light. She was smiling at him slyly as she took hold of the torn sleeve, and between her lips was a needle and thread.

"Don't wriggle," she told him severely. "I'm beginning. And put something in your mouth so that I don't sew up your mind, too. You'd better keep that at least."

Everyone began to laugh.

"Look here," Rada went on. "Get yourself a wife so that you have someone to mend for you, instead of going about all rags like . . ."

"Like what?"

"Like a gypsy.

Shibil scowled. The women glanced at one another fearfully. "I'd marry," said Shibil. "But the girls won't have me."

"Bah, they'll take you. Such a young bachelor!"

"Well then, take me yourself."

"Who? I? Runs through the valley, ties up his shoe, what's that? A *haidout*. No, not for me, I don't want a *haidout*."

Shibil scowled again. Rada encountered the pleading eyes of the women and hurriedly corrected herself.

"Well, well, I might take you after all. Only you'll have to ask Veliko the *kehaya*."

And after a silence she added: "And the *kurserdar* Murad Bey, too. . . . Ready. Do you see how I've mended it?" she said dropping the sleeve. "That's to remember me by. May you wear it in health."

Shibil looked at her and laughed. They spoke a little longer, then the women set off, and Shibil accompanied them down to where the wood stopped and the plain began.

It had been spring when that happened. Only here and there in the hollows there were fresh beech leaves, the other trees had only buds. Shibil had returned to the mountain, still smiling, while the other *haidouts* followed silently, their eyes on the ground. A raven fluttered by overhead, cawing—a bad sign. Shibil did not notice it, but the *haidouts* clustered together muttering. A woman had crossed their path, a pretty woman, and all that boded no good.

Some time passed and it grew warmer. The wild sloes blossomed, the pear trees were covered with leaves, and one fine day when the sun shone and the air was warm, the cuckoo sang. As the custom was Shibil began to count in order to see how many years he had to live yet, but then he began to think of his own years, and it seemed to him that he was already old. He thought of Rada and smiled. What a strange mixture, he thought, of woman, child, and imp. And how well it all suited her: if she said anything it was wise; if she did anything it was nice. And he saw her as he had seen her when she held the needle and thread in her mouth, looking at him, and he sighed; not a needle but a knife, and anyone would be glad to die on it.

It was just then that some merchants passed and the *haidouts* had stopped them. Frightened, as yellow as wax, they could hardly hold themselves in their saddles as they waited for Shibil to speak. But Shibil did not make them open their bags nor did he look to see what they had in their belts. He began to beat about the bush, talking of this and that; he mentioned Veliko the *kehaya* and at last spoke of Rada. The *haidouts* looked at the ground, burning with shame. Shibil let the merchants go, accompanied them a part of their way, and called out loudly to them to carry his greetings to Rada.

The *haidouts* said nothing to Shibil; they dared not look him in the face. And when at evening they returned to the Blue Rocks among the eyries, and Shibil lay down and fell asleep, they remained about the fire talking. The mountain was still the same, their lair was safe enough. And yet they were restless and glanced about them fearfully. If a twig crackled, they thought somebody was coming. And they bent closer together, whispering and glancing at Shibil as he turned about in his sleep, groaning and muttering something. Then they rose and got themselves ready for the journey. They did not kill him, but they ran from him as though he was stricken with plague.

Shibil remained alone. And then the money from the royal treasuries that he had plundered, the rings torn from the fingers of the living and the dead, the gold and silver from monasteries and churches—all the wealth he had gathered and hidden in caves and hollow trees—everything began to flow toward the house of Veliko the *kehaya* in the shape of gifts for Rada. Rich gifts for every greeting she sent him. And then he received a message that made his head swim: Rada was calling him to come down to the village; her father had given them his blessing. Murad Bey had pardoned him. And as a token that his word was good the *kurserdar* had sent him a rosary of amber from Jerusalem.

For a long time Shibil considered whether it was not a trap. He had given away everything he had. And the forest now was covered with green, heavy and dank, the grass in the glades had shot up, the peonies, the dittany, and the fairy flower were in bloom. The scent of lilac and of lime trees lay in the valleys. And when the bell of the stag echoed through the wilds and the ring doves cooed in the

Old Wood, it seemed to Shibil that the stone on which he laid his head in the evening was hard and his gun heavy. He could hold out no longer and set out for the village.

When he started from the Blue Rocks it was noon, and when he reached the road below and looked back the mountain peaks and the rocks were reddened by the setting sun. But the eagles were still wheeling above the white screes and the rocky walls of the ravines, those eagles who were accustomed to carrion and who, perched on some rock, had often torn human flesh. Dusk was falling, bluish mist was gathering in the valleys, and over the hills crept long shadows. The mountain lay silent and brooding as though looking after Shibil and asking "Whither?" His heart grew heavy within him, and the worm of doubt gnawed at it. He sat down on a stone and considered.

Once again he passed everything through his mind. When he raised his eyes again the moon had risen. It was another world that Shibil saw before him: the mountain had changed, spread out, broad and clouded; it had smoothed out like a blue wall wrapped in a veil of white. The woods cowered in dark shadows, coolness was wafted from the clearings, and white mist spread over them, twisting, writing some sign with a line of fire, some secret word, then disappeared. And deep down in the valley something was singing—could it be the river?—singing so softly, so sweetly.

Shibil looked before him, reflecting. Like short yellow wires the moonbeams were broken in his eyes, flashed and twisted together in an indistinct form that kept appearing and disappearing. But Shibil saw clearly two eyes that looked at him, a smile that drew him on. He rose, following those eyes, and looked back no more.

Three cautious knocks, a softly whispered "It's me, Mustafa," and the door was opened. He entered his father's house. On the hearth the fire burned, and shadows played on the walls. On the butts of Shibil's pistols, his cartridge cases, the tassels of his wallet, danced the reflections. Tall and manly, the house seemed too small for him. He met his mother's eyes and read the alarm in them.

"Mustafa," she said, "why have you come? Will you go there?"

"I shall go."

"You will! When?"

"Tomorrow."

The old woman knew that it was useless to insist or try to change his mind. She crouched down by the hearth, clasping her knees in her arms and wailed: "Mustafa, for three days the guards of the *kurserdar* have been casting bullets and whetting knives; they feel them on their fingers to see if they are sharp; if you drop a hair on them they will cut the hair in two. And they twist their mustaches and look toward us. . . . Mustafa, something bad is going to happen."

Shibil turned and looked at her, but his glance was such that she did not know whether he had heard and whether he had understood, and she said no more.

But Shibil was unbuckling his belt, taking off his pistols with their gilded butts, his Damask knives, his cartridge cases worked with silver, everything which was now a heavy and useless burden for him.

Up at the coffee shop by the church at the open window sit the *Kurserdar* Mustafa Bey and Veliko the *kehaya*. The Bey is scowling, silent and thoughtfully sucking his hookah. But Veliko the *kehaya* is merry, he walks about the room, and the seat of his wide Turkish trousers waves as he moves. From time to time he takes a watch as big as a turnip out of his colored silk cummerbund, looks at it, and puts it back again. Then he rubs his hands and says: "Everything is arranged, Bey *effendi*. Don't you worry, the wolf is in the trap."

On the table before the *kurserdar* are two kerchiefs—one white, one red. Those are the signals for the guards hidden in ambush. If the Bey waves the white kerchief from the window, it means mercy; if he waves the red one, it means death. And they wait and look toward the street. No one is to be seen. Rada has not come out before the gate, nor can one see Mustafa coming. Veliko the *kehaya* can contain himself no longer and hurries to his house.

"Eh?" asks the Bey when he returns.

"Everything is in order. She has put on her best clothes, a scarlet satin waistcoat, a dress of blue silk. Just as when we sent her into the mountain. And just like a woman, she's preening herself in the mirror, smoothing her eyebrows and laughing."

"What's she got to laugh at?" says the Bey angrily. "Doesn't she know what's got to happen?"

"She knows. How should she not know?"

"Did you tell her everything?"

"Hm. . . . Well, not everything. How could I? But no. I told her everything, everything. Do not worry, *effendi*. It is all in order."

Another hour goes by. Nobody comes. Veliko the *kehaya* runs home again, stays away longer this time, and at last comes back.

"Eh?" asks the Bey.

"Drat it all! Something else now. In tears. That old witch his mother has been there. If I'd caught her I'd have taught her something. She's been, *effendi,* and God knows what she's been babbling to her. 'I won't let them touch a hair of his head,' she says, 'I'll run away with him to the mountains.' Eh, women, women! That's the way with them. Oh, well, I've settled her. She'll come out. You'll see her there at the gateway this very minute."

The *kurserdar* strokes his beard and says nothing. Blue rings of smoke twist and curl about his head.

And then Rada stood in the gateway; from below came up Mustafa. The *kurserdar* and Veliko the *kehaya* run to the window and hide behind the curtains, watching with bated breath.

Mustafa walks along the middle of the street. On the roofs and fruit trees shines the sun. Far away, at the end of the street one sees the mountains where Mustafa was king. He carries no weapons. But what clothes! A suit of blue Wallachian cloth, braided with gold. Slim and tall, somewhat gaunt, somewhat sunburned, but handsome and gallant. In his hands a rosary of amber and a red carnation—the rosary from the Bey, the carnation from Rada. He is close now, looking at Rada and smiling.

The Bey kneads his white beard and mutters.

"What a fellow! What a handsome fellow!"

"The kerchief, Bey *effendi,* the kerchief!" cries Veliko the *kehaya.*

"What a fellow!" repeats the Bey, lost in admiration. "What a handsome fellow!"

Veliko the *kehaya* grabs the red kerchief and runs to the window. The Bey seizes his hand.

"No *chorbadji,* a man like that must not die!"

"And my girl? My honor?" screams Veliko the *kehaya* as he tears himself free and waves the red kerchief from the window.

The muskets ring out. The window panes rattle, the houses rock, a black shadow seems to fall on the earth. Shibil stands still, terrible and handsome. He tears the rosary, the carnation he still holds as he folds his arms and waits. A moment or two—enough for the guards to reload. A sharp scream comes from somewhere in the lower quarter. Shibil does not stir. Another scream from the gateway of Veliko the *kehaya.* Shibil turns: it is Rada. She runs to him with outstretched arms as though to save him; he spreads his arms as though to embrace her. The muskets ring out again, Shibil falls first on his face, then turns over. Rada falls beside him.

And everything is quiet. The sun splashes the cobblestone.

Like a fleck of blood between the two corpses lies the red carnation.

From the window of the coffee shop by the church somebody is desperately waving a white kerchief.

Translated by MARGUERITE ALEXIEVA

The White Swallow

Even as he was calling off the dogs, Peter Mokanin could tell that this unknown peasant had not turned aside merely to pass the time of day, but that he was driven by some misfortune. That was why he lost his temper with the dogs, swore at them, beat them off, and then turned to look at the peasant again. By his dress he could tell that he was from somewhere near Deli-Orman. A tall, big man, but poor he was, and poor he had always been, that was plain. His shirt was clumsily patched, his belt frayed, and his trousers, too. He was barefoot. Otherwise, a man like a mountain to look at him, but Peter Mokanin quickly judged him and decided that he was one of those soft, slack folk, of whom one says they would not hurt a fly.

The peasant greeted him muttering something like "Good day to you, how are you," but it was clear that his thoughts were elsewhere, and that other cares were on his mind. And looking ahead somewhere and pointing with his arm, he asked if that was not the way to the village of Mandjilari and how far it might be. Peter Mokanin told him, and it was only then he noticed that a horse and cart were standing in the road. The peasant had left the cart to come to him. On it crouched a woman, her hands thrust inside her smock, the ends of her kerchief hanging loose for ease. It was hot, but Peter Mokanin knew that when a peasant woman left her kerchief like that it was not the heat, but something else that worried her. At the back of the cart, half covered by a rug, and with her head on a pillow, lay another woman, younger, probably a girl. She was looking to one side, and her face was hidden.

"You seem to have sick folk," said Peter Mokanin.

"I have, my girl is ill."

The peasant looked towards the sheep resting in the meadow, his unseeing gaze, full of care, fixed on them, then it wandered.

"Eh, this lass of mine," he said, "a bad business."

"You're not from these parts—where do you come from?" asked Peter Mokanin.

"From Kuchouk-Ahmed, Maderha they call it now, near the Big Rock. I've been this way before. I go from village to village selling clay. Fine clay we have in our village. It's good and the women buy it; then, when I get down to the coast I buy fish or grapes or whatever comes. Thank God, it feeds us, if only this hadn't come to us."

He sat down on the ground and, taking out a leather pouch, began to roll a cigarette. Peter Mokanin sat down beside him and saw his thick, hairy fingers trembling as they pressed the tobacco.

"We've had no luck with our children," the peasant began. "Two of them died as little tots, and only this one is left." He looked toward the cart. "She's been our one ewe lamb. I've gone without things myself, to give her clothes, so that she shouldn't feel it when she saw the other girls. And God has let us keep her till now. But she's changed of late. There's nothing wrong, she just fades away. Her mother says it's hard for her seeing her playmates all married and she still a maid. 'What ails you, lass,' I tell her, 'your chance will come, too. Why d'ye look at the others?—They're well off. The young men today are all like that—they're for rich wives. But you'll marry, too, don't worry, you're not too old yet?' "

"How old is she?"

"Getting on for twenty. She'll be twenty come Michaelmas."

"Eh, but she's young, the maid."

"Of course, she's young."

The peasant stood quiet again, regarding the sheep blankly. From close by the shrill chirp of the cicada was heard in the heat.

"This summer she begged me to let her go harvesting. We're poor folk, needy folk, but seeing her so thin and ailing, I was against it. 'Please, dad, let me go. I want to go along with the other girls.' Well, since it was like that, I gave way. Now what happened, I don't know, for I wasn't there. They slept in the fields, and they rose in the fields—that's what she tells me. Once, they reaped the whole day, and at night they ate; then the lasses sang and laughed together; and then they lay down to sleep. Nonka, that's my girl, lay down, too. 'I lay among the sheaves, dad,' she tells me, 'under a stack, sheltered, and wrapped myself up. And I feel asleep. Suddenly I felt something heavy, something cold, here on my breast. When I opened my eyes—a snake!' "

"Now then!"

"Yes, a snake, curled round and asleep on her breast. She cried out then, terrified, she grabbed it and flung it away."

"Flung it away! Ay, that happens sometimes at harvest. But it didn't bite her, did it?"

"No, it didn't. The snake lay on her breast and she flung it off. So she told me. Was it a dream or was it the truth—I don't know, for I wasn't there. But from that time the girl doesn't thrive. Look at her—she's withering like a flower. Her breast hurts her. 'Here,' she says, 'here, dad, where the snake was, it hurts, it hurts.' "

"Eh, that's a queer thing," Peter Mokanin was amazed. "But where are you off to now? Are you taking her to the doctors?"

"Doctors! How many doctors have seen her! No, now we are going to . . . h'm . . . how shall I tell you? If you ask me I don't believe it, but womenfolk, you know. . . . Then she's sick, the poor lass." His voice quavered and he was silent. He stood there, tugging at his mustache, then at his long-unshaven beard, rough and grizzled. There was no need to tell Peter Mokanin that every gray hair was the scar of some trouble.

"Last evening," continued the peasant, "some of our folk came up from the harbor. They were talking about something—how should I know what it was? Well-to-do folk—perhaps they were joking. Then Stoenitsa came running up. She's the girl's godmother and she's a fair gossip and one of those that know everything. 'Gounyo,' she shouts from the door, 'you're in luck, man, you and Nonka.' 'What is it?' I say. 'Kolyo and Penyo, old Sider's sons, have just come from the harbor,' she says, 'and they say that a white swallow has been seen at Mandjalari. Quite white, like snow!' 'Well?' I say. 'Well,' she says, 'you fool, and don't you know what a white swallow means? It appears,' says she, 'only once in a hundred years, but whoever sees it, if he's ill, no matter what ails him, he's cured. Gounyo,' says she, 'off with you! Quick! Don't wait! Take Nonka!' The lass began to cry. 'Oh, can it?' Her mother took it up and we have come."

"But is it true?" asked Peter Mokanin. "Where is the swallow?"

"Didn't I tell you? It's been seen hereabouts."

"White?"

"Snow white."

Puzzled, Peter Mokanin turned and looked down the road. Every day the flock took its noon rest in the meadow, yet it seemed to Peter Mokanin that for the first time he noticed how many swallows were perched on the telegraph wires. But that was not strange;

autumn was approaching, and the swallows and the storks were gathering to leave. There were so many swallows there, and they clustered so thickly that the wire was stretched and weighted like a rosary. So many, but all of them black.

"That's why I came to you," said the peasant, relieved and encouraged. "I thought I'd ask you, perhaps you've seen, perhaps you've heard. . . ."

"I haven't, friend, I haven't. A white swallow? I've neither seen nor heard of it."

But Peter Mokanin bethought himself that he might make these folks despair, and he added: "But there may be one. A white buffalo, a white mouse, and a white raven there are. There may be a white swallow, too. And there must be one since you've heard of it."

"Who knows?" sighed the peasant, "if you ask me I don't believe it, but womenfolk, you know. . . . Then she's ill, the poor girl."

He got up to go. Touched, Peter Mokanin rose also to see him off and look at the girl. As they reached the high road the mother—a sallow, worn-out woman—looked at her husband, even from the distance, trying to read from his face what he had learned. The girl lay still, her head turned to one side, watching the swallows on the wire.

"The man says the village is near," said the peasant. Hearing his voice the girl turned. She was very thin: her figure, wasted away by illness, hardly showed beneath the cover. Her face was like wax, but her eyes were still bright, still young and smiling. She looked from her father to Peter Mokanin.

"Nonka, this friend has seen the swallow," said the peasant, throwing an uneasy glance at Peter Mokanin, "and it's in the village there. Now if we can only see it, too!"

"Shall we see it, sir?" asked the girl, and her eyes brightened.

Something rose in Peter Mokanin's throat and threatened to choke him, his eyes dimmed.

"You'll see it, lass, you'll see it," he began to pour out all at once. "I've seen it, lass, and you'll see it, too. I saw it with my own eyes, such a one, a white one, all white, like snow. And you'll see it, lass. God grant you may see it and get better . . . and you'll see it, for I saw it with my own eyes. Eh, but you're a young maid. I tell you, you'll see it and you'll be well again, lass, never fear."

The mother wept through closed eyelids. The big, tall peasant coughed, took hold of the horse's reins, and led it forward.

"God keep you," Peter Mokanin shouted after them. "The village is near. Keep to the wires, keep to the wires."

He stayed there on the white high road for a long while, gazing after the cart. He saw the mother with the black kerchief, the dying girl lying by her, and the tall peasant striding along, leading the small horse. And above them, between every two telegraph poles, the swallows were flitting away and then returning to perch on the wires.

Thoughtfully Peter Mokanin turned to his sheep and started again on the rough shoes he was making of untanned horsehide. "A white swallow," he pondered, "would there be one?" And something stuck in his throat, hurting him. And dropping the awl, he gazed at the sky: "God, how much trouble there is in this world. . . ."

And again he gazed after the cart.

Translated by M. MINKOV

Iliya Volen

(1905–   )

Iliya Volen was born on October 13, 1905 in the village of Uglen, Loukovit district. He received his education in his native village and in the theological school in Sofia. He studied Slavonic philology and literature at Sofia University and worked as an office clerk. His first poems were published in 1924 in the *Dionysius* magazine. Later his works appeared in Anton Strashimirov's *Vedrina*, in *Zlatorog*, and in other magazines. In 1934 and 1935 he edited *Detsko Znamé*. Now he is editor on the Bulgarski Pissatel publishing house.

He has published the following books: *Black Fallow* (1928); *God's People* (1937); *Wild Souls* (1954); *Wolfish Times*, a play (1956); *Between Two Worlds*, short stories (1958); *Selected Works* (1959); *Zlatan's Dream*, short stories (1960). He has also written a book for children, *Joy at Home*, which was first published in 1942 and has been reprinted several times.

Groudka

Sviden leaned on the wedge which he was making for the front part of the cart and gazed at Groudka. She was shaking out some black clothes she had washed and was hanging them on the wattle fence of the sheep pen, rising on tiptoe and humming a song. At one time, their eyes met. He bent his head and went on shaping the wood. Groudka gave him an artful look and opened her mouth to say something, but suddenly turned around and became absorbed in her work. Sviden chopped on for a while, then after looking at the wedge through half-closed eyes to make sure that it was perfectly straight, his eyes fell on Groudka again. She was already hanging the last garment on the line. When she saw that Sviden was still staring at her, her eyes sparkled playfully, and she laughed, musically but quietly, as she always did. Sviden smiled, too; he spat on his palm and set to work vigorously on the wedge. She went up to him—big, plump and beautiful—and said to him laughing: "Do you think I look better now? . . . In this white blouse, I mean?"

"You do."

"You like me better like that? But what about Maroushka, the Black Man's girl?"

Sviden drew his brows together and bent over and touched the lower end of the wedge. Groudka stood before him looking still bigger than before, and her eyes glowed with an artful and merciless fire. She laughed again, and this time her laughter was soft and long. When she stopped laughing, she bent her head over one of her sleeves and began to brush it with her hand.

"This white blouse . . . I like white clothes, you know. They're prettier."

"They make you look gayer," Sviden replied, with eyes fixed on the ground. "Those black ones," he added, raising his eyes to the wattle fence, "you must have got tired of them, while you mourned for the master."

"Well!" Groudka exclaimed, looking at Sviden with half-closed eyes, "what a man you are! How long you have been at this wedge! The sun's already high up in the sky, but you're still hard at it. Haven't you got any other work to do? Black clothes, white clothes, indeed!"

Sviden stirred and began to look about restlessly among the chips, trying to start up the conversation, but she neither listened nor looked at him, and continued scolding him: "That maize that was taken from you from last year's crop the other day, you can make it up from the new lot today. Call Danka to help you at the shelling machine. . . . Black clothes!"

A chip which was not like the others caught Sviden's eyes, and God knows why he picked it up and began to break it to pieces.

Just then a shaggy little puppy came trotting along from the barn, went up to Groudka, and joyfully wagged its tail at her feet. She did not notice it, because she was still scolding, and stepped on it. The puppy gave a squeak. Groudka turned around and kicked it. The puppy rolled away, squeaking harder than ever. Sviden frowned, turned aside, and began to chop the wood faster. Groudka made for the threshing ground, threatening the dog: "You *will* get under my feet! I threw the other pup out in the gardens, and I'll throw you there, too, see if I don't! What use are you to me? Wretched pups! You *will* get under my feet."

A lanky bitch came up to the puppy and began to lick it, glancing timidly toward the threshing ground.

When Sviden stopped to catch his breath, he turned his eyes to the clothes on the line and stared at them for a long time. Drops of black water were oozing down the wattle fence and dripping on the ground.

On the following day the entire village went out to bring in the maize. The previous spring Groudka had distributed part of her maize fields to sharecroppers, so now she wanted to bring that crop in first. She called Danka Ivanitsa, who was one of her sharecroppers, and went to the Two Pools with her. The soil was stony at that place, and the maize ripened the earliest there. During the day Sviden did his mistress' share and piled it under the upper shed, where they husked the cobs every year. In the evening, after dinner, a lamp was put under the shed, a fire was built, and all of them sat down to husk. Granny Gena, Groudka's mother-in-law, who was failing and was on the way to the other world, so to speak, came out to do some husking, too. The children did not want to go to bed, either.

Groudka sat between her mother-in-law and her little son. Maize cobs popped on the burning coals, and a kettle of choice ones was boiling on the fire.

"Why did you throw away that one, granny?" the boy asked. "It's like milk, and you threw it away. Let me see!" And he crept over the husks to the piled cobs. "Oh, look at what she's done!" he exclaimed, showing the cob to his mother.

Groudka glanced at Sviden and drew her brows together. A smile curved her lips. "What are the mice to make their nests from next winter? She ought to be put away. She can't see, the poor woman, but she's anxious to husk. Go on, husk away!"

Sviden smiled. Groudka moved closer to him and turned to the boy who was sitting between them: "Will you sit next to your granny, dear, to husk her cobs? She can't see well, poor thing! That's right!" she said, settling next to Sviden. "Over there, where I sat, I had to twist myself all the time in order to reach the cobs."

Meanwhile, the boy sat by his grandmother. Granny Gena stopped husking, gave him a short look askance and snapped at him: "What've you come for?"

"For the cobs you've been husking. I'll clean their silk."

"What silk?"

"The silk that's on them. You can't see it."

"I can do it myself. If there's silk, I'll clean it myself. You're not going to do it for me."

Groudka heard her mother-in-law's last words and nodded to her child to stay where he was. The children hung around their grandmother to help her, they quarreled for the baked cobs and wrestled in the husks. Groudka and Sviden husked in silence. At one time, Sviden muttered something, as he bent over a cob, and Groudka raised her face to him.

"What is it?" she asked.

"Nothing. The silk here."

"I thought you said something to me."

They were silent again. Groudka often glanced at him, and once she said, as she looked at him: "What kind of a cob is this one here?"

"A crushed one. Its top has been crushed. Looks like a scraper," and Sviden began to laugh, moving the cob like a scraper.

Groudka drew back. The dimples on her cheeks trembled, her eyes blinked and she began to laugh: "They'll see you," she whispered.

Sviden stopped moving his hand, gave her a long look and a wide smile, and said: "I just wanted to show you how you scoop the dough when you make bread, but you. . . ."

Their eyes met again, happily.

"Let's see who can husk faster, Sviden! Let's see who'll be beaten!" she cried, laughing softly.

Sviden whistled and shook his head, meaning to say that he agreed, and they began to husk as fast as they could. The boy left his grandmother, turned to the two to watch their game and, secretly, gave his mother barer cobs. When Sviden saw that he was outdoing her, he began to work more slowly to let her beat him. When they got tired and stopped, he stretched out his right arm, shook it, and touched his shoulder. Groudka asked wearily: "Why are you touching it? Have you sprained it by any chance, working so fast?"

"Oh no! But when you went home this morning, I carried all the baskets alone. From our pile and Danka's, I wanted to help her, too. 'I'm too old,' she said. 'And I've carried it alone up to now.' So I gave her a helping hand."

During this race Granny Gena and the small girl fell asleep. Groudka awakened them and took them home. Sviden and the little boy were left at the shed. And when they were left alone, Sviden dropped the cobs he was husking on his lap, locked his hands at the back of his neck, stretched himself and cast a thoughtful look at the sheep pen. It could not be seen; the night had blotted it out. Only the poles on its wattle fence were sticking out, against a cold, gray strip of sky, spangled with large autumn stars. At one time something rustled beside him. He looked around, and when he saw the boy sitting next to him, his eyes brightened. He took him on his lap and caressed him with delight.

At the place where Granny Gena had worked, the pile had not risen very high, so when Sviden started husking again he seated himself there. When Groudka came back she took her old place, so that she found herself somewhat behind him. But she took her cobs from the same place as he. They husked the cobs and talked. As Groudka threw the bare cobs, she hit him once or twice on the back on purpose, and pretended to have done so unintentionally. Sometimes she gave him the thicker cobs to break them and said: "Why should I strain myself when there's a man next to me! Take this one, too."

He took them, bent forward, and broke the cobs.

"See what a weakling you are! Your arms are fatter than mine," he answered once.

"You're right, Sviden, let's see. Let's measure them!" she said, stretching out her plump red arm.

Sviden stretched his out, too.

"It's plumper, of course! A man's hand can't hold it."

Groudka laughed.

He took hold of her hand above the wrist and tried to join his fingers around it, pressing it with all his might. Groudka laughed heartily, and moaned, moving her shoulders and looking at him with sparkling eyes. When he let her hand go, the boy jumped to his mother. "Let me try, mother! I'll do it, I'll do it! You'll see that I will."

Groudka winked at Sviden and stretched her hand out to the child.

It was late. The child wanted to sleep, and Groudka took down the lamp and took him to bed. The light of the lamp swayed in the sheep pen, crossed the courtyard, and vanished. Sviden was going to sleep by the maize to guard it from the dog.

When the lamp was taken away and only the fire was left in the shed, the sheep pen grew lighter. Sviden could see the scattered cobwebs and baskets. He remembered that he ought to give some husks to the buffaloes, so he jumped up, filled the basket, and took it to the lower shed. When he left the buffaloes and came out into the yard the light in Groudka's room had already gone out.

Sviden roamed around the yard for a while, then he stopped at the cart, crossed his hands on the rail, and raised his eyes. The sky above him was studded with stars. They were scarcer and bigger in the lower parts, but the higher he looked, the denser they grew, and there were both big ones and smaller among them. And when he gazed at a place which looked emptier, minute stars made their appearance before him like dust. The whole multitude of stars blazed up and shimmered as if they were worried and were waiting for something to happen.

A big star was shining in the middle of the sky like a diabolical green fire, and three more big ones were shining beside it, as if they were guarding it. Often a falling star crossed the sky, leaving a shower of golden feathers behind it and seeming to perch on another branch, after which the stars grew still more uneasy and quivered more than ever.

Something touched Sviden's elbow; he started and turned around. The heifer was standing at his back, trying to reach his sleeve with its tongue. He put his arm around its neck, brought his face to its cheek, and fondled it. It stood with its legs wide apart and lifted its tail. When he stepped aside, it stood in its place for a while, rubbed itself on the cart, and made its way to the shed.

Sviden glanced at Groudka's window, and God knows for what reason, roared like a buffalo himself, in which he was highly experienced. The next moment he was ashamed of himself and quickly entered the sheep pen. There he lay down by the cold fireplace, lit a cigarette, drew on it once or twice, and gave the kettle with the cobs a push. His thoughts carried him to Groudka again. They went astray for a minute or two, but went back to her again and again. And as he thought of her, he often reached out unconsciously and pushed the kettle. When he had finished his cigarette and was stubbing it out in the fireplace, the door of the sheep pen gave a creak, and before he had raised himself on his elbow, he heard Groudka's voice: "Heavens, how big it is! Are you asleep, Sviden? . . . Come, come out! . . . Look at the moon! It's rising, but it looks terrible! . . . How big it is!"

Sviden jumped up in agitation. Over the dark forests to the east, the moon was rising in the sky, as if it came from a hot furnace. It was deeply chipped, lean and blood red, and it stood over the treetops, which seemed to have come to life under it, fixing its gaze like a witch on the dark village. Sviden looked at it for a while, then he looked around and said rather embarrassedly: "Well . . . what of it? Just the moon. It's growing smaller, that's why. A moon like any other moon."

"It's a moon, Sviden, but it frightened me. It looks so horrible, so red! As if it's full of blood. And it stares at you like a man!"

Sviden turned his eyes from Groudka to the moon and back again.

"You . . . you've brought something," he said, nodding at the black cauldron in her hand.

"Who, I? Oh, it's nothing, Sviden. It's water for the maize cobs, you know. When I lay down to sleep someone seemed to whisper in my ear. They'll burn without water, I thought, so I got up. See how I've come . . . in a . . . petticoat and a bodice. But just as I got to the door, it was there," Groudka explained, turning to the roof of the barn. "Look at it! It's still standing there, looking at us. The cat!"

When they made for the shed, she said to Sviden, who walked before her: "Poke up the fire, so that we get a fine blaze. It's so dark here, I'm afraid."

He knelt by the fire and lit it, while she stood behind him, talking: "I thought you were asleep, but . . . that's what I thought: Sviden is asleep already, but I'll go in quietly, not to awaken him. And you haven't lain down at all. Aren't you tired, or perhaps you've something to think about?"

"Think about! What do I have to think about! I gave husks to the buffaloes. And the weather is so. . . . There are so many stars shining, one can't fall asleep," he answered, and sat down to brush his knees.

"So many stars shining!" Groudka exclaimed with a smile. She poured water on the maize cobs, pressed them down with her fingers, and put a log on the fire, and when she had finished her job, she stood up, looked at Sviden and said: "When you mentioned the stars, you reminded me of something. Do you know that there are certain sicknesses—when the stars and the moon begin to shine, the sick person. . . ."

Sviden had turned his back to her—he was poking the maize husks with his hand—and replied: "Sicknesses! As I said to you, I gave husks to the buffaloes and stopped in the yard to look around."

"To the buffaloes!" she said, laughing cheerfully. "Was it you that made them low when I was going to bed?"

Sviden suddenly stopped poking the husks. Then he began to mix them with both hands and crawled away on his knees.

Groudka did not take her eyes off the man. They glowed with a cold, gay, diabolical fire; she smiled again and again, and her smiles were like flashes of lightning. Her nostrils moved with excitement, her unbuttoned bodice rose high, but it was open. She stayed like that for a while, then stepped up to him and said: "Are you making yourself a bed for the night? Tell me, Sviden! Why are you poking the husks?"

He turned around and sat down again.

"Yes, a bed for the night. I want to find a flatter place," he replied, without raising his eyes.

"All places are flat here under this shed. Let's see if it's soft enough."

She seated herself on the husks, jumped up and down on them and said in a gay voice: "It won't be bad. It's soft. Oh, oh, it's very soft!" she repeated and jumped again. "Won't you feel cold with the buffalo rug? Well, it's your own fault, you should have taken a bride."

Sviden stirred anew. "A bride. When Danka and I were coming back from the maize field, Vulko the widower caught up with us and walked along with the cart. Danka said to him: 'Why doesn't Groudka marry you? You've got only one child. You'll take care of her land.' He laughed at this."

"Let him laugh! He laughs, but he asked about me after the fortieth day of your master's death. I won't have that man! Such a lean fellow! I'll send him packing, too. I'm not dying for him!"

Groudka moved closer to Sviden and lay on the maize husks. "I know whom I'll take," she said. "Danka! She's got her own worries, too! Wait a minute!" Groudka rose from the maize husks and put her hand on Sviden's knee. "Did Danka say something about me after I left you? . . . Because I went home so early?"

Sviden did not move and looked at her with warmth in his eyes. "Well, she did . . . 'She didn't take the basket on her back even once,' she said. 'I have to carry it alone with my old bones all the way. I've rubbed my back sore. And she wouldn't even lift it for me, but told the child. She doesn't pity even her child. She doesn't seem to have any heart at all. She only takes care of herself. Wealth makes one selfish, you know. Her father was rich, and now she has even more.'"

Groudka laughed.

"Of course I'll take care of myself and not of her. The land is my own, why should I work, too? I needn't have gone at all, if I didn't want to. Why did her husband go abroad to earn money? And she wants me to help her!"

Groudka's eyes shone above Sviden and trembled like stars. She pressed close to him, as she reached out to take a cob, and when she had taken the cob, did not move away. She put the cob straight in her lap and husked it on one side, pressing it.

"Well, but what kind of a woman am I, Sviden? I didn't touch the basket at all. She did all the work with her daughter."

Sviden turned this way and that, not knowing where to look, and said quietly: "I didn't help her either. She and her daughter did all the work."

"Didn't you help her at all? I thought you said that your shoulder. . . . Oh, what a fellow you are!"

Groudka dropped on the maize cobs, gave him a soft, quiet smile, and half-closed her misty eyes. Dimples appeared in her cheeks, she beamed with joy, and her face blossomed like a rose. Sviden looked at her with eyes full of devotion.

"Today she didn't want to cut the big pumpkin we found near Penyo's field. She hid it for herself. 'I've earthed it up,' she said, 'let my children feast on it.' And she asked me not to tell you about it."

Groudka rose from the maize cobs: "Did she, indeed?" she exclaimed. "I'll teach her a lesson, that I will. I won't take her on as a sharecropper again. Let her see what it is to have no bread!"

"Don't take her on! Let her see! Let her be!" he repeated as if he were bewitched, in a faint and broken voice, in which there was a touch of pain.

Groudka was looking at him. Her white teeth gleamed coldly as she smiled, and her lips, full and blood red, as they seemed to him, quivered slightly. She fixed her eyes on Sviden's and brought her face up to his. He suddenly remembered the rising moon and drew back, but Groudka threw herself on his neck and they both fell onto the husks.

The moon, already still and pale, shone high up in the sky, and the earth with its plains, hills, and forests, slept as if it were enchanted, muffled in a milky, bluish haze. A rooster crowed in the distance, then another one followed, and from all parts of the village the roosters sent their call up to the skies—shrill, piercing, and strange. As he lay on the maize husks, Sviden awoke out of weariness and turned to Groudka. She felt his gaze, turned to him, and gave him a quiet smile. Her face was soft, gentle, and kind. He stretched out his hand and stroked her rosy cheek. She smiled again and said in a weak and drowsy voice: "The roosters are crowing already. I must get up."

She rose to her feet, leaning on Sviden, and set off. Nobody heard when she left the sheep pen and entered her house. Sviden did not feel like getting up. He continued to lie in his place, and his thoughts wandered here and there; then he dozed off and they scattered. He began to dream of the things he thought about. At one time he felt cold and got up to set his bed to rights. And as he did so, he nearly stumbled on a cob which was only half husked.

The following morning Sviden got up, removed the husks and silk from his clothes, and entered the house smiling. Granny Gena was lying awake on her couch by the fireplace, while Groudka was raising the baking hood with the tongs to see if the bread was baked. Sviden stood in the middle of the room and said: "I slept too long this morning. You, Groudka . . ."

Groudka dropped the hood, burned herself and began to scold: " 'You, Groudka!' What's this 'You, Groudka! . . . Groudka!' We'll sleep until noon, shall we? Hurry up, go and fetch water, while the bread bakes. Take the yoke with the water jars. Go to . . . to the millrace."

"Sleeps, sleeps, always sleeps!" Granny Gena moaned angrily in a singsong voice, while Groudka was scolding Sviden.

Sviden frowned, put the yoke with the water jars on his shoulder and went out. When he came back, there was sweat on his face. Groudka approached him, peeped at the water, frowned and said, without looking at him: "You can go home, if you like!"

"Yes, I will. I haven't been home for a long time. I'll go!"

"Stays a bachelor!" Granny Gena mumbled again. "Won't take that girl, what was her name, the Black Man's daughter, to do his washing, but just stays a bachelor!"

Groudka went to the fireplace with a mocking smile on her lips.

"He'll take her in the end, but let's see to it that we don't lose her. Let's hope she'll say yes," said Groudka, turning to Sviden. "Go and tell Danka not to wait for me. Let them go and pick the cobs. Today I'm going to stay at home to clean the house. You'll be there, and keep your eyes open when you divide the maize, for she. . . . I'll teach her a lesson when I see her!"

He left while she continued to give him orders.

The next morning the sun poured its rays on the window; they trembled on the wall opposite, above Sviden. His rug had fallen on the floor. He had tossed back his head and was sound asleep. There were a few of a woman's fair hairs on his pillow. The door of the room opened quietly, and Groudka's big figure appeared on the threshold. She smiled, stood there for a moment, then went up to the couch, bent over Sviden, seized him by the chin, and shook him. Sviden stirred and opened his eyes. She still held him, laughed and said to him: "You, lazy Turk! I've been up for a long time! What kind of a man are you? It's a holiday all right, but just the same . . . the sun'll burn your eyes! And the rug! How can you sleep like that, as if you were fighting someone in your sleep!" And she bent down to pick up the rug.

Sviden slowly sat up, put his feet down and got up. His face was tired and crumpled.

"The rug . . . I must have thrown it off. At one time I felt it was. . . ." But he did not finish his sentence and was lost in thought.

Groudka put the bedding in order and said: "The nights are already growing cold. It was quite cold last night, and you got uncovered."

Sviden was silent. When they made for the door, he lifted the wet shirt on his breast and his back, and wearily dragged his feet. Out in the yard, Groudka stopped and stared at the white road which ran over the opposite hill, toward Rakitino.

"I'm sorry for you, Sviden!" she said thoughtfully.

"Why?" he asked lazily, looking around the yard.

"Just because I'm sorry for you. You're kindhearted and clever, but . . . have you been to Rakitino recently?"

"Not since last spring, when we took the wheat to the station. Why do you ask?"

"Well, I just asked. A person gets up in the morning, and doesn't know what may happen to him in the evening," she added, still deep in thought.

Sviden stopped looking around the yard and stared at her in surprise. She caught his gaze, started, and made for the house; he followed her.

The children were not up yet, and Granny Gena was still in bed, with her back toward the door. She stirred, but did not say a word. Sviden washed his face and sat down by the fire. Meanwhile Groudka had poured hot water into the bread trough and began to scrub it with a scraper.

"I wonder why you are scrubbing it now!" Sviden said, with his eyes on the bread trough.

"I'm scrubbing it because I must! I haven't washed it a long time. It's disgusting, how dirty it is. People may come. So I decided to give it a scrubbing," Groudka replied, her eyes on the bread trough, too. She was silent for a while. Then, leaning on the scraper, she raised her face toward Sviden.

"D'you know what I heard this morning, Sviden, as I was throwing the rubbish out away? This morning I heard that Voika, your neighbor, is getting married. They sent her a matchmaker last night, and she'll be getting married on Wednesday."

"Getting married? To Stoyan, I expect. Why haven't I heard anything?"

"Not Stoyan, no! But Naiden Popsky."

"Oh, to Naiden! To Naiden! She was in love with Stoyan, but now . . ."

"She loved Stoyan, but is marrying Naiden. Well, Naiden's a much better match. As to Stoyan. . . . Everyone seeks his like, you know," and Groudka bent over the bread trough again.

Sviden saw to the cattle, did some work in the courtyard, and made for his mother's house to change his clothes. All the way home something bothered him. He was sad and oppressed, but did not understand why.

On the next morning, he went to the fields to sow. Everything he did during the day was wrong. After unharnessing the buffalo cows, he did not know where he had left the yoke. He spilled the grain from the sack two or three times, and even cut one of the buffaloes with the plowshare in the evening. After plowing, he took the buffaloes down to the valley by the small market garden where he had left the cart. Groudka had come out at sunset to cut the cabbage and was waiting for Sviden to load the cart. Sviden began to carry the cabbage in the basket which Groudka lifted on his back.

"Carry it, carry it," she said at one time. "For we may need it next winter . . . for the marriage feast."

Sviden carried the basket without saying a word. When he came back, she teased him again: "Do you know, Sviden, that a widow in Piperkovo married her farmhand? If you were in his place, what would you do? . . . She liked the boy and married him."

"She must have been crazy. He isn't her like."

Groudka laughed her bell-like laugh and looked artfully at Sviden through her long eyelashes. Sviden's face brightened, and Groudka went on hurriedly, in a breathless voice: "He isn't her like! Why shouldn't he be, for Heaven's sake? What a queer fellow you are! She is rich, but he is young and good; everything comes handy to him. If she took a widower with a whole lot of children, would she feel happier, do you think? Or say, without children, but from another village?" she added with a half-concealed smile, "whom she doesn't know and he turns out to be a spendthrift? She knows this boy. And most important of all, she'll have a young husband. Is it a bad thing to put wealth to hard work? Two virtues together."

Sviden had put his head on one side and was looking at her with wide-open, blazing eyes.

"Well, it would be a good thing. Well," he replied, wringing his fingers and shifting his eyes now to the cabbage, now to Groudka, "it's not so much for the . . . I don't care for the wealth . . . it's something else that I like, something else. Shall I cut a cabbage for you?" he asked unexpectedly.

"Wait, you'll give me one later," Groudka replied quietly, bending a little and stretching her hand out to Sviden, who was kneeling over a cabbage and staring at her. "What did you say? Something else, something else. Not the land, but that other thing. That's why everyone seeks his like. That woman must have been crazy to marry her farmhand. Do you remember that man who said he had come for the buffalo cow? The tall man, from Rakitino? He did not come for the buffalo cow, he came to see me. My brother went to see him yesterday. And he liked him. He's coming again. We're getting married. I've found my like. Why shouldn't I?"

Sviden had dropped his head and was scratching the dry earth around the cob with his nails.

Groudka straightened up and cried to him: "Come on, cut me a cabbage! Cut it and clean it for me. Don't take it so badly! . . . Oh, how hungry I am, I'll crunch it up at once!"

Sviden cut the cabbage and began to peel it. As he was removing the last leaves, he dropped it and the knife and cut his finger. There was a red drop of blood on it.

Groudka bent down and took it; she wiped it with her palm once or twice and greedily took a bite with her strong white teeth.

After supper, Sviden walked around the yard for hours. And when he went to his room, he did not fall asleep at once. He tossed and turned, deep in thought. He did not know when he fell asleep. At one time he had nightmare. He dreamed that he had not yet gone to sleep and was lying alone in the bed where he used to sleep as a child. And as he lay there he did not notice that a big man whom he did not know had entered the room. Sviden was frightened. The unknown man had raised his sharp shoulders, locked his hands in front of him, bent his head, and was staring fixedly at him. His eyes were vague, like those of a madman, and his lean face had deep, ugly wrinkles on it. There were repulsive white locks in his low-cut black hair and unshaven black beard. "He must be mad," Sviden thought, shivering. "If the door had been locked, he couldn't have entered the room." And while he was thinking this and trembling with horror, the unknown man moved forward with big strides, sat on his breast and began to strangle him. Sviden cried out and woke up. He found himself trembling all over, his heart throbbing violently. He rose in his bed, looked around the room and thought in a fever: "If the door had been locked, the man couldn't have come in. But it was only a dream! . . . How awful he was! . . . It's better always to lock the room. Good Lord, it was only a dream, wasn't it?" Sviden thought, annoyed, but still trembling as before. "How he stood by the door!" Sviden jumped up and stared right at the corner: "What's that black thing over there? . . . Oh, I . . . it's the cabbage, of course! . . . We piled it up there last night . . . the cabbage. . . . Little by little he quieted down and came to his senses; he realized that the unknown man was a dream. Since he could not sleep any more, he got up and opened the door. It was nearly dawn. The sky had grown pale, and there were only a few stars in it. The bitch was playing with her puppies in the yard, and the buffalo cows were stirring in the shed.

Groudka soon married the widower from Rakitovo. He came to live with her, took all the farmwork in his hands and, when St. Dimiter's Day came, refused to hire Sviden again. Sviden felt exhausted and sickly and was in no hurry to find another job. When he felt better, he harnessed Danka Ivanitsa's cows and went out to sow the fields she had not managed to sow, as well as his father's. He spent the days partly plowing and partly lying in the sun, for such was his job.

One morning he went to Groudka's house to get the rest of the money for the work he had done for her. He was planning to go to a doctor in town. As he entered the yard, he saw Groudka and her husband talking angrily at the bottom of the yard with their backs turned to the gate. Sviden stopped by the wattle fence and listened.

"Danka Ivanitsa! I said it once, and that's that! I'm not going to give her my field as a sharecropper. I wouldn't even give my sins to that woman!"

Sviden grew pale.

"A woman's mulishness!" the husband answered angrily. "Why shouldn't I let her have it? When I sowed the field at the Two Ponds, I saw how well it had been worked. Why shouldn't I let the poor woman have it since she's asked me for it?"

"Because I said no! I won't let her have it. Let her beg for it!"

"I'll not be guided by a silly woman like you!"

"All right, we'll see! . . . I'll send you packing, too, and farm my land as I wish."

Sviden staggered and stretched his hand back toward the wattle fence, but he pricked himself on the thorns and fell to the ground. A thin stream of blood oozed from the corner of his mouth. Somewhere beside the wattle fence, the bitch was sniffing the air and whimpering sadly.

Translated by ELENA MLADENOVA

Svetoslav Minkov

(1902–1966)

Svetoslav Minkov was born on February 17, 1902 in Radomir. He received his secondary education in Sofia and later studied philology at the Sofia State University and commerce in Munich. He worked as a librarian at the Co-operative Bank, and took a diplomatic post in Tokyo (1943–44). After September 9, 1944 he edited the cultural page of the *Otechestven Front* newspaper, then worked in the Bulgarian Cinematography and as chief editor of the Bulgarski Pissatel publishing house. He contributed to *Hyperion, Bulgarska Missul, Zlatorog, Literatouren Front, Izkoustvo*, and other periodicals. He has translated many books into Bulgarian, including the tales of Hans Christian Andersen. Minkov died on November 22, 1966.

He is the author of the following important books: *The Lady with the X-Ray Eyes*, short stories (1934); *Stories in Hedgehog Skin, Monkey Youth* (1942). Books for children: *The Miraculous Money Box* (1934); *The Candy Girl* (1935); *The Fox in Disguise* (1936); *The Little Moon* (1954); *King Sleepless*, tales (1956); *Tales of Sheherezada*, authorized translation (1959).

The Begonia

The stranger rang the doorbell. Somewhere within the walls of the house a sound like that of a fly caught in a cobweb was heard. It was followed by light footsteps. A key clicked in the lock and the door opened.

An old woman with a shawl flung over her shoulders stood on the threshold. On her small feet she wore huge woolen slippers, and her gray hair had a faint silvery radiance in the darkness.

"Good evening," the man said. "Have you a room to let?"

The woman cast an inquisitive glance at the stranger, trying to judge by his appearance whether he would pay his rent regularly. She carefully examined his crumpled tie, faded hat, and worn-out clothes; but she could not bring herself to say that the room was already taken. For several months now it had been vacant; tenants were difficult to find. Moreover, very often people in worn-out clothes were much more regular in the payment of their rent than those wearing silk shirts and new hats with small feathers stuck in the bands.

"Come in!" the old woman said, ushering the stranger into the house.

They walked along a dark passage and entered a room with green walls. The man looked about the room, like an experienced tenant: a bed, a wardrobe, a table, chairs, an upholstered sofa—everything old, worn-out, shabby and almost dilapidated with long use. Among this motley assembly of old furniture only two or three pictures on the walls lent a somewhat insipid freshness to the room. They portrayed women who, pretending to be innocently bathing in the open, were smiling the wicked smiles of night-club dancers. The stranger took a deep breath of the stuffy air, saturated with the musty smell of old chests and dressers, approached the window, and cast a distracted glance at the back yard of a tall building with many balconies and windows. He liked the room and its gloomy atmosphere. Obviously he was used to living among wardrobes with opaque mirrors, creaking beds with bottomless springs, and plush chairs and sofas which seemed to despite man, incessantly haunting him with a nail which would suddenly pop up. The visitor came to the middle of the room and asked in a hushed voice: "Isn't there a washbasin?"

"No," the woman replied. "There's one in the kitchen."

Then they began to talk about the rent. During the conversation both the landlady and her visitor disclosed some details about their personal lives. A widow, in receipt of a small pension, the woman had to let a room to make both ends meet. Her husband had died a few years previously. She had a married daughter in the country and a son in America, in Detroit.

"Have you ever heard of Detroit?" the woman asked.

"Yes; America has plenty of immigrants from all over the world," the stranger replied, trying to conceal his ignorance.

He told her that he worked in a private business which only paid him a small wage. The woman finally agreed to let him have the room at a reduced rent, providing he paid it regularly. Finally, she asked him if he had many friends, and if so, if they were likely to visit him frequently. The new lodger said he lived a lonely life and had no friends. After work he was in the habit of going straight home; he was as quiet as a fly, he said. The old woman was overwhelmed with joy. As quiet as a fly! This tenant suited her perfectly. And as so often happens with newly acquainted landladies and lodgers, the woman and the stranger felt a particular liking for each other. She offered him some jam; he blinked in embarrassment, but swallowed the jam, and examined the portrait of the landlady's son in Detroit. And he paid for the room in advance.

On the following day the man took his luggage to his new lodgings—two canvas trunks packed with clothes and several pieces of worn-out furniture. Suddenly the room took on an entirely new aspect. A pair of old slippers appeared on the small carpet in front of the bed; a jacket with frayed sleeves hung on the chair, and a winter coat in the wardrobe; and some aluminum cups, a tin spirit-lamp, and several spoons and forks began to rattle on the table. These clothes and utensils seemed to strike the invisible roots of a new life, the shoots of which were just starting to grow in the room.

The new lodger seemed to be a tidy man. With the permission of the landlady, he drove a few nails into the door, on which he hung a towel, a cardigan, and a cap. Finally, he carefully inscribed his name on an empty visiting card, wrote underneath "Ring twice!" and fixed it under the front doorbell. He was perfectly aware that nobody would call for him and that the injunction was quite superfluous; but like every living man he had his own idiosyncrasies, and had got used to putting such inscriptions on the doors of all his previous lodgings, without giving much thought to the fact that people had long since ceased to be interested in his personality.

The lodger left the house early in the morning and returned at dusk. Sometimes he ate in his room. He brought a piece of bread and something wrapped in paper, spread a white napkin on one corner of the table and ate slowly, lost in thought. Should there happen to be a crust of bread or a piece of salami left over, he would carefully wrap it up in the napkin and place it in the drawer of the table. A frugal person, he did not even throw away the crumbs, but collected them in his fingers and crunched them up.

In the evening, before going to bed, he would sit by the window, watching the tall, gloomy back of the neighboring house. There, exactly opposite him, within the frame of a window which threw a faint yellow light in the darkness, he saw, as if on a screen, always the same picture: a young man playing the violin. The window opposite was shut and he could not hear the music. The violinist appeared to be a beginner. He stubbornly beat time with his whole body, his hand pulling the bow uncertainly across the strings. The same picture could be seen every evening; it was as invariable as the lodger's habit of watching it with indifferent persistence.

What was this fifty-year-old man, with his bald head and colorless eyes, thinking about? Did the youth with the violin remind him of his past? Perhaps he himself had once played the violin and had hopes of becoming a musician? Children run after butterflies, trying hard to catch them; when they grow into adults they often don't even notice them. A young man dreams of noble goals; but soon his hair turns gray or quite unexpectedly begins to fall out, his face becomes wrinkled, and his hands become as thin as the legs of a bird. He sinks into the gray monotony of his daily existence, invisible to his old acquaintances and unnoticeable even to himself. The question arises: Was the lodger indeed living, in the real sense of the word? Estranged from the world and indifferent to current events, he seemed completely devoid of feeling. His daily life was bounded by the road between his lodgings and the office, the cheap restaurant where he occasionally had a meal, and the dilapidated laundry where they washed his clothes. On holidays he used to go for a walk, but would soon return to his room, afraid that he would catch cold if he stayed out any longer. He was incessantly haunted by the fear of catching cold, and it always seemed to him that he was in a draft or that the wind was blowing dangerously against him. He felt safe only when watching, dully and senselessly, the tall wall of the opposite house, with its numerous balconies and windows, staring at the boy with the violin and patiently waiting for him to switch off the light, so that he might switch his off too.

One morning, when he was just setting out for the office, the landlady stopped him in the front passage and told him she was leaving for the country in the evening to spend a few weeks with her daughter, who had had a baby and needed her help. She asked him to lock the front door and turn off the main tap in the kitchen every night and morning.

Left alone, the lodger followed his landlady's instructions strictly. He religiously kept the front door locked, and turned off the water at the main.

Then came a day when something quite extraordinary happened. It was a Sunday morning. The lonely man was making his coffee on the spirit-lamp when suddenly from the far end of the passage he heard the drawn-out buzzing of the doorbell—once, twice! It goes without saying that this meticulous man reacted quite naturally to this most unusual phenomenon, as if every day the bell rang twice for him. He went to the front door and peeped from behind the curtain. There was no one outside. He opened the door and saw a letter on the threshold. He bent down and lifted a blue envelope bearing his name and address from the ground.

Anyone in his place might have been at least slightly surprised to receive his first letter for years on end; might have grasped the invisible link between the world and himself, and felt the low-voltage current running in the mysterious chain which connects people even when they are utterly lonely. But this man seemed to be devoid of feeling and imagination. He calmly opened the envelope, produced the folded sheet of paper, and read it from beginning to end.

It was from his landlady. She asked him to water the begonia on the window sill in the drawing room. In the kitchen, on the shelf above the sink, he would find a white pitcher, in which the water should be taken to the plant. There followed another reminder about locking the front door and turning off the water at the main.

In the distant provincial town the old woman had not ceased to think about her house, about the begonia in the drawing room, and the white pitcher in the kitchen. Why had the flower to be watered only with the white pitcher? Because the landlady would not accept even the slightest change in the daily routine of her life. The objects in her house had acquired a special meaning for her. They had become intertwined with her life and now played the leading role in it.

Without hesitating a moment, the tenant went into the kitchen. He took down the white pitcher, filled it with water, and went to the drawing room.

There, in the mysterious dusk of this intimate museum with its old family portraits, the stranger stepped forward as in a graveyard. It was quiet in the room, where two candlesticks and a clock with a worn-out dial glistened on a sideboard, and at the far end a cold mirror reflected a faint light. Each object emanated something inexpressibly sad which enveloped the whole room in an invisible cobweb, creeping over the face of the portraits and pressing against the leaves of the begonia, which was beginning to wither behind the dusty windowpane.

The long monotonous days followed each other. Life went on as usual. Housemaids giggled in front of other people's doors, and children went running up and down the stairs. The lodger moved like a shadow and carefully watered the begonia; while many miles away his landlady no less carefully bathed her grandchild, who was just beginning to look out on the world with wide-open eyes.

Translated by **KRASSIMIRA NONEVA**

Armand Barouh

(1908–   )

Armand Barouh was born on July 15, 1908 in Sofia. Barouh left school at the age of fifteen and worked first as an office clerk and then in a textile mill, a bakery, and as a mechanic. In 1941 he was arrested and spent nearly three years in the Yeni Köy concentration camp, where he translated Tolstoy's *War and Peace* into Bulgarian. From 1944 on, Armand Barouh has devoted himself to writing.

He has published the following short story collections: *Carnations and Shoes* (1936); *In Pursuit of Happiness* (1937); *Hearts* (1945); most of these stories have been collected in *Short Stories* (1961). He has also written the novels *Fateful Autumn* (1960) and *The Ralevs* (1961) and the novelette *The Darker the Night . . .* (1963), as well as several plays, literary and theatrical criticism, some of which has been collected in *Man on the Stage*, in *Literature and on the Screen* (1958), and the literary and historical essay *M. Y. Lermontov*, which has had two editions (1941 and 1947).

Reb Yossl

"There are many large stars in the sky, but more of the small ones; they are sprinkled like salt over the Milky Way. There are many rich people in the world, but more of the poor. Even the weakest eyes see the large, heavenly bodies. But God created Paradise for the poor, because no one thinks of them here on earth."

With these words Reb Yossl taught his five children. He repeated them every day, because he feared they might not believe him any more.

God's aged servant knew when to read each prayer and how

to celebrate the Passover, Yom Kippur, and Shabuoth, but he forgot that the rent was paid early each month and the torn shoes of Zilli, Mendle, Sofka, Lolichka, and Haimo needed mending. For nearly half a century now, the municipal synagogue had been paying him less than a porter earned, and the old man rightly believed that only the Lord God of Sabaoth knew that the poor existed.

Reb Yossl was poorest among the poor, and for this reason he did not worry about his earthly duties. All his hopes were turned toward Heaven; for scores of years he had pondered over the secrets of the Torah, and on his face, which had withered in his faith in the heavenly orders, there was a look of anger. He liked to teach that hatred, love, joy, and wrath should not disturb pious souls; and the thought that the poor might grow rich by some miracle and lose their right to enter Paradise made him shiver.

"Children," Yossl would say as the family sat at the table, "you should not irritate poverty with compassion or alms, should Fate wish to punish you by making you rich. If you have no supper, do not envy those who have. Poverty is God's gift and the doorway to Paradise."

His children listened, but did not believe that the angel who stood guard at the big Gate of Heaven would let their father go in, dressed as he was in that shabby, patched coat, not a single inch of which had remained clean. The old man felt lonely in the silence that his sons and daughters maintained in his presence, and he preached with growing zeal: "In Heaven, my children, the last shall be the first, and the first. . . ."

Yossl believed in Heaven's justice because he had supporters. Father Antiochus was a believer like himself. He was the abbot of the local monastery, from which Reb received honey three times a year. The holy man fed piglets and kids, but he sent Yossl only honey, for bees were God's favorites and gathered their sweet nectar from flowers, among which there was not a single *trepha*! Every autumn Antiochus put one of Reb's letters of thanks in his hermit's bag, in which the old man assured him that he would not grow rich for anything on earth and when he died they would meet each other in Paradise.

Yossl wanted to go to Heaven as early as possible, for he knew he would be happy there and would not have to endure his wife's insults, at least as long as she was on earth. Besides her virginity, she had also given him thirty gold pieces, a straw mat, a green rug, a kettle, and a series of love cards. Reb married Leah because he was an obedient son. His father, the ancient Moisl, felt that his death

was approaching and wanted to go to Jerusalem, but the ticket to the
holy place cost twenty gold pounds. Moisl died as a holy man, but
Reb Yossl remained on the sinful earth.

Leah never forgot her pounds. For twenty years now she had
been adding small stones to the Sabbath rice. When she heard them
crunching on her husband's teeth, she scolded him for buying bad
products. This was the revenge of a woman who had seen neither
youth nor joy. Yossl would spit out the stones and thank God that
they were small, for they could have been large and broken his remaining teeth. Leah would then taste the joy of a sufferer avenged
and ask for some of her own pounds to be able to cook soup from a
fat chicken at least once.

Thus the years passed by. Leah bore children each winter,
and they died more often than they survived. Yossl read his prayers
with still greater zeal and simply would not realize that one could
not live only with the thought of God. Two prayer books fell to
pieces in his hands.

As far as he remembered, Yossl had not seen any change in
the world except the two small windows they had opened on the
narrow side of the synagogue, and the fact that his wife had stopped
sleeping with him, and that his house had filled with children. Leah
bathed them and did their washing, made bread, did the housework,
and cried very often. Yossl was not annoyed. She would thirst and
would come to him again—where else could she go? At night, when
he stretched out a hand as he was wont to and did not find her there,
he thanked God for not having sent him a still more cruel punishment.

The cruel punishment came of itself. Haimo and Sofka died.
Reb did not buy them medicines because he thought that God was
testing him. The children caught whooping cough and often went
blue in the face. When they began to gasp, Leah dipped a goose quill
in kerosine and smeared their throats with it, but it was too late.
Yossl read the burial service without tears, and the burial, like all
honest burials in the world, was finished hurriedly. While they cried
and sat on the rugs for weeks at home, another calamity befell them.

Lolichka was already thirteen years old. Her breasts could be
seen and her red hair had become curly and fluffy. The girl loved to
read books about the stars and distant worlds. One morning the
neighbors found her dead under the minaret of the town mosque.
The Moslem imam, Selim, who spent his days at the coffee house
opposite Reb Yossl's home, had long taken a fancy to the red-haired
girl. He lured the child with chick-peas and red candies. Then he

promised to fulfill Lolichka's wish to look at the stars from a closer distance.

Selim did not consider himself worthy of nirvana, and for that reason he valued earthly joys. He took Lolichka to the minaret. While they were climbing up, the girl felt the dry hands of the imam, ran up the flight till she reached a small window giving on to the stars, and threw herself down. At the cemetery, while he was seeing her off to Paradise, Yossl thanked God that his daughter had not given her heart to Mohammed but had died as an upright Jewish child.

On the day of Lolichka's death Mendl stopped talking to his father. No one had ever bothered about the boy, and he expected nothing from anyone. He had had smallpox six years earlier, and it had left his face so deeply pitted that Mendl was ashamed to have people look at him.

He played in the back yards all alone. Sometimes he even hated himself. At such times he broke whatever stood in his way and threatened to flee from his father's house and get married.

Zilli did not threaten anyone and never lost her temper about anything. When she went to work at the hairdresser's shop of Madame Margot she bought many rings, poured Eau de Cologne on her clothes, plucked her eyebrows, and returned home at dawn when Reb went out for the service. Leah waited for her daughter every evening, beat her, and shut herself up in the kitchen with her. The two women used to cry for all they were worth there.

But Yossl was blind for this misfortune, too. He did not see anything but his prayer books. Leah tried to speak to him about the children many times, but Reb merely waved his hand and went to the synagogue. Leah remained at home alone with her worries. Before she had understood how meaningless her life had become, she found no other comfort but to cry for the dead and the living. Since the day she had buried her youthful hopes, each day of her life had become a burden for her. She knew that her husband believed she was his punishment. He complained of her in his prayers and thanked God that he had not made him a woman, that Leah was not unfaithful to him, and that she had not poisoned him with rat poison, but confined herself to tormenting him with small stones. Yossl had failed to realize that she had a woman's heart, that she was a mother and was suffering for her children, who had died like May flies. Nor did Reb notice Zilli's existence either.

This girl reached her seventeenth year and married without anyone's blessing. The father only learned about it when she appeared before him in a wedding dress at the synagogue, next to a tall man with red eyebrows. Reb shivered with the wrath of an offended father, but he remembered that a holy man was bound to be meek. Consoled by the thought that Zilli had to marry some day, anyway, he married the couple, thanking God for not having sent him a more severe trial.

A week after this wedding Reb learned that his son-in-law was ready to do anything for his wife, Zilli, provided she freed him from the marriage oath. And it was then that the most terrible thing happened.

Leah went mad. She screamed all day long, cursed her husband, and neither cooked, washed, nor cleaned the house. Then she packed her clothes and went to live with her daughter. Yossl did not know what she did, but a couple of months later, when she returned home, a rumor spread in the neighborhood that the Yossls were going to have a grandchild and the son-in-law was crazy about it. Leah stayed at home only a week, without speaking a word, and disappeared one night. Some time afterward people said she had gone to work at the Bourgas swamps.

Reb Yossl began to get his prayers mixed. It happened from time to time that he married and buried people with the same prayer. One day, when he saw Mendl stealing into the cellar with a woman he didn't know, Reb felt like a fading star that no one had noticed; he thought the time was approaching when he would leave this world, and knew no tear would be shed for him. From that moment on Yossl spent nightmarish hours. For the first time he remembered that he had lived sixty years, that Leah had been a healthy, rosy-cheeked girl, like all the good-looking Jewish girls; for the first time he shed tears for Lolichka, Haimo, and Sofka, for Mendl and Zilli. And rebellious thoughts rose in his heart: Was not God cruel?

But Reb regretted these sinful thoughts and thanked God in his prayers for having ordered his life to pass quietly, that he might not die in torture and disgrace, that he had not suffered all the evil there was in the world. Yossl thanked Jehovah for not having sent him on earth many centuries ago when people crossed the Red Sea carrying thousands of sins on their shoulders and redeemed their imperfection by wandering in the desert for forty years.

Yossl did not understand that even without having crossed the Red Sea and wandering in the sands, he had spent his life in a desert.

Consoled by and reconciled to all his calamities, one morning Reb Yossl entered the synagogue as usual. It was early spring, and

many young people wanted to marry. A man dressed in tight bor-
rowed clothes glanced bashfully at his beloved girl and wiped his
eyes with a silk handkerchief.

Yossl started to sing the wedding hymn, but suddenly
stopped in the middle of it. He shook as he did when pronouncing
the prayers of thanks. His knees bent, and he fell dead at the feet of
the horrified couple.

Translated by ELENA MLADENOVA

Serafim Severnyak

(1930–)

Serafim Severnyak was born on July 10, 1930 in the village of Gorna Lit-nitsa, Turnovo district. He majored in literature at Sofia University. He has written the following books: *Farmers,* short stories (1952); *Kinsfolk,* short stories (1954); *Ten Short Stories* (1957).

The Stone Pigeons

There were always pigeons in the square in the middle of which a slim obelisk towered high like a crozier—the pedestal of some royal head in bronze from the Middle Ages. The pigeons swooped down in feathery flocks like shimmering fans and carpeted the large green flagstones, hopping about on their slender legs and tilting their heads coquettishly at the generous passers-by who threw them food.

The pigeons were not afraid of the people. They hovered about their shoulders, swarmed about their feet, occasionally gazing at them with eye aglitter in their velvety heads. Then the pigeons would suddenly dart away, leaving behind only the silken rustle of their wings and the happy wonder of the people who watched them fly away over the rooftops of the old Renaissance houses and disappear.

Only a small flock would stay behind, perched on the granite cornice over an ancient oaken door studded with metal disks.

We had passed by here every day, but it was only toward the end of the first week that we noticed the pigeons. They were carved of white stone, as big as the real ones which would drop from the sky and then rise from the square. Time and the rains had given them the light gray color of the living pigeons. Their frozen pose betrayed a hardly perceptible troubled movement. They took no notice of the hands scattering crumbs right beneath them and regarded the world and men from the height of their unusual and intriguing monument. They stood motionless, yet as alive as a memory.

We would watch them, lingering awhile and then, seized by an indefinable but deep excitement, we would dive into a coffee place nearby. There were many cafés around the square. Displaying no inviting signs on the outside, they hid in the basements of the ancient houses and welcomed their customers in the half-light of their geometric vaultlike ceilings and booths. The cafés smelled of strong southern coffee. Stillness held sway in the cozy little rooms. No snatches of conversation were to be heard, and inasmuch as people felt the need for communication, they would exchange a soundless word or two across the tables, as if the human voice had no place in the impenetrable, yet hospitable silence. It was only occasionally that the soft sound of music, created by a great composer born in this city a hundred years ago, would float up from the old grand piano.

We sat at the bare deal tables, sipping our coffee which the espresso machine had just expelled from its nickel-plated beak as we wondered if we could not, somehow, bring a portion of this silence to our own noisy and graceless taverns at home. We thought that this kind of quiet was probably responsible for the proverbial patience with which the people had restored this ancient part of the city brick by brick, ravaged by the mindless murderous invaders during the war.

There was not only a great deal of history in the restored Gothic steeples of the churches, in the bronze and iron bars of the windows, in the stifled echo of the narrow squares and in the frosted glass of the street lanterns. There was also a great deal of love. The kind of self-sacrificing and long-abiding love which conquers bondage and keeps great nations alive.

All this had been seeping into us day after day. However, our curiosity had been roused through some strange law of impressions and thoughts forming the question: Who had carved the flock of stone pigeons upon the granite cornice on the square, and why?

We often passed people right under them. Somebody perhaps knew their exciting story, but we felt that it would be an act of sacrilege to ask questions here, with everything standing like a mute and painful memory. It was for this very reason that we suppressed our southern talkativeness and let the quiet of the cafés engulf us completely.

So, naturally, we were surprised when one afternoon, at the Krokodil Café, an elderly gentleman asked us in an even and quiet voice if there was a vacant seat at our table. We answered in the affirmative.

There were many empty places about; as a matter of fact, there were whole empty tables, and maybe that's why I thought I somehow knew the man who took a seat directly opposite me.

"You are foreigners, aren't you?" was his first question.

"Yes, we are . . ."

Silence fell as the initial conversation between strangers petered out.

Then he said: "I guessed that much by the lady's profile." He bowed to my wife in confusion. There really was something Oriental about the line of her eyes and nose. "And also by the fur coat," he smiled. "We don't have such coats around here. There is fur, but it's not good and it's quite expensive."

I felt slightly put off. We had been asked, I don't know how many times, at shops, restaurants, and hotels, whether the fur coat was not for sale. The man sensed this and hastened to explain: "I don't want to buy it. I only want to talk with you for awhile. If you don't mind, of course."

We both gave a slight, respectful bow followed by a few minutes of polite silence. Women are always better at conversation. So I was not surprised to hear my wife's voice: "You come from this city, don't you?"

"Yes, madam."

That started off our conversation this time. The man rose, kissed my wife's hand, shook hands with me and introduced himself. We cannot remember the name, but it predictably had a few typical combinations of "zh" and "sh" sounds in it.

"I was born in this city and I've lived here ever since," the man said. "I didn't leave it even during the war and the occupation. Besides Kant, perhaps, I'm the only man in the world who's never left his home town." The man smiled again and lapsed into silence.

I had a close look at him. He was a big man, his hair was gray and thinning, and there was a transparent blueness in his eyes which had begun to lose their luster with the years. He could have been sixty, seventy or more. Despite the warm air in the café, he wore a knitted brick-red scarf around his neck which pleasantly matched his brown topcoat.

"I know all about this city," he said. "I know it so well that I worked as a consultant to the restoration teams for ten years. Whatever you see here was my life for years and years on end. Then all of it went up in smoke before my very eyes in a matter of days. I'm happy I've lived to see the liberation so that I could have a share in the restoration work."

"Will you have something to drink?"

"No, thank you. Coffee will do for today." He put his hand on his coat where his heart was.

"How about a glass of Bulgarian wine?" I suggested. "One can get the best Bulgarian wines here."

"Oh, they're very expensive here. You needn't order anything as I'm not fond of alcohol."

"But our wine is not alcohol," I joked. "It's made of sunshine and it's very nutritious." I called the waiter and ordered three glasses of "Mavroud" wine. I even told the man a funny story about Mavroud and Khan Kroum. He laughed heartily.

"You know," my wife began, and I knew she was going to ask him about the stone pigeons, because I, too, had been thinking about them. "We would like very much to know the story about the pigeons."

Our new acquaintance did not respond right away.

"It seems there have always been pigeons in this city," he said slowly. "The books of our oldest writers mention them. Many artists have painted them. Even composers have named some of their songs after them."

"How about the ones over the door, to the left of the monument?" my wife was quicker again.

This time the man's silence was more protracted. "It's a long story," he said finally. "They're made of stone, but they're more real than the others."

They turned on the lights, and although there were no overhead fixtures, as the lighting came from discreet niches in the walls, the wine in our glasses sparkled with violet opalescence. They were crystal glasses with long stems, and the sparks gleamed along the edges. The man talked on but his voice did not disturb the stillness. On the contrary, his soft timbre seemed to blend perfectly with the silent communication with the other tables and with the warm aroma of coffee in the air.

"The invaders first drove the people away. Then they tore down the houses and blew up the bridges, sparing only the column with the royal head and the pigeons. As was their wont, the birds would fly over the smoldering ruins and alight in the square. But there was no one to feed them any more. Sudden explosions and sporadic gunfire would frighten them away, but only temporarily, and the pigeons would fly back again. Their flocks grew thinner, their cooing became subdued and disquieted, but their habit of alighting on the green flagstones did not change. Someone's invisible hand would throw them crumbs of bread from time to time. The town went on living amidst destruction and death. . . .

"An old woman, one of those souls determined to die in her own bed, no matter what, would give them the remnants of her humble meals. There are such old women," the man smiled. "They do not recognize war, they are unafraid of occupiers. With one foot in the grave, they possess the inner freedom to do whatever they please. One might say that old woman only lived to feed the pigeons —a town can do without houses, without streets, without lights— but what kind of a town would it be if there were no pigeons which have alighted here for five hundred years and old women to feed them?"

I beckoned to the waiter again, but the man firmly placed his hand over his glass. "Even a glass of wine is too much at my age, sir," he said. "Even if it is sunshine and not alcohol . . . the sun can warm you with one single ray, with one single particle of light."

The story of the pigeons was evidently over, but I wanted so much to hear more, so I said: "Perhaps there ought to be an inscription or a plaque in memory of that old woman."

The man eyed me with genuine amazement: "But we put the pigeons there, didn't we?"

There was such hidden vigor in his voice that an involuntary tremor passed through my wife and me.

"Does it really matter what the name of that old woman was or what she looked like? Sir, men are mortal, and it is only their deeds that live on after them. Names and faces are forgotten, and none will be the poorer for that. But it would be frightening, indeed, if their deeds sank into oblivion."

The chords of a melody by the composer born in this city came from the grand piano. We were silent because we knew that the music of a genius could be appreciated only as one would appreciate a ritual, or the organ music in the stone cathedrals of this old and young city. Then we said good-bye and went out into the open.

The square was deserted at this time of night. The wind had risen. Solitary passers-by occasionally crossed the square. The granite pedestal rose lonely and meaningless with the bronze royal head from ages past shining upon it. No pigeons alighted on the green flagstones.

Speechless and tense, the stone pigeons huddled together on the granite cornice over the door studded with metal disks. We walked past with our eyes fixed on the small motionless flock. Soft footsteps echoed behind us as we walked away.

Translated by GREGOR PAVLOV

Diko Fouchedjiev
(1928–   )

Diko Fouchedjiev was born on July 16, 1928 in Gramatikovo, Bourgas district, in a family of workers. He received his elementary education in his native village and attended secondary school in Bourgas. He majored in law at Sofia University in 1954.

He began his literary career in 1955, when his first short story was published in the *Vecherni Novini* newspaper. Later he contributed short stories, essays, and novelettes to the daily press and literary periodicals: the dailies *Rabotnichesko Delo* and *Narodna Mladesh*, the *Septemvri* and *Plamuk* magazines.

He is the author of several prose works: *A Wolf's Dreams*, a novelette (1961); *Spring Juice*, short stories (1963); *The Sky over the Veleka, An Angry Journey*, novelettes (1965).

Spring Juice

My friend Georgi had told the bus driver beforehand to let me off at the calfshed, which was more than one kilometer away from the bus stop. The village houses were so scattered that even, as he put it, "If you were to beat the wedding drum, or toll the death bell, nobody would hear anything."

Georgi had come out to meet me. He shook my hand firmly and waved to the driver. The bus ground on, and the two of us were left on the hay-strewn asphalt road.

Several village boys stood across the ditch with snowballs in their red hands. Their ruddy cheeks and the trampled snow bore evidence of an interrupted fight.

"Let's go," Georgi urged and slipped a shining pair of pruning shears into his pocket. "We promised we'd be the ones to take care of the garden round the calfshed. It's noon right now, and the next shift has arrived."

We set out along a well-beaten path through a large orchard. The black boughs of the trees had been pruned; here and there the trunks showed white under the peeling old bark, which now on the threshold of spring the trees did not need any more. The bark was drying and a tart tang lingered in the air. A white-breasted bird with a long tail alighted in an apple tree. It pecked at its feathers, then looked at us inquiringly, and flew off. The path was almost dry, but the soil was crumbling in places and Georgi looked critically at my shoes.

We descended toward a creek, across which the house of my host could be seen. A patter of steps along the path was heard, and one of the boys caught up with us.

"Uncle Georgi," he said, as he waded into the snow, keeping his eyes fixed on me, "I'll come along to your garden to cut a willow stick for a bow."

"It's not the stick you're after, I think, but it's all right!" Georgi said, looking at me.

The boy was freckled; a lot of freckles were sprinkled in particular around his nose and eyes, and a smile seemed always to be hovering on his clearly outlined, full-blooded lips. Two tiny silk brooms dangled from the star on his fur cap—a white one and a red one. This badge of spring would probably stay there throughout the whole season.

The boy walked on the snow and the black swollen earth and kept scrutinizing me. But when we approached the creek he ran up in front of us and crossed over to the other bank on a thick willow bole, which served as a bridge. He remained there, to watch the way we would pass.

A dog started yelping behind the high wall of the yard. Georgi opened the gate and we entered. A grayish-brown wolf-hound pup sat on a rickety wooden table under a little shed by the gate. When the dog saw us it barked again, wagging its tail uncertainly, and jumped down clumsily. The dog whined for a while at its master's feet, sniffing at me, too, and rose, placing its front paws against the boy's chest. The boy stroked its ears, then he started running about the yard and the pup after him.

"It's a wolfhound. When it grows up they'll stiffen," Georgi said, referring to the pup's ears, which were flopping to all sides.

With a yelp it caught up with the boy and jumped against his chest again. Then the boy flung a thin stick. The pup retrieved it, but when the boy tried to snatch it up the pup leaped aside looking at him roguishly, and scrambled ahead. They went romping about for some time, engrossed in their play, until they tired. The boy started for the willow trees. The pup followed him, still leaping around his feet or attacking some imaginary enemies in the dry grass under the fruit trees.

The white rustic room was somewhat untidy, but the kitchen range radiated warmth. On the open oven door there was a dish with a fat roasted hen in it.

"Make yourself at home," my host said and began bustling about. "My wife is staying with her sister in town for a few days. The working season is drawing near and she'll have no time later on. We'll knock up a meal with what we find."

Soon the room was in order and my host laid the table, which was covered with a white oilcloth: the hen, a lump of cheese as thick as a brick, boiled eggs, red peppers pickled in oil and vinegar and kept in a jar, paprika and tomatoes in brine, and sauerkraut. Broth of giblets and dried paprika was warming in a big green pot, the kind used at village weddings.

He poured brandy into a coffee pot and put it on the range. The room filled with the aroma of apples.

"Hey," Georgi shouted from the window to the boy. "Come on in."

"I'll go on home," he answered hesitantly.

"Come on, we'll go hunting afterwards."

That settled the boy's hesitation, and he came in carrying the sticks. The pup squatted down in the yard opposite the window. Georgi took out some food for it and came back. He turned on the radio and while drying his hands on a towel, he asked: "Do you need anything else?"

"No, nothing."

"I wanted to treat you to some stewed rabbit, but I couldn't get out these days," he said as he sat down at the table. "We'll go over to Gloginina Spring as soon as we're ready. You'll have a chance to see our land, and we might perhaps shoot something. The rabbits are a bit dazed in early spring."

We finished eating and Georgi sent out the boy to bring in the sheep, while he himself set about making a bow. The boy showed up after awhile among the apple trees, driving four sheep with lambs before him. He carried the smallest one in his arms, while the mother tripped obediently after him holding her head low.

"Seems to me that one is bloated," the boy said, pointing at one of the sheep, as he put the lamb down on the ground.

Georgi caught it and felt the belly. "It's nothing. Let's be off."

The pup started whining and followed us. Georgi looked at the pup, then at the boy, and taking up a little chain with a collar he said: "All right, I see you don't want to stay behind."

The pup yelped with joy and scrambled out. It tumbled about, stuck its muzzle into the snow, then it sneezed and began jumping about its master, trying to lick his hand.

"We'll strike off up the Virbinka," Georgi went on after some reflection. "We'll have to wade in mud otherwise, until we reach the wood."

Virbinka was the name of the creek. It flowed between old willows, and this beautiful and poetic name fitted it very well indeed. The peasants had cut off the boughs of the willow trees and now long slender sticks were growing out of the thick trunks. They would cut them again, and the sticks would grow anew on top of the gray hollows, in which not a spark of life seemed to have remained. But the river would revive these hollows, because it liked to chat with them and contemplate their tender leaves in its mirror-like surface—until the gray fall, when the leaves would start falling and the water would begin to carry them away like little barks of gold.

The young saplings gleamed, now bright green, now auburn, and the bursting buds showed their fluffy points.

"The spring juice is already flowing," Georgi said.

The creek ran foaming, swollen by the melting snow. But its force was already spent, and now the water that lapped its bed was bluish-gray, as if the freshly peeled bark of a tree had been immersed in it.

The banks were green with the constant moisture and water squirted from under our feet. The boy and the pup kept running and gamboling on this soft carpet, skipping over the creek in the places where it was narrow enough. Georgi watched their play indulgently.

The creek took us higher and higher up. Successive waves of long gray clouds arranged in a pattern of stairs drifted in the sky. The snow in the balk furrows of the slanting plain before us looked like stairs, too, and I had a feeling that we were climbing some endless staircase. The earth stretched out streaked with snow, bloated with water, and in the black sections the tiny needles of the winter crops showed timidly green.

The fields and the orchard ended, and taking leave of the creek we set foot on firm ground. Far ahead a gray-looking sunny meadow spread out near a young wood. To the left a large sheep flock nibbled at last summer's dry grass. A huge shaggy mastiff bounced out of the flock and reached us in several bounds. The pup ran up to meet it and they stood facing each other, wagging their tails. The mastiff approached, sniffed the air, and stretched out its large paw. The pup was waiting for just that, and it jumped on top the big dog and they began scuffling. The mastiff rolled over on its back, while the pup kept hopping on it and biting it, until it realized that we had moved off. It gave a short bark and ran off, to join us, its ears flopping.

When we started through the wood the overcast sky opened a slit to the west, and the sun shone brightly through the narrow blue opening. It was as if the earth felt some sudden relief, and the remains of the snow began to glitter. A yellowhammer chirped unexpectedly in the thicket, at first timorously, but then ever more loudly and confidently.

We started cautiously through the wood, which opened into glades and bare thickets here and there. By Georgi's order the boy had tied the pup, which now walked alongside obediently but discontentedly. The wood became quite sparse, and we met only clusters of low shrubs and hawthorns with black little pellets on their branches. There was a smell of drying foliage and also of something light and barely perceptible, coming from the melting snow.

Georgi stopped abruptly before a shrub and made a sign with his hand without turning back, and I all but bumped into his broad back. The boy instantly slipped between the two of us and craned his thin neck forward.

By a nearby hawthorn shrub under which a small patch of snow showed white, there was a little rabbit. It was young and inexperienced and sat on its hind legs facing the bright spring sun, rubbing its eyes, as if the rays were blinding it. Then it bent down and nibbled at something. It listened attentively and rose again, facing the sun. It seemed as if the little rabbit could not have its fill of watching this bright marvel, which laughed from its blue window and warmed it. The rabbit had forgotten the sun during the long cold winter, when it trembled with fear and cold in the thorny bushes, frightened by the icy animosity of the surrounding world. And see, now this world had suddenly become warm and friendly.

The blue eyes of the boy were wide open, and all the freckles in his face were laughing. Nothing could tear him away from this rare sight—nor us, two grown, rough men, for that matter. Out of the corner of his eyes he saw the black barrel of the gun, which Georgi held pointing down. He touched the barrel and whispered imploringly: "Uncle Georgi, let me watch it a little."

The little rabbit was hopping about, rubbing its nose with its little paws, and chewing. A tiny bird flitted by, and the rabbit gave a start and huddled motionless on the ground. Yet on not seeing any danger, it rose and started hopping about anew.

The boy watched, gripping the chain of the pup. Georgi turned to me and pointed at them with his eyes. The pup did not budge, but it was obviously tense and timid. This small wolfhound, whose ears were yet to stiffen, who would become predatory and fierce, was puzzled by this gray furry thing, which was hopping and tumbling about on the grass. We stood by, too, like the pup and the little boy. We were children like them, like the spring, which was stripping its garments of snow, taking off its baby dress.

Then the pup stirred impatiently and whined.

Sitting there as it was on its hind legs, the little rabbit made a somersault of surprise, then it jumped up and darted away, its ears low on its back.

"It's off!" the boy shouted in a high and frightened voice. Everything in him was aglow; the freckles, his blue eyes, and the motley pullover under the crossed suspenders.

"I couldn't hit it, anyway, it was too far," Georgi said.

"Come on, it wasn't far! Didn't I see its whiskers, they were that long!" the boy showed by spreading his arms.

We moved on through the wood, but we had already forgotten all caution. The boy unchained the pup, and it began to run in and out of the thorn shrubs, digging up last summer's dry leaves in the sunny places while sniffing loudly at the transparent air.

In a little dale Gloginina Spring poured forth a thick grayish spurt of water. About a score of big-uddered cows were lapping noisily at the two troughs, while a man, leaning on a staff, kept shouting at them. He noticed the gun, looked us over and said: "No kill?"

"We didn't try, really," Georgi replied. "We'd gone out for a stroll and I took the gun along just in case. I haven't been carrying it for quite a long time."

The boy was about to say something, but got hold of the spout instead and stooped down to drink. Limpid drops of water started running down his chin.

"I, too, took them out for awhile in the fresh air," the man said pointing at the cows. "They're pretty old, but they romped like calves. They feel the spring."

There were mud stains on the foreheads of some of the cows.

Toward dusk we started back for the village. The boy did not stop commenting on the encounter with the little rabbit, adding more and more details. The tired pup trotted after him obediently.

The blue streak to the west was growing wider, and everything around gleamed bright. Golden light poured down lavishly from the setting sun like so much gold dust.

Translated by ANDREI DANCHEV

The Woman Who Walked About the Sky

The sun stole in through the narrow little window of the chapel in the evening. It drew the images of Saints Constantine and Helena out of the half-light. The kindly eyes of the saints saw nothing—the soft radiance only meant the end of the day.

Nouna, the *Nestinarka,* was unaware of the only moment in which the setting sun entered the dark chapel. She lay face downward, quite exhausted, in front of the iconostasis. The float light was burning, but the saints did not look at the woman in black in its light, for it had tired them. The woman did not see them, either. She was remembering the previous night, when the elder had left the chapel and locked the door, and she was seeing other things.

The fire-dancer was unable to rid her mind at once of the dry rattle of the key in the lock. It reminded her of the people outside, of the warmth of the spring day, of the breeze that swayed the treetops. The feverish whisper of her prayer rose to the rafters, dark with age, filling every corner, but it could not stifle that sharp sound, or wipe out the visions that crowded before her closed eyes. She thrust her fingers under her black kerchief, seized her white hair, and struck her forehead on the stone slab in front of the iconostasis. The chapel was filled with sound, the float light went out, and she sank into a black and soundless wilderness.

In its immeasurable distance a faint light was lit, which set out toward Nouna. As it drew nearer it grew stronger and stronger, and she saw the sun quite near, and in it the images of Constantine and Helena. The saints smiled kindly on her, then the sun flew to pieces, which melted into the black wilderness. Only the two images were left. They grew and seemed to flow over, and their radiance replaced the sun, which had gone out, filling every corner in the white walls of the chapel, which was as small as a tomb. Wonderful music echoed in Nouna's soul, and it was like the cry of a newborn babe, like the cries of a thousand newborn babes, like the cry of mankind, being born. The music echoed in the white tomb, coming in waves from the womb of the earth and from the abyss of the sky, and Nouna, listening to it, no longer saw or remembered anything.

Again the dry rattle of the key in the lock was heard, and the music stopped as if the string from which it came had broken. Nouna bent her head still lower, whispered her prayer more feverishly, and the music rang out again. The door was opened, and a rectangle of evening light fell at the end of the white tomb.

The elder's steps echoed softly in the chapel. He stood over Nouna and touched her shoulder.

"It is time," he said.

She felt the touch, but was listening to the music and had not the strength to rise.

"It is time," the elder repeated.

Nouna rose to her knees. She crossed her hands over her flat breasts and fixed her eyes on the images of Constantine and Helena, which shone like the sun.

It seemed to her that she saw the image of her father, of her grandfather and of all the others of her family whom she did not know, and who, standing one beside the other, grew more and more blurred the farther away they were. They looked at her gently, smiling, like a child of theirs, like their flesh and blood. She tore her eyes from the icon; the images set out before her, and she followed them, listening to the music.

The elder called to the door: "Kostadincho!"

A boy in a clean white shirt ran into the chapel. After kissing the icon, he took it and stood before Nouna. The boy fixed his empty gaze on the mud floor; his lower lip, thick and moist, hung loosely, and a tiny clear drop gathered on his chin.

Nouna placed her hand on the boy's matted hair, then pushed him toward the chapel door. She followed him and drew herself up to her full height.

She looked around the sky. It was already growing dark, and

she felt the warm wind, which was borne under its vault, and dropped over the listening forest, whispering about something with it. Birds were flying under the sky, and soft music was heard from the wind and their wings. It mingled with the music of the chapel, but this only lasted a moment, because it was different, and could not really blend with it. The wind frolicked, and the birds flew about, and the song of the forest rose to their musk—the song of the green grass and of the flowers, the song of the spring waters. The solemn harmonies of the mighty symphony rose from the earth and the heavens and flooded everything with their sound.

Nouna now listened only to this music; everything else disappeared. People crowded the meadow in front of the chapel. They were her children. Standing there, motionless, men in reddish quilted jackets and fur caps gazed at her; old women dressed in black, their headkerchiefs pulled well over their eyes; young women with snow-white kerchiefs and gaily embroidered smocks, holding babies in their arms; bareheaded girls and boys, who were silent, their eyes fixed on the chapel.

They were quite a large crowd, but for Nouna they were just an insignificant living mass under the high blue sky of the Strandja Mountains.

This throng of people lived on poor land, fighting it tooth and nail to scratch out their bread. But even the poorest have their holidays, and their forebears had bequeathed to them the day of Constantine and Helena at the end of spring. On that day, their bodies rested, and in their primitive souls the belief took root that the days ahead would be better. The icon had little to say to these people who never went to church. But they looked at Nouna and believed in her. She worked in the fields with them, suffered with them, and had borne children like them. And on that day alone, when, more eagerly than ever, their souls sought support, they found it in her, because she was the strongest of them all. In this lean woman, who can hardly have remembered that she was a woman, there lived a hardy and insubmissive human spirit, of which life is born and all the heights men ever reach along their way.

Nouna stood with her arms before her, barefooted, with cracked and roughened soles, as hard as hoofs. She was stern. She looked at her children, and the vision of those unknown people whom she had never seen, whose daughter she was, crowded her eyes, and the solemn music of life and of human love echoed in her soul.

The elder never took his eyes off her, as he stood beside the boy with the icon. He was an elder, but he waited for an order. Nouna nodded to him.

The crowd swayed and stirred. The bagpipe struck up, and its shrill notes were broken by the beats of the big drum.

Nouna set out after the boy with the icon. Stern and silent, the crowd made off along the road to the village.

The bagpipe shrilled on, and Nouna, her gaze wandering over the boy's head, listened within herself. All other sounds died away in the dusk of the spring sky, and the shrill tones of the bagpipe were wafted over the crowd, like the cry of a newborn babe, like the cries of a thousand newborn babes, like the cry of mankind, being born to the echoes of thunder. They rent and tore the clouds and water issued from them, and spring rivers murmured over the earth. Then abysses gaped from which fire blazed. The water put it out, and in the burning steam the white swords of lightning crossed, and there was fire again, and water. When the fire in the abyss went out, the water withdrew into the narrow beds, and sang, quite calm again. It was strange, but the water sang.

Nouna listened to the song of the water and saw the grass sprouting, the trees putting out leaves, the streams foaming over boulders and weirs. She was seized by an unearthly lightness which she had experienced only once in her life: when she had given birth to the first of her nine children. It was spring then, as it was today. The young mother had dropped down on the hard earth and had seemed to fly high up toward the sun, not feeling the weight of her body—an endless emptiness, in which the first cry of a newly born man brought her back to feeling.

The world seemed reborn then. Birds flew in couples under the bright sky, and a quiet love song came to her ears from the forest. Time had been unable to efface from her memory those distant days in which Nouna had born her first son. She saw him as a little boy, when he had gone to pick periwinkles for the school holiday. The bushes with long green leaves were covered with pale pink blossoms. As they were breaking the tender branches they suddenly heard a crash, and a stag flew past them, breaking the periwinkle with its strong horns. The child was not even frightened. He merely dropped the branches in surprise, and Nouna seized him in her arms. And that long winter with the deep snow, when she and her husband were returning with the child from a neighboring village. Her husband feared nothing when his ax hung from his arm. The night was white and warm, but the snow wasn't melting. They went down into a small valley, quite near their own village and suddenly stopped dead in their tracks: black figures were jumping around a big beech tree, and they heard growling. With his back to the thick trunk, a huge black boar was fiercely fighting a pack of wolves.

Her husband took the ax from his arm, put Nouna and the child behind him, and the three took cover behind the nearest tree. The furious animals did not sense them. A white whirlwind eddied around the beech tree; the boar seemed to have grown into the earth; he snorted and turned his bristly head this way and that; but from time to time he squealed loudly and piercingly; his long, sharp tusks flashed among the bristles.

Nouna's husband gripped his ax firmly and stepped forward when the ice in the valley cracked beneath the herd which had come to the boar's aid. Dark pelts showed up against the snow, squeals and howls were heard, and the wolves scattered. The herd grunted around the boar for awhile, and he led them up the glen. They set off, too. The snow was steeped with blood. From the forest, to which the wolves had fled, came a long, sad howl that broke off suddenly as if something had torn it.

"It's over," her husband said. "The boar wounded him badly, and now the others are going to eat him up."

He tucked the child under his warm hooded shepherd's cape. That was long ago, his firstborn was already an old man, but spring is spring, and the brooks in which the torn sky is mirrored flow along, drawing wonderful music from the stones.

Nouna was listening to that music. It blended with the shrill tones of the bagpipe and fitted the whole world, piercing the fire-dancer's soul and every cell of her old body, filling it with strength, so that Nouna's bare rough feet did not feel the stones and pebbles on the road, and quivered to the roll of the drum, seeking for the rhythm in the shrilling of the bagpipes. Her fingers thrust into her waistband, her lips firmly pressed together. Nouna walked along, trembling, never taking her eyes from the dark sky above the boy's head.

The crowd entered the village along a narrow street, scarred by torrents. The footsteps of the people behind her made their way into Nouna's consciousness. The low houses with big, low-hanging eaves echoed every sound that struck their oak walls. The footsteps whispered in Nouna's mind, and she saw the fathers, grandfathers and most distant forebears of these people, of her children, crawling like ants along this endless road, being born and dying, in happiness and pain. The windowpanes behind the old wooden gratings moaned at the rolling of the drum, and it seemed to Nouna that the sky was moaning, stretched out above her. No, it wasn't moaning, it was thundering rather, and the woman's body absorbed it, quivering to it, so that she could not control her hands, thrust into her waistband, and her feet which stumbled along the uneven road; a lament, a moan, a cry was rising in her throat, which was to open the floodgates of all that had gathered in her body and in her soul since the birth of the first living cell.

The pyre had burnt down on the crooked little village square, and its embers cast a vivid glow around it. The windows of the surrounding houses were ablaze. The villagers formed a living ring around the fire.

Only the boy with the icon stood before Nouna now. The tones of the bagpipe grew shriller and faster, and the old woman hurried around the fire after the boy, trembling and panting. She circled it once, twice, three times. Her hands and feet shook unrestrainedly, her throat contracted and relaxed several times, and suddenly she raised her head to the black, starry sky and a half-smothered cry was torn from her breast: "V-v-v-uh! V-v-uh!"

A black wall swayed before her, and a whisper rose over the square: "The icon! The icon!"

The elder made a dash for the boy, took the icon, wrapped it in a white scarf, and handed it to Nouna. She seized it in both hands and held it close to her breast.

The elder drew the boy aside and stood beside him in the first row.

"V-v-uh!" the cry, strong and sharp now, was torn again from Nouna's breast.

It drowned the shrill tones of the bagpipe, and she heard it no more. She danced in a small semicircle about the fire and stepped on to it. Her bare feet plowed through the thick layer of embers, and a shower of sparks rose from it. Nouna suddenly felt that this was not fire, but the fiery disk of the sun. It began to rise smoothly and bore her up above the low houses, over the dark summits of the mountains, high up toward the starry sky. The sun was shining, and under her feet everything grew radiant; she saw the crowd of villagers with shining faces that seemed to be cast of metal; the windows of the houses were no longer ablaze, because it was broad daylight down below, the brightest day of all her life; she saw the old houses, the little fields over which she had bent her back since childhood, the periwinkle bushes, and the shining bands of the brooks in spring. Everything was down there, beneath her feet, fertilized by her hand,

and watered by her sweat and that of her children. The land and the forest and the water submitted to her will because she was a human being and her children were men. And if weariness crushed their bodies, they still lived and struggled, because weariness could not crush their will to be men.

Nouna closed her eyes and the sun went out. She felt nothing because she was not treading over the embers but was walking over the black sky and stirring up the starry embers with her feet. She crossed the sky from end to end. Convulsively she clutched the wooden icon to her lean breasts, but the images painted on it vanished from her consciousness and she could no longer see them. The faces of her children stood living before her, surrounding the fire, gazing at the stars, which flew from under her feet, and listening intently to the shrill tones of the bagpipe and the roll of the heavenly drum. The more she danced over the fire, the rarer the tremors which shook her body grew; the noose around her neck was loosened; her sharp cries gradually turned into low moans. The springs which moved her hands and feet, which kept every muscle of her old body tense, seemed to break quite suddenly, and Nouna felt completely exhausted.

She staggered once, twice, reached the edge of the circle of fire, and fell into the arms of two men. A second before, she had dropped the icon onto the embers and her white smock had caught fire, but she had no strength left to think about it. One last shrill note of the bagpipe reached her consciousness. But no, it was not the bagpipe, but the cry of a newborn babe, who had drawn its first breath in this world. The cry with which all those who had come before her had come into the world, and all those who would come after her to triumph over every being that stood in their way, because they were men.

Translated by MARGUERITE ALEXIEVA

Boris Aprilov
(1921–   )

Boris Aprilov was born in 1921 in the Black Sea port of Bourgas. He began writing when he was a senior at secondary school and has had his works published in the local daily *Bourgaski Far*. In 1946 he went to live in Sofia, where he published the following collections of humorous stories and feuilletons: *Worries* (1953); *The Cheek of It* (1955); *Knock Out* (1959); and *Pirate Romance* (1967). In 1958 his comedy *The King Goes to War* was produced at the State Satire Theater in Sofia. He has also written two humorous novels for children: *Lisko's Adventures* and *Lisko's Adventures on Sea*.

The theme of the sea recurs in Boris Aprilov's recent works: *The Sea Belongs to All* (1963); *The Touch* (1966); and *Autumn Dunes* (1968).

Blue

You can't know anything about such a hopeless state. You probably know what it is to be hopelessly in love with a woman, or to wait for someone fatally ill to come home, or to be up to your neck in slander; but to wait hopelessly for two whole months on a desert shore by a fishless sea, with the rain pelting you and winds bursting the veins of your eyes—that's a hopeless state you can't know anything about. It's tragic because whether you are lying in the tent or on the ground one and the same thought is at the top of your mind: somewhere in that miserable water there are fish, and if those damned fish were to get caught in the net, then thirteen families would smile, thirteen people would know why they had been stuck in the desert.

I was with them every day. They hated me. Every time they

100

pulled out an empty net and shoved it in the sea and then pulled it out empty again, they hated me the more. At one point they began to rub it in. "Hey, look, Mr. 'Bad-luck,' look, we lower the net and then we pull it out and there's only the net! Look—what an empty net!"

"I see," I said to myself, "but why rub it into me, rub it into yourselves; twiddle your thumbs, you scoundrels, since you've chosen the worst spot to fish!" They were an uncommonly nasty bunch, and I hated them from the bottom of my soul. They didn't want to see me around because they regarded me as "Mr. Bad-luck." They were loathsome and narrow-minded fatalists, and they were bad craftsmen, not worth their hire. To them I was a spectacled Mr. Bad-luck in a jacket, with a transistor radio set in my hands, come to bring them bad luck. Even if I had had no glasses, even if I had had no transistor, they would have hated me all the same. The fools didn't know what to hate! At night I banged furiously at my type-writer. I knew that the fishermen could hear me. I wanted them to hear me. I wanted them to think that I was getting on well with my work. Well, I wasn't! I banged at the keys because I hated them. I hated everything, even the reed cabin I lived in. Let the clatter of the typewriter exasperate them—for the first time in my life I hated a whole group of people.

Maybe they intended to beat me up. Fine! I'd decided to accept the challenge. A couple of hooligans, notorious in the town on the big bay, worked in the brigade. Both of them had spent a year in prison, and I started carrying a knife in my pocket. I kept going to the shore where I watched them spread the seine to dry; and when they pulled it out I was there too, at a distance of ten meters, always warmly dressed, with a full stomach and a cool expression on my face.

"You're getting on their nerves," one of the amateur fisher-men warned me.

"How?" I wanted to know.

"Don't hang around."

"I can't help it that they're good for nothing!"

The man who wanted to protect me from something shrugged his shoulders and left me.

It was an unusually bad autumn, but one day the weather cleared to such an extent that it amazed me.

I continued to hang around the fishermen. I didn't do it out of thickheadedness. Please understand—if I went away and they filled the net, I'd be done for. It would get around and I would be stamped as "a man who chased luck away." Then nobody could help me.

To watch them, I sat at the foot of a large sand dune that protected me from the wind. Whenever I gazed at the horizon I thought I saw the curve of the planet. The sea had recovered its tender soul, the wind swept lovingly over it, and the sky rose high— I expected it to open up at any moment and show its notorious secrets at last.

The good weather shattered my adversaries. Demoralization crept up on the brigade: there was drinking, fighting, and malingering; and there was a terrific row with the barman who refused to sell them drinks. In spite of that, they got hold of some brandy. Two of the men, not giving a damn anymore, got some gasoline and started a wholesale bombardment of the waters. The others began to envy them. Under their pressure the captain refused to give the boat to the poachers, and that gave rise to a free-for-all. It never came out who was against whom. Next day I noticed that all of them were black and blue.

Even now, when I look back on it, I wonder how it happened that I didn't get beaten up in the confusion. They didn't even set fire to my cabin. Maybe they were too busy with each other. Somebody did take a punch at me, though. And who do you think it was?—the cook. It was past midnight. I was walking along the path when I stumbled and fell over a body. Whoever it was rose, crawled over to me and looked me over.

"Oh, so it's you!"

I felt his fist hit my mouth. It was a signal for all the devils to wake within me. All my secret hatred flew into the muscles of my hands. I couldn't strike, but I managed to grip my fingers tight around my attacker's dirty neck. My strength doubled when I realized it was the cook. He had taken me by surprise with his quickness, but now he was down next to me and didn't move. I was no gentleman. As soon as I got up I started kicking him furiously. Then I went off to the sea. I waded in, scooped up some water, and bathed my bleeding mouth.

"Look at him, standing in the sea and gargling!" someone said. There was no need for me to turn around. It was the two jailbirds.

More and more fishermen appeared. They stood on top of the sand dune forming an outline against the clear, starry sky. They arrived one by one and stood in a row till they were all there except for the captain and the cook. The constellation of Orion hung low above their heads and I (strong in my irony) for a moment thought what a beautiful creation man is, born to conquer the deep and to stretch up to the stars. I had been drinking Scotch at the town bar, not the contemptible grape brandy of the fisherman, fit only to rouse their lowest instincts.

"Hey, you writing man," somebody shouted, "who gave you the beauty treatment?"

"You haven't got a cook any more!" I shouted. "You had one, but now you have no one to cook for you because I strangled him!"

"He cooked slops!" another gave his loud approval. "Good for him!"

"You don't know how to work the sea!" I shouted, though I could not see their faces (the sheen of Orion was more brilliant than their thick, musty, clay mugs). "You're bad fishermen."

The row on the sand dune stood still. I had no idea what they'd decide to do. One thing I knew: they couldn't reach me, try as they might. I was a better swimmer than any of them. With an imperceptible motion I unfastened my watch, dropped it, and covered it up in the sand with the tip of my shoe. Apparently they hated me a lot, since they had come for a final settling of scores.

"He's crazy!" someone said.

"You can say that again," affirmed another. "What can you expect of a person who leaves Sofia and comes here to live in a cabin!"

People who are going to attack you don't talk that way. Then it dawned on me that I was very drunk and that only a man full of Scotch whisky can get into such a foolish position. The fishermen hadn't come to beat me up, they had come to cast the net.

"You're good for nothing!" I shouted, not knowing why I had to say it.

"Do I beat him up?" asked one of the former prisoners.

"Let it go till morning."

The captain shouted up from the boats. The fishermen started off in that direction, laughing. I dug up my watch, blew on the crystal several times, and shoved it in my pocket. I couldn't see the fishermen any more; only their voices reached me—some instructions from the captain and the splash of oars. There was a cool western breeze, the usual land breeze which always died down at dawn.

You don't know how I hate writing about fights. I hate books about the sea and fighting because the two are often connected. But such were the facts with those loathsome scoundrels. What was I to do? Should I run away? No, I had to stay. Even if they beat me black and blue. In my drunken head I decided to fight the next day

till I fell. It's funny, but that night I breathed free and happy and felt
like swimming and singing. The sea slept at my feet, bodyless and
transparent as the air. The water and the air had blended into a single
soft substance, and any moment fish would be swimming beyond the
veil of it; the stars were like millions of bubbles—the oxygen of the
universe. On such a beautiful and incorporeal night all creatures
must be good, they mustn't fight, they mustn't swear, they mustn't
threaten. I sat down on the sand and thought of man. Not in an
abstract way as you would suppose. Now, in this tender mood, I
could even think of the cook, and the two hooligans, and the whole
brigade as men. This concession that I made in the name of good
saddened me. These fishermen were inhabitants of the raggedy quarters of mankind, vile and loathsome scoundrels! . . . It's funny, but
you don't get a headache from whisky! . . . They wanted to destroy me because they hated not only me, but everyone who was
better spoken and wore a jacket.

The captain's boat disappeared in the dark blue void. Now I
could see only the outlines of those still on the beach. They were
holding the right end of the seine. The boat had to go far out, to
close off a large area of the sea and then come back to the beach.
There should be fish in that great horseshoe of net, ropes, and cork.
But there wasn't going to be any. When luck is bad, it's bad. I don't
think there is a more magic rhythm than the splashing of oars in the
stillness of the night. This rhythm is sweetest and most lulling when
the nets are being cast.

At last the boat reappeared. It emerged from the space directly opposite me, with a whisper of oars, a muffled roll of the sides,
and a quiet hissing of ropes. In vain I waited for it to touch the
shore. Something held it back.

High above, the constellations made their gigantic chesslike
moves. I was in a hurry to take their coordinates as to the North
Star—a favorite occupation of mine. A small comet scratched the
sky and went out high above the North Star; below it another comet
died away, and when I linked the three points, I got an amazingly
straight line, whose extension passed through the bow of the boat. I
tried to read some omen in this, but what? I had no time to think.
There was rising excitement among the fishermen. They began talking loudly in wild and excited voices.

"Let's get to shore first!"

"Captain, let's loosen the rope!"

"Shut up!" shouted the captain.

"Now there is silence for you!" In all probability the captain was making a decision.

"Make for the shore!" he snapped at last. "Loosen the rope!"

The rope hissed sharply. Now I could see hands freeing the rope, and I heard it whine when it touched the side of the boat. The bow touched the sand. Several pairs of boots went into the water. The fishermen skillfully pulled the boat out and grabbed the rope. Then all took hold of it. Someone swore and announced that the net wouldn't budge, but the rest had already felt the pull.

"That does it!"

"Quiet!" shouted the captain.

"It must have got caught somewhere."

"Shut up!"

The men at the other end of the net, who had stayed ashore, were also excited. The captain made for them. Midway he stopped and lighted a cigarette. I anticipated the worst. Jammed the way it was, the fools were going to tear the net and the most shameful finish was in store for them. A fit reward for a couple of months' despair. The captain vented his ire on the other group and then came back to us again. Holding on to the rope, his people dug their feet in the sand.

"We've rounded up about a hundred mines!" said someone jokingly.

"There aren't any mines here," answered the captain, not catching on to the joke.

"That's the end of the net," remarked another. He swore, and I'd like to tell you how, but since swearing is forbidden in literature I won't.

I thought that the most discouraged of them were ready to drop everything and beat it. That night the fate of the brigade, which would inevitably fall apart, was being decided. To tell you the truth, I sobered up. I started wondering whether I should get away before the tragedy or stay to the end! It was clear what was happening. My hardheartedness melted away. I was sorry for my enemies. Wasn't I, too, like them, a man with cares and thousands of troubles on my head? The effect of the whisky wore away. There was a sour taste in my mouth, and I felt like crying. Now they could beat me up like a dog, they could crush me in their fury, that wasn't the worst; I was tormented by the thought that I had brought bad luck to people. I recalled other, similar occasions. I ruthlessly picked them out of my past, like a sadist, and I felt sadder.

Is it enough to despise yourself at such a moment? There was something worse; what can bring more despair than to be the man who bears bad luck; the man who spreads it the way some do joy and optimism. . . . The sea and the sky darkened, the bright spots in life dimmed, the rotten life that people like the fishermen and I lived.

A loud silver wave rose on the quiet, shallow water; it slid toward the shore and splashed along the dead sand.

"Fish!" cried one of the former prisoners.

"Fish!" affirmed another.

I ran up and waded into the water. The second wave of the bubbling sea hit my ankles. Several fish were tossing on the sand strip. I stopped and picked up one of them.

"Fish!" I waved it over my head. "Fish!"

The shallow water bubbled. Hundreds of fish tossed about in it. For a moment I felt that I was standing in the rapids of a river and that the fish counted not in hundreds, but in thousands, and that all of the space closed off by the net was in motion.

Instinctively I sought a free space at the rope; my palms touched wet hands, the hands of the others. I felt the captain's breathing in my ear, very close, in my very ear, as if he meant to bite it off. His breath smelled of beer and garlic. The panic-stricken shoals of fish plunged to the deeps, and the surface of the sea settled. The net slowly approached us with the speed of clock hands. We spread out, climbing the sand dune; there was room for everybody at the rope. We longed for a bit of solid earth beneath our feet! We had the feeling that we were hauling in the whole of the earth, with the skyscrapers, the Cheops Pyramid, and Chomolumgma. There was a slight hue of pink in the sky; the sun was being born below the horizon, and the nearby stars were dissolving in its rays of light. I let go of the rope and set off for the tents of the independent fishermen. I staggered but kept on and bumped into the cook once again.

"It's hard pulling," I told him.

"What?" he said, holding his neck where I had gripped it.

"Lots of fish!" I added.

"Where?"

"In our net."

"Whose net?"

"Your net."

He hurried off toward the brigade. I turned to tell him that I was going to fetch more people, but the cook had vanished.

Nobody wanted to come. Everyone wanted to sleep; they

needed strength for the morrow. Only one came with me, a strong young fellow with a handsome, manly face. Several times I stopped to wait for him to catch up. He had no idea what was up, nor where he was going. I think he was still asleep; maybe thought that he was dreaming a beautiful dream about plenty of fish. When we neared the seine, the man woke up and said:

"What's this, where are you taking me?"

"To help a little," I said.

"Help who?"

"The fishermen."

He swore at me and turned back.

The ends of the seine were already on the sand. The fish were one next to the other and tangled up in the net. The gills and tails that had given them life and motion had now trapped and killed them. The net was slow in coming out of the sea, the dawn was slow in breaking, the bodies of the fish were slow in reflecting the light, and we were slow in pulling. Occasionally we looked at the frightened shoals that set the water in motion; we wanted to make sure that we weren't dreaming. Why shouldn't I admit it? I was done for. My hands dropped the rope, and my feet wanted to run away. Finally, when I couldn't go on any more, I dropped on the soft sand dune. I felt its coolness and crawled to the dry grass along the edge of the dune. I rested a bit and then made for my cabin. I don't know why, but the first thing I picked up was the transistor radio set. Somewhere to the east mankind was waking up—whole countries were getting up. Simple rhythmical music; men's and women's voices; a piano and morning exercises. I flopped down on the bed and smiled: come and have a go at the net and you won't need setting-up exercises.

I must say that I slept for two or three hours. Later I was sorry about that and am still sorry, because I can't get over the feeling of having missed the best part of a film, the bravest part of a book. The pains in the palms of my hands woke me up. The music for the morning exercises had vanished. Brahms was thundering over the radio. The sun shot in through the small window. I ran out along the path and stood on the sand dune as usual.

The motor of the big boat was throbbing. Its white sides were reflected in the soft water. A white boat took cratefuls to the deck: the hull, the foredeck, and the stern of the big boat were crammed with fish; it sank to the bulwarks.

There were huge piles of mackerel on the sand. The worn-out fishermen were freeing every fish from the net and piling them in the crates; the captain washed the crates in the sea, and then the silvery bodies of the fish gleamed with a rich metallic glow. The independent fishermen helped somewhat but were more quick to put some fish aside for themselves; after all, why not? Far and wide along the shore there were thousands of mackerel. Many peasant women had come to fill their aprons with fish; in return, they handed bottles of brandy to the fishermen (a well-tried trick of the local inhabitants). The fishermen stopped their work to drink but had no strength even for that, collapsing with fatigue and lack of sleep. The women were the only black spots in the landscape. The seagulls, millions of them, were snow white in the sun; their very screams were white; the air was white; and the second big boat that came out of the blue was whiter than all else. The birds dived down and carried away fish; the boats of State Fishing carried away full crates; the women carried away fish; the independent fishermen carried away fish; everyone carried fish away, but the piles of fish got no smaller.

I took hold of the net once again and began to help. A chap with red cheeks and mustaches worked next to me. I looked at him and recognized the barman.

"Did they say how much they've caught?" I asked.

"About fifty tons," answered the barman. "No one has caught so much with a seine."

One had to shout because the seagulls and the mews were screaming in concert. Maybe their screams could be heard up to the skyscrapers, the Cheops Pyramid, and Chomolumgma.

The barman helped conscientiously, but have you any idea how much a barman can put aside for himself? He took some, the peasant women took some, and the seagulls and the State took some; friends and strangers, who came God knows from where, took and took fish.

The faces of the two bullies had slackened with fatigue. You could see how their beards had grown. I looked at them and wondered: why had those two boys been to prison and wasn't it all a miscarriage of justice?

"And you couldn't get any sleep either for all of us."

I turned my head, the captain was speaking to me.

"Go and lie down!" he added. "This won't get finished even by tomorrow."

"The palms of his hands are in ribbons," said one of the hooligans.

"A writer, eh?" shouted someone from the side.

The fishermen laughed, and you can imagine what an effort it was for them to laugh at such a moment. They were all ready to crumble to the ground, and they still had a day and a night of work ahead of them. It's a hard job picking fish out of a net. You have to be deft so as not to tear them. Still, their job was easier than mine. They only had to watch their hands, while I had to watch their hands carefully and take in the whole picture, too. Because it is seldom that one can see a picture of a sky and a sea completely bathed in joy, a magnificent picture set to the music of Brahms. For the first time my radio set was at one with nature. The best part of it all was that the seagulls snatched the fish from the hands of the men; the peasant women, like penguins in their dark native costumes, carried the fish in their aprons; the boats, the barman, friends and strangers —all carried away the fish. At one time I even fancied that the sky made off with some, and the sea, too. There was enough for everybody and plenty left. The controllers of State Fishing had thrown up their hands: How would it ever be possible to collect the whole catch? I also had to look at the horizon, because on this beautiful day you could see very far and if you looked well you could almost see the sharp curve of our planet. The tired-out captain smiled, and the fishermen smiled. And you know how winners smile, don't you?

Translated by ROUMYANA ATANASSOVA

Konstantin Konstantinov

(1890–   )

Konstantin Konstantinov was born on September 2, 1890 in Sliven, where he finished secondary school. He graduated from the Faculty of Law at Sofia University. For twelve years he worked as a judge and for the next twenty-two years as a law consultant for the Co-operative Bank and the Napred Co-operative Centre in Sofia. He began writing in 1908. He has published more than ten books: short stories, a novel, travel notes, memoirs and essays, besides eight books for children. He has translated more than forty books by French, Russian, and Soviet authors, including *Madame Bovary* by Gustave Flaubert, *Til Ulenspiegel* by Charles de Coster, *Charmed Souls* by Romain Rolland, six books by Antoine de Saint-Exupéry, many books by Alphonse Daudet, Emile Zola, *War and Peace* and *Hadji Murat* by Leo Tolstoy, *Fathers and Children* by Ivan Turgenyev, *Short Stories* by Nikolay Gogol, and the *Ninth Bank* by I. Erenburg.

His own works have been translated into Russian, Serbo-Croatian, Greek, Turkish, French, Italian, and other European languages.

He received various literary prizes both before and after September 9, 1944. For one year he was chairman of the Bulgarian Writers' Union. He is now living and working in Sofia.

Day By Day

A young woman was leaning against one of the windows of the Central Hotel and looking outside. A wet October afternoon had closed in on the little town. Until the day before the days had been sunny—the last fine days of autumn—calm, warm, clear. But all unnoticed in the night it had begun to drizzle, and now the hills, the eaves of the houses, and the park at the crossroads were enveloped in what looked like watery dust while a thin layer of black mud glistened on the ground.

Moving slowly along the street there were heavy drays, long oxcarts with their shafts up, speedy cabriolets, ridiculously high and all painted yellow, packhorses with panniers, behind which strode men wearing fur caps. Next day was the fair, the big autumn fair, and all the people from the surrounding villages were streaming to the big square that was used as a fairground, just on the outskirts of the town.

Leaning out of the window on the first floor of the hotel, the young woman was looking with curiosity at the unceasing, noisy stream of traffic below. But she felt the damp air grow chillier and she withdrew from the window for a moment, to wrap a knitted rose-colored shawl round her before she went to lean against the window again. From time to time, a hardly perceptible smile flitted across her face, as she saw some man pass by below and motion to her furtively. Tinka was the chambermaid at the Central Hotel, known to almost everybody in the town. With her short fair hair, big, indolent, roving brown eyes, and the clear white skin of a woman well nourished and brimful of health, she showed up to advantage with the rose-colored shawl in the dark frame of the window. Standing there she looked like one of those big, many-hued pictures that were stuck to the barrel organs.

A muddy old bus, heaped high with cases, sacks, and bundles, stopped with a roar at the other side of the street, near the automobile agency. One after another, the passengers with their clothes all rumpled, got out, took their luggage, and lingered a bit by the bus, confused by the throng of people in the street. Tinka, looking down at them from above, suddenly remembered her arrival in the town two years before. It had been the same kind of rainy day and a policeman had stood by her side. It had been a terrible and shameful moment for her. Then that plain-clothes man from Sofia had found her in the police station. He took her from there and brought her to the hotel where he had evidently fixed the matter up beforehand. In the hotel, they told her that they would engage her as a chambermaid just to please the plain-clothes man. The conditions—board and lodgings free, and, as far as the rest was concerned, she had only to get enough to live on out of it. They looked her over from top to toe with those dull, gloating, clammy eyes, which she already knew from Sofia.

Later, whenever she tried to remember this first hour, she never succeeded. In her memory everything about it was disjointed, mixed up, one thing merging into another, as in a dream. But suddenly, that same evening, as soon as the proprietor of the hotel and after him the plain-clothes man had come to her, her confusion and fear had vanished. She had understood that everything would be more or less all right and, indeed, her life had gone on smoothly after that, without trouble, even pleasantly. Her little single room, near the staircase, was small and dark, but she had it to herself. There was a boy to do the rough work, and she had only to see to the bed linen and to be at the disposal of the guests who came to the hotel. Word about the new chambermaid immediately went round the little town, but she kept a high price on herself and received only a select clientele. The plain-clothes man, who had fixed it up to have her established here and who continued to keep her under his protection and patronage, came to her twice a week. She received him amiably, as a friend, but with a little fear and with the wish to please him. And although he was an ugly young man, quite depraved and with a bad smell in his mouth, she was rather proud that he came to her. After all, he was the only person here with whom she had been acquainted before she had come to the little town, and she knew that her life in the hotel depended on him. Sometimes she rendered him a friendly service by lending him money, and she did not grudge it, or resent having to do it.

"See how well I've fixed you up, Tinka," he would often say. "Listen to me and you won't do the wrong thing."

Tinka made an effort to estimate whether she had really not done the wrong thing. No, of course, she had not. The memory of her life till two years before kept coming into her mind. Her sister's little house near the sugar factory in Sofia, the poverty that got worse every day, the knitwear workshop where six other girls like her worked. All of them had already passed through the hands of the small, fat proprietor of the workshop, and her turn came too. After him, there had been that handsome chauffeur, who used to take her to a cinema, then to a café, and after that to his lodgings. Finally, that house in the center of the town, where one of her girlfriends had taken her on one of their days off. Unknown gentlemen came there and treated them to caviar, vermouth, and cakes, and they paid the girls well. She passed herself off as a pupil in the School of Agriculture, and she was able to dress herself a little better, to wear silk stockings, and to buy chocolates for her sister's little girl. This went on until one evening the place was invaded by plain-clothes men, who took everybody to the police station, detained the girls two days, and then interned them. Then one day her future patron, the plain-clothes man in this little town, saw her in the corridor of the police station and succeeded in establishing her here in the hotel.

All that seemed to her to be very far away now, although she had forgotten nothing. Now she was easy and quiet, for a long time had passed without any trouble, and everything had worked out all right. The plain-clothes man had disappeared a long time since. But she had no longer any need of a patron, she herself knew the town and time passed, one day after the other, each one the same, replete with food, lazy, half-dark like her little room which had only one small window opening onto the corridor. She had already grown up and filled out, and she was a big, beautiful young woman, with a leisurely, voluptuous way of walking, which attracted men. She had even saved some money, but she herself didn't know of what use the money was to her, except to buy clothes with and to send from time to time to her sister. Sometimes, when she was alone at night, a kind of depression would weigh down upon her, and she became sad without understanding why. Once she remembered a colored printed-cotton dress in which she used to go to the knitwear workshop, and she began to weep. The next day this mood had passed and again, day by day, the time began to slip by.

In the corridor the bell rang, brisk steps could be heard, and doors were being opened. This cut short Tinka's thoughts. Guests were coming to the hotel, and Lencheto, her fellow chambermaid, who came over from a neighboring town to the fair, whenever there happened to be more work than usual, was receiving them. Lenche was a funny girl. She always wore a short black dress, well above her knees, and her sinewy legs, which looked like bottles with very narrow necks, were always in black silk stockings. She had a very slender waist and wore ribbons on her big ruffled head with the plucked eyebrows. She looked exactly like a fast-moving insect, with a half-wondering, half-hurt, and, at the same time, whimsical expression on her face. The two of them got on very well together, they did not envy each other and they did not hinder each other. Each one of them had her own parimeter: Tinka received the regular customers and the local people, while Lencheto busied herself with the chance guests and the fair people.

Dusk was falling and the rain kept on drizzling. The little town was completely enveloped in moisture. In the boza shop opposite a light was burning. Tinka got up to shut the window and all at once she smiled playfully. Down the street, at the cigarette kiosk, an elderly, very respectable-looking gentleman was standing and looking up stealthily and making a secret sign. One of the local well-to-do, he was stout and slightly paunchy, with a short mustache, and well dressed. Tinka winked at him and smiled again. That morning she had been at the public baths, and it so happened that his wife had been sitting on the other side of the bathing fountain with their daughter, who was three or four years old, and the wife of the apothecary. Tinka knew both women by sight, but she could never have imagined that without clothes they were so shapeless and ugly. The wife of the apothecary was a dark, scrawny, elderly woman, with wrinkled skin and gray hair that was, however, red at the roots. The other woman was young, fair-skinned, and hairy, with hanging breasts and a sunken abdomen with many folds in it. Only the little child, as fragile and rosy as Farfor china, looked like a wonderful, naked doll. The two ladies had looked at each other before deciding to take the places near Tinka; they had said something in a whisper, looked all round to see whether there was not some other place free, and at last, with dissatisfied, sharp faces, had sat down. All the time while she had been washing herself, they had been casting quick hostile looks at the young woman, who had noticed this and very calmly continued to examine them from top to toe.

She knew their husbands all too well. The one who was now down in the street was always pompous and untalkative, with noisy, lascivious breathing, and banknotes in one pocket of his trousers, and in the other—a key ring with a lot of rattling keys. He was generous and attentive, and she even found him pleasant. The apothecary was bent and bald, with an oily smile and unpleasantly soft, warm hands which had a smell like that in a hospital about them, and which counted out small change like gram weights in his drugstore. She had looked at the women then, remembering how their husbands stole into her room like thieves, and still more stealthily slipped out again. She understood these husbands very well and had suddenly felt proud. What man could like such scarecrows? She had combed her hair back, looked in the mirror at her small, still well-preserved breasts, and smiled to herself. At that moment the child had unexpectedly slipped and would have fallen on the tiles, had not Tinka sprung across and caught her before she fell. Her arms had embraced the delicate, wet, little body and had unconsciously pressed it to her. Suddenly, like a warm wave, a long-forgotten feeling had overwhelmed her. So years before she had felt when she bathed the little daughter of her sister, and now something strange and ununderstandable rose in her breast, which made her want to cry, although she felt no grief.

The women had started in fear and taken the child away from

her quickly, while the mother had said in a dry voice: "Thanks . . ."

After a little while she had turned her head and added with a twisted smile: "You are the young lady from the Central Hotel, aren't you?"

Tinka had nodded: "Yes, madam . . . the chambermaid from the Central."

The other woman had examined her with her eyes and gone on: "What a good skin you have—like a fifteen-year-old girl!" Then, as she turned to the wife of the apothecary, she had added angrily: "There's good reason for the men to like you."

Tinka had stood up and begun pouring water over herself to rinse down before going out. She had tossed her hair back again, standing up straight in front of the two women like a wonderful statue of a beautiful, well-built woman. Now it had been her turn to smile: "It is not because I am young, madam, that men like me. It's something God's given me!" She had stopped speaking and giggled provocatively. "Everyone likes what is beautiful—what can I do about it? No matter whether it's a man or a woman, everybody wants what is beautiful!"

She had rinsed herself once more and clattered away proudly with her clogs as she made her way to the door. She remembered that little happening now, and felt highly amused. She shut the window and went down to the kitchen to have her supper. The people were hustling and bustling in the corridors, carrying their suitcases up the stairs, and in the yard the bells of the barouches and carts were jingling. Someone spoke to her in the darkness: "Hello, Tinka! How are you?"

She peeped into the restaurant through the kitchen window, which was separated from the restaurant by a glass door. The whole place was full of clamor, the rattling of plates and glasses, tobacco smoke, and the smell of cooking food. Tinka cast her eyes over the crowd, searching for acquaintances. Yes, there they were, they had already arrived, most of them commercial travelers, the pleasantest guests that came to the hotel. This was the beginning of their season. Through the whole of the autumn, winter, and spring they would come and go, with their enormous, heavy, leather-strapped brief-cases and strong suitcases, bulging with every possible kind of sample. They almost always came in groups as though they had got scent of each other, streaming from all the different parts of the country, noisy, generous revelers, bringing the only variety there was into the monotonous life of the hotel. Tinka was on friendly terms with all of them. They were simple, good-natured and gay.

They knew a great many towns and people, and they had a gift for telling stories about interesting things.

There was Popeto already, as mouselike as ever—small and long-faced, with his brightly colored peasant-kerchiefs and printed cottons. That was limping Palamarov over there, too, with his razor blades and celluloid goods. And Lalyu Gabrovets had also arrived, bringing two cases full of ladies' handbags and purses.

Tinka gave them a friendly nod through the window and said: "Hello! I'm glad to see you! But where are the others—Subcho and Karakash?"

"Oh, they're coming, too . . . tomorrow or the day after—they'll be along for sure," Palamarov replied. "I met Karakash the day before yesterday, in the station at Stara Zagora. 'Well, so long,' he said, 'I'll be seeing you at the fair.'"

Tinka took her plate of food and a slice of bread and went upstairs to her room. Her face was serene and happy. She did not need the others, she only wanted to know about Karakash. Tomorrow, or the day after! Eh, thanks be to God! How many months she had been waiting for that autumn fair. She sat down on her bed in her little cramped room, which smelt of "Perfume d'aventure," and looked at the colored postcards pinned up on the wall without seeing them. From one of the other rooms came the muffled affected sound of Lenche's raised voice, mingled with that of an uncertain, troubled man's voice. Drops of rain were pattering on the windows. The engine of a motorcar was droning below in the square, but the car did not start. She sat there on her bed so lost in her dreams that she forgot to eat her meal.

From when had she known Karakash—that tall man, long past forty years of age, with the red birthmark covering the whole of his left cheek, in his old sheepskin coat with the lambskin collar? She could not remember very well, it seemed to her that she had always known him, because for ages now she had considered him as somebody very close and dear to her. When she saw his stooping figure, loaded with cases on which the letters "D. M. C." were struck—he was selling that firm's sewing thread and embroidery silk —when she heard his husky voice and looked into his gray eyes, which looked as though they were faded, she was always filled with a feeling of gladness. He was a strange fellow, this Karakash. All the others here called her "Tinka," only he couldn't get it right, and always said "Tinko." And even this gave her pleasure.

One evening, at the beginning of their acquaintance, when all the other guests had gone to bed, he had slipped into her room on tiptoe. His hands had been trembling then, and his eyes had looked feverishly excited and uneasy. He was smiling guiltily and keeping an ear bent all the time to the door, as he came up to her and tried to put his arms round her. Tinka had got up, put back her hair, ready for him. Saying he would take off his coat, he had begun fumbling in a troubled, uncertain way in his pocket out of which two photographs had fallen to the ground. He had bent down to pick them up, rising again very, very slowly, and when he turned his face toward her, his eyes had been shining with unshed tears. He had been flushed all over, as red as the birthmark on his cheek, and putting on his coat very quickly, he had sat down on the bed, near the undressed woman. She had looked at him in astonishment, waited for a little while, and then said impatiently: "Well?"

He was breathing heavily, sitting silent with the two photographs trembling in his hands.

Then the woman had spoken for the second time: "Well, now! What are you waiting for? Hurry up, I'm sleepy!"

He had heaved a deep sigh as he turned to her and said quietly: "Lie down, Tinko! I'll go."

"Why, what do you take me for, making game of me like this?"

He had looked at her again in his gentle, quiet way and handed her the photographs. "Look, this is a photograph of me with my wife. And that girl is my daughter. She's still at school. Seventeen years old."

He had stopped speaking for a minute, then gone on: "Don't be angry, Tinko! Take this," he said, putting a hundred leva* into her hand, "and buy yourself a pair of stockings as a present from me. I don't want you to think that Karakash is making fun of you. Well, now good night! Go to sleep, sleep well."

The stooping figure had got up and stolen quietly out of the room. She had sat gaping in astonishment, without understanding a thing, then suddenly the whole thing had seemed strange and laughable to her, and putting away the money, she had gone to sleep.

The next evening, a few of the guests had been throwing a party in one of the rooms of the hotel that had been taken by two commercial travelers and a miller, who was a townified peasant. The waiter was hurrying to carry up bottles of wine to them. Popeto and Lalyu were having a game of cards and playing for money, Karakash

---

* When the leva was only one-tenth of its present value

was watching the game and smoking his cigarette through a reed-holder. The stout miller, flushed from drinking, was sitting on one of the beds between Tinka and Lenche, with an arm round each of them.

Suddenly Tinka had let out a shriek and jumped up, almost weeping: "Stop it, I tell you, stop it! You've pinched and squeezed me black and blue already!"

"Come here! For God's sake don't be so silly!" the man had shouted. "I pay for the wine and for you! Come over here! . . ."

"I want neither your money nor your drinks! Off you go to your wife in the village!"

Tinka had turned up her sleeve and shown a big blue bruise above her elbow.

Karakash had turned to the drunken man and said: "Listen, Neno, don't do that to the girl. Look what you've done! Do you think it doesn't hurt her?"

"Shut your blasted mouth!" the raging man had shouted, as he jumped and flung his glass at Karakash's head.

The others had intervened, and the landlord had come flying upstairs. Tinka had fled to her room and locked herself in. They had left Lenche to calm down the turbulent miller.

Tinka remembered that evening. From then on Karakash had been completely devoted to her, although nothing more had happened between them. Quite a long time had passed since then. He used to come to the town, stay a few days, and then go away again. The last time he had been there, he had dropped in to see her before starting.

"Let me tell you something, Tinko. Look, do you wish to get away from here? This job's not for you, you're a good girl."

She looked at him, kept silent, and then laughed derisively, tapping her head with her finger. "Karakash, are you in your right mind? Where in the world could I go to, away from here?"

"Tell me only whether you want to. . . . You can leave the rest to me. It can be arranged. In autumn my cousin is opening a knitwear shop in Roussé. He needs somebody who understands the business. Someone he can trust. You're a good girl, I know you are. I'll arrange for you to go into the shop. Only wait a little. When I come to the fair in autumn, I'll take you away from here—straight to Roussé."

He had patted her on the back, with a grin on his rust-colored, unshaven face, and then, taking up his case, had clattered down the stairs.

Months had passed—one, two, then five had dragged by. Each new month had appeared to be longer than the last. Sometimes it had seemed to Tinka that the whole thing had been a dream—she had never thought that she could expect anything else. Formerly her life had been just the same as it was now. How could everything suddenly change! And yet she knew for sure that Karakash had not been lying and romancing her. At other times she would even picture to herself the little knitwear shop in the strange town, where no one knew her. She imagined herself standing behind the counter, the noise of knitting machines, that well-known pleasant sound which she had forgotten, in the room behind the shop. At such times, she would go into her little room, lie down and shut her eyes. She wanted to weep and to laugh at the same time. Then she used to go through the daily grind of her duties, as if she were in a half-dream, never flying off the handle at anyone, never bargaining even with the worst of the customers, putting up with everything with a dreamy smiling expression in her big, gentle eyes, which were like those of a young heifer.

The next day the rain stopped. The little town looked bare now that the trees had shed their leaves. It seemed old and faded, as if a rot had set in. On the fairground they were putting the last touches to their work, laying out their wares and getting the swings ready. In the circus tent, which was already pitched, they were nailing something together while the hungry oxen, tethered unharnessed by the carts, were mooing uneasily. A cold dampness had pervaded everything, making things look more miserable and depressing than ever, but the throng and traffic was getting bigger all the time. Twice Tinka slipped over to the fairground, wading through puddles, looking at the booths, and the circus caravan with its chimney smoking there behind the circus, and she also went through all the streets. She could not sit still anywhere. That night she was sure that Karakash would arrive. In the next three days she would have an awful lot of work, the hotel was packed with guests . . . but this was the last time for her. In three days' time, there would be the little shop with jerseys and vests hanging outside. Another town, another life, which, in spite of everything, she could not imagine.

Toward evening, Sheytana, the salesman for aniline dyes, arrived. He was cold but, as always, jocular and gay. He was young and smart in his waterproof overcoat and gloves. He drank a couple of brandies, one after the other, rubbed his hands together and bent over toward Tinka.

"How are you getting on, Miss Tinka? Will you have a glass of brandy with me?" He tapped for the waiter. Then Tinka began questioning him too.

"But where is Karakash? Everybody's already here, but he's missing."

"Ah, so you're interested in Monsieur Karakash Chervenii, are you? Don't worry! He's coming with the trans-Balkan bus. I saw him yesterday morning. He's got all smartened up—he's bought himself a new waistcoat with a catskin collar."

Tinka went up to her room, looked once more at her clothes, folded and already in her suitcase. The evening passed away unnoticeably into the night. Downstairs the place was ringing with the racket and clatter of the guests. Here, upstairs, a separate company of timber merchants and cattle dealers had taken one of the rooms. Lenche was with them. They had put on the gramophone and from time to time there came great bursts of laughter from there. Lenche had already come twice to call her—they wanted Tinka to go to them.

"All right, I'll come. I'll have something to eat first and then I'll come," she answered frowning. She was out of humor that evening. She wanted to have nothing to do with chatter, noise and drunken men.

She went into the kitchen and, without sitting down, got a bite of something to eat. At one moment a mud-spattered policeman came in, stopped by the table, where the chief of police was taking his supper, and reported something to him with a worried face. The chief got up at once, and knitting his eyebrows, asked aloud: "Was it the trans-Balkan bus? Were there any casualties?"

"Yes, sir, there were three. The road caved in at the turn near the sixteen kilometer point. Two people were killed on the spot—a child and that commercial traveler, the Jew Karakash. The third died while we were getting him from under the bus."

The policemen went out at once. The noise in the restaurant died down. Tinka leaned against the wall—everything suddenly began swaying around her and her ears buzzing and ringing, then she heard nothing more. She heard neither the wailing and shrieking of the people around, nor the voice of Lenche who had come running to call her again. At last, as she came to herself, she heard the landlord, who was shaking her by the shoulder and saying: "Have you gone deaf or something? For goodness' sake, stop being so foolish! The customers are asking for you upstairs . . . they're getting angry. What are you waiting here for?"

Tinka looked at him with vacant eyes, neither moving nor answering. Then he pushed her toward the door out of the kitchen, and she set off across the courtyard, swaying from side to side as she went. Going inside the hotel, she got hold of the banisters and began going slowly up the staircase, stopping on every step, as if her feet had turned to lead. Without thinking what she was doing, she bent and put her garters to rights, and then went toward the room at the far end of the corridor, from where the sound of laughter and the clinking of glasses could be heard.

Translated by MARJORIE HALL

PART II

National Consciousness:
Rebellion—Hope—War

Anton Strashimirov

(1872–1937)

Anton Strashimirov was born on June 15, 1872 in Varna. He received his elementary education in his native town and then attended secondary school in Razgrad and agricultural school in Sadovo. For two years he attended lectures on literature and geography in Bern (Switzerland). Upon his return to Bulgaria he was appointed secondary school teacher in Vidin and later in Bourgas and Kazanluk. In 1900 his play *The Wedding in Bolyarovo* was staged and somewhat later another play, *Vampire*, was produced.

Strashimirov took part in the Macedonian revolutionary movement headed by Yané Sandanski and made friends with Gotsé Delchev and Krustyu Assenov. He edited the Macedonian newspaper *Reformi* (1900–1901). In 1901 with Stoyan Mihailovski and Kiril Hristov he founded the literary magazine *Nash Zhivot*, which appeared, with some interruptions, for six years until 1912. In 1902, he was elected national representative for the opposition. For one year he edited the *Demokraticheski Pregled* magazine with Todor Vlaikov and Iliya Georgiev.

During the Balkan Wars he took part in the marches of the Sofia division to Chataldja. His experiences of that time provided the material for his novel-chronicle *Whirlwind* (1922).

During World War I he became correspondent for Army Headquarters and visited all the fronts. On the basis of these experiences he wrote several books about war. After the war he began reading public lectures on literature and folklore, and edited the magazine *Nashi Dni* (1921) and *Bulgarska Obshtodostupna Biblioteka* (1922–23). The bloody suppression of the September 1923 Uprising shook him, and he pronounced the now famous sentence "They butchered the people as even the Turks did not!"

Strashimirov died on December 7, 1937.

He wrote the following important books: *Laughter and Tears*, short stories (1897); *Time of Reckoning*, a novel (1899); *Autumn Days*, a novel (1902); *Vampire*, a drama (1902); *Crossroads*, a novelette (1904); *Meeting*, a novel (1904); *Wars and Liberation* (1916); *A Book of Bulgaria* (1917); *Horo*, a novel (1926).

Soura Bir

I

The east began to glow behind the dark outlines of Souha Gora; color played over the eternal snows of Shar Mountain, and the folds of night receded over Kobilitsa and Lyubotrun. Soon small pink clouds were floating over the high heavens, now growing light, and the east blazed up, a fiery brilliant red. A wonderful radiance poured over the southern folds of Shar Mountain, where the lovely valley of Tetovo lay; the pearly forest dew and blue haze of early morning melted into a thin rosy mist in the flaming light of dawn, and only Abduraman's Towers, in the middle of Tetovo, rose out of it, and—far away at the foot of the mountain—the copper cross of the big monastery at Krainish.

A fiery July day broke, and Shar Mountain stood out clear with its snowy summits, sharp crags, and dark recesses.

Seven armed horsemen appeared at early dawn along the granite ridge above Krainish. They were on their way down to the monastery. At their head rode a broad-shouldered man who seemed to disappear in the brilliance of his clothing. On his head he wore an Albanian cap around which a fine silk kerchief was wound; a close-fitting jacket of gold-embroidered scarlet blazed from under his unbuttoned tunic, magnificent in its gold braid; its empty sleeves hung over his shoulders, thrust out by the heavy swordbelt around his waist, from which bristled the mother-of-pearl hilts of various yataghans, daggers, and revolvers. The six horsemen, who followed him in single file, were long-faced Albanians, simply dressed and well armed.

Not a man in the Shar region but would have recognized in this alert company the bandits who were the masters of the snow-capped mountain. Their leader was Soura Bir, the fierce chieftain, at whose door the authorities in Skopié laid scores of murderous deeds against the families of pashas and beys alone.

He was going down to Krainish now, the secular patron of whose rich and famous monastery he was.

The monastery was awakening to the new day. It was a fortress. A high and inaccessible rectangular wall surrounded its spacious courtyard. In its midst rose the tall stone church, and beyond it three huge lath-and-plaster buildings, which had been destroyed by fire so many times that the population of the monastery's ten villages had grown used to building them up again. The abbot, Father Danail, was a semiliterate, but wily fellow, who having once won the favor of Soura Bir, now lorded it in his fashion under the bandit's wing. The monastery had sixty servants, whose work was directed by Father Ignatii, an unlettered coppersmith, who had turned monk after having been refused the hand of a girl he had caught sight of over a wattle fence in his youth. He now worked day and night, forgotten by the world, living in a dark little cell near the workers' shed. There was also a watchman, Father Martirii, a huge young monk who began to drink as soon as he rose from his slumbers, drank himself into a stupor after a good meal, and then went to sleep again. He was only sober when bandits attacked the monastery; on such occasions he armed the servants with guns and, with the coolness of a commander, opened deadly fire on them from the walls of the monastery.

Besides these three, the monastery was inhabited by Father Maxim, Deacon Avksentii, and Schoolmaster Dammé. Father Maxim had graduated from the Kiev Seminary, and the exarchate had sent him to Krainish to take over the management of the monastery, and to raise the prosperity of the region with its wealth. But soon after his arrival Father Danail delivered him to the Albanian bandits, who returned him after some time, out of his mind and coughing badly. He now wandered around the monastery's spacious courtyards, muttering crazed words and coughing helplessly. Whenever he met Father Danail, the poor seminarist timidly shrank from him, while the abbot crossed himself. Deacon Avksentii had finished the high school in Salonica, and had taken the oath of the revolutionary movement on a dagger, and he had managed to take the vows under Father Danail, simply in order to clear away all the "carrion" in the monastery as opportunity arose, so that he might buy weapons for the whole of Macedonia with its wealth. He had killed a man, it was said, on the eve of Easter, and read the Easter service next morning.

The only man whom Deacon Avksentii trusted was Schoolmaster Dammé, who had moved from the village to the monastery on that account. In 1895 he had been around the Pirin Mountains with the revolutionary bands, then he had gone to Switzerland to study; but his father, Nasté, the old baker in Tetovo, had been so badly beaten up by Zindil Chaoush in Tetovo, that he had died, so Dammé had to come back and look after his young brothers and sisters. He had taught in Tetovo, but, unable to adapt himself to the subtleties of the policy pursued by the Bishops Suffragan there, he had retired to Krainish, worried and even frightened. Dammé was afraid of Deacon Avksentii, but was never separated from him, just as a man, grown wise in years, does not separate himself from his youthful dreams, although he already fears them.

The first servant to open the big iron gates of the monastery that day caught sight of Soura Bir and his band winding down from the ridge above. The servant paled, bowed down to the earth, and quickly turned back.

The band of brigands had stopped at the river glen above the monastery. Like a virgin's breast, the glorious bosom of Shar Mountain revealed itself to their eyes. Far to the south, the shady pass of Gostivar let the blue waters of the Vardar into the valley, where they flowed eastward to Souha Gora, washing it on the north and disappearing into the dark forests there. Once these waters, with the brooks formed by the eternal snows, had made one of those mirrors of water here, such as all snow-capped mountains have to reflect themselves in. They had now forced a way to the sea and had left a southern garden at the foot of Shar Mountain, sunk in greenery, amid which like a rocky island rose that nest of pashas—Tetovo, with its unending seraglios, lost in water, shade, and flowers.

Soura Bir was gazing about him. His eyes were caressed by the blue sheen of the water and the velvety green of the gardens. But the bandit was gloomy. His round, olive face was tense; his fine black mustache curled like a sickle around his lips; and the look in his dark eyes, sunk deep beneath his forehead, was enough to arouse horror. He was a man of about forty. In his right hand he held a Martini rifle. If the Sultan from Stamboul himself had appeared now from somewhere, without bowing down to the earth before him, Soura Bir would have given the order to cut him down.

The proud bandit finally raised his head and looked up at the white cone of Lyubotrun. A small black cloud had perched on the very crest of the mountain, like a fierce eagle. "It sticks there," the bandit thought. "Does it bode good or ill for me?" And he spurred his fine black stallion.

At the monastery gates the band was welcomed by all the fathers and servants. Only drunken Father Martirii, whom they did not awaken, and Schoolmaster Dammé, who had locked himself in his room, were absent.

Soura Bir nodded condescendingly in answer to the deep bows of those who welcomed him and raised his arms slightly. Two of his band helped him dismount, and with oriental tact Father Danail flattered him and led him away to the open galleries of the central building, onto which, tier upon tier, the cells opened.

"Priest," said Soura Bir, heavily, "the day has dawned for me with a black cloud."

"The breezes will drive it away, my lord!" said Father Danail, grinning at him as he cast a glance at the snow-capped summits.

"And it's not a good omen, priest," Soura Bir added. "I've reached the age of forty. I'm finishing my fortieth year today; and I've decided to marry today . . . but this morning I saw—a black cloud on the mountain."

The fat abbot did not know what to make of these words. Soura Bir had appeared in the Shar region about ten years ago. He was not an Albanian and did not know the Albanian language; nor did he behave much like a Turk, either; no one remembered his having cast a glance at a woman to that day. One rarely heard of a pretty belly dancer from Gostivar having been taken to his konak up in the mountains. Moreover, it was said in Gostivar that Soura Bir had never yet smiled at a woman. Where had he come from? It was said that he had buried a wife far away in the lands by the Danube, but it was known, on the other hand, that he had come to these parts from Stamboul.

So Father Danail was perplexed now. The bandit usually spoke in Bulgarian, a language he had learned, not very well, from the Turks and Albanians hereabouts, and it was only occasionally that he spoke in good Turkish. The wily abbot had noticed that Soura Bir only spoke Turkish when he was in one of his better moods. The bandit was addressing him in Turkish now, and the abbot rubbed his hands as he answered: "Pasha, the monastery is yours: How many guests are there to be? How many rams am I to slaughter?"

They had already reached the middle gallery. The bandit stretched out on the soft cushions, and the abbot knelt behind him holding a hookah.

"The Hodja of Avratlar," Soura Bir said with a smile, "appealed to me some days ago, saying that he had a most beautiful girl, and that he would give her to me if I took blood for him from Haidar Bey in Gostiva, who had killed his brother's son. Yesterday we went down to Haidar Bey in Gostivar and killed his daughter's child. I sent a man this night to the Hodja in Avratlar, he is to meet me here today, with the bride."

The fat abbot gaped at him, then placed the hookah, which

Soura Bir was sucking at, on the ground, and bent over the railing to shout: "What are you about there? Hurry up and slaughter nine rams, the fattest ones! Ha, and tell Father Avksentii to come here!"

The Albanians had placed themselves along the stairs, Martinis in hand, standing like bodyguards, with their eyes fixed on their leader. Deacon Avksentii and Father Maxim soon appeared on the stairs.

"Avksentii," the abbot ordered, "take the Chieftain's men to the front gallery and come back." The Albanians bowed to the earth before Soura Bir and disappeared at Deacon Avksentii's heels.

Crazy Father Maxim bent double before the awesome visitor and began to cough.

"What's the matter with that fellow?" asked Soura Bir, frowning.

"He's beyond hope, my lord; he's lost his mind and has a deadly sickness," the abbot answered, sadly.

"You speak well," Soura Bir remembered something, fumbled in his cartridge belt, drew out a leather purse, and took out a folded envelope with big seals, saying: "Send for the schoolmaster! As to that poor devil," and he pointed to Maxim, "I've got a hakim up at my place for him . . . the Vali's hakim from Skopié. I've brought him here to treat a childhood friend of mine. Have someone sent to fetch them, too, priest."

II

Under Plocha, one of the crags of Shar Mountain, the icy brooks of the snows form a small lake that is as clear as a tear. It is hidden amid the rocks which rise up to the skies. Years ago leafy poplars grew around that lake, caressing the dry brows of the rocks with their tips. And along the ridge looking down on Krainish three mountain buildings were perched, each of them two stories high: the living rock formed their backs; their fronts were built of stone slabs, with holes for windows; and their roofs were terraced gardens. The middle one was the higher and was thrust forward over the lake: its upper floor had latticed windows, and its roof had a floor of oak boards surrounded with pots of all the flowers which grew from the Danube to the Aegean Sea. This was Soura Bir's pleasure ground: he rested and drank his coffee here, looking down on Krainish, Tetovo, and Gostivar, and enjoyed the sight of the red trout in the lake.

The sun had now risen in the blue sky, bathing the whole earth in its light.

"Eh, Yussuf Aga, I nearly turned Turk once myself," said a

man dressed in a black frock coat and a top hat, somewhat low in the crown, as he stood in the middle of the terrace, with a bottle of mastique brandy in his hand.

He was Doctor Zacconi, the trusted friend of Hafuz Pasha of Skopié. Three days ago Soura Bir had seized him in his home in Skopié in the middle of the night, and brought him here. Zacconi had been terrified at first, but he had been given plenty of food and drink, and a huge sick man to treat, who was sitting at his side now. This man's name was Yussuf, and his face was the color of the earth, as if he had risen from the grave; wounds made by chains were still unhealed at his wrists, showing that he was just out of prison. His back was broad enough for two men, and his broad face was taken up by a fair mustache, so big and bushy that it reached his shoulders. But this mountain of a man had a hacking cough, and his broad chest rumbled like a hollow tree in a storm.

"You're a merry little fellow," he now answered Zacconi, sucking at his amber cigarette holder.

Zacconi was indeed in a gay mood. He felt very comfortable in Soura Bir's konak, although not as well as he had felt in the various inns and pleasure houses, the konaks and seraglios he had known, from Egypt in the south as far as Wallachia and Moldavia in the north. For there were no women here, and that was all that Zacconi lacked. But he was old, his small eyes watered amid perfect clouds of wrinkles, there were no teeth in his mouth, and only a few scanty locks of hennaed hair were left above his ears. He was thought to be a Greek and he himself considered himself a Christian, but he had made such a muddle of all the Christian tongues he knew that he only spoke Turkish fluently.

"No, how much merrier I used to be, how much merrier!" said he, grinning from ear to ear, as he rolled a cigarette; he began to tell his tale.

It had happened in Silistra. Zacconi was a doctor there, under another name, of course, for the Bulgarians pursued him because of his friendship with the Turks. And while he was in Silistra there was a regular war raging in the forests of Deliorman between two peoples of the same faith, the Kazulbashes and the Turks. The Kazulbashes were fine fellows, who ate pork and drank wine, because such was their custom. They had no truck with the Turks, although they spoke the same tongue and belonged to the same faith. The most learned hodjas were sent to them from Stamboul, but all in vain. One of these Stamboul hodjas had settled among the Kazulbashes of Akkadunlar, with his harem and his three daughters, and it so happened that the foremost of the Kazulbash bachelors, Lefidji Redjeb, fell madly in love with one of these three daughters. She was as lovely as a rose in a garden and had an eye for Lefidji, who was as lithe as a dappled stag. Finally the hodja got wind of something and one night took his daughters to a purely Turkish village. But the watchful bachelor discovered his intentions and got his friends together; they attacked the hodja in the forest and carried off the girl.

Then the men of the Turkish villages rose and went for the Kazulbashes, and the war was on. Zacconi was a merry fellow and he wanted to see the Stamboul lady who had been carried off, so he set out from the town with the troops that were sent to chase the Kazulbashes. But as soon as he had carried off the lady, Lefidji had his wedding that same night in the forest, according to old custom: he raced his bride to an old oak tree in a small meadow; then they chased each other around its trunk and lay down. Whichever of the two, the man or the girl, ran the faster and caught the slower one, became the master, and his word was law all their life. Such was the Kazulbash custom. Lefidji outran his bride, picked her up under his arm, so to speak, and dashed through Deliorman to collect a group of Kazulbashes and defend himself against the Turks and the troops. They fought him for a whole month! He went into battle like a dragon—sometimes roaring like a madman, sometimes crying, and sometimes singing songs—and aiming at the flesh, always at the flesh. All wondered at this young chieftain, and made a song about him, singing of him and his bride as "Dejkli Gyuzeler" or fighting beauties.

Zacconi moved his toothless gums and with rare eloquence recounted as in a song the wonderful epic of the enamored hillman. Nor did he notice that Yussuf, his patient, shivered slightly, restlessly twirling his big mustache and casting troubled looks at him. Zacconi raised the bottle of mastique brandy to his lips, smiled and went on with his tale, telling it to the wind which blew from the mountain.

And at last the troops and the Turks got the better of the fighting beauties: they slew or captured Lefidji's band and took his bride away from him; only he, though covered with wounds, was able to slip through their fingers. He soon forced two kingdoms to busy themselves with him, for he began to seize herds of horses and cattle and flocks of sheep all over the roads of Deliorman and the Dobroudja, piling up money and saying that he would cover the judges in Silistra with silver to let his mates go, and that he would cover the Hodja from Stamboul with gold to give him back his bride. Hey, it was madness in that handsome, fighting lad, the kind of madness one hears about only in songs! Lefidji was a rich man's son, he had studied at the Roushdié in Silistra, and wrote such letters to his father, in such terms that when they were read in court later, everybody who heard them wept. "Unfortunate Father," Lefidji wrote, "you, whose feet I am unworthy to wash, and whose name I bear out of your mercy, you, whose word I cannot break, dearest father and parent, do not curse me, for I shed tears that sear my cheeks, and inconsolably lament and suffer from deep wounds. . . . Was I born a homeless and unfortunate wanderer? Or have I no father or mother, or have I no brothers and sisters, or have I no family and friends, no roof, no faith and no honor? A rose was I, my father, a rose, tender and green, and a nightingale perched on my sprig, a sweet nightingale, a songster, lovely and true. Oh, they have wounded my nightingale, father, and caged it; my sprigs and my branches are broken, winds lash me, father, bitter winds, and only the thorns have been left on me. . . . Sweet father, parent mine, whose feet I am not worthy to wash, only do not curse me, the unworthy and unfortunate!"

Zacconi delivered the filial letter of the enamored hillman in the most touching words and put so much of his heart into his narrative that he burst into tears at the end. But Yussuf only shook his head, and once he coughed so hard that he seemed to be tearing his broad hollow chest.

The courts cast Lefidji's mates into prison for twenty years each, and condemned him to death by default. His father returned to his village and died of grief within a week. After that Lefidji went mad. He began to attack people even at the fairs. In the meantime Zacconi himself was treating his bride at the hodja's house in Silistra. She was so beautiful that there was none to compare to her in the whole world. And Zacconi decided then to adopt Islam. He wasn't afraid of Lefidji: he would flee to Constantinople with the lady and become a Mohammedan. And that would have happened, for the first beys in Silistra were on his side and had persuaded the hodja to give his consent. The beauty only needed to recover somewhat from her state of fear, grief, and shame. But they also had to wait for her to give birth to her child by Lefidji. Well, and this incomparable beauty died in childbirth! She bore a girl and the child had lived, the Hodja had taken her back with him in Constantinople. Nothing more was heard after that either of the Hodja or of Lefidji: as soon as the Hodja had left, Djenkli Gyuzel, the handsome fighting lad, had disappeared. His supporters had probably slain him, because he had amassed countless wealth; and it was a known thing—as soon as a bandit grew rich—his supporters did him in.

Zacconi gazed about him sadly for some time, wetting his lips with the mastique brandy; the bottle never left his hand. He did not once let his eyes rest on Yussuf, the sick man, who had bent his head, staring in front of him and shaking it from time to time. But suddenly the huge Turk sighed and said: "Well, hakim effendi, you have traveled over much country . . . you have visited many lands . . . tut, tut, tut."

"That I have, Yussuf Aga, that I have; and that's all I'll have to remember in the end!"

"And now let me tell you something—Djenkli Lefidji is alive! He's alive! Look," and Yussuf showed his wrists, "it's for him I wore the chains for sixteen long years!"

Zacconi gaped at him and went white. But just then one of the monastery servants appeared from the foothills of the mountain, bringing Soura Bir's command that Zacconi and the sick man should come down to the monastery, for the wedding guests were expected there from Avratlar, Soura Bir was marrying the youngest of the Stamboul Hodja's girls, and nine of the fattest rams had been slaughtered. Zacconi jumped for joy and forgot his fears again. "I love a wedding, hey!" he cried gaily.

But Yussuf Aga frowned. "You go down," he said. "I don't want to."

"What, Yussuf Aga, not when the Chieftain has sent orders?"

"Don't you bother about me; I've got one foot in the grave."

"Damn it!" cried Zacconi with outspread hands, "but I tell you, Yussuf Aga, in a week's time you'll be as sound as those rocks, you'll be as radiant as the sun, and as merry as the fish in the lake! I tell you this: take my head if I'm lying!"

The poor sick man smiled, and in a little while they set out for Krainish.

III

At the monastery they were preparing for the wedding. Soura Bir sucked his hookah, lying on the gallery of the middle and most spacious monastery building, while his band were sitting in a circle on that of the front building, which was something like a wing of the middle one. The back wing of the monastery was taken up by the cells of the monks, and among these was Schoolmaster Dammé's room. He taught in the village and behaved in such a way that neither good nor ill could be spoken of him. Dammé was one of those young people who respond to heroism, but who, if left to themselves, spend their lives unnoticed by anyone. As a rebel, he had fought, rifle in hand, in the Malashevo region in 1895, and he had fought coolly and fearlessly, but yet in such a way that no one noticed him. He was not plotting anything against the Turks now, though he still avoided them like the plague, and was never without a sharp dagger in his waistband.

Soura Bir's appearance that morning confused Dammé; his soul revolted at the idea of humoring a Turk; but he was not quick-witted enough to hide his dislike with flattering words. So he had locked himself up in his room. When, somewhat later, he was sent for to appear before the brigand, Dammé paled. He cleaned his dagger every morning, but had never thought of using it, and only had a vague feeling that if the need arose, he would know how to send Soura Bir himself to hell with it. That was why Dammé shivered now, settled his dagger well in his waistband, and went.

"Come, schoolmaster, come!" Soura Bir said to him in broken Bulgarian without looking at him. "Why do you hide yourself? We don't eat people."

"May your shadow never grow less, Chieftain Aga," Dammé replied, bowing low to him. "I am a poor schoolmaster, and I stick to my job!"

"You have studied much, eh? Read me this letter!" said Soura Bir, handing him the envelope.

Dammé took the letter with trembling fingers. Rapidly he went over everything in his mind, but he knew he had sent no one any letters. However, the big envelope bore a German heading and the seal of the Bosnian Bank. The young man drew a breath of relief, his blue eyes smiled and he said: "I shall be able to read this letter, Chieftain Aga!"

"Well, let's see!" the bandit said waving him away. "Read it and then I'll send for you."

Father Danail signaled to Dammé to withdraw, as the wedding guests had appeared in the distance, coming from Avratlar; gypsies with pipes and drums walked ahead of three covered carts. The monastery was alerted again. Only Avksentii and Dammé did not appear; they were in a dark cell facing the back courtyard, next to the gun room, beyond which, in another cell, the drunken Martirii lay snoring. Dammé was just finishing Soura Bir's letter: it was some kind of a monetary paper in his name, from the Bosnian Bank in Saraievo.

"He'll be the ruin of the monastery!" Deacon Avksentii was

saying with affected emotion. "The news will travel to Constantinople, that bandits celebrate their weddings here."

Dammé was reading the paper. He had long since forgotten
what little German he had once picked up in Zurich, and all he could
make out was that the paper was about some three thousand liras.

"What are we to do, eh?" Avksentii asked, tapping his shoulder.

"Let me be!" answered Dammé and pressed his hands to his
head. It seemed to him that it was clear: they were sending Soura Bir
three thousand liras from Austria.

"What is it?" Avksentii asked, in wonder.

"Let the monastery burn, Avksentii, let it burn! It's all up
with Macedonia, brother!" And he explained how he had guessed
the contents of the German letter to Soura Bir. The young deacon's
mood suddenly changed. That young man had donned the monk's
garb to serve Macedonia. But love of his enslaved country had
blended in his mind with the images of the heroic apostles of liberty,
who had fanned the fire in his bosom from his earliest childhood.
And the words, that it was all up with Macedonia, meant to Avksentii that those apostles would vanish from the face of the earth, those
men for whom he felt a blind reverence, and for whose cause he was
ready to steal, set fire to anything, poison or kill, and sacrifice himself. For the young deacon, those apostles personified honor, wisdom, scholarship, glory, and greatness. It was only behind them that
the image of Macedonia shone forth like a radiant cloud. The apostles and Macedonia—that was all the world held for him. And the
day would come. Deacon Avksentii, Dammé, and thousands of
others would soar like kites, and at one stroke they would tear to
pieces the black veil of bondage; it would be such a miracle that all
those people beyond Rila would be amazed and the whole world
would gape in wonder. Avksentii looked upon himself as an animated weapon for the achievement of this end. And the mere idea
that it was unattainable cut through all the chords of thought and
feeling in the poor deacon. His eyes now started out of his head; he
went white and clenched his teeth. Oh, the Germans, Austria—they
might frustrate everything! They would bribe those bandits, like
Soura Bir; they would stir up everything in Macedonia; and then
suddenly they would occupy it as they had done with Bosnia and
Herzegovina.

It was a long time since Dammé had been so moved. He was
silent because, as always, he could find no plan in his own head about
what should be done in these terrible muddles of life. But Avksentii

tapped him on the shoulder again. "Dammé," he whispered in a sinister voice, "let's set fire to the monastery tonight, shall we?"

"Why?" Dammé asked, hesitating.

"To burn them all!"

"And the monastery?"

"Let it burn, too!"

They fell silent. Dammé frowned; he was troubled and held his tongue. But the deacon added, incensed: "Get rid of those curs who are digging our graves for us! Soura Bir must die! He and his bloodthirsty rabble, let them go up in smoke!"

And the young deacon stood there, trembling from head to toe, intoxicated with his decision, like a child. A little while ago he had been preparing a completely different plan. He had decided to persuade Dammé to escape to Tetovo that night. Several of the pashas there were secretly against Soura Bir and were persuading Zindil Chaoush, the terror of Tetovo, to rise against the master of Shar and take him captive. And Avksentii had calculated that if they learned there that Soura Bir was celebrating his wedding at Krainish, they might call out the troops and take him. Father Danail, the abbot, would then be carried off to Skopié. Avksentii himself would see to that, and with a couple of journeys between Skopié and Tetovo he would have the monastery in his own hands and . . . Salonica and Bitolya, too, and Sofia itself, would have moved over to Krainish.

Avksentii now decided to do the whole business on his own. Yes. He would not bat an eyelid. They should burn . . . let them: let the servants burn along with the bandits, even Father Danail, and all of them, all of them.

In the meantime the drums and pipes were already deafening the monastery courtyards. Soura Bir had settled himself in the abbot's big parlor and awaited the wedding guests there. The bandit was restless. Fear seemed to have come to life in his hardened spirit. He had only experienced that feeling once, sixteen years ago, when he had shouldered his gun for the first time, to go out to battle. The last ten years of his life he had spent like yesterday, when he had gone down to Haidar Bey in Gostivar, and had killed his daughter's child. Soura Bir—either at another's request or when his spirits were low—used to go down to the crossroads with his terrible band and amuse himself with people's feuds and their lives. If it happened that he had spent a quiet summer, he would be sad in the winter, so much so that he would disband his men and disappear. They said that in such winters he wandered alone to Constantinople and even around the regions of the Danube. But if Soura Bir spent a turbulent summer he became idle and hospitable in winter, and then they brought belly dancers to his mountain konaks from Gostivar. There, slender, temperamental, and shamelessly half-naked, they would sing and dance their wild dances before Soura Bir the livelong night. The bandit would suck his hookah, lying on his cushions, his eye bloodshot, staring at the voluptuous belly dancers and cursing . . . cursing them and spitting to one side.

All who knew Soura Bir felt that this terrible man hid a deep wound in his soul, a wound that he never complained of and never sighed over, of which he never spoke to anyone and which he seemed to avoid thinking of, but which could be read in his eyes, in his behavior and in his bloodthirsty deeds. Soura Bir had no friends; he was feared, flattered, revered, and served; people were true to him only out of fear and were bewitched by his courage. And he seemed to be necessary, this powerful man, to those people about Shar, so different from each other and so hostile to each other. No one here had any respect for human life, and among them he who also despised this life was the first. Soura Bir was such a man. He cared nothing for the whole world, but woe unto him who cared nought for him! Soura Bir neither laughed at anyone, nor was angry at anyone, nor sought anyone; but before him everyone had to smile and bow. And people smiled before him, bowed to him, and made use of his terrible right hand, although each one welcomed with secret delight the frequent rumors that Soura Bir had been killed.

When, fourteen years ago, he had appeared here for the first time, there was much rivalry between the Albanian and the Turkish brigand chiefs. But they all yielded pride of place to him; he was enthroned as Soura Bir the Chieftain, and soon people ceased speaking of him as a wonder: all that he did and all that he could do no longer aroused either amazement or indignation. Years ago, Selim Pasha of Tetovo had offered him twelve of his loveliest odalisques to bring him blood from Mukdu, the Derebei of Prizren. Soura Bir came down one night then to the pasha's seraglio, asked to see the girls, gazed long at them, and said: "There is no beautiful girl among the living, Pasha!"

And he had gone. But a week ago the old Stamboul Hodja of Avratlar had thought of it, and first of all men here offered Soura Bir, not horses, nor riches, nor mistresses, but a bride, according to the canon. If the Tetovo pashas had heard of it they would have laughed the naïve hodja to scorn. But Soura Bir himself did not laugh.

And there he was, waiting for the promised bride. The hum of voices grew louder outside on the broad galleries, the whispering of women reached Soura Bir's ears in the parlor—the bride was being led into the next room, and the door to the gallery was opened. The wedding guests entered, the white-bearded Hodja of Avratlar, with three beys, led by Father Danail. They advanced with low bows, sat down, with the exception of the abbot, and began to exchange greetings.

"Soura Bir, Chieftain," the old hodja began in a quavering voice, "twice has evil befallen me in my lifetime: once, sixteen years ago in other lands, when I was still young, so that I defended myself, and now for the second time. I thank Allah that I met you, so that I shall not die with my eyes open with enmity for Haidar Bey! It is the custom here for the men not to be fearful, and I have lived here for the last ten years without meeting with evil and without doing evil to anyone. And now, in my old age, you have saved me from shame, Soura Bir, Chieftain. And I am poor, so that I have little with which to pay you back. My pain was of my heart, and my requital will be of my heart, too: I bring you a cartful of dower, women's embroideries, and I bring you a bride, the firstborn of my firstborn daughter."

Soura Bir was not listening. He seemed restless. The woman's voice he had heard outside seemed to have troubled him. He remembered the small black cloud on Mount Lyubotrun and frowned; then smiling slightly beneath his mustache, turned to Father Danail and said:

"Priest, something tells me today that I am about to do evil: tell me, what is sin, according to your giaour canons?" And without waiting for an answer, he rose, signaled to the abbot, and went out. Once outside he said to him: "Ask the guests to sit down to lunch, then take the women out by the back stairs so that no one sees you and bring them up here."

And he disappeared along the narrow passages toward the end wing of the spacious building. Just then the horses of Zacconi and the sick Yussuf appeared along the ridge above the monastery. Soura Bir waited for them at one of the staircases, and when they entered the courtyard, he called, happily: "Brother Yussuf, come, come along!"

No one in this region had ever heard Soura Bir address anyone in that way.

A little later the two men sat down side by side on the upper gallery, and the sick Yussuf said: "I shall die here, Redjeb! Why didn't you leave me there, in our part of the country? You said he was the Vali's doctor. He's a cur! He was the one, the healer from Silistra, when I was tried!"

"Who?" asked Soura Bir, bristling.

"He told me this morning, he was the one . . . he knows everything, all about you, the Stamboul Hodja . . . they called him in for the lady, he said."

"What?" gasped the bandit.

"He knows everything."

"Does he know about the hodja?"

"What about the hodja, Redjeb?"

"Where is he? I've been looking for him these sixteen years!"

The sick Yussuf blinked, and said: "What need have you of him, Redjeb?"

"I have a child, Yussuf!" Soura Bir whispered, dropping his eyes, and a slight evil smile played beneath his mustache.

"Aha," Yussuf said, remembering. "The cur spoke of it: the lady died in childbirth. She bore a girl. The hodja took it away with him on his flight to Stamboul."

And they fell silent. A little later, twisting a straw in his hard fingers, Soura Bir explained: "I set out for Stamboul in those days. I only took Kyutryulyu with me, you know he was true to me. But one night, above Edirné, he found me asleep, cut my throat and robbed me. A shepherd brought me back to life and healed me. And so I came to Constantinople, Yussuf Aga, bloodless, ragged and unarmed. If one wasn't mad, one would go mad at that! And I was taken there, some of our people took me and cast me into prison. A foul world!"

IV

The abbot took the guests out to a table laid under the chestnuts in the courtyard, then he took the women—two of them—out through the back court to the upper gallery where Soura Bir awaited them. And as he passed the cell in which the schoolmaster and the deacon were, the two young men eagerly fixed their eyes on one of the women he was leading, who shot them a glance of her black eyes.

"Where's that eunuch taking them?" Avksentii muttered through clenched teeth.

"And how lovely the little one is!" stammered Dammé.

"But she's still a child, brother!"

"D'you know?" cried Avksentii, starting up with a horrified face. "She may be a Bulgarian!"

And the two young men exchanged horrified glances. Then Avksentii dashed out, saw where the abbot had taken the women, returned to the cell, cast aside his cassock, clambered up into the uncovered attic, and was lost in the darkness of the maze of smoke-darkened rafters.

But Soura Bir, in whom his talk with his sick friend had revived memories of his unfortunate youth, waited, frowning, to see the beautiful girl he had been promised, to whom, after so many years of a grim and bloodstained life, he had decided to yield the impulses of his harshly controlled flesh. Father Danail appeared on the stairs, uneasy, passed with quick steps, bowing low, and the two women stood before Soura Bir. One of them was old and bent; the other was the bride they had brought him. The bandit fixed his gaze under the girl's yashmak and started: it divided and revealed the beauty's face—milk-white cheeks, with strongly marked cheekbones; scarlet lips with dimples at the corners; and black eyes with thick lashes.

Soura Bir was dazed, though not by the girl's beauty. He gaped in amazement; then, seeming embarrassed by something, bent his head and signaled to the women to enter the room, shivered and turned pale.

The women entered the spacious room indicated to them, where, on a low divan lay the diamond earrings, bracelets, necklace, and fine sash which Soura Bir had placed there. On the threshold of the room, the girl caught sight of them and, turning, cast Soura Bir one of those glances out of the corner of her eye which are the dangerous love speech of oriental women.

The bandit now caught fire. At the first glance the girl reminded him of something that seemed like a vague image from an old dream. Then the grim brigand chief paled because it seemed to him that the girl strongly resembled his bride, buried so long ago. But now, after the girl's fleeting womanly glance, Soura Bir caught fire; he slowly rose to his feet and stopped as if to assure himself of something, and before his eyes he suddenly saw a glance . . . out of the past, a glance cast on him by his bride, wounded in the last bloody battle sixteen years ago, and lying at his feet, covered with blood.

It was only for a moment. The grim man's powerful flesh proved stronger than the painful memory. And a little later, when he went in to the women, something stirred in his breast, and an evil exultation seemed to lay hold of him. The stormiest of his past days revived in his memory: he was flying along on horseback; two soft arms were wound around his neck; warm breasts were pressing close to his right arm and quivering while a hail of bullets flew over his head, whistling shrilly and cheering his spirit with their sinister laughter.

A greenish light from the shady back yard of the monastery filtered into the room through two windows. On the divan next to these windows the old woman was decking the bride. As Soura Bir entered she withdrew to a dark corner of the room, and there her shadow grew still, like a mysterious watchman. Soura Bir advanced and mutely stared at his bride. She smiled at him—a beauty of barely fifteen—but trained in harems: alluring, yielding, and ready for a husband. Her eyebrows were painted; black patches had been placed on her forehead and near the dimples in her cheeks; her hair, black and abundant, was contained by a small flat fez, on which long strings of coins had been sewn, and the numerous pigtails into which it had been plaited fell over her shoulders; her white silk yashmak covered her costume; under it she wore a satin bolero, which fitted her waist tightly, half covering the belt of her wide satin trousers. She submissively folded her arms below her breasts and looked, smiling, at the brigand with her velvety eyes. The scent of a garden flower and the sensuousness of mature flesh emanated from her.

"What do they call you, my beauty?" Soura Bir asked in a muffled voice, touching her dewy cheek with his palm.

She moved shyly and said: "Gyulsyumé."

The bandit drew his hand away. He was astounded by the strange coincidence, for that was the name of that beauty of Deliorman, his first bride.

"What did you say?" he asked timidly.

The girl moved again and now placed her hand confidently on the bandit's breast, saying with playful shyness: "Why, I told you: Gyulsyumé."

This time Soura Bir heard only her voice, soft and alluring. He put out his hand again and raised her face; she turned, as if to avoid the touch of his thick fingers, but did not draw away, turning slightly to lean her shoulder against his breast. Then the flattered man took her in his arms and, seating her on the divan, sat down beside her and gazed long upon her with love, delight, and suppressed wonder.

"I love your name, Gyulsyumé, I shall love you, too," he said

at last with a slight tremor in his voice, and, kissing her forehead, he
went out.

Two eager eyes were watching through a crack in the ceiling.
They retired when Soura Bir left the room. The watcher was Deacon
Avksentii. He disappeared again in the dark attics of the spacious
building. Dammé was waiting for him below, but Avksentii did
not return for a long time.

V

"Better never have been born if the monastery does not lie in
ashes tomorrow!" said Deacon Avksentii when he went in to
Dammé at dusk. He had unloosed his cassock; under it a gray rebel's
jacket was visible, tightly belted at the waist.

"Oh, drop it!" muttered Dammé, troubled, staring at the
jacket; "why, you've got a rebel's uniform."

Avksentii strode restlessly up and down and in a little while
stepped mysteriously in front of Dammé, bent down to him, and
said in a muffled voice: "With that little Turkish girl up there, I'll
build everything up again in a month's time! But this night . . .
H'm, there'll be fire and the sword!"

"But do you mean to carry her off?" Dammé asked, gaping at
him.

The two young men had been living in this region, where it
was hard to see a woman's face, for the last two years. And the
shadow of the Turkish lady, who had been brought to the monastery, had troubled both flesh and spirit.

Quick steps were heard outside, and the fat abbot appeared at
the door. "Go along, schoolmaster, the Chieftain has sent for you!"
he said, and stared at the confused young men. But, suspecting nothing, he went on: "He may ask you about the letter—have you read
it? We are heating the bath for him. But there is one thing that
bothers me: the man with the Chieftain, the sick man—one would
say he wanted to know more about the Hodja of Avratlar—they
seem to have come across each other before, and now they're staring
at one another, and the sick man keeps fumbling with his sword belt.
They'll be flying at each other's throats before we know where we
are . . . tut, tut, tut!"

"Let them burst, abbot!" muttered Deacon Avksentii, "are
you the one to care for that—he, he, he!"

"That I'm not, deacon," said Father Danail, "but. . . ." And
he vanished in the darkness, followed by Dammé.

Soura Bir was sitting with his bride on the upper gallery of

the back wing. Stars already covered the sky, and there was a wonderful radiance over the eternal snows of Lyubotrun. But Gyulsyumé was smiling, restless, warm. And Soura Bir, stroking her hair
with his hard palms, was bemused by her breath, calmed by the stillness of the wonderful night, and stared out at the wonderful radiance over the eternal snows. His forty years; his passions, desires,
and sorrows, held in leash until that day; his courage, pride, and
hatred of mankind; his visions of blood by day and his dark ravings
in his sleep—all now seemed to be melting in a crystal cup, melting
slowly, drop by drop—and the more dazed the brigand's mind grew,
the more powerfully his broad chest heaved. The girl's wonderful
eyes, her dewy cheeks, and her burning young body seemed at times
no longer outside his being; they vanished before his eyes, and he
felt them within him—he felt them in an intoxicating stream of
boundless sweetness. Soura Bir was torn away from his past and felt
so distant from the dead that he did not even suspect their shades,
and from the living he was separated by such a strength of desire
that he lacked memory.

Fourteen years ago, when an Albanian bandit chief had taken
him out of the prisons in Constantinople and brought him to the
Shar region, he had had to unravel the entire network of his spirit,
linking the quick and the dead. And as soon as he himself became a
chieftain he went to Constantinople and to the forests along the
Danube: he had sought his daughter, bought his mates out of the
prisons, rewarded the shepherd who had saved his life, buying him a
farm, and had also found his treacherous mate Kyutryulyu. Oh, that
was the last dark knot of his life. Kyutryulyu was master of a big
farm on the shores of the Aegean Sea, bought with the three bags of
liras he had stolen from Soura Bir; he had a large harem, and pashas
and beys were his constant visitors. One night Soura Bir descended
on him with his band, slew his visitors, burned his farm with every
living thing in it, and carried Kyutryulyu off alive to his konaks in
Shar Mountain. Here he feasted him for three days and three nights
with pipes and drums, with singers of love songs and belly dancers.
Soura Bir made him merry as befitted an old and faithful comrade.
Then he led him out to the top of the rock opposite his arbor above
the little lake and nailed him alive to the granite, that the sun might
burn him, the winds suck him dry, and eagles and their eaglets tear
his flesh.

Gyulsyumé's breath was on his face now, and for the bandit
everything, the entire universe, was gathered in the dewy image of
this spring blossom. Soura Bir had never in his life oppressed his

nature with fantasies, devoid of flesh, bodiless and passionless. He had never dreamed. But even the loveliest belly dancers of Gostivar filled him with disgust because in his soul and body he had preserved the sweetness of the waking dream he had lived through together with that image which had vanished from the earth, and solely because of which he had begun his first murderous war against men. It was the disappearance of that image from the earth, and later the treacherous knife of a friend who had played him false, that had made him a savage beast, ravening on the human herds. He lacked a tiny drop of joy to make him shake his mane like a lion and spread his wings like an eagle in the sky.

Happiness now flowed over his softened spirit, and his breast swelled with it. And when Father Danail coughed on the stairs leading to the back court, Soura Bir playfully raised his bride to her feet with one hand, and almost involuntarily said to her: "May you live long, little lamb!"

Then he sent her into the room and clapped his hands so that the schoolmaster, whom Father Danail had brought, might appear before him.

"Have you read the letter, eh?" Soura Bir asked him from afar.

Dammé flushed scarlet; he told him what he had understood in the letter from the bank, but something else was troubling him, so he added: "Please heaven, Chieftain Aga, that those who honor you be your good friends."

The bandit smiled: "Eh, schoolmaster, what bad friends could those people be to me?"

"Pardon me, Chieftain Aga," Dammé answered, "they are in another kingdom, and the two kingdoms are like two beys, they chase each other to fight. . . ."

Soura Bir frowned. "Schoolmaster, you have studied much, eh?"

"I have, Chieftain Aga."

"But you're a poor man. Look to your poverty, schoolmaster, look to your poverty. What does it matter to you, if two kingdoms are fighting?"

And putting a hand to his waistband, the bandit brought out a purse in which there was a clink of coins, handed it to the schoolmaster and said: "You'd better get married! Get married while you're young!"

And he laughed out loud. It was the first time in his life that he had ever given alms.

VI

The moon had already risen over Souha Gora and was gazing at her own reflection in the waters of the Vardar River. The courtyard of the Krainish Monastery rang to the gypsies' pipes and drums, amid which a throaty singer of love songs raised his voice, singing Turkish songs one after the other, as playful as proverbs. From the middle galleries incessant wedding shots broke the crystal stillness of the moonlit night. They came from Soura Bir's faithful men. Seated at the table together with the other wedding guests the wild Albanians still kept their guns in their hands. The hodja of Avratlar sat to the left of them with his people, and opposite them, to the right of the Albanians, squatted Yussuf Aga, the sick man, with Zacconi next to him. That old sinner was trying to be at ease here, too, but something hindered him: Yussuf was gloomy and bristled every time he looked at the Hodja of Avratlar. Father Danail had correctly noticed what he had told the deacon and the schoolmaster; the sick Yussuf seemed to be trying to recognize a former enemy in the hodja of Avratlar.

When the wedding ceremony was over, the Hodja of Avratlar had taken the bride by the hand and said to her: "Little lamb, you know no father, you remember no mother: from now on your husband will be both father and mother to you." Nobody had paid any attention to the words, least of all Soura Bir. But now that the newly married pair had withdrawn to the upper gallery and the wedding guests were left alone, Yussuf Aga, as yellow as a quince, and frowning, stared long at the white-bearded hodja, and finally said to him: "Hodja Effendi, I shall ask you something: why did you say that the beautiful lady *knew no* father, and *remembered no* mother?"

The hodja half-closed his small blue eyes, flushed slightly and said: "His honor will forgive me: the lady is my daughter's child, and it is not in my heart to speak of how she came into the world and why she knows no father and remembers no mother."

Yussuf was dissatisfied with the answer and began to cough. After that they did not speak a word to each other, but the sick man was on the watch for the hodja's looks and stared at his face.

But Zacconi had observed everything, and this hostility disturbed him. He listened to the singer's playful songs, was carried away by them, and would have liked to sing himself. Finally the Hodja of Avratlar fixed his eyes on Zacconi and asked him if he had been in Stamboul. This question suddenly loosened the old wanderer's tongue: he began to speak of where he had been, what he had

done, and what he had seen; he began to speak and had no intention
of stopping. And the old hodja listened to him, shaking his head,
hinting that he, too, had been to those lands, that he knew the regions near and far from the Aegean Sea to the Danube, and from
Bosnia to Egypt. Then Zacconi lifted his voice and sang of a boat on
the Danube at night, of the beauty of the land along the Danube, and
cried: "Hodja Effendi, I spent my youth by the Danube! And I saw
people there, daring and handsome!"

The sick man heaved a sigh. His gloomy look was now fixed
on Zacconi. But the gay ne'er-do-well was quite carried away. He
patted the sick man's shoulder and said: "Take heart, Yussuf Aga! I
will cure you. Hey there! Long live Soura Bir the Chieftain—fire,
brave men!" And raising his voice, he looked kindly at Yussuf Aga,
adding: "Yussuf Aga, I have it in my heart to shout for another
hero . . . give me leave!"

"Shout what you will!" the gloomy Yussuf muttered through
clenched teeth, turning aside.

"Long live Djenkli Lefidji!" cried Zacconi. He wanted to
please Yussuf, but the latter did not so much as look at him.

"Hah," said the Hodja of Avratlar, sharply: "what Djenkli
Lefidji are you talking of, my master?"

Zacconi drew himself up. "There is only one Djenkli Lefidji,
Hodja Effendi," he replied. "He warred on two kingdoms along the
Danube."

The hodja's face suddenly changed, he seized his white beard
and muttered: "A faithless cur! A savage Kazulbash! Half a pig!
And their origin is of the giaours!" And turning away he spat.

Here something happened to the sick Yussuf. He bent his
huge body forward, stretched an arm out to the hodja, his lips quivered, horror appeared in his face, he stuttered, and hoarse words
broke from him. "A-ah. . . . He carried your daughter off, Redjeb
Lefidji, didn't he?"

And the eyes of the terrible Turk grew bloodshot.

But the hodja seemed not to understand; he only grasped the
reference to his daughter's former shame with Lefidji, and flushing
scarlet he cursed him fanatically: "God slay him!"

The Yussuf gaped in amazement, pointing with his left hand
to the upper gallery where Soura Bir was with his bride, and tried to
say something. But he was trembling all over and his eyes grew
misty; unable to speak a word, he choked in a terrible fit of coughing. Confusion broke out among the wedding guests; the sick man
was fighting his cough, but his hand pointed to the upper gallery, as

if he wanted Soura Bir to be restrained from something. He seemed
to have said this twice with his darkening eyes, but no one understood him. And in the end the impatient man grew furious: his eyes
grew a little clearer, a dash of foam appeared on his lips, he bent
double, got the better of his cough for a moment, and suddenly a
revolver flashed in his hairy right hand, and was aimed at the hodja.
It was only for a moment; the revolver began to belch forth bullets,
but they scattered aimlessly, for the sick man's hand dropped, his
eyes grew misty, the cough he had suppressed by force burst out, his
huge breast shook, and suddenly he fell forward. For a while he lay
there twitching and then was still; only his thick left mustache
turned red and clung to the ground in a pool of clear blood.

They all shuddered at this sudden appearance of death among
them.

VII

A subdued murmur spread over the monastery and then all
was hushed. The Albanians retired to the room set aside for them,
saying to each other: "See, and we brought him a doctor all the way
from Skopié." The wedding guests from Avratlar did not question
the hodja about the sudden quarrel, but comforted him, saying: "He
raised his hand to take another's life, and the Lord took him by the
nose, and he died on the spot."

And as they had all eaten their fill, they soon fell asleep. Only
Father Danail and Zacconi remained awake. The abbot's rosy face
had suddenly withered; he laid the dead man out, closed his eyes, put
a cushion under his head, and lighted a taper. But Zacconi was holding his head in both his hands, wailing that there would be no life for
him now—he knew that—woe to his children in Stamboul and to his
orphans in Wallachia. The poor ne'er-do-well bewailed himself in
his own way: he grieved for his several families, left in several lands,
and in their name he was preparing to beg the terrible Chieftain to
spare his life. Father Danail sighed and from time to time consoled
Zacconi, without understanding his laments.

And night was advancing.

Suddenly in the darkness someone began to giggle. The abbot
started and, recognizing the deacon, grew angry: "Have you gone
out of your mind, deacon, what is it?"

"A taper for a Turk—ha, ha, ha!" giggled Avksentii drawing
nearer. "Are you reading prayers for him, Father Danail?"

Father Danail suddenly realized his error, seized the taper
from the dead Turk's head and, putting it out, began to scold the

deacon: "Go to bed!" he cried to him. "Soura Bir will hear us, and for one thing he'll do to me, he'll do two to you!"

In the meantime, Soura Bir, alone with his bride on the upper gallery, was beginning to lose his thoughts in a terrible riddle. Gyulsyumé had dozed off on his knees, and he was looking at her. It was strange: today, after sixteen years, that same Gyulsyumé, light and quivering, with whom he had once flown, fighting his way through the forests of Deliorman, seemed to have come to life in her features, her name, and her body before Soura Bir. Gazing upon the face of the sleeping beauty, the bandit raised his brows in amazement at times, but smiled immediately: he had never lived in dreams, so that now, sober as ever, he sought only to enjoy the wonderful resemblance, trying to drive from his spirits the threat, which arose as a feeling of fear at something mysterious, which might work miracles, and blend scores of years into one, link events that had occurred beyond hill and dale, foretell a fall, a wreck, death to someone, or bring the dead to life!

At last Soura Bir felt his head grow heavy. His gaze wandered abstractly, and he reached out a hand to wake the beauty asleep on his knees. But his body had had its fill of caresses, and he felt deep down within himself a strange turmoil, so he rose and with measured steps went out. The curved sickle of the moon stood high over the snows. Soura Bir glanced at it, merely to measure the time, and then set off to exercise his body, to rid his spirit of its unrest and voluptuous ecstasy. He was ignorant of what had occurred on the gallery below; the shots from Yussuf's revolver had sounded like the last wedding shots and had not aroused his suspicions. With measured steps he went down the broad staircase, making straight for the entrance to the lower gallery. And only at the lowest steps did he hear someone whispering; he stopped in surprise and in a moment saw Father Danail before him.

"May you live long, my lord," the wily abbot said sadly. "Yussuf has died!"

The bandit seemed to start. Immediately behind the abbot came Zacconi, who fell on his knees and wailed: "Spare my life, Gaazi!" And rising, he began a solemn speech of high-sounding praise and flattery. The late Yussuf's sickness was nothing; it could have been blown away with a breath, but. . . . Zacconi related his talk with Yussuf in the mountains that morning: the secret quarrel between the Hodja of Avratlar and Yussuf that evening; and his own sincere wishes for a long life to the unknown Djenkli Lefidji. Eloquently the flatterer raised his hand and continued:

"But what was my amazement, Soura Bir Aga, when the reverend Hodja of Avratlar jumped upon me and shouted: 'Unworthy one! The Warrior Lefidji was of another faith!' Then Yussuf Aga grew furious and spoke terrible words to the hodja. 'Stamboul Hodja,' he said to him, 'was it not you whose daughter the glorious Lefidji Redjeb carried off?' "

Soura Bir swayed on his feet. But Zacconi noticed nothing and continued: "God is my witness, Prince and Chieftain: the reverend hodja was wrong. He bitterly cursed Lefidji, and then Yussuf Aga, in a rage, drew out his revolver and began to fire, and because he was in such a rage he fell upon the ground and expired."

The old windbag made his voice quaver at the last words and, falling on his knees, begged again: "Mercy, my lord Chieftain. I have children, poor little orphans!"

Soura Bir was writhing. He remembered as in a dream the hodja saying to Gyulsyumé: "You know no father, you remember no mother. . . ." And now, as Zacconi fell on his knees before him, the bandit groaned and overcoming the horror which was racking his whole body, he kicked the wretch aside with terrible strength, turned on his heel and, raising his arm over his head, Albanian fashion, returned with rapid steps to the upper gallery.

Father Danail led the cringing Zacconi away to his room to sleep, but, although he was dying for rest himself, he took a sip of rakiya to refresh himself and went back to the gallery.

The moon was already hiding behind the white crest of the mountain, and the night closed its eyes in a last slumber before the dawn. The abbot stopped in a daze at the entrance, and in a little while Deacon Avksentii appeared like a ghost behind him.

"What, are you still about, Father Abbot?" he muttered through clenched teeth in a strange voice, and in the darkness one could notice the glint of a dagger in his hand.

But the worried abbot scarcely glanced at the young deacon. "Go away!" he cried, "get out of the way! The Chieftain will be down in a moment."

And Deacon Avksentii, who had crouched as if about to hurl himself on the abbot like a kite, now muttered: "Ah, is he still awake?" and disappeared in the darkness of the passages. Just then steps were indeed heard coming from the upper gallery.

It was Soura Bir who, as never before, was walking on tiptoe. The bandit came toward the abbot, his head bent. "Get me the hodja." And then he covered his forehead with one arm. Hot needles seemed to be burning his body. If there had been any thoughts beneath Soura Bir's hard skull, they must have been drowned in blood now, and his consciousness must have left him for ever. For at that moment he felt that the hot needles which were pricking his body would soon clutch his heart, and it would be terrible then—more terrible than it had ever been in the world before.

The old woman upstairs, whom he had just questioned, had told him little, but all she knew: Gyulsyumé bore the name of her mother, who was buried in distant lands.

That must be an invention. Or was there a mockery in it? And finally . . . whatever it might be, it should not touch Soura Bir and his bride! The bandit threw out his chest, and his whole body quivered in terrible strength. That morning a small black cloud over Lyubotrun had troubled him, and now he would have laughed in the face of the very devil. He would even have been delighted if Satan had appeared before him; he would have hacked him to pieces . . . or he would have chained him to Mount Lyubotrun for a terrible death . . . or he would have nailed him to the death rock opposite his konak and aimed at him morning and evening with his Martini, all his life.

Standing there, furious and sinister, Soura Bir was ready to crush the misfortune that had befallen him with unearthly strength. But all around him was dark and empty.

And then Father Danail led the white-bearded Hodja of Avratlar out from one of the cells and, leaving him at the entrance, disappeared. The bandit stood motionless for a while. Then something burst in his chest, he seized the hodja, bore him out on to the gallery in a couple of strides, and showed him Yussuf's prone body.

The morning star had risen, the radiance of dawn was playing over the east like a smile, and the shadows of the night began to vanish.

Themselves two shades of night, the two men stood facing each other on the gallery, frozen to immobility: they might have exchanged some words, then a sudden whirl, as if something had shaken them, and the beginning of a hoarse cry was throttled: in Soura Bir's terrible grip the hodja's white head straightened out, his feet were raised from the ground and so he died as though he had been hanged. Then Soura Bir gave a shake of his iron right hand, and the hodja's corpse crashed onto the boards beside Yussuf's body.

The cocks crowed in the village.

VIII

Soura Bir stood motionless in the middle of the gallery. He did not feel the passing of time. His clouded reason seemed to be trying to grasp something which eluded him. At last he shook his head, as if to escape a dreadful vision, and went down into the courtyard with resolute steps. He probably did not realize what he intended to do, but his intention was carried out as if he were fully conscious. With measured steps he made for the back wing of the buildings, where, beneath a shelter, the horses were tethered. Suddenly smoke began to pour over his head from between the lower and the upper floors of the lath-and-plaster buildings; tongues of flame crept out here and there. But Soura Bir saw nothing. Soon a wave of smoke struck his face, and he felt the heat, but he did not seem conscious of it and only hastened his steps. A moment later, as he passed along by the wall, something tripped his feet, and a rifle clattered onto the stones. He bent down to pick it up and noticed a red light under the stable roof, and through it the shadow of a man moving among the horses. Only then did the bandit start, trying to pull himself together, and immediately his stilled fury of a little while ago rose up again. He picked up the rifle, felt it over and was now really surprised—it was his own Martini. He was all on edge. Something mysterious was going on around him; a red tongue of flame curled up from a dark corner of the shelter, quivering in the darkness, and in the blood-red light of the flame Soura Bir caught sight of a saddled horse. He looked again: it was his own stallion.

And before he could collect himself, from the darkness something black hurled itself upon him like a kite. It was only a second— the unknown assailant was flung back—then with lightning speed Soura Bir drew one of his huge weapons, swung it, and someone's body fell to the ground.

"Cursed night!" the bandit said aloud, seizing his bloodstained yataghan in his teeth, and swiftly approaching his black stallion, which had probably been led out and saddled by the dead man. He untethered it, looked around him in horror and, springing into the saddle, galloped toward the monastery gates.

As never before, they were open. Beside them, in the darkness, stood a man. It was Dammé, the schoolmaster. The appearance of Soura Bir startled him, and he ducked behind the wall as the bandit galloped past without seeing him, headed for the mountain. Dammé stood there astounded. He had agreed to help the deacon in one thing only: to hide the Turkish lady in the village if Avksentii succeeded in rescuing her from the fire. Soura Bir, he thought, must fall to the deacon's dagger or else perish in the flames.

In his heart of hearts, Dammé had little faith in this plan of Father Avksentii's. He had always thought that Avksentii would break his head in such foolish business because he did nothing with his reason, and dealt only in boldness and what he took for cunning. And now that Soura Bir had so unexpectedly left the monastery safe and sound before his very eyes, Dammé gaped after him in amazement, mixed with furious resentment at the deacon.

For the monastery was already on fire. The flames were licking the wide middle galleries, and the lower floor of the building was full of pale smoke. Avksentii had carried out his dreadful intention.

Dammé stood there, on tenterhooks, and felt like running away to the village, running away and hiding. The purse of liras which Soura Bir had given him was in his waistband. With that money, the young man could settle his impoverished family and make for Bulgaria himself. He had already thought of this; he had not told the deacon of the money he had been given. But nevertheless, he had stayed on to help in this terrible business. Dammé would not have admitted to himself why he had done it, but today for at least a minute he had considered: if they could carry off Soura Bir's little bride, then . . . Dammé might cross the border into Bulgaria with her, baptize her, and marry her.

The young man hesitated for the last time now; the longing for the Turkish girl that had laid hold of him, Avksentii's plan, and the monastery, flaming at all four corners—everything was still confusion in his mind. He started and stared through the gates at the terrible fire now raging in the monastery; it was deserted and horrible there now; dark clouds of smoke enveloped the galleries, and sinister flames tore through the smoke.

And suddenly Dammé was seized with horror. Where was Avksentii? He could not know that Soura Bir had left and that the girl could be carried off now. Dammé shrugged his shoulders and dashed toward the fire; it seemed to him that he caught sight of the abbot's horrified face, but he did not stop; he ran round to the back courtyard, which the fire had not yet reached, and found himself at the stairs leading to the upper gallery that Soura Bir had occupied during the day. Dammé was sure that he would find Avksentii here. But before starting up the stairs he peeped into Father Martirii's cell, where he thought he heard steps. The drunken monk roared out to frighten him and burst into laughter. In spite of his irritation Dammé called out: "Run for it, the monastery's on fire!" and without further delay hurried up the stairs. The fire had been started from several points, so that now the flames were leaping up from under the galleries of all three buildings at once. But the stairs were still free, and Dammé hurried on with eyes starting out of his head as he measured the waves of flames already leaping up to the place where Avksentii was to have been. The young schoolmaster was so certain that the deacon must be up there that it did not even enter his mind to be afraid of the fire: he hurried along, calling "Avksentii, Avksentii!" softly. Then, remembering that Soura Bir was not there, he called out aloud.

In the meanwhile Soura Bir's horse bore its stunned master up the breakneck paths of the mountain. Blood flowed down the bandit's left hand, wetting his fingers; he had repelled the deacon's attack with that hand. His right hand now held the Martini on his knee; it, too, was bespattered with blood; it was with that hand that he had cut down poor Avksentii. But Soura Bir felt neither his wound nor himself. He probably only vaguely realized one thing—that he was on his horse and that he was going home. However, the horse soon made a long detour around a precipice, then stopped and neighed timidly: from below the mountain came the glare of the terrible fire in the monastery. The bandit shivered and leaned forward for a moment. Then something stirred in his breast, and he felt a terrible pain, as if the flames down below were searing his right hand. And with madness in his eyes he turned his horse and galloped back.

In the monastery, Dammé, up on the highest gallery, where he was calling Avksentii, heard a woman's smothered scream. Flames were already dancing over his head, and he began to lose consciousness of what he was doing: he dashed in the direction of the screams, pushed the half-open door, and stopped. The women were timidly huddling by the door hiding from him. Behind them, at the other end of the room, the floor was already burned through, and smoke and flames were pouring through the holes. Dammé turned away his eyes, and not boldly, but insistently called something to the women, pulling at the girl to take her out. Both women began to scream; the old woman jumped on her feet and stood before Dammé all a-flutter; it was obvious that the two women did not want to be touched by a Christian. Dammé grew confused, but just then a strong wave of clear flames crept up over the balconies, and something crashed. The girl, who was cowering at the old woman's feet, rose in horror, opened her eyes wide, and shrieked. With one shove Dammé thrust the old woman back, toppling her over, and seizing the girl in his arms he disappeared amid the flames, making for the back stairs.

Just then the monastery bell began to ring wildly with sinister insistence, spreading alarm through the night. The abbot, Father Danail, had been the first to discover the fire, because, after Soura Bir's terrible murder, he had been unable to sleep. But dazed and frightened, the fat monk was unable to realize the flight of time, and moreover, he supposed that the fire was the work of the bandit. So he fled first to the courtyard, and to the worker's shed, where, quietly rousing Father Ignatii, he warned him to make no sound; then they woke the workmen in the same quiet way and kept very still. They heard the horses neighing in their shed and, imagining that Soura Bir was about to withdraw with his Albanians, feared that they would all be slaughtered by the maddened bandit. But the flames grew bigger and crept up over all the galleries. The women's screams could be heard from above, a terrible noise came from the room where the Albanians were, and still there was no sign of the terrible Chieftain. Then Father Ignatii, who had done more than anyone to enrich the monastery, could contain himself no longer, and without asking the abbot's leave dashed forward and began tugging angrily at the bell: let the village be aroused, let old and young run to the rescue and drag from the monastery's cellars all that could still be saved.

In the back yard, the flames were just beginning to curl down from the eaves. Drunken Martirii had been left without his supper that night, and when the startled Dammé called to him that the monastery was burning, the huge swollen monk cried, laughing: "Aha, that's fine; that's the stuff to give 'em!" and went out to watch the flames, laughing and shouting: "Ha-ha-ha! Burn away, burn your fill!" A little later he blundered scowling into the cells again, and disappeared for quite a time, till finally he emerged carrying poor crazed Father Maxim: it was only to the poor crazed seminarist that the drunken monk showed any gentleness or kindness. He carried him to the stone walls of the courtyard, far from the fire; then, fetching a stepladder from somewhere, he propped it against the wall, climbed up, and facing the fire, sat down, crossed his legs, and lighted a cigarette.

The fire delayed the dawn. In the monastery courtyard it was as light as day, but all around the night seemed to have grown darker.

Suddenly Martirii caught sight of a human figure, holding something in its arms amid the flames, making for the head of the stairs that led to the back yard. Martirii fixed his eyes on it and recognized Dammé, then he sensed the woman's flesh and his lust was inflamed: he followed Dammé intently. Could the intrepid young schoolmaster save himself with his living burden? Twice, before reaching his goal, Dammé fell, as if his foot had gone through the floor. Finally, with a desperate movement, he threw the girl over his shoulder and began to crawl on till he found himself, head foremost, above the well of the staircase. Another step and they would have fallen. But the flames had not yet reached this spot, and the girl caught hold of the banisters, shrieking faintly. Dammé sat down on the uppermost step, and then—Martirii grinned as he watched—then it was as though the girl were leading Dammé: he must have been burned by the flames, for he was doubled up with pain and barely managed to get down.

Martirii began to scramble down his stepladder, too. And soon, in the glare of the courtyard, under a row of elm trees, the two parties came face to face. Sitting on the ground beside Gyulsyumé, who was standing, Dammé saw Martirii advancing on them, with his thick neck outstretched and his brutish eyes starting out of his head, and Martirii realized that Dammé had grasped his intention and shook his drunken head, smiling uncertainly.

"Get back, Martirii, I'll kill you!" Dammé called to him from a distance, drawing his dagger and rising painfully to his feet.

Martirii stopped for a moment, grinning broadly, but soon advanced again.

"Don't be a fool, Dammé," he drawled. "If I get my hands on you, I'll tear you in two."

They did not hear that the noise of the peasants who had gathered in the outer court had suddenly been stilled, nor did they hear the frightened neigh of a horse behind the flames. Martirii shook his head angrily and was already staring with eager eyes at the girl as she timidly cowered behind Dammé, when suddenly, from between the tall elms, Soura Bir appeared on his horse, which was rearing with terror. The gold-embroidered garments of the brigand shone dazzling in the glare of the flames, but there was infernal horror in his dark face and his bloodshot eyes. Dammé shuddered and turned to stone as he stood; Martirii only gaped in amazement. Soura Bir turned his horse with the speed of a whirlwind toward Gyulsyumé, who screamed and cast herself at the hand outstretched to her. In a flash the girl sped through the air like a fairy and was swung onto the saddle in front. Then the terrible Chieftain cast a quick glance at Dammé and Martirii, but no spark of comprehension lighted his face. He only fumbled mechanically in his waistband, tossed them a purse full of coins, and turned his horse. Martirii came to his senses and seized the money, then he jumped over the monastery wall and was lost in the darkness. Dammé helplessly followed Soura Bir's flying horse with his eyes, as it skirted the fire, dashed out into the forecourt through the crowd of peasants, and out at the gates toward the mountain. Everyone there believed it was he that was responsible for the fire and followed him with a shower of curses: "The Lord slay you, mad cur! May lightning strike you!"

The terrible fire shocked even the inhabitants of those regions, accustomed as they were to horrors: there was a general outcry against Soura Bir. A strongly armed detachment of troops arrived from Skopié on the second day and surrounded the bandit's konak in the mountain. But they only found poor Gyulsyumé there —Soura Bir had left. Gyulsyumé told them that he had brought her here on his horse and had not spoken a word all day long; he was very terrible, so terrible that she had pretended to be ill, and kept her eyes closed. But in the evening he had begun to pace the length and breadth of the terraces, tramping up and down the stairs, spending a whole hour up on the roof garden and crying out so fiercely once that Gyulsyumé had been frightened. At last he had come down to her and spoke, asking her about her father and her mother, and then suddenly he had burst out most terribly, telling her that he himself was her father, and they would go away to a distant land, where he would build her a marble seraglio and marry her to the handsomest boy in the world. Gyulsyumé had listened; she had not eaten a morsel the whole day, and now she saw that Soura Bir was growing more and more terrible. In the end she could endure no more: she had screamed for all she was worth and fainted. She remembered nothing more, not even when she had come to her senses, and did not know what had become of Soura Bir or where he had gone.

From that day on the terrible bandit chief vanished completely. That summer the peasants built the Krainish Monastery up again and placed a new stone cross behind the church over Deacon Avksentii's grave. Of Dammé the peasants heard that he had crossed into Bulgaria. And the people at the Bishop's See found Father Martirii in the pubs of Veles, drinking up the bundle of liras which Soura Bir had thrown him.

Translated by MARGUERITE ALEXIEVA

Yordan Yovkov*

(1880–1937)

Heroes' Heads

"1876, May 7.—On Friday a rumor
spread throughout the town that several lads, young Bulgarians, had raised
their standard in the Balkan Mountains. . . ."

From the Chronicle of Hadji Kiro
Tabak of Sliven

At the foot of the steep hills, on which groves of ancient oaks stood
on a black arc, the village had remained unchanged for centuries. So
had the mountains around them, the meadows on Dobromeritsa and
Botsour, the crags and valleys of Gurmovets where, if anyone
shouted, the echo repeated his voice up to seven times running.
There were many more old and unchanging things there, but people
forgot about them and, whenever there was any talk of anything of
long ago, they would speak either of the poplar tree in the Beliznenska district or of Roussi *Sapoundjia*.

No one knew how old the poplar tree was. Although its top
had withered and it leaned to one side, it did not fall as some people
expected. Neither did Old Roussi age. He was in the habit of sitting
outside in the street on the bench under the white wall of his house,
dozing there in the sunshine, or gazing at the Balkan Mountains
opposite. People remembered him thus for years. Quite near, in the

* For biographical data, see p. 41.

next-door yard, stood the poplar tree, and its withered top pricked
the sky like a pitchfork. In the evening the leaves of the old tree
would quiver like butterflies, and its shadow would stretch out
across the square to the white wall under which old Roussi sat.

While most of the peasants had already put on European
clothes, Old Roussi still wore gray baggy trousers and a red waistband. In summer he went about in his shirtsleeves, beautiful white
shirtsleeves which recalled his craft and seemed to praise the soap he
made. But that was in days gone by. Once Old Roussi's craft had
been wrapped in impenetrable mystery, but now that everyone
knew how to make his own soap, his business had taken a turn for
the worse. Nonetheless, no one had ever heard him complain; somehow or other he managed to make both ends meet. His sleeves were
just as clean and white as ever, and he still found time to take a rest
out on his bench—as he used to do long ago.

That is how Old Roussi was sitting that spring. He sat and
wondered what of all the talk that was going around the village
could be true and what could not. Women's chatter he did not believe, but he himself had noticed that the *chorbadjis* got together at
the Church Café and whispered to each other in an anxious way.
Every morning Ali the *Soubash* came out in front of the *Konak* and
stood for hours on end, gazing up at the mountain summits, then
down along the cobbled streets of the village. Meanwhile, the *zaptiehs* sat on the stairs in the yard of the *Konak*, scowling and savage,
their rifles in their hands and their horses ready saddled and waiting.
Something was happening, something was being prepared, but
where, and by whom—that was what Old Roussi did not know. Neither, apparently, did Ali the *Soubash*.

Old Roussi had noticed another thing, too. The little cobbler's shop belonging to his son Miloush was along the same white
wall under which he sat. One could see its wide open door and a
small window ajar, no bigger than a hole. For some time past, Penko
Dodovanyak had taken to coming to the shop very often. What did
he want of Miloush? Dodovanyak had about ten children, all barefooted; he had no need of shoes, he was a loafer, and spent days
roaming around the Balkan Mountains, looking for buried treasure.
He was a poor man and needed money, but what did he want of
Miloush?

In the evening young people came to Miloush. They came; so
many of them gathered that the little shop could not hold them, and
then they would go into the house. Miloush led them; Miloush com-

manded them. Old Roussi saw no harm in this. "They're young
people," he thought. "They're of one mind; why shouldn't they get
together?"

Not that Old Roussi was quite unaware of what was in preparation. He, too, had heard something. He knew that dark days were
ahead of them, that a storm was brewing, not just any kind of a
storm at that, but a hurricane—when the sky crashes and forked
lightning flashes across it, as if dragons are falling, when eagles fly
ahead of the clouds, leading them. At such times hail the size of
stones may fall and nothing is left whole. That was the kind of storm
that was brewing. What Old Roussi didn't know was whether it
would pass by, missing them, or hit their village, too.

This is what he was thinking about on his bench. Once, when
he had gone into the house, he had passed by the room in which
Miloush used to shut himself up with his visitors. They would sit
there till cock-crow, and were either as silent as the dead or sang so
loudly that the tiles fell off the roof. Old Roussi stopped at the door
and looked through the keyhole. He looked and started: in the
middle of the room stood Miloush—his Miloush in *haidout* garb,
with white puttees wound high up his legs, and bound with crossed
black string. On his head was a fur cap with a little lion in front, and
in his hands a sword. Behind him others were drilling with rifles. Still
others were squatting near the hearth casting bullets and making
squibs. Old Roussi understood it all.

The next morning he sat down on his bench again, gazed at
the Balkan Mountains, and smiled. "You know all about it," he
wanted to say, "but you hold your tongue." From a distance it
looked as if he were dozing, but he was merry and he nearly laughed
aloud when he saw Ali the *Soubash* looking around on all sides, and
seeing nothing. The *chorbadjis* seemed comical to him, too, when he
saw how their full-bottomed trousers swayed as they walked, and
how they got together, whispering pompously to each other, as if
they held the world in their hands. "You don't know anything, anything at all!" Old Roussi thought. "It's all up, it's over. Turkey will
fall!"

And he remembered that among the many rumors going
around the village, he had heard that two monks had slept at the
Metoh overnight. They had had a book with them, found at a monastery on Mount Athos, in which it was written that Turkey would
fall. And as it was written thus, thus it would be. And that was
that.

Old Roussi clearly saw which way the wind was blowing. He

was afraid, but at the same time he rejoiced. Otherwise, everything
went on its usual way. It was fine sunny weather. The Balkan Mountains were lovely; green forests encircled them below, growing
darker at the middle, while the highest crags, cutting into the sky,
were blue as always. Above them white clouds had halted, looking
like towers. To the village, too, spring had come. The foliage of the
fruit trees was thick and heavy, somewhere above the dry walls the
lilac blossoms hung blue, or one saw the yellow of acacias in blossom. Barefooted lasses ran from gate to gate with scarlet tulips stuck
in their hair. It was warm and lovely weather. It was always like
that when anything was brewing.

But in broad daylight and in such lovely weather, it seemed to
Old Roussi that nothing could happen. What he had seen through
the keyhole seemed a lie to him. Perhaps he had only thought he had
seen it! And although he seemed to have taken root on the bench, he
rose and made for Miloush's little shop. He wanted to have a look,
and find out.

Old Roussi took his stand at the little window. Bent over his
counter, Miloush was working. Before him stood an old woman.

"So, as I told you, Miloush," she was saying through her tears,
"mend them. But mend them nicely, soundly. And for the price I
told you, don't ask me for more, Miloush."

A young woman entered, her cheeks plump and rosy, ready
to burst, her brows slender and arched, like leeches. She placed in
front of him a pair of fashionable, black slippers with brass heels, and
began in a great hurry: "Take them, Miloush, take them and mend
them, mend them first of all. I need them. But listen, Miloush, mend
them soundly, and nicely. And don't ask me much for them!"

Old Roussi laughed. The old woman's tearful eyes gleamed,
too—she was laughing. The young woman blushed like a peony,
looked around, touched her kerchief, her dress—she did not know
why they were laughing.

"So you, too, don't want him to charge you much, eh?" Old
Roussi snapped, and he wasn't joking, either. "Well, the old woman
is poor, at least, but you? Your father-in-law is rotten with money;
he's got gold coins enough to weigh them by the bushel!"

"Speak up, Miloush, for I'm in a hurry," said the young
woman, offended.

Miloush raised his head. His shirt was unbuttoned—his strong
manly breast showed under it, and his neck, like the bole of an oak
tree. His face was somewhat pale, and freckled, his small fair mustache turned up at the ends, but his eyes were kind. They were blue

eyes with little black bars in them—the same eyes as Old Roussi's.

Miloush picked up the shoes which had been brought to him, looked them up and down and said: "So you won't give me more, is that it? Very well, so be it, I'll mend them."

And he smiled, a smile that was his best promise. The women knew this and did not haggle further. The young one dashed out and ran across the street in the sunlight. With moans and sighs the old one followed her. Old Roussi, too, went back to his bench. "He doesn't care about the money," he thought about Miloush. "He just does his best to mend well for everybody."

A few more days passed. Miloush was working. There was a fence opposite and next to it an apple tree. Lyutsa, the neighbors' daughter, often appeared there and looked toward the little shop. In the evening Miloush used to go to the fence under the branches of the apple tree and talk to Lyutsa. The poplar tree looked black and still taller, and behind its branches the moon shone like gold. Old Roussi would sit on his bench, pretending that he saw nothing, but the heaviest thoughts of all came to him at these moments.

Day would dawn, and the same thing would be repeated. Ali the *Soubash* would come out in front of the *Konak* and look around. Dodovanyak would come to the shop as he had done before. He would simply appear from somewhere, ragged and dusty, with a pointed cap of kid's fur on his head and his pock-marked face. It was clear that he had come from the mountains. He would stop, look to the left, then to the right, and disappear into the shop like a hamster disappearing into its hole. He would sit there for a long time, but when he passed Old Roussi, he would look at him as if butter would not melt in his mouth. This once made Old Roussi angry, and he stopped the man.

"Well, Penko," he said, "shall we be chopping them off?"

"Chopping them off? Chopping what off?"

"The cabbages." *

"What cabbages, Granddad Roussi?"

At last Old Roussi told him what cabbages, and so loudly at that that even Ali the *Soubash* could hear him, who, as always, was standing in front of the *Konak*. Dodovanyak started, looked Old Roussi straight in the eye, and realized that he had nothing to hide from him. From that day on he always stopped to see the old man, too. The two of them would sit on the bench, gazing at the mountains and talking. People saw them, but did not know what they

---

* Contemptuous name for the Turks, some of whom wore green turbans.

were talking about. They only saw that from time to time Old
Roussi would gesticulate, as if he were chopping something off. Or
else he would make soothing gestures, as if he were calming Dodovanyak and saying: "Wait, wait a little longer!"

But it was hard to wait and endure, for times were growing
difficult. Omens began to appear, too. In the Beliznenska district a
cow had given birth to a two-headed calf. One evening the moon,
although it had risen white and pure, suddenly grew dark and as red
as blood. And earlier—some believed this and some did not—in the
church, when it was quite empty and there was no one there but the
boy who assisted *Pop* Roussko and handed him the incense burner,
Saint Nikolai, the miracle-worker, came down from his icon and
talked to him. All sorts of other tales went the rounds of the village.
What didn't people say, most of all the women?

Old Roussi was calm. Everything, he thought, had its right
side and its wrong side. If the omens were bad for some, they were
good for others. Good for Bulgarians, bad for Turks.

One evening Dodovanyak came to him, but he was in such a
hurry that he only managed to say: "They're coming! I left them at
Koush Bounar. They'll be here tomorrow!" And he vanished in the
shop to see Miloush. The hammer fell silent. It was heard no more.

But Old Roussi looked up at the Balkan Mountains. They
seemed larger and higher than ever, bristling and terrible, as if they
were about to speak. Old Roussi crossed himself three times. He sat
on his bench till it grew dark. At the top of the poplar tree the
branches were bending and rustling—a sign of bad weather.

The weather changed. Mists came creeping down from the
north across the hills, drowning the black summits of the forests as if
in a sea, tearing away from them and fleeing to the Balkan Mountains. It grew dark as at dusk, and it was very cold. The men put on
their greatcoats; the women, their short jackets trimmed with fox
fur. And they all hurried as if they were being driven on by the
wind. If two or three met by any chance they would quickly exchange a word or two and then separate. Fear and anxiety was on
every face.

Ali the *Soubash* stood before the *Konak*. But the *zaptiehs* had
come down from the stairs and, with their rifles slung over their
shoulders, held the reins of their saddled horses.

About noon all the men and women who happened to be out
in the streets suddenly began to run in all directions. Shutters came
down with a rattle, doors were banged. Tailors, saddlers, and grocers

shut up their shops, turned the keys in their locks, and ran for their homes. The streets grew deserted; the village seemed to die. The mists crept lower down and the forests rustled more ominously.

Then, in the middle of the village, at the Threshing Ground, many people appeared—the black figures of men—and above them stretched out by the wind flew a green flag. Stoïl *Voivoda* had come down from the Balkan Mountains with his lads.

But most of the men were shepherds in the Dobroudja, and the village was not thinking of rebellion. The few men who were left were peaceable craftsmen; there was no courage in their hearts. They all hid. From behind the drawn curtains, through the cracks of gates and fences, they looked with their wives at the green flag as it fluttered against the dark clouds, and waited to see what would happen. There was no one in front of the *Konak*—neither Ali the *Soubash* nor the *zaptiehs*.

For a second or two the village seemed dead, as if it had been struck by lightning. Then a song rang out. Some men were singing as they wound their way down the narrow streets, but they were not to be seen. There they came: five or six men with rifles. A tall man marched at their head—Miloush, Old Roussi's son, in *haidout* garb, scowling, his red hair blowing in the wind. The men who followed him strode along soldier-fashion with blazing eyes, inspired and intent, singing as they came. But Miloush, tall, trim Miloush, raised his rifle from time to time and shouted: "To arms!"

The men, hidden in their houses, bent their heads; the women wept. They watched the lads marching through the village alone, going up to the Threshing Ground and stopping by the green flag. There the black figures were now gathered in tight straight ranks. They were bareheaded. Against the darkness of the clouds, *Pop* Roussko's vestments shone golden, and when the howling of the wind died down, the long-drawn-out chanting of a prayer was heard.

Regularly, from house to house, through the courtyard gates, across garden walls and fences, the news was handed on, as if over a wire. A Turk from Gerlovo, who had come to sell flour, had been killed. All the Turkish gypsies had been locked up and were going to be slaughtered. But then came the worst rumor of all: the *haidouts* were going from house to house and forcing the men out. The frightened tailors and saddlers sought safer hiding places. But the curious eyes of the women never left the cracks of the gates.

Then they saw Old Roussi—tall, slender, white-haired. He must have been in a hurry, because he had not managed to wind his red waistband around his trousers, and had come out with the cord that held them up still showing. He was gay, smiling, striking his arms with his hands—such was his habit—and humming to himself: "Tsum-tsum-tsumunum! Tsum-tsum-tsumunum!"

Some of the women overcame their fear and emerged from their gates.

"Christ is risen, good folk!" Old Roussi called to them. "Congratulations on your kingdom! And long life to it!" And turning, he pointed to the Threshing Ground, saying: "Do you see them? They're our own soldiers! Tsum-tsum-tsumunum! Tsum-tsum-tsumunum!"

Suddenly his brows drew together in a frown, his face grew dark, he waved his arms and cried: "To arms! To arms!" Then he began again: "Tsum-tsum-tsumunum! Tsum-tsum-tsumunum!"

No one could believe that this was Old Roussi, who had dozed for years on end on his bench. They didn't believe he was drunk; they thought, rather, that he might be mad.

But Old Roussi made the round of almost the whole village. Then he went back to the Threshing Ground, rejoiced at the lads, and rejoiced at Miloush. At one moment he started, for he realized that he still had work to do. After having told the news to his own village, he had to tell it to the neighboring villages. And, without delay, just as he was, with the rope that held up his trousers still showing, he seized a *yamourlouk* from somewhere, and set out across country.

The cold wind had to pierce him, the peasants to whom he brought the glad tidings had to scold him, and threaten that they would tie him up and hand him over to the *zaptiehs*, before he came to himself, and collected his wits. Then he turned back. The first doubts shook his soul. Before his eyes a miracle was taking place: the fine drizzle that had been falling since morning had turned to sleet, and now snow was falling. "Why is the weather like this?" Old Roussi wondered. "What will become of the lads?" And he hurried back to the village, battered by the blizzard and the snow, which was falling like a white veil over plain and mountain.

As he entered the village at one end, the band left at the other, along Vlassyo's road. Old Roussi stopped and stared around: the flag had dropped, and the black figures swayed wearily as they made their way up the hill with difficulty. Above them the forests were black, and frozen branches swayed over the whitened earth. The flag disappeared from sight as did the last man in the dusk and the blizzard. Old Roussi bent his head and hurried back to his house.

The following day he was seated on his bench, gazing at the white Balkan Mountains. Everywhere thick snow dazzled his eyes. White snow and green leaves—that was a wonder never seen before. Old Roussi wrapped his fur coat around him, gazed at the Balkan Mountains, and his eye seemed to ask: "Why did this happen? What will become of the lads?"

Now the worst hours began for the village. The Sultan's soldiers were advancing on it. The *chorbadjis* were on the alert. Old Neiko Barouchka, the wisest and most honey-tongued of them, was sent to welcome the Pasha, bow down to him and tell him that the village was not to blame, and that the *haidouts* had come down from the mountains. Dobromeritsa grew black with men, like an antheap. Over there the Gerlovo *Yourouks* had stopped, their heads wrapped in huge turbans, with ropes wound around their waists—for the loot. But the *chorbadjis* begged the Pasha hard and were ready to give anything to save the village. The Pasha kept his word and did not allow the Gerlovo *Yourouks* to attack the village. But they still stayed at Dobromeritsa—a black and terrible rabble amid the white snow around them.

Old Roussi sat motionless on his bench, staring before him. He cared not a whit for the Gerlovo Turks, nor was he troubled by the cares of the *chorbadjis*. He gazed at the mountains, staring at paths and ravines, straining his ears to hear if shots would be fired anywhere in that winter stillness. "Winter in May," he thought. "That's bad. They'll be caught by their tracks, like hares."

He sat there in the same way the following day. The Gerlovo Turks had gone, and where they had been at Dobromeritsa, there was a big black circle, as if a herd had lain there. But fear still weighed over the village. Old Roussi was, perhaps, the only person who dared stay outside.

Unexpectedly, a noise was heard at the end of the village. It rose higher, grew, and invaded the village like a storm. Drums, shouts, and songs were heard, and amid it all the long-drawn and whining melody of the *zourlas*. There they came; they appeared at Burdo: horsemen at the head, then wave after wave of foot soldiers. And long poles rose above them, and on the poles human heads had been stuck. Old Roussi seemed to lose consciousness. The *zourlas* wailed, the drums thundered. There—was that a shout, or the howling of a pack of wolves? Then again those sharp, terrible blows on the drums, as if a keen sword were striking the village, whistling and flashing in the sunlight and amid the whiteness of the snow. Like a black river the horde flowed through the village, with those terrible poles swaying over their heads.

Old Roussi turned his gaze to the mountains. His eyes saw nothing, his hands shook.

When he looked toward the *Konak* once more, the horde of *bashi-bazouks* had stopped in a circle, while the poles with the heads had been stuck in the ground on the square. Sinister and terrible saplings appeared to have grown out of the snow.

A public crier was sent around—his voice choked with fear and pain: everyone was to go and see the heads, and say whether he knew any of them.

No one went. Then the *zaptiehs* set out and began knocking on doors. They saw Old Roussi on his bench and dragged him off. He drew near the poles, shuddering and pale. He raised his eyes, he saw the head on the first pole and recognized it. The earth shook beneath his legs. "Miloush!" he almost cried out, but the word froze on his lips. And he swallowed his tears and drew himself up. He passed by all the poles, looked at them, and turned and looked at the Pasha. His eyes were cold and calm.

"Do you know them?" the Pasha asked.

"No, *Aga*, I do not know them. I do not know any of them."

And he set out for his home, tall, slender, his hair white, as white as the snow on the mountains. He stared before him and was silent. When he passed by Miloush's little shop, his heart contracted. A black raven had perched on the withered top of the poplar tree and was croaking. Lower down, behind the wooden fence, under the apple tree, someone was looking through the cracks toward the *Konak*. And Old Roussi heard Lyutsa's voice:

"Oh, dear Lord, it's he . . . Miloush, dear Miloush!" Old Roussi heard this, but he did not start, he did not turn.

It was spring again, the meadows were green once more, the Balkan Mountains were beautiful again. Old Roussi sat on his bench thinking: "What was all this for?" Miloush's little shop was shut, and his hammer was still. In the evening Lyutsa would pass by on her way home from the fountain, and quietly, with restraint, as if only the two of them were to hear, she would say: "Good evening, Granddad Roussi!"

Dodovanyak would come to see him, too. One evening, when the Balkan Mountains grew dark and stars shone above them, he whispered to Old Roussi: "A bigwig came to Sliven: he gave orders to have the heads of the lads put away, and not to leave them on the rubbish heaps, but to have them buried in the Bulgarian cemetery. In the evening some women wanted to go and light candles there. They weren't allowed to. *Zaptiehs* were placed on guard with orders not to let anyone in. But when dusk fell . . ."

Dodovanyak lowered his voice still more: "But when dusk fell and it grew dark, float lights dropped from heaven. I was told this, Granddad Roussi, people saw it with their own eyes. A float light on each grave. Like stars . . ."

"Good evening, Granddad Roussi," Lyutsa said.

And Old Roussi seemed to hear that same voice, long ago, in the distance, crying: "Miloush, dear Miloush!" And it grew weaker and weaker, as if the echo of Gurmovets were repeating it seven times running.

As if it had been awakened from a dream, the old poplar tree, a hundred years old, stirred its leaves, shook its branches, and rustled softly.

Translated by MARGUERITE ALEXIEVA

Ivan Vazov

(1850–1922)

Ivan Vazov was born on June 27, 1850 in the town of Sopot. At first he went to school in his native town, then in Kalofer where he studied under Hristo Botev's father, Botyo Petkov, in 1865.

In 1870 Vazov left for Rumania and went to live in Oltenita with his uncle, who was a merchant. At the same time he began to contribute to the *Periodichesko Spissanié* journal. Here it was that his poem "The Pine-Tree" was printed. It is believed to be his first published work.

In 1877 Vazov joined the Central Charity Committee (similar to the former Central Revolutionary Committee) and became its secretary. After the Russo-Turkish War was declared, the committee decided that their mission was completed and issued an appeal to the people to support the Russian army.

During the war Vazov was in the service of the governor of Svishtov Naiden Gerov. Later he was transferred to Roussé as a clerk for special services and a translator at the governor's office. Here he made friends with Lyuben Karavelov. Owing to an illness he had to seek employment at another place more suitable for his health, and he accepted the post of president of the district court in Berkovitsa (1879). His stay in that town coincided with one of his most productive literary periods.

In the autumn of 1880 the Berkovitsa District Court was closed down and Vazov settled in Plovdiv, then the capital of Eastern Rumelia. He was appointed deputy and member of the permanent council controlling the government, at the same time devoting much time to social and cultural work. In 1882 he began the publication of the *Naouka* magazine, in which some of his works, including his first prose pieces, appeared. In Plovdiv, he also served for some time as the editor of *Narodniy Glas* newspaper. At the end of 1884, the publication of *Naouka* was discontinued. In the following year, 1885, Vazov undertook, with Konstantin Velichkov, the publication of the *Zora* magazine, of which, however, no more than five numbers appeared.

In 1884 Vazov traveled through Constantinople, Thessaloniki, and Athens to Italy, where he spent the longest time in Naples and Rome. The result of this trip was his collection of poems, *Italy* (1884).

In connection with the Union of Bulgaria and Eastern Rumelia (September 6, 1885) Vazov experienced some disappointments, because he was a member of the so-called Union Party, which came to power and pledged to support the Union, but later failed to support it. Very soon, however, his attention was wholly occupied by the Serbo-Bulgarian War. In the general patriotic upsurge, he found himself on the battlefield. But with the countercoup following the dethronement of Alexander of Battenberg, his situation as a Russophile became precarious. He was forced to seek political asylum in Odessa in 1886.

In Odessa Vazov was given a warm welcome by the Bulgarian émigrés, but soon grew intensely homesick. Under the pressure of his memories he began writing a prose work which was to become his masterpiece—the novel *Under the Yoke*.

During the following period of his life Vazov devoted himself entirely to writing. During the first decade of this century he worked mainly on historical subjects, and during the 1920's his attention was mostly occupied by the events of World War I. He sang of the courage of the Bulgarian soldier. His last works frequently show traces of chauvinism. On October 24, 1920 the seventieth anniversary of the author was celebrated, and he was given the title of "people's poet." Vazov died on September 22, 1922.

His works have been collected in twenty volumes published from 1955 to 1957 by the Bulgarski Pissatel publishing house.

Old Yotso Is Watching

When I remember our fathers, forefathers, and relatives who passed to another world before our country's liberation—before seeing the bright rays of liberty—I often think how astonished and happy they would be if by a miracle they could wake from their eternal sleep in their graves, emerge into this world, and take a look around. How startled they would be by every unfamiliar and incredible aspect of life which would surround them and to which they would feel alien.

But the poor souls will never rise again and never enjoy the miracles of liberty to which we have grown so accustomed that we view it with indifference—liberty which they never dreamed of in their wildest fantasies!

No, they will never rise again. No one ever has.

But there lived a man who died on the eve of the war of liberation and who did not rise again, but could relish such a resurrected person's astonishment at the sight of liberated Bulgaria without experiencing the disillusionments of living people with sight.

He was eighty-four-year-old Yotso.

He lived in a remote mountain village of only several homes, nestling in a high shady fold of Stara Planina above the Isker gorge.

Old Yotso, a simple but shrewd old man, had experienced the hard life of a serf with all its hardships, wretchedness, and hopelessness, and had the misfortune suddenly to lose his sight in his home town at the age of sixty-four, just on the eve of the Russo-Turkish War.

He remained alive but was dead to life and light, with a secret longing still burning in his heart to see "the Bulgarian thing," as he called liberated Bulgaria!

Only images from the dark past lived in his heart. A host of memories of life in bondage—horrid and evil memories—lived in the old man's still vigorous mind. He could see in his mind what he had once seen with his eyes: red fezes stood out clearly in the darkness, turbans, whips, fierce Turks with cruel faces, a long night of bondage without ray of hope or happiness—he had been born in it and he died in it.

The echo of war hardly reached those then inaccessible Balkan highlands. The war began and ended, and its salvos never resounded in the rocks of the forbidding Isker gorge.

Bulgaria was liberated.

And Old Yotso was liberated: people told him so.

But he was blind, he could not see Liberation, nor could he feel it. For him Liberation was expressed in the words: "There are no more Turks." And he felt there were none.

But he was longing to see "the Bulgarian thing," to enjoy it.

In the humble peasants of his village, in their conversation, thoughts, and concern for their daily bread he sensed nothing particularly new. They were the same people with the same passions, misfortunes, and poverty as before. He listened to the same babble and noise in the pub; heard the same village rows; felt the same struggle against need and nature in this forsaken, barren, and remote place, far removed from the world.

Sitting under the branches of the gnarled oaks in front of his plot with a lifeless look, dreamily directed towards space, he would ask in surprise: "Where is the Bulgarian thing?"

If he had had sight, he would have flown like an eagle to see what there was in this new world. "It is now I need my eyes!" he thought bitterly.

To see liberated Bulgaria was his constant wish. This thought overshadowed all else. The din of the life around him left him indifferent and impassive; everything was so petty, insignificant, commonplace, a mere nothing. He was afraid he would die before finding out what "the Bulgarian thing" was like; or that he might lose his wits in old age without becoming acquainted with this marvelous thing.

One day—it was in the fifth year after Liberation—a rumor spread in the village that the chief county officer was arriving, who knows by what hidden ways of God.

This news stirred the village.

Old Yotso's poor old heart was moved; his soul was roused by a sweet and burning emotion he had not experienced until then. Now he would see "the Bulgarian thing"! Really see it!

He inquired what sort of a man this important person was, what sort of a *maimourin*. More knowledgeable peasants told him that the chief officer was something like a *kaimakamin*, like a pasha.

"A Bulgarian pasha?" he asked, breathless with emotion.

"Bulgarian, what else!" they answered.

"Our own? Bulgarian?" he again asked in astonishment.

"Do you want him to be a Turk, Yotso?" the peasants answered pityingly, since they had seen chief officers and more important people in Vratsa—no one had been as far as Sofia.

But Old Yotso was not satisfied with this answer. He asked how importantly the man was dressed, how he walked, whether he carried a sword. They told him.

"You say he wears a sword?" And he sighed happily.

"We shall see him when he comes," his old head would think as it wagged.

The important person arrived and was put up at Denko's. Denko's house, the only presentable one in the village, with its two stories plastered with mud outside, its small windows, one of which had even glass panes, with its narrow flight of stairs on the outside, was chosen to accommodate the visitor.

Old Yotso ran towards Denko's, knocked with his stick on the wicker gate, and called: "Denko, is the visitor here?"

Denko saw him and frowned: "He's here, Old Yotso. What have you come for? The chief officer's tired, leave him alone now!"

"Tell him to come here for a minute!" said Old Yotso and

tapped with his stick across the yard, making for the stairs leading to the porch.

"Why the hurry? What is it, what do you want the chief officer for?" asked the host.

"Nothing, I want him, so . . . you tell him: 'Old Yotso, the blind man, wants to see you!' "

"You want to see him?" Denko smiled bitterly and thought to himself: "You'll see him when you see your mug in the well."

But the old man insisted. He was already tapping his stick on the first step of the stairs. His old head was shaking. The host went in and told the chief officer that a childish blind old man wanted him.

"What for?" the important man asked.

"He came to see you."

"To see me? And you say he's blind?"

"He went blind five or six years ago." And he told him how Old Yotso had suddenly lost his sight when the Russian brothers were coming.

"He was a well-to-do and a reasonable man," Denko added, "but the Lord willed he should lose his sight somehow. Now he looks but does not see. He's almost a dead man. Why doesn't the Lord take him! It was a good thing he had some property—some land and cattle—so his son and daughter-in-law are looking after him. He's very well looked after."

"How interesting!" said the important man. "Let him come in! No, wait, better let me go out!" And he went out and came down the stairs.

By the click of his boots Old Yotso recognized that it was him, the Bulgarian pasha, and he took off his cap.

The officer saw in front of him a man white-bearded but still sturdy, with a large, sunburned, coarse face, a worn-out vest, and trousers tied with string. His whole body was shaking. He stood in a humble posture with his white head bowed.

"What is it, granddad?" the chief officer asked kindly.

The old man raised his head and turned his lifeless eyes to him. Only the muscles of his big face twitched nervously.

"Is it Your Honor, son?"

"It is I, granddad."

"The pasha?"

"The very same," the chief said with a smile.

Old Yotso drew nearer to him, put his cap under his left armpit, took the man's arm, fingered the stuff of his sleeves; with trembling hands he touched the silver-braided epaulets on his shoulders, then stood on tiptoe and kissed them.

"Dear Lord, I have seen!" said the old man and made the sign of the cross, and with his sleeve wiped away the tears gushing from his dead eyes.

Then he bowed low and said: "Excuse me, son, for troubling you!"

And, tapping his stick, he went out bare-headed.

Again uneventful and unhappy days set in for him, again the deep darkness of blindness in which only one vision with its twinkling radiance shone like a bright star: the Bulgarian chief officer, the pasha! To the old man it seemed that for the first time in five years he had been able to see for a minute and had seen "the Bulgarian thing," a ray of "Bulgaria," and he was fully convinced there were no more Turks and there was freedom in the world.

Apart from this event, everything was as before: he met the same people in the pub and listened to the same arguments and gossip. Life around him went on in the same way, with its worries, toil, and petty struggles. He took no part in them; they were alien to him and he was alien to them. He had only one happiness and it sweetened his dark life—the awareness that Bulgaria was free. And when sometimes he would take note of the local animosities and quarrels he wondered why people embittered each others' lives when they should be always cheerful and happy, because everything was Bulgarian and there was freedom. Why, they had sight! They should be happy!

"One would think that it is they who are blind and I who can see," he thought. And he would sit under the oak trees listening to the sound of the Isker way down below, and the thought that it came from afar and had probably seen greater things made him happy. And time passed.

One day Old Yotso's heart was stirred by a new emotion. The only soldier from the village had returned on leave.

"How did he come? Is he in soldier's uniform?" Old Yotso asked in agitation.

"Yes, in soldier's dress," was the answer.

"With a sword?"

"You should just hear it click, Old Yotso!"

The old man rushed to Kolyo's son: "Young man, are you there?"

"What do you want, Yotso?" asked Old Kolyo.

"Where's the soldier? I want to see him."

Kolyo called to his son to come out so Yotso could see him, and he smiled proudly. The soldier came out.

The old man could tell it by the sword clicking on the stones. He rushed forward and shook the nimble hand that the soldier thrust cheerfully to him. Then he touched his thick overcoat, buttons, and cap, and he took the sword and kissed it.

After that he looked at the soldier with his lifeless gaze and astonished face, down which two tears ran. "So now we have a Bulgarian army?" he asked, trembling with joy.

"Yes, we do, Old Yotso, an army and captains and our own prince," the soldier answered proudly.

"Won't he pass this way sometime?"

"Who? The prince?" and both the soldier and Kolyo laughed at Yotso's ignorance.

And Old Yotso asked about the Bulgarian palace in Sofia, about Bulgaria's guns, Bulgarian ceremonies and everything. And, as he listened to the marvels the soldier related, it seemed to him that a sun was rising somewhere deep in his soul, casting light on everything, and again he saw the green mountains and barren peaks with eagles perched on them and God's bright world, splendidly beautiful!

And the inspired soldier went on talking about all manner of marvels.

"Oh, what a shame! It's now I need my eyes!" the old man would say.

For a long time Old Yotso cherished these impressions. To this remote village no outsider came from the new Bulgaria to add a new streak of happy emotion in his heart. No event broke the even life of the village, not even a remote semblance of the seething life of Bulgaria. The political tremors that deeply shook the entire country one after the other were not reflected by the peaceful sky of the village. No newspaper reached these few poor homes, for no one could read; there was no teacher, for there was no school; there was no priest, for there was no church; there was no policeman, for there was no village council; and, besides, the winter with its snow and mud cut off the difficult contact with the world for seven months.

They heard only faintly about the war with Serbia in which the only soldier in the village perished. Only vague, indefinite rumors reached them that something was going on beyond the mountains, but what it was nobody knew. In their struggle to earn their hard underbaked rye bread there was no time for both toil and curiosity in the dark minds of these dark people.

And Old Yotso lived in the undisturbed peace of his village, ignorant of world events.

Little by little he sank into apathy about everything that surrounded him, into a mild mood approaching senility. For hours and days on end he would sit pensively in the shade of the oak trees listening to the dull roar of the Isker, his lifeless eyes staring aimlessly into space.

It seemed nothing new would come from outside to draw his soul out from this slow and quiet dying.

But such a thing did happen.

Rumor spread that a railway would be built through the Isker gorge; engineers were already taking measurements there. This rumor reached Old Yotso's ears and, as if with a hammer, struck and shattered the lethargy of his soul. In the depths of his mind a sleeping memory awoke. In his youth he had heard from a wealthy man in Vratsa, Mano by name, that pashas and important people and Frenchmen had said it was impossible for a train to pass through the gorge—that it would be throwing millions and millions to the wind. "What? A Bulgarian railway?"

He couldn't believe it. A railway? Through this gorge, through these steep places where even a horse could not find a foothold? Where goat's hoofs could hardly balance on the sheer slopes? "A big power had not dared to do it, so how dare we?"

But the rumor persisted; it persisted in stirring the blind old man's imagination; it occupied his mind—in all else remaining in a state of infantile good humor.

But one day they told him the building of the railway was to begin. The peasants went to work there down by the Isker.

The old man wondered. "They have obviously found more knowledgeable engineers somewhere—it's a big world—are they French again?"

They told him they were Bulgarians.

The old man was stunned. "Ours? Bulgarian engineers? But pashas and Frenchmen said it was impossible! So you say we have people more skilled? But what about the millions, the thousands of millions Mano used to talk about?"

"We've got millions, too. If you've a beard, you've a comb!"

Old Yotso's heart was brimming with admiration. An army, pashas, guns, a prince, skilled men, and millions, and marvel upon marvel.

Now "the Bulgarian thing" seemed to him great, powerful, immeasurable. His weak mind could not grasp its entire grandeur. Until then the symbols of "Bulgaria" for him were the district officer's epaulets and the soldier's sword he had touched and kissed. Now everything impressed him, astonished him with its power, and filled his heart with pride. Bulgarian hands were cutting mountains; Bulgarian minds were inventing things for one to ponder over and marvel at!

Where was Mano now, for Yotso to see what he would have to say?

When he heard the first detonations among the rocks which were being blown up by the charges, he wiped his eyes on his sleeve because they filled with tears.

From then on his favorite place to stand was the rock about fifty feet away from his plot, overhanging the deep gorge of the Isker, which thundered from the feverish labors.

From morning till night he stood on the rock, listened to the din, the detonations, the striking of picks on the earth, the rumble of wheels, the bustle, the confused sound of the exertions of the giant enterprise.

The railway was completed and began operating. With trembling heart Old Yotso heard the first sound of the train's whistle, the rumble of the wheels on the rails.

How the "Bulgarian train" whistled and thundered! It was as if Yotso was reborn again; he was a new man.

As the time for the train approached, he would regularly go to the rock to hear the whistle and to watch the Bulgarian train roaring through the gorge.

The railway was connected in his mind with the notion of free Bulgaria. In its thunder it spoke to him of the new Bulgarian era. As before, there was nothing in the village to remind him of it; only the whistle proclaimed it. And when the time came for the whistle, Yotso dropped everything and rushed with his stick to the rock to watch.

Passengers gazing from the carriage windows at the pictur-
esque bends of the gorge were amused to see a man standing on the
slope opposite and waving his cap. It was Old Yotso. It was his way
of saluting the new Bulgaria.

The peasants of his village grew used to seeing him every day
on the rock and would say with a smile: "Old Yotso is watching. . . ."

This man, dead to life, was reborn at the echo of the train and
was cheered by it like a child. It was the only embodiment of free
Bulgaria; since he had never seen a train in his life, his imagination
pictured it as a giant flying monster belching fire from its mouth,
roaring and thundering with incredible force and speeding through
the mountain, spreading news of the power, glory, and progress of
free Bulgaria.

His blindness and kindness had, like armor, preserved his soul
from the disillusion of its somber aspects, like the disillusions which
we, people with good sight, experience.

Happy blind man!

Often a new railway guard, amazed to see an old man always
on the rock at the same time, waving his cap at the flying train,
would ask the peasants entering the third-class carriages at the next
stop: "Who's the man waving his cap from the rock? Is he crazy?"

And the peasants would usually reply: "No, it's Old Yotso
watching. . . ."

One evening Yotso did not return home. In the morning his
son went straight to the rock to look for him, since he thought perhaps he had fallen into the ravine.

But he found him dead there, cap in hand.

Yotso had suddenly died as he greeted the new Bulgaria.

Translated by ZHANA MOLHOVA

Vesselin Andreyev

(1918–   )

Vesselin Andreyev was born on February 16, 1918 in Pirdop, where he received his elementary education. He finished secondary school in Sofia, and studied law at Sofia University. He first published in 1934 in *Bulgarska Rech* periodical and contributed to several other periodicals: *Suvremennik, Zhar, Horovod,* and *Zarya.* He edited the *Akademik* and *Srednogorska Missul* newspapers. Between 1941 and 1943 he went underground and worked in the resistance movement. In September 1943 he became a partisan, and in 1944 he was political commissar of the First Sofia Partisan Brigade Chavdar. He wrote the text for the march song of his detachment. After September 9, 1944 he was chief editor of the *Narodna Voiska* newspaper (1945–49) and of the *Literatouren Front* newspaper (1949–55). He worked for some time with the army writers' group at the Army Political Headquarters.

His publications include the following books: *Guerrilla Songs,* poems (1947); *In the Lopyan Forest* (1947); *There Is Moscow in the World* (1951); *Guerrilla Gift* (1959); and *Guerrilla Stories.*

One Night, One Day . . .

The low, laden sky seemed to be pressing heavily upon the damp darkness. Although Kamen had known these places ever since he was a child, he just missed bumping into the barrier at the level-crossing. He nudged his comrade, and the two of them soft-footed their way back to the patrol.

The column was following not far behind.

"Here we are, Comrade Commissar. The village lies just beyond the railway line."

One could hear the rearmost end of the file swearing in undertones as they stumbled into the compact bunch of men who had come to a sudden stop.

The Commissar whispered his last instructions to the men, then laid his hand on Kamen's shoulder: "You stay here with Raicho and Pesho to cover our rear. Keep your eyes peeled . . . no, what's the use in this pitch darkness. . . . Better keep your ears open!"

The order was so unexpected that Kamen gasped. The Commissar could not see the surprise on his face, but he caught the note of alarm in his voice.

"What's wrong? You took it for granted you'd be in on the raiding part, didn't you? Naturally . . ."

"But I know the village . . ."

"And the village knows you, too. The later they catch on to things, the better: we can invent any cover for you—a soldier, or a soldier on furlough. You've drawn up a chart for us, we'll manage!"

Should he tell him the truth? No, not in a couple of words, anyway, you never could tell how he would take it. He was so rash —but suppose something happened? Kamen finally mumbled: "Comrade Commissar, the mayor . . . he's not a bad sort. True, he's a bit stiff-necked, but . . ."

"What makes you think of the mayor? If he's a mayor, he's no good . . ."

"That's true, but everybody's not the same . . ."

"All right, all right. Cut it out, my boy."

The thirty-odd men disappeared one after the other into the darkness, their soft steps died away, but Kamen still stood peering after them.

"Well, are we going to hang about like this? Let's have your orders, they've left you in charge!"

Raicho was an old hand in the partisan movement, and he was sore that a novice should be commanding him.

"So you're envious, are you?" Kamen would have liked to snap back, but he was worrying about more important things just then. He instructed his two comrades to walk a hundred yards up and down the track and then come back to the grade crossing, while he strode down the road. It was better that way; he would be alone.

The noisy silence was full of invisible, yet intense life. The air was heavy with the pungent aroma of humid soil and rotting grass. The rivulet, swollen with melting snow, was babbling noisily, and the murmur of the water came to him like the sound of inarticulate human speech. Something intangible, springlike, enlivened the night —not spring itself, but a premonition of it.

That he was straining to catch every sound did not interfere with his thoughts. "I should have told them earlier. But I thought I'd do it in the village, if it was necessary. Now I've got to take it . . ."

He was back at the crossing again.

"All quiet!" his comrades whispered, then they parted again.

"All quiet . . . for you, yes. Ask me how I feel! If only Venko were here, he knows all about it . . ."

His comrade Venko had left for somewhere in the direction of Isker with the other partisans from his village. Kamen had found the battalion camping in the chalet below Mourgash Peak. They had taken him on trust, for he knew the password. Venko had told him to join them up in the mountain. But among these unknown people full of a bitter and legitimate hatred of the enemy, he had been afraid to admit that his father was a mayor.

The barking of dogs startled him. "They've got wind of them. I hope they make it . . . and the old man . . . I only hope they don't do him any harm! If anything were to happen, I'd never forgive myself . . . but he's to blame. 'I've been an honest man all my life and now you've disgraced me!' I'm supposed to have disgraced him! And with what? By joining the partisans! But isn't it a disgrace to be a mayor? After all, he's only got himself to blame."

His anxiety, however, was mounting. Kamen quickened his pace and did not wait for his comrades at the grade crossing.

They took possession of the village with surprising ease. As soon as the policeman in the building of the village council heard the word "gendarmes," he opened the door, sleepy and unarmed. He expected to be cursed or reprimanded for being absent from his post, but the partisans thanked him in a biting manner and his jaw went stiff at this politeness. The forest and field guards were caught napping in their homes. The "public force" had preferred not to take any chances on such a treacherous night.

The raiding party stood concealed near the walls of the village council in combat readiness.

The Commissar sent a few people to fill the rucksacks with food from the co-operative store and dispatched ten or twelve men in pairs to find bread and to invite the peasants to a meeting, while he himself, with two partisans in the uniforms of soldiers, started for the mayor's house.

The house was small with wooden shutters and a stout oak door. They knocked, then listened for the creaking of bedsprings or the padding of bare feet on the floor. There was not a sound. They knocked again.

"Sir, the captain wants to see you. You're to say where we are to billet the company!" The Commissar tried to pass for a simple-minded gendarme.

Not a sound. . . .

Pressing himself against the wall, the mayor held his breath. Alarming thoughts were whirling through his head and he had not slept a wink; ever since the fierce barking of dogs had startled him, he had done nothing but walk up and down and smoke, smoke and think. When he heard the thudding of heavy boots, he stopped dead by the window. Through the crevices in the shutters he could see nothing in the pitch darkness outside, but stationed there he could hear better what was going on.

What were those gendarmes doing there in the dead of the night? Had they not set the partisans' homes on fire already, had they not interned so many people and seized everything they could lay their hands on? Perhaps they already knew about Kamen. . . .

There was a knocking on the door again!

"Come on, sir, wake up, the captain's waiting. And he's got a temper, and not half. . . ."

The voice did not distract him from his thoughts, it was as if it had nothing to do with him. They probably knew. The telegram had been received last night, it must have reached the police. No, let them come in the morning. It would be different in the daylight. And suppose they set his house on fire? You never knew with them, they might do it. Especially if the plain-clothes men had come. They would do it without batting an eyelid—they had beaten Sando to death, and Latin, and even Grandpa Stanko! No, they wouldn't dare, after all he was the mayor there. . . . Ah, that Kamen! He'd bring order to Bulgaria! "I hope at least I've done more good than harm to people . . . but the disgrace of it?" he thought. "A deserter from the army! He'd deserted from the army, not the police."

Outside the Commissar was wondering: "Why doesn't he open the door? Or, maybe, they have a password. Most likely he's not in." He decided to come straight to the point—there was nothing to lose with it, anyway: "Listen, sir, we're not gendarmes but partisans. Open the door if you don't want anything to happen to you. We only need the key to the secret archives."

The mayor could hardly help letting out a cry. The neighboring villages were full of gendarmes and then, suddenly—partisans? No, these must be plain-clothes men. They were testing him. All right, their old Uncle Ranghel knew a thing or two.

"Comrade Commissar, why all this courtesy?" sang out an impatient youthful voice. "Let's set his house on fire, he'll rush out then all right, like a rat."

"We are not gendarmes, are we?" came the Commissar's stern answer. "Such talk doesn't become you!"

"Do they ever show any pity for us?"

"This isn't a question of pity. And, besides, who do you mean by they? Do you know him? Kamen said he was a good man. The devil only knows, he might really be out—let's go!"

In his anger—they had lost so much valuable time!—the Commissar forgot that many of the new partisans had kept their real names. The mayor leaned his head on the wall, his hand pressed hard against his heart. It seemed to have disappeared, leaving a painful void in its place. When the steps had died away, he took out a coarse blue handkerchief and wiped his face for a long time. Then with unsteady steps he went to get the jug of water. His face was wet, his lips dry. He drank thirstily, as if he had never seen water in his life. Then he lit a cigarette and sat on the bed. He inhaled deeply, hiding his cigarette in the hollow of his hand, and the tobacco did not taste strong enough.

"Kamen said he was a good man . . ." The joy had surged up in him so suddenly that he was still unable to accept it as true. And what a row he had had with Kamen when he was leaving! "You are no longer my son!" "And you are no longer my father!" Kamen was his youngest child, but the mayor was a hard man and did not want to admit even to himself that he loved him more than his other children; he considered this unfair, but could anyone deceive his own heart? Maybe he was with them, too. Was he perhaps in the building of the village council? His feet sought and found his rubber shoes and he put them on. He threw on his sheepskin coat and took his cap. What else had he to take? Yes, some bread! And a little cheese and bacon.

He got everything ready and then sat down again. "Has anybody told you that Kamen is with them?" he thought. "If he had been in the village, he would have come home. He ought to have come!" And the pride which prevented him from understanding Kamen's ideas rose up in him again. Why didn't he come? Perhaps he wanted his father to go and bow and scrape to him. Nothing doing! Or perhaps he didn't trust his own father? "You're a mayor," Kamen used to keep hammering into him, "you're a mayor, understand! Who is going to believe that you have been honest?" It was his pride again that kept him from confiding in him and telling him that, since the atrocities had started in the neighboring villages, he had wanted to quit, but the authorities had mobilized him as a civilian —it seemed that those who had graduated from the university were not very eager to serve in this primitive village. But these people here, these partisans, had trusted him, they had not done anything to him or his house. He thought it was strange calling them "*these people*," although he had never inveighed against them. They were simply strangers to him, and he did not want to rise up against the State. But in all justice it must be said that the boys who had run away from the village to join the partisans were good boys. Kamen, too. And then, the words: "We are not gendarmes, are we?" They had pride. Had there been anything to prevent them from burning down his house? It would be interesting to see them, to speak to them. But how could he possibly hand over the keys to them?

The village bell chimed three times and set the dogs barking again. They were probably leaving.

He smoked another cigarette, then snatched up the small bundle.

The sky had cleared up, the big stars shone as if they had been washed. He stole along in the shadow of the houses away from evil eyes, listened, then went on again.

A disturbing silence reigned in the village square.

He trod on something soft and bent down to pick it up. Naturally, they were doing it everywhere—they had burned the lists of goods scheduled for requisition, the tax accounts.

His room was in a mess and involuntarily he felt vexed. He hated disorder! He struck another match. The safe was locked, but they had taken the secret archives away. The money was still there with a note on top of it. "We understand that these funds are for the compulsory seizures exacted from the peasants. They are to be paid for everything immediately. Political Commissar Voinov." Well, they even issued orders! And they had not made the mistake of burning the list of the amounts due to the different peasants. They had done what they had wanted to do without his help. The tax collector must have assisted them, he had the second key to the safe.

He entered the rooms of the clerk and of the guards, unconsciously looking for some trace of Kamen.

Outside a leaflet rustled at his feet. He picked it up, opened his sheepskin coat. "Dear peasants, today is the militant Day of Labor. . . ." The match was burning down and he glanced at the signature: "General Staff of the First Battalion of the Chavdar Brigade." He slipped the leaflet into his pocket and looked around. So that was it—it was May Day today—that was right, today, the dawn was about to break. He stared: two flags with their flagpoles crossed flew from the chimney in the light wind. The tricolor—he could distinguish the white strip on top quite clearly, and the other, a dark one, probably a red one—their banner. He almost started to go and pull them down, but remained where he was. Climbing up chimneys was not for one his age. And it was not only his age. So, they had raised the national flag, too.

The village square was still silent and disturbingly quiet. His soul felt empty and anxious. Above him rose the dark mass of the Balkan mountains: that was where those whom Kamen had joined were going to. Far away, down in the plain twinkled the lights of the village of Bogrov—the headquarters of the others, who were going to hold him to account in the morning. And he was alone in this immeasurable night, alone in the silent village, alone under the cold stars high above. Where could he go to? To the mountain? They wouldn't have gone very far yet. But he realized quite clearly that he could not join them. If he had only managed to see them.

In his hands he still held the small bundle. No one needed it now.

They had a long way to go that night, and as soon as they left the village the Commissar stopped his men so that they could have a bite to eat. They immediately started to chatter excitedly.

Kamen swallowed big mouthfuls (for two days his stomach had been gnawing at him), but he did not enjoy the food! There was not a morsel of his father's food in it.

As soon as they met at the grade crossing, Misho began to get at him: "So he's a good chap, your mayor, is he? We've been kind enough not to set his house on fire . . . or perhaps we've been silly."

Nothing bad had happened after all! He was alive—but his joy did not last long—nothing bad, eh? He'd barricaded himself in like a. . . . And he would most likely have opened the door to the others!

His secret alienated him from the people who shared their bread with him, and Kamen took the conversation for a personal accusation against himself.

"The Shopi will always be Shopi! Zacchari Stoyanov* was right when he said that it would take five hundred years for the Shopi to wake up!" Itska, a partisan since the autumn before, said in a philosophical strain.

"What's wrong with the Shopi?" said a man from one of the neighboring villages.

"What's wrong? Everything. Do you know how they welcomed us in the Pirdop region? The whole village turned out into the square. There were cheers, embraces, flowers. You're so touched with such things you'd like to cry. And here we couldn't even organize a meeting."

In view of that night's happenings, they could find no convincing retort and moreover they were feeling the shyness of novices in the presence of the old partisan. Nevertheless, some voices were raised in objection to what he had said:

"And who gave you the bread you are eating now?"

"Look here, Itska, didn't you see what happened the day before yesterday, just below Mourgash? Two hundred new recruits got together, and all of them Shopi."

"Why don't you try to understand: the people have not yet got inured to all this arson, these internments and killings. Some of them didn't even want to believe that we were partisans."

But Itska did not give in easily: "All right, all right. As you're all Shopi, you'll naturally stand by your own folk. But when they understood who we were, why didn't they come out?"

"We can be satisfied that as many turned out as they did. You've slung your rifle, my friend, over your shoulder, and off you go to the shelter of the thick oak trees! But tomorrow they'll be in the bloody hands of Kocho Stoyanov." †

The Commissar saw that he would have to intervene. "Easy there! Be quiet, you're not in the camp. What's all this nonsense you're talking about, Itska? Think what you're saying: the gendarmes had hardly left the village and in we walked, straight off. And Docho Hristov ‡ had been boasting that he'd exterminated us to

* Bulgarian writer and historian, author of memoirs on the April 1876 uprising against Ottoman bondage.

† An army general, commanding the anti-guerrilla activities in the district of Sofia.

‡ Then Minister of the Interior.

the last man. Tomorrow he'll be raging mad, for he'll be the joke of everybody. But how did we manage to pull things off? Thanks to our links, to those in the village who help us—they informed us immediately. Our links there are Shopi. That's clear, isn't it? You may be a partisan, and a good one, but don't show off in front of the people!"

Itska lapsed into silence, and the men began murmuring with approval. Kamen felt ashamed and angry with himself: he had not come out in defense of the village, his own village. And again it was because of his father.

It was only at daybreak that the mayor was able to get to sleep and when he heard a jostling sound and a shout of "The captain is asking for you!" the sun was already pretty high in the sky and he had the feeling that he'd just gone to bed. He rubbed his eyes, but the nightmare did not disappear: a noncommissioned officer and two gendarmes. They were absolutely silent, their rifles ready, as if for a hand-to-hand fight.

They led him away as if under arrest.

Soldiers and policemen were hurrying to and fro in the square. When the peasants, who appeared here and there in the neighboring streets, saw the mayor amid the pointed bayonets, they looked at each other. But the half-innocent, half-sly expressions could not be wiped out of their faces immediately. After all, you didn't see such things every day: five venturesome chaps, balancing themselves with their arms, were stepping gingerly along the slippery wet roof of the municipal building, as though performing a ritual dance around the damned flags, which fluttered with all the morning brilliance of their colors. The gendarmes were afraid of partisan tricks. Finally, spurred on by the captain's curses, they got hold of the chimney stack and furiously threw the flags down into the mud below.

The policemen, the tax collector, the forest guard, and the two field guards were sitting, looking very woebegone, in the mayor's room. The partisans had locked them in the cellar, advising them not to make a sound until morning, and now they regretted having taken heed of this advice. This reassured the mayor a little, for it meant that they had not seen him during the night. But they had at least some sort of justification for not having called the gendarmes, whereas he had none. In one corner of the room the storekeeper in charge of the co-operative store was moistening a bluish-violet swelling on his temple with a towel. He had been naïve enough to say that the partisans had paid for everything they had taken.

Two green-and-yellow army cars growled threateningly and suddenly fell silent in the middle of the square. An aged general had appeared, followed by several officers in combat uniforms, all of them silent. For part of the way they had been escorting the units which were detailed to follow the partisans.

"Bring the mayor here," the general hissed, without addressing anyone in particular. His aide-de-camp saluted and hurried off.

The general started walking about slowly—five steps forward, five steps back. "Your coolheadedness ought to inspire your subordinates with confidence in you," he thought, "that's true, but the devil himself could not stand this sort of thing. Mass flight to the maquis. Blow after blow. In the last two days alone they've struck at Sarantsi, Negoushevo, Dolno Kamartsi. And now, here! And what treachery—on the eve of May Day!" The general felt personally offended: he was in charge of the blockade, he had made the plan for it, he knew from cowardly deserters where the brigade had been formed. But he had got on the job too late. And now he was in the idiotic position of a blindfolded man senselessly waving his arms about without touching anyone, while getting blow after blow himself on the back of his head. And he had troops, gendarmes, policemen, special agents, the "public force" at his disposal. But as it is only human to find fault with others, he was raving against "that man" (he was thinking of the Minister of the Interior), who had declared in the newspaper that the partisans on Mourgash had been liquidated.

The general had a sound position and he could permit himself some latitude . . . in his thoughts: The blockhead! The chatterbox! Whom did he think he was going to deceive? The Germans, so that they would keep him in power a little longer? That very day the whole of Sofia, the whole of Bulgaria would know about it. Perhaps the general was exaggerating, but not very much. Quite a number of workers and evacuees had left for Sofia that morning. He would have stopped the train, would have isolated the village, as if it had been infected by the pest, but they had kept him in ignorance a whole night! There were no proper people in authority—they were a rabble. The army had been away for one single night, and they had made a mess of everything. In the whole village there had not been a single patriotic and courageous man to slip away and dash to Bogrov! The infection had caught on everywhere, and it ought to be nipped in the bud!

He came to a stop. They were bringing the major culprit.

When the mayor saw him, he gained new hope. It was a good thing that it was the general and not those bastards. He had heard that people were afraid of him, too, but still, he was an older man, a representative of the authorities who bore responsibility.

With a cigarette in his leather-gloved hand, the general was beating out a measure with one of his feet. Now and then painful shivers passed over his sallow, ashen face. His brows were puckered.

"Well, Mister Mayor?"

"At your orders, sir!" He took off his cap and clicked his heels slightly.

"My orders will come later," the general muttered. "Now I am putting questions. Why didn't you put up any resistance to the bandits?"

"But how could we possibly do so, sir? With one policeman and two field guards? And besides, they had seized them."

"Like that, eh?" he cried, furiously crushing the end of his cigarette under his boot and coming a step forward. "And you, Mister Mayor, are you a scarecrow or the representative of the law here? Why didn't you call upon the public force, the patriotic Bulgarians? Why didn't you put up any fight yourself?"

Last night's happenings, those strangers, "he is a good man," everything now seemed to him as beautiful and as distant as a dream. And this power here, real and threatening, was closing in and tightening its tentacles round him. But they probably did not know about Kamen, and he was endeavoring to find a way out.

"Since these"—he managed somehow to swallow the exact word that sprang to his tongue—"since these things started here, I have absolutely no authority. Every gendarme has greater authority than I have."

"Shut up . . . or I'll kill you! Are you trying to slander the army?"

And in order to remain true to his principle—to be always coolheaded—he started striding around. Then he snapped curtly and malevolently: "Why didn't you call us?"

He had been expecting this question for a long time, but he was not ready for it and said simply: "These people cut the telephone wires."

The general stared at him for a moment, then approached and struck first with one hand, then with the other, without taking off his gloves. In the heavy silence the slaps resounded with a dull and hollow sound.

The mayor stood there as if he had grown out of the soil, broad-shouldered, white-haired, his face darkened by the sun and winds of six decades. The scar, left by a shrapnel wound, which cut down his left eyebrow and gave a crushed look to his nose, now covered with blood, pulled his lips into a bitterly insulted and disgusted grin. His stiff shoulder, where the old wound had been, was a little higher than the other one, and he was bristling all over, shocked, yet keeping his dignity. The general instinctively turned his eyes away from the eyes filled with moisture and hatred. He considered himself a soldier and was a little sorry for having struck an old front fighter.

"Sir, I have been through two wars, and nobody has ever dared . . ." He was panting, his wrath drowning his words: "I will not forgive . . ."

The general felt easier; he had an excuse now. He waved the peasants away (he felt it was vexing that they had seen even so much) and planted himself in front of the mayor, his hands clasped behind him and his neck stretched up and poking out of the collar of his greatcoat, a stooping figure with a wrinkled nose.

"So you won't forgive, will you? 'The Peo-ple'—you call the robbers people, eh? The bandits?"

The mayor was silent. These stinging blows suddenly revealed many things to him, things he could not fathom or did not want to believe. Why had he blamed the smaller fry, the captains, the agents? He had thought that they were officious and were exceeding their authority, and that this was where the evil lay. No, that was the way they had been taught to act! Look at this man now, with the horsy head. He was the authority. He was the state. He was the army, of which he, the mayor, had talked so much. And he was striking him with his gloves on—he was squeamish, the fastidious ass.

The tax collector suddenly appeared. Puny and shabby, he touched his greasy cap with his fingers and pulled himself up to attention in a comical way, with the unrealizable longing of the noncombatant: "Sir, allow me to report!"

The general looked him over with aversion. "Now, where had this fellow come from?" He could not stand puny people, perhaps because he himself was not of a Herculean build. The tax collector managed to keep up his military pose for only a short time; then he resumed his natural appearance. He made a furtive sign to the general with his finger and winked nastily with both eyes:

"Could we go just a little aside . . . something confidential."

No, he was not all that naïve. The general would forgive him this familiarity. Without the mayor noticing it, he had read the telegram about Kamen's desertion. Why should he remain a tax collector all his life, when he'd got a chance of becoming a mayor?

The general did an about-face and started toward his victim like a real victor. Until that moment he had been showing off as a thunderer, but a secret doubt had been gnawing at him: "This country is lost," he thought, "when even the mayors have become such scoundrels." That was something too complicated and too terrible for his mind to cope with. But now everything was simplicity itself again: the mayor had been talking that way not because he was right, but because he was guilty.

"Aha-a-a! So you've been hiding it, have you?" the general hissed, as he gripped the chin of the white-haired man and jerked his head painfully. "Your son a bandit, a deserter, and you . . . a traitor," he sought for a stronger, more killing word and found one that he liked very much— "a perfidious traitor . . . a perfidious snake!"

He dusted his gloves and made a gesture to the officers: "His house, get to his house right away and burn it down! And shoot him!" He had finally calmed down and started for his car.

"Let me at least take my things out. They are my goods and chattels, why should they burn?" the mayor said most unexpectedly.

The general stopped short; this sounded to him like the quintessence of mockery.

"Are you an idiot, or what?! Your trip to the next world will be easier without luggage."

It was only now that the mayor realized everything. And before thinking what he was doing, he moved a step forward.

"What do you mean? Without a law court?"

This was an accusation, not a request. The general felt it and he was obviously only too pleased to come back, and placing his clenched fists on his hips and swaying to and fro on his toes, to declare:

"I am the court! I am the law. Without appeal and pardon. How do you like it?"

With his legs apart and his head thrown back, as if to protect himself from some evil smell, the mayor looked much taller and stronger than the general. He, at least, felt that way. No muscle quivered in his face, even his scar was as pale as his cheeks. Only his fingers trembled slightly and he clenched them and pressed them to his body soldier-fashion. He looked over the heads of all of them toward the mountain. How could this general possibly shoot him?

Why? Who had given him the right? If he carried on in this way, he would shoot everyone in Bulgaria. He nourished a faint hope that this was not going to happen now; perhaps it was never going to happen; but two gendarmes were already standing on each side of him and their bayonets stuck out above their heads. Was it true that he was going to die in a short while? This could not be true! "You're alive," he thought, "there is nothing wrong with you and then, all of a sudden—the end! And with no guilt either?" But the two men with the bayonets were waiting. Should he beg for pardon? Perhaps . . . perhaps they would, at least, put him on trial. . . . Hm, he was mayor and he had not been able to do anything for three absolutely innocent people the captain had taken away. The captain had not heeded him in the least; why should this one here do it—"Without appeal or pardon"—what was the use of humiliating himself?

The general kept swaying on his toes, probably expecting to have precisely this pleasure, but the mayor did not move; he only lowered his eyes to the level of the general's and looked straight into them: "Monster . . ."

The general shivered, stopped swaying on his toes, and an evil expression crossed his face, but he controlled himself with an effort and started laughing aloud. Then he turned and walked off in the direction of the cars.

It seemed to the mayor that he was running away.

He was walking through the village in which he had spent all his life and through which he was passing for the last time, and he was taking his last farewell of it. His wife had passed away. In good time, too, so she did not have to see him now. They were going to meet again, if such a meeting place existed. Gatsé and Milena were somewhere in Sofia, they knew nothing. It was better that way, for how could they say good-bye to their father while he was still alive? But Kamen must be somewhere near. Yes, he had to say good-bye to Kamen.

But there was no one about. It was awful when there was no one near you when you were dying. Were there no human beings alive in this village?

Through a rotten broken-down fence he caught a glimpse of Grandpa Stamen and his daughter-in-law. He shouted involuntarily: "Good-bye, folks. I'm going . . ."

The daughter-in-law raised her hand over her eyes and stood still. In one hand Stamen was holding a hatchet and in the other the wedge he was whittling at. They gazed at him and could not understand whether *he* was escorting the gendarmes or *they* were escorting him.

"Good-bye, I said. If you see Kamen, give him my love! Tell him I sent him my love."

He turned his head away, his sound shoulder trembled a little. He only heard: "Good-bye, Ranghel. But look here . . . what's happening?"

The gendarmes had received no orders not to allow him to talk, but to be on the safe side they gave him a slight shove. In any case, that was all he needed. A few muffled gulps held back in the throat, a few painful tears wiped out before they trickled down his face, sufficed to relieve a man going to his death. Fortunately, they were decent people; Stamen's nephew was up there, in the mountains. They would understand everything.

They stopped him just outside the village, near the dung-heaps. Was this where he was going to end? In the garbage! Wait, what was it Kamen used to say? . . . "On the dunghill of history!" "Big talk!" he had answered then. And now—a nice sort of history —on the village garbage heap!

"Listen," he wondered what to call them. "Couldn't we possibly move a little farther on, into the meadow?"

"The order said here," the smaller gendarme said guiltily.

He looked at them for the first time. There might be a little kindness in them, too? And he suddenly shuddered at the awful thought that they might do the same thing to Kamen . . . "The order said . . ."

"Isn't it all the same to you where you are going to kick the bucket?" asked the other.

"But you surely know the words of that rebel song: 'My shirt should be washed and clean . . .'"

"Well, you're not a rebel, are you?" the tall one looked him over with mocking eyes. That was the last insult they could fling at him. But it no longer touched him.

The small one cut in again: "Well, if he insists. But you are not going to run away, are you?"

The sunshine was sweet and drowsy. The sun-capped Mour-gash Peak glittered as if it were made of glass, then disappeared veiled in the shadow of a small cloud. The forest, rusty at the top, was coming back to life at the foot of the mountain. The meadows and the winter crops were bathed in a soft greenness. The strong breath of the awakening earth filled his nostrils, poured into his body.

All his life he had labored on this land, and now he was going to lie in it. It knew him and would accept him as its own, as a laborer. He was no mayor! If he had consented to become one at the time, it was because he had thought that he could do some good. And he had done good, too. The people remembered. He believed that if everyone was honest, justice would prevail. But he had been mistaken, very much mistaken. It appeared that Kamen had been right. And he had not gone out last night. If he could only have gripped Kamen's hand.

When they came to the spot, he was ready. He took off his fur coat and stood in his shabby homespun coat, his mud-soiled trousers and his rubber shoes. He felt miserable only because he was going to die silent. He had heard how the captured partisans died: singing, shouting "Long live . . . ," smiling. He could not understand them, but he felt something: you needed something more to do it that way than your conviction that you were an honest man. This night and this day had been sufficient to bring him here, to the meadow. But the day and the night had been too short to get as far as Kamen.

Nevertheless, he was calm. He was dying alone, but not lonely.

It seemed incredible to him that the small pale lights could hit him with such shattering power. But it was only for a moment, the moment in which every feeling of pain disappeared.

Translated by V. IZMIRLIEV

Georgi Karaslavov
(1904–   )

Georgi Karaslavov was born on January 12, 1904 in the village of Debur, Borissovgrad (now Purvomai) district. He attended a postal and telegraph school and then a teacher-training college. He took part in the September 1923 anti-Fascist uprising. He studied agronomy at Sofia University, but after organizing a students' strike he was expelled in 1928. Later he studied agronomy in Prague, working on construction sites at the same time. While there he wrote his first novel, *Sporzhilov*. For his book *The Village Correspondent*, he was tried and imprisoned in the Sofia Central Prison.

After Bulgaria's liberation from fascism he became director of the National Theatre and editor-in-chief of a literary magazine.

Georgi Karaslavov has published many collections of short stories, numerous novels and plays. He describes life in the Bulgarian village following the defeat of the uprising in 1923, revealing the effects of the economic crises, poverty, and antagonism undermining traditional peasant morality and virtues.

Among his more outstanding works are the novels *Sporzhilov* (1931), *Thorn-Apple* (1938), *Daughter-in-Law* (1942), and *Ordinary People;* the novelettes *Tango* and *Father's Sin;* and the drama *A Stone in the Marsh.*

The Portrait

The herds were slowly wending their way home. Their muffled bells jingled in the air, the sound spreading over the flower-strewn meadows where carefree children romped and played. The old teacher had once loved to listen to those sounds which signified the rebirth of life for him. Each sound was a flower breathing, each tone a shower of tranquillity and gold. Now he neither heard nor listened. Neither did he see the children searching in the blooming bushes for the four-leaf clover of their childlike wishes. His soul had sunk into a quiet desperation. The spring of his joy had run dry forever, the sun of his days had dropped down into a hopeless night, and his last source of consolation and cheer had been cruelly wiped out. He now resembled a deserted flour mill with the dust of a drab existence drowsing in its corners. The bloodied finger of dark foreboding had branded his nights with sleeplessness, and his eyes had had the tired soft look of velvet for days on end. But now the eyes were dead and humbled, the cheeks were hollow, and the soft wavy hair showed gray from under his black hat.

Why has this all happened, dear God? Why? It could have been otherwise . . . it could have been . . . but Dragomir was so thickheaded—he wouldn't listen to reason.

"Troubled times have come upon us, my son!" his father would warn him. "People have an obsession to kill each other off as if they were hypnotized! Who is to return them to brotherly love and peace? Who is to check them? Some day the world will quiet down again, but how bitter for those who have died in vain! Tend to your own business! The time of partisans is over . . . isn't it?"

"The world is not what it used to be, you're right," Dragomir was busy packing and he answered without looking up. The son well understood his old father who had supported him through college with such difficulty. One more year and the old man would see his son climb up to the highest rung of the social ladder—he'd be a physician! Then the old man would be able to relax, and his only care would be the education of his young daughter Slaveika. She was a high school student in the town near by. But anxiety-ridden days had arrived. The old man sensed the tremors of a formidable volcano, and he shuddered at the thought of his beloved son, the apple of his eye, being trapped on the edge of the crater. He knew him well, only too well. The tornado would descend howling upon them, and it would destroy Dragomir because he did not know how to crawl! Could he sidetrack him, keep him to himself, not let him finish his studies under the pretext that he had no money? No, he couldn't do that, his son was not a child. The old man grew gentle and tender, and seemed to become reconciled to it all.

"These are hard times we're living through, Dragomir!"

"Yes, they are, father."

"Human life is not worth a straw these days."

"It's a civil war."

"The devil it is! They're killing each other over the big bone."

"They're fighting over the bone, but they're not killing each other over it. Mankind has reached a certain stage of development when it is going to take a leap forward, a leap of regeneration."

"Stuff and nonsense! All of it!" the father retorted in anger. "It's too late you've learned those things. Once they held water . . . but not any more . . . if you only tended to your own business . . . nobody has ever profited by politics. Today . . ."

"Today—that is the question," Dragomir answered back. "Yesterday all cowards passed as heroes. Tomorrow that same type will do a lot of breast-beating about his bravery. No, I don't want to be taken for a great hero! I'll only be what I have to be—an honest person."

"They'll bash in your head."

"If it's unavoidable."

The father flared up.

"Whoever needs your poor head, son, who?"

"Those who do not stop to choose their means."

"You know they're beasts, don't you?"

"They're worse than beasts, blind in their death agony as they are. But I can't play dumb and it will be a godsend."

"For whom?"

"For you . . . if I survive."

Dragomir shut his suitcase and straightened his shoulders, the flame of deep-seated and unshakable confidence burning in his eyes. The father waved his hand as he shuffled to the grapevine and slumped down onto the big wicker chair.

"So that's—for me. Only God can put some sense into him." He gave a deep sigh.

They said nothing more that day. At dusk Dragomir came up to his father. "Father, I'm leaving tomorrow."

"Since the time has come—you must go."

They parted in the morning. Days of ominous presentiment and nights of endless nightmares set in. Long letters full of advice went into the mail. The son wrote seldom and then in a short, restrained way. He wouldn't argue with his father or cause him unnecessary anxiety. The father suffered, and the strangest thoughts went through his mind. Only memories of his own remote and beautiful youth coming alive in his consciousness would revive him. "We all trod the same path . . ." he would wave his hand. "Stubborn, impressionable and intelligent as he is, he can't think any other way, he can't go against himself. And he's right."

But he immediately came up with a start as though he had betrayed himself and hastened to stifle the flash of frankness. Did this involuntary admission spring from profound love or from the still undying national feeling of the old teacher? Had he also once been ready to sacrifice his life and shed his last drop of blood for the nameless gray masses suffocating in poverty and darkness? Who had murdered the sacred urges of his young heart? Who had trampled upon his ideals of truth, beauty, and freedom in the mire of life? Why was his soul bogged down today in criminal indifference?

These questions crowded through his overheated mind, vanishing into the recesses of a temporary truce, leaving his consciousness quivering and bleeding.

Winter came on, then Christmas, but Dragomir failed to come home. The old teacher spent the long holidays working with young Slaveika. They went over literature and history lessons and did problems in mathematics together. "It's his last year at the university . . . all those exams . . . it's not easy for him," the teacher thought.

"Your mother, God rest her soul, had a talent for languages," he said to Slaveika. "Dragomir has taken after her. He learned French well at high school. You're like me—you love to do math."

At the end of the vacation the girl caught a cold. She was bedridden for a long while, and the old man was taken up with new worries. Dragomir was pushed into the back of his mind, the political struggles receded and the world melted away, leaving only the sick girl's pale face and her deep, dark eyes to haunt him.

"Child," he would whisper, choking with tears. "Dear child . . ." The doctor reassured him, but the suspicious father took his attitude for professional indifference and his heart was heavy with fear. When the fever dropped and the girl felt better, his mind was somewhat eased and he was so happy he did not know what to do.

Slaveika left school and stayed at home in the village. The teacher seemed to find forgetfulness in looking after his daughter, and he lost sight of what had troubled him day and night. His mind was completely at rest. "Your brother will come home in the summer and both of you will go on a holiday somewhere," he would tell her. "Then you'll get stronger and you'll go back to school next year. What's left? Only March, April, and May." And he would count the months on his fingers.

The warm February days wore on. As never before, summer seemed to be working hard to overtake spring. The slushy March days came and went, and Easter drew near. But the teacher was once again deeply disturbed. The newspapers carried alarming headlines, stretching his nerves to the breaking point. Once again the nights were filled with dire forebodings. With strange feverishness he waited for the letter which would bring him the consolation he needed so much.

"Simon, if there is anything for me, please bring it to me right away!" he would say to the postman three times a day. He waited for the mail all day long, making the school secretary open it, while his shaking fingers rummaged through the letters and newspapers. There was nothing. His head drooped, his eyes went out like dead embers, and the rapiers of hope and uneasiness clashed in his heart.

Then he would read the sensational news items, his heart trembling within him. If something had gone wrong, the papers would surely print it . . . yes . . . they would. But did they always? The old man tried to subdue his fear as he shook his head in disbelief. And yet he waited and waited. One day the news struck. "Suicide of a medical student, Dragomir Dimitrov." Details followed, suppositions and interpretations—dull, cynical, and stupid—newspapers! No, they were lying, exaggerating. He was alive . . . alive! The old man ran around like a madman, searching for the truth. The news item was a lie! It was a printer's error! He went to town only to be told that his son had refused to surrender and had killed himself, or had been killed, fighting. Under the circumstances, it was immaterial which.

His eyes grew cold in their deep sockets, the sun plummeted down into bands of black crepe, the sky darkened, and the earth collapsed like a bloated corpse into the icebound region of Death.

Unable to bear up under the blow, Slaveika grew pale and once more took to her bed. The old man was stunned by her illness and pretended that he could endure the irreparable loss with courage. He asked his fellow teachers, the young women, to keep his daughter company, while he himself stayed out of the house. After the painful lunch breaks he would take his pupils out into the open fields. He would find a solitary spot and let the tide of painful memories overtake him. His eyes were blind to the green carpet of the boundless fields, his ears were deaf to the sounds of spring, and his soul failed to drink in the freedom of the wide-open spaces. But his heartache was less intense out here as though scattered like invisible powder over the waves of the fathomless bread-bearing sea.

"The universe is unfathomable and human beings how insignificant," he often thought. Here was a bug crawling at his feet. How he wished he were a tiny gnat, a little animal this earth of ours was so generously blessed with! Why had nature been so unjust to man burdening him with brains to think with and nerves to feel with! "Is it a sin to think like this?" the teacher was roused from his reverie, looking about him to see if anyone had read his thoughts.

His pupils romped and chirped like birds around him. A little boy, his thumb in his mouth, came up to him a little uncertainly: "Sir, are we going home soon?"

"Yes, we are, little one!"

The teacher rose looking at his watch and walked up to his pupils, already falling into line. They started on the way back. The young mischief-makers walked in silence, and none would strike up a song. The wide black band on their teacher's sleeve confused their little hearts. They knew why he was so sad and silent, and they did not dare to look into his eyes.

"Poor children . . . only they can understand me, only the little ones."

The remote memory of a slender young figure in short pants choked him, and his eyes swam in moisture as he looked over the disheveled little heads. The line drew up to the village like a funeral procession, songless and cheerless. The teacher said: "Now, children, you go straight home and don't bother anyone on your way!"

He walked along the bridge over the small river and climbed up the deserted and narrow lanes to the school. The postman came out of the municipal office and called out to him.

"Mr. Dimitrov . . . there's a registered letter for you."

"A registered letter?" the teacher whispered.

His heart leaped and his hands shook. A registered letter? Whoever from? Was it good news? Yes. Could he get any worse news? He signed for the letter, tore the envelope open nervously, and his eyes were rooted on the small sheet of paper. It was a typed letter and its content was brief and clear. But the teacher refused to grasp its meaning.

"It's a mistake . . . it's somebody else's letter," he faltered, staring at the envelope. It bore his address—the words were printed distinctly and precisely. He unfolded the sheet of paper again and spelled it out: "This is to inform you that you have been dismissed and are barred from teaching for the rest of your life."

It was only then that the teacher noticed the crooked signatures sticking out like two tongues. Yellow little circles struck his eyes, his fingers opened and froze, the letter fluttered down to the ground, touching the point of his shoe. He took a step forward and leaned against the wall, looking around him in dismay. The tall belfry wilted like a taper and went crashing down on the road; the white chimneys of the junior high school spun around, broke in two, and vanished into thin air; one of the walls tilted and began to come down, pulling down the wire fence with it. Then it rammed into the two-storied house under construction, crushing it to the foundations.

"This is . . . my reward . . . my reward!"

A giant maw had suddenly opened up swallowing the village, the cornfields, the world.

"No school, no summer salary . . . my sick little girl. . . ."

The sun was sinking in the west. The herds of cattle were coming home from pasture, raising clouds of dust and disappearing through the open, dilapidated gates. Carts loaded with willow branches creaked by. Outsmarting the drivers, children caught out brittle sap-filled sprigs to make whistles with.

With his long pole the horseherd goaded his horses along, as they neighed and snorted. The plaintive bleating of young lambs shrilled over the village.

The old teacher walked along, heartbroken, oblivious of the teeming life of the spring evening. The good-natured peasants greeted him respectfully and passed on, puzzled by his woeful countenance. Was he ill? Why did he avert his eyes so? Had anybody hurt him? What had happened? It was Dragomir . . . they knew.

The teacher walked on slowly, trudging under the burden of the cruel blow. What else did the future hold for him? Why was he being punished so cruelly? Why did they want to kill the poor firefly, the only tiny source of light in his bleak existence? Was it because he had fathered a son who had burnt up in the fire of a glorious quest to bring happiness to the suffering? Was that the reason? Yes, that was it! Then he would take up the challenge and drink the bitter cup to the lees! For the sake of his son's sacred memory, he would not lower his head before anyone, nor would he beg anyone for help.

Stillness hung over his courtyard; the beehives, stacked like huge gray turtles alongside the high wall, had quieted down. Sla-veika's voice came from behind the house. "Easy, now, easy!" She was closing up the two goats for the night after they'd come in from pasture.

The teacher made his way up the stairs and into the parlor. Sharp spasms of pain cut through his body. The corners of the room were flooded with anguish which momentarily caught him in its invisible net. He slumped down on the sofa, lowered his head, and closed his eyes. He wanted to be alone, all alone in the house and the world. He did not wish to think of anybody, and he wanted none to remember him. He wanted to be alone so the tears of his inconsolable grief might flow freely.

Then the old teacher raised himself up to gaze at Dragomir's portrait on the desk, right under the big framed one of his dead mother. He saw two big rounded eyes—the sign of goodness and courage. Richly waving hair wove a garland around the youthful head. Self-sacrifice had been an undeniable human duty to his son. The thin, barely visible wrinkles on the brow shone with the faith of prophetic insight. The slight nervous twitch, which had lent conviction to his words, seemed to hover around the corners of his mouth.

"My son . . . my son . . . you were right and now I understand you. But I never admitted it when you were alive, and now it is too late."

The teacher stared blankly into space, reeled, and leaned against the table. His eyes darkened and took on the open and indifferent look of a drunkard.

"You were right," he kept murmuring. "But I was a father and afraid to admit that you were. Forgive me. Forgive me. Now I know . . . they don't choose their means . . . today . . . a short while ago . . . I understood. My son . . . my son. . . ."

Gropingly he stretched his hand, took the portrait, and pressed it against his chest, sobbing uncontrollably and disconsolately.

Translated by GREGOR PAVLOV

Emil Manov

(1918–   )

Emil Manov was born on July 29, 1918 in Sofia. He was educated locally and graduated from the Faculty of Law of Sofia University, after which he worked as an office clerk. He was first published in 1936 in the *Ouchenicheski Podem* newspaper and later contributed to the *Svetlostroui* and *Svyat* newspapers and to the literary collections *Prag* and *Antena*. He took an active part in the anti-Fascist revolutionary movement and was sentenced to life imprisonment. After September 9, 1944 he was political officer, vice-president of the Committee for Culture, deputy editor-in-chief of the Bulgarski Pissatel publishing house, and secretary of the Writers' Union.

He has published the following books: *Young Heroes of the Patriotic War* (1946); *Captive Birds*, memoirs from prison (1947); *The End of the Delis*, a novel (1955); *The Little Flame*, short stories (1957); *A Doubtful Case*, a novelette (1958); *A Day Is Born*, a novel (1959); *Steep Slopes*, a novel.

Vanya and the Statuette

I

For all its strangeness and imperfection, human memory is splendid and very intelligently constructed. True, its watertight compartment does not always succeed in preserving great and unquestionable facts, nor does its largest filter always sift out particles of pettiness and insignificance. In this sense its points of contact with the memory of history are negligible. However, living memory often selects and keeps alive what the living need. Memory leaves it to time to tell the difference between greatness and pettiness, while it awaits the opportunity to revive a faded memory, a forgotten thought or merely a sound which will bring the complex music of the present closer to us, rendering it more comprehensible.

Some time ago my friend Danail T., a sculptor who is in a very ambivalent position (critics tend either to decry or praise him, unable to decide whether he is a realist or a modernist), presented me with one of his works. Danail is the only friend I have my own age who regularly honors my birthdays. The rest of my friends skip them occasionally, but I am not angry with them: in the long run, if an event occurs every year and over a long period of time, people naturally get tired of observing it, even if they cherish the best of feelings for you. I am not angry, I am even grateful to them, inasmuch as after the fortieth such anniversary birthdays begin to lose something of their charm.

Danail brought his present wrapped up in an old newspaper, handing it to me solemnly with the traditional wish that I might live twice as long as I had. I thought that if his good wishes came true I ran the risk of becoming immortal. Just imagine what it might be like, if, for example, on your seventieth birthday you had another seventy years ahead of you, or if you were one hundred and forty years old and knew that you had another hundred and forty years in store, and so on. When I explained to him why I had laughed, Danail shrugged his shoulders.

"What can you do! Life is full of clichés, old and new. This one is not the worst, so don't gripe!"

We gave each other a bear hug, slapping each other's backs as custom has it, and I hastened to tear the newspaper off his present and to put it on my desk. It was a nude, the figure of a girl done in baked clay, tawny and brown, with a small head and long legs that still had the rough imprint of his hands. At first sight there was nothing unusual about the figure; it was one of Danail's many "maidens" and "Young Communist League members." But it was precisely this contrast between the rough marks of the sculptor's fingers and the slender rushing lines of the whole figure that betrayed a special airy charm. Beneath the rough surface of the body, as taut as a bow, was hidden a nimble lively strength, a desire to soar; the head, thrown backwards, implied an abandon to light, and it was only the slightly bending knees that exhibited a powerlessness to overcome the earth's gravity. This girl's figure aroused both joy and anguish cleansed of all petty everyday feelings, of all selfishness—it evoked the joy and anguish of true art. On the other hand, it possibly reminded us of our youth and of things long since dead and gone. As no other guests had come as yet, Danail and I stood gazing at the figure, each sunk in his own thoughts.

Then something quivered and stirred in my memory as I took my eyes off the beautiful present. "Listen," I said, "do you remember . . . Diana the Huntress?"

"Which Diana? I don't remember."

"That copy of the goddess, the one we found in the merchant's house."

Danail knit his eyebrows as he rubbed his high, balding forehead. I was sure he had remembered it right away since one never forgets such things, but he had lost a great deal of his straightforwardness over the years.

"Oh yes," he said after a fairly long pause. "Only it was no copy but the crazy invention of a semiliterate high school student. I sincerely hope my present did not remind you of it."

"You wouldn't have become an artist if you weren't so touchy," I replied.

We exchanged a joke or two and had a good laugh over them. Thus our favorite game began: "Do you remember this, do you remember that?" which took us back to the beautiful hours of the past, and we lived through them again. This time the game revived a twenty-year-old story, but the story started an argument.

The moment the exclamations had subsided and the memories had faded, Danail sighed with a smile. "We were such naïve youngsters in those days."

"Why naïve?" I countered, little suspecting that this would rub him the wrong way. "We were what we had to be. Each period creates the type of men it needs."

Danail regarded me with a mixture of condescension and annoyance, and he started proving to me that the revolution had never needed fools, just as it did not need them now—a truth I had no intention of disputing, but with which I could not quite agree, inasmuch as an angry resignation sounded in his contention. It was high time, he insisted, as he stroked his luxuriant mustache, that we became wise and realized that not all that glittered was gold and that the time of showy flamboyance had long since gone. On my part, I contended that if everybody grew wise, that is, if the wise reconciliation with reality, which he so urgently recommended, came about, the world might as well stop turning and grow moldy into the bargain.

"Much do I care about the world," Danail said tersely. "Nobody can set the world right. People will be people, and things over which I have no control I leave to fortunetellers."

"What about this statuette? Why did you make it?"

"Well . . . I don't deny that the world is exciting . . . as far as form and space go. I made the statuette because you needed something to fill that space with over there." He pointed to an empty space in the bookshelves as he took the statuette and placed it there. "Please spare me your gems of puerile wisdom and don't strike the ground with your hat—it isn't sanitary."

Thus our argument moved round and round the familiar circle of well-known and irreconcilable truths of life. We were generously furnished by life with occasions for similar arguments, and we often delved into the same facts only to arrive at different conclusions. Danail loved to make fun of me for not minding my physics and semiconductors and for trespassing from time to time into the sphere of philosophy, a field crawling with authorities and full of trouble and headaches for this very reason. My civic spirit made him predict a gloomy future for me. In fact, I do think that Danail was not so deeply convinced in his skepticism, but he belongs to that category of men who, irritated by the contradictions of life, the stronger they defend their views, the stronger they doubt their validity.

He stood before me, tall and thin, his face lean from too much work and bachelorhood, looking at me with friendly irony in his big blue eyes. But I saw him the way he had been twenty years before, when we had just gotten out of jail. In those days he was no more a Communist than he is today, but he thought us Communists the only sensible people and vehemently hated fascism. He was jailed because I was arrested in his room, and they found a rubber stamp for forging identity cards on his table. He was an art student and he had fashioned the stamp so artfully that even the police admired his skill. Their generosity of feeling cost him quite a lot—to this day he wears scars on his fingers—but the police, too, had a problem on their hands as Danail was well known for his fiery temper.

In those days he was as handsome a man as they come: slender-waisted and broad-shouldered, his glossy black hair tumbling over his forehead, from under which his bold eyes sparkled, his mouth was big and well shaped, his bearing rough and domineering. A great many female hearts fluttered when his eyes met theirs and even when they didn't. He was a bit peculiar even then and as soon as we joked with him about it he would flush and say that sculpture was his only love. I cannot say how true his statement was. At any rate, I had never seen him go out with a girl before he met Vanya. Then he fell in love head over heels, as the saying goes, and I keep thinking that had it not been for that ill-fated statuette, he would probably have become a loving husband and father and not an inveterate bachelor and the Don Juan his colleagues say he is. Perhaps he wouldn't claim that the world interested him only in terms of form and space. Who knows?

Incidentally, there was nothing extraordinary about the story of the statuette, and its interpretation greatly depends on one's point of view.

II

We met Vanya on the first day of freedom—even a little earlier—and this is how it happened.

An amnesty for political prisoners was declared on September 7, 1944, and on September 8, both Danail and I left the prison walls behind us in the town of "S." We were set free at dusk, since our family names were somewhere toward the end of the alphabet. The Fascist authorities in the town still went through the motions of being alive and had not abandoned formalities. They had sifted us through one by one throughout the day, looking over our case records and handing us certificates instead of the lost identity cards.

When we passed through the iron gates, the crowd of relatives and friends in front of the jailhouse had thinned out. A few young men shook our hands, congratulating us on our release and advising us to hurry and catch the evening train. We thanked them, slung our bundles over our shoulders, and started out, our hearts hammering with the thought that we would be in Sofia and home by the next morning.

But things took another turn. In the town square we ran into Ivan, a veteran political prisoner, to whom we had said good-bye but a few hours earlier. He was a local man, one of the leaders of the town party organization, who had been thrown into jail only two months before and they hadn't had time to sentence him. So he appeared before us with his broad, slightly uncouth figure, his hands raised to stop us, thus playing the role of Destiny for us.

"Where are you dashing off to? The railroad station? No trains are running." He took us aside as he lowered his voice. "You'd better put off your departure until tomorrow; the Fascists are astir around the railroad yard, and they may be up to something. There's a rumor they tried to sneak an infernal machine into the noon train." We put up some resistance. We were dying to see our families, having waited nearly two years for this day, and Ivan's misgivings did not duly impress us. "Another thing, we have no place to sleep in this town," I added.

"Don't worry on that score," Ivan replied. "I won't let you go and that's that. We'll find a place to put you up."

He scratched his graying shaggy hair, thinking, and then looked once and then again at a girl in a white blouse and black skirt, standing to the side. The girl had been with him when we ran into him, and I took her for his daughter. While we talked with Ivan she kept looking at us, but with no visible interest. Her swarthy, slightly elongated face, with a little dimple on her chin, hid an attractiveness and yet the cold and forbidding reticence of one not given to talking. This impression was further strengthened by her black, knitted eyebrows.

"Vanya, come over here!" Ivan called to her. "Meet these comrades." The girl held out her hand without saying her family name and without smiling. "Where do you think we should send them to spend the night? How about Charakchiev's?"

"I've already taken three people over there, there's no room," Vanya answered in a singsong voice, strangely at variance with her stern and detached look.

"Then you'll take them home with you."

"But you know . . ."

"I do, but what of it!" Ivan smiled. "I know you're going to have a girl staying with you. All four of you have reached marriageable age and something might come out of it. Come on, don't frown because the boys are already blushing." A shadow of a smile flitted across Vanya's face, and she nodded. We gave up our resistance, although "the old man's" caution seemed uncalled for to us.

"Take the comrades home and then come around again," said Ivan. "You'll find me at Simitchiev's."

"All right," Vanya said.

We followed her obediently. When we got there it had grown dark, and behind the black hump of the mountain there blinked the three familiar stars which I remembered from the window of my cell. Vanya's room was in the lower section of the town, near the barracks. Our hostess lived alone in the only attic room of an old two-storied frame house. By the way, in this particular case "room" sounds almost luxurious: it was, in fact, a cubbyhole with a sloping ceiling which let you stand erect only in the middle, with wooden beams barely plastered and a small one-wing casement leading up to the roof. One could hardly squeeze one's head through that casement. The worldly comforts of the cubbyhole consisted of a mattress on iron legs and two rickety chairs. Vanya's entire wardrobe hung on a few wooden boards with nails instead of hooks, and there wasn't even a rag rug on the clean floor, which had begun to decay. I had grown up in an attic room in Sofia and I well knew the ugly face of poverty, but I had never seen anything like Vanya's poverty.

I deposited my bundle and my coat on the floor near the door, exchanging glances with Danail. Vanya interpreted our confusion in her own way. "You don't have to worry about the sleeping accommodations. We'll fix something up." She left the room, but Danail kept holding his things in his hands.

"Listen, brother, we'll only make it harder for the girl," he said. "I can't, upon my word."

"The girl won't perish this one night. We mustn't look ridiculous," I said as softly as I could, afraid that Danail might grow obstinate. "Ivan said there was another woman staying with her, so it will be easier both for her and for us."

Vanya returned after awhile. She dragged in a limp straw mattress and a piece of old green velvet, frayed and faded, which had obviously done service a long time before finding its way into the cellar. She spread out the mattress behind the door where the ceiling touched the floor, covered it with the velvet, and stood up, pleased with her job. "The landlady loaned it to me," she explained. "As you can see, it's a royal bed, though you'll find it a bit narrow."

For the first time Vanya smiled, and her smile took our breath away. She changed in an instant. A hidden spring of light seemed to gush forth suddenly and generously from her heart, as though someone had flung open shuttered windows at a stroke, flooding the room with a rich wave of sunshine and air. I noticed that Danail was more violently shaken than I was because, all of a sudden, he started fumbling for his cigarettes.

We were silent, and Vanya's smile faded away so quickly that I wasn't sure it had ever appeared at all. Now she stood watching us with cold surprise in her eyes.

"It will not be very comfortable, but I can't offer you anything better." She spoke in an unexpectedly abrupt tone, and a certain hostility was visible in her dark eyes. Now it was our turn to be surprised. This girl positively had no knowledge of herself or of others, for that matter, and she knew nothing about psychology. I thought she must have lived in utter loneliness to bear herself like this with two strangers. Danail tried to persuade her that the bed was of no matter to us, since we had slept on cement floors before, and that we could easily have passed the night at the railroad station without causing her all this trouble.

Vanya merely waved her hand, narrowing her eyes haughtily, as if his words did not merit an answer, and Danail fell silent. He even smiled in embarrassment as if he had said something stupid. That was really a most unusual occurrence, because once he got an idea in his head it was no use arguing with him. Besides, he never forgave anybody for such a display of disregard. Once, in prison, he had asked the Principal Overseer about something—if I remember correctly they had detained a letter of his at the Central Office. The overseer was busy talking to a subordinate and he didn't bother to answer him. This happened out in the yard, in the prison square during our daily walk. Danail politely repeated his question, and since the other again ignored him, frowning as if an annoying fly were buzzing around him, Danail reached out, grabbed him by the shoulder, and turned him completely around. "I'm talking to you, blockhead!" he said quietly, but so distinctly that everybody heard him. For some time the Principal Overseer stood gulping air like a fish on dry land hooked with a single jerk of a fishing rod, while Danail watched him with indescribable pleasure in his light-colored eyes, like those of a highwayman debating with himself whether to spare his victim's life or not.

Of course, he was put into solitary confinement, and they cut down our daily walk by half while Danail paid for his unreasonable pride. He came out of the solitary looking much thinner twenty days later. The comrades rebuked him for his rashness; he apologized and looked sorry for what he had done. Unfortunately, right after the incident, he came across his tormentor in the corridor. He passed him, his hands buried in his pockets, whistling a tune from "Cavalleria Rusticana." Back he went into solitary confinement, this time for a week. Then the performance was repeated, and I don't know how the competition between Danail's health and the methodicality of the jailers would have ended had not our comrades threatened our Orpheus that they would demand his transfer to the criminal section. He was compelled to compromise: he exchanged "Cavalleria Rusticana" for Boudyoni's much more modern march. The jailers threw up their hands in despair and pretended they were satisfied.

One way or another, we stayed on to spend the night in Vanya's cubbyhole. Her guest also arrived, and as she was an elderly lady who could have been our mother we felt less constrained.

Vanya brought in some freshly baked bread and yellow cheese, un-rationed as she boasted, and then she went out looking for Ivan. We ate and talked with the elderly comrade. The Soviet army had already entered Bulgaria, and momentous events lay ahead. We were very excited and talked for a long time in the dark after going to bed . . . so we never knew when we sank into sleep and when Vanya got in.

We woke up at about nine o'clock the next morning. The two women had left. The guest's suitcase was also gone. We jumped up from the mattress and started packing excitedly, although the Sofia-bound train wasn't due until noon. But some sort of unusual noise was coming in from the street below. There were sounds of shouting, and a male voice boomed hoarsely over the radio. We stopped to listen.

We ran to the small casement. The street was not visible, as the wide eaves of the roof obstructed our view. However, the artillery barracks could be seen across the road. There, on the wide, flat grounds, between the dormitories and the stables, soldiers clustered around, without formation or order, merging into groups and bustling about. The scene very much resembled the prison yard of the day before. No commands were to be heard and not a single individual voice was raised, but a buzzing like a beehive in distress reached us. Several officers stood by the archway watching the scene from afar. Danail and I had never been in the army, but it did not take us long to realize that something extraordinary was afoot.

We exchanged glances and rushed outside without a word. We bumped into Vanya on the wooden staircase, almost knocking her down. She seized our hands and started shaking them. "Comrades, you slept right through the revolution . . . in Sofia . . . our people . . . the Fatherland Front. . . ." Her voice trailed off, and she leaned against the wall to catch her breath.

A minute later the three of us were running along the streets of the town, overtaking multitudes of men and women also hurrying toward the town center. Before we had reached it we were told that our people had taken the Town Hall, that the Mayor and the head of the garrison had fled, and that Ivan needed us. The rest of the conversation, if it could be so described, consisted of exclamations, bits of broken laughter, and pregnant pauses in which we tried hard to check our excitement.

Those first hours of freedom will never be erased from my memory. We walked in the September morning filled with joyful anxiety and feeling like children. Nothing held us back to the past;

we were like newborn babes or like soldiers in the heat of battle who had nothing to lose or leave behind, while somewhere, just around the corner, an all-embracing glowing world, wide open and warm, beckoned to us. And I knew this was the state of mind of my companions, too. Now I am even surer, as I have gained better knowledge of myself and others, that in days of overwhelming happiness or shattering calamity, we all become better and more generous. The petty parasitic passions favor the slough of success and the frictions of a stabler everyday life.

We pushed our way into the square. The entire town had gathered there. There was a buzz of talk as the people patiently waited for someone to appear on the Town Hall balcony and address them. For the time being the balcony was deserted, with some shadows flitting across the glass doors behind it. Not a single policeman or soldier was in sight. Three armed men—with a carbine and two hunters' rifles—stood sentry at the entrance of the building. The man with the carbine recognized Vanya and let us through.

Upstairs, stern-looking and erect, Ivan sat at the mayor's desk in the room with the glass doors. Some fifteen men and women crowded around him. Ivan answered questions, calling somebody on the phone, giving instructions which people hurried out to implement, making way for new arrivals. Four men conferred in a corner, and Ivan kept going up to them, bending over their heads.

Finally he noticed us. "You're right on time!" he cried. "Go and take over Police Station Two. This comrade will go with you, and he'll take charge there. Take a gun in any case." He started toward the balcony to make his speech.

We were given Italian rifles which hardly worked; but they showed us how to handle them, and we were off to establish people's power in the town. It was not difficult. At the police station we were met by a mustached sergeant, yellow with fear, who clicked his heels and never took his hand off his visor. He reported that everything was under control, that in the morning the Fascist chief of police had given himself up and was now locked up. The police were all accounted for and gathered in the dormitory, and so were the mounted police. We were informed, in the way of extraordinary events, that a mare's back had been bruised and that the culprit had already been punished accordingly. There was nothing for us to do here. We left the newly promoted chief in charge and rushed back to the Town Hall for a more serious assignment.

Thus, on the very first day, we three became an operative group for emergency assignments, so to speak. In the evening Danail and I sent wires to Sofia, informing our families that we were safe and sound, but that we would be delayed for another few days. Ivan kept us from going and anyway, we'd have found it awkward to leave with so many things still to be done.

Of course, not everything went as smoothly as it had at the police station, but let us leave aside the ups and downs of our activity in the town of "S." I'll only add that we had all kinds of assignments, like arresting some local Fascist criminals and searching out rich men's hoarded supplies of olive oil, smoked hams, and other foodstuffs which the Germans had not managed to take off. We loaded the stuff onto a truck with the aid of the owners who had "forgotten" to declare it, and turned it over to a public-owned warehouse so that the people could share it. Once they asked us to search a transit train, another time to hold a meeting with high school students. Generally speaking, during those few days we "ran errands" for our revolution, and our pride knew no bounds.

In the evening we would get together in Vanya's cubbyhole. Vanya would order us out into the small corridor and we would stand there in the dark until she had gone to bed. This procedure was repeated in the morning as well. We, on our part, did not undress before going to bed, simply lying down as we were, in our clothes, covering ourselves with our topcoats. We usually stayed up late and talked despite the fatiguing day, in order to sort out our impressions and calm down a bit. In fact, it was Vanya and I who did all the talking while, seated at the small table, Danail would draw in his sketch pad, from which he never parted, only putting in a word or two from time to time. Sometimes his pencil would go on drawing lines in his sketch pad mechanically as his eyes lingered on Vanya longer and longer, and it was not difficult to read the meaning of those glances. He would either prop up his forehead with his hand, ostensibly engaged in drawing, or watch her between his fingers, forgetting there was a third person in the room.

In brief, it did not take my friend more than two or three days to be up to the ears in love with Vanya. She was not indifferent to his qualities, either. She would be talking with me, but her attention would stray to Danail and she would more and more frequently laugh out at a joke, astonishing us with the beauty of her voice. What was more, sometimes I would become the butt of their flashing wit, and in their solidarity—subjecting my person and my acts to critical scrutiny—they would indirectly confess their love for each other, little caring about my self-respect. Anyway, it did not suffer much. In Sofia I had a girl whose letters I kept in my luggage, in a special cardboard box, and I found a way to get at it every night.

Vanya was not always talkative and gay, even during those days of delirious happiness. At times, while we were doing something together or resting, she would suddenly grow quiet and change completely. Some hidden pain, some evil deadness would creep into her eyes, and she would become cold and brooding as she had been when we first met her. Her face would strain and grow homely as if she were desperately trying to ward off the attack of a cruel pain. At first Danail and I pretended not to notice this and refrained from showing undue curiosity. Later, as we grew closer, I decided it was better to be guilty of tactlessness rather than of indifference to a comrade's suffering.

One evening—I think it was the fourth day of our stay in the town of "S."—I could not contain myself any longer and asked her if she was all right or if she was suffering from some illness.

Vanya did not answer right away. She sat in her white blouse, sewing a large brown button on her winter topcoat. She raised her head and looked at me, knitting her eyebrows as if she had not understood my question, and I became embarrassed.

"Oh . . . it's nothing," she said slowly, as if excusing me. "This happens to me from time to time. It's fatigue. I've been like this since childhood. I grew up alone and was often ill."

"I see. You were left an orphan at an early age."

"I have parents; they're still alive. But I wish they were dead."

Her peculiar state was gone as if banished by my question, and she answered with such cold and detached calmness that I shivered. Danail towered over the table as he drew his face near hers.

"Are they . . . Fascists?" he asked in a low voice.

"No," Vanya answered. "My father even took part in the Vladaya rebellion once."

"Then why are you talking like this? Parents are parents." His words sounded reproachful. Vanya stuck the needle into her coat and then she threw it aside.

"Why shouldn't I? They never asked when they had me, and I am not obliged to forgive them," she replied in a harsh voice. "If I've become a decent human being, I certainly don't owe it to them."

That evening we learned Vanya's short but sad story. She told it in dry, cold tones as if filling out a questionnaire, without trying to smooth things over or evoke sympathy.

Vanya had been born in that same town and had never been elsewhere. In his young days her father had been a teacher in the neighboring villages, but after he came back from the front, he became a watchmaker and made a good deal of money. He was always out for a good time and used to say that the war had taught him how to live. He got married late, at thirty-four, and Vanya's mother was eleven years his junior, the daughter of a furrier. She had never finished school and had been strictly brought up. All went well for some time. But when Vanya was a first-grader, her father suddenly vanished from the town without a trace. What the reasons were for his disappearance, nobody could ever say. At any rate, the gossiping went the rounds. Some thought he had been murdered and buried in a secret place; others said he had emigrated; while others claimed he had fled from his wife whom he couldn't stand for reasons nobody could explain. His friends said that before he vanished he had often spoken of "a lack of air," that he had become withdrawn and downcast and that was the only factual comment in all the talk.

Vanya's mother fell ill or tried to poison herself, Vanya didn't know which. She spent a long time in the hospital and when she came out she found out she had become an outcast. Her parents blamed her for failing to keep her husband and considered her disgraced for having become "the talk of the town" (this made Vanya think that her mother had really tried to kill herself). One way or another, they forbade her to visit their home as did her entire clan. She did not have courage enough to look for a factory job, blinded as she was by petty bourgeois prejudices, as Vanya put it. For a time she tried doing Bulgarian embroidery at home, working for a Plovdiv merchant, but the work was exhausting and did not pay well. Then her mother took a job as a waitress in a café, probably from sheer desperation or wishing to scandalize her relatives. That was the beginning of her fall. At first, the café-owner began paying her visits at her house, then a lieutenant from the garrison came along, until her bad reputation was irrevocable. Vanya was left to her own devices: she starved and suffered from lack of sleep; she was washing and scrubbing floors when she was barely thirteen. In the summertime she worked in a tailor shop, but she never left school and enrolled in the high school. From the very start she became friends with our Young Communist League members there; this shaped her life and saved her from the degradation of her home.

Meanwhile, at the outbreak of the war, her father unexpectedly returned—old, decrepit, with a wooden stump where his right leg had been. He forced his way into the house, since his wife did not want any part of him, and after chasing her lover away, he restored what he called "his legitimate rights." That was the most trying period for Vanya. To the poverty and shame in which she had lived until then, were added endless scenes of drunkenness and violence, often terminated through the interference of the police and their neighbors. Both husband and wife drank. Her father told tall tales about France and Istanbul where he had lived and where, in Pera, a truck had rolled over his leg, laming him for life. At times he would explode into fits of rage, accusing his wife of "unfaithfulness"; at other times he would slobber and crawl at her feet, begging for forgiveness. During the war Vanya was seized by her nervous fits and at last was taken in by the parents of a schoolmate of hers. Thus she never went back home again. As soon as she was back on her feet, she left high school and got a job as a weaver at a textile mill. There she completely devoted herself to the cause.

Vanya fell silent and I sneaked a look at Danail. His index finger was drawing imaginary lines on the blue paper covering the table. His tightened lips had paled and his eyes had narrowed as if he meant to strike somebody any minute.

I rose and went out into the yard to smoke a cigarette in solitude. I leaned against the old poplar tree next to the fence. The tree towered high into the still night, motionless and straight, like a spear. The sky overhead was clear and starry—almost oppressing me with its serene purity. Poor Vanya! I had started that conversation in vain, and she had dug into her past in vain: you could not talk about those things without pain. The past was over and done with, and it was no use going back along its muddy paths and calling to account the weak who had failed to steer clear of the mud. I also thought that for all the ugliness in their lives, for all their beastliness to Vanya, her parents were more to be pitied than despised.

I waited for Danail to come out into the yard as he did every night before bedtime, but he didn't come. I went back to the cubby-hole and found my roommates sitting side by side. Danail held Vanya's hand, lightly caressing it with his fingertips. They both looked up at me with such pure eyes that I wasn't disconcerted.

That same night Vanya went to stay with a girl, a textile worker, leaving us her attic room until our departure. I was left alone with Danail. A silly argument arose over the bed. He insisted that I sleep in Vanya's bed and would not listen to my objections. Since obstinacy was not Danail's prerogative, we went as far as casting lots. The bed fell to him. However, he ignored "the finger of Fate" and stretched out full-length on the straw mattress, threateningly showing me his fist. I had to give in. If I had known his inner turmoil that night as I do now, after all these years, I would not have persisted. But that night we said nothing more to each other. He did not like to talk about himself, and I was in love myself and too young to penetrate the lofty logic of his feelings.

The next two days we saw Vanya only by chance about town and at the public cafeteria where we ate lunch and dinner. She was no longer a member of our group; she was working at the town committee of the Young Communist League. She came to the cafeteria surrounded by young men and women, and we realized how well liked and respected she was by the young Communists who had just come out from underground. They clustered around her, and she talked business with them, now smiling, now frowning and stern-looking. She was like so much radium bursting with energy. Whatever she did or whoever she talked with, she was constantly watching for Danail, and she would become livelier and more energetic as soon as she spotted him. If she was late in joining us at our table, Danail would separate her from her friends with his typical rough directness, bringing her by the hand to our table.

"Let go of me, this is a violation of my personal freedom," Vanya would protest, but not very vigorously.

"He's to blame," Danail would nod my way. "He was the first to teach me that man is not free from society. So quiet down!"

"It never occurred to me that one could justify tyranny with historical materialism," Vanya laughed. "They're waiting for me over there."

"So are we," Danail would answer, unruffled. "After all, we have greater privileges over you than those kids."

"Privileges! And who are you?"

"A half-baked sculptor and a half-baked physicist who's now exploring the aggregate state of the soup."

They bandied jokes as I gulped down my soup with the feeling that I was the odd man out. But I did not dare leave them alone because they would have been furious. They enjoyed the game like the foretaste of happiness: they hadn't as yet tasted the raspberry jam (it's my favorite kind of jam, so it popped into my head first), and for the time being they chewed the cud, ruminating on their gastric juices. The metaphor may sound crude and would undoubtedly arouse the indignation of a poet, but it is very precise.

Those were days of intoxication with freedom, with the feeling of absolute security in the future, with youth—ours and the country's. To Vanya and Danail those were days of intoxication with the eternal and unique birth of love. Now, twenty years later, I know for certain that such a fusion of personal happiness with common joy, of spiritual light with the sun's explosions is a phenomenon as rare as the birth of a genius. Otherwise even man's brightest hour contains a grain of poison which often sprouts in future years into a rank weed of doubt and disappointment, casting a shadow over the very memory of happiness.

Danail and Vanya questioned nothing. They were still children in their feelings, and those were days of an exuberant faith in man's potentialities, often overstepping the bounds of what one would call common sense. In fact, it now seems to me that Vanya was closer to common sense in those days, and that the grain of poison, if there had been any, was festering in Danail's heart.

It was about mid-September. I approached Ivan and jokingly tried to persuade him that people's power had been firmly established in the town, that the Fascists had all been taken care of, and that every empty space on house fronts and walls had been adequately filled with slogans and posters. In other words, our further stay in the town was no longer required. Ivan agreed, approved and . . . delayed our departure by another two or three days. He wouldn't let people go once he'd gotten hold of them.

The same day we finally fired our Italian rifles. We, together with a former partisan, a beardless young man nicknamed "the Terror," were entrusted with the arrest of a merchant, a onetime representative of a German sewing-machine firm. He was suspected of having collaborated with the Gestapo and of informing on Communists. It was late in the evening. When "the Terror" dropped by to fetch us, Vanya was visiting with us in the cubbyhole, and she volunteered to come along with us.

The merchant lived in the upper section of the town, near the vineyards, in a beautiful two-storied villa. On the suggestion of "the Terror" we walked lest we should make a noise. However, in the courtyard of the villa a big shepherd's dog raised bedlam and no matter how hard we tried to shut him up, he strained at his chain, barking ferociously and hoarsely. A window lit up on the upper floor, a shadow darted across it, and then the lights went out the same instant.

"Quick!" "the Terror" commanded.

Vanya and Danail ran around the house as "the Terror" and I rang the door bell. Two shots crashed above us by way of an answer. We pressed ourselves close against the door. "The Terror" fired a round of his machinegun toward the second floor, and I, too, fired my rifle, more for courage than anything else, since there was noth-

ing to aim at in the dark. A second later shots resounded from behind the villa, and we both rushed in that direction.

Vanya and Danail were already leading the captive; he was a
tall man, his shirt all torn at the chest, and dressed in his pyjama
bottoms. He had tried to escape through one of the rear windows.
The former merchant held up his left hand, his right hanging limp at
his side: he had been wounded in the shoulder, but he kept silent
without uttering a groan. His big face was white and immobile.

"We have to search the house," Danail said. "There may be
somebody else hiding inside."

"Here you, hand over the keys, Mister!" "The Terror" said.
The prisoner raised his head slowly. "The keys are upstairs,
on my desk," he said softly. "There's no one inside."

"We'll see . . . where's your family?"

"They're not here."

"The Terror" scratched his head. "This is my decision," he
said in soldier-like fashion. "I'll take him along and you check the
villa. Wait for me here!"

We followed instructions. Danail and I climbed in through
the open window, turned the lights on in the house, found the keys
and opened the door for Vanya. There really was no one in the
house or in the basement underneath. We found no important documents although we shifted the furniture about and tapped on the
walls as we had read they do in detective stories.

"If he's the Gestapo man, he wouldn't be so crazy as to leave
evidence against himself, would he?" Danail remarked profoundly.

"Yes, we seem to be dealing with a dangerous character," I
agreed.

Common sense and iron-clad logic sometimes play all kinds of
tricks on us. We learned later that the "dangerous character" had
made a pile during the war as a black-marketeer, but his connection
with the Gestapo and the police was never proved. On the contrary,
relatives of our political prisoners in the town testified in court in his
favor: he favored the English and had helped them with food and
money. He himself stated that he had not shot at us but into the air
to frighten us away and escape because he feared bad times were
ahead for the bourgeoisie. Nonetheless, he was sentenced to two
years for having fired those two shots.

The villa was new and lavishly furnished. The lower floor
contained a huge living room, a nursery and pantries, bathrooms,
and the like, while the bedrooms, a study, and a guest room were on

the upper floor. The wood paneling on the walls, the modern upholstered furniture, the Persian rugs, the lighting, paintings and
ornaments—all the interior decoration was exquisite and costly,
obviously designed by a good decorator, and not even Danail had
anything to say against it. As for Vanya and myself, we stood there,
our mouths hanging open, as though someone had suddenly flashed
Aladdin's lamp before us.

I noticed that Vanya, who was usually very active on our
assignments, shied away from the search this time. At first she wandered from room to room with us, watching us move the furniture
and pictures on the walls in our search for a secret safe. We raised
mattresses and rummaged in the wardrobes, and finally went down
into the basement while she remained up in the living room. When
we returned we found her in a strange posture. She was leaning
against the wall by the large French window, gazing into space and
clutching at the collar of her frayed winter coat. Her lips were half-
open, and her face was pale and contorted as if she had just seen
something frightful.

She gave a start when we entered and straightened up as she
let her hand fall to her side without a word. She was probably weary
with all she had gone through. Danail and I were also tired, and we
lost no time in relaxing near the big fireplace which had a roughly
hewn green marble front.

"Vanya, sit down and take a rest!" said Danail, drawing another armchair up to his.

"I don't want to sit down," Vanya said in a shaky voice.

"Do you think that mines have been planted under the chairs,
or what?" Danail laughed.

Vanya merely shook her head, with the same timid and in-
credulous expression in her eyes. She crossed the living room cautiously as if walking on broken glass, came up to us, and leaned
against Danail's armchair just as cautiously. I had the feeling she was
afraid of touching the green upholstery.

"The life these people lived here," she said in a hushed voice,
"you can hardly believe it."

"That's a fine thing!" I said. "As if you didn't know some
people lived like this?"

"Of course, I did!" Vanya smiled pensively. "But it's another
thing to see it for yourself and actually touch it."

She was regarding a statuette placed on the mantel piece—a
white marble Diana, big-breasted, her classical drapes in falling lines
and with a bow in her hand. Vanya drew nearer to have a closer look

at it. Danail rose, picked up the statuette, and began tossing it up and down on his palm.

"You'll drop it!" Vanya cautioned him.

"So what! That's exactly what it deserves! The only thing in bad taste in this room. Just look at the beautiful landscapes on the wall and then at this monstrosity. The obscene jest of an erotic which our rich man took for an *objet d' art*."

Tapping it lightly, Danail replaced the statuette in her place. I didn't like the statuette either, although I did not quite agree with the categorical opinion of my friend. However, I said nothing because I didn't know much about sculpture anyway. As for Vanya, she kept looking at the abused goddess of hunting, and I saw a hard, cold look appear in her dark eyes. Her glance fixed on the statuette, she slowly said: "Whatever you say, I do like the statuette!"

Danail gave her a look of surprise. It wasn't, perhaps, the words so much as the cold finality in Vanya's voice that threw him off balance. He even made an involuntary gesture with his hand as if to stop her and save her from some unwise act. Then he lowered his head: "You're joking, aren't you?"

"No, I'm not," Vanya said. "What's wrong with it? It's beautiful!"

Danail's light-colored eyes again traveled to the statuette, but he said nothing. He lit a cigarette and resumed his seat, silent and downcast. Next to the fireplace Vanya stood staring at him, her eyebrows slightly knitted, and there was an almost triumphant look about her, at least so it seemed to me. I could not tell why, but that look depressed me.

"The Terror" had come back in the meantime. We sealed up the villa and started back to town. All the way back Vanya and Danail did not exchange a word.

That night it was pretty sad in the cubbyhole. The lamp had long since been turned off and, tossing from side to side, I tried to go to sleep as Danail smoked cigarette after cigarette at the open window. I saw the glowing end of his cigarette in the dark, and it drove all sleep away. I was hot and felt tense. My thoughts were far away from here, back home, with my family and friends. I jumped out of bed and lighted a cigarette from Danail's.

"Why don't you go to bed!" I grumbled with annoyance.

"I will . . . but do you think she really liked that figure, or did she talk like that on purpose?" he asked.

"I think she said it on purpose to make you mad." I wanted to calm him down but I was beginning to get angry. "After all, there's nothing tragic in the fact that one doesn't know much about art, is there? That's no reason why you should be all on edge! Millions of people in the world right now couldn't care less about your Dianas and Venuses!"

"One may not know much about art," he objected, "but that's no reason to go into a trance over such mediocrity. Incidentally, that's not what's worrying me."

"What is it, then?"

He shrugged his shoulders, threw his cigarette away, and began undressing.

In the morning somebody knocked on the door, waking us. It was Vanya who had come to get her beret, as she explained outside the door. She waited in the small corridor for us to get dressed and then she came in, unusually subdued and silent. She said hello, took her beret off the nail and stopped, twisting it in her hands. She looked like a child who had misbehaved. I tried to strike up a conversation with her and asked her to sit down, but she refused. Danail was silent, fiddling with his sketch pad as if she were not in the room at all, and I felt terribly embarrassed.

Finally he ripped a sheet off the pad with a drawing on it, and handed it to Vanya. "Please, take it as a souvenir. I apologize if I insulted you." He spoke with an unhappy smile on his face as if he were parting with his life. Vanya's face blanched. She did not even reach for the sheet of paper, and I could see it was a drawing of her head—the sketch of a somber visage, like Vanya's in the grip of one of her "fits."

"Are you leaving?" only her lips asked.

"Tomorrow," Danail answered.

Vanya took the drawing without looking at it, and her shoulders quivered.

All of a sudden, Danail seized her up by the hand and drew her to him. "Will you come to Sofia with me?"

"You know I can't right now. The comrades won't let me go."

"When?"

They did not need anything else. The two beamed as they looked into each other's eyes as if that were the most exciting sight in the world. I grabbed my towel and slipped out.

When I returned to the room Vanya was already gone. Danail told me that she felt shy in my presence and hadn't waited for me. The two had agreed to get married in Sofia in a month. He spoke with a scowl on his face, without looking me in the eye, and he smiled only after I had offered my congratulations.

Then he smiled and challenged me to a fight boot to boot and had the satisfaction of knocking me down in the first thirty seconds.

Danail was that kind of a person—a man of quick decisions—and this sometimes scared me.

No, he was no adventurer as some comrades in prison had claimed, especially after that business with the Principal Overseer. That was rather a youthful confidence in his own evaluations and his own strength, a rare willingness to pay for his mistakes to the full extent. He was capable of striking somebody, and later, aware of his transgression, he bowed his head awaiting punishment. That was the kind of person he was in those days. He has retained some of this, but a lot has been blunted by his collisions with people who are disinclined to endanger their decorum, preferring to have someone else's head battered.

Thus, the last day of our sojourn in the town of "S." came upon us. We were to leave on the evening train. We packed up, stopped at some government and Party offices to say good-bye to our comrades and at lunch time we were in the cafeteria supposedly to meet Vanya there. She was late. We waited for her until three o'clock, but she failed to turn up. Danail was worried. I told him I supposed she had been detained at the town committee of the Young Communist League for a meeting or some other urgent business.

We went over there to look for her. She had been there but was not expected back in the afternoon, and we got the address of the textile worker in whose house Vanya was lodging temporarily. Neither she nor her hosts were there. They hadn't yet come home from the textile mill.

"Maybe she's waiting for us in the cubbyhole while we've been running around all over town," Danail suggested.

We dashed off in that direction. She had in fact been there as the landlady told us, but she had not left a message. It was past four-thirty, we still had more than two hours until train time, and we again headed for Vanya's friend's house. The house was locked up as it had been the first time, but a neighbor told us that at noon Vanya, the textile worker, and her husband had moved. When we asked her where, the woman mentioned the name of the merchant we had arrested and went into a detailed explanation of how to get there.

We did not wait for her to finish. Twenty-odd minutes later, gasping for breath and perspiring from our unforeseen chase all across the town, we pressed the doorbell of the familiar house. A young man in overalls opened the door for us. His face was smeared with grease and iron grit. He asked us in as soon as he realized we were looking for Vanya: "Come on in! . . . She went out with my wife for awhile, but she asked you to wait for her. Will you excuse me, please, while I go and wash up?"

He opened the door to the living room, let us through, and closed the door behind him without suspecting the surprise that was in store for us: the living room was absolutely bare. That isn't quite a correct statement since a seascape, forgotten as it was, still hung on the wall as though ineffectually trying to cover up the barrenness of the room. It was the only article left of all the furnishings. They were all gone—the rugs, the two divans in the corners, the big bar of walnut wood, the serving tables and armchairs, the flimsy red curtains on the French windows. Even Diana's ill-fated statuette was missing from the mantelpiece.

I exchanged glances with Danail, and then burst into laughter —it wasn't very polite of our host to ask us into this wasteland of wood paneling and parquet flooring.

"Well, that's the expropriation of the expropriators for you," Danail commented. "Only I don't see a single chair to sit down on . . . I'm dead beat."

"Neither do I," I said. "Let's walk around while we enjoy the seascape." I joked but I felt my heart tighten. Not that I was sorry about anything, but the desolation of the huge room rather depressed me.

Washed and freshened, the young worker joined us shortly afterwards, and we asked him where all the luxury had disappeared to. Most of the furniture had been confiscated for office use, it turned out, and some smaller things had been given to Vanya and to his family. Vanya's room was downstairs and theirs was upstairs, on the second floor. The rest of the rooms had been locked up until further notice.

"Vanya arranged the deal," the young man said with admiration. "A very capable girl. We had never dreamed of such a house. But why don't you sit down?"

Slightly shaken by Vanya's efficiency and by the strange question of our host, we smiled in silence. He cast a look around, and his face assumed a somewhat baffled expression. "I'll be damned! There were two soft chairs around here just a little while ago! I wonder where they are! Did anyone take them away?"

"Not while we've been here," I said.

"That's funny . . . I'll ask my wife when she gets home. Meantime come upstairs to our place and sit down awhile."

"We'd better wait in Vanya's room," Danail said.

"You could do that, too," the young man agreed.

We left the living room. He showed us to Vanya's room, waved his hand in a friendly manner, and climbed up the staircase patting the shining wooden banisters with satisfaction. Our friend's room was locked, but the key was in the door. Danail turned it and the door opened.

Alas, we could not sit down here either. There was simply no room to sit down: we stood on the threshold without even trying to squeeze inside. The former nursery was a big square room, and the two children's cots, the two small tables, the wardrobe, and the heap of toys were all there—it must once have been a spacious and sunlit room. But now my first impression was that it was impossible to cross over from the door to the window.

My eyes were first arrested by the two green armchairs, the "soft" chairs as Vanya's co-lodger had called them. Here they were, next to the door, placed one atop the other to save space. A magnificent carpet (during the search we had caught a glimpse of it in the merchant's study) lay rolled up at our feet. In the left a big, three-wing wardrobe with a full-sized mirror covered almost the entire wall of the room, not counting the children's wardrobe on the other side. The middle of the room was taken up by a big table piled high with enameled and aluminum kitchen utensils, a cut-glass wine service, and a myriad of ladies' odds and ends: vanity boxes, carved and poker-work, powder compacts, perfume bottles, a mirror with an exquisite silver handle, scissors and brushes, a set of silk underwear, and what not. Three or four dresses and a lady's topcoat with a Persian collar lay flung on the cots. In a word, the room looked more like a second-hand shop than a place to live. The objects were heaped high and strewn about as if in the heat of fever, with a blind Cyclopean passion. Over all this cornucopia of wealth, on the tall wardrobe, there stood the statuette of Diana the Huntress. She seemed to be watching us from above, with scorn in her sightless eyes.

Oh, Vanya, Vanya! We shouldn't have come in here, Danail and I—at least, he shouldn't have! We should never have opened that door, especially not those first days. Maybe a few years later, having gained more experience and shed some of our adolescent illusions—then we might have been able to bear that sight. Then we might have waited for you and said good-bye.

I fearfully stole a glance at my friend's face. He seemed to have shrunk away and dried up. Aware of my eyes, he came up with a start and walked over to the wardrobe. He lifted his hand and pushed the statuette off the edge. It fell on the silk underwear on the cot with a thud, but it did not break.

Then Danail seized the statuette and smashed it against the floor with all his venomous strength.

III

What is a major and what is a minor event in a man's life? Someone might prick his foot on a thorn and die of infection. Another might spend months and years in the trenches, amid the explosions of mines and shells, might be hospitalized for months afterwards, and have the shrapnel cut out of his body and have his flesh stitched, and yet survive. If he loses his right arm, he is happy to be able to earn his living and stroke his children's heads with his left; if he loses his eyesight, he is content to have his head intact so he can think.

Not any of these happened to Danail. He is alive and in good health today, but he has no children. He works in his studio, and only sculpture has meaning in his life. But he lacks something—perhaps the ability to look at things in a generalized and detached way without which great art is unthinkable. I don't believe that the incident with Vanya is the only reason for his failure or for his decision to remain single; and yet what to me and to many others was merely an unpleasant episode was something of far more importance to him. Maybe his misfortune comes from the fact that he regards the world with the sensitivity of an artist and not with the detachment of a philosopher and a historian.

As for Vanya, I used to think of her very often in the first years after the Liberation, and the more time went by, the more I was convinced that Danail had judged her much too harshly—almost as harshly as she had judged her own parents. It is hard to walk along a muddy road and keep your shoes clean. And then, there come moments in a man's life when, overtaken by passions unsuspected by him, he loses self-control and does things which seem incredible to him afterwards.

Vanya had spent a joyless childhood and then, with no forewarning at all, from the drab hell of poverty, she had suddenly found herself in the comfortable and dazzling paradise of that rich man's home.

Nevertheless, Danial does not agree with my point of view. He still believes that the outburst of such passions has its deep and lasting causes and even more lasting effects, and that under certain conditions these passions can become the mainspring of one's behavior. In this mainspring, as ancient and tough as the roots of couch-grass, he sees the roots of evil.

After all, everybody is entitled to his own views, isn't he?

Translated by GREGOR PAVLOV

Peter Neznakomov

(1920–   )

Biographical notes written by himself

I was born on October 12, 1920 in the town of Sliven. My father is an engineer and my mother a secondary school teacher. I received my secondary education in Bourgas and Sofia. I also finished an army school in Sofia, and started writing and publishing in 1946. My first stories were printed in the humorous paper *Sturshel*, on which I have been working for the last nineteen years.

I have written the following books, most of them collections of humorous stories and feuilletons: *Another Friday, Humorous Stories, White and Black, Innocent Stories, In Those Days, Margaritka and I, The Petrovs, Atilla the Scourge of God, Après Nous le Déluge, Iron Men* (written with Miron Ivanov), *An Old Dream, How I Became a Hero, A Sleepless Night*. My humorous story "The Miracle in Vuobrazhaevo," and a new volume of humorous stories under the title *The Mysterious Ship*, will soon appear.

PETER NEZNAKOMOV

The Painlevé Case

Already in the early morning one could tell that the long cold winter was on its way out. For the first time since we had been here, the timid March sun peeped out over the strip of pine forest, pouring its light over the wide, snow-covered yard of the holiday house. It was still cold, but there was a barely perceptible tang of spring in the air. The tiresome gray of the sky broke apart, a perfect swarm of tousled sparrows alighted in the middle of the yard, and it was extraordinarily pleasant to listen to their excited and disharmonious chirruping. About noon, the rainpipes began to drip, and the first runnel of muddy spring water began to slip past the yellow, dirty wall of the rest house.

It was a shame to stay indoors on a day like that and to hug the capricious stove.

So there I was, sitting on a bench in the lee, with my fur-lined jacket off, my eyes blinking at the unaccustomed light, my lungs pleasurably inhaling the fresh air, redolent of melting snow, and filled with an ineffable sense of well-being. Along the flags of the path, now showing beneath the snow, came the fat, gray holiday-house tom stopping to sun himself, stretching himself out with delight, and winking at me with one eye, as he looked at me with the air of an accomplice, as much as to say: "Not too bad, eh?" Stanka, the housemaid, ran past between the two cottages, with blankets and sheets over her shoulder, laughing for no particular reason, and leaving one wondering if that were the same sluggish girl who lighted the stove every morning with a sulky face, and who swept the rooms out any old way. Ivan, the cook, came out of the open door of the kitchen. He looked at the sparrows, which had flown up to a tree, and called gaily: "Darn it all! What's eating you this morning?"

In the caressing look on his rough freckled face, in the warm brilliance of his slightly crossed eyes, one read the peasant's pure, unadulterated joy, inherited from his forefathers, at the wonderful awakening of the earth in spring. Then he noticed me sitting on the bench and, probably ashamed of his feeling, so clearly expressed, bent down, picked up a handful of the sticky, wet snow, and threw it at the cat.

"Just look at him basking in the sun, the lazy bones!"

The cat jumped aside in a fright, scaled the fence, and glowered down angrily from there. Ivan seated himself on the bench beside me.

"Well, that's the end of this winter," he said, authoritatively. "There didn't seem no end to it, the way it was dragging out."

I nodded. Then we both fell silent for a long time—it was so pleasant here in the sun that we didn't feel like saying a word.

From behind the cottage came a song. "Co-o-o-ommander hero, hero Chapa-a-a-yev . . ." sang a high ringing tenor. A strong, merry whistle and the song was taken up by numerous, somewhat hoarse voices, which, however, sang in harmony. A squad of soldiers passed down the muddy road beyond the fence, on their way to the baths. A cocky young sergeant with a fair mustache was in charge, his cap perched jauntily on one side of his head, his legs encased in the most highly polished boots I ever saw in my life. He nimbly jumped the puddles in the road, and despite his severe look, as befitted a commander, his face clearly showed how pleased he was with himself, his boys, and the three stripes which shone on his shoulders. His squad passed on, but their song could still be heard in the distance, and in it, too, the approach of spring was clearly to be felt.

"Singing like blooming larks," remarked Ivan. "There weren't no songs like that in my time."

He looked up at the clearing blue sky, and sank in thought, and, knowing him pretty well by now, I knew that he was about to tell me one of his stories, with which he had so often amused us as we sat around the stove in the evening with a saucepan of sweetened rakiya warming on it.

"Ever been in the army?" he asked suddenly, still gazing up at the sky, as if he found something of great interest there.

"I have."

"The old barracks?"

"That's right, in the old barracks."

"Eh, then you've more or less got an idea and a conscientiousness," said Ivan, who was fond of using words which he didn't always understand properly. "Well, well, that reminds me of a spot of trouble we had in 1941 at the Turkish frontier. Or it happens you're busy, eh? Wanting to rattle away at that typewriter of yours."

"I've nothing to do today," said I, settling myself more comfortably on the bench. "Carry on with the story. But . . . are you sure none of the dishes'll burn?"

"Don't you worry about that," Ivan said, somewhat offended. Then he was silent for some time, for effect, a habit shared by all good raconteurs, and finally he began:

That year, forty-one, I mean, there was some kind of a fuss in the international situation. The Huns they had gone through Greece, and the Turks was restless. They said as how they'd been massing troops at the frontier . . . dislocation they calls it in military lingo. All very well, but our lot never wants to be outdone. So one morning we hears the signal for assembly. And the order comes, for Her Royal Highness Princess Eudoxia's entire Artillery Regiment to form up on the parade ground. Usually we cooks just stays in the kitchen, carrying on with our manipulations . . . we wasn't reckoned as soldiers in them days. But now the mess sergeant, Stoyu, he comes along roaring at the door:

"Come on you b—— louts! Can't you hear the signal, or d'you want me to unbuckle my belt. . . ."

There was five of us cooks in the regiment then—picked men, all of us. With a kick here, and his belt swung there, Stoyu got us out onto the parade ground. We stood to 'tention at the left flank, wondering what was up now, if it had got as far as us cooks. We looks around, and there was the officers walking gloomily up and down in front of their companies, with their sabers rattling against their spurs, and their eyes all looking thunder under their visors. The N.C.O.'s was running along the ranks, pushing in the boys' bellies. "Throw your chest out!" they says. "Fix your eyes on one spot and don't move an inch, damn you!"

So it wasn't just for the fun of it. And so it turned out. The regiment commander comes along, and the band strikes up, and we goes through the whole ceremonial all right and proper. Regiment all present, someone reports to him, and waits for orders real submissively. The commander takes his stand in the middle of the parade ground, and sets to: "Men," he says, "the decisive hour has struck. . . . the Treaty of Neuilly," he says, "and so on and so forth. . . . "We must remember," he says, "the great behests of Simeon the First . . ."

And other fantasies of that kind. We wonders what it's all about. Are we going into the war or aren't we? And the commander, he roars on: "Orders has come," says he, "from His Majesty the King of United Bulgaria, for our Artillery Regiment, Her Royal Highness Eudoxia's Own, to move with all speed in a southerly direction, and to do its duty, should that prove necessary, to the last drop of blood. On this occasion," says he, "three cheers for His Majesty and all the Royal Family!"

The officers roars for all they're worth, keeping one eye on the ranks, to find out, that is, what the mood and the morale is. And the morale, you might say, was in the lowest degree. Most of our boys was reserves called up—one with a young bride at home, another with a field as hadn't been ploughed nor sown, another with a horse as had been requisitioned—all they needed was this—to move in a southerly direction and shed their last drop of blood. Well, they dismissed us at last. And then, crickey you should've heard the commotion. Get the guns ready, and the hosses spruced and their backsides shaved in squares, and get marching rations for five days. And the officers cursing for all they was worth, and whichever way you looks somebody exercises with the belt. There wasn't the pedagogics and psychologics in them days—if you wasn't on the run all day, if you didn't click your heels just so, you got it in the neck. That was all the military science they had. Anyways, we finally got loaded onto the vans and sets out in a southerly direction as per order. How it went with the others, I don't know, but there wasn't hardly nothing left of us cooks. We'd stop at a station, say, and next thing there'd be, the officer in charge coming prancing up to the last van where the kitchens was.

"Hey," he'd say, "you bags of tripes, you, what sort of a mess is that you've cooked for the commander again? Don't you know, he's got an ulcer in his guts, confound you! I'll have the skin off your backs."

Go and tell him if you dare that the provisions is moldy, that Sergeant Stoyu and the t'other mess sergeant has built houses out of them provisions. He'd never listen to what you said, he'd never think as you was flesh and blood, he just went for you with his sword.

At last we gets to the end of the journey. We unloads the guns and the luggage, we occupies the lines we was ordered to—bare hills, without a scrap of shade to rest your soul in. They attaches our artillery detachment to the Twelfth Infantry Regiment. And then we has to set up camp. First it was to be here, then there, and at last they chooses a dry gully. The common soldiers makes dugouts for themselves, and tents was pitched for the officers. We, as belonged to the staff, we builds an officers' mess with a cookhouse, staff offices, and a hut for the C.O., with all conveniences.

Our C.O. was Major Ivan Rankov. And a worse fellow I never hopes to set eyes on. P'raps you've heard of him? You haven't? Eh, he was a proper devil, I tells you. About forty years he might've been. A lean son of a gun, dark as they makes 'em, and with green eyes, like a cat. I've never been able to stick 'em since that time—cats. They always remind me of that chap. He wore a gold ring on the finger of his right hand, a skull and crossbones, it was; and I don't know if he got a nervous breakdown, or there was a screw loose with him from the start, but he always struck out for a fellow's face with that ring. He wasn't married, the swine, and the women fell for him right and left. In Sofia, even married women would visit him in his quarters. The devil only knows what they saw in him! He treated 'em badly enough, just as if they was dogs. But that's beside this matter. And the soldiers was as afeard of him as if he'd been a snake. And no wonder—there was never a good word to be heard from him—nothing but cursing and: "Take so many days C. B." * He was fond of the rakiya, too. He'd get drunk once a

---

* Confined to barracks or guardhouse.

month regular, and when he was lit up, God help you. All the staff
went about on tiptoe, not to disturb one of his nerve centers, and
you wouldn't see as much as a bird flying within three meters of
his hut.

And we staff men got the worst of it. Sometimes he'd happen
to send for me in his hut. I'd go in and salute, clicking my heels, like
it says in the rules. I'd look at him—there he'd be, sitting on the cot
in his breeches and his pyjama top, and tapping his boots with his
whip. And his cat's eyes would move all over you, and you could
never know what his head had hatched.

"Private Gandjoulov Ivan."

"Here, sir."

"I know you're here. Now tell me, Private Gandjoulov Ivan,
what you imagine yourself to be, as you walk over this sinful earth?"

I'd straighten up before him with me hands glued to the seems
of me breeches and yell: "Private, sir, of Her Royal Highness Eudoxia's Fourth Artillery Regiment. Staff Company. At present carrying out the duties of cook at the officers' mess."

"That's a lie," says he. "You're no private." And tap he goes
with the whip on his boot, grinning all over his face.

"I am a private, sir!"

"And I tell you you're no private!"

"Then I don't know at all what I am, sir."

"You're a mangy crow, that's what you are."

Suddenly I feels aggrieved. Why crow!

"That I'm not, sir!"

"A-a-ah," says he, getting up from the cot, "so according to
you, your C.O.'s lying, eh?"

"No, sir! Not at all, sir!"

"Well, then? Are you a mangy crow or aren't you?"

I could see as things was taking a nasty turn, but I holds my
tongue.

"Answer me, can't you?" says he, "or don't you know Bulgarian?"

I holds my tongue again.

"Well," says he, "as you're ashamed of your own language,
you can stand in the sun for two hours, in full battle kit. And you'll
keep the sun off me when I have my nap. Now get out, or I might
hit you."

And that's the kind of game he was always up to. He just
loved being offensive and plaguing folk. So we called him "the Mosquito."

Another time he decides to have an air bath. He strips to his drawers and shouts: "Private Gandjoulov Ivan, take the groundsheet and the ladder. We're going," he says, "to swallow some ozone. It invigorates the whole system, and partikerly what pertains to the ladies."

So I takes the double painter's ladder from headquarters and a groundsheet and off we goes, the two of us, behind the hayricks. He stretches out between a couple of ricks and swallows ozone, that's some sort of gas, and I perches up on top of that there ladder, and holds the groundsheet over him to keep the sun off. And God help me if I falls asleep and drops the groundsheet on his head."

"You're under arrest," he shouts, "you dirty bolshie, consider yourself C.B.!"

So off I marches to the guardhouse and sits there enjoying the quiet and taking a look at my shirt to make sure I haven't picked up any vermin, and presently along comes Anton, his orderly, with a release. There wasn't no one else to cook for the major, d'ye see. And he liked to guzzle, he did, and always wanted dishes, y'know, and there was I, the only one as knew how to cook 'em.

That "Mosquito," he only had one weakness. I don't know where he'd picked 'em up, but he had two roosters, big, fine, red birds, Rhode Islands, they calls 'em, a foreign breed. Each one of 'em musta weighed a good nine pounds apiece solid meat, without the wings. I still can't make out why he was that fond of 'em. P'raps every soul, no matter how sinful, needs a spot of love. He called them roosters Panlevy and Loyzhorzh.*

"There's a pair of Anglo-French ministers of that name," he says, "but that's no matter for the likes of you."

"Yes, sir," says I.

So, as I was telling you, he was fair gone on them roosters. Sometimes I'd go into his hut to take him his breakfast, and what do I see—there he lies in his stocking feet on the cot, reading the "Army rules" with one hand stretched down, and Panlevy and Loyzhorzh pecking corn out of it. He'd even give them sugar—out of the stores, of course.

And they was right fond of him, was them damn birds! As soon as they heard his voice in the distance, they'd run to meet him, flapping their wings, as if the Lord's anointed was coming.

And Anton and I, we had the devil's own dance with them Rhode Islands. One evening, say, we'd just have rolled a couple of fags of homegrown baccy, and be having a quiet smoke, to get some

* Paul Painlevé and Lloyd George.

relief, and we'd hear "the Mosquito's" voice from the hut: "Where are you, blockhea-eads?"

We puts out our fags and runs in to him. The roosters was on his knees, trying to peck at his ears. "Why isn't Loyzhorzh in a happy frame of mind today, you damn Huguenots?" he says.

"I really can't say, sir!" I answers alone.

His orderly, Anton—he came from northern parts, and was killed at the front later, poor devil—was frightened out of his wits. Whenever the major shouted at him, he lost his tongue. He just stood there mooing, and not even the mother that bore him could ha' telled what he was saying.

"What d'you mean, you really can't say! Have you had orders to take most partikerler care of these roosters, or not?"

"Yes, sir. There was nothing the matter with the rooster all day, sir. This morning, sir," I says, "he woke us up, and after it grew warmer he chased the hens, sir. . . . If," says I, "he was indisposed, sir, would he be running after females, sir? He ate well at lunch."

"What did he eat?"

"Why," I says, "what he usually has, sir, the officers' food, sir. He had a cutlet fried in breadcrumbs, sir, and sautéed potatoes, sir, and custard . . . "

"H'm . . . just look out, won't you, 'cause if anything happens I'll hack your head off. Get out of it, now, 'cause the roosters don't appreciate your B.O. And tell the doctor to come at once!"

And so along of the major it came that we begins to hate them Anglo-French ministers like poison. And the truth of it is they lived for all the world like ministers with us. There wasn't no baths for the soldiers for months, and they was all full of vermin in the trenches, but them freemasons, we had to wash them in warm water, and wipe 'em on special towels with monograms on 'em, we even had to choose hens for them, as they wasn't to carry on with just any old hen what might have ticks and lice. And whatever we did, Anton and I was always to blame, we was always called Huguenots and what not, and they was always right. Well, says I to myself, this can't go on. I'll find a way to do for 'em.

And one day, sure enough, I did. "The Mosquito" wasn't there that morning. He'd gone off to watch some kind of exercises. I was making a veal stew in the kitchen, and I wasn't in the best of moods. I'd had a letter from the wife the day before. The child was ill, she wrote, the doctor wanted a mint of money (they fleeced you good and proper in them days), the landlord was down on 'em for the rent—in short—the sort of harmony to put your teeth on edge.

There I was, slicing onions and wondering what we was doing in that Godforsaken spot, on them bare hills, with anything in an officers' uniform calling you names and making life a misery. And I was in a temper, I felt like taking my cap and making off somewheres. Just then, into the kitchen comes Panlevy and starts strutting around, swelling with his own importance, you'd think he owns the place. I takes no notice and goes on slicing onions. Okay but he's out for trouble. All of a sudden up he flies onto the shelves and brings down the saucepans, and on top of it all he looks at me out of one eye, for all the world as if he was laughing at me, as much as to say: "Look, I does what I likes, and you can just stew around your old stove and do your duty to the Royal Family!"

To tell you the truth, I lost my temper, though it wasn't the creature's fault. "Get out," I shouts, "you blankety-blank minister . . . get out before I throws you out!"

But he wasn't one to take no notice. I might as well be talking to the wall. He even brought down another saucepan. "A-a-ah!" I cries, "you would, would you," and I seizes the poker. I goes up to the shelves gentle-like, and then I swings that poker. . . . I swipes him one on the head, or on the back, I don't really remember. He falls down to earth, squawks once or twice, beats his wings, slips behind the cupboard, and grows quiet.

"Ha," says I, "has that learned you something?" And I goes on slicing onions and not paying any attention whatever to him. I even feels a kind of relief. Just as if I'd swiped the major himself on his dirty mug.

Presently Anton peeps into the kitchen. "Ain't there anything of the officers' food I could have a bite of?" he asks.

Poor devil, he did like a tasty morsel.

"Why," I says, "just take a look at the frying pan, Anton. Over there, on the cupboard. But," I says, "don't you go getting too busy with it! The other day you stowed away three good pieces of meat and 'the Mosquito,' he got darned suspicious. See you don't get me mixed up with any guardhouses!"

His eyes grows bright, and off he goes to the cupboard, and begins exploring the frying pan, looking for a bit of fat; and suddenly he draws back. "Hey, Ivan, what's happened to the Panlevy?" he asks.

"Nothing. He's just had a little aperletic fit." And I grins at him.

Anton bends down, and I hears him begin to moo, something I couldn't understand. Then he straightens up and points at the cupboard with his eyes fair starting out of his head. To tell you true, I begins to feel a melancholy stealing over me, too. "I haven't been and gone and swiped him too hard," says I, "have I?" I runs up to the cupboard and what does I see? Panlevy with his legs stiff and sticking up, has given up the ghosts, as the old folk says. Now if it was one of our hens it would have been clucking around the parade ground by then, but those Rhode Islands, it don't take much to do for them. A weak breed.

So there we stand, Anton and I, over the corpse, staring at each other. What's to be done now?

"Oh," Anton says presently, "there won't be no room for us in these barracks. That madman will shoot the lot of us, for sure."

I near loses me own mind at first, but after a bit I pulls myself together. "We won't get far with moans and groans," says I. "Either you pulls yourself together, or you gets out, take your choice. I'll deal with 'the Mosquito.' All that's wanted of you is to keep your mouth shut. Mum's the word, entirely, d'you hear?"

Anton heaves two or three more groans, and departs somewheres. And I goes into action. First, I gives that Panlevy a thorough medical checkup. I takes a good look at him, and sees there ain't no serious bodily harm from the blow. He had thick feathers, and there wasn't a mark on him. Then I goes and pours a bit of rakiya down his throat; I always kept a bit of reserves in the kitchen, hidden away for the times when I gets to missing the wife. Then I sticks Panlevy under me apron and makes for the Major's hut. I looks around—not a soul in sight. Then I throws the bird in through the open window, and with a stick I pushes over the rakiya bottle, standing on the table. The bottle breaks, and there's a big puddle of rakiya round that blasted rooster.

"That's the ticket," says I. "Now we'll await the farther appointments of destiny." I goes back to me kitchen, and carries on, as innocent as you please. But me heart, y'know, it beats quietly, and next thing I know, it's up in me mouth. So I wasn't that easy in me mind.

After lunchtime I hears the rattle of horses' hoofs outside, and orders being given and somebody shouting: "Where are you, you dawdling blockhead?" In other words, exercises was over, and the major was on hand. I stands there on tenterhooks, with me ears wide open. Half an hour goes by—nothing happens. Suddenly I hears—not a voice, brother, more like a roar, as if someone was having his throat cut: "Private Gandjoulov Ivan! Where are you, you herring-gutted son-of-a-bitch?"

"Now," says I, "we'll see the action. Hold on, Ivan."

I runs to the hut. The major is standing in the middle of the hut, in full field uniform, staring at Panlevy. His whip is tapping his boot, and, leaving everything else aside, that tapping was more than a man could bear.

"Yes, sir!"

He turns and looks me up and down. "A-a-h, so it's you, Private Gandjoulov Ivan Stankov, is it? So you've turned up, have you? And how come you to salute with your cap off?"

I touches my head—sure enough, I'd forgotten me cap in the alarm. A bad beginning, thinks I: "Beg pardon, sir!"

"No pardon!" he roars. "Now tell me what's happened to Panlevy?"

"I couldn't say, sir!"

"Speak up! Who killed him?"

"Couldn't say, sir, I'm sure! This morning he was crowing all over the yard, he and Loyzhorzh had a scrap . . . he had his breakfast. . . . Then he disappeared somewheres."

"Where did he disappear? Look me straight in the eye! Dolt!"

"Yes, sir. I really couldn't say where he disappeared, sir."

"And could you say where the guardhouse was, eh?"

"Yes, sir."

"Who killed Panlevy?"

Here I looks down and pretends to see the carpet for the first time. "But," says I, "is he really dead, sir? Perhaps it's the rakiya as. . . ."

"What rakiya?"

"Why," I says, "the rakiya what's spilt on the floor. He was a mite high-spirited, he may have pushed the bottle over without wanting to . . . and if," I says, "he took it for water . . . it's quite strong, that rakiya, sir, it might even kill a man. And that rooster it wasn't as big as all that."

"You leave the rooster alone, and see I don't give you a thrashing." But I could see he'd softened a bit. He picks the cock up from the floor, and puts his nose to its bill.

"It's true, he does smell of brandy. Dammit! Why did I leave that bottle out!"

He begins to puff and blow, and little by little I retreats to the door. "He's took the bait," I says. "I've got off, he's forgotten me." And I grows bold. "Am I free to go, sir?" I asks.

But he never hears me. He paces up and down, stepping in

front of the cock, putting a hand out to touch it, but not touching it, only moving his fingers in the air. He was hurt, that's clear. There's no denying it, he loved that Panlevy.

I stands there, watching him, then I asks again: "Am I free to go, sir?"

Only then does he raise his eyes and take a good look at me. "Ah," he says, "you're still here, are you? Enjoying the sight, eh?" And suddenly his face grows terrible, all twisted and ugly, and such a look of evil in his eyes it makes me shudder. "Get out!" he says. "Escort yourself to the guardhouse, and tell the sergeant, my orders is to keep you there till you rot. Tell him I'll come and see in person if you've rotted. Now repeat the order!"

"Yes, sir. You said I was to report to the sergeant as he was to keep me in the guardhouse until I rotted, and you would come and see in person if I had."

"Right," he says. "And be thankful I didn't shoot you!"

"Yes, sir. Thank you, sir!" I says.

"Get out!"

So off I goes, rubbing my hands at having got off so lightly. "Well," I says, "that's all over. I'll have a rest in the guardhouse from all these alluminations." I goes to the sergeant, and tells him as the officer had ordered me C.B. till I rotted.

The sergeant, he just laughs. "What for, Gandjoulov? You haven't burnt his food, have you?"

"Not at all, sergeant," I says. "Panlevy has perished of some tropical death, so he's took it out on me."

The sergeant's smile freezes on his face. "What!" he cries. "You don't say! There'll be no life in the batteries for a week at least, all because of that there Rhode Island."

"I really don't know, sir," I says.

So they puts me in the guardhouse and puts a sentry to guard me, like I was a deep-dyed criminal person. But before ten minutes was over, along comes Anton, to rot, too. So I begins to question him. "What happened?" I asks. "You haven't let anything out, have you?"

And he just sits there, trembling, and not able to speak a word of sense. I only gets one thing out of him—he hasn't got off scot-free either. He got beaten because of the bottle. Why's he left it in a place where the bird could upset it!

A couple of hours later the sergeant comes along, and says, frowning without looking at me: "Private Gandjoulov, you're released! The major has sent for you!"

"Why, sergeant?" I asks. "I haven't rotted yet."

"I don't know," he says. "He's sent for you. He's in one of them moods." And he keeps his eyes off me.

Now I doesn't like that at all. What does he want me for now? I wonders. Has he found out the rights of the matter? Okay, but if he wants to beat me, he'd have me brought under an armed guard; why should he release me? So I makes for the hut, wondering and wondering, and me feet, they're the most sensitive part of one y'know, always pulling me back. At last I says: in for a penny, in for a pound! And into the hut I goes. At first I don't see nothing—outside the sun's just going down, and it's dark in the hut—but in a minute I'm considering the nature of things. So Panlevy is lying on the table. Next to him is the empty rakiya bottle, and the major is sitting on the cot, with his collar unbuttoned, holding his head in both hands, as if he's having hard work keeping it in place.

"Oh dear," I thinks. "He's done himself proud! Now all kinds of allegories is to be expected!" I reports that I'm appearing at his orders—he never moves, just mutters something down his nose. Then after five long minutes he drops his hands, looks me up and down with his bloodshot eyes, and says, indistinctly:

"Private Gandjoulov Ivan, in this army . . . you're the only man who undersssstands me . . . and," he says, "I ressspect you highly, you ass. . . . So I order you without delay or loss of time to find me a pickax and a spade! Before the sun goes down," says he, "the deceased must be buried with all honors and salutes. Carrrry on."

There was nothing for it. Orders is orders. I finds a pickax and a spade, and appears before him for further orders.

"Follow me!" he says. He picks up the cock and carries him like a child.

I follows him, and though I feels like laughing, an inner voice says to me: "It's too early to laugh, Ivan."

We gets to the hayricks, and there was some small bushes there. The major walks up and down along them, chooses a place and says: "Dig here," he says, "a foot and a half by two!"

So I begins digging to the measurements given, and he sits down ten paces away with the cock on his knees, saying never a word.

"Ready, sir!"

"Ah," he says, "so the hour has struck! Then take the mortal remains, Private Gandjoulov Ivan, and place them carefully in the grave! And if, by chance, you've mistaken the measurements, I'll rip your ears off!"

I takes over Panlevy, and shoves him into the hole. And the major rises heavily, sways, and—now what can I swear by—three paces from the grave he stands to attention, takes off his cap, and bows his head. Then he sees me there, leaning on the spade gaping at him, and roars: "Hats off, atheist!"

"Eh," says I, "I'll take off me cap, it's no great matter." But that there humoresque was tickling my funny bone so, that I all but laughed in his face, ha-ha-ha. And a good thing I held my noise, eh, for I saw him fumbling with his holster, and the next thing he draws his revolver. "Now, Ivan," I says, "is the time to be as careful as Mother Nature has taught you to be—for he's under the influence of alcohol, and before you knows it he'll have shot you down." I stands as still as still can be at his back, just as if I wasn't there, not moving, not breathing. And d'you know what it was all about? That drunkard wants to give his cock military honors. He raises his revolver and . . . bang . . . bang . . . bang . . . fires three shots in the air. Then he puts the revolver back in its holster, and says quietly to me: "Cover him, Gandjoulov Ivan!"

Well, them words was a relief. "Yes, sir!" I says.

And he stands there frowning. "Don't shout so, you uneducated piece of beef! Don't trouble this solemn moment!"

So I covers the grave over more or less, and he paces gloomily up and down.

"Have you finished?" he says, "have you resigned the body to the earth?"

"Ready, sir! The Lord be merciful to Panlevy!"

"Now leave me alone!" he says. "Scram, before I've counted three!"

That's all I was waiting for. I runs straight to headquarters. From a distance I sees the staff soldiers talking anxiously and gesticulating, and when they sees me, they all surrounds me and begins to hug me.

"Are you alive?" they cries. "Eh, we were like to lose our minds because of you. When we heard them shots, we says: 'He's done for him, "that Mosquito" . . .'"

"Done, your grandmother!" I says, grinning. And I tells them the whole story. They were like to die of laughter. Only Anton—they'd released him, too—stands there sadly.

"What's the matter with you?" I asks. "You ain't mourning for that Anglo-Frenchman, are you?"

"Not likely!" he says. "I'm only sorry for all that meat. His drumsticks alone must have weighed a couple of pounds apiece."

And suddenly a bright idea strikes me. "Come on, brothers," I says, "put your hands in your pockets! Let each one give what he can!"

"What for, Vanka?"

"Why," I says, "to buy some wine in the village. We had ought to honor the dear departed, too. We ought to have a wake for him. I'll provide the meal. And you, Anton, go to the mess sergeant and get two pounds of rice, not the moldy stuff they gives us . . . the officers' rice, tell him the major wants it. His digestive track is out of order, and he's ordered boiled rice to doctor it."

Anton realizes how the land lies, and grins from ear to ear. He goes to the mess, we sends a runner to the village for the wine, and I slips back behind the hayricks, finds the grave, undigs Panlevy and takes him into my kitchen. I smells him, and there ain't nothing wrong with him. I pours boiling water over him, plucks him, cuts him up into portions, and puts him in the oven. I'm working, but I'm laughing, too. "This case," I says, "has paid for all the troubles I've had in barracks."

After supper the major and the other officers goes to the village to drink, and we, the lower ranks of the staff, gets together in the cookhouse, locks ourselves in, covers the windows with greatcoats in case, and eats up the deceased, as the saying is, bones and all. We drinks to his rest, too. And to tell you the truth, I've never eaten anything with such relish. And they all keeps saying: "Come on, Ivan, tell us again how you buried the minister!" So I tells the story again, and they laughs fit to split their sides. All very well, but it turned out that too much laughter brings bad luck.

Next morning, it was Sunday. The major gets up late . . . liverish . . . disgruntled . . . the very devil. Loyzhorzh goes in to him, to be petted, and gets kicked for his pains. Anton takes him his breakfast, and gets it thrown at his head. About 11A.M. he comes out and starts on his round of the camp. The weather was fine that day, the sun was shining and there was a light breeze. All very well, but there was the feel of a storm in the atmosphere, it don't smell healthy. At other times, Stoyan, the bagpipe player, would strike up a tune, and the boys would dance a round dance . . . to forget their troubles a bit, but there was nothing of the sort that day. Everybody lies low, and there ain't a sound to be heard.

So the major set out on his rounds of the batteries, and I can feel there is something up. The others tells me afterwards what it was all about. He don't like the line of the trenches. We've been sitting in this Godforsaken hole for two months, and he'd no fault to find with them so far, and now—they won't do. They have to be made according to some German model or other. "Fill them in!" he orders. "And dig new ones five meters further back!" Just to bother the men. He strikes three of 'em in the face with his ring, and even shoves two of the second lieutenants in the guardhouse, and he calls Grozdan the sergeant, what was his right-hand man, a "kangaroo." The sergeant complains afterwards.

"Now, I'd understand it if he called a private by that French word," he says, "a private is a kangaroo by nature, anyhow. But me," he says. "Who give him the right to call me that? I can't remember the time when I wasn't in uniform. What kangaroo," says he, "has three stripes to his sleeves, I asks you?"

About noon the major shows up in the cookhouse. He sniffs around here and there, tastes the food, and frowns. "What kind of a mess have you cooked for us again?" he asks.

I stands to attention with my ladle. "Veal," says I, "with belvedere sauce, sir. And the soup," I says, "if I may speak, sir . . ."

"You've no call to speak," he says. "I've tasted it, haven't I? It's just a mess."

"It's no mess, sir. This kind of soup . . ." It hurts my feelings proper to have my cooking run down.

"Hold your tongue!" he shouts. "When you talk to me, you're to hold your tongue!"

And the hand with the ring balls up into a fist. I swallows the insult and holds me tongue. He sniffs about some more, and goes out. And I'm just thinking that I got off easily this time, when I hears a roar from outside: "Private Gandjoulov, come here at once! Qui-i-ick!"

I runs behind the cookhouse. There he is, standing by the rubbish heap and pointing at something with his whip. And his mustaches aquivering like they was alive.

"What's that there, Private Gandjoulov Ivan?" he asks. I looks in the direction given, and I grows cold all over. Right on top of the rubbish heap lies two long cock's legs . . . and there's nary a local breed as has them long spurs. Last night, after the wake, in the flurry, I goes and throws them there. What now?

"I'm asking you, Private Gandjoulov, what's that over there?"

I swallows hard and clicks me heels. "Hen's legs, sir. We had chicken soup with spaghetti the other day, sir, if you remember."

"Hen's legs, eh? Just hand them over."

I hands him the legs, but how only I can tell. He looks them over carefully, then gives me a look from under his eyebrows.

"Now look here, Private Gandjoulov Ivan," he says, "these aren't the late Panlevy's legs by any chance, are they?"

"I really couldn't say, sir!"

He does a bit of thinking. "As you can't say," he says, "be so good as to fetch a spade, please!"

"Sir," I says, trying to talk him out of it. "How can it be Panlevy? Didn't we bury him last night? It's a sin . . ."

"Be so good," says he, "as to bring me that spade before I shoot you! Right about-turn! March!"

I sees there wasn't no way out of it, and I runs for the spade. I runs, but it feels as if my boots had lead in 'em. We sets out for the hayricks. We finds the grave by the bushes.

"Dig," he says, "be so good as to dig!"

I begins to dig, but I digs to one side, and only scratches the earth, so to speak. He stands over me, watching me like an eagle.

"Don't waste your time, you Babylonian bastard! I give you three minutes."

I begins to dig with more energy, but there wasn't no sign of any Panlevy. And he just peers into the hole, and says with a twisted grin: "Dig," he says, "dig away! You'll dig here for the rest of your life, but you'll find that rooster for me."

I digs up a few more spadefuls, then I takes my courage in both hands, and speaks up, come what may: "There ain't no sign of our Panlevy, sir," I says.

"A-a-ah," he says, "is that so? Very odd. Can he have come to life again?"

"I really couldn't say, sir. He ain't here."

"Or p'raps," he says, "an angel come down from Heaven and took him up to paradise, eh? But," he says, as far as my memory of Holy Writ goes, it's only the soul that's resurrected, and the body is left in the grave. What have you to say on the matter?"

"I couldn't say nothing, sir. I ain't had no eddication."

And that's when he exploded. He takes me by the collar, and shakes me, yelling: "Listen, you bastard, tell me who ate Panlevy. I'll not leave a sound bone in your body. I'll make mincemeat of you! Who was it?"

"I really couldn't say, sir. Might have been a fox, sir."

"I'll fox you," he says. "Who was it?" And he brings his whip down across my face.

"Nobody has et him, sir."

"Who was it?" And he hits me again. This time it hurts like sin, and I tastes something sweet, blood must have flowed from the cut.

"Who was it?" He begins to hit at random. The sight of the blood maddens him. But I grows stubborn, too. "I'll die here," I says. "I may never see my child again, but I shan't tell you. But I'm not going to forget this beating. And the time'll come when I'll pay you back." He beats me, I can't remember how much, and finally he stops, he's tired.

"Now run and get me those bolsheviks of the staff," he says. "Let them see what a sight you are, and think what's coming to them. And then tell them to fall in in front of my hut, in the shape of a letter 'U.' That rooster," he says, "I'll get him out of your buttocks if I have to."

I gets the staff men together, and tells them how the land lies on the way. "We'll all have to take a thrashing, but if there's a Judas among us as gives the show away, he'll get what's coming to him afterwards!"

We forms up as he's ordered in front of the hut, and waits. I looks at the boys, and feels quite calm. They've all got their lips pressed together, and their eyes is shining with hate—you wouldn't get a sound out of 'em if you was to flay them alive. Then out comes the major, whip in hand.

"Welcome," he says, "you bastards! We'll have a little talk, you and I. Right about-face!"

We faces about.

"Move away five paces from each other!"

We moves.

"If any of you moves so much as an eyelid," he says, "you'll be on your way to the other world. Got it?"

Silence, as if we'd decided on it beforehand.

"Got it, I ask?"

Silence again.

"Aha," he says, "this smells of anti-state ideas, too . . . So, so, so . . . now we'll find everything out, with the help of well-tried methods. I've long had my suspicions," he says, "that someone was up to mischief here. . . . Shall we begin, eh?"

And he stops at the first of us, Mitko, his name was, a telephone operator, a clever kind of bloke, always reading books . . . he's a bigshot in Sofia these days. He served in the army and was promoted last year, he's a lieutenant colonel now . . . sometimes I meets him in the street, and he always laughs when he sees me. "Do you remember Panlevy, Ivan?" he asks. "Course I do," says I. So, as I was saying, the major hauls up behind him.

"Now, me lad," he says, "if you're still true to your country, tell me," he says, "without any more fuss, who ate Panlevy?"

"I really can't say, sir." Down comes the whip on his head. Well, that boy Mitko, he goes scarlet. I expect he'd never been hit before.

"And don't you know now, traitor?"

"I don't know now, sir." Down comes the whip on his head again.

"But you know how to read books, eh? Don't think the sergeant hasn't reported to me. And," he says, "I shall be going into your business more thoroughly. I'll cut out all sources of infection."

Then he goes on to the next man, and gives him a few cuts, and so on down the line. He hits us, and we keeps quiet. And that was the odd thing about it, when the major hits me tayte-à-tayte at the hayricks, it hurt me, and I was that sorry for myself, I nearly lets out a groan, for the shame of it; but now, in a collective situation with the same amount of blows, I do not feel nothing. I even feels lighthearted. . . . There's some philosophical sense in that, too, eh? That's what it is.

So the major hits us to his heart's content, and sees that he won't get nothing for his pains. Then he goes wild, and draws his revolver. "I'll destroy you," he says, "like flies, you bastards . . . and on top of it all, I'll be thanked for ridding the earth of you." But none of us stirred now either. One of us may go, we thinks, but only a wet spot'll be left of you afterwards.

He threatened us, he cursed us, but he daren't shoot. He was frightened by our backs, for not one of 'em was bent. Then he sends us to the guardhouse.

"Let them stay there, on nothing but water," he says, "until their bellies sticks to their spines!"

But Mitko, what possessed him I don't know—at other times he always held his tongue—suddenly stands to attention and cries: "Please, sir," he says, "allow me to report! There's no such punishment in the regulations. It isn't legal."

Well, and doesn't that major go wild then.

"You impertinent rascal," he says, "you're not to teach me what's legal and what isn't. This is the law in barracks." And he shakes the whip at us. "And if you're not pleased," he says, "complain to the C.O. of the regiment! He likes to flay such legal-minded bastards himself! Now, march to the guardhouse!"

They sticks us in the guardhouse. There was hardly room for the lot of us, we was nine men. At first we is silent, each one looking for a corner to make hisself comfortable, and stretch out his legs. And Mitko says: "Well, we held out well, boys, didn't we?" And he laughs, well pleased with hisself. At hard times like these, he always laughed. "One has to realize, that all by himself a private is nothing. But if we stick together, we can become such a terrible force that the major and all those above him will go to the devil. Wise men," he says, "have said so. . . ."

And he goes on to tell us things of that kind . . . but not right out. I listens to him, and thinks, I've heard them tales from schoolmaster at home in the village. You leans to communism, brother, but you're still careful, testing the ground. Never mind, be careful, yours ain't an easy job, you're wanting to overthrow a kingdom. And afterwards, when you get to know us better, you'll find out as the soil is ready, it's only waiting for you to sow the seed. People like the major have plowed it for you.

And what do you think, two days later, while we was still in the guardhouse, Hitler goes and attacks Russia. So I tell you, that's how our business began, with that there Panlevy. He got us together, and because of him, our eyes was opened to the other thing.

Ivan fell silent, stroking his chin thoughtfully, as if all he had lived through was passing before his eyes again.

"But today," he said, giving me a smiling look, "the boys sings right merrily, and the uniform don't weigh on them! You can see at once, there's respect for man, affection."

"And what happened to the major?" I asked.

The cook's face grew stern. "He got his deserts," he answered briefly, and somewhat reluctantly. "He didn't get out of it. And now, I'll be leaving you, brother. We've sat here talking, you and I, but there's work to be done. I'm not on holiday like you are."

He got up and vanished in the kitchen. A little later his gay humming could be heard from there: "Oh, little lassie mischievous. . . ."

The sparrows were still cheeping in the tree. The cat went back to his sunny patch. The inhabitants of the holiday house were returning for lunch. And I sat there on the bench, going over various parts of the sad and comical tale of Panlevy and smiling. And the day seemed sunnier than ever to me, and the earth's spring awakening reminded me now of that terrible force of the people, of which Mitko, the telephone operator, had talked so simply and so well to the silent and smarting privates in the lockup.

Translated by MARGUERITE ALEXIEVA

Svetoslav Minkov*

(1902–1966)

Laughter in Ramonia

"Not long ago an epidemic of
laughter broke out in an African
village near Lake Victoria, affecting
all its 200 inhabitants. The epidemic
was caused by some unknown virus."
Ghanaian Times—Accra

Deep midnight silence enveloped distant Ramonia. The moon, large
and yellow, was now vanishing into the depths of heaven, now
climbing the crest of a cloud and shining in its full radiance. The
ocean was gently caressing the shores of Ramonia, lulling the small
island state into blissful sleep. Everything seemed to be sound asleep:
palms, gazelles, leopards, snakes, butterflies, and people.

Suddenly the silence was broken by gunfire, the rattling of
machine guns, and the thunder of shells. Lampur, the capital of Ramonia, bristled in alarm. Human shadows flitted about in the dark,
sneaking along the walls and, after a short struggle with the guards,
forced their way into the government buildings.

In the morning Ramonia awoke under the bayonets of a new
dictatorship. A military junta, headed by General Gardubal Suarez
Tabaneira, had overthrown the autocrat Juan Oliver Chakarachat,
and seized power. Oliver Chakarachat himself was lying in a puddle
of blood in front of his magnificent residence, while his loyal fol-
lowers were swaying gently from the branches of the surrounding
trees. Such was the established custom at a change of Ramonian
government, and if Gardubal Suarez Tabaneira ever fell from
power, he would be expected to play his part in the same ritual.

* For biographical data, see p. 69.

After having firmly seized power in his hands, General Tabaneira introduced a whole series of reorganizations and innovations,
which were aimed at eliminating all the shortcomings inherited from
former regimes. The moment he set foot on the magic carpet of
power the new dictator organized the customary vigilant army
against the Communists (in Ramonia as everywhere else there appeared to be a plentiful supply of them). Some Communists were
summarily executed, and others were thrown into prison; those who
had succeeded in hiding were outlawed and declared to be more
dangerous than wild animals. A loyal descendant of the Spanish in-
quisitors who once burned heretics and apostates at the stake, the
general in the blood-stained boots wrote his name in history as a
famous executioner of thousands of Ramonian Communists and
other patriots.

It is difficult to give here a full list of the reforms carried out
by this benevolent despot. They included compulsory visits to
churches and sports stadiums (a sound mind in a sound body) and a
complete ban on trade with red objects (red roses, red cabbage, mo-
rello cherries, Moslem fezes, scarlet toreador's mantles, etc.), the
color of which might involuntarily remind people of the accursed
communism or serve as propaganda against the government. The
present story will focus the reader's attention on only one excep-
tionally important reform which, being unique of its kind, immortal-
ized the name of its initiator. But to make the need for this reform
clear to the reader, let us first say a few words about the Ramonian
people.

In Ramonia the Ramonians danced their beloved Ramona folk
dance. For them the Ramona folk dance was the same as the *ruche-
nitsa* dance is for the Bulgarians, the czardas for the Hungarians, and
the tango for the Argentinians. Not only did the Ramonians dance
the Ramona, but since time immemorial they had been in the habit
of joking, telling anecdotes, and laughing. Yes, they loved to laugh—
freely and from the bottom of their hearts—as if a ringing stream
was irresistibly gushing from their throats. For the Ramonian, laughter was a source of vital force, an outburst of inborn joy which made
him forget all his hardships. Deprived of his laughter, the Ramonian
would pine away, withering like a flower growing in the shade. On
the other hand, if you made him split his sides with cheerful laughter
and then threw him into an inferno, his laughter would take him on
its radiant wings and bring him back to life.

Now you might imagine that there was nothing very alarming about this laughter of the Ramonian people; but like every other

dictator, General Tabaneira wisely discerned in it the dangerous elements of sedition and secret resistance. That is why, after turning over the problem in his mind for a long time, the leader of the military junta decided to promote laughter to the status of a state monopoly. One day in all the streets, squares, and public places in Ramonia, the following decree was posted, carrying the force of a law:

DECREE
ON LAUGHTER AND THE CONTROL OF ITS PROPER USAGE

I.

In view of the now frequently encountered phenomenon known as *Laughter*, which leads to the slackening of morality and established custom, and constitutes an alarming threat to the moral integrity of the Ramonian people, the following practices of this particular luxury are

FORBIDDEN UNDER THE PENALTY OF THE STRICTEST PUNISHMENT

1. Laughter for personal reasons, in all its forms and varieties, as well as any incitement to laughter such as tickling, the presentation of comedies, vaudevilles and farces, the dissemination of jokes, anecdotes, banter, etc.
2. The publication and dissemination of any humorous works, including cartoons portraying prominent statesmen and public events in an unfavorable light.
3. The gathering together of more than two persons at places and under circumstances conducive to the open perpetration of the above-named crimes.

II.

To satisfy the natural needs of good-natured laughter, which is useful for the health, promotes digestion, and maintains the good cheer of the Ramonian people,

I ORDER:

4. That in the different parts of the country, state circuses and satirical companies be established and the necessary administrative and disciplinary measures be taken to ensure mass attendances at all performances.
5. That for the same purpose the publication of a state satirical newspaper be started, with a view to illuminating every home in Ramonia, without exception, with officially sanctioned humor.
6. That for the correct implementation of government policy, a separate Ministry of Laughter be set up and entrusted with the elaboration of a detailed plan for action within the framework of special regulations.

The undertakings implementing the state monopoly of laughter, as indicated in paragraphs 4, 5, and 6 of the present order, shall not be subject to penal sanctions, but shall be fostered by all methods of public propaganda.

The present decree shall come into force as from the date of its publication in the official State Bulletin.

(Signed) *General Gardubal Suarez
Tabaneira,
Supreme Leader of Ramonia*

Crowds of curious Ramonians flocked in front of the posted decree, holding a lively discussion of the wise decision of their supreme leader. Taking advantage of the still-existing freedom (for the publication of the decree in the State Bulletin was delayed for unexplained reasons), everybody hurried to have a good laugh for the last time. Many of them, though unknown to each other, set out in groups for the nearest coffee shops, restaurants, and bars to make merry together, while the more cautious ones gathered in their houses, seeking comfort in silent drinking and occasionally bursting into a kind of furtive and satanic chuckle.

But finally this interregnum ended, and the decree became immutable law.

As might be expected, the Ramonian Ministry of Laughter, although housed in a pretty small building, ill-suited for such an important institution, developed a feverish activity. Previously this building had been a monastery, in which a dozen monks, half-blind and half-deaf with age, had been slowly burning out like wax candles. When General Tabaneira announced the reform which he was about to introduce, the holy fathers took shelter elsewhere, and the monastery was rapidly reconstructed to house the Ministry of Laughter.

The new establishment put forth its first spring leaves, its young roots eagerly sucking the juices that would give life to its future bureaucratic activities. Typewriters started rattling, files began rustling, and the once-monastic labyrinth was filled with chiefs, deputy chiefs, secretaries, advisers, and all kinds of other officials. Odd as it might seem, although entrusted with such invigorating tasks, all the officials in this Ministry were (perhaps the better to enforce their weight and authority) stern and sullen men who pursued their activities as if at some funeral establishment which busied itself with the saddest rituals and burial ceremonies. Even Don Salvator Barboza, the Minister of Laughter himself, appeared to be an inveterate melancholic who had apparently never laughed in his life. But how could one judge the true nature of a man by such superficial signs?

In all fairness it must be admitted that the army of officials in the field of state-controlled laughter, despite their apparent coldness, were burning with the selfless enthusiasm of authentic bureaucracy, the flames of which, although invisible, illumined the strenuous activity of the whole Ministry.

How were the state-controlled undertakings, as directed by the Ramonian Ministry of Laughter, received by the masses? To our deep regret, it must be admitted that despite the immense efforts on the part of the organs of the Ministry, its superb control, and the energetic co-operation of the police force, which firmly encouraged full attendance at the circuses and other places of official entertainment and helped to ensure the population-wide circulation of the satirical newspaper, *Ramoniana,* the masses were not amused by state-controlled laughter. We have already mentioned that the Ramonians were cheerful people and loved to laugh; but as soon as the state supplanted their own form of laughter with its more purposeful, regulated variety, they began to wane like flowers in a sunless place. Before long, not even the faintest smile was to be seen flickering over their faces.

It is true that the Ramonian places of entertainment resounded with the well-paid and correct laughter of petty state officials trembling for their posts, and with the self-satisfied giggling of the ruling circles. But it was not quite like the genuine human laughter that comes from the bottom of one's heart. That kind of exhibitionism was punished with imprisonment, forced labor, and death.

But something happened to bring this state of affairs to an end. It was one of those wonderful mornings when the sun shines in a pale green strip between the sky and the ocean, rising magnificently from the water and shaking its fiery mane to illuminate the coastal palms with a purple light—a sight which may be enjoyed only on the luxuriant green shores of Ramonia.

On this particular morning a tall, broad-shouldered Negro with a very dark face and very white teeth landed from a Mexican ship. He had a raincoat flung over his shoulder and carried a small suitcase in his right hand. From his passport, which was stamped by a Ramonian border official, it became evident that the Negro was a citizen of the former imperial colony of Tombo, recently liberated and proclaimed as a free independent republic, with its own state coat-of-arms.

After having observed the numerous customs formalities, the Tombonian set out along a broad street and soon found himself before a small bar with wicker tables on the sidewalk. He sank into a wicker chair. When the waiter brought him his glass of whisky and soda, even before taking his first sip, his face suddenly contorted in a nervous spasm, his pupils widened, and a muffled grunt escaped from his throat. Then the Negro burst into a fit of hearty laughter, giggling irresistibly, to the surprise of the passers-by who stopped and looked at him in amazement.

Soon a curious crowd thronged in front of the bar—sailors, fishermen, vendors of oysters and octopuses, porters, prostitutes—a whole cross-section of the port, eager for sensation. And as the stranger continued to laugh ever more violently and irresistibly—and remember that such laughter constituted a violation of the law—a number of eager uniformed policemen and plain-clothes men soon arrived at the scene of the crime.

Diligent guardians of public order and undoubted practical experts on all violations of the laws, these government representatives promptly established that the Negro had long since passed the peak of forbidden laughter (indicated in the special schedule as laughter of the tenth degree).

The policemen seized the law-breaking Negro, who continued laughing ever more provocatively, and, despite his desperate resistance, succeeded in pushing him into a closed car.

The investigation of the strange case revealed that the Negro had fallen victim to the *Endvara yokusheka* disease, which is caused by a peculiar virus which attacks the nervous cells and provokes irresistible laughter. The symptoms of this mysterious ailment have never been fully explained, but Professor Mitsu Vakamatsu, who happened to be on a visit to Ramonia, declared that similar epidemics of irresistible laughter had been observed in almost all the emerging nations which had been liberated from colonial oppression; and that the disease was caused by a virus which the professor considered should rightly be called the freedom virus.

Additional information indicated that the disease was highly contagious—easily transmitted from one person to another. The chain reaction of the laughter virus was confirmed by the fact that the policemen who had fought the criminal and escorted him in the car arrived at the local police headquarters in the same disgraceful condition. When they appeared before the police chief with the laughing Negro, their own sides were splitting with laughter, and they were unable to explain what had happened. While the police official was trying to unravel the mystery, he suddenly twisted his face in a sour grimace as though ready to sneeze, and then burst into the well-known fit of irresistible laughter. From him the torch was

carried to others, flooding the whole country in a wave of laughter.
In vain did the Ramonian authorities try to raise a barrier
against the swelling torrent of the mass epidemic; in vain did General Tabaneira personally issue order after order, threatening the Ramonian people with a foaming mouth: "Stop laughing at once!" But
how could laughter be put in chains, and a whole nation thrown into
prison because for no fault of their own they had been affected by
the Tombonian epidemic!

Among various other methods of treatment which were tried,
someone proposed that experiments should be made with the Bulgarian nivalin preparation, a tested remedy against spasmic phenomena.
Although it gave rise to faint hopes of salvation, even the wonder-working extract from the snowdrop proved powerless to quench the
Tombonian laughter.

Gradually the epidemic spread all over Ramonia. It penetrated
deep into the masses; in fact, it mainly affected the ordinary people.
The big tycoons of the rich ruling class hid in their magnificent
palaces and villas and remained unaffected by the epidemic because
it was transmitted only through physical contact, and the Ramonian
rich in general avoided all possible contact with the rabble.

We should not fail to note, however, that the ordinary Ramonians bore their frequent attacks of laughter with equanimity, and
were by no means unhappy. Regrettably, they seemed to prefer
these fits of free laughter to the official commodity ordered by the
dictator.

General Tabaneira, who was a very religious man, had a
weakness for appearing before his people, and paid a weekly visit for
this purpose to Saint Benedictus Cathedral. One Sunday morning he
set out for church, escorted by a suite who cleared the road ahead of
him of ragamuffins and suspicious poverty-stricken types. The general humbly listened to the Sunday liturgy, to the blessing of Bishop
Ignacio himself, and ordered his men to drop a silver coin in the
plate of each beggar waiting at the church gate. Then, pleased that
he had fulfilled his duty, the prominent worshiper returned to his
residence, signed a couple of death warrants, and began to examine a
newly received foreign magazine which contained a portrait of himself in full dress.

But the leader of the military junta had hardly turned the first
few pages before he suddenly felt dizzy, and immediately afterward
burst into a loud fit of giggling. The two officers of the guard on
duty in the next room immediately scurried in to him; but the general continued to laugh irresistibly, staring at them and unable to

utter a word. No doubt, his fatal passion to appear before the ordinary people had been the sole reason for his falling victim to the seditious epidemic.

His domestic servants (the general had no relatives) scampered about in alarm, while the agitated officers dialed telephones, and confidentially spread the alarming news. In a few minutes the best Ramonian doctors arrived, followed by all the Ramonian ministers. The general's residence was surrounded by three lines of guardsmen and turned into an inaccessible fortress.

But General Tabaneira continued to roar with hoarse laughter. He tossed about like a wounded beast, banging the desk with his fists. Suddenly he pointed to his belly, confessing with horror-stricken eyes that the dangerous Communist virus had taken hold of him. Then the poor man again burst into a nightmarish fit of ringing laughter. The doctors gathered around him for a consultation at which different Latin names were mentioned, but suddenly they, too, burst out laughing. They were followed by the ministers and the two officers on duty, and soon the whole residence resounded with powerful laughter, which shook the building to its foundations.

By noon General Tabaneira was swollen with excitement; his face was suffused with a dark flush, his pulse accelerated rapidly (120–150–180) until finally the poor fellow, unable to endure the suffering of genuine laughter, exploded, leaving behind not even a trace of himself. Some said that he died not of laughter, but of the fear of having become a Communist.

That is how General Tabaneira disappeared from this world, unable to wait for the next coup d'état in Ramonia, and therefore unable to play the traditional role in the selection ceremony as his predecessor had done.

Anything can happen in Ramonia. After the dissolution of General Tabaneira, leader of the military junta, the state power was seized not by a general or a president, but by a sultan. He had a golden turban and a harem of beautiful women. His name was Djanabet II.

The character and pursuits of the new head of state were quite different from those of his predecessor, General Tabaneira, and he showed no leanings toward reform. After having ascended the throne, freshly gilded after its removal from the state furniture storehouse, he wisely scratched his wavy beard and decided the destiny of his people with a single sweep of his hand. He entrusted the monopolies with unlimited power of exploiting the country's lead mines, oil deposits and refineries, banana plantations, and other natural resources, and he placed his army under the command of experienced officers. Besides the right to live in luxury the Sultan introduced simpler procedures for executing Ramonian Communists and reserved for himself the right to sign execution orders.

It goes without saying that Djanabet II repealed the decree on laughter and all the other undertakings of the former dictatorial regime. He did away with the Ministry of Laughter, dismissing all its sinister officials. In Ramonia's capital, Rampur, he allowed one state circus to remain; but here the main parts were no longer played by clowns and performing monkeys but by beautiful women acrobats, equestriennes and animal-tamers who enjoyed the personal protection of the Sultan himself.

The strange epidemic of laughter which had swept the country disappeared as suddenly as it had arrived. It has been observed, however, that ordinary human laughter has ever since preserved certain elements of the mysterious Tombonian infection.

Reclining on soft cushions, Sultan Djanabet II continued blissfully smoking his hookah, drinking coffee and sherbet, and watching football matches on television. He made no attempt to interfere with his people's constitutional right to laugh and to go hungry.

And the hungry Ramonian people went on laughing in the Tombonian way, secretly whetting their daggers, and continued to dance the Ramona folk dance.

Translated by KRASSIMIRA NONEVA

PART III

Modern Mentalities:
City, Factory, Town

Orlin Vassilev

(1904—   )

Orlin Vassilev was born on December 4, 1904 in the village of Vranyak, Byala Slatina district. He finished secondary school in Vratsa and studied diplomacy at the Free University in Sofia. His first works were published in 1927 in Anton Strashimirov's magazine *Vedrina*. Later Orlin Vassilev contributed to the newspapers *Missul, Literatouren Glas, Vestnik na Zhenata, Douma, Shtit*, and *Literatouren Pregled*. He was the editor of the *Svyat* newspaper (1933–34), which was suppressed by the censors and started appearing again in 1935 under the name of *Prostor*. He also took part in the editing of the *Kormilo* newspaper (1936). For some time he was secretary of the National Library and manager of the City Library in Sofia. He was also on the editorial staff of the *Patriot* newspaper, edited by Kroum Kyulyavkov (1944). After September 9, 1944 he was director of Radio Sofia and was editor of the *Literatouren Front* newspaper.

He has published the following works: *The Fire Ring*, a novelette (1928); *The White Path*, a novel (1929); *Simple Hearts*, short stories (1939); *A Haidouk Never Feeds His Own*, a historical novel (1937); *Life*, short stories (1944); *Alarm*, a drama (1948); *Love*, a drama (1952); *The People's Voice*, short stories (1952); *Happiness*, a drama (1953); *Selected Works* in five volumes (1957–58). Books for children: *The Wild Forest* (1936); *Bitter Bread*, tales and stories (1937); *Tooth for Tooth*, a historical novel (1944); *The Fearful Monster*, selected works for children and adolescents (1956); *The Clever Ducks* (1958).

Null with a Capital Letter

Among the many different types of people met with in the transition period, I am the most seldom encountered. Perhaps, I am even the only one of my kind, unique. That is why I have remained not properly looked into, known only to myself. It is namely this that has awakened the temptation in me to make an analysis myself of my psychical being. (And why not exult secretly once more? A victory over other people, unshared with anyone, and unknown to anyone, like drinking on one's own, brings a certain enjoyment to the heart. There now, I had only to mention the word "victory" and I got the first foretaste of my enjoyment.)

I am a complete and absolute null. A null with a capital letter.

(I make this comparison not to demean myself—oh no!—but to define the category I am in, and to emphasize and show my personality and my social value.)

As is known, the word "null" comes from the Latin *nullus*, which means "not any"—nothing. And I am just such a nothing. All my attempt to become something—in poetry, fiction, drama, journalism, even in the public and organizational hierarchy—I am sorry to say came to nothing. It is true that nature endowed me richly with a good memory, willpower, industriousness, go-getting, and spider-like patience—even with a faultless taste for what is beautiful. But unfortunately because of some unjust and evil equilibrium, nature did not give me that magic thing that either you have or you haven't: talent, the divine power of creating what is beautiful—both as a sensual palpable image, and as something throbbing with immortal life. The moment when, in rising aloft to the abode of art, I realized that something irreplaceable was lacking in my talent, was a crushing, positively crippling moment.

I had already let my hands drop in futility—to the devil with all my false hopes: I would plunge forever to the very bottom—become a house-painter, an odd-job man for electricity repairs, a clerk, one of the mass—when I discovered that I bore within me the potential greatness of a Null.

In himself a Null is really just a nought. But a mysterious, fascinating nought. If it is put after the figure one, for instance, it makes its value ten times greater. (In such a case is it fair that this power to be multiplied many times over should belong only to a one? Without the addition of this wonder-working nought it would remain only one of the simplest ones.)

The first incentive to become aware of myself as a Null was given me by a woman.

I love women, indeed. Namely women—in the crowd, in the flock. Especially if they are not only beautiful but also desirable and sexy. The still almost scientifically unknown sensual biocurrents—from their mouths, their chins, their necks, and so on—charge all my cells with a feeling of bliss, as electricity charges the lamellae in a battery (surely the rams in the midst of their flocks have similar feelings, and the pashas in their harem).

Alas! My times are monogamous—I am forced to take only one out of the flock. It is true I have the most beautiful, with the most sex appeal—as fiery as a filly, intoxicated with herself, and intoxicating everyone else with her stirring femininity. She is one of those rarely born beauties—arrogant and self-confident, who take it as their natural right that every man they meet should fall before them entranced to be trampled in the dust under their stalking feet, beautiful as any screen star's.

If it is a matter of trampling in the dust, I am ready to trample —in the concrete and abstract sense of the word. But what is the good of it? Everyone of us, even those of us who are most madly in love, always cherish at least a faint hope that, if not tomorrow, then some other day, after years, we shall make the loved one respond to our feelings (give love for love), through our doglike devotion, tender feelings, and the like.

Clever and honestly sober in judging things concerning myself, I cannot allow myself to be misled in this way. Nadya will never be able to love me no matter what my feelings, my sacrifices, my feats of heroism may be. I mean she will never begin greeting me with a rush of joyous light in her eyes, laying my head on her left breast to hear the melodious throbbing of her heart and finally sinking in the oblivion of complete self-forgetfulness. There is something which no social order and no homilies about love and brotherhood will ever be able to make right: for my sake even in the future with communism realized, Nadya will never treasure up any of the sacred relics of love—a flower stolen in the park, a cigarette case covered with a drawing of a heart, pierced by Cupid's arrow, a lock of hair, a hieroglyphic note.

Unlike other people, I myself know very well that I am an unpleasant man, and not only from the woman's point of view. I am short, with a large, rounded behind, and my head planted right down in my shoulders, with a mouth like a sheatfish's, with coarse lips, and with shifty little eyes, hidden deep under the sinuous bones. Some kind of a sour smell, like that of a polecat or billy goat, and disgusting for other people, comes from the deep, open pores in my skin. My voice is hoarse and my laugh squawky like a goat's bleating. Why in the world should this glamor girl have preferred me, when goodness knows how many handsome guys used to crowd around her—students, fellows from the science institutes, dons, married and unmarried, plus a whole legion of admirers who weren't working in any of the institutes or at the university. And each one something special, the only one of his kind—clever and talented, with a present and with a future.

When I married her, however, her affectionate attachment, and even her love were not all that necessary for me in the classical sense, as depicted in literature. (That kind of sentimental relations between men and women sprang up in comparatively recent times, when French chivalry was flourishing in the twelfth and thirteenth centuries. There were no such sentimental relations in antiquity— the throbbing, fiery flesh did not thrust into its heart, the thought of what was male and what was female to such a degree as now.) I was looking for compensation; I would procure for myself what I could not get as my natural lot. The greatest, most glamorous beauty among the young people in Sofia should belong to me as my wife and companion (in the literal sense): to lie near me and to go about with me. When walking through the streets with her, when entering a café in the foyer of the theater, I had to feel how every single person turned around to look at us: "Just look at him, that stinking billy goat! How ever did he get hold of that wonderful-looking woman? What invisible qualities can he have in him, the old sly dog?"

Quite a nice feeling, don't you think? (I ask as if I were talking to someone. But this story of mine is only a top-secret monologue for my own moral satisfaction and esthetic enjoyment.)

I began, whenever opportunity offered, and even when it did not, to appear before the girl I had picked out: I went to lectures that were quite useless for me, to meetings, on excursions, and I joined their canteen for my meals. If I saw an empty chair at her table (it was very rare), I immediately wormed myself into it. How could they have refused to let me sit there? It was a free chair in a public establishment. I never gave anyone a hint that I was courting her. In the most flagrant manner, I neglected even the usual conventional customs through which courtesy is shown to women—for example, holding her coat to put on. In spite of this, with the eternal instinct of the female, it is impossible that she had not got some faint inkling of my secret, spider-like expectations. Otherwise, she would not always have sprung away from me so instinctively, as if I had been a spider, indeed—with dread in her eyes, with irritation, and with barely concealed disgust.

But is there an impregnable fortress in this world? The clever conqueror has always found a little traitor's gate. Like all beautiful girls, in whose head their grandmothers and aunts have kept on hammering the same thought—"Ah, you charming little mother's angel!"—Nadya had grown up in the expectation that everybody would spread carpets before her feet. She had read five books and a half, had remained simple and, as far as literature was concerned, half-ignorant, but like many other glamor girls, she had entered a higher educational establishment not to study agronomy or veterinary medicine, or something like that, but art, of all things! To judge and adjudicate the complicated combined collective work of dramaturgy, stage-managing, and acting—of the theater in general, in whose chariot, as is well known, are yoked all the muses—from Melpomene to Calypso.

Womanly charm—come to the rescue!

Eyes, skin, lips, chin, neck, etc., emit your magic invisible fluid!

So by actively switching on all her charm she had, somehow, managed to get through to her last university test, her diploma thesis.

But now what? I looked at her in the canteen. Her slender body was moving uneasily in her chair, and she was crumbling her bread. She was fiddling with her fork, not bothering about her food, and she even forgot the repugnance she felt for me. And she spoke to me first: "Oh, my goodness! What shall I do? I must begin writing it, and I've got absolutely no idea in my head."

I was jubilant: there it was, the little gate! "Well, that's a nice thing! Now see here—your face has lost all its brightness. . . . Can there be anything easier than that diploma thesis of yours? Only tell me what theme you've got, and the instructions of your consulting tutor. He surely gave you some kind of an examination synopsis."

"He gave me one, of course. It's here in my bag."

"Show it to me, please!" I said, passing from the formal Bulgarian "you" to the familiar "thou."

The muddled girl stretched out her hand toward her bag, and I moved to the chair next to hers: the mighty Null, the nought, was added to an insignificant one.

Nadya graduated in art with distinction, but her advancement did not stop with that. Her articles on the most intricate problems were published in the appropriate magazines, and there could hardly be any responsible meeting of the institute at which some decision had to be taken without first hearing her enlightened and competent opinion.

Her salary was good. But quite a bit began flowing in from different sidelines: pay for articles, reviews for the use of institutes, consultations, and so on.

It is unnecessary to inform you explicitly that she was already my wife—the sweetest, the most desirable—and my companion on the street, in the cafés, in the foyers of concert halls and theaters (turn round, ye envious ones!).

But I was speaking of something else. . . .

Archimedes wished for a point of support to lean on, in order to turn the earth over. And for me it was necessary only to have someone else's thought, no matter of what kind, someone else's elementary text, an initial conflicting position, and my brain ignited and sprang into action—completed its development, enriched itself, saturated itself with fine details. Or it would shorten, shift, smooth out, and polish, until it had cleared up the nebula and given a firm form to the shapeless mass.

Now the time came for my triumph.

It has not been said elsewhere, but the following discovery should be known as my original contribution to the science of writing: the discovery, namely, that the transition period is a period of editing.

The heralded era of the equality of all men was welcomed by many with the plebeian conviction that all people had to be leveled down till they equalled them in ignorance. They felt it would be advantageous to pull down the whole of culture from the crest of the world wave to their own level, rather than that they themselves should breathlessly struggle and splash toward the crest. "When we've done our little bit toward bringing the victory, why shouldn't we find places for ourselves in alluring and profitable sectors of intellectual activity?" they thought. "Don't we see that the state grudges nothing in fostering and training more and more skilled cadres? Geniuses don't drop from heaven. Let us cherish the hope that while they are wasting paper on thousands of trashy books, they will fertilize the soil for the flourishing of what is desired and has been long expected. What would happen to the host of editors, if they decided to let only the good ones, the really useful ones, work? Ha! ha! Let those who know how and can, hold and guide our hands. We will scribble something or other, and they will lick it into the shape that their much-praised norms and rules demand."

I haven't sunk so low—I work with people who have got through the first stage of becoming knowledgeable in literature.

Sometimes I myself make a suggestion to them: "Listen, why

don't you write a play? Do you know what a demand there is for plays now? A positive gold mine in them! It could be on a historical subject. Or it could be about geologists—there's a theme that's both contemporary and romantic. My suggestions are at your disposal, without my having any claim to co-authorship."

At other times, I would sit down over their manuscripts and begin to expand, pare down, add to. When I would begin to read aloud the clean, retyped pages of the manuscript, tears of tenderness would gush to the eyes of the authors. (From the realization of the great understanding shown by their own minds, from the deep emotion of their own hearts.)

"Right. . . . It's just right so! You've altered it a tiny little bit, and it's become marvelous . . . simply marvelous!"

"Thanks. I'm glad you like it."

"You're simply born for an editor."

"Oh, thanks! You're very kind!"

There are translators (for the most part scientific ones) who don't know any language—neither a foreign one, nor Bulgarian. And that's just why they are able to grab the translations. And the grabbing is what is important. The rest is just a game. (Sometimes we go fifty-fifty, and sometimes sixty to forty. And their position is strengthened, and I collect what is due to me.)

Orders pour in half on the sly, the others wholly secret, but there are always too many for even my motor-like industriousness to cope with.

Well, my name is not on the book covers, on the theater bills, or in the catalogues—but what does it matter? Aren't the authors of national legends and folk art unknown? Is the name of the inventor written over the machine he makes? Finally, in the future radiant times will not the noble creators relinquish the right to have their names on their works, give up this individualistic habit, this leftover of a private-owning society?

The name! What of it!

Don't I live with the best-looking and sexiest little woman in the most beautiful and most elegant flat in the center of the town? It isn't a flat—it's a poem—the simultaneous creation of five arts. My collection of books is unique, and I shall make just the same kind of collections of stamps and pictures.

We have a housekeeper, with a white housemaid's cap.

My relations with the Figure Ones are not only on a pecuniary basis, I mean to say not only "You have written it for me, you have edited it for me, here's your money and you can go." Oh, no!

Between us there is, so to say, some spiritual affinity. We become something like intellectual foster brothers: through sin we are bound together forever. There has not been a single occasion on which I have asked for a favor, or for someone to put in a good word somewhere for me, or for my wife, or for someone else, one of my friends or relations, and been refused. Even very interesting things have occurred: I myself have sometimes become the intercessor on behalf of my eminent patrons. For example, when I drop in at the publishing house or come across some editor I know on the street, I cry something similar to what I cried out to Mangurov:

"Oh, Mangurov, how do you do! Well, if I'd gone specially to look you up, I couldn't have dropped in on you at a more favorable moment. I wanted to warn you that the Figure One is frowning about something. You've become so engrossed in those new things you're putting out that you've begun to forget the gold mine of Bulgarian sociology. Why don't you let a volume of his studies through to the press? The libraries will always buy up the copies, even if nobody else does. That is singular!"

Those editors who can refuse outright are few—the chaps I was talking to knew very well that in half an hour's time his words would be passed on, directly or by telephone, to the right place. Afterwards the editor would extricate himself. Figure One would peck at him with his beak on the sorest place. (Of course, behind the screen of some points of principle.) That was why he was filtering his stuff, somehow, in a very balanced way.

"Well . . . yes . . . it wouldn't be bad to think it over. We'll talk about it in the director's office."

In a flash, I would alter all my plans for the day and dash toward the said creative study (I had free access to it at any time of the day or night): "Do you know, boss, I've got some good news. (He and I have been using the familiar "thou" for a long time.) I mentioned a collection of your sociologistic works to Mangurov. It is a good idea, isn't it? And not only an idea—God forgive me—but it will also bring in quite a nice little sum of money. I shall be happy if I am the reason for one of your books to come out. (My dear Figure One, why do you pretend to be so selflessly indifferent?)

"The money, old chap . . . oh, don't think about that. . . . But see, if there is really a chance of the book coming out."

"Of course it'll come out! It's only necessary that you personally drop in at the publishing house."

But did they say I had to?

Say it? Well, you know how they hum and haw. Anyway,

old fellow, strike the iron whilst it's hot. And he seized his overcoat and set off to strike the iron. Somebody might ask: What was there in such transactions for me? There was quite a lot in it for me. If the sociologistic writings, or any others, were still not in shipshape order, because of the actual demands of the moment, I would immediately get busy over them—working like a Negro on a colonial plantation. If, on the other hand, the composition, on the whole, was already in trim, I would drop in to see him later, just at the most suitable moment, to get a copy of the book with his grateful signature and to ask him among other things to lend me a little money. (Not ten leva, of course—it was a matter of a bigger sum.)

"What about it? Will you let me have it?"

The host surveyed me in silence, but his eyes expressed his eloquent admiration.

"Ah, the accomplished scoundrel! How brazenly he's demanding to be paid for putting in his good word and arranging the matter!"

No, morality had not completely disappeared. Some of them would fumble in their purses and give me the loan which I would never pay back. (If the fellow in question had not paid, which of us would have been the greater scoundrel?)

Well, now they despise me. If they have important guests, they don't invite Nadya and me. I am conspicuous by my absence in general gatherings of the most eminent people. But if it is a matter of contempt, my contempt is greater, and I have more grounds to be contemptuous, for I play with my cards on the table and don't pretend to be a virtuous young man. Who would take from me the right to be jubilant when I read articles of praise, with just those passages quoted that I have written with my own hand?

And I, as a Null (if that word can be used), have some consciousness of my contribution to intellectual development: How many works would not have seen the light of day if I had not put into them a small part of my untalented personality?

They threaten me with communism: they say such people as I will disappear then. First of all, there's still time till then; secondly, the prophecies after Christ have not always come true.

Yes, I really could vanish, and that before communism comes. But for that it would be necessary to be exposed, delineated, and shown as a type in literature, so that the public would recognize me, as they recognize criminals after all their distinctive features have been announced. The name "Null with a Capital Letter" would remain then as the byword for them.

Fortunately the writers, even if they see me as I really am, will not describe me in their books. There is a hard, unamendable law in their esthetics: to tell about what is typical in our actual life. And I am absolutely not typical. I am an exception, a small beast of prey, a jackal, a survival of the past. If anyone, however, should decide that he'll get me by the throat, my people, the Figure Ones, would be the first to go for him. "What's this evildoer daring to say against the builders of socialism!" they would say. "So many works have been written, so many splendid heroes created! Don't let him get away with such slander!"

So, protected by mediocrity and esthetics, I live and flourish. I am expecting to get a car. Although there is a danger of becoming conspicuous, of attracting people's attention (a jackal in a motor car), I am in a hurry to buy one—chiefly because of Nadya. Something is happening to that woman. Whenever I return home after her, I always find her with red, tear-bleared eyes. We already sleep in separate rooms, but, in spite of this, I can hear how for whole nights together she turns and rolls about in her bed, lights the lamp, puts it out and then lights it again. And she reads, reads. . . . She has enrolled in courses for lessons and has taken a private teacher to learn two languages at once (she is not stupid and she had a good memory: I was not a little astonished one day to hear her prattling in English to a guest in their institute). It is a sad thing that she doesn't want to have a child. (She would tear out her own insides rather than bear a child of mine! She is surely horrified by the thought that it might resemble me—outwardly and inwardly.) However, the most worrying thing is that she seeks my help ever more rarely—she is trying, the unhappy creature, to get down from my back, to attempt to stumble across the black, fallow land of art alone. That is why I decided to get a car. The women of our time love cars.

(Ah, that verb "to love"!)

But what if a new love should really appear in her life? Or rather, not a new love, but her first love, for, up to now, she has never experienced love at all (our relations have only been a physical sticking together of a one and a nought). I wonder whether the fiery flesh in her bosom won't get the better of her—won't break off my dear little Figure One from me, and push it into the enticing abyss of sentimentality?

I've simply got to get a car as soon as possible!

Translated by MARJORIE HALL

Pavel Vezhinov

(1914–   )

Born on November 9, 1914 in Sofia, Pavel Vezhinov graduated from secondary school in Varna and studied philosophy at Sofia University. His first works were published in the *Zhoupel* newspaper in 1932. He contributed to the *RLF*, *Shtit*, *Literatouren Pregled*, *Izkoustvo i Kritika* and other periodicals, and took part in World War II as an army writer. After the war Vezhinov was on the editorial staff of the *Sturshel* newspaper and the *Septemvri* magazine. At present he is working as scriptwriter for the Bulgarian cinematography.

He is the author of the following books: *Unpaved Street*, short stories (1938); *Days and Nights*, short stories (1942); *At the Post*, short stories (1947); *Second Company*, short stories (1949); *For the Honour of One's Country* (1949); *In the Field*, a novelette (1950); *The Arid Plain* (1952); *At the Helsinki Olympics* (1953); *The Traces Remain* (1954); *Our Strength*, short stories (1957); *Incredible Stories* (1958); *Far from the Shore* (1958).

The Boy with the Violin

I

The day was damp and gray, but toward evening the sky over Mount Lyulin cleared a little and the soft red of the sunset glowed in the windowpanes. The boy with the violin, his back to the window, sat watching the reddish reflection on the television screen. In the cold twilight of the room this was the only spot of warmth, all the other objects having lost their color in the shadows. The red velvet of the armchair in which Dady sat now looked quite brown. Dady's hair, too, looked brown and his green eyes showed dark, but the reflection had caused the fanatic's pallor of his face to assume a slightly warmer hue.

"Anti-matter is a fact," Dady said, staring hard at the boy. "This is not merely a fact of logic. I've seen the photo of a particle of anti-matter."

The boy was thinking about something else, and answered absently. "I haven't read anything . . ."

"They don't write about it, indeed!" Dady replied sharply. "Why? I just don't know. It is actually a brilliant confirmation of dialectics."

Interpreting the boy's silence in his own way, he added in a tone of exaltation: "Just imagine, everything in this world is plus and minus. There can be no plus without a minus and no minus without a plus. One has to stop and think about it."

"Dialectics, that's all right," the boy said. "But doesn't this contradict materialism?"

"What?" Dady asked, narrowing his eye insidiously.

"Well, this anti-matter . . ."

"Nonsense!" Dady said with assurance. "Matter as a philosophical concept is something else. Don't you understand? Subjective-objective. The point is that anti-matter exists objectively." Dady straightened himself up a little, his eyes shining as fanatically as before.

For a second the boy forgot the frightening thoughts crowding into his mind. "What is a plus and what is a minus? Is that also objective?" he asked uncertainly.

"Of course!" Dady said in dead earnest. "It all depends on the direction of movement."

Right at this moment the deep bass chimes of the clock sounded in the corridor. "So soon?" thought the boy in despair. The sound died down slowly as if it were water filtering through the crack under the door. As the chiming sound died out, he said in a rather calm voice, "Dady, I must be off."

"Where to?"

"I have a violin lesson."

Dady made a face. "Your father really surprises me. Such an intelligent and serious person. Doesn't he realize that this is a period of reason and not of sentiment?"

"Just the opposite," the boy said nervously.

"Just the opposite?" Dady repeated, as though he did not believe his own ears.

"Just the opposite, of course!" the boy exclaimed abruptly and somewhat roughly. "Who believes in reason? No one. No one at all."

While Dady was gaping at him he quickly went out of the room. No, he shouldn't have done that, he had acted too badly for words. This evening should not have been different from any other, in tone or action. No nervousness, no jumpiness. The boy entered the kitchen and turned on the light. The chill dampness coming from the open door of the small balcony made him shiver slightly. He switched on the boiler and then carefully closed the narrow door to the balcony. All the windows in the building across the street were still dark. Her window was also dark. The boy stood still for a couple of minutes hoping that the window would light up suddenly and a slender woman's figure emerge in the space of light. She would face the mirror on the wall and raise her arms to fix her hair. This would make her figure look more slender, and the beautiful curve of her breasts would become more visible under her thin pull-over. But there was no movement in the dark window; the room with the light-green walls was probably empty. His heart, too, was empty when he started back to the room.

In the foyer the boy stood still again. Should he wear his top-coat or his raincoat? Maybe the topcoat, because they would spend a long time there and he would be cold. But the Italian topcoat of camel's hair color was very expensive. Passers-by turned to look at him when he wore it. No one must look at him tonight; no one must notice him or remember him.

When he went back into the room, Dady was standing near the French window pensively looking outside. Although he was only one year the boy's senior, Dady looked as tall as his father, only he wasn't so broad-shouldered. His legs were downright massive. His trousers, stretched as tight as Christmas sausages, had long since become too short for him, and his large, bony ankles showed from under the cuffs. "What a figure," the boy thought, "and what a su-permind." Someday perhaps Dady would be running an academy.

"Let's go," he said softly.

"Let's go," Dady echoed, thinking of something else.

A quarantine notice with a red cross on it and a penciled in-scription "Measles" hung upon the peeled wall on the first floor. Half a dozen children, all of them curly-headed and olive-eyed, lived in that apartment as in a rabbit hole. Almost every month the quarantine sign was up there, and parents in the apartment house were at their wits' end about how to protect their children from contagion.

The boy with the violin lifted his hand from the bannister and put it cautiously into the pocket of his raincoat.

They parted company at the entrance. The sidewalk was damp, and the yellow leaves from the chestnut trees stuck to it thickly like mosaics. A white cat walked gingerly on the wet flagstones, like a woman, stepping lightly on the tip of its soft little paws. From time to time her white whiskers touched the flagstones squeamishly, but her eyes were on the alert. As the boy drew nearer she quickened her steps, crossing the street with elegant leaps. Only on the opposite sidewalk did she turn around and look at the violin carefully. Perhaps the violin had frightened her more than the boy had.

At that hour few people were out. At dusk passers-by did not stare at each other and that was all to the good. At first he had the feeling that everybody knew the truth and this depressed him. It was better not to meet people, not to see human eyes. Thus the violin moved along its senseless way more calmly. But upon approaching the apartment house where Vas lived, he noticed a large group of people clustered around the entrance. All of a sudden the violin seemed to weigh heavier, and his step fell light and short. What could this mean? Nothing! Of course, nothing! Nevertheless he came closer carefully, ready to turn back at any moment. A man separated himself from the crowd, his gray unshaven face wrinkled in a scowl.

"An epileptic fit," he mumbled under his breath.

The boy was about to pass on when he remembered the motto of the fraternity: "Harden yourself!" Cautiously pushing his way through the crowd, he reached the innermost circle. Lying on the ground was a young man; his face was stiff and it had a deathly pallor. One of his cheeks had been grazed in his fall and blood had collected in the wound, but it was not trickling down his face. He was wheezing dreadfully and shook convulsively from time to time. When the boy retraced his steps out of the crowd, his face wore the same color as the sick man's. He was aware of an irrepressible nausea. What if Vas should pop up out of somewhere and see him in this condition? The boy walked slowly to the corner and then back again. He believed he had regained his normal color again, and his hand firmly clutched the handle of the violin case. A "First Aid" ambulance sped past him and stopped short at the entrance. Without stopping to see more, the boy started climbing the stairs slowly.

As soon as he pressed the bell Vas showed him in as if he had been waiting behind the door. His face seemed quite calm, but a feverish gleam lurked in his eyes. Vas wrenched the violin from the boy's hands and thrust it quickly into a closet. His burning eyes lingered on the boy's face for a moment.

"What's the matter with you?" he asked, displeased.

"Nothing," the boy said.

Vas frowned and turned his head. The glass door to the hall was lit up, a radio was on inside. Vas half-opened the door and said in a loud voice, "I'm going out."

"All right," a woman's pleasant voice answered from within. "When will you be back?"

"In a short while."

Yes, in a short while. Or in a long while? Nobody could tell. Vas shut the door and started for the exit headlong. The boy caught him by the elbow: "Aren't you going to put anything on?"

"Oh yes, sure," Vas murmured in confusion, adding angrily, "it isn't terribly cold after all."

Just the same, he put on his school topcoat and this made him look taller, almost as tall as Dady, but much thinner. His face shrank in size, and the pink rash that covered his narrow forehead stood out more conspicuously. Vas put on a woolen ski cap and walked out without looking at the boy. For some time the two of them climbed down the stairs in silence. On the ground floor the boy could not hold back any longer and said with some trepidation, "A man fainted outside."

"What was it?" Vas asked briefly.

"I don't know. An epileptic."

"That's why you were so pale before, wasn't it?" Vas said contemptuously.

The boy did not answer. The ambulance had carried the epileptic away and the crowd had long since dispersed. They took a short cut along a narrow street, so yellow with fallen leaves that the paving stones were hardly visible. Flocks of sparrows chirped wildly overhead, and dry branches swayed as if they were alive in the late dusk. Vas stopped and looked around for a stone, but seeing nothing handy, he walked on in somber silence. There were some stones at the end of the street. There the paving stones had been taken out and arranged in two heaps near the curb, while the shallow canal dividing the street into two, was covered with moist yellow sand. A car which had strayed into the trap came back zigzagging between the two sidewalks. As the car came nearer the boy noticed that the man at the wheel was very fat and probably had found it difficult to turn his head and look back.

"Fool!" Vas said with contempt. "To think they give a driver's license to people like that."

The boy was silent again. This might have been all right coming from anybody else, but Vas, of all people. . . . Once Evgeni had suddenly given Vas the steering wheel without any warning. And although the car moved along, it zigzagged more or less in the same way as the one that had just passed. Evgeni watched in silence; on his left cheek there was a jeering smile, immobile as though carved with a chisel. The headlights of the car lit up now the left-hand side, now the right-hand side of the road; the shaft of light brushed against the trunks of trees and flooded the shrubs with brilliance. All of a sudden a huge bus shot out of the curve of the road, its headlights blinding them.

"Turn off the switch," Evgeni shouted.

Vas did not understand what he was supposed to turn off—the engine or the headlights. He went numb at the wheel, and the car moved left, into the path of the bus. Keeping his presence of mind, Evgeni snatched the wheel and sharply turned the car to the right. But he could not steer well and the new, shining "Opel" foundered into the gutter. As far as Vas was concerned, the incident ended with a slap, but they could not pull the car out. What was more, there was no time. Other headlights twinkled in the distance, and the approaching car might stop to help them. Then, of course, the people would immediately realize that the boys were no drivers at all and that the car had been stolen. They merely switched off the engine and vanished into the dark forest. Evgeni walked ahead. They could hear his quick, confident step in the darkness. Still frightened, Vas bumped hard against a tree but this time he neither cursed nor complained. They made a small circle in the forest and came out again onto the highway close to the railroad tracks. The stoplights of a car glowed red and immobile near the scene of the accident.

It was then that Evgeni slapped Vas. He hit the boy hard and sent him reeling. "You're nowhere," Evgeni then said darkly. "You're just a good-for-nothing!"

The incident ended with that, but Vas was never trusted with the steering wheel again.

Now they were slowly walking along the boulevard near the canal. The lamps on both sides of the canal were on, but their light was lost in the dense branches of the trees. Just the same, it wasn't completely dark. Below in the canal the muddy water ran fast, noisily splashing against the wet, stony bank. There were no people on the benches, and the dark figure of a passer-by was rarely to be seen. They crossed the lane and took the wide path along the hedge-row growing on the bank of the canal. Here it was darker, and the splash of the water was louder. As they approached the spot they spied the figures of a man and a woman seated on one of the shadiest benches. That was bad, as they were not more than a hundred meters away. Vas slowed down.

"Let's sit down," he suggested. The bench was damp like all the rest, like the path, like the yellow leaves of the trees, like the lampposts. They sat down in silence. The other bench was a mere five paces away from theirs. The boys could clearly see the figures, but the faces were lost in the shadows. The man was rather big, and his shoulders looked broad and massive. He had spread his raincoat on the bench, and the small woman had nestled into it so that only her shoulders and her hair could be seen.

Vas put his thick, moist lips against the boy's ear. "They'll go away if we keep sitting here for awhile," he whispered.

The boy did not reply right away. "What if they sit down you know where?" he finally asked with some anxiety.

"They won't."

"They may! There's no lamppost there."

That was true; the night before they had deliberately broken the lamp with a sling. Vas grew silent. While hesitating what to do the man on the bench shouted at them: "You, youngsters, get lost, will you?"

His voice was rough and unpleasant. The boys got up immediately and went down the path in silence. When they were some ten steps away, Vas turned around and shouted venomously, "You, ram!"

The tension of his figure showed that he was ready to take to his heels at any moment. But no answer came from the man's direction. The two boys again walked under the boughs of the trees to which birds, black and on the prowl, had come to perch. A cat darted out of the darkened canal bank and stopped for a second in the yellow circle of lamp light. She looked at them, and the boys saw a big dead rat hanging from her mouth like a limp rag. For an instant they stopped short in disgust. The cat ran away and was lost in the shrubbery. It was not a good omen—and the cat had crossed their path on top of it all.

"If she eats the rat she will drop dead," Vas murmured vengefully and let the boy be the first to cross the danger line.

Soon they sat down on their bench in the shadow of the big tree. The day before there had been two benches here, but in the evening Evgeni and Vas had shifted one of them farther down the canal. From this place they could see the dark clearing in front of the little house and part of the boulevard to the right and left of it. But the tiny house itself was below ground, and only the black cement roof with its two short pipes for ventilation showed above ground—a public toilet. The men's section was just opposite them. Worn, slippery stairs led down directly into the place itself, which was damp and poorly lit by a single electric bulb. Although the bulb was protected in a wire netting they could always break it. However, after some deliberation they left it as it was. It must not be completely dark in there.

"Evgeni's late again," Vas complained.

That was not true. Evgeni was never late. They had probably come too early and that wasn't good either. Many times Evgeni had tried to drive home to them that in such cases one had to be absolutely punctual even if, at first glance, there seemed no sense in it. The boy looked at his watch but could see nothing in the dark. As he was about to go to a lighter spot, Evgeni arrived.

As always, he came calm and silent and sat down next to them without saying hello. He smelled slightly of tobacco and of something else which the boy felt without being able to define—something strange and masculine which his own father almost imperceptibly also had about him. Evgeni took out his cigarettes immediately, and the boy stared at his face as Evgeni clicked his lighter. In the the flame his face looked older; he was frowning slightly but he was calm. His face with the broad cheeks, the heavy-set straight nose and the cruel light in his eyes had always frightened the two boys, but at the same time, it had inspired in them feelings of strength, security, and obedience. This man was not of their kind; there was something iron-like about him, yet strangely enough, he had chosen them to give his friendship to. The boy had often thought about it, but now he was merely aware of the waves of calm which radiated from his heart and into his fingers. He also felt how Vas was losing control of himself in his petty willfulness and his angry spirit. Perhaps that was the way it should be to have everything come out all right.

Evgeni smoked in silence. In his stiff, dark raincoat he always struck them as armored, rigid from the waist up. Now he was sitting more erect than usual because of the object he was carrying in his right pocket. He was carrying it in that pocket, the boy knew. The tip of his cigarette glowed evenly, the smoke spreading cozily around them. He was thinking. But what could he be thinking about when everything had already been decided? Never before had Evgeni gone back on anything he had made up his mind to do.

At last, looking straight ahead he spoke in a low voice. "Now, let's get it clear for the last time. If anybody is not ready, let him back out now."

The boy held his breath, feeling a vague sense of panic and yet the sweetness of freedom. Never before had Evgeni talked to them like this; never before had he looked for their consent.

"Of course, we're ready!" Vas said nervously.

"You speak for yourself," Evgeni said dryly. "Villy?"

"What?" the boy started.

"Your father doesn't know anything about this yet, does he?"

"No, he doesn't."

"I'd get the money in two or three days," Evgeni said. "So, that's not the point."

"How will you get it?" the boy asked in a low voice.

"I know how. I'd pinch the professor's headlights."

"That won't bring enough," the boy said hesitantly.

"Don't you worry. There's another iron in the fire. So, that's not the point."

The boy was quiet. What did this soft, strange voice signify? Maybe Evgeni himself had thought it over and was now looking to him for help in saving his pride. Before thinking twice he blurted out involuntarily, "Maybe that's better."

Evgeni jumped to his feet so fast that the boy nearly gasped. Evgeni was furious, his voice shaking. "You skunk!" he said in a hollow voice. "You damned coward! Get away from here!"

Vas, who was looking toward the clearing, caught him by the sleeve.

"Evgeni!" he said in a frightened voice.

"You hear me? Get away from here at once!"

"Evgeni," Vas said again.

Now Evgeni realized everything and looked around. A man was coming toward the small building. He seemed old. His gait lacked confidence and his step was short. Evgeni sat down again. The old man climbed down the stairs slowly, holding on to the wall carefully, as if the steps were made of smooth blocks of ice. When he disappeared into the dark opening, Evgeni turned to the boy and said in a changed and calm voice: "Now, you make yourself scarce!"

"I won't!" the boy exclaimed in desperation. "You promised."

"I promised, but you lied to me."

"I've never lied to you."

"You did! Why did you back out?"

"I haven't backed out. I thought you wanted it that way!"

Only then did Evgeni turn and looked at him attentively. "I didn't," he snapped but it wasn't the same ruthless voice any more. "I was only testing you."

"I didn't understand. I thought you wanted it that way."

"How can I want such a thing? I am not like you," Evgeni said gruffly. After he thought for some time, he added darkly, "Go away."

The boy got up suddenly and started for the sidewalk. Nothing remained of his feeling of freedom, not even the memory of it. He felt terribly hurt at that moment, and nothing made any difference to him now. He crossed the dark clearing and stopped on reaching the sidewalk. His sense of loneliness and rejection was so piercing that his feet would not carry him. He would not go anywhere; he would stand here no matter what they did! He would stand here even if it upset their scheme.

The old man emerged from the dark aperture as if rising from a grave. His face looked emaciated and sickly like the face of a man after a grave illness. However, he did not look poor, his overcoat was made of expensive material, the woolen scarf around his neck was fine and new. What if it was *him*! He shouldn't be like this! Or perhaps he should be just like this, do you hear, poor little soul—harden yourself. Now it's all the same.

The boy clearly saw Vas get up from his seat and approach him. The old man had gone, vanished into the darkness of the boulevard on his feeble feet.

"Come over here," Vas said in an unfriendly tone.

"Are you calling me?"

"No, Evgeni is."

The two went back to the bench. Evgeni was still smoking and looking at the ground.

"You can stay," he said dryly. "But Vas will go down with me. You'll cover us from the outside."

"All right," the boy's voice was muffled.

But that was a real blow. Never before had Evgeni preferred Vas to him. The three of them were above everybody else, but Evgeni knew very well where the idea came from. Evgeni knew very well who had invented the motto which they all obeyed.

At that moment a man headed for the dark clearing. They had seen him passing with his lumbering gait under the lamppost. He was a huge man dressed in a very tight and frayed overcoat which was buttoned up at the front. He wore a blue cap, close about his head; and a wretched bluish face, puffy with unhealthy flesh, was visible from under the cap. In the clearing the man halted and doubled up as if with a sudden abdominal pain, then he rapidly climbed down the stairs. The boys exchanged glances.

"No," Evgeni said briefly.

II

The one they chose came from the southern end of the boulevard. It was 8:40 and the red bus had just drawn up at the bus stop. The diesel engine was dying down in the distance when they discerned a light-colored topcoat and yellow leather gloves. When he passed under the lamp they saw his face for a second—a handsome masculine face but somewhat dark and upset. The man was in a hurry. He hesitated for a moment in the clearing, then he started for the stairs. The right-hand side of his topcoat bulged with some object they could not see.

The boys exchanged glances again. Although it was very dark, they seemed to understand each other with their eyes.

"Come on," Evgeni said.

For a split second the boy felt sick, as though someone had hit him in the stomach with a fist. When he rose from the bench his mouth was full of salty saliva and his knees trembled slightly. In his consciousness there was nothing—neither thought nor emotion—only infinite emptiness outside of time. On the sidewalk the boy came to himself and looked around, first to the north, toward the bridge, and then to the south. There were no people anywhere around, and only the green lights of the bus flickered in the distance. As if in reply, blue light flashed over the bridge and blue electric sparks dissolved into the darkness: a street car was passing by.

Evgeni nodded and descended the steps. Nothing could be read on his immobile face. On the third step Vas slipped and hardly managed to keep his balance. Evgeni merely clenched his teeth and let him go first. When they reached bottom the man was standing against the wall which dripped with water. Vas stood next to him, but his hands shook so badly that he could not unfasten the two lower buttons of his coat. Evgeni was still standing behind Vas, gazing at his broad back with the softly drooping raglan sleeves. The topcoat and the hat were light gray, and the edge of a wool scarf showed yellow above the collar. Without thinking further, Evgeni took out the lead pipe from the right-hand pocket of his coat and struck with all his might. The blow fell exactly where it was meant to, in the fold of the hat.

The man's legs gave way, and he sprawled on his back on the dirty floor. A surprising sound of broken glass filled the narrow place. After that, silence fell again, broken only by the sound of the gurgling water as it ran down the smooth wall. The yellow electric bulb enclosed in the wire cage shone unblinking from the ceiling. As he bent down over the man, Evgeni became suddenly aware of the pungent smell of cognac which was what the man had carried in his pocket. The boy continued searching the man's pockets without taking his eyes off his face. It did not look like a dead face, although it seemed quite lifeless and stiff. Opening the topcoat Evgeni saw a bunch of yellow flowers, crumpled but still fresh. They weren't in the pocket, the man had just held them close to his body with his elbow. Evgeni unbuttoned the jacket, too, and swiftly searched the inside pockets. In one he found a wallet and in the other an identification card, but the wallet felt rather thin, as if empty. He wanted to look into the back pocket of the trousers, but the man was on his back. It was only then that Evgeni looked at Vas. He was standing with his glassy eyes over Evgeni's head, his small face resembling a shrunken lemon.

"Help me!" Evgeni said through his teeth.

But Vas did not seem to hear him. With difficulty Evgeni lifted the heavy body and thrust his hand into the back pocket. Precisely at that moment the man opened his eyes and looked directly at him.

Evgeni straightened up abruptly.

"Run!" he said hoarsely.

But Vas did not budge. Evgeni struck him in the chest with his fist, and only when he began running did Vas follow suit. The man lifted himself up on his elbows and a muffled cry came tearing from his throat. The two ran out as if lashed by a whip.

They must not run—this they knew in advance—they must leave the place with a calm, steady step. Without seeing anything around him, Vas crossed the road and came to the other sidewalk. He was to head south toward the stadium and then turn into the first street to the right. Evgeni's way lay in exactly the opposite direction, to the north whence the two boys had come. After Evgeni had made ten steps he realized he was still holding the lead pipe. The bridge from which he was supposed to throw it straight into the canal was still far off, and the piece of iron, wrapped up in woolen cloth though it was, burned his hands as if it were red hot. Without stopping he threw it into the shrubs and quickened his pace.

At this moment the man in the light-colored coat climbed up the steps, reeling. Blood ran down his face and had already filled his right eye. Horrified, he spread out his mud-covered hands and shouted with all his might for help.

To the boys the cry was as loud as if somebody were rolling an enormous barrel down the granite paving stones of the boulevard. "Catch them!"

Evgeni and Vas ran as fast as they could. Villy turned round and saw the frightful figure waving his hands and shouting incoherently. Only one thought churned in his mind: he must not run. But as he turned around, he spotted Vas's thin, lean figure tearing down the boulevard not far from him. His legs seemed to weave under him, the tassle of his ski cap jumping crazily on his head. Not a soul was to be seen, only the lone headlights of a car glimmered weakly in the distance. A moment later the headlights glared blindingly and sped forward. Vas approached the crossing, slowed down for an instant, and then vanished around the corner. A little later the boy saw a motorcycle rapidly turn the corner of the same street.

However, he had no time to think about all that. Someone was running after him. The boy could hold out for a few more seconds, but when the steps sounded quite close to him, he desperately lunged forward.

"Catch him!" someone gave an awful shout behind his back.

The boy kept on running. He did not know where he was going, nor how far he would get. He was running blindly straight on, followed by the dreadful steps. He was not thinking any more, he was not expecting anything; he only knew that he had to run for dear life—the faster and the farther the better. The steps behind him suddenly died down, but the ringing voice again reached him, "Hold him!"

Two dark shadows suddenly emerged from the darkness of the street. The boy bumped against them, lost his balance, and fell. Two strong hands grabbed and raised him in the air, and as he again felt the ground under his feet, he saw a blood-covered face and two eyes mercilessly fixed on his own.

"It's him!"

"It wasn't me!" the boy screamed in despair.

A resounding slap sent him to the ground, but a moment later the hands picked him up again. Now the blood-spattered face was quite close to his and, horrified, the boy became aware of the man's hot breath.

"There were two of them!"

A woman he could not see was shouting indignantly behind his back. "Shame on you! What kind of grown man are you, beating a child?"

"You keep out of this, Comrade," somebody said roughly.

"Shame on you," the woman was screaming. "You're drunk on top of it all."

Suddenly she fell silent. First, she had seen the wet mud-covered back, then the hands. But when the man turned his head and she saw his blood-stained face, her mouth gaped and she noiselessly stepped aside. The boy in the raincoat wrenched himself free but he was grabbed by the hair, and the frightened woman hastened away.

The motorcycle driver caught Vas more or less at the same time. He was a short, broad-shouldered assembly worker, shorter than Vas, dressed in dirty overalls and in black leather gloves. To come abreast with Vas, he slowed down and drove close to the curbstone. At this speed the motorcycle functioned badly, and the coughing of the exhaust drowned his words: "Stop . . . stop! You rotter!" But Vas ran on like a blind man. It never occurred to him to turn off the road and into a courtyard. At that moment a fat man with a bandaged leg, wearing felt slippers, came out of a building and stopped indecisively. Vas could have passed him but in his panic decided to cross the street. The motorcycle caught up with him exactly in the middle of the road. With the impact of the front wheel, the driver drove down on the brakes. Vas fell on his face and the engine of the motorcycle went dead. As the man with the bandaged leg drew closer, as timidly and indecisively as before, he saw a dumbfounded young man trying to balance his motorcycle and a boy screaming and kicking his feet against the pavement.

Then Evgeni was captured. The man and the girl on the bench had heard the shouting; the man had got up and stood in the shadow of a transformer tower quietly waiting for the boy. Evgeni spotted him at the last moment, managed to shake free of the strong hand that had grabbed his lapel, and again ran along the boulevard. The chase went on for another twenty paces. The man ran a little faster and, catching up with the boy, he tripped him with his right foot. Evgeni swayed violently and sprawled on the sidewalk. When he rose, blood was spurting from his nose, but his look was so fierce that the man was taken aback for an instant. Evgeni used this moment to pound his pursuer madly with his fists. However, his advantage lasted only a few seconds. A policeman who came up to the scene of the incident put an end to the fight.

In a little while he took the boys to the police station.

III

Everything was in place in the room—both the people and the objects. Only Villy's chair was vacant. The family was having lunch. This family always had lunch in silence, but now one could not even hear the slight rattle of dishes. Not even the talkative dark woman who worked in the kitchen uttered a word. In the room she maintained a somber silence, but in the kitchen she wiped the tears from her eyes with the palm of her hand. Her dry mouth with the bleached hairs above it was tight with anger. "All this has happened because they leave the child all alone at home. Don't the have money enough that they must both go to work?"

But in the room again the woman was struck with pity once more. She had been working here for many years, she had got used to the family and was sorrier for them than she was for herself. Nevertheless, today, she did not know whom she felt sorrier for. Maybe for the mother who hardly touched her food. Maybe for the father who seemed to have suddenly grown old and shrunken. Despite everything, she thought, he conducted himself well, this big and calm man who had such confidence in himself. Since he had come home he had not raised his voice once, and he had not made a single remark. Generally he never raised his voice, but his calm, cool stare sometimes weighed heavier than the cruelest of words. When he entered the house everything would become quiet, and the boy would immediately stop his violin playing. The woman liked this. She did not like parents to pet their children and to shower them with kisses. A father was always a father, and if the others did not fear him just a little, everything went to the devil. She had always believed this and she was sure she was right.

At the table only Sashka was eating with appetite, as usual. She was ashamed of it, but just the same she went on eating. In the morning she had gone to the university without breakfast. She had not dared ask her father for money, and she never asked her mother for money. She had gone hungry all morning, on account of Villy, of course.

She did not feel sorry for him. With all her heart she wished she could love him and pity him on this day, but she could not. She was scared by the wickedness of her heart, but instead of sorrow, she felt some vague and bitter satisfaction. They loved him more—she knew it in her heart. They did not show it openly, but she was aware of it. This was perfectly natural for Olga, but why was it true of him, too? Olga was not her real mother and Villy was her half-brother. Here, she had only a father but Villy had a mother, too. He had their love, he had everything. Then why did he do it? Even if they were so blind, they would surely realize something now!

As a child Villy used to be ill quite often. She would stay at his bedside for hours and hold his burning hand. In those days she loved him dearly. The boy loved her, too. But those two spoiled everything. They would call in three doctors to his bedside; they would walk around the room with frightened eyes and send the maid to the chemist's every other hour. But when once she herself fell ill, Olga merely sent for the district doctor and that was all. It all began like this, the thing which divided them, and he was to blame for everything.

Sashka felt her father was watching her now, too, with some hidden anxiety, but coldly and searchingly at the same time. Never before had he looked at her like this. He rarely noticed her, spoke with her in an absent-minded way, and never listened to the end of what he had asked her about. While she was at high school, he never knew which grade she was in. When he signed her high school report book he fleetingly looked over her marks, and no paternal satisfaction ever appeared on his big face. He seldom smiled at her. He had only once stroked her smooth brown hair—the day of her graduation dance. It was a wonderful day, because of the caress and all. Her dress, which had been made by Olga's dressmaker, had been the prettiest dress in the class. It was the most expensive one, too—she knew that. He never spared his money for her, he gave her a lot more than he did Villy. Yes, a lot more. Then why didn't he love her? Why was he looking at her today so furtively and anxiously?

The phone rang. She saw everybody at the table tremble. The dark woman, her hands full of plates, stopped on the threshold. Her father cast a silent look at his wife. Without saying a word she rose and started for the desk. From the back her figure was like a young girl's, her slender legs moved gracefully on the carpet. Sashka knew very well she would never be as beautiful as Olga. She would never be as smartly dressed, nor would she ever manage such pretty hair-dos.

Olga picked up the receiver. "Who's calling him, please?"

They answered something at the other end. She covered the mouthpiece with her hand and said softly, "It's the General."

The father sighed and rose from his chair. It was the General. He recognized him immediately.

"This business is very unpleasant, Georgi," the General was saying. "There is no misunderstanding. Your boy was in it, too. The three of them have made complete confessions."

The father swallowed dryly.

"Unfortunately, this is a fact," the General went on. "To top it all, there's a whole gang of them."

"What does that mean?" the father asked dryly.

"Well, they have formed an organization of their own," he laughed. "It's a good thing they didn't kill the man. As I understand it, he left the hospital today."

"Might I see him?"

"Whom? The man?"

"No, Villy, my boy."

"Villy!" the General snorted. "Listen, Georgi, as long as you give them such names, they'll carry on like this."

"I named him after Vladimir Ilich Lenin," the father said a little tersely.

"Well, then, it's too bad for the name. You can see Inspector Donev at about five today. I've spoken to him and he'll be waiting for you."

"Thank you, Nikifor," the father said with restraint, stressing the name. "I'm sorry for the trouble I've caused you."

He was about to hang up, but the voice on the other end of the wire buzzed again, "Listen, listen. . . ." The father frowned, but again put the receiver to his ear. "Listen, don't worry yourself to death," the General was speaking in a changed voice. "After all, we'll do something—we won't let your boy go to the dogs."

"Thank you," the father said with genuine sincerity this time. He replaced the receiver and stood next to the desk, deep in thought. He had forgotten about the others; he was not aware of the impatience with which they were waiting for him to speak.

"Well? Will they let him out?" the maid asked from the threshold.

"They will," he said softly.

"Oh, thank God!" the woman exclaimed, overjoyed, and walked out of the room.

The father walked across the room and sank into the armchair next to the television set. He looked so crushed that the heart of the girl quivered with pity.

"He was really part of it all," he said in a muffled voice. "He admitted everything himself."

Olga went awfully pale, tears welling up in her eyes.

"Will they let you see him?"

"Yes, at about five today."

Olga rose abruptly from her seat and stumbled to the bedroom. But the girl hardly saw her, she was watching her father. She had never seen him so weak, defeated and unhappy. She had never seen him so helpless. Maybe she had never seen him so justly punished. He slumped down, the collar of his blue jacket riding up to cover his short neck. He seemed far away from here, people, his home, he was all alone with his unhappiness. Suddenly her father raised his head and looked at her sharply.

"What have you done to your face?" he asked angrily.

She started with surprise and touched her face with frightened hands. "I—I don't know!" she stammered. "Nothing!"

"Nothing! There's powder on it."

That was true, she really used powder. But the powder was of the finest quality, the natural color of a suntan.

"I'm asking you!" the father said crossly. He had never used this tone to her.

"I—I have a very bad complexion," she said timidly.

"What complexion are you talking about? You're not grown up yet. You're just a young girl."

"That's what you think," she thought with hostility, looking down at the floor as though he could see through her eyes and into her mind.

"Where did you get the powder from? Did you get it from Olga?"

Powder from Olga—what an idea! "I bought it," she said in a hurt tone.

"So this is what she's been spending her money on, the young miss," he said with a frown. "Now go and wash it off."

Since Sashka did not budge from her seat, he added: "Do you hear me?"

She got up and started for the kitchen obediently. The maid was doing the dishes in the porcelain sink, the Czech chinaware clinking pleasantly in her experienced hands. She did not turn to look, but she knew who had entered the kitchen. It was only with the girl that the maid talked as with an equal.

"They'll let him out, why wouldn't they let him out," she mumbled. "All kinds of robbers are walking the streets, but they have to go and pick on a child! They should be ashamed of themselves."

Sashka stood behind her without saying a word. The woman turned round.

"What's the matter with you?"

"I want to wash my face."

"Isn't there a faucet in the bathroom, too?" the woman asked snappishly.

There was a faucet in the bathroom, but the hot-water tap

was out of order. Sashka didn't say a word, she merely stuck out her tongue at the maid's back and went to the bathroom. She washed her face carefully, wiped it dry with the snow-white Turkish towel, and looked into the mirror. Her skin was really shiny and porous, but even this could not spoil her mood now. What a silly and funny father she had! She had been powdering her face for a year and he had only noticed now. She certainly had a very silly, a very funny father!

IV

The staircase to the second floor of the police station was steep, narrow, and led straight to the entrance. He had never seen such an old house with such rotting wooden stairs. As he climbed up they gave under his feet and let out a thick muffled sound as if they were living beings. The entrance door was framed in attractive and antique-looking stained glass, and the brass handle was sculptured into a small lion's head. On the right-hand side there was a bell, dark with the passage of time, which had evidently fallen out of use. He hesitated for a second, then he went in.

The smell of mildew which had assailed his nostrils on the staircase was here mingled with the pungent ammonia odor of the lavatory. The corridor lay before him, long and deserted, with the same kind of decayed wooden floor. On the left side were the windows overlooking the courtyard, on his right side were the doors, all of them in the peculiar stained glass he had once seen at Schönbrün. What eccentric had erected this place and what whim had made him combine the expensive stained glass with the cheap wooden doors? He had no time to reflect on this. He slowly walked along the corridor, carefully reading the names on the doors. He read the name "Donev" on the third door. So, it was here. What if the boy was inside? Taking a deep breath, the father knocked and went in.

A long, perplexed face looked up at him.

"Are you Comrade Tanev?"

"That's right!"

"Wait outside awhile, please."

The man went into the corridor again. Right on this door one of the old panes was broken and was replaced with an ordinary one. Now he involuntarily looked through it and saw part of the room. An unkempt man was seated on a yellow wooden chair and was dumbly moving his lips. He had not shaved for a week, his face was oily, and a tuft of matted hair stuck up, hornlike, on his head. His entire appearance, subdued and cringing, bespoke a man who had stopped resisting and was now ready to let them squeeze any information out of him they wanted.

The father swiftly shifted his gaze to the window. Down below, by the fountain in the yard, two policemen wearing patterns were laughing throatily and splashing water as if it were midsummer. "Can what is going on behind the glass be a daily routine to anyone?" he thought in horror. For a moment his own misfortune paled into insignificance. His own appearance seemed to rebuke him mutely. His cheeks were close-shaven and well-fed, the gray coat could not quite conceal the unwelcome corpulence which had filled out his suits over the past few years. Or maybe this was merely the beginning of something much worse? Whatever the unshaven man had done, right at this minute he felt guilty before him and shame-faced before his own person. Below, the policemen had finished being playful and were rapidly walking toward their dormitory, their pattens thudding along.

The entrance door opened and in walked a drunken man and the policeman who had pulled him in. The two went the length of the corridor and entered the last door. Keys, locks, and bolts were heard to click and then it was quiet again. There was no doubt that they kept the detained over there.

They called him in ten minutes later. A young man in a sports jacket led out the arrested man. Casting a brief look at him he said, "You can go in."

His voice was unfriendly; it was as though he were dealing with one of his clients. The father frowned and pushed his way through the open door. There was only one vacant chair in the room, the one on which the man with the grimy face had been sitting. Behind the chair and against the wall were disorderly piles of shirts wrapped in cellophane, shoes, material for women's dresses, a transistor radio. The father hesitated for a second.

"Please, sit down," the Inspector said in a tired voice. "I'm sorry to have kept you waiting."

The father slumped down into the chair. The man sitting opposite him was quite young, in a brown suit which had become shiny and shrunken with wear. His small, pale face was unshaven, his eyes still somewhat absent. The father could hardly suppress his irritation any longer.

"First, I would like to ask you a question," he started off in a muffled voice. "Where do you keep the boys?"

"In the detention room," the Inspector returned.

"And you think this has educational value? Keeping them there together with drunks and thieves?"

It was only then the Inspector seemed to wake up and look at him attentively. He did not appear either surprised or alarmed by this question. A ghost of a smile played in his eyes for a fraction of a second. "I beg your pardon," he said calmly, "but don't you find it awkward to talk about education?"

"Nevertheless, I'd appreciate it if you answered my question," the father said irritably.

The police officer leaned back against his chair. "Comrade Tanev, unfortunately, we do not have two detention rooms," he said dryly. "Anyway, they are in a separate room."

"Yes, thank you. That's what I wanted to hear." He unbuttoned his coat unconsciously, then buttoned it up again nervously. The officer was still watching him calmly.

"Besides, the boys know a lot more than you imagine," he said. "And if you are now here, it's because you couldn't imagine it in time."

The father stared at him. This young man could really talk and he could really be well mannered. His irritation slowly evaporated. "You are probably right," he said tiredly. "But if you were a father, you would hardly have been different from me."

"I surely would have been different," the officer smiled faintly. "And not because I am more intelligent than you, but simply because one has a much better view of things from here."

"I am afraid you see only the bad side here."

"No, on the contrary," the young man replied with animation.

The father did not say anything. The meaning of the man's last words was lost to him, he couldn't make him out. While he was silent, he was aware that the Inspector was watching him rather frankly and openly.

"To tell you the truth, you don't at all look like a man who can be severe with his child," he started again. "I guess you hit him rarely."

The father looked at him in shock. "I never did!" he exclaimed. "Never!"

"Never!" the young man repeated pensively. "But I suppose you know the difference between physical and mental cruelty."

"I don't understand you."

"All right, let's not talk about the most trivial quarrels and threats. But take haughtiness, for example! Imagine that your boss, if you have one, were like that. Wouldn't that be cruelty?"

"Yes, of course," the father nodded.

"Groundless suspicions, disregard. Or the arrogance of thinking that all men are unworthy of you. Excuse me, but I am not preaching to you, and I am not questioning you."

The father was silent. He wasn't lecturing or questioning him. That was more than clear.

"I'll answer you in two words," he said. "I have never been rude with the boy. The things you have just mentioned are foreign to my nature. Or at least, I think they are. But I loved my son and took good care of him."

"And you showed it?"

"No, I think it is infinitely more dangerous to spoil children that way than behaving a bit sternly with them."

"Or coldly?"

"I think I expressed myself correctly."

"Sometimes people who express themselves correctly judge themselves incorrectly," the Inspector said pensively.

The father nervously straightened up in his chair.

"You are on the wrong track," he said a little impatiently.

"No, I am not on the wrong track, Comrade Tanev," the Inspector answered calmly. "Do you know what pushed your son into crime? Fear! The boy was afraid of you."

The father became aware of trembling. There was such conviction in this man's voice, so calm and so ruthless.

"I don't believe it," he said hollowly. "I have never frightened him with anything."

"That's what you think! But fact is fact. You yourself should know how you frightened him. All right, not with cruelty. Maybe with excessive principles. With excessive requirements. Or with excessive notions of virtue. Or maybe with your own excessive prestige in his eyes. But one thing you have to understand. The boy was afraid of you."

"If this is true, then it is hateful," the father said. "This is what I have hated most in all my life, frightening or intimidating people! To me this is a complete negation of our principles."

"Yes," the Inspector said darkly. "But here are the results."

The father once again fell silent. The Inspector leaned his worn elbows on the desk.

"I'll give you the facts, Comrade Tanev," he said. "And you judge for yourself. Do you remember having given the boy some money twenty days ago? For his violin lessons?"

"Yes, of course."

"How much did you give him?"

"Four hundred leva."

"That's quite a sum," the Inspector said. "But it was four hundred leva. Do you know what happened? He did not give the money to the professor at all. He spent it. Of course, he did not spend it by himself, but with his friends. They thought they could make up the money, but couldn't. During the last two weeks the boy did not even see the professor. He simply took his violin and went out with his friends. They thought and planned and this is what they did. Why didn't your son come to you? Why didn't he confess everything? Why was he silent? Because he was afraid of you."

The Inspector was silent for a moment and started to search his pockets. The cigarette pack he fished out was empty, and he pushed it to the edge of his desk with annoyance. The father got up from his chair and offered him his pack of cigarettes. The young man took a cigarette with a sad smile.

"I'm that fatal type of inspector who offers his victims cigarettes at critical moments," he said. "And since there are too many critical moments with that fellow who was here before you, I have run out of cigarettes. To tell you the truth, this plays the devil with my budget."

"Oh, it's nothing, go ahead and smoke my cigarettes," the father said stupidly.

"Right. I'll consider that an unofficial bribe."

"I'm sorry, I expressed myself badly," the father said.

"Early this afternoon I called on your son's teacher. To tell you truly, she shocked me even more than the canal incident. It is not only that for a long, long time I hadn't seen such a brainless creature. The worst thing is that she was shocked to the marrow. Why? That's difficult to explain. Because of cowardice, pedagogical hypocrisy, the most primitive ideas about education. She didn't have a single thought of her own in her head, not to mention conscience or feelings. I hope you know her well."

"No, I haven't even seen her."

The Inspector's face flushed red. "That's just fine," he said. "And I thought. If it's violin lessons, then you naturally get a professor, if the boy is down with fever, then again a professor runs to his bedside. But why should you care who shapes his thoughts and feelings?"

"Of course I care!" the father frowned. "But the point is we have no choice."

"But you never took the trouble to meet her."

"As I have no choice, she does not interest me."

"That's not true," the Inspector said. "That's exactly what

she lives by, the lack of interest in her. But it doesn't matter. I asked her a couple of questions about this and that. Of course, each of her opinions must be read very carefully. Her ideals are the informer, the crammer, and the pitiable cringer. From this point of view, she doesn't like your son, of course. This is to be expected. He is really a very intelligent and sensitive boy."

"He is rather uncommunicative," the father said.

"No, he is sensitive. Even morbidly so. He was the one to invent the motto of their fraternity: 'Harden ourselves.' Do you understand the meaning of that? To exist you have to harden your soul and your feelings. But against what? The boy has no answer to this. Against everything, he says. But this isn't so. Perhaps against the fruits of her education. Or maybe against the injustice he has witnessed even in his own home."

The Inspector became silent. The father was silent, too.

"I don't know what he has seen in his home," he said at last. "But I assure you it's a most ordinary home."

"That's not quite true," the Inspector said. "As I understand you have remarried."

"Yes, that's right . . . but the boy is by my second marriage."

"And yet perhaps you love your daughter more? And maybe you have been unfair to your son?"

"No, no," the father protested. "The opposite is rather the case. But I never let this show."

"Oh!" the Inspector mumbled. "Children are often more observant than grownups. And since as a rule they don't react, we are apt to think they don't see anything. But they react in their own way. And sometimes they become embittered in their own way."

"The boy has had everything," the father said, and his voice now sounded much more confident.

"They had common funds," the Inspector said. "But those funds were very low. Did you give him money? I mean an allowance?"

The father thought for some time with a frown on his face. "Boys always ask their mothers for pocket money," he said. "In general I haven't been very generous in this respect. Of course, the reason is not that I am stingy. I don't think it wise to give children a lot of money because it spoils them."

"How about the girl?"

"I have been more generous with her. But she is a university student. I wouldn't like it if somebody else paid her checks in coffee shops."

"You worried yourself in vain," the Inspector said. "Modern young men don't suffer from excessive scruples on that score."

"And just the same . . ."

"Perhaps in this way you made up for your insufficient attention as a father."

"Maybe that's it," the father said dejectedly.

"Whatever it is, this is hardly important. The boy is not petty. And he is not envious. Maybe he was a little lonely, which explains his sensitiveness. . . . Maybe . . ."

The Inspector became silent all of a sudden, and his eyes searchingly rested on the father. "But why should I be trying to interpret your boy's character?" he said bitterly. "What's the use of it? It is you that should try to understand him. Otherwise you'll never be able to help him." The Inspector looked at his watch and suddenly asked: "Do you want to see him?"

"Yes, please."

"I strongly doubt if this would be of any help."

"Please!" the father said, greatly agitated.

The Inspector pressed a button. His thin and unshaven face was dark and careworn.

"I wanted to ask you about something," the father said.

"Go ahead!" said the Inspector.

"There were three of them. Do you consider them equally guilty?"

"Would you feel better if he were less guilty than the others?" the Inspector asked with a frown.

"Well . . ."

"In the assault itself, no!" the Inspector said. "But generally speaking, yes. The three of them are equally guilty and at the same time equally innocent. You most probably think that your son has fallen prey to somebody else's bad influence."

"Do you rule out that possibility?"

"I don't go along with the idea that your son is a weak-willed fool," the Inspector said, and the man was aware of a note of irritation in his voice. "Evgeni is in fact a boy of exceptional will power and character. That's his misfortune. We are confronted with such a paradox—what is a source of pride in most cases is a misfortune in his."

"I believe he's a lot older than my son," the father persisted.

"Yes, he's two years older. He had personal power over the boys, this I don't deny. But to make a scapegoat of him is to close our eyes to the truth. The three boys have come to this each in his own way."

The young man in the sports jacket entered the room.

"Bring in the boy, please," the Inspector said.

The young man cast a dismal look at the guest and went out.

"He's taken a dislike to me," the father said.

"Don't expect anything else," the Inspector said. "He has his own theory. According to him the parents should be sent to jail for the crimes their children have committed. It's not a bad idea. It would make parents really stop and think."

The Inspector spoke jocularly, but there was no mirth in his eyes. The father did not hear him. He was listening to the footsteps dying away in the corridor. He heard things in the stillness that followed. Over there bolts and locks were probably clicking and opening. Now the boy was standing up with frightened eyes. Now he was starting off watched by the others. Now he was walking along the endless corridor with the old decayed floor. Now . . .

He heard steps, but they were the heavy footsteps of a man. No matter how hard he listened, he could not catch the lighter footsteps of the boy, too. They came closer and closer, then they halted. The door was suddenly flung open and the boy stood on the threshold. His face was very pale, his clothes wrinkled. There was some matted hair on his forehead. The man in the sports jacket stood frowning behind him.

The boy did not see him. He was looking at the Inspector, his eyes trusting and calm.

"Come on in, Vladimir," the Inspector said softly.

The boy closed the door and saw his father as he turned around. Every muscle on his face twitched imperceptibly; his lips quivered; only his glance remained fixed and unmoving like a wax doll's.

"Aren't you going to say hello to your father?" the Inspector said.

He started forward automatically. Now he could see only a yellow face tense with grief. He also saw tears running down the hard cheeks. Then he stopped. The father lifted his hand and put it on his shoulder.

The boy drew away abruptly, turned his back on him and, doubling up, he dropped to the floor. The two men leapt to their feet in fright. They could not see the boy's face hidden in his arms, they could only see his shaking body. They tried to get him back to his feet, but his body convulsively contorted and again he fell to the floor. Neither of the men could tell whether the boy was sobbing or writhing in a fit of nerves. It was impossible to see his face.

The Inspector straightened up. "Go. Please leave the room."
The father looked at him with unseeing eyes.

"Do you hear me?" the Inspector asked impatiently. The father started for the glass door obediently. Out in the corridor the Inspector said: "Go home now. And don't be afraid. The boy will calm down faster if you are not here."

The father wiped his face dry with a clean, neatly folded handkerchief, and then, without uttering a word, he walked slowly along the empty corridor.

V

Night had fallen outside, and a soft dark rain pattered on rooftops and sidewalks. Few people were passing by. A young woman was standing under a balcony holding a closed umbrella in her hand. A car, shiny with the rain, drew up at the curb, the woman ran out on her high heels and vanished into the open door of the car. When the man reached the balcony he stopped. The car had disappeared. Its smooth roof had gleamed for an instant under the lamppost and then it had dissolved into the night.

But the man had seen nothing. Water was streaming down his temples and cheeks, but he was not conscious of it. He was looking into himself. The memory was so clear as if everything had happened only yesterday. The man questioning him was in a blue policeman's uniform, his face purple with blood, and his eyes round and yellow like a bird's.

"What were you doing in front of the theater?" the policeman had asked.

"I was demonstrating," the boy said.

He was really only a boy, with short hair and in a crumpled high school uniform. Large spots of dried lime showed white on his trousers and jacket.

"What?" the policeman did not believe his ears.

"I was demonstrating," the boy repeated a little lower.

The policeman raised his hairy hand. When the boy got up a whole waterfall thundered in his ears. "I'm asking you. What were you doing in front of the theater?"

The boy was silent. The policeman squinted his eyes contentedly and smiled. He was in a hurry; this small victory was quite enough for him. "If your father hadn't begged me, I would have beaten you black and blue," he said. "Mihal, let him go!"

The plain-clothes man led him along the corridor. A winding staircase with white marble steps descended from the first to the ground floor. He remembered only the first step. The next moment the plain-clothes man pushed him, and he tumbled headlong downstairs from step to step, trying in vain to clutch at something.

Outside the night was shimmery and warm, there were a lot of people around. He walked without looking at them because he was ashamed. His cheek was grazed, a stain of dried blood showed red on the green collar of his student's jacket. The boy did not go home to his father who had interceded for him. For several months now he had not been home. There were a movie house and a small neighborhood restaurant in Lozenets where streetcars screeched around the curve of the line. There he ate four *kebabcheta* and drank two large glasses of beer. The beer made him dizzy, and his knees turned so soft that he could hardly climb up to his attic room.

The boy lay and smoked. He lighted one cigarette from another and extinguished the butts on the heel of his shoe. The white night shimmered through the small rectangular window on the roof, birds shrieked in the forest. Away in the distance, behind the roof of the Seminary, Mount Vitosha raised its rocky summit sprinkled all over with the light gray ash of moonlight. The boy could not sleep. The immeasurable sweetness of freedom was mingled with the nightmare of the past two days. He could see the muzzle of the heavy machine gun behind the Town Hall and the soldiers' helmets gleaming cold behind it. He could see the running feet and the foam-covered mouths of the horses. In the warehouse the policemen were beating those that had been arrested with large clubs and were breaking slabs of coal against their heads. People screamed in the dark, the motors of police vans roared in front of the entrance. They spent the first night in a courtyard, one next to the other, on the bare ground.

When he woke up it was a brilliant sunny day. Tears streaming down his face, his father was seated near his hard bed. The boy held his breath; never before had he seen him so deeply moved. Even in the store his father had always been harsh with his customers and never allowed them to be capricious and choosy. Not many people walked into the semidark store crammed with glassware and hardware. The boy did not dare say a word; he lay curled up and frightened in his bed.

"Come on, get up and let's get going," the father said.

The boy was silent. No matter how fearful he found his father, the police agent was much more so. But now the distressing thing was that his father was weeping.

"I won't go anywhere," the boy said.

"Do you want to stay here?"

"I want to go my own way. That's all I want."

The father was no longer crying, but his cheeks were still wet with tears. "What is your way, son?" he asked in a crushed tone. "Is this your way: to climb up scaffoldings with buckets full of lime?"

"Why not?" the boy asked. "Your god also climbed up a hill with a wooden cross on his back. And for nothing. I'm at least building houses for people."

The father took down his eyeglasses and without shame he began wiping his reddened eyes. With the eyeglasses off, his face appeared quite bare and helpless, as though all his severity were contained in the gold rims of his glasses. The boy felt his heart sink painfully.

"Houses for people!" the father sighed, still holding the glasses in his hand. "And for whom am I building your house? On the prettiest and quietest street in Sofia? With such a wonderful view to the south, toward Mount Vitosha! What have I saved money for, whom have I stinted for? For myself? I wanted you to live in a fine clean house with lots of sunshine in it! And now you want it to go empty."

"I don't want anything," the boy said passionately. "I want nothing from you. I don't want you to save money or to build houses for me. I want you to understand me and let me go my own way. I don't know where exactly it will take me, but I certainly know yours leads nowhere."

The father dried his face with his handkerchief. The rain softly knit a wet dark curtain on the iron railing of the balcony, the water ran down the sidewalk and washed clean the withered leaves. This is what the boy in the high school uniform had said to his father, and now he could not make out how these words could have been born in his mind. There were many things he could not remember or understand. He was walking the street again as the rain wet his hair and face and slowly ran down his neck. The house his father had built was not far off. Big new homes had been erected in front of it and had hidden part of the eastern and southern sky. Only a view of the western sky had been left to the house with the soft backbone of Mount Lyulin behind which the autumn sun was setting like a bloodstained yolk. Many things had changed and grown old without his noticing them.

The father pressed the doorbell lightly and walked into his own house which the man with the gold eyeglasses had once built for him. The corridor was plunged in darkness. The room, too, was dark, but at the back the television screen showed its dead green shimmer. Over the back of the armchair he saw the delicate shoulders of his daughter and her smooth hair, which gleamed in greenish reflections. The girl did not turn her head to see who had come in; she was watching the television screen. The father drew near in silence and could see her pretty chiseled little nose with the brittle open nostrils. At that moment he wanted very much to stroke the shoulders and to touch the smooth hair which he hadn't touched for years. He sighed and sat down on the small ottoman next to the glass table.

The girl turned around.

"Is that you?" she asked and again looked back to the television set.

A building was on fire on the screen and long green flames shot out of the windows. Men in shiny rubber cloaks were pouring jets of water over them.

The father was silent. But his grief throbbed so unbearably that he said in a soft voice: "Aren't you going to ask about your brother?"

The girl gave a start and turned to him. "Are you coming from there?" she asked.

"Yes."

"Will they release him soon?"

"Probably. But is that the most important thing?" he asked.

The girl had flushed crimson in the dark, but the father did not see it.

"Did he ask about me?"

"Of course. The first thing he did was to ask about you."

"I will take care of him when they let him out," the girl said.

She was again watching the screen. Cloaked policemen were running about and throwing tear-gas bombs at a dense crowd which was slowly retreating toward the back of the square.

The father kept silent for awhile, his shoulders drooping. Then he asked softly, "Where is your mother?"

"I don't know," the girl replied.

Why hadn't she at least waited for him, he thought in confusion. Could the price of her tears be so low? You could never understand whether one wept for somebody else or for oneself. On the screen tiny black figures crawled along the thick network of farmsteads. Invisible welding machines were showering sparks like the sparks of candles on a Christmas tree. It was not interesting, but the girl kept on watching. Maybe she just did not want to talk with her father. Or maybe she did want to but she didn't dare. They both kept silent, then the father rose with a cold heart and started for his study slowly. The television set buzzed behind him, and molten steel hissed around the feet of the people like a stream on fire.

Translated by GREGOR PAVLOV

Spanish Cholera

It was for the first time that I was coming to this little resort station, which was nestled among barren yellow hills and among vineyards that appeared blue in the distance. Standing at the window I felt boredom, like so much engine steam, beginning to cloud my good mood which was that of a holiday-maker. The smell of heat, of yellow, crumbling earth, and burned grass irritated my city nose and made me frown. And actually, what the devil had sent me to this open country dying of heat? My kidneys, it seemed! But they could have waited somewhat, after all. Each stage of life has its earmark, and mine had not yet reached that of aches and pains.

The train made a few more turns along the scorched stubble-fields and pulled slowly into the little station which, by the way, was the last stop. I caught a glimpse of a white kiosk with a red roof, looking like a fresh mushroom in this hot wilderness; a few cab drivers, their whips hanging limp to the ground; a militiaman, his tunic all wet with sweat, painstakingly saluting the black waggons. There was the clash of buffers and then the train stopped. When I set foot on the platform it became still worse as a hot downpour from the sky brought up a sweltering heat from the basalt pavement with tenfold intensity. A heavy smell of rotting vegetables came from the waggons.

"This will drive me into an early grave!" I thought in despair.

It was only then that I noticed more people had poured out of the train than I had expected. They were mainly peasant women in blue, yellow, and pink skirts, in bodices and colored kerchiefs, in rubber shoes, in slippers and even in pattens. In their hands they held baskets and bunches of multicolored flowers so withered with the heat that God only knew why they clutched them between their dry fingers. There were a few townswomen and almost no men if one didn't count those that dragged their feet under the weight of imaginary ailments. Anyway, I knew that the resort was mainly for women—preferred and recommended for ages to women who came for the special cures required by their sex.

And now this crowd started hurrying somewhere energetically; some were even running. Involuntarily submitting to the others I, too, put my lank legs into motion. And just in time, too, since the bus was overcrowded, but a smart jump put me in the last of the vacant cabs. Thank goodness! But the cabman lingered somewhat, unwilling to start off with only one passenger. I sent a cheerless look over the bony back of the little old horse and, bent as it was, I thought that with two passengers in the cab it would probably go no farther than the graveyard for horses. At that moment I heard a contralto voice: "Ilinchev, could I also? . . ."

I looked in the direction of the voice in surprise and felt my blood go cold in spite of the heat. You Spanish cholera, what quick-witted devil had sent me so precious a present in this heat? It was my colleague Marinova, with whom I worked at the plant. I saw that the mocking look of her gypsy beauty—Moorish nose and curved eyebrows—did not in the least seem to have been affected by the journey. She looked as fresh as if she had just stepped out of a cold shower.

"Were you on the same train?" I asked, amazed.

"What other train is there?" she said, laughing, and handed her suitcase to the cabman.

"How is it I didn't see you! Where will you put up?"

"At the Trade Unions Home."

Marinova seated herself to my left, while I instinctively moved a bit to the right. I could swear she was aware of it, and her face brightened up even more. The cabman waved the whip, and it cracked as if coming against a board.

"So, that's it," I mumbled. "And what is it you are going to cure?"

There was hidden malice in my question, but she paid no attention to it.

"My gall bladder isn't quite right."

"Naturally!" I thought gloatingly. "What amazes me is that you still have a gall bladder."

She seemed to have understood my thoughts, for she threw out casually: "How can it be in a good state with the engineers we have!"

I looked at her in anger. If there were a description for her it would read: "Always the same!" What an irritating creature. I am chief engineer at the plant, loved and respected by everybody. How many times they have tried to get me into the Ministry—but I wouldn't go. There is no other plant like ours, and nobody knows his job better than I do. The director knows that quite well and holds me tight by the tails. Only this empty-headed creature . . . had she been director this cock would long have flown the coop.

But my colleague, who had evidently forgotten her words, was gazing with curiosity now to the right, now to the left of the cab.

"Isn't it beautiful," she was saying quietly to herself. "How much everything has changed! . . . Are you coming here for the first time?" she turned to me.

"Yes, for the first time . . ."

"But it's hardly recognizable!"

And indeed the resort was not so bad as it had seemed from the train. We passed by a park with huge trees. Beautiful villas sunk in verdure ranged along both sides of the road. Lightly striking its hoofs against the asphalt, the horse drove us under the vaulted arch of the ancient Roman gateway—so wonderfully made I craned my neck to see it. It was really worth seeing! And if Roman emperors used to travel months to the place, why should not an ordinary engineer waste half a month in it? Then there came gardens, bridges, huge trees with heavy shadows . . . there would not be any dying here.

But the Trade Unions Home was built on a steep, barren bank. I don't know where the tradition came from to build these homes in Attila's trail, where no grass and no trees grow. But then the stairs seemed to be taking you to the temple of Osiris—you had to do twice as much climbing as was reasonable.

On the top landing instead of a priest there was a man with an unfriendly, pimply face who seemed to have been attracted by the clattering of the cab. He gave us a suspicious look and asked: "Are you a married couple?"

"Not at all!" I started in surprise. "Only fellow travelers."

"I see," he mumbled under his nose.

It is hard to describe the rich scale of intonation in this single sound. In it were both doubt about a glib lie and suspicion about the true character of our relations. The threat that he would in no way let the morals of the rest home be undermined was mixed with contempt at so naïve a revelation as was our simultaneous arrival. After we had left our identification cards at the office he said grimly: "Lunch will be in half an hour! Be punctual!"

From the glance she gave him it became quite clear to me— you will have a hard time of it, comrade! In three days she will look through your books, inspect your stores, push into your kitchen to weigh the rations, and take a good look at your cultural program in which she is sure to find remnants of bourgeois culture. You'll soon see, soon be convinced! I didn't feel like warning him—the rhinoceros did not deserve a better fate. The rhinoceros evidently did not sense danger, for he took the liberty of saying: "I lock up at ten! Don't you complain if . . ."

She said nothing, only gave me a portentous look. It's coming, I thought to myself, much pleased.

My little room was lovely, with one bed that shone delicately white. The window overlooked a valley with a thick growth of trees beyond which was a long string of fortress walls, now strong and massive, now showing the inroads of time and man's destructive hand. I would probably have had a happy stay here had I not fallen so fatally upon the Cholera. I was sure she would not let me be.

In fact, she was the only person at the plant who felt obliged to pester me at meetings. There would always be something in my work she didn't like, something not up to the mark, something more that she wanted. No matter what I did I always felt on my sensitive spots the invisible goad of her words and reproaches which were ready to prick me even when I felt most safe. I thought I would at least be rid of her here, but here she was.

The bell rang, and I almost jumped in my seat and rushed down the stairs with a faint heart. Amazed at the way the bad lot succeed in forcing their will upon the good and the meek, I climbed down the white stairs poked at by the brusque orders on the walls: "Don't spit . . . Don't touch . . . Don't throw . . . Have respect . . ." I stopped a minute to see what was to be respected. And it turned out to be the tranquillity of my neighbor. That was all right, but why hadn't that pimpled bossy character tried to have respect for my dignity? As it is, I don't have the habit of spitting or touching, and as for respect . . .

I noticed that despite my speed, the holiday-makers had already seated themselves around the tables. I, too, sat down at one of the vacant tables. While the waitress was serving me the soup I had time to reason that the soup could hardly be hot if the girl could keep her thumb in it so long.

"May I?"

It was none other than Marinova, naturally. And why did she ever ask permission when she never waited for an answer?

"Everything so well arranged!" she exclaimed in a voice that seemed to me quite unsuitable to express delight. "With simplicity and good taste!" But seeing the director's frowning face as he passed by the table, she added, the ghost of a smile playing on her face: "Except for that grim fellow, naturally."

In fact, at that moment I found my soup much more sour than it actually was. But what right of all people did she have to say it?

"I think," she went on, "so much money has been spent to create a pleasant atmosphere for the people, and here he is spoiling it all with his appearance."

Now this, I thought, was the last straw. "It's true. But don't you think you're a lot like him?"

She looked at me flabbergasted.

"I? Like him? . . . Why on earth?"

"Just think about it."

The remark evidently spoiled her mood. She didn't say a word during the meal. When we were rising she asked diffidently: "What do you think of having a swim? There's a lovely swimming pool."

I didn't want to, but I accepted the invitation. I felt a bit guilty for the remark I had made about her. Luckily the swimming pool was not far away, and there were only a few people there at that time of the day. She seemed to me so very different in the bathing suit—slim and supple, like a young girl. I wonder if it's not malice that melts extra fat? Instinctively I took a good look at myself. Although I was thin, my belly, yellow-white like cow cheese, hung loose, and my thighs were outright skinny.

Marinova swam for a quarter of an hour and then came over to me. As she sat down, a breath of coolness and freshness came from her wet body. Her face was smiling, her eyes calculating.

"So I look like the manager?" she asked gaily.

The tone of her voice surprised me. "Well, in a way," I mumbled, ill-at-ease.

"In what way, for instance?"

"In what way? Well, just like him you always probe and try to find fault with people."

"So that's it, eh?" she said thoughtfully and her face took on a serious expression. "But even if it is so, I have never done it for a mere nothing."

"That's how he thinks of himself, too," I said. "He also imagines it is all being done in the name of peace and good order for the sake of others."

She looked at me, smiled, and jumping up, made for the pool again. I watched her slim back in surprise—she was not herself. She didn't scold, didn't start an argument, or turn on me for being insulting. On reaching the pool she dived into the water gracefully and disappeared under the blue surface. A fountain of diamond spray shone bright in the sun and was gone. After a short while her head came up from the water and she cried: "Come on in! You can't imagine how nice the water is."

I got up and, looking at my cowlike belly, made for the pool.

She did not come down for dinner, and I was depressed. She might be malicious, she might nag, she might be anything, but after all she was a human being and life is impossible without people. Where to sit, whom to talk to? They were all strangers to me here; nobody knew my work, my thoughts. I was finishing my dinner when the manager came over to me and casually threw our identification cards on the table.

"Yours," he said, "and your lady friend's."

In the last word I once more felt a wealth of intonation in his voice. I flew into a rage, but I differ from others in that my mouth goes numb and I can't say a word. I took the cards and opened hers in spite of myself. It was only then that I remembered her name was Olga. Naturally it was Olga.

That night I went to my room feeling unhappy.

The following morning Olga came to breakfast in a new dress and was smiling affably. It was a real wonder . . . was it only in the factory that she was such a nag? Did she in fact have two faces—one for work and the other in outside life? While I was trying to make her out she explained her absence the night before.

"I usually don't eat in the evening. I stay up reading till late anyway, and if I put food in my stomach I simply couldn't sleep at all."

"Now, now!" I mumbled condescendingly. "It's clear enough that you are losing weight."

"I, losing weight?" she asked in a voice which sounded quite sincere.

"Surely! That at least is clear enough."

She tossed her head. "No, you can't lose weight by going on a diet," she said firmly. "You can lose weight by burning inside, by never being indifferent to anything about you."

"It's all right to burn," I said, "as long as you don't burn at the expense of others."

She understood and smiled: "Now you see who likes to pick quarrels. Is it me or you?"

From then on we took all our meals together and went to the swimming pool together. I stretched in the sun, swam, and was happy to discover that the layer of fat on my belly was slowly disappearing. Something like virility appeared in my gait, and my body become more solid. I so much wished she noticed the change, but she said nothing.

While sunbathing on the coarse white sand we often talked about things at the plant, the people there and their doings. Her evaluations of people seemed to me amazingly correct, and that was what worried me. If she could see them all in a true light, what was the guarantee that she had been wrong concerning me? What if there was some reason to her remarks at meetings, and her invisible goad with which she kept pricking me constantly?

Once, talking about the production process of our special dyes, she told me something that made me gape.

"How do you know this?" I exclaimed in excitement.

"I read it in a German magazine," she said.

"Was it long ago?" I asked.

"Two weeks ago."

The answer made me feel relieved, though not quite.

"How idiotic," I sighed bitterly. "And I thought I had invented it myself."

She gave me a suspicious look.

"And what has that to do with our work?"

"Well—can't you see?"

"I can't."

I explained it to her briefly. And her face lit up with excitement and pleasure. "We must introduce it!" she said, stepping along the white sand in a fury of activity. "The minute we get back."

That night we went back delighted. But the following morning she came to breakfast, her face dark, her spirits low. First I kept silent out of tactfulness but at length I couldn't hold out and asked what the trouble was.

"We must not sit together any more," she said scowling. "People are beginning to talk."

"Talk about what?" I asked.

"You know what they are talking about."

Had she looked in my direction she would have seen the fright in my eyes. But she did not. Yes, we would have to look to appearances.

"What does it matter when it isn't true?" I said, as calmly as I could. "As it is, there is absolutely no truth in it."

"There isn't," she uttered cheerlessly. "But we are not alone in this world; there are also those we live with."

"You are the last person who should think like that," I said, raising my voice. "We should try to think honestly and live honestly. Only those who have no respect for themselves live to please the petty gossips."

"You're right," she nodded, her face brightening up.

That evening as if to put this maxim into practice, we went to the beer garden together. We had a drink of beer first and then a bottle of Karlovsko wine. To those who are not used to drinking this is not little. We cheered up and did some dancing. I even heard myself humming in time with the orchestra. How long had it been since I had allowed myself such liberties? God only knows! We were naturally late and started back at about midnight.

I will never forget that night! It was warm, the stars shone big upon the black southern sky. We were walking back along the path by the valley where fireflies twinkled and night birds called out from time to time. I felt somehow younger and self-assured, and my thoughts were fast and clear. It was a long time, since my young days, that I had felt so good. It was probably this self-assurance and sense of being free inside that gave me the courage to ask with casual gaiety: "Now honestly, Olga, tell me, why have you been so persistently down on me at the factory? Do you really think I was the most incompetent of them all?"

I was aware of her face flushing in the dark.

"On the contrary!" she said, warming up. "I thought you were the most competent."

"I can't quite make out this logic," I admitted.

"It's not a question of logic in this case," she went on after a pause, "but of conviction. What I honor most of all in the world is talent. Not goodness, not sincerity, not impeccable diligence nor conscientiousness, but talent. I may be wrong, but I think we owe everything to it. We all live from the fruit of its thoughts and inspiration. If the world were carried on the shoulders of the sincere and the diligent alone, life would not move one single step ahead."

I did not quite agree with her, but I was delighted. These were far from being the thoughts of a woman.

"Isn't that so?" she asked.

"Let's say . . ."

"No, that's just it," she said with conviction. "And that is why talent obligates us more than anything else. The talented person is marked. He has no right to give in, or become reconciled, or retire into himself! And that is exactly what you do. Nobody thinks you are not a good engineer, but you vegetate and become reconciled to what you have achieved, and you never look up high. You shouldn't be just an engineer, but a man of science, an inventor. Your whole being should burn with your talent. This will add brightness to your eyes, it will make you younger. How old are you?"

"Forty-two," I said quietly.

"But you look much older than that. It is because you've become reconciled. And this is what I can never do. And watching you waste away your talent I protest and grumble."

Some time passed in silence. On that memorable night I felt deeply the bitterness of her words. Finally, I spoke up diffidently: "Maybe you're right, Olga. But I have always regarded modesty as the greatest virtue. I seem to have compared myself with the ambitious and the covetous instead of with the scientists and inventors." We talked for a long while, going around the yard wall three times.

"We must go in," Olga said at last, realizing how late it was.

The front door was locked of course. I was immediately seized by timidity: What would the pimply man say? What explanation would I give him? I was all for going back to the park and spending the night on a bench. But in the meantime Olga had already pressed the button good and hard.

The manager appeared almost at once as if he had been waiting for us in the dark little room. There was an air of reproach about him which was so telling that I crouched where I stood, wishing to turn into invisible vapor then and there. He unlocked the door, examining us from top to toe with silent contempt, and grumbled: "Aren't you ashamed of yourselves! And both of you married people!"

Olga, having come in first, stopped short as if hit on the forehead with a hammer: "You are a pitiful pithecanthropus!" Her voice trembled with indignation.

"Watch your words, Comrade!" the manager said, but his voice lacked firmness.

It seemed to me that a small explosion flashed up in her eyes.

"Get out of my way!" That voice could have killed a man. I saw the manager move with a start as if some powerful eight-cylinder car had loomed before him at top speed.

Reaching the first landing she smiled at me, stretched her hand, and said, "You are right! Maybe I am wicked but only with the wicked."

I stood at my window for some time in the dark, staring into the thick darkness that had settled at the bottom of the valley. Fireflies still flitted about out there, night birds still called out hoarse and unceasing. Wicked? No, anything but that. Now I could safely admit what I had long since felt—she really was the most pleasing woman I had ever met. And she had the clearest view of life.

About ten days later we arrived at the Sofia station together. She had sent a telegram to her husband to inform him of her arrival, but I, for some unknown reason, had not ventured to wire my wife. Her husband was a little younger than I, quite tall and handsome. He gave her a rather casual kiss and gave me a still more casual look.

"This is my colleague Ilinchev," she said, introducing me to him.

"Ah," he exclaimed. "Olga has often talked to me about you."

Her smile was not bad.

As I had expected, my wife was at home. After the first spontaneous burst of joy and surprise, she became silent. The atmosphere seemed to be charged with something I was to be blamed for. In order to conceal my embarrassment I began to talk about the resort, the manager, and the two barrels of mineral water I had drunk. I had the feeling that she was not listening attentively but was keeping something to herself. It was toward nightfall. Dusk was slowly falling, the miscellaneous city noises, so very different from those at the spa, came through the open window. She fried some eggs and put them on the table, but did not sit down.

"I hear you were not alone at the spa!" she said suddenly.

"What do you mean?" I asked, blinking.

"It's for you to say . . ."

"What is there to say? It's only that there was also . . ."

"Was it by mere chance that it all happened?" she asked, looking me straight in the eye.

Without anything to feel guilty about, here I was feeling exceedingly uneasy before her searching eyes.

"You're crazy, Magdalena," I said.

"I'm asking you, was it by mere chance that you were there together?" she said in a firm voice.

That startled me. "Good God, but you know quite well what our relations with her are, don't you?"

"That is just what I want to know." Her voice suddenly grew soft, her eyes went moist. Now that was even worse than if she had screamed.

"Magdalena, I swear to you, our being in the same shift was pure accident. I was even scared when I first saw her there. What could I have in common with that Cholera!"

I still can't understand how I got out the last word. And why? Maybe it was that cursed timidity of mine, or pity, for I didn't want her to shed tears in vain and lose confidence in my fidelity. Whatever the reasons, I despised myself to death. My heart ached as if pierced with a sharp poisonous needle.

But that very word seemed to have had some magic effect upon Magdalena. Truly she grumbled and asked questions long after we went to bed. I lay in the dark for quite a long time. Was it by her side that I had lost part of myself? Was it that love of hers, quiet, uncomplaining, and tranquil, that had taken away part of my power of resisting and going ahead? And what mattered most, would I go backwards? Or would I start, though with twists and turns, along the glowing road I had so clearly seen on that dark night of the fireflies?

That night I could not understand anything. All I knew was that I was exceedingly sad.

Translated by GREGOR PAVLOV

Stoyan T. Daskalov

(1909–   )

Stoyan Daskalov was born on August 22, 1909 in the village of Lilyache, Vratsa district. He finished a secondary school in Lom, a teacher-training college in Shoumen, and studied Slavonic philology at Sofia University. For many years he was a teacher in his native county. His first works were published in *Svetlostroui*, in 1930.

He contributed to a number of periodicals, including the newspapers *Zemya* and *Zarya*, *RLF*, *Kormilo*, *Brod*, *Echo*, *Akademic*, *Zhoupel* and the magazines *Bulgarska Missul*, *Zlatorog*, and *Izkoustvo i Kritika*. He edited the children's magazine *Rossitsa* before he took part in World War II as an army writer. Later he edited two more children's magazines: *Zvunché* and *Drouzhinka*.

He is the author of the following books: *Sorrow*, short stories (1935); *Under the Shepherd's Cloak*, short stories (1941); *Yard*, short stories (1943); *With One's Own Folk*, short stories (1946); *The Lipovanski Mill*, a novel (1951); *One's Own Land*, a novel; *The Change*, a drama (1953); *Road*, a novel in three parts (1945–55); *Water from the Monastery* (1958); *The Stoublen Linden Trees*, a novel (1960); *When Love Begins*, novelettes (1961); *Birds of Paradise*, short stories, and many other works. Books for children: *Dewdrops*, short stories (1937); *The Young Volunteer*, short stories (1946); *Stories for Pioneers* (1953); *Rogousha's Bell* (1953); *Tracks through the Fields*, short stories for children and adolescents (1959).

A New Attitude Toward Life

It was not until the very end of March that old Panto was operated upon, and although he had not fully recovered, he was discharged from hospital and was brought in an ambulance right here to this hamlet in the mountains, where they told him not to move for another ten days if he wanted to frisk about like a boy afterwards.

The mountains had doffed their cloak of snow, and the warm spring wind had cleared the ground of ice. The meadows were already green, the bells of the flocks tinkled, and the old man pictured them to himself occasionally nibbling at the grass, occasionally gamboling about, all day long. His heart filled with tinkling sounds as though it, too, were a bell, so that finally he felt like starting up, snatching up his shepherd's crook and his hooded cloak and going up into the hills. Old Panto had herded sheep all his life. He knew no rest, prowling in the fields at night like a vampire, spending the night where dusk had fallen, coming home with his flocks only when day had dawned. But lately he had suffered intensely from his pains, and his steps had become faltering. For that reason he had consented to an operation, hoping that his ordeal would be soon over. But, lying in bed now, he felt fettered, cut off from life; each day he asked his nephew, a boy he had adopted after the death of his wife, to look after him in his old age: "What has become of that lad of mine! Go and get him on the telephone again."

Pante, his nephew, had written a long letter to Sofia and had telephoned more than once. His son kept on promising, but was somewhat slow in making good his promises. The old man was pining away, thinking of him. He had four daughters, three of whom had married and were now living in other villages, but his favorite was his only son. He had made every sacrifice to educate him and was glad that he had married and had a good job. He had not seen him for a long time, and that made him most unhappy. Perhaps the sick always behave like this, especially in cases when death is so probable. In their desire to see their loved ones again all is forgotten and forgiven.

The old man refused his food, he could not sleep, tossing and turning, moaning and groaning: "Go and see . . . isn't he coming? The people of the co-operative farm may have detained him to repair their machine-and-tractor station."

Pante knew that his uncle had not arrived, but still he went out, made the round of the village and came back to reassure him: "He has not arrived yet. But you get some sleep. When he arrives, he will come here."

The old man often started from his sleep: "I'm certain that was the sound of a car engine. Go and see if he's coming."

His nephew went out, sleepy, in the middle of the night, strained his eyes in the darkness, listened, and came back anxious to go to bed again.

"That is the Pluskalo—it's the snow water thundering."

The old man could hardly wait till dawn. Through the small window he saw only a patch of blue sky and nothing more.

"Has the oak put forth leaves?"

"Yes, it has."

"And he is not yet here. Has anything happened to the lad? Has he had an accident?"

One morning he said: "I heard a blackbird singing. The blackbirds have come back, but he is not yet here. I've stared so much that my eyes are growing dim."

To the father his son was now like the song of a bird, like the spring generously covering the green meadows with crocuses, cornflowers and violets. And when at last the sound of a car unexpectedly disturbed the peace of the remote hamlet, old Panto almost jumped out of bed, so surprised that he could hardly ask, "Is that him?"

"Yes . . . in his car!" his nephew flattened his face against the windowpane, his eyes open wide and sparkling.

"I'd rather have seen him bringing a buffalo for me to drink milk straight out of the gourd." Old Panto relaxed after the long tension; he seemed to have fallen to pieces on his mattress.

"You lie where you are!" his nephew warned him, and left him alone.

Swarms of children were running along beside and behind the car. Some bolder spirits ran ahead of it, as though luring it on like a strange animal which they were coaxing into a stable with a corncob. By the well in the middle of the village a big, spare, raw-boned woman came running up with a pitcher full of water in her hand, shouting:

"Stop! Stop!"

"Peter, take your sister for a drive. She has brought you up and washed your nappies. Jump in, Sofika!"

Sofika, whose son had been adopted by old Panto, pressed the palm of her hand against the front of the car.

He stopped. He opened the door, but before his sister could get in, some urchins had somehow squeezed their way in; they began calling him uncle and getting under his feet. He shut the other door, through which some other children had stolen in like weasels. Some clambered onto the trunk, others onto the hood. His sister, stooping so as not to strike her head, struck the pitcher against the door and the water spilled over her skirt and the car.

"Bother these kids! You can't . . ." she splashed water over the car out of her cupped hand, as though out of a ladle.

"Good-bye!" people shouted. "May cars multiply! May all villages be full of cars!"

Her brother shut the door of the car and moved away slowly, while she clutched the handle of the broken pitcher, as though it were possible to repair it, whining all the time.

"What a pity, a new pitcher, I bought it at the fair!"

Young Pante came out of the old slate house, his shirt unbuttoned, although there was still snow on the brow of the Ostri Peak, and, on seeing the car with all those children in it, as though it were a cart going to a wedding, he opened the gate wide.

"Get out all of you!" the people shouted, but no one got out and his sister said, "What's the use of a car if it does not take me to the house where I was born? I'm staying put."

"Well then, there's nothing to do but to push it. And the ground isn't so bumpy here."

But the car managed the steep slope without anyone's aid, and it roared into the wide yard. The young man, so long awaited, at last appeared standing erect, neatly dressed, big and robust like the oak which Panto pruned every year and rejuvenated. At once his bare-headed nephew took the suitcase from his hands, while he began looking around at the yard and the house.

"Look at your house! Look at it for the last time, because we are going to pull it down. We are going to put up a new house," his sister Sofika shouted.

He saw the bricks and stones piled up in the front garden and the beach rafters ranged under the shed and fastened with wedges so as not to warp.

"But you mustn't stand aside and do nothing!" the peasants butted in and blurted out what she had left to the last moment. "There should be a place you could come to and sleep. Not alone like you are now, but with your wife and family. Why didn't you bring them to let them see the old man, so as not to forget their roots? You know the saying about people with no roots."

He only smiled at somebody here and somebody there. What could he say to so many people at once! Some of them he knew from childhood, others he had forgotten about, yet others he recognized but could no longer tell who they were, and the majority he had never seen in his life.

"Brother, brother, you have forgotten us village people!" his sister said with a sigh, when they had detached themselves from the uninvited guests and started for home.

As the lady of the house accustomed to receiving cherished

guests when they reached the door, she suddenly went back, snatched up some green cuttings from the chopping log, and brought them into the kitchen where she was now to begin that hard, thankless work which is the lot of woman, but which, at the same time, is the soul of hospitality.

"How lucky old Panto is to have a son like you, both an engineer and a car owner!" People shook hands with the engineer pellmell, detaining him in the yard to speak to him about their private affairs. When they had admired him sufficiently and he had heard enough complaints, he locked the car and left it for old and young alike to admire.

Pante, who had been rubbing the soiled number plate with his hand, followed him with his suitcase up the stone steps. "I'll wash it with soap afterwards so as to get a shine on it!"

"How is he?" the engineer inquired calmly, even gaily, after his father's health.

"He has lived to see you take him for a drive in your car!" the adoptive nephew nodded joyfully. "He was on the mend, but when they told him that you were coming in your car, he had a relapse. I called Pakyo to shave him, and this morning he wanted to get up and put his Sunday best on for your sake. It is quite true that old people are like children. I gave him a suit of clothes, but he did not want it. 'Give me my full-bottomed breeches,' he said. 'I have worn them all my life and I will die in them.' "

The son was stirred when he stood on the veranda from where he could see the straggling hamlet stretching over hills and valleys. Between the trees, in sunny spots, he glimpsed the cottages, isolated or in clusters, scattered like stray cattle. But here where he was, at the deep fork of the mountain, they formed a more compact mass—the center of the hamlet.

"Do you know that a road has been built to the Pluskalo, so that we may go there by car? The old fellow says that if you take him there he'll recover. 'I have been dying,' he says, 'to drink of that cold water out of my cupped hands!' "

The waterfall tumbled down like a white belt from the Ostri Peak. He caught a whiff of moisture, and the spray seemed to refresh his face, hot from driving. Pylons had gone up between the Pluskalo and the hamlet, their wires glittering like yarn on iron looms. The son looked at the peaks and the ravines he had wandered through, the winding paths he had trodden in his bare feet, but his memories were like the clouds scudding across the pale sky—they did not touch him. It was probably the pride of at last owning a car and returning in it to his village where he had ridden on donkeys and on horseback that prevented any other feeling from taking possession of him. With the same coolness, even indifference, he walked across the passageway and entered the room where his father lay sick. As soon as he opened the door slightly, he saw in the bed in the twilit corner a haggard face gleaming white, like a piece broken off a wall. The son crossed the earth floor, went and took the dropping hand which was like a network of protruding yellow veins, similar to osiers, and kissed it. He felt its hardness on his lips and a smell of sourish musty dampness and decay. Something stirred in his breast, but his heart did not melt within him. The disagreeable, offensive smell coming from his father proved stronger and, incredible though this may seem, killed all sympathy in him.

He sat down silently at the bedside, brooding for an inexplicable reason on himself. He had broken with the village long ago. He could not come back, even if he wanted to. Such was the nature of his work—it would hardly permit him to return even once a year. While he was a bachelor, he used to pop over more often, but after his marriage, the children born to him bound him like chains to the new home and impelled him in a new direction. But his coming in his car now seemed to have made amends for everything, and he began to think about the place he was to go after his return.

"Well," a guttural sound startled him.

That was his father's voice. That was the tone of voice in which he often used to ask questions.

Wearing a new sleeveless jacket and full-bottomed trousers, his father lay at full length, looking eagerly at his son, full of admiration. His hands felt his knees trembling. He ran his tongue across his dry lips, pushed at his drooping mustache, knitted his brow, and his even, white soft hair stood on end. He wanted to say a great many things at the same time, but could not.

"I am a bit late," his son replied.

The father was eager to hear what the fatal cause of the delay had been.

"The car isn't broken in yet, that was why I was late," he added, whereupon the old man heaved a sigh of relief. "And how are you?"

He did not address him as "dad," and his conscience pricked him for losing the habit of using this affectionate word, there being long since no one he could address by the word "mother."

"My head's been buzzing with no end of things. My daughter-in-law, I said to myself, or the children must be ill, that is why he is so late. Or something has happened on your way here, the roads being slippery and your car being like a buffalo that is not used to being harnessed, may not have been able to manage those hills and has fallen over a precipice."

"I have arrived safe and sound."

"But where is . . . I feel like getting up, but I am not allowed to. We really need a cow buffalo. That would be a support for the household, while you . . . a car!"

He had heard the car drive in perfectly well, he had heard the dying sounds of the engine under the window, and something keyed him up. He had all but gone to the windowpane and flattened his face against it. The old man pictured it to himself in the empty yard of which the cattle had been driven never to return, and it seemed to him to have filled the vacuum left by the cattle. He listened now to the confused babble of voices, and his heart felt younger. The tortuous veins on his arms had swollen up and were twitching now. His dark complexion and his tan were returning. His cheekbones, cut here and there by his shave, had reddened. His cheeks bulged out, blood-red. His Adam's apple twitched, showing that he was gulping back his joy in silence.

"A wonderful thing!" people said, admiring the new car, and he heard everything. Children whistled, pushing their hands through the side window.

Adults tapped the body work and shouted in raptures:

"The way it sings!"

Others slammed the doors.

"Like stone!" yet others pressed their feet against the tires, dazzled:

"They don't cave in!"

"Oho, it hasn't done much—even less than two thousand kilometers. It is still locked."

"With the lock on, it is like a young bride in her veil. He will appreciate it fully when it has been taken off. Then he will be able to drive it in any gear he chooses."

His son was the only man of the village to have bought a car. That made the old man feel proud and strong, helped him to rest on his elbows and might even help him to get up and see with his own eyes how people in the village reacted to the car. From his bed he recognized people by their voices.

"This costs as much as all working days of the village added together!" a hollow voice boomed out.

And the old man said: "This is Netsko! He is a disgruntled man and such he will remain for ever. That is what happens when you are born feet instead of head foremost."

"He has had to sweat away for it," somebody ventured quietly.

"Do you hear, that is Dinyo! He is a just man. He is the only one in the village with a ready answer for everything. He stops your mouth with one word."

"Where are you climbing to, Toshka?" a woman's voice was heard. "Get down! They can see your thighs and you are no longer a child! That chap, Pante, will give you a good thrashing."

"Blessed Calitsa! She will drive them away from the car like a whirlwind."

Pante's voice, now joyous, now angry, could be heard above everything. The nephew was jealously keeping the kids off.

"Hey, why have you nestled down in the trunk like a young stork?"

"That is the Bosatsi brat," old Panto nodded his head menacingly. "How many times have I thrashed him, but he is as pigheaded as his father is."

"Don't touch, this is not an Easter egg! You'll scratch the paint. Keep back, or else I'll give you a clout."

But, however much he protected the car, the admiration and the curiosity of the villagers was so great that laughter and shouting filled the yard, and although the old man told his son to go and see that no harm was done, he wanted the noise to continue a long time, all through the night, so that it should banish solitude and despondency.

Suddenly the noise invaded the room he lay in.

"Well, Panto, you don't believe it, eh?" the voice of Natsko was heard, that sullen character who gave vent to his ill will in public but sang a different song here.

"The car has come. It is only waiting to carry you round like a Hero of Socialist Labor."

"Leave him with his buffalo cows. He prefers tending and harnessing them."

Some shook hands with him, others with his son, shaking their heads, expressing in this way their gladness or their envy.

"The old man said once that he might die without seeing his son, but he didn't expect to see him bursting with health and driving not a bullock cart, but a Russian car," Calitsa the sharp-tongued shouted, all but lifting up the old man: "Get up and have a look at it!"

"Well, there is plenty of time. Let him lie there now. He'll have enough opportunities to drive in it," Dinko cut her down to size.

The old man's eyes shone, shifting from man to man, until they came to rest on his son.

"What have you brought for your father?" Calitsa shouted, as though she were on very intimate terms with Panto's family and might scold and speak her mind. The son got up, startled, open the suitcase which the villagers were examining with curiosity, eager to see what the learned son had brought for his sick father.

"Here, father, Lena has sent you these pyjamas."

"Oh," a woman exclaimed, with a note of pity in her voice, expecting probably that the son would bring all Sofia in his car.

"Why, it's all right. Let old Panto wear pyjamas, too. How soft they are! They won't chafe him the way his full-bagged trousers do. If he wears full-bagged trousers now, does that mean that he should wear them all his life?"

"How nice their design is! He can go around in them in the village."

Some of them laughed.

"When I was on holiday this summer I saw foreigners coming down from their rooms in pyjamas, walking about in pyjamas, taking their meals in pyjamas. So why shouldn't old Panto go to the restaurant as well, and have a drink?" Dinyo snapped. The son took out a bag of oranges. He peeled one, cut it up, and served it to his father, using the peel as a saucer.

"You had better gobble it up yourself. Your father, poor man, will only fiddle about with it staining his clothes and not really enjoying it," Calitsa said, her eyes fixed on the rose-colored fruit covered with a thin rind as if with a layer of fat, and she stared unflinchingly until the old man had sucked all the sweet juice.

The relations' children plundered the oranges and made short shrift of the sweets.

He had also brought for his father a suit of clothes and a pair of shoes.

"Poor lad, he has bought them as though for a dead man," Calitsa whispered mournfully, putting her palm to her cheek. "Both the clothes and the slippers are black."

"Well, he is an old man," Dinyo shouted at her, startling her and putting her to shame. "Do you want him to buy rosy-colored things for his father? Considerate they are, both he and his wife. It is a pity we have no such considerate relatives—our relatives don't care for us."

Dinyo, too, had a son living in a town.

"Enough of this!" younger Pante shouted. "Leave grandfather alone, he's tired. Let him rest."

"Yes, yes, let us give father and son a chance of chatting alone together. What are we doing here?" Calitsa led the women out, the men trooping out after them, and all the confused babble of voices was heard again down in the yard, around the car. Pante stood guard again in the yard, while inside father and son conversed alone together in low voices.

"What color is it?" old Panto asked.

"Green, father, green."

"Crane's-bills, and woods, and grass are also green. The color of youth! A good color." The eyes of the old man seemed to see green. "And how many people can it hold?"

"It is a four-seater. Quite good enough for us."

"But, with your mother-in-law you are five!"

"Well, the kids are still young, so there'll be room for you, too."

"Aha! But does it go fast?"

Thirsting for motion, the old man seemed to be sweeping along in his bed.

"Thirty-five horsepower, father."

"Dear me, it must be a mighty thing then! We have been harnessing up to ten pairs of horses, but thirty-five! It will kill you, my son," he turned around, resting on his elbow.

"No, it won't! The car runs at your own sweet will, either fast or slow."

"But who drives it?"

"Why, me of course! Do you think it is more difficult than engineering? Lena has learned to drive, too."

"Do you let her handle that wheel?" the old man raised himself up, alarmed.

"Yes, she manages. She sometimes goes for a drive with the children."

"But that is dangerous! Don't let her do it, she may get killed! Women are like butterflies, flitting about everywhere. They are very fickle and capable of anything."

"On the contrary, Sofia is full of women driving cars, and most accidents are caused by men, because they are too big for their boots, while women, being more timid, are also more careful."

"Don't let your wife drive, anyhow," the old man said.

Although he did not approve of his daughter-in-law, he was glad that she could drive a car.

"The boys will learn how to drive, too, but I shall not live long enough to see that," he said, his eyes filling with tears.

He was a hard man and did not want to let his son see that having been cut up by the doctors here and stitched up by them there, he had become soft and was crying like a child. His son had turned away to the window, so he took advantage of that to brush away a tear from his eyelid with his thumb. He resumed at once: "How much did you pay for it?"

"Three thousand, father," his son replied, as though that were a small amount that could be scooped up at will like a bushel of corn from a barn.

"Where did you get all that money? You could buy a horse with it. Have you run into debt?" The old man had fixed a searching look on him. "If so, it may be seized and sold at a public auction."

"No, father, no, I. . . . We, both of us are working, and I receive bonuses for overfulfilling the plan. This year I also got a prize for a money-saving innovation that saves the State one hundred thousand leva."

Everything was clear to the father thus far. After that, when his son began to speak about his specialized field, he only heard the words—they only soothed his hearing without reaching his consciousness. He was very happy, he could listen like that all night long. Wasn't the car, which was the key to everything, out in the yard?

"Why didn't you leave it under the shed," the old man was worrying. "It may start raining and, besides, there are all sorts of people about. Someone may damage it out of sheer spite. We haven't even got milk, he may say to himself, while he has a car. There! It stands in the yard like a lonely bride. Anyone may be tempted."

"You can count on me," his nephew shouted menacingly. "I'll keep guard all night long and will crack the head of anyone who dares."

Peter drove the car under the shed. They had just started dinner when Commissioner Vitko appeared. They placed him at the middle of the table. All the time, instead of eating, he reported at length to Peter about the state of the population of the mountain villages, as though they were his responsibility.

When he was gone, old Panto said to his son: "Take him tomorrow in your car to the Pluskalo. You may take me there afterwards, but you should take him there first."

"Take poor old Kina, too!" the boy said, laughing.

"Why not? She is the oldest member of the family and she's not long for this world. Let everybody see that you don't give yourself airs and graces, and don't keep away from ordinary people."

They asked Peter where he was going to sleep, whether in the small room where he had slept as a child and as a young man, or with his father.

"Here! Make up a bed for him where I am," old Panto said, and he made no objections.

They soon spread a rug made of goat's hair on the couch, brought the bedclothes from the small room, and the son lay down over against his father. When the tramp of feet about the house had died away and the old man was sure that everybody had gone to sleep, he began to whisper to his son in a low voice, confidentially, as though confessing his sins: "Has your sister Sofika been asking you for money for the new house?"

"This car has cost me a pretty penny, so where am I to find any money for them?"

"They were wanting me to persuade you to help them. He has got a flat and a car, they say, while we haven't got anything. Your sister wants her share of what your mother left. They say that your mother left everything to you, thus enabling you to receive your schooling, while they . . . you received your schooling at their cost, so they want you to pay them back."

The son sighed and yawned.

"She complains to you of me, then, does she? They want to build a new house and so they are about to pull the old one down, but I'm not in favor of doing that. As long as I live, let it stay, it does not interfere with anyone. But they say: either-or."

"What do you mean by that either-or?"

"They have given me an ultimatum: either I should do whatever they want me to do, since they are looking after me, or I should come to live with you. I said: 'let Peter come, and we shall see what is going to happen.'"

The son had not expected these complications. He said, as though they did not concern him: "You stay in the old house, and let them build a new one if they want to."

"But what they are anxious about are the building materials."

They said a few more words, but as both of them were tired, one from anticipation and excitement, the other from the strain of traveling, their voices soon grew fainter. It was the son that became silent first. After having seen and heard his father, he relaxed. At first he found the couch too hard. However thick the rug might be, still the planks were too much for his ribs. It was as if he were lying right on the rough ground. He was used to a soft bed and an eider down in Sofia, and was annoyed with himself for agreeing to this discomfort, but he could not move in the middle of the night; he had to stick it out until morning. On the morrow he would take the old man for a drive, and then good-bye to the village! There was a stale smell in the room, a smell of smoke, of earth floor coated with dung. The old man slept in his woolen clothes, and his sweat smelled of greasy wool. He was also annoyed by the wheeze of the old man's cough. He was an engineer and could stand the rumble of machinery and the grating sound of lathes, but this chest, wheezing continually now, bored his skull like a gimlet; he seemed to be bitten by fleas jumping about him. The rug felt rough; he felt as though he were lying on stubble, and it was so heavy that he seemed to be buried under sheaves of corn. He tossed and turned, but only groaned slightly from time to time so as not to let his father feel that he was uncomfortable.

In his heart of hearts he knew that he could not return any more to this way of life, to begin to wear full-bottomed trousers again as he had done once and as his father still did. He had become used to sleeping in the car, he could stand the smell of gasoline and grease, but with this smell of mold coming from the rotten beams he could not sleep a wink. Dust from the crumbling ceiling seemed to be falling into his eyes. He wanted to open the window to let fresh air in, but was afraid that the old man might catch cold. He tossed and turned, his mind full of new projects; he seemed to be setting out on new journeys, and fell asleep. He reviewed his life in his sleep, while asleep there was nothing to irritate him: everything was beautiful as a realized dream.

Old Panto, too, reviewed his life, only not in his sleep, but awake. He only thought about Peter. He was born small, smaller than normal, bluish and thin-faced. They were afraid he would not survive, they were not lucky with their boys. They persuaded him to make a present of a silk shirt to the Virgin Mary, and he contributed a sheep as an offering at the ceremony at the Tutina Pear Tree.

Although he did not believe in these customs, still he did all the old women of the village told him to do. The child remained alive through his own strength. He was their last child, so they looked after him and fed him better than they had done the others. When the time came to go to high school, he was a puny but healthy boy. He went out with his father to tend sheep in the mountains, and when he got caught in the rain, old Panto wrapped him up in his hooded cloak and brought him back home as though he were a wet lamb.

At night, when he lay asleep, his mother used to get up and cover him with the rug if he had kicked it off, and after her death, whenever Peter came back home, Panto used to get up himself as she used to do and go to the small room to see if he was well tucked in. If he had thrown back the rug, he covered him gently, tucking its edge deep under the mattress so that he would not kick it off a second time. It had become such a habit with the old man that now, although laid up, he wanted to go and see his son asleep. It seemed to him more urgent than ever, for he thought that Peter had become effeminate. While he was here in the mountains, the air invigorated him, but there in Sofia, he had become paler and more susceptible to disease. It is so easy for a scholar to catch a cold and, before realizing what the matter with him is, to die. The old man was horrified at the thought that his son, who had to live, might catch a cold and die instead of him, who had more or less lived out his life already. The car in the yard made him feel happy. Why should he interfere with what made him feel happy? The old man was uneasy even if his son was only suffering from a headache. How would he manage that steering wheel? It was not a whip; it demanded a strong hand. How would he release those thirty-five horses? How would he stop them on a slope? If he slept uncovered all night long, the cold would weaken him, his trembling hands wouldn't be able to manage the wheel, and the car might fall over a precipice. Peter, his son, his heir, killed!

"Peter, Peter!" he shouted gently two or three times, so as not to startle him, but his son was fast asleep.

The old man saw in the dark his son a child again, stark naked, barefoot, his chest bare, shivering, shriveled up, the cold spreading all through him, penetrating through the tender skin, piercing his heart. Old Panto could stand it no longer. He threw back the covering and got up. He groped his way forward hesitantly and, having reached the bed, he passed his hand over the body of his

son from the feet upwards. When he reached his head, he found that
his son had pushed the rug back just a little and one of his shoulders
and his neck were uncovered.

"I knew, I knew," the old man whispered. "Yes, yes . . ."

He covered him gently, bent over him, listening to his warm
regular breathing, and kissed him. In his opinion, a peasant, a rustic
wearing full-bottomed trousers could only kiss his child when he
was sleeping. Reassured now, groping his way carefully so as not to
crash into the table or the chair, he made for his bed. Through the
window he saw the morning star which, too, seemed to be rejoicing
that the first car had come to the village and in the yard of the Panto
family. He saw it covered like a weary mare under the shed, and
smiled. He imagined himself sitting again in it, in good health, releasing the thirty horses, and the car flying along. "Stop!" he shouts, but
Peter laughs: "Don't be afraid!" He releases the other five horses,
too, and the car seems to be leaving the ground and flying upwards.

Suddenly the old man felt a sharp pain, he tottered on his thin
legs and collapsed. When his son jumped out of bed in alarm his
father was lying huddled up by the window. Beside him lay the
striped pyjamas which had dropped off the pillow and which he was
probably keeping for better days. On the white wall attached to a
nail, the black clothes he was to put on next morning were hanging.

"Father, what are you doing up?" his son started shaking him,
but the father had passed away. "Because of the car? Just to see it?
Ah, why did I have to bring this car!" his son was shouting, not
knowing that his father had died of love for him.

"What have you done, uncle?" Pante rushed in from outside,
and caught his breath. "I have been watching over him for such a
long time, and you've caused his death in one night. Had I slept with
him this wouldn't have happened!"

The women started up, alarmed, and neighbors came in
throngs.

"It's the doctors that were the death of him. If he had not
been to the hospital, he would have lived to be a hundred."

"That will do. He was fated to see his son own a car and then
die. He saw the new ways with his own eyes. Let us close them
now."

The house was filled with crying, subdued at first and then
swelling to a pitch. A candle was lit over the head of the dead man.
The flame flickering, flooding his face with a yellow light. His son
was looking at his dead father, wondering why he was not crying
like the rest. He was dumbfounded. Even strangers were crying,

while there he was standing apathetic, cold. If he had been wounded, he would not have shed blood, let alone tears.

"Aha!" some one said. "Look at him, he is not even crying."

"Cry, man!" someone whispered timidly, embarrassed himself at daring to suggest that to him. "He killed himself crying on account of you, while you . . ."

He wanted to cry and was angry at not being able to do so. He asked himself why it should be so. One of his dreams had been realized—he owned a flat and a car in which he could ride wherever he wanted, he felt proud, free, on top of the world. But while that had been happening, a great change had imperceptibly come over him. He was still a sociable man, but somehow he seemed to have lost something valuable—he did not know what its name was, but it was the feeling of sorrow. Was not that also true of his love for his wife? In his mind's eye there stood out scenes which paralyzed him and prevented him from being moved.

The flame of the candle flickered, and he saw the face of his wife under it and yet could not cry. Was not his love for her also insensible? Of late he had treated his wife like a mere acquaintance, usually meeting her by the car. His home was to him just kitchen and bedroom. His life, his emotions began away from home. At home he lived without feelings, without even a laugh. He could not think of any intense experience he had undergone. A life without depth or drama, without light or shadow: a shallow, superficial life slipping away untidily.

The flame flickered and he saw himself under it. It seemed to him that his wife would shed no tears over him, nor, for that matter, would his children. They had grown estranged from him and had no love for him. When he was seriously ill, his big boy only laughed, had no time for him, never inquired how he was. He discovered the same coldness and lack of emotional depth in others around him. But so far he had never thought of himself from that point of view. He remembered himself a different man—a strong branch of his family, heavy with affection as with fruit. When had he scattered that fruit of his soul, rendering it so barren that it could not even produce one tear for his father? What was that new attitude toward life?

"Grandfather, grandfather, you could not take a drive," Pante was sobbing.

"You may at least carry him to the graveyard in the car, brother, so that we all have something by which we may remember it," his sister felt faint. "This car has become his hearse."

He was afraid that when he carried him in his car and all the villagers were weeping he might not be able again to shed a tear. He realized that he had been devastated so much while preoccupied with readjusting and mechanizing himself, that his heart remained unmoved by sorrow—it had lost its elasticity, it had become nothing more than a contracting and dilating ball.

He started crying in his anguish at not being able to cry for his father.

It was only on the day after, when it was all over, that he cried so much that he wetted the steering wheel, the car stopping in the middle of the road as though because of floods.

Translated by ROUSSI ROUSSEV

Maria Groubeshlieva

(1900–   )

Maria Groubeshlieva was born in the town of Kyustendil in 1900. She finished secondary school in Sofia and began writing her first poems in the 1930's. Her early poems "Bread and Wine" and "Pagan Songs" are in the lyrical mood, whereas the later "Arrows," "Bridge," and "Street" treat some social themes, and the anxieties of life in the big city.

Similar subjects are dealt with in her short stories "Married People," "Down the Slope," and "At the Threshold." Her novels *Adverse Wind* and *Enemies* are a criticism of city life. Her novels *Brig on the Sea* and *Through a Needle's Eye* have been translated into Czech, and her book of short stories *Joys and Worries*, into Russian.

She has written about thirty books, including some for children: *The Little Negro Bigger, Our Dairy Farm, The Two Brother Bear Cubs.* A number of her poems, short stories and other works have been translated into many languages.

Maria Groubeshlieva is a Dimitrov Prize laureate, and she has been granted the title of Honored Cultural Worker.

Second-Hand Shop

In the large but stuffy shop, the smell of coffee, moth balls, and other scents hung in the air. Stray sunbeams that had managed to get past the imported dressing gowns, nylon slips, shawls, and pull-overs that decked the window, played on the walls, and were reflected on the polished surfaces of the guitars and mandolins that hung there. These chance reflections seemed to give the shop a still more bleak and gloomy aspect. To the left, behind the counter, hung lamé evening gowns, blouses embroidered with beads, transparent raincoats for men and women that gave the impression of hanged people. To

327

the right, were beetle-like brown and black vacuum cleaners, washing machines, and squared-off newly enameled refrigerators and electric ranges.

The young salesclerk behind the main counter clearly stood out in the semidarkness in her light blue white-collared uniform.

"Excuse me, miss."

"Which one? This red one? Two hundred and twenty leva."

The clerk quickly reached up, took down a leather bag hanging on a nail, and handed it to a plump young woman.

"And you, sir, have you decided about the razor? As you wish. The accordian costs three thousand two hundred leva. Yes, it's German."

Her light eyes scanned the articles and the hands and faces of the customers who pushed and craned their necks, elbowing their way to the counter piled with goods.

A tall, rather stout gentleman, with graying hair, stood aside, holding a big rectangular parcel, patiently waiting for the girl to free herself so as to offer her his merchandise. It got oppressively closer in the shop, and the mixture of various smells was choking him; besides, his own waterproof coat smelled strongly of rubber.

He loosened his tie and his elbow accidentally jolted a guitar that was hanging behind him. A faint ring filled the clammy air.

The girl asked him politely: "Why are you hanging back, sir? You have been waiting a long time!"

The man smiled and nodded pacifyingly, then as he turned to look at the guitar the plaster over a boil on his neck came off. He frowned, stood respectfully in the same place, and continued to wait.

However, the customers were in no hurry. They fussed about at the counter with nerve-wracking deliberation, handled the goods, asked questions, and as one group went out another came in.

The girl eyed the patient customer with surprise. When at last only two girls, who were choosing lipstick, were left, the man came awkwardly forward and began to unwrap his parcel. The clerk eyed him with curiosity. He was neatly dressed, with the casual elegance of a man who had once lived in luxury. His steel gray, cunning eyes, though somewhat faded, were sharp and self-confident.

"An old Viennese clock, a real antique," he said, placing the rectangular box on the counter, sighing with relief. "Every hour this little door here opens, and this little couple turns around three times to the melody of an old waltz. It is a wonderful thing, I am sorry to part with it."

The girl looked at the door and the minute ivory figures: a lady in a pink crinoline and a cavalier in white stockings and a white wig.

"It works, doesn't it?" she asked, running her thin fingers automatically over the smooth surface of the ebony clock, studded with mother-of-pearl around the dial, which had gold carved hands. "How much do you want for it?" She lowered her eyelids, and her lashes shaded half of her pale, peach-skin cheek.

"Four thousand, only four."

The girl lifted her eyes. "If I can get that price. Shall I write out a receipt?"

"Yes, do, and please sell it as soon as possible. I'm rather pressed . . ."

The girl started writing quickly and in a minute handed him the receipt.

"Keep calling. I'll place it here, where everybody can see it, below this Venetian mirror."

She lifted the clock and, stretching her arms, placed it on the shelf behind her. Her slim figure curved in at the waist.

The man swallowed and his eyes followed her hand which gracefully brushed the lock of fair hair that had fallen across her forehead. His eyes stopped on her open face, but suddenly he seemed to recover himself. He nervously stuffed the string from his parcel into his pocket and shifted his glance.

At that moment soft music was heard. The small door on the clock clicked and opened, and on the square platform in front of it the romantic couple turned freely. The astonished girl stared at the dancing figures.

"How wonderful!" she smiled, and her eyes smiled, too.

An elderly salesclerk came over from the other counter, and she, too, glued her eyes on the dancing couple.

"Oh, and how sweet the music is, isn't it?" the fair girl said and looked at the man sympathetically. "What a wonderful clock! Aren't you sorry to part with it, sir?"

The man shrugged his shoulders and replied dryly: "What can I do, my girl? There's no other way. I'm glad you like it, too. Good-bye. I'll keep calling, then."

And he walked quickly and somewhat guiltily to the door.

The two women studied his neck where the plaster had come off and the belt that hung on either side of his coat.

Next day, around noon, a small, elderly woman with thin black hair, so thin that the parting in the middle was like a white ribbon, came into the shop quietly as a bird. Her lusterless eyes were puffed and bluish, but they were warm, kind eyes—velvet soft. She stood in front of the salesgirl, out of breath, looking at the clock above the round Venetian mirror, and she asked in a German accent: "Excuse me, miss . . . when they have brought here my clock?" Her voice quavered as if it would break at any moment.

The girl shrugged her shoulders stupefied. "A gentleman brought it yesterday, madam. I didn't know."

The woman licked her dry lips and interrupted the girl with a kind smile: "My husband . . . I say nothing . . . it is his, after all, is it not? Please sell it not. I will bring receipt today. That clock for me a dear souvenir. Wedding present from my father. Please keep till tonight, will you?"

The girl looked at the lady warmly and attentively; she shrugged her shoulders again as if seeking advice from two customers who were looking at a gay Spanish shawl.

"Yes, madam, bring the receipt and I shall give it to you at once, don't worry."

The small woman folded her unbuttoned and rather worn coat about her, thanked the girl profusely and, with her small steps, quietly went out of the shop. The girl followed her with her eyes and then looked around at the clock behind her as if to make sure that it was still there.

"How upset she was, poor thing!" she said to the customer, as she took the shawl from her hands and put it in the box before her. "You find the shawl a bit expensive? But it's well worth the price. Too bad!"

The door kept opening and new customers kept coming in. The girl stooped and looked for what was wanted in the drawers of the counter and readily answered questions to the right and to the left, polite and smiling. Her straight, bright, golden hair darkened from moisture over her temples. The ladies who looked at the goods cast furtive glances at her and nudged each other: "Look how lovely she is, look! A real beauty!"

The girl was used to being liked and somehow wanted to thank the customers for being so delighted; she served them still faster and tried to be polite even with the most fussy shoppers.

Yet, she seemed to be far away from the shop. She kept looking at her cheap wrist watch. Vasko would come any moment now to see her off on the tram. She smiled at her thoughts. She always seemed to be in a hurry to get home. Yet she always let three or four trams go by until finally she would jump onto the already moving tram and wave good-bye to Vasko from the platform.

There were not many customers that day. She was even able to sit down for awhile on the chair behind the counter and dream about the color film starring Gerard Philippe that she and Vasko were going to see in the next few days. He had promised to find tickets at all costs. Nearly closing time! A few more minutes to one o'clock! And there he was, in his clean trench coat, with his clean-shaven face, standing in front of the window and looking at the small Swedish radio set. The girl smiled and looked out and her face brightened.

A deep male voice started her out of her dreams: "I'm asking you for the third time, miss! Why is the upper part of this pen loose? Is it broken?"

The girl smiled guiltily, took the pen from the hands of the customer, and tried to tighten it. Then, handing it to him, she said jokingly: "It doesn't need force but skill!"

The man looked at her with desire in his eyes and pretended that he couldn't close the pen; he purposely lingered before the beauty and wanted to stay a little longer in the shop. But she did not understand; she forgot that yesterday he had spent half an hour trying to put a flute together. How could she know that he had never touched a flute in his life!

She looked at her watch; it was one sharp.

"We're closing, sir. Will you take it? I'm sorry, but. . . ." Tired, she took off her uniform and stood there in her red-checkered rayon dress. The man placed the pen in front of her and began uncertainly: "I'll probably buy it tomorrow, Miss. Would you allow me . . . for quite a time now I have . . ."

But the door of the rectangular clock swung open, and the two dainty figures stood on the platform. The waltz beat its three-quarter time; the empty shop was filled with the soft, ringing music; the crinolined lady began to circle.

The man raised his eyes and looked at the wonderful clock. The door of the shop opened and Vasko stood by the counter—tall, sun-tanned, displaying two rows of white, regular teeth. He shook hands with the girl and casually made his way to her behind the counter. He even took her net bag with red peppers.

"What did you say, sir?" the girl asked the customer. "I didn't catch . . ."

But he did not want anything any more; he frowned at the young man, wiped his hands in his handkerchief and replied casually: "Tomorrow, I'll come tomorrow . . . for the pen."

Then he went out and stood in front of the window, pretending to look at the objects there.

INTRODUCTION TO BULGARIAN LITERATURE

The young couple started quickly toward the market hall, and he looked after the slim figure of the fair beauty. The young man walked close to her, holding the fingers of her free hand.

At that moment the customer felt someone tapping him on the shoulder.

A tall man stood before him and said breathlessly: "It seems that I've just missed the clerk!"

The other one smiled: "Have you come because of her, too? You know, Papazov, she pretends to be inaccessible, what do you think?"

"Oh, you!" Papazov waved his hand. "It isn't the girl at all. I have something for sale here, you know." And he peered through the window. "Yes, it's still there. I want it sold quickly because I'm in a bit of a tight spot."

The younger man took him by the arm and, bending close to him, whispered: "In Hungary things are going fine. It's a terrible business, I tell you! The workers in the plants are slaughtering the top Communists like so many chickens, like that!" he sawed the air with his hand. "A blood bath . . . things will change here, too, now . . ."

"Not so loud, not so loud!" Papazov nudged him, coughed loudly and looked around: "You do jabber a lot! It's all right for you, but do you know how I spent those seven months in there? I don't want to go in again. Who knows, though," he added, regretfully, because things might not end exactly as Lichev wanted them to. He carefully fingered the plaster over his boil and automatically straightened his collar.

"Look here," continued Lichev, "since our papers, too, admit that Minszenty will become prime minister and Count Esterhazy will get back half of Hungary . . ."

"They can give Esterhazy the whole of Hungary, dear boy, but you won't get your factory back. I don't want to live with illusions."

When a militiaman quietly passed by them, both men started, and saying "good-bye" quickly, they set off in different directions.

Papazov noticed great excitement in the streets and in the tram. People were talking and waving their hands. They denounced the barbarity of the rebels in Budapest. That they should turn such a beautiful town into ruins! There were others, too, who bent over, whispered quietly, and understood each other with looks.

"Great events are really taking place," Papazov thought,

troubled and joyful at the same time. Chills ran up his spine when he remembered the endless months behind bars. What for? For his foolishness in believing the empty promises of an empty-headed priest. Thank goodness that Ann backed his alibi then, thank goodness that she agreed to give false evidence. Papazov was deep in thought. No, no! He would never get mixed up in such a mess again! Especially now that he had managed to find work. That Lichev! He was convinced that the old order would come back. Well, let's hope so! Who turns his back on good luck! But he . . . he wouldn't put his head in any noose. Let things turn out as they would.

Papazov did not wait for the tram to come to a full stop, and in spite of his heavy figure jumped off neatly. He went a hundred paces and entered the wide entrance of the darkened apartment house, starting up the wide and comfortable stairs. The walls were scratched with pencil and chalk; here and there he saw names scratched with a penknife. He knitted his brows involuntarily when he remembered the onetime clean entrance of the apartment house. Once upon a time only he and his wife and child lived on the first floor.

He panted up the few steps and went into the living room which now resembled a furniture store. They had put lodgers in every one of his rooms, and each boarder had put some piece of unwanted furniture in the living room. There was a wardrobe, a green kitchen cupboard, a cooking range, and even a white rocking horse. Almost every night Papazov bumped into this pile of furniture when he crossed from the living room to the bathroom in the dark.

The living room smelled of onion stew. "That slattern is cooking," he said to himself, thinking about the young bride living in the room with the bay window, his onetime dining room.

Upon entering his own room he found his wife in tears again. She sat at one end of the couch, with her feet tucked below her dressing gown, whining like a cat.

"Stop it!" he shouted and threw up his hands in disgust. "If you want that silly clock so much, here is the receipt, go and get it. Since you've made a laughingstock of me in the shop."

He nervously began to fumble in his small breast pocket.

"Go and get it and then get the food cans ready for prison; you have plenty of experience already . . ."

He handed the blue receipt to her, his hand trembling, but she pushed it away and began to blow her nose. Papazov went on trying to put the receipt in her hand, quite sure that she wouldn't take it.

"Go on, take it!" he insisted. "It'll be even better for me. I'll know one thing. I won't have to tremble every day that there might be a checkup, that an overdraft might be discovered in my accounts, or something or other. Look here, Lotte! I'll go and give myself up! I'll tell them that two people can hardly live on six hundred leva. There, get your clock back and live with your memories!"

The woman got up quickly, blew her nose again, and went to the other end of the room. "Look here, Sava, understand. You've already sold everything and I am not cross. But the clock, the clock . . . souvenir of happiest years. And you know what pains in stomach . . ."

Papazov coughed spitefully. "How couldn't she have learned to speak the language correctly in twenty years!" he thought as he lit a cigarette, comfortably sitting in the dirty, raspberry-colored armchair. Opposite him, in a flyblown frame and slightly tilted to one side a picture by Veshin had survived. Below it was a picture of Lotte, a wonderful thirteen-year-old girl, taken on the day of her confirmation. Her rabbit mouth disclosed large, overlapping teeth. She reminded him of his ten-year-old daughter, Virginia, who had been killed by the bombs. Sorrow gripped his heart which had hardened after the tragic death of the child.

Papazov sighed, turned his head and, in order to blunt his sorrow, said: "Come on, Lotte, let me have something to eat, I'm dying!" He stared at his fingers yellow from tobacco and followed the smoke rings creeping up the velvet curtain. "Do you know what's happening in Hungary?"

While she was laying the table he quickly told her what he had heard from Lichev. Lotte gasped and exclaimed and asked him whether these events would have any consequences here as well. A comparative peace pervaded her small world. Was it possible that this peace would be broken, that her husband would be in some sort of danger again, after she had become resigned, long ago, to the privations and even to his growing indifference?

"I'm not a fortuneteller, how should I know! It would be wonderful! This red plague has raged long enough. What about those idiots, the students, have they paid their electric bill or do I have to pay it again?"

"They haven't," said Lotte timidly. "But today I not let them use my hot plate." She pressed her stomach with her hand and frowned.

"That's right, why should they! Don't let them have anything any more! Let them get out of my house!"

Lotte ate without any appetite, occasionally doubling up with pain, and furtively looking at her husband.

When he stopped talking she asked him quietly: "What if you not get that price for . . . ?"

"I hope to get it," he said, breaking a couple of green walnuts in the palm of his hand and beginning to peal them.

"What if a checkup come before?" Lotte asked again, quietly, almost inaudibly.

"What if? What if? Stop it! Only questions. How should I know!"

The woman recoiled, fell silent, and after awhile went to the kitchen to get some water. He looked at her impersonal figure in the beige-green dressing gown, swallowed, frowned, and thought: "A moth! A real moth! Insignificant and quiet as a moth!"

For a moment he imagined her as she had been when he first met her at a reception in Vienna. He was military attaché then, and Lotte had just come back from her Paris boarding school looking like a fairy in her white net dress. The daughter of a factory owner, she had the best of candidates, but she had chosen him. But then she couldn't help choosing him. He was young, interesting—the Viennese girls were mad about him. He tested her feelings. He used to say: "In Bulgaria the women weave rugs and bake their own bread." He scared her; he wanted to hear that she loved him all the time, that she preferred him to all the rest. And she answered with a smile: "All right! I'll weave rugs and I'll bake bread as well!"

But her life in Bulgaria was not good. The smart general staff officer soon had enough of her and got mixed up in many love affairs. Lotte cried, nagged, and threatened she would go back to her country. But that was long ago. Later, she could not even threaten that she would leave him, because the only other member of her family, her father, committed suicide, and Sava lost the faint hope that she would one day carry out her threats. Their daughter, Virginia, was killed in the ruins of the school Sancta Maria. Then came the spy trial. They kept Sava for quite a few months in the preliminary hearings. The worries and the fears. At the time of the trial she was taken to the hospital and had an ulcer operation; when she came home she found Sava out of prison.

Lotte came back from the kitchen with a jug in her hand and found her husband stretched out on the couch, puffing lightly and snoring now and then. She put her cardigan over his chest and curled up at the end of the couch again. Her face, usually an ashy gray, was purple from crying and her disheveled hair stuck to her tear-streaked cheeks. The dishes were still on the table. She did not dare make a noise, fearing she would wake her husband. There was still something left of her onetime doglike loyalty to him.

When the porter knocked at their door for his money, Lotte gently pushed him into the sitting room and whispered: "Please come later. Now he rest!"

When he heard Papazov snoring, the porter smiled and went out on tiptoe.

When Papazov went to the second-hand shop two days later at noon, the clerk was not very polite.

"Nobody is interested in your clock, sir, except your own wife. I don't dare offer it either, because I'm waiting for her to come and fetch it."

Papazov smiled sadly, sighed, and leaned a bit tragically on the counter. "Look here, miss, I haven't told my wife how things are really. She is very ill with an ulcer. She must go abroad for an operation, but what about money? Which is dearer, the clock or her health? Right now she is in the hospital again."

He spoke clearly and straightforwardly, like a child, and finally even she grew sad. "Can you imagine," he continued, the same sad note in his voice, "I had to promise her that one day I would buy the clock back, so that she wouldn't be sorry for it. And I am sure that I shall never be able to do it in spite of my most sincere wishes."

The girl looked at him warmly and with interest.

"So I am to sell it. All right. Then I can tell you that a foreign diplomat liked it, but he offered only two thousand and eight hundred."

Papazov became thoughtful. He shook his head and threw up his hands helplessly: "If there is no other offer I'll have to agree."

"You have a very nice wife," said the girl with bitterness in her voice. "I did hope you could fix your affairs some other way so that she could keep her clock. I'm so sorry for her, poor thing!"

Papazov threw up his hands again with a still more tragic expression on his face.

The girl looked at him and said anxiously: "You know, the man is a regular customer. Call me up tomorrow at noon."

At about ten in the morning, the bookkeeper of the co-operative where Papazov worked called him from the next room and said in a sour voice: "A strange woman wants you on the phone. She is rather excited."

Papazov thought that they were ringing up from the hospital and quickly passed by the clerks.

The girl was on the phone.

"I've fixed everything, Mr. Papazov. The customer was firm at first, but then he paid a little more, so now you will get about three thousand three hundred levas. You can come and get the money at once. You know where, don't you? Yes, yes . . . the second floor."

After work, Papazov decided to go and see the girl. At first he thought of buying her some sort of present, for she had got him nearly five hundred leva more, but then he decided against it: "She might be offended. He would simply thank her now and another time."

There were many people in the shop, and he quickly uttered a few words of thanks. The girl sent her regards to his wife and saw him off with a smile. It was getting close to seven, and the customers began leaving the shop one after another. Papazov left, too. At that moment Lichev came around the corner, holding two black roses.

"Oho! What about your clock?" he asked, strongly smelling of wine. "It's a pity, really, it was a lovely thing. It was only last night I learned that it was yours. How is your wife? I have not seen her for a long time."

Papazov frowned. "Don't ask . . . cares and worries . . . she must have an operation again. Three-quarters of her stomach is out already, and now again . . . doctors, injections . . . I took her to the hospital the other day."

"That's life," Lichev sighed and gently looked at his roses. "It's easier for me . . . I'm alone." And he winked cunningly.

"So you're still at it," Papazov gave a knowing nod. "You're wasting your time—the girl has a boyfriend—a technician in a machine-building plant."

"Well," Lichev gave an oily smile, "it depends on the force of the argument."

Suddenly Papazov burst into hoarse laughter. "Are the two roses your argument? Look, if you still had your factory. And if you were at least twenty years younger!"

Lichev took it badly and thumped his old friend on the shoulder: "You mind your own business. Your old pal isn't headed for the scrap heap yet! And here," he smacked his pocket, "there is still something left. Let things be. And you see I was right? Budapest is in ruins! Nothing is left of the town of our youth. Do you remember, Sava, what fiery Hungarians we were in love with then?"

Papazov sighed and asked very quietly: "They say that the Soviet Army has withdrawn completely. Is it true?"

"They do, they do," Lichev laughed. "But what more there is to come! Get your uniform ready! So long, now."

He looked at his roses again and shook hands with his friend: "We'll wait and see. *Servus!*" *

Papazov brightened and tried to remember what Lotte had asked him to bring her on the following day. "Yes, a towel and some soap!" As he went off he saw Lichev through the window, gazing at the fair girl. "Fool!" he thought, and set off quickly along the street.

After he had gone, the girl issued a receipt to an elderly lady for a tapestry in a rectangular gilt frame and reached up to put it in the place of the antique clock. Then she took off her uniform, put some lipstick on, and quickly combed her hair with a big, yellow comb. It was five to seven. Vasko would be coming any moment now. He told her over the phone that morning that he had managed to get tickets for the evening.

When he saw her alone at the counter, Lichev stood in front of her and gave her the flowers with a gallant flourish.

"I take the liberty of offering you these roses!" he said, stuttering a little, because the wine he had drunk in the pub had gone to his head in the stuffy shop.

The girl did not take them. He faltered for a moment and then lightly placed the roses before her.

"From my garden. I have a lovely garden in Krasno Selo."

The girl gazed at the beautiful flowers, deliberating what to do. She did not notice Vasko, who had come in and was standing a bit to the side. Lichev did not see him either, because his eyes were on the girl.

At last she looked at the customer, knitted her brows, and said dryly: "Look here, mister! Take your flowers. I'm only an ordinary employee, a salesclerk, and I wouldn't . . ."

"Well," Lichev interrupted her with an oily smile, "you sell and sell only second-hand things . . . but you yourself are the best bargain in this shop . . . a thing which unfortunately is not for sale!"

As the girl drew her breath in indignation and bent forward to answer, Vasko stood up before Lichev and gave his coat lapel such a strong jerk that one button flew off and fell to the floor. Two

* Good-bye in Hungarian.

clerks from the other counters ran over and stood ready behind Vasko.

"Scum!" muttered Vasko. "Not everything in here is for sale, but everything has to be paid for!"

Lichev stepped back and bumped into the mandolin on the wall. It gave a hideous ring and crashed to the floor. It was then that the girl understood what was happening; she screamed in fright and picked up the mandolin to see whether it had been broken.

One of the clerks took Lichev by the sleeve, while he was puffing, looked at the place where the button had come off, and coaxed him out of the shop. The girl gripped Vasko's hand and pulled him behind the counter.

Out on the street she burst into tears: "Why did you pounce on him like that? I could have got rid of him myself. A good thing that the scoundrel left . . . Oh, Vasko, Vasko . . . look, we'll be late for the movie."

The boy gripped her elbow gently: "I can't go along with you, Donka!"

"Why not? Didn't you say . . ." She looked at him, her eyes full of tears.

"I must stand sentry tonight! You know, Donka. Now, with these events, anything might happen and our people . . . like that one you didn't let me punch in the nose."

The girl pressed closer to him: "Will you be alone on guard?"

"No, usually there are two sentries. Why, are you afraid? Everything is quiet here, but we must, just in case. Isn't that so? I have the tickets. You'll go by yourself. I'll come and pick you up at twelve—the second part of the film ends then and I'll be relieved at twelve. Then I'll see you home."

Clutching the wad of bank notes in his pocket with one hand and holding onto the backs of the seats with the other, Papazov made his way through the crowd in the tram. When he reached the stop and got off, the street swarmed with people who were talking excitedly about the football game that had just ended.

Papazov turned off along Evlogi Georgiev Street and looked round when he stopped before the iron fence of the yard shaded by trees. He quickly checked the wad in his pocket, then the ten hundred-leva bills in the innermost compartment of his wallet, and looked at the only illuminated window of the small house that was the window of Ann's room.

On entering, Papazov banged the wad of money angrily on the table.

"Rogues, Ann! When they see that a man is hard up they simply rob him! They say they sold it for one thousand eight hundred and what with the taxes . . . I've simply been robbed! Such a valuable antique!" He wiped the sweat off his forehead and stood in the middle of the room.

The tall, dark woman with thick, converging eyebrows frowned a little, came forward, put her hands on his shoulders and said in a throaty, contralto voice: "Never mind, thank you, darling! You acted like a gentleman! I'll pay this much, and I'll manage somehow to put off for the rest."

He put his arms around her waist and then ran his hands over her rounded shoulders.

Ann wriggled out of his arms, giggled coquettishly, and then asked in a matter-of-fact voice: "So, how much did you say?"

"Exactly one thousand six hundred and thirty."

She took the money, deliberated whether to count it or not, then put it in the drawer of the table and pointed to the armchair.

"Sit down, Sava! You will have some cognac, won't you? Have some candies. Do! They're quite fresh." She placed a box of multicolored candies on the table in front of him and stopped to take out the bottle of cognac from the sideboard.

The lace of her slip showed through her pink nylon blouse and further up the pearl button of her bra shone. She looked like a young schoolgirl in her short black skirt. Thick red hair fell in big waves over her back.

"What lovely hair!" he thought and remembered Lotte. "Ann, I forgot to tell you that Lotte had an operation today."

Ann quickly turned round, glass in hand. "Is that so? And how is she?"

Papazov took the glass. "The nurse rang up. She told me to speak with the doctor, but when I tried to contact him he was on rounds."

"Cheers!" said Ann and touched glasses with Sava, staring at him with her slightly set apart, doll-like eyes, with fans of fine wrinkles around them. "Her health!" she added, and sipped at the cognac.

Then she took a couple of candies and with her cheek comically bulging, said gaily: "How näive she is, poor thing! To tell you the truth, in her place I wouldn't have believed you so easily about having an overdraft. First of all, I'd have wanted to know why you had drawn that money out."

Papazov smiled and thought of the hundred-leva bills stored away in his wallet.

"It wasn't all that easy, you know. She cried a lot."

"Why don't you ring up and ask how she is? What was the number? Shall I dial it for you?"

Papazov became thoughtful. After all, it did not seem right to ask about his wife from the house of his mistress.

"No, don't. As it is, I'll be going home tonight. I'll ring up from my place. When will your contractor be coming?"

"It's nearly eight now. He said at half-past." Ann looked at the clock on the wall. "When I see him off I'm going straight to bed. You know how strenuous these last few days have been!"

"Well, everything is fine, now!" he sighed. "Though only half of it, but still! A good thing that there was that diplomat to buy it! Nobody wanted it. When will your apartment be ready?"

"I'll move in the spring. This is the last installment. Oh, Sava, when I come to think of it, what would I have done if you hadn't helped me? Oh, dear, what's the matter with you? You have a new boil coming, on your cheek now."

He fingered it. "Yes, I'm beginning to feel the pain . . . never mind . . ."

Ann sat opposite him, her legs crossed, greedily breathing in the cigarette smoke, gracefully flicking the ashes into the crystal ashtray. There was dark down above her upper lip.

"You've got down all over you . . . like a devil butterfly," he murmured caressingly and reached over to pat her knee. "Your hair is so thick . . . a real jungle."

Papazov noticed her quick look at the clock on the wall, which pointed to eight sharp.

"Shall we go to the nightclub tomorrow?" she asked with a pretended, childish desire. "Tonight we'll have a good long sleep and we'll be fresh. I'll hand in the hats I've finished tomorrow, and I'll rest the whole day."

He looked at the three dummies with ladies' hats, arranged in the corner on the counter among piles of multicolored material.

"Isn't that gray one your model?"

"Yes, it is, you do remember! My model. The customer liked it on me and ordered the same."

"But she'd need to have ordered a head like yours, too," Papazov flattered her. Ann laughed deep in her throat and once more looked at the clock.

Papazov caught her glance again and got up.

"Well, I'll be off. You don't seem to care about having the contractor meet me here, do you?"

"Why? Stay if you wish! But he'll only gossip afterward!"

She, too, got up, and Papazov quickly kissed her forehead, her cheeks, and her lips.

In the passage he met a young man with a black mustache and thought: "The contractor . . . but didn't she tell me that he was old?" Then he heard Ann's voice welcoming him.

Papazov stopped at the door and hesitated, but finding no excuse to go back he continued through the yard. The sand crunched under his feet, and he did not hear Ann open the window. Her voice made him start.

"Sava," she said with a smile, "when you get in touch with the hospital, give me a ring to tell me how she is, won't you?"

He stopped, unable at first to understand her question and then replied politely: "Yes, yes of course."

He waved good-bye to her and thought: "You can't say that she isn't kind." He turned to look at her once again, but she had disappeared from the open window. "But why, after all, did she deceive me about the contractor being an old man?"

He walked deep in thought and found himself in front of the local restaurant.

He went in intending to have a quick meal, but an old friend of his was there and ordered a pint of wine, filling Papazov's glass as well. They touched glasses and drank to old times, and then they both kept refilling their glasses. Papazov complained bitterly to his schoolmate: how he had spent seven months in prison during the preliminary hearings; he even told him that "a very noble lady" (he didn't mention Ann) had saved him then, and he mentioned among other things that his wife had had an operation that day; finally, both of them began to discuss the Hungarian events.

Papazov's eyes became filmy from the wine; it was almost ten o'clock. They both got up.

"My wife and daughters will be coming back from the movies and they haven't got a key," groaned the friend, and Papazov went to see him off. It turned out that his friend lived next door to Ann.

His friend was lost in the entrance of the big apartment house and Papazov stared at Ann's dark window. Just as he was thinking that she was fast asleep, the light suddenly went on in her room. At first, Papazov was pleased. She was awake, wasn't she complaining of insomnia all the time? "Why shouldn't I go up and have a chat!"

But he remembered that he had to ask about Lotte before midnight. He hesitated a few seconds and began walking back and forth by the gate. He looked at the window again but saw that it was dark once more. An unpleasant feeling came over him. What was going on up there?

He decided to go up to Ann's and find out when he heard hollow steps in the overgrown yard. Some twigs cracked. Somebody had got caught in the briar. A tall man stopped at the gate, clicked his lighter, and his face, with a thin, dark mustache and a cigarette stuck in his mouth, was illuminated. Then he looked around suspiciously and set off with a firm, sure step along the street.

"The contractor!" Papazov told himself and stood motionless. Then he spat angrily. Now he knew for sure that that could not be the contractor and leaned heavily against the fence.

"I'll go up and wring her neck," he said aloud, feeling a sharp pain below his stomach. "And I'll get my money back! Vile and treacherous snake. So that's whom she was waiting for, that's why she kept looking at the clock so often . . . faithless viper . . ."

A large raindrop hit his nose. There was a smell of ozone in the sultry evening air. Papazov still couldn't leave the fence. "I'll ask her for my money, too . . . but what if she says: 'Was that a small favor I did you then, my friend? Do you know how long you stay in prison for perjury?' Yes, she was sure to say that. He had better go away and be quick about it. We're even. I've paid her off for the favor."

A second, a third raindrop fell on his face. A wind blew up. A window banged nearby. Papazov began to move and looked into the yard. Ann's window remained dark, closed and impenetrable. The moon, chased by a herd of white clouds, raced across the sky. Then, it suddenly sank into a fluffy avalanche of clouds and then came the downpour.

Papazov wore only a hat and jacket. He pulled his collar up and his hat down and quickly made for home. He had sobered quite unexpectedly. Was it because of what he had experienced or from the cold shower of the rain? He pounded down the street. A young girl in a blue transparent raincoat hurried in front of him, her feet wobbling on her high heels. The raincoat rustled in the wind, blowing out like a balloon, while the rain splashed hollowly against it.

When Papazov entered his room, soaking wet, he found the blanket on his bed drenched. He had forgotten to close the window when he went out.

"I'll sleep on Lotte's bed," he thought and patted the other bed. The damp air and the smell of walnut-tree leaves came in through the open window. Now he had a headache from all the wind and dampness. He went to the sideboard and poured the last of the brandy into a water glass. He drank it slowly, thoughtfully, in sips, and sat down wet as he was in the armchair. He closed his eyes and sat there a long time without thinking about anything. When he opened his eyes he noticed a slight steam rising from his knees. "I'll catch cold," he thought, and got up to change clothes.

The telephone rang out quietly and brokenly. Papazov started and quickly picked up the receiver.

"Yes, yes, I had asked them to ring me up, but I wasn't at home. Doctor Levchev? Hello! I rang you up twice today but you were on rounds. Yes? What's that?" Papazov sat down in the armchair, tired.

"I'm ready to hear anything. Is she dead? No? Thank goodness! Yes, I can take it, of course . . ." He listened with a strained face, his eyebrows knitted, as if he had frozen to the armchair in his wet clothes. Then he asked in a voice that was not his own:

"So they closed her immediately. What does that mean? Are you sure? None of us suspected anything of the sort. So there is no hope? Well, I won't give way. Thank you. So, she'll be out in a week. Oh dear, what a misfortune. Yes, I'll remember. Good-bye. I'll come round early tomorrow morning."

Papazov replaced the receiver noiselessly. Nothing mattered any more now. Yes, yes, he would be able to keep it from her . . . let her believe that everything will be all right from now on.

Papazov looked out through the window. How the wind tossed and bent the branches of the old walnut tree! He listened to the rain pattering on the window panes, and through the irregular splash of the streams of water he occasionally heard the clatter of the tram making a right turn. The sky was yellow. The moon shone beneath the clouds.

The brandy he had drunk had completely dulled him. He had a vacant look. Suddenly he noticed the rectangular white spot on the wall where the Viennese clock had hung many a long year. Papazov began to sing quietly, inaudibly. Maybe he was not singing, but he could hear the soft strains of the waltz which year after year had counted off the happy and bitter hours of his life. He began to cry. The tears ran down his cheeks and chin in wide streams and dropped to his jacket.

He was not crying about Ann's disloyalty—to hell with her! —nor for Lotte who was doomed. He grieved for everything that was going away with them, for himself, for his own peace. The room was empty and as untidy as it had been when he had taken

Lotte to the hospital. Lotte had never been a good housewife. In spite of that, he had always been able to rely on her to iron his shirts and to cook a meal, though it was always tasteless and saltless. Now he would have to eat at a canteen or make the round of the restaurants, as Lichev did. And the disorder at home would grow and grow, and there was no salvation! He could not go to Ann's any more and sit in her tidy room, and relax in the armchair. That low character with the mustache would probably make himself comfortable there.

Hatred overwhelmed him, and from the dregs of that hatred a dull, and hardly suppressible feeling began to grow: he wanted to jump and scream and break the few things that were left in this room.

Suddenly, thoughts about Ann crept into his brain. He seemed to see her again in the window frame, leaning on her elbows, smiling, kind: "When you get in touch with the hospital give me a ring and tell me how she is!" Base vermin—pretending to be sorry for Lotte! She wanted to find out what his mood was and whether he suspected anything. While he, the fool, fell for it, and calmly went to eat meatballs!

He suddenly got up and picked up the receiver. Hadn't she asked him to call her up? He dialed the number and when he heard her deep, throaty voice, he shouted harshly: "Now I know that you are a base woman. That's all I wanted to tell you."

He heard an inaudible and vague exclamation over the line and immediately banged down the receiver.

At that moment, the wind outside wildly tore a branch off the walnut tree. It fell and crashed on the roof of the garden shed.

Papazov jumped. No! He could not stay in this room any longer. He would go out and take a breath of fresh air. Let the wind blow at him, let the rain beat him . . . He put on his overcoat and went down the stairs. Standing in the entrance, he looked about the street. The rain had stopped, but the water noisily drained away in the gutter. Papazov set off aimlessly. He found himself near the Zoo. The sad and lonely roar of a lion completely set his nerves on edge, and he started along the tramlines. Then he ran after a tram, jumped onto it, and soon found himself by the Mosque.

He saw a crowd of people and wondered where they were coming from. The bright advertisement of the Macedonia Theater for "The Red and the Black" reminded him that the performance had just ended. "I had promised Lotte to take her to see this film, and now see what happened," he said to himself, and instead of feeling sorry, his hatred increased. The people buzzed around him, talking loudly. He started off among them with the hope that further down along Zhdanov Street he would find the solitude he sought, and from far off he saw the illuminated window of the second-hand shop. Like a night moth drawn by the light, he automatically made for it. He did not want to think about anything; he wanted to walk and walk till he fell from fatigue and went to sleep wherever he was, even if it were on the street itself.

The brandy and the several pints of wine he had drunk with his friend in the pub dulled his brain even more. The lampposts rocked before his eyes. When he reached the window of the second-hand shop, it seemed to him that a slim, tall woman hid in the entrance to the cinema.

Papazov stood in front of the lighted window and stared. Yes, there was the radio—it hadn't been sold yet. There was the big doll, too, with the ringlets, which a young woman had left in the shop once. There, too, was the electric shaver belonging to a student who hadn't succeeded in graduating in Prague.

Papazov leaned on the wall next to the window, his legs trembling.

"I'll go and strangle her," he thought. Hadn't she been satisfied that because of her apartment he had sold the blue carpet from his sitting room, Lotte's pearls . . . treacherous and avaricious woman! It was because of her that he had stooped so low as to sell his goods in the shop.

Then Papazov remembered Lichev's words, "Get your uniform ready!" Oh, if only that time would come! How would he wring the neck of that good-for-nothing woman. How he would make her crawl at his feet!

He saw the tall woman come out of the theater-way and wave to somebody on the other side. A slim girl, with fair hair, down to her shoulders. Papazov got up, gazed at the pretty, longish face and was dumbfounded: it was Donka, the fair salesclerk! A bright, forgotten feeling touched him. As she passed by him her elbow nearly brushed against him, but she was looking ahead and did not recognize him.

Papazov saw that Vasko, the technician from the plant, was coming toward her quickly, the lapels of his wet trench coat flapping. His warm feeling disappeared immediately. An inexplicable fear of the girl took hold of him. He quickly went into an entrance and hid in the shadows.

The young man stopped by the girl, out of breath, took her in his arms and cried joyfully: "Was I late, Donka? I'm sorry. I have wonderful news for you."

The girl, who was tired of waiting, looked at him distrust-fully. Vasko kissed her on the cheek and held her away from himself.

"The Hungarian counterrevolution is over! A new government has been formed in Hungary—a Communist one. Our reactionaries will dream of millet again as hungry hens do." *

Papazov, who had caught every word, swallowed painfully. He was offended and disgusted at the joy of these two young people. He felt that they were the ones who were hindering his life, that it was because of them that he would be forced to carry on his old hard lot, like a tortoise its shell, to go to the pawnshop and sell everything down to the last needle in his bare house, even the coat on his back.

"That's wonderful!" Donka cried, but her words were drowned by the rumble of a car passing noisily along the adjoining street. Then she stood on tiptoe, put her arms around the young man, and began kissing him with abandon.

Papazov pressed back against the wall so as not to be seen. His envy at the happiness of these young people replaced the fine feeling of gratitude toward the young girl, which up to yesterday had burned in his heart. Everything in him now brimmed over with hatred. Hidden in the dark entrance, he didn't dare move. The street was completely deserted, and nobody disturbed them; he had become an involuntary witness to their endless kissing.

Raindrops fell on Papazov's shoulders from the drainpipe. He moved aside, but one drop fell on his bare neck, and he shivered from the cold. Unexpectedly, the girl saw him and whispered: "Let's go."

They set off, arm in arm, toward the tram stop, firmly pressed against each other.

In spite of his hatred for them, it seemed to him that life itself was going away. What was he going to do from now on? Where would he go? Home, in the deserted house, where Lotte would come back tomorrow to wander like a shadow between the room and the kitchen. And when she disappeared—he knew that day wasn't far off—what then?

Papazov looked up and down the deserted street and, feeling an unbearable burden on his heart, he dragged his feet homeward.

Translated by ROUMYANA ATANASSOVA

* A hungry hen dreams of millet—Bulgarian proverb.

Bogomil Rainov

(1919–   )

Bogomil Rainov was born in 1919 in Sofia. His father was a professor in the history of art. Bogomil Rainov majored in philosophy at Sofia University.

He has published the following books: *Poems* (1941); *Love Calendar* (1942); *A Journey into the Weekday*, a novel (1946); *The Man at the Corner*, short stories (1958); *A Rainy Evening*, short stories; *Night Boulevards*, short stories and poems.

Rush Hour

A quarter past six. The traffic jam along Boulevard Magenta had reached its peak. It was just the turn of the city tide, when people fled from downtown, from the dank offices, from the concrete cages of office buildings. Thousands of cars crowded along the main thoroughfares to slink off toward the quiet residential districts or distant suburbs.

The traffic jam started in the boulevards. The red lights would flash up at the corners so as to let the cars from the side streets pass. But the stream of cars barely managed to get started before the lights changed and it would be the boulevards' turn. The whole swarm of cars would rumble into first gear and be set in jerky motion. One minute, two minutes. Then the red light would flash on once more, and again the swarm of cars would stand motionless in clouds of bluish smoke.

From his high driver's box Claude could see the entire congested street. The cars rushed like an avalanche down the steep incline of the Faubourg Saint-Denis, and for a brief second he felt they would crash one over the other, fall to pieces on the boulevard, and block it right up to the top floors of the buildings.

Claude glanced at the clock above the steering wheel. Fifteen minutes late. Fifteen so far, probably twice that by the time he reached the last stop. That would mean more trouble with the inspector. At first, when he was new on the job, he used to grumble and try to excuse himself.

"Why, d'you think I invented traffic jams?"

But they always cut him short: "If you're in Paris, you'll have to put up with traffic jams. If you can't, go back to Lyons."

Actually why not go to Lyons or anywhere else, for that matter? It didn't matter much, if it weren't for the old woman.

The file of cars was closer now. A small space opened up before the bus. Claude shifted into first gear and slowly stepped on the gas. Just then an open sport Simca overtook him on the left and darted into the empty space. He took his foot off the gas, let in the clutch and unclutched again. There was a woman in the Simca. Of course. Fools like her would wedge themselves in anywhere—no rules for them. The driver looked with irritation at the woman's careful hairdo and her neatly shaved neck. He suddenly wished his arm were three times its normal length so as to be able to give that arrogant neck a good slap.

The green light was on at the corner. Claude made ready to let in the clutch. A hopeless business. Before the first cars got started and those after them followed suit—before the whole line of traffic got moving—the red light would come on again.

That is just what happened. Still, the lines made some headway and Claude advanced fifteen meters. The stop was near by, beyond the red light. Just when the way would be less congested, the bus would have to stop to discharge passengers. And before he could start it would be congested again.

The driver leaned on the steering wheel and tried to think about something else. He had a good view of the whole street from his glass cabin. A long time ago, in the early days, he enjoyed sitting so high up and driving this great big machine which made the cars look like cockroaches. He would turn the steering wheel to the left and right with bold, sweeping motions of the arms, overtake the cockroaches, and take up a convenient position before them. Let the cockroaches watch out; it was up to them to take care, he wasn't afraid of their smashing the bus.

Then one day Claude lightly grazed a little Renault. Just grazed it because it had wedged itself right under his very nose and he hadn't been able to stop short. There was a crunching sound like that of a shell breaking, and the back part of the car was suddenly gone, crushed like a paper bag. Even before he realized what had happened, a crowd gathered around his cabin. Two policemen dragged a frightened, fat gentleman from the car. Red faces belched forth insults and abuse.

"How much longer will such sadists be allowed to drive and get off scot-free?" a skinny old woman shouted.

"Get that beast of a man down!" the skinny old lady's husband urged, pointing to Claude with a long French loaf.

There followed endless arguments with inspectors, fines, and court inquiries. When Claude finally took his seat behind the steering wheel again, he was almost paralyzed with fear. The bus no longer seemed to him a safe machine, but a strange creature with an unbridled will of its own which might any minute rush upon the crowd on the pavement or a fragile car. That day the roadway from Vincennes to Clignancourt seemed to him very long indeed. It seemed endless, longer even than that terrible Algerian highway his military truck had slithered along with Rommel's artillery raising fountains of sand all about him. When he reached the end station, the sweat was pouring down his face, and his shirt, drenched with perspiration, was sticking to his back.

"What about a drink?" asked Léon, the conductor.

Then on seeing his face, he cried: "Why, what's the matter with you, old man? You don't mean to kick the bucket, do you?"

But all that soon passed. Claude now drove his bus without fear but also without any pleasure. He began work with indifference and waited for the moment when he'd find it revolting. It would come after the first few hours. An unpleasant metallic taste would gather in his stomach, and his head would be completely befogged. He would feel sick.

"It's because of the gasoline," Claude thought to himself. "The burned gas. The other one is pleasant, it has a nice smell."

The fumes really were poisoning his lungs. The cars crowded around the bus and gave out a stench of gray vapors. Sometimes he would shut the window, but then the cabin would fill with a still more horrid smell of burned oil.

Even now he was feeling sick. He raised the window, then shut it again. Perhaps it wasn't only because of the fuel. The weather had something to do with it, too: foul weather, looking like rain all day and not getting around to it. Wet-looking, leaden clouds hung low above the sheet-iron roofs. The summer afternoon looked more like an autumn evening. Here and there one could see a cheerless yellow bulb casting a dim light through a window. The city looked smokier than ever, old and ugly like a worn soiled garment.

Claude unbuttoned his collar, leaned back, and sighed. Forever that red light. The familiar sense of exhaustion and complete hopelessness came over him. He felt that the traffic jam would never end and that he would sit there forever immobile in that motionless crowd.

At long last there was a stir. The driver let in the clutch and got started almost when the cars ahead of the bus did. One must always stick very close to the cars in front; otherwise, the minute you make ever so little room, some cheeky clod is sure to displace you. Claude slowed down at the street crossing, raised the right traffic signal, waited a minute for a little space to clear before him and, pressing the steering wheel with both hands, brought the bus to a stop right by the curbstone.

"Gare de l'Est section!" Léon's voice announced from behind.

"If we start at once," Claude thought, "I'll manage to make at least twenty meters more. But we shan't start."

He could hear Léon arguing with the passengers: "I said only five. The bus is full up. That's that, Monsieur. Do you see, that's that!" The gentleman grumbled out something unintelligible, probably explaining he wasn't just anybody. Léon, greatly irritated, tugged away at the strap of the signal bell.

"You may ring for all you're worth," Claude said to himself. "You don't expect me to drive over the roofs of the cars, do you?"

Léon had an easy time of it. Of course, he did stand all day long, but time went much faster. And above all, he wasn't alone. He argued with people about the fares, gave now this, now that lady a smile, quarreled with passengers at the entrance, and so time flew. But Claude sat cooped up in his cabin all alone. He was always alone, even when he was not in the cabin. He sometimes told himself he must really do something about it and stop being like that. At other times he thought it was no use. Probably everyone—all of us— shared the same fate. A sentence, a remnant of his school days, recurred to him: man is born and dies in solitude. It really must be so. He had felt it for the first time at Dunkirk.

He could not get Dunkirk out of his mind. He had only to shut his eyes to draw a mental picture of the wide, wet beach left by the low tide and of the thousands of little figures running toward the sea. Then suddenly the air would grow thick and heavy—it was the noise of the planes' motors. The first German Stukas rent the air with their sinister wail. There followed the thundering explosions. Claude could no longer see anything. He lay on the beach, face down, mechanically clawing at the sand. He was weighed down by a wild longing to diminish in size, to disappear into the earth, the deeper the better. There was nothing in his head but "it's over." And he was alone, horribly alone. And every one of the thousands lying all about him was alone.

The driver passed his hand over his face and looked at the street once more. After the memory of Dunkirk, the scene struck him as being less repulsive. It was always like that. Claude had noticed it and made use of it. Whenever he felt particularly blue he would shut his eyes and remember Dunkirk. He knew that later, when he opened his eyes, the present would seem less awful. Almost bearable.

See, even the green light was on. Sluggishly, row after row, the column got going. So did Claude. He tried to keep up a distance of a span or two between himself and the cars before him. It was dangerous. If the cars stopped suddenly, the bus would rush on them. One had to be very careful and not think of anything else. All the better. When one is busy, time passes more quickly.

The green light was still on. The policeman at the corner was probably gaping at something, or was having an argument with some headstrong driver. That was all to the good, too. Let him have it out with the man. If he carried on a little longer, Claude could just make it to the bus stop. But such miracles do not happen, especially during rush hour.

The green light went out. The yellow one flashed up, then the red one again. With the bus stop a mere hundred meters away. It was always like that.

He could hear Léon's voice at the back: "I tell you, it's not the bus stop, don't you see?"

"Much I care about your bus stop!" a woman shouted. "Get out of my way so I can get off!"

"You'll get off at the bus stop, like everyone else."

"Goodness, what an obstinate fellow! Will you or won't you get out of my way?"

"I certainly shall not. There are regulations."

Léon had an easy time of it. With all his arguing the day passed more quickly, while Claude sat there alone in his cabin. He was alone at home, too. When he entered his room, he had the feeling he was entering his grave. The room had no window. Or rather, it had one, but it was blocked by the wall of the house next door, and all one could see through the panes was unplastered bricks. He would turn the switch and the place would fill with a dim yellow light. The weaker the bulb, the lower his electricity bill would be. Claude would put his shabby bag on the table and take out his supper. A piece of dry salami, some cheese, part of a crushed long French loaf and half a bottle of wine. Supper was the leftovers of his lunch. He got his food from the big *Monoprix** in the boulevard. On the stalls outside the shop they displayed the cheapest food. Salami at 90 francs, cheese at 65 francs per portion, wine at 70 francs. That added up to 250 francs including the bread. Claude couldn't afford to pay more. Sometimes, for a change, he would get a small box of sardines, but that was irrational. Nothing was left over for his supper, and even if there was, there was no way of taking it home.

He would spread a sheet of old newspaper on the table and sit down to his meal. He did not feel like eating. That revolting metallic taste would appear again. Someone seemed to have stuffed his stomach with brass shavings. Claude would uncork the olive-green bottle and swallow a long draught. The copper taste would grow fainter, and the bus driver's head would be suffused with warmth. If he had more money he would drink a whole bottle every evening. Even two bottles, like Bernard the Bottomless. Bernard the Bottomless was his roommate. He was nicknamed thus because of his capacity to go on drinking endlessly. Claude knew that Bernard was even that very minute sitting at the counter of the corner café. Léon and some of the others were probably there, too. And they were probably throwing the big red dice to see whose turn it would be to pay the next round of drinks. Claude could also have gone to the café, but he knew he wouldn't go. He wouldn't have enough money for his needs, and it didn't do to be given a treat without treating the others. He would go to bed as usual and that would be the end of it. That was probably why his friends in the neighborhood considered him a contrary fellow.

"You were born to be a gravedigger, buddy, not a bus driver," Bernard used to say to him sometimes. "Bus drivers are jolly fellows."

"You have an easy time of it," Claude thought to himself. "Anyone can be jolly with two liters of wine in his belly." But he said nothing at all.

When he finished his supper, Claude would painstakingly

* *Monoprix:* one-price shop (author's note).

scoop up the remains of his meal and throw them in the bucket. Then he would go to bed. Before falling asleep, he would turn the pages of the crumpled newspaper he had brought in his bag together with the bread and the salami. It was Léon's newspaper. Léon read it during lunch hour and then gave it to Claude to improve his mind. Léon was one of the comrades. Claude was unaffiliated, and all these struggles seemed to him a hopeless business. He went out on strike because everybody did, and besides there was some sense in striking. You demanded a ten-franc raise, and if the company was driven into a corner it would pay up. But that other business was hopeless. If anything came of it, it would do so without Claude's support. But nothing would come of it.

Outside, somewhere in the dark, a clock was striking ten. The driver folded the newspaper and put out the light. Bernard would probably turn up in a little while. He usually came home drunk and in the mood for long talks. And Claude didn't feel like talking. What's more, the fellow was usually so soused one could hardly follow what he said. What was the use of living with such a person? One might as well be alone. He was, to all intents and purposes, alone. The only advantage was that Bernard paid half the rent; that was all.

The green light had been on for two minutes already, but Claude hadn't started yet. Some greenhorn in front had probably let his motor die out. Any old fool who didn't even know where to look for the clutch could get a license. You only had to grease the inspector's palm and pocket for it. No license is as good as a big bank note.

The column moved forward very slightly. So the greenhorn had got his engine started after all. Claude let in the clutch and started with the rest. The green light was still on but might stop any minute. The bus just managed to reach the crossroads when the yellow light blazed up. Claude only stepped on the accelerator more energetically and dashed across the suddenly vacated crossroads. The policeman at the corner tapped his finger on his forehead, as much as to say "Are you mad?"

Claude was pleased. It was a dangerous maneuver, the column from the cross street might have come crashing down on him, but you saved five minutes this way. He raised the direction indicator and stopped short at the bus stop.

"Barbès Rochechouart," Loén's voice rang out.

"What a dirty hole, this Barbès Rochechouart is," Claude

thought. The crossroads looked still darker and gloomier than the huge, grimy concrete bridge which spanned it. Only a narrow strip of sky was visible between the tall, dingy buildings and the great bulk of the bridge. And now even this strip was pressed down by the wet clouds, as if someone had stopped up the chink with dirty rags.

Suddenly the pavement shook as if an earthquake had hit. The windows of the bus rattled. The noise of the traffic was drowned in the thundering roar which came upon them unexpectedly from above. For a second, Claude had the same painful vacant sensation in his chest he had felt there when the bombs were falling at Dunkirk. It lasted only a second, then he relaxed again. It was the trolley rushing along the bridge overhead.

At both corners across the way there were large and squalid cafés. The façade was lit up by red, the interior by white and blue neon lighting. Young men and peroxide-blondes hung around the long copper-plated bars. Claude knew they were all a bad lot, but still he sometimes envied them. It was pleasanter to lead even that kind of a life than to spend the whole day at the steering wheel in the midst of a traffic jam. You spent one hour selling smuggled cigarettes at the corner, then two hours playing cards with friends over a glass of pernod. Then you sold more cigarettes. Or something still easier: you picked someone's pocket in the crowd. At a small risk, with a little luck you could give yourself a whole week's leave. Or else the easiest solution of all: your girlfriend would be making money upstairs in the hotel room while you spent your time in the warm café, having a drink now and then. No, that wasn't the easiest way. At least not for Claude. He imagined that the girlfriend was Jacqueline, and he simply couldn't stand the thought. But the other way was easy enough. On condition, of course, that you could do it, on condition that you had it in you to do such things.

Léon had long since rung the little bell, yet Claude somehow could not get started. Cars were creeping all around, overtaking him, making sharp turns right under the nose of the bus, without leaving even space enough for him to start. They took no precautions, yet he had to be careful not to damage them. At last he seized the opportunity when the traffic was thinning and stepped on the accelerator, but just then a large green Cadillac overtook him and planted itself right under his very nose. Claude braked hard. The bus jolted terribly, as if it had crashed into a wall, and stopped short a few inches from the Cadillac. Just then the stream of cars came to a standstill again.

Claude thrust his head out of the window: "Think you're very smart, hey? You're lucky I hadn't really got started. Otherwise I'd have made mincemeat of you and your dirty limousine!"

A young man with a brazen, puffy face sat in the car. A woman in a white coat was lounging in the seat next to him. The man looked ahead of him, with an expression of indifference as if the abuse was not meant for him.

"I'll teach you a lesson, you fat brute!" Claude thought. He turned the steering wheel with all his might and shifted the wheels on the spot. As soon as the traffic thinned out, he would make a slight turn, come in line immediately, and the Cadillac would see his back. He looked at the couple in the green car with growing irritation. "Pretending not to see me, the bluebloods! Well-bred people pay no attention to mere bus drivers."

The woman waved her white-gloved hand capriciously, as if pointing to something. The man bent slightly toward her to hear the question. They weren't hurrying anywhere on business. Nor were they on their way home. They'd probably go up to Montmartre to have a binge up there and go dancing. And yet they had to forge ahead, and yet they were short of time. Now Claude could wait, and the eighty people behind him, they could wait, too. The common herd has nothing to do, they can wait.

The line in front of him began to move slowly forward. From his cabin Claude could see this motion slowly approach him. He had let the clutch in and sat with his foot on the accelerator. The minute the two cars before him swung forward, he started, too. The Cadillac was just one second late, but that was enough. With a skillful maneuver Claude overtook him and blocked his way. "You'll creep right there behind my back. Dirty aristocrats!"

The traffic gathered speed, and the bus rushed through the dark arch of the bridge. Then lights appeared again through the windows—the bus was running down Boulevard Barbés. From here on the traffic thinned out a bit. Claude nearly always managed to get to Château Rouge without waiting and to make up a minute or two of his delay. He would manage to now.

He stepped down on the accelerator and shifted into third. But during this short delay someone again overtook him. It was the green Cadillac. The fellow had decided to teach him good manners. Once he had passed the bus, the Cadillac drove on at a provocatively slow pace, thus forcing the bus driver to slow down. Claude was seized with an almost irrepressible desire to rush upon the impudent brute and to hurl him somewhere on the pavement together with pieces of his limousine. To give vent to his irritation he pressed the horn, although it was prohibited. The harsh wail of the siren made the Cadillac speed up jerkily, but its driver immediately regained his composure and slowed down again. The puffy youth poked his face through the window and gave Claude a brazen look, as much as to say, "You'll know better next time!"

That was too much. Continuing to drive the bus automatically, the driver in his turn put his head through the window, and, in an effort to be heard above the noise, shouted: "Now listen, you dirty dog, you bloody bastard! You'll pay through the nose for this trick—just wait till we stop. I'll teach you a lesson all right. I'll teach you such a lesson that first thing you know you'll be on the sick list in a hospital, you lousy little millionaire!"

The bus had to stop at the corner because of the red light. The Cadillac rushed off somewhere ahead of him. But Claude continued to call its driver names louder and louder, and more fiercely, stuttering in his vain attempts to think of something still more offensive and still dirtier. He sat like that, up in his cabin, in the midst of the roaring traffic, shouting to himself without anyone hearing him, till finally he exhausted himself and calmed down.

He breathed more freely now. His irritation was spent, and all that remained was the fatigue and the nausea. He wiped his face with both palms, as if washing something off, then leaned back and let his arms hang limply down. He would count till eight, no, till ten, and the green light would go on again. Claude started counting slowly to himself. The green light did flash on. But he no longer enjoyed this game. In the first place, he was so used to it that he nearly always guessed right. In the second, there no longer was anything to wager on. He used to wager on Jacqueline before. Or on whether they would find lodgings within a month, and all kinds of other things besides.

The bus was moving along in its lane again. In a little while Léon's voice would ring out: "Château Rouge." But it didn't. He was probably taken up with the passengers. What Claude heard was the ringing of the bell—the starting signal. "You could've got a move on instead of ringing so hard," Claude muttered almost audibly. "Now you'll have to wait a good long while."

At Château Rouge the streets met from six directions, and they were all chock-full of cars and trucks. The column from Rue Custine seemed not to have stopped on time and had jammed the whole square. Two policemen, their faces distorted with shouting, were threading their way among the cars, gesticulating angrily. The green light had long been on at Rue Poulet, but the column couldn't get started because the road wasn't free. Someone in that direction lost patience and started up a long, drawn-out tooting. Others followed suit, and in a moment the entire Rue Poulet became a seething mixture of scores of thin, low, piercing, and bass voices. A little later Rue Des Gens took up the pandemonium, then Boulevard Ornano, and finally all six streets together. The policemen waved their batons about wildly, and angry faces appeared in car windows, mouths awry with vituperation. People came out on the balconies of the surrounding houses.

The wailing of the horns grew ever more shrill and piercing. The city seemed to be pouring out all its irritation accumulated during the day in this unbearable metallic scream. Anyone who felt in any way disgruntled could pour out abuse at will in the general uproar. Thoroughly insignificant people, whom no one ever bothered about, entered the fray in a state of great excitement to lend a hand here and there, to give advice, and to feel for a brief second that they weren't utter nonentities after all. Housewives, bored with their humdrum chores, poked their heads through the windows to see how it would all end, with the secret hope that it wouldn't end too soon. A traffic jam was at all events better than nothing.

Claude continued to sit in his cabin with his elbows propped on the steering wheel. There was a time when he, too, took part in the general commotion, telling people off and giving instructions. But that was long ago. Now he just sat back and wondered how long the traffic jam would last.

Suddenly it struck him as rather strange that he should sit there in the thick of such an uproar and feel lonely. The sound of many hooters filled the entire crossroads, abuse was bandied back and forth, hundreds of human faces appeared one behind the other, yet Claude felt as lonely as ever, lonelier than Robinson did on his island. He was seized with an absurd sense of unreality: Could it be that all this, the tall, grimy house fronts at the corners, this inextricable turmoil of cars and pedestrians, the wailing hooters, didn't really exist? Perhaps if he rubbed his eyes, he might see his mother with her kindly tired face bending above his bed as he awoke from a dream, and saying: "There, there, Claude my boy, you'll be late for school."

It suddenly seemed to him he could catch the faint, half-forgotten smell of toast and freshly brewed tea. There followed the refreshing sprays of the cold water, breakfast, then a few minutes of play with the cat. The cat was really a tomcat, but for some unknown reason he had been given the name of Margot, which he bore with resignation.

"For goodness' sake, leave the poor creature alone, you'll be late."

"All right, I'm off. Just give me two sous, will you?"

"Two sous?"

"To get myself a roll in the long break."

"Where am I to get them from? You know perfectly well that we're not well off."

After all, one could manage without a roll. The school gave you a sense of security. If they make you study, it follows that you're needed, which means that you're expected somewhere. Claude didn't know, neither did he care very much where he'd be expected. Personally he would rather become a cowboy, or at least a Red Indian. . . .

The driver rubbed his eyes with the palms of his hands and straightened up. The grimy buildings at the crossroads hung out over him. No, he wasn't dreaming, and all the rest belonged to the distant past.

A small black van had managed to creep up to the corner across the way. A number of policemen jumped out of it, headed by a superintendent wearing a peaked cap decorated with white piping.

"Now, let's see what these fellows will do."

While the policemen walked about among the cars quieting the drivers with tickets and threats, the superintendent took up his stand at the crossroads and, with a series of sharp gestures, began giving directions.

Claude followed the movements of the man with white piping and immediately realized he knew his job. The first thing the superintendent did was to order all vehicles in the third lane to draw back, to allow the clearing of the square. To achieve it the maneuvers had to begin further back, as far away as the neighboring streets, but there was no other way out. Claude knew from the very beginning that if the policemen only wandered about the crossroads, they couldn't set things right. This fellow knew his business and began from afar.

Once the left side of Barbès became less congested, the chief constable let the cars from the Rue Custine, which had filled the square, enter along it. Then he once again stopped all traffic and waited for the right side of the Boulevard Ornano to clear to give the Boulevard Barbès the green light.

Claude stepped on the accelerator and was the first to rush

across the crossroads. Ahead, the boulevard was free from traffic for more than three hundred meters. This opportunity was not to be missed before the confusion spread to the next cross street. The driver engaged the second gear to the very end, changed into third gear, and a minute later the dangerous corner was behind him. "If only I could get on like this to Marcadet," Claude thought, although he knew that was out of the question. The jam had probably disrupted the traffic for miles around. The confusion spread like the rings made by a stone thrown in the water. The traffic had only to be blocked somewhere for five minutes for everything to be in a turmoil three districts away. And when the streams of cars from the place of the original traffic jam finally got disentangled, they were stopped by fresh traffic jams in the vicinity, which they themselves had caused. Claude could already see the cars crowding up ahead of him. He slowed down, chose a more convenient position, and stopped in his turn. A brief glance at the crossroads assured the driver that the traffic in this part of the city was not disrupted, but simply congested. He wouldn't have to wait an age to get started again.

Claude cast a hostile look at the crowd of shining coupés. The majority were black Citroëns. Gleaming black as they were, they reminded him of a swarm of large, clumsy cockroaches, crowded together in a dirty corner. And while he watched the cockroaches, he was once more conscious of that depressing loneliness—something —a vacuum he wanted to throw out of his chest, and instead it would spread until he was quite overcome with it.

Claude often felt like this after that business with Jacqueline. It didn't come on at once. At first it was pain; the emptiness came much later.

Jacqueline worked at the *Monoprix* shop where Claude bought the food for his lunches. She was the assistant at the stand for provisions outside the shop and had remembered Claude by his invariable request: "One salami and a box of Camembert cheese, please."

When there wasn't much of a crowd, Jacqueline found time to smile and say: "My goodness, what are you doing! You're sure to ruin your stomach with your everlasting salami!"

"What do you expect me to do?" Claude would mumble. "If I had a beauty like you at home, I . . ."

"And why shouldn't you? Who prevents you from having one?" At this point the conversation usually came to an end. There were people around, and Jacqueline was far too busy for idle talk.

On one occasion, however, there were no customers and Claude managed to answer: "Lovely girls like you are after rich men."

"That's sheer nonsense," Jacqueline answered. "That's the invention of some men who aren't popular with women."

"Like me," said Claude.

She looked at him. Claude had a smooth, clear face, soft thoughtful eyes and a very boyish look about him. But a big boy with a peaked cap and a bus driver's uniform.

"I don't know," said Jacqueline, smiling. "If a fellow like you asked me to go to the cinema, I don't know if I'd refuse."

That evening they went to the cinema for the first time. They went many more times after that. They sat in a corner of the upper balcony, held hands, and kissed. Claude didn't remember a thing about the films. All he remembered was the rounded warm shoulder under the soft pullover, the smooth cool skin of her cheek against his, and the scraps of meaningless conversation which one nevertheless didn't forget.

Claude no longer had his lunch behind the bus stop, with his bag spread out on his knees. He had sandwiches with Jacqueline at the corner café. The sandwiches were a little more expensive, but then he could spend the whole lunch break with Jacqueline. That way they had a quiet hour to look at each other and talk about many things, principally about lodgings.

At first they thought of living in Claude's room for the time being. But when Jacqueline saw the little room with the window facing a brick wall, she dropped her eyes and said in a disappointed whisper: "But this might as well be a grave!"

"I told you it wasn't anything much," Claude answered, embarrassed. That minute he himself felt that if they were to begin their life like this, it would be spoiled from the start. So they decided to look for a room elsewhere.

The old man, Jacqueline's father, gave his consent to the marriage. He was a railwayman and was still working.

"A railwayman and a bus driver," said the old man, "they're much of a muchness. We're all of a kind. And if anyone has money, it simply means that he stole it. The more he's got, the more he's stolen. And that's a fact."

The mother never said anything. Claude realized she kept silent because she was against the marriage. Sometimes he even sympathized with her and saw her point: it wasn't easy to raise such a beautiful daughter and give her to a bus driver. Claude agreed that he wasn't worthy of Jacqueline, but did one give up one's good fortune, simply because one didn't deserve it? They simply had to find lodgings as soon as possible; everything else was sure to be solved somehow or other. But no lodgings were to be had. What they did find were terribly expensive.

"Don't get discouraged," Jacqueline kept saying. "We'll look around a little longer. As a last resort we always have your room to fall back on."

And he set his mind more at ease. A room, even though it had no window, meant that things weren't completely hopeless.

Then Jacqueline was moved to another, a more central branch of the *Monoprix* stores. She was a good worker and deserved the raise. But now they could no longer have lunch together, pore over advertisements for rooms to let, and discuss their plans. Only the evenings remained, yet it was past eight o'clock by the time Jacqueline got home from downtown. They went to the cinema or sat with the old folks, because one couldn't go to the pictures every day. Claude felt ill at ease in the company of the old people and also because of Jacqueline's talk.

"You should see what well-dressed ladies do their shopping at our store. It's most extraordinary that such ladies should enter the *Monoprix!* Ladies in mink coats and crocodile leather shoes!"

"Mink indeed!—What nonsense!" exclaimed the railwayman with a snarl. "Clothes are worn to keep one warm, and not to attract people's attention. That's what I think."

"What you think doesn't matter one bit," the mother put in. "Clothes in general and your blue overalls are very different things. If France has become world famous, it's because of the clothes."

"Come now," said the old man angrily. "Much you know what has made France famous. Only thieves wear your smart clothes; they can only be bought with stolen money."

"You seem to take everyone for a thief except ragamuffins like us."

Claude held his tongue and shifted uneasily in his chair. He felt this family scene had quite a different meaning, that everything actually converged on him, and that what the old man really meant was: "My girl, don't stuff your head with such nonsense. Just know your place."

While the old woman kept saying: "Let the child go her own way. Much good that bus driver is to her."

He looked at Jacqueline furtively to see if she reacted in the same way. But Jacqueline was entirely absorbed in her impressions of the day: "A little while ago, just before closing time, a woman came in. I wish you could've seen her clothes, Mother! A tobacco-colored camel's hair coat, a high-raised collar!"

Far ahead the cars began rumbling, but the movement took a long time to reach Claude. "Ten meters at best," he figured, "and then another stop." However, he wasn't able even to cover five meters. At the last moment the gearshift got stuck and before he let the clutch in again, the right-hand column got started and blocked his way. The bus, which had only just started, braked hard alongside the pavement.

Claude again turned his thoughts to the affair with Jacqueline. Actually there was no point in thinking about it. Since nothing had come of it, it was useless to think about it.

At first things went on almost as before. Then little by little they began seeing less of each other. Once she'd say she was tired, on another occasion she said she'd promised her girlfriends to go out with them or she'd extra hours at the shop. When they went to the cinema, Jacqueline let Claude hold her hand, but she was entirely engrossed in the film. She rarely asked about the room, and then only as a mere formality, to fill in some of the frequent pauses.

Claude kept saying to himself that possibly he was stupid, but not as stupid as all that. He realized that the district around the opera house was a far cry from the suburb. Rich, elderly gentlemen, younger ones, too, for that matter, hung around the shop in quest of love affairs with the shopgirls. The shop assistants were always pretty girls, and affairs with them cost them less than adventures with some fashion model or night-club singer.

"One of those scoundrels must have got hold of my girl," Claude thought. "And if he hasn't, he will. It's child's play, with Jacqueline dreaming of nothing but fine clothes."

He knew Jacqueline was too good for him. She was too beautiful for a bus driver. She had every right to possess so many things he didn't have. He felt ashamed and helpless. What could he do or promise except the room with the wall-blocked window?

"Come, tell me, don't you love me any more?" Claude had asked one evening as they were leaving the cinema.

"Oh Lord, Claude, stop asking such silly questions!" Then, a few steps further on, she'd added in a gentler tone: "Of course I love you, but don't you see we have no prospects at all? Not even a dim chance of having any. You can't even find a room."

"We did have a last resort," Claude thought sadly. But what he said was: "I am still on the lookout for one. I was told today rooms were to be had in Saint-Denis."

"Yes, but when? You've been looking for one all these months."

"Shall I be seeing you soon?" Claude said when they parted. He wanted to say, "Shall I be seeing you tomorrow?" but couldn't screw up the courage to at the last moment.

"Yes, but not for the next few days, if you don't mind. We're fixing the shop up for Easter, and I'm terribly busy. I'll look you up when I'm free."

Claude felt the end was probably not far off, but didn't realize it had actually come. Jacqueline never looked him up again.

One evening some time later they met by chance in front of the café. It was still cold and Jacqueline was wrapped in a soft, yellow, camel's hair coat.

"Why Claude!" she exclaimed, as she stopped him, somewhat embarrassed, and held out her hand.

Equally embarrassed, he tried to smile, casting a sidelong glance at her. But this Jacqueline of the high upturned collar, the sleek fashionable hairdo, and that whiff of a strange perfume seemed somehow remote and inaccessible.

An awkward pause followed. Then Claude said almost without a hint of reproach: "So you did finally get your tobacco-colored coat."

"Yes," she replied. "I saved up for a while. What are you doing?"

"Nothing. What am I to do? Nothing."

And so they had parted. Then he had seen her once more, for the last time, but from a distance, through the shop window.

The column of cars moved on again. This time Claude had loosened the gearshift beforehand, engaged the first gear and was only waiting to step on the accelerator. The bus started, almost touching the car in front, passed the crossing, and stopped at Boulevard Ornano.

"Marcadet-Poissonier, section!" Léon's impressive voice rang out. He always announced the main stops rather solemnly.

"Many people get off here," Claude thought, remembering, "and that means a long halt." It didn't matter much—the worst was over by now. Ahead, as far as one could see, the boulevard was full of cars, but they were on the move. The bus had gotten out of the traffic-jam zone.

Léon tugged at the bell. He was ready. If there were no further delays to the last stop it meant they would get away with half a run's delay. With a delay of one run and a half during the day, it amounted to a total of two runs. There was no avoiding a quarrel with that fellow the inspector. Let's hope that would be all.

As he approached the second cross street of Boulevard Ornano, Claude looked to the right by force of habit. That's where Jacqueline's former *Monoprix* was. A young girl in a blue apron stood before the provisions stand in front of the shop, but it wasn't Jacqueline—just a young girl he didn't know with a pale, freckled face.

"Why should it always be like that?" he wondered. "Why do the rich deprive the poor of everything, including even their pretty girls?" If a good-looking girl turned up, less than a month later she was sure to be sent to a central store. The suburban fellows could do without beauties.

Claude remembered the shop window of the *Monoprix* near the opera house. It was the day before Easter, and his shift had an afternoon off to do their shopping. Claude had already done his. A piece of salami, a box of cheese, and a tin of sardines because it was a holiday. He had the whole afternoon to take a walk. He took a bus and got off at Les Pyramides. He knew he would get off there, although he hadn't thought about it beforehand. There at the corner Jacqueline's *Monoprix* glowed in its red and white neon lighting. It was drizzling, and people hurried into the shop through the all-glass doors. Claude threaded his way through the crowd around the shop windows and looked in. At first he could not distinguish anything, for it was very light and full of people. Then he saw Jacqueline. She stood behind the sweets counter in her blue overalls. All assistants at the *Monoprix* shops had such overalls, but that particular blue seemed to be made specially for Jacqueline, for her olive face and dark auburn hair. Dressed as she was in her overalls, she appeared to Claude once more like the Jacqueline of old days, who was so dear to him. The people at the shop window jostled against him and prevented him from looking.

"Look here, my lad, if you aren't going in, you might as well make room for others," an old man grumbled behind his back.

Claude stepped aside and once more almost glued his face to the pane. Jacqueline was far away, but he could clearly see her hands move above the counter and her face turn this way and that toward the circle of customers. There, now she was going to smile. She always raised her eyebrows like that before smiling. Now she was fingering the brooch on her bosom. She always fingered her brooch like that when she was figuring something out. Now she was pointing with both hands in this direction and that, as if she were saying, "choose for yourself, after all."

People kept bumping into him, and he had to step back several times. Then there was a downpour and the crowd dispersed. That was all to the good. Claude now stood alone in front of the shop window and was free to gaze as long as he pleased at the sweets counter. Jacqueline unexpectedly turned her head and looked toward the street. He quickly withdrew and turned the corner. And the minute he had turned it, he felt that the city was suddenly growing dark and deserted. There was nowhere else to go, and nothing to do. He felt cold shivers down his back, for he was soaking wet. The words of Bernard the Bottomless came to his mind: "When you feel blue, get a drink." He did not feel like drinking. He did not feel like doing anything. There was no point in it.

"Simplon!" Léon's voice rang out from behind.

The bus had reached the next to the last stop. The working day would soon be over. But the thought didn't cheer him up. "Tomorrow will be Sunday," he reminded himself by way of encouragement. But this, too, failed to cheer him. To him all Sundays smelled of carbolic acid and of a hospital. . . . The Sundays. . . .

Léon was tugging away at the bell nervously and all that ringing meant: "Hey, old boy, sleeping, are you? You're a fine fellow, this is no blinking time to sleep." Léon was in a hurry to leave work. His throat was parched.

Claude started and, changing into second gear, raised one hand from the steering wheel and lowered the other window. He was gasping for breath. Ahead of him, between the two long rows of zinc-covered roofs, with chimneys and lightning rods sticking out of them, was the same lowering, stopped-up, wet sky. If only it would finally make up its mind to rain.

The Sundays. . . . It meant getting up late in the poisonous air of the little room, filled with the sour alcoholic breath of Bernard the Bottomless. There followed coffee, of that brand, the cheapest brand which smelt of soot and carbonized sugar. Then it was time for Claude to prepare for his trip. He put on his best suit, in which he used to go the pictures with Jacqueline. The trousers in front, right along the crease, were almost threadbare; but there was no hole as yet, and in any case it wasn't noticeable. Next he would don his peaked cap and take the little package of acid drops left on the table the night before. They were cheap and lasted long. It took quite a long time to suck one. Bernard was still asleep. Claude looked enviously at the calm, puffy face of his friend, then went out, quietly closing the door behind him.

On Sundays the buses passed every twenty or thirty minutes, and he had to change buses many times before reaching the Salpêtrière. Claude would change from bus to bus, waiting for ages at the stops, standing a solitary figure in the deserted Sunday streets. At long last he arrived at his destination. He would pass under a large grimy archway and find himself in a wide, paved court. That was the Salpêtrière, or "the morgue of the poor," as it was called. Claude knew the way—the third pavilion, second floor. From the very entrance hall of the dank, yellow building with the peeling walls he was greeted by the deathlike smell of carbolic acid blended with that nauseating sickly smell of pus. The third pavilion, second floor. Claude entered the ward filled with long rows of white beds. The eighth bed from the door. His mother tried to sit up; her head, swathed in a white towel, trembled slightly on her slender, sinewy throat.

"Claude, darling, here you are at last. Did you have to wait long at the stops, sonny?"

He kissed the cold, wrinkled skin of the cheek, and replied that he hadn't. As always. Then he would sit down on the chair placed there specially for him. The old lady told him all about her affairs—about who had died, and how badly the nurse behaved to patients. "Let's hope she has much to tell me, otherwise there'll be nothing for us to talk about."

He listened and kept his eyes fixed on a spot on the bedstead where the paint had come off, the spot thus formed looked just like the map of France. Whenever he sat there, he always looked at that peeled spot.

Finally his mother had no more to say and asked him about his news.

"There's nothing new, the same old story," Claude would answer.

"You haven't found a room yet?"

"Not for the time being, but we're bound to find one sooner or later." His mother didn't know that the romance with Jacqueline was over. There was no point in telling her.

"Of course you will, sonny. I even have a hunch it'll be settled very soon. You must get together at last and settle down to a real family life."

Claude kept looking at the spot with the peeled paint. It really was just like a map.

Then the old woman would heave a weak sigh and say: "Oh, if only the Lord would have mercy on me and let me die so I should suffer no more and give you no trouble."

"Don't talk like that," Claude would answer, shifting uneasily in his chair. "You know that you'll get well. You don't give us any trouble at all."

"I know very well, my boy. I know how much money goes for the hospital bills. And I see you have no clothes to speak of. How I wish some kind person could give me something, to make me die in a minute and have done with it all."

Claude would mumble some comforting words, with a tired glance at the spot. Then they would sit like that in silence, each absorbed in his own thoughts. The tall, old-fashioned, sad-looking window gradually grew dark. The building opposite looked death-like and distant in the gathering dusk.

"I brought you some sweets," Claude would say, to break the silence. "Of the cheap kind, but they're refreshing," he would add because the little packet made an extremely poor show, crumpled as it was after being in his pocket. There would follow a little squabble over the unnecessary expense. Then came the moment of parting, once more the return trip, once more the deserted bus stops, once more the room with the walled-up window and the yellow bulb.
. . .

The bus left the boulevard, made a wide turn along the square and came to a stop in front of the glass-made end station.

"Porte de Clignancourt!" Léon called out from behind, more cheerfully than before. And to leave no shadow of doubt, he added: "Last stop!"

Very soon he poked his head through the little left window, looking at Claude. "What about it, shall we have a glass?"

"I don't feel like a drink," Claude said. "I'll wait for the next shift."

"As you wish. See you tomorrow morning, then. So long."

"So long."

Claude sank back in his seat with fatigue and looked at his watch. Five to seven. So he had half a run's delay. With the delays of the day, it added up to two. There would be trouble. A stream of damp air came through the windows. The muddy drooping trees on the boulevard beyond the square began swaying to and fro. Suddenly the rain came pouring down from the lowering sky. At long last.

The gloomy, ugly square of the suburb grew still darker. Under the streaks of rain, the grimy low buildings looked almost black. The café at the corner was lit up with a dirty greenish light. "It's Sunday tomorrow," Claude remembered, to cheer himself up. "I'll sleep late." Sunday, well, what of it? He felt sick and that empty feeling inside him was spreading again. He dropped onto the steering wheel and closed his eyes.

The splashing of the rain reminded him of the pelting drops on the wet yellow beaches. The howling of the wind increased and was swelled by the roar of the sea waves. Then suddenly the air grew thick and heavy. The explosions. The whole earth shook with them. The sinister roar of the sirens rent the sky. One, two, three, no end of them. The guns on the cruisers cracked alarmingly from the ocean. And in the uproar, the high, evil shriek of the Stukas. Claude pressed himself against the wet sand, with trembling knees and deafened ears and the sole thought of digging himself in, of sinking, of hiding from the universe which was crumbling all over him.

He opened his eyes. The square was quiet and peaceful. The green café blazed at the corner. The rain calmly pelted down against the windowpanes of the bus.

That was better. One could breathe once more now.

Translated by THEODORA ATANASSOVA

Dragomir Assenov

(1926–   )

Dragomir Assenov was born on May 15, 1926 in Mihailovgrad and majored in law at Sofia University. His first works were published in 1945 in the *Dounavski Otechestven Front* newspaper, appearing in Roussé. He worked in the editorial office of the same paper in Roussé and later as editor of *Rabotnichesko Delo* and other newspapers. At present he is chief editor of the *Rodna Rech* magazine.

He has published the following books: *Conscience*, short stories (1956); *Our Platoon*, a novelette (1965); *The Roads Don't Cross*, a novel (1959); *Brown Horizons*, a novel (1961); *The Big Stone House*, a novel (1965); and *The Fruit of Winds*, a novel (1966). In 1964 his first play, *Birthday*, was acted, and in 1966 his second, *Roses for Dr. Shomov*, was performed.

A Strict Upbringing

We returned home as pale and downcast as if we had commited a crime against our child. We both felt that we were being ridiculous, but the irritation that had come over us on our way back did not lessen. On the contrary, it grew so much that both of us were ready to burst out at the slightest provocation. I lit a cigarette in order to calm myself and began to pace the room, keeping an eye on my wife. I was sure she would take it out on me.

And then, after spending some time on the balcony as though indifferent, she stood in the doorway, threw back her hair and looked at me defiantly (a pose I knew only too well). I shrugged my shoulders, and in my voice there was uncertain though perceptible irony: "What is it?"

"I told you that we should have given him his light pyjamas, not his flannel ones. . . . He'll be too hot."

I tried to keep my temper and explain everything reasonably to her, as befitted the head of the family: "Up in the mountain the nights are cold . . ."

My wife gave a killing, soundless laugh: "You talk as though he were in the Himalayas."

"Nevertheless, it's Vitosha . . ."

"Oh, stop it! It's hellishly hot outside!"

"All right!" I agreed reluctantly, ready to give in. "It's visiting day on Wednesday, and we'll take up his light ones. He'll just have to bear it till then."

She sat on the settee, silent, but finally could contain herself no longer, and her words flew at me like wasps, sharp and fierce: "I don't know how you imagine his upbringing, but lately you have spoiled him completely. Our boy doesn't know the meaning of 'no'; he has no taste for work; and he has no pity for anyone. My dear, your son will become such an egoist that you'll wonder what to do with him! He lives in a family of intellectuals, but does not like books—do you understand where all that will lead him to?"

"I do!" I tried to turn the conversation into a joke. "Lately, children's literature hasn't been all it should be . . ."

"Fiddlesticks! And don't try to joke everything away! He's lazy, he's not independent, he's artful—don't such qualities give you a start?"

"Why don't you go on and call him a rogue?"

My wife gave an indignant cry, went to a corner of the room, and didn't utter a sound for a long time.

"From now on, I'll take him over!" she said decisively. "Spartan ways, a plan for the day and a sense of responsiblility—that's what he needs! It's time he stopped living for his own pleasure; let him find out that life can also be hard and difficult and that one must fight! Only then will he grow into a man and not a parasite or a drag."

"That's the spirit!"

My wife shot a suspicious glance at me: "Are you joking?"

"Great God, no, I admire you! Only . . ."

"Only what?"

"Only I hope you stick to your principles! After all, he obeys me more than . . ."

"Because you beat him!"

"I haven't slapped him once in the past three years!"

"He's scared of you, that's why. The important thing is that he should obey you without being afraid of you!"

"I haven't noticed him obeying you more; you two quarrel like equals. Where is the respectful distance between mother and son?"

My wife stood up offended, her lips quivering. But I had gathered momentum, and my anger poured out in torrents: "You've spoiled him, not I. You've made a milksop out of him. A sniveler! So he's lazy, is he? And why? Because you do everything for him. . . . He isn't independent . . . how can he be independent the way you follow him around?"

"Stop it!" she said through clenched teeth.

"I won't stop! Since we are going to discuss his upbringing . . ."

"Stop it, I tell you!"

"Pedagogue! You feel sore that he's away from you for the first time and you take it out on me! Do you think that I don't know who Pestalozzi was!"

My wife turned on her heel and went out, banging the door. That was that. The day was ruined. I sat in the dark room and listened: a strange, heavy, and dense silence filled the house. There was not a sound, not a creak; it was as if there wasn't a living soul around. I was angry. Not because of my wife, naturally! Tomorrow or the day after we would make it up—our quarrels didn't last longer—but tonight we were both nagging each other to get rid of the irritation from the parting, from the heat.

I missed my little mischief-maker! I missed him because there was no one to scold and threaten to break the TV set, if only to get rid of William Tell and Robin Hood, which were so much alike and so dull that they made you sick and tired; that there was no comfort for you at home and everyone was in your way and took up your hours for rest and meditation; that a man's system needed some vegetables as well as bread and cheese and if he didn't eat some salad you'd pull his mulish ears for him! And a hundred other dear trifles which the presence of a child creates and which you notice only when they don't exist or when they begin to disappear.

In the morning we parted sullen, without exchanging a single sentence, but toward noon, in spite of everything, my wife called me up.

"Have you come to your senses?" I began ironically, with as

much haughtiness in my tone as I could manage. "I'm ready to listen to your excuses!"

She sighed mysteriously into the receiver and then said: "I'll be late tonight . . ."

"Is that so. Why?"

"I have a meeting with the doctors from the ward."

"Fine!" I decided, as I replaced the receiver. "I'll go and see him—it's about an hour by bus."

I was frightened by my intention: only one night had passed, and my son had warned me expressly not to visit oftener than the other parents!

. . . "I don't want to be laughed at!" he said, though something sad and confused shone in his eyes: "I'm a man already . . ."

"That's right, you're a man!" I encouraged him, trying to remember whether I had been so ambitious at nine and a half. Then I had an idea. He wanted a penknife to cut sticks with, as all the boys at the camp were feverishly preparing bows, arrows, and lances. Why shouldn't I fulfill his wish?

I left the office early, bought a box of cookies, too, just in case, and set out. On the bus I felt fine and in high spirits, but when I took the path and entered the damp wood below the meadows, where the dormitories and the dining room were, I was troubled and my heart beat faster. What if he should be upset? What if he should refuse to stay and want to come home?

My son spotted me from afar and frowned, his eyebrows gathering threateningly above his snub nose: "Why have you come?"

"Say 'hello' first and then . . ."

"Hello! Why have you come?"

"You asked for a penknife . . ."

He lit up, his face brightened—impatient, joyful: "Have you got one?"

"Yes, I have . . . it's an old type, with a bone handle . . . it cost four leva . . ."

"Let me have it!"

"Be careful not to cut anyone, it's sharp . . ."

My son carefully took the precious gift, put it into one of the numerous pockets of his jeans, and nodded benevolently, almost warmly. I took advantage of the break and asked casually, indifferently: "How are you? How are things?"

He sniffed scornfully and clicked his tongue: "All right!"

"And the food?"

"I eat up everything—even the *tarator**—you know that I don't like *tarator*, don't you?"

"Hm! Do you sleep in the afternoon?"

"I rest . . ."

"Anything wrong?"

"No. Everything's great! Everything."

My son looked around nervously.

"Come on, go back, because they'll make fun of me. They poke fun at feminine boys . . ."

"What are these feminine boys?"

"Crybabies . . . that can't do without mom and dad . . . and that wear white underpants . . ."

"I see!" I scratched myself knowingly behind the ear. "That's how it should be! If you're homesick, you remember the number of our . . ."

"I won't feel homesick!"

"Bye-bye!" I pressed his hand and added rather confused: "Don't tell your mother that I came to see you!"

He smiled as artfully as a grownup: "Don't be afraid. I won't!"

The bugle sounded, and my son ran off toward the flagpole. I started back, satisfied and hurt at the same time. Did I really know my child? Wasn't I a bit disappointed by his self-importance and high spirits?

And then I gaped, surprised and shaken: toward me along the path was coming a familiar figure, stooped a little through fatigue.

"Spartan ways!" I roared, outraged. "A plan for the day! A sense of responsibility! What are you doing here?"

My wife stopped, dizzy and speechless. In the net bag which hung below her bag swayed the inevitable cookies and a bag of apples.

"Well?" I came closer. "What about the meeting?"

"It was postponed," she mumbled, and her lids moistened from the strain. "So I decided . . . he wanted a penknife, didn't he?"

"He already has a penknife!"

"Did you bring one?"

"I did . . . I don't envy you, you'll catch it from him."

My wife was downcast: "Was he mad about you coming?"

* *Tarator:* a cold soup prepared with yoghurt and cucumbers.

"He was furious. Maybe he's right—don't think that our son is a feminine boy!"

"A feminine boy?" she was puzzled. "What does that mean?"

Then she bit her lips and looked at me helplessly. In her eyes I read the same fear that had come over me; was it possible that our troubles and cares were old-fashioned and foolish?

The wind blew from the mountaintop, and we caught bits of the energetic melody that was the signal for assembly: up there they were lining up for roll call.

Translated by ROUMYANA ATANASSOVA

Lyuben Stanev
(1924–   )

Lyuben Stanev was born on December 4, 1924 in Plovdiv in the family
of an office clerk. He graduated from secondary school and from the
Higher Medical School in his native city. He has been living in Sofia
since 1950. Since 1953 he has worked, with short interruptions, as editor
at the Feature Film Studio.

He has published the following books: *Penicillin*, short stories
(1952); *Smoke over the Valley*, sketches (1954); *The Laskovs*, a novelette
(1956); *The Pledge*, a novelette for youngsters (1956); *Cold House*,
short stories (1957); *A Woman Lies Awake*, short stories (1962). He has
also written the scripts for the films *The Little Girl* (1959) and *The Tsar
and the General* (1966).

A Visitor

The financial inspector Georgi Kalkanov threw the last bill on the
huge pile of documents and glanced at his watch. It was six o'clock.
Imperceptibly the noise in the neighboring rooms had died down,
and now only the rhythmical thudding of machines could be heard.
Through the window one could see the new as yet unplastered sections of the large plant, which was where the noise was coming
from. "They're working round the clock," Kalkanov thought.
"Why all the rush? As if they were afraid the work might run
away."

A satisfying thrill of impatience went through him. Let them
work. "He himself was free, wasn't he?" And Kalkanov again recalled the unknown dark-haired woman he had glimpsed that morning at the bus travel agency. All day long, while going through the
account books of the plant, he had been thinking of her, alternately

reproaching himself for not having stopped her there and then consoling himself that she could not vanish into thin air. That evening he would track her down. Now the endless, tiring day was over at last, and he could leave the smoky office.

"Have you finished?" the chief accountant asked with surprise, when Kalkanov rose from his chair.

"Of course, I told you, finished by six. That's how we do things in Sofia."

As a matter of fact, Kalkanov had made rather short work of the auditing, so as to be off earlier. There were five or six hours till train time, and these last hours of his business trip filled him with tense excitement. Now he could stop being a financial inspector second-class, the dull husband and father of three grownup children. Now he could be himself, an interesting man with graying hair, his face still fresh and smooth. At such times he was overcome by an intense desire for life. He was afraid that he might miss something, that he might waste the short stretch of time, that he might return home without carrying with him the remembrance of some new adventure, which would fill his days till the next business trip.

Kalkanov signed out and put on his raincoat. "Now I'll have a shave and then straight to the main street," he thought. "She'll no doubt come out for a walk."

"If you haven't anything on for tonight, I could stand you a drink," the accountant said uncertainly.

"Thank you very much, but I'll have to look up an aunt of my wife's," he replied, and as he held out his hand to the accountant he tried to imagine whether this fat, clumsy man had ever been unfaithful to his wife. "Who knows, for all his shabby and diffident looks, perhaps? . . . No, no, out of the question," Kalkanov decided suddenly, and this caused him to feel pity for the accountant.

"And don't overwork," he smiled and tapped the other on the shoulder. "Spring is just around the corner."

The man gave him a puzzled and somewhat hurt look and instantly Kalkanov was bored to death with him. He took leave and went out.

It was the season of the year when winter is already gone, but spring has not set in as yet. A gusty wind blew from all directions, carrying the smell of melting snow. On the black, naked boughs of the trees small pink buds gleamed as if in challenge. The town itself, with its new unplastered blocks of flats, its gardens and alleys still barren of grass, sprawled out beneath a ring of mountains and seemed to be waiting eagerly for the green dress of spring. And spring was near—perhaps just beyond the rounded ridge over there, above which a piece of blue sky shimmered, as if reflecting the azure of the nearby warm sea.

Spring had not yet arrived on earth, but it was already sparkling in the eyes of the people about him, particularly the women's. It seemed to Kalkanov that every woman who passed gave him a look full of meaning, and that she wanted to tell him something. With every such mysterious glance the inspector felt a momentary giddiness. He recalled the dark-haired woman and unconsciously hurried his steps. Her eyes, too, had dwelt on him this morning, but Kalkanov had perceived quite distinctly the quick and cautious glitter in her big eyes, which was not due solely to the spring. He had just arrived from the neighboring town and was getting off the bus. She was walking along the pavement, well-built and erect, holding her beautiful head high. Their eyes met, the woman stopped hesitatingly, gave a half-smile, then she lowered her eyes and moved on. Kalkanov felt his knees give way. It was a long time since he had aroused the interest of such a charming and seductive woman and it turned his head. When he recovered, the unknown woman had disappeared around the corner. Then he set out for the plant with his blood suddenly rushing to his head, and the firm decision not to leave before having seen her once more.

After a shave and a shoeshine, Kalkanov went off toward the main street. In spite of the wearisome day he felt fresh and pleasantly impatient. In a little while he would come across her, he would slowly stop in front of her and give her a friendly smile: "Well, here I am. . . ." He was not thinking of her reply, because he was used to easy conquests. And he had heard wild stories about this town. Kalkanov hurried on, confident that it was enough to see her and everything would fall into place.

But there was no trace of her in the main street. He walked up and down several times, then he stopped on the pavement. Hundreds of unknown faces passed before him, and his ears resounded with shouts, whistles, and shrill laughter. The smell of pumpkin seeds and of a multitude of human bodies reached him. All this reminded him of the several years before the Day of Liberation, when he worked as a teacher and used to be on duty evenings, patrolling the streets for belated schoolboys. It was a pleasant and carefree time. People did not overwork then and preferred to enjoy life instead. Kalkanov still cherished the pleasant memory of a couple of young schoolteachers who were full of the devil.

The spring night was falling quickly, yet the dark-haired

woman was nowhere to be seen. The financial inspector grew worried that he had wasted the evening. What is more, he had become ravenously hungry. He glanced around for the last time and started for the nearest restaurant. Perhaps he would come upon another woman there—she was not the only one in this town, after all.

But the restaurant was full of men. They were sitting in twos and threes or in larger parties at the tables, drinking and talking noisily. Kalkanov sat down at a corner table and inspected the place with boredom. Suddenly he gave a start. A young woman wearing a black apron and a tiny white cap came out of the kitchen. She was carrying a tray loaded with plates and bottles. When she reached the cashier's desk she gracefully bent over, extending a slip of paper held between her lips. Then she started to move among the tables to serve her customers.

Kalkanov was stunned. Yes, this was the woman who had haunted him all day long, for whose sake he had been hanging about the streets for two hours—a waitress in a restaurant. At first he was displeased, as if he had been cheated. But on scrutinizing her more attentively, he discovered that she was still as beautiful and attractive as in the morning—with the tiny cap perched roguishly on her black hair, the apron snug to her body, and the white frilled shoulder straps, which put her high bust alluringly into relief. Kalkanov livened up.

While waiting to be served he did not take his eyes off her lithe figure. She was at the tables in the farthest corner of the restaurant. The woman threaded her way among the chairs with difficulty, occasionally leaning on a client's shoulder, so as to clear a table or put something on it. Frequently some customer would get hold of her hand and draw her to himself, whispering something in her ear, while the others would laugh artlessly. An obliging and amiable smile kept hovering on the face of the woman, as if to say: "I know you well enough. When you're sober you're good boys, but when you drink too much you get impossible." Kalkanov sensed this smile, he saw that the woman was conducting herself very properly and nevertheless he felt a vague annoyance, as if somebody else's hands were reaching out for something that belonged to him. "Once she sees me everything will be all right," he thought, and kept shifting in his seat and craning his neck, to catch her attention.

And then at last she saw him. She was carrying an overloaded tray as she passed by his table. Kalkanov noticed that her face flushed and that the same flame that had scorched him in the morning lit up her dark, moist eyes. He nodded to her and she looked quickly away, but the next moment she returned his look and smiled without restraint.

A hot wave surged to the inspector's throat and spread slowly and sweetly all over his body. Everything was quite clear now. It was true, this adventure was going to be different, there would be no need for smart talk and ambiguous allusions. This woman could favor him with hot sensual delights and selfless affection, and this was more worthwhile than the shallow airs of some silly provincial girl.

His dinner before him, Kalkanov greedily started eating the tasty grill. From time to time he let his eyes wander to the other end of the room, and as soon as he met her glance he smiled familiarly. She responded in the same manner and then hurried about her work, unconsciously fixing her hair. After a while the woman approached his table and said: "Good appetite!"

Her voice was deep and it quivered. "She's excited," Kalkanov thought with pleasure and mumbled his thanks.

"Do you like our town?"

"Very much," he said, looking at her with his eyes half-closed.

"It's a pretty town," she affirmed.

They fell silent. From across the room came an impatient voice: "Danche, bring us a half of wine!"

The woman shrugged her shoulders and moved off reluctantly. Kalkanov looked at her figure with appreciation. "As if hewn out with the smallest of chisels," he thought. And while he chewed the juicy meat with his strong white teeth, he felt a wild scalding desire pervading his body together with the juice.

The restaurant was slowly emptying. Kalkanov glanced at his watch. One hour before his train. "I'll travel tomorrow," he made up his mind suddenly and tried to imagine the coming night. He did not know where exactly they would go, but he somehow saw quite distinctly a snow-white pillow, on which splendid black hair fanned out.

"We're closing now," her tender voice startled him. She stood at his table, watching him curiously and affectionately. Kalkanov smiled.

"Supposing one hasn't got a place to put up?"

Her face grew serious.

"Have you really no place to go to?"

"So it seems."

She became embarrassed.

"It's true, our hotel is always crowded."

After that a few wrinkles formed and disappeared quickly on her forehead. She looked aside with concentration and then said hastily: "Wait outside in the park. I'll be with you in a minute."

Kalkanov did not ask any questions; he only nodded slowly, feeling his blood race. While he waited on the park bench it occurred to him that next month he had a job to do in a nearby town. "I'll come over again," he thought happily and suddenly began humming the tune of an old-fashioned popular song off-key.

After a while the woman appeared, and they set forth down a dark, narrow street. Now she was dressed as in the morning, in a simple but well-cut coat, and again she stepped along proudly, with her head held high. As Kalkanov was somewhat short, he kept rising on his toes. For a while both were silent, but then she laughed and asked: "How did you recognize me? I thought you'd forgotten me."

He gave her a bewildered look, but did not betray himself, mumbling: "Eh, how could I forget you!"

At the same time he started racking his brain feverishly. "Where could she know me from? . . . There was a Danche several years ago in Varna, but she was a blonde and worked at the post office. . . . Strange, indeed." They entered a still darker street, and Kalkanov smiled suddenly. "This is a good one on me. She must've been a waitress in Sofia, and she's come to make more money here. That's where she knows me from, of course," he reassured himself and even began to think that he had seen her somewhere.

"In any case, you haven't changed in the least," the woman went on. "I recognized you immediately, the very moment I saw you in the morning." She was speaking in a loud voice quite freely, with no fear that somebody might spot them.

"Where's she taking me to?" Kalkanov thought and wondered at her easy manner. "Is she so experienced at this, or is it out of embarrassment that she's doing it? Well, there are such types and maybe they're the most interesting ones . . ." At the very thought of the next several hours the inspector's blood tingled and his fingers trembled. He gulped down the saliva that filled his mouth and on getting nearer the woman, he tried to take her arm.

She did not notice his motion and asked loudly: "Are you still at the commercial school, Comrade Kalkanov?"

Kalkanov froze in his tracks. If somebody had struck him on his head with a brick he could not have been more taken aback! So that was it! She was a former pupil of his. He should have thought of that earlier, when he realized that she knew him.

He drew back quickly, overcome by a complex and unpleasant feeling. He himself could not decide whether it was anger or regret, whether his conscience had spoken up unexpectedly or whether he felt sorry for himself because he'd grown old. But soon all this dwindled away before the apprehension that he might have given himself away and he answered hurriedly in an artificially careless voice: "It's a long time since I left the school. When did you graduate, Danche?"

"I couldn't graduate, don't you remember?" she replied with astonishment, and a cold edge seemed to have come into her voice. "I only went as far as the fifth form."

"Yes, yes," Kalkanov mumbled, disturbed by the sudden change in her tone.

"Perhaps she suspects, after all?" He winced when he thought of the way she had been behaving over the last two hours. "Where on earth is she taking me to along these dark streets? What if she's connected with the militia? One never knows—they say they're mostly that sort in restaurants. What possessed me to pick up a waitress!"

Kalkanov looked about, but he could not make out anything in the dark. At the same moment he tripped on a flagstone and exclaimed with pain.

"Did you hurt yourself?" her voice reached him from quite nearby, and now it was again warm and solicitous. "Now wait, I'll take your arm. It's very dark here."

She slipped her hand under his elbow and led him on with assurance. Kalkanov began to recover. Wherever they might be going, this walk along the deserted streets was anything but unpleasant. She held his arm firmly, and through the texture of the raincoat he could feel the warmth of her long fingers. From time to time, when the track between the upturned flagstones became very narrow, he clung to her firm shoulder, and her hair would just graze his face. Neither said a word, as if the only thing on their minds was to get out unharmed from the dark, excavated streets. Whether it was due to the proximity of her body or because he had again recalled her smiles and glances in the restaurant, Kalkanov recovered his composure again. "No, no, she couldn't be from the militia," he decided. "She wouldn't have behaved in such a way and she wouldn't have brought up the school. . . . Well, what then?" A bold conjecture flashed through his mind. As a matter of fact, why not? After all, she was a waitress in a town to which people had flocked from all over the country, and where money was flowing like water. True, he had been her teacher years ago, but now they were only a man and a woman who had taken a fancy to each other, and the rest was only a coincidence, which could even speed up their intimacy. And on clinging tightly to her again as if quite by accident, he asked impatiently: "By the way, where're we going?"

"Why, home, of course!" she exclaimed. "I couldn't let you sleep in the street, could I?" There was a gay and mischievous note in her voice that made him giddy.

"There, what a thing!" he thought. "Well . . . come to think of it, why not—one must be ready for anything. This promises to be even more interesting."

They reached a new building and Danche opened the door: "Come in, please!"

She hurried on ahead of him. Kalkanov looked around and began to climb the stairs uncertainly, marveling at her confidence. After a while he entered a narrow anteroom and began to unbutton his raincoat.

From behind the nearest door came a low male voice: "That you, Danche?"

Kalkanov gave a start, his face drained of all its color. He stepped back unconsciously and glanced quickly at the door. He expected that she, too, would lose her head, but Danche seemed quite unperturbed.

"Come on in! We've a visitor," she called toward the bathroom. The door opened and a young, extraordinarily broad-shouldered man appeared in the doorway in an undershirt. His large hands and his bristling hair were wet.

Kalkanov felt faint with apprehension. What if she had brought him to this giant in order to teach him a good lesson.

"This is my husband, just back from work," the woman explained. "Mitko, this is Comrade Kalkanov. I've told you about him —he was one of my teachers."

The financial inspector relaxed. "Whew! The ideas that will cross one's mind!" he thought and grew angry at his own cowardice.

The husband shook hands heartily with the guest. Kalkanov measured his powerful muscles with admiration and looked away. And then his eyes came to rest on the mirror before him. It frightened him. He looked infinitely miserable and unhappy. His face was pale and sharp, with two deep old-age wrinkles running under his lips. "You're a fool, my dear fellow," he cursed himself silently, "a bloody old fool, who'll imagine anything. She's got a mountain of a husband. How would she set eyes on you, you dried-up dwarf!"

They entered the bedroom. The furniture was new and gave out a pleasant smell. In the room there was a double bed, a large closet, and a radio. On the windows hung checkered curtains.

Danche started bustling about. She offered him a chair, wiping it with her palm, although there was no trace of dust on it. Kalkanov watched her guiltily from the corner of his eyes. Now, in the light, with her husband, she seemed a very ordinary and modest woman. He remembered his quite recent thoughts and designs and felt guilty. "How could I make such an error in judgment!" he thought. "Is it that I've grown to know women so little?"

"My wife has told me about you," he heard his host's voice and saw that they were alone. "It was you who tried to persuade her father that she should not be taken out of school! And you spoke about her to the director, too."

Kalkanov blinked with surprise. He had forgotten. He searched his memory, and suddenly a thin girl with burning eyes, which looked at him with pain and timid hope, emerged in his mind. Now he remembered quite distinctly how he had told the director that the poor peasant girl, so thirsty for knowledge, should be given help. "So it was that same girl in coarse cotton stockings that he has met now after so many years!"

Kalkanov inclined his head, overcome by a sudden yearning for something beautiful and clean that he had lost long ago. For the first time he felt old and superfluous; he wanted to be another person so as to be able to look those people in the eyes with an open and honest mind.

He did not notice Danche as she entered the room and stood by him. "We couldn't agree with my husband," she started to speak a little haltingly. "I think it would be best for you to sleep in the other room, but he says that the bed is short . . . as if everybody's the Maypole he is!"

Kalkanov was startled, brought back abruptly to reality. It was only now that he grasped the reason for his presence and what his prospects were. While walking along the dark pavements, he had been thinking of everything but this. He had overlooked the simplest explanation. The woman had taken him to her home because he had told her that he had no place to sleep. And when it occurred to him that he had to stay all night long with these people whom he had deceived so cruelly and was going on deceiving, Kalkanov shuddered.

"My wife gets up early and she'll wake you," Mitko's voice

floated to him. "While here you can rest as much as you like. I'm going to work on the afternoon shift."

"Perhaps Comrade Kalkanov won't find it very convenient to sleep in the same bed with you," Danche spoke up.

Kalkanov raised his head slowly. He did not get the exact meaning of their questions, but he could tell by their anxious expressions that they wanted, though at this late date, to repay him for his onetime kindness. And it was far more because of this than because of their words that Kalkanov felt so mean and disgusted with himself. Now he only wanted to sink into the earth, to escape both from people and himself.

Translated by ANDREI DANCHEV

Youth

The morning session was over. The chairman of the district court, Ivan Palaveyev, a meager, stooping man with sunken eyes and knit eyebrows, who years ago had been forced into marrying a local girl, entered his study. He felt tired and worn out. In all three cases this morning the contending parties had been Turks. They understood Bulgarian, but feigned ignorance in order to mislead him. Palaveyev had sworn that he was not going to learn their language and thus had to rely on stupid interpreters. As usual, not one of the lawyers had offered any help. "If you choose to be a devil you can fry alone," their cunning smiles seemed to say. Of course, they dared not tell him this to his face. Outside the court they feared and avoided him, but Palaveyev knew that they spread jokes about his notoriously nagging disposition and that among themselves they called him "The walking paragraph." It occurred to him that a new colleague had arrived, and when he thought how they would prejudice her against him he got still angrier.

There was a knock at the door. Palaveyev threw on his coat, because he was ashamed of his thin and ugly arms. Without waiting for an invitation, a young broad-shouldered man in gabardine trousers and a dark blue shirt entered the room. A thin woman with gray-streaked hair and her best dress on came in after him. The boy quickly walked up to the desk. His face shone with solemn self-confidence.

"What is it?" Palaveyev asked coldly.

"It's only a little thing, comrade chairman," the boy started to speak with excitement. "We want to marry, but she's still under age, so they sent us to get a certificate."

Palaveyev gave the woman a puzzled look, and it was only then that he noticed a very young girl at the door in a rather short silk dress and with two rows of black pearls on her thin neck. She watched him with that cool and somewhat astonished expression with which young girls look at older people, whom they find uninteresting. In spite of her pearls, the waved hair and the high-heeled shoes, something childish and immature emanated from her long and skinny legs, her narrow shoulders, and the barely budding pointed breasts. Standing somehow half-turned toward the wall, with one leg to the side and her head inclined, she resembled a small, frightened calf.

"Hm, aren't they crazy?" Palaveyev thought to himself. "Still smell of milk and want to marry!"

According to the marriage law the chairman of the district court had the right to grant permission for the marriage of minors. Palaveyev had had other similar cases before—mostly Turks, who were only too willing to get rid of their numerous female progeny as soon as possible. He usually granted this permission without even consulting the parents, as the law recommended. This time, too, he decided to "pass" the newcomers, but it was his habit to badger them a little before doing so.

"Where do you work?" he turned to the boy.

"In the electrolysis section of the plant."

"Why did you have that fish tatooed on your skin?"

The boy looked at his arm with the mermaid tatoo and said nothing.

"How old are you?"

"I was born in 1939."

"And the bride?"

"She was born in 1941, comrade judge," the woman spoke up. "She'll be seventeen St. Dimiter's day."

"She's the same age as my Velichko, then," Palaveyev thought. He asked: "Isn't she going to school?"

"No, she works in the factory."

"I see, so you were afraid they'd miss their chance, and now you're in a hurry to marry them off, is that it?"

The mother and the boy smiled and lowered their eyes. Only the girl continued to stand motionless with her eyes fixed on Palaveyev. Now her expression showed astonishment along with a silent rebuke, the way a child looks who disapproves of a grownup's actions. "Now, look at her, isn't she severe," he thought. Palaveyev felt slightly put out, and he suddenly wanted to take her down a peg or two.

"You haven't by any chance already . . . ," he started, without taking his eyes off the girl.

She knit her black eyebrows, and there was a short, sharp flash in her eyes. And though she showed in no other way that she understood the implication, Palaveyev was nonplussed.

"Oh, no such thing, comrade judge," the mother spoke up again. "The boy is going to the Soviet Union. They're sending him to specialize there—that's why we want to have them married."

Palaveyev cast an envious glance at the boy. "Just out of diapers, and already bound for specializations!" he thought. There were those with important posts for years and had never been abroad. He felt a vague annoyance, and a desire to nag overcame him.

"How long will he be away?"

"Six months, comrade judge. Before that they'll take their holidays. They were given holiday cards for Varna."

Palaveyev imagined how the young people had been dreaming all summer long of this honeymoon at the seaside. Then he remembered how dull had been his vacation spent at the bedside of his ill wife, and his annoyance grew. "Where's her father? Why hasn't he come with you?" he asked.

"He's a reservist, comrade judge, and was called up the other day, on Wednesday."

Palaveyev smiled maliciously. "So you decided to push ahead with the marriage, before he came back, is that it?"

"Why, my husband knows," the mother replied with animation. "They work in the same brigade with the boy. He even wanted to have them married in the spring, but . . ."

"These matters can't be settled just as you like," Palaveyev interrupted her. "It's my duty to question both parents."

"But it's all right with him, comrade judge!" the woman ejaculated. "Couldn't I, on my own . . . ?"

"His signature must be here, black on white, too."

"Well, but how if he's absent?"

"You'll have to wait for his return. There's no reason why they should marry today of all days."

The woman stared at him unbelievingly: "Now that's a fine thing! We've got everything ready for the wedding—is it right, just on account of a piece of paper?"

Palaveyev shrugged his shoulders and opened up his newspaper.

Silence fell. Only the labored breathing of the boy could be heard. A clock struck somewhere. "I mustn't forget Tsveta's medicine," Palaveyev thought, and he felt that the girl continued watching him. "What a cheeky brat!" He got angry. "Does she think her being a factory worker is going to put the fear of God into me? Her fiancé going to the Soviet Union: big deal! That's what the hurry is all about—not to let the big fish slip away."

"It's no use your waiting," he said, without lifting his head from the paper.

The woman started imploring him again; the boy, too, said something in a shaken voice, but Palaveyev was not listening to them. He wanted very much to see what the girl was doing. Finally he could not restrain himself and looked at her. She was still watching him with the same inquisitive and concentrated expression, as if lying in wait for him. Although she had not moved from the door since she had entered the room, Palaveyev had the feeling that she was reading every thought of his and this unnerved him.

"Make an exception, comrade judge," the woman went on again. "Don't spoil their happiness. You were young, too, once, just remember that!"

Palaveyev gave her a crooked look and burst out suddenly: "Much good there is to remembering! Tomorrow they'll want a divorce!"

At this point the girl crossed over quickly to her mother, swaying somehow strangely, and said hollowly: "Stop begging!"

Then she made several steps toward the desk. As she walked, the upper part of her body swayed from side to side, and her heels tapped irregularly on the floor.

Palaveyev drew back in bewilderment. The girl was lame. So that's why she'd stood motionless by the door. He suddenly experienced an unpleasant, guilty confusion.

She reached the desk and said quietly in a low voice: "You're a cruel person. You've probably never loved anyone. You may as well know, though, that you won't keep us apart. We'll get married without you." After that she started for the door, limping, but mid-way she stopped and, turning her head, she added: "And we'll never divorce!"

Then she went out hurriedly. The others slipped out after her.

Palaveyev was dumbfounded. It had all happened so unex-pectedly that he still could not grasp it completely. He could not understand what had upset him most—the sudden outburst of the girl, the hard words she had flung at him, after she had kept silent all the time, or the fact that she was lame. He saw her again, as if in life, the way she had swayed toward the desk, and a chord of pity and fearsome guilt struck his heart. How could he have behaved so cru-elly to the unhappy girl! But would I have treated them differently, if I'd known that she was lame?" Palaveyev thought, trying to relieve his conscience. Why hadn't she told him at the beginning, why hadn't she stirred earlier? Was she so much ashamed of her deform-ity? . . . No, she was not ashamed, he decided suddenly, remember-ing each movement of hers. And it wasn't pity she had expected from him. What strength and pride there was in her eyes, when she stood before him uttering these words!

Palaveyev looked into space, and an old ache, buried for many years, stirred in his heart. It was only now that he realized why the visit of these people had so upset and irritated him. "Hadn't it been the same with him, years ago, when he was on the point of leaving his home town and had to part from his fiancée? If he had thrown his lot together with Elena then, he wouldn't be here now, married to a sickly, unloved wife, and perhaps he would not have become sullen and carping. Who had crossed him?"

He went to the open window and looked at the new red roofs. Over there, somewhere beyond those roofs, was his wife's house. One night Palaveyev had entered it as a lodger and he had never left it again. It sometimes seemed to him that it had all been a dream. On the third day after his arrival, he met Tsveta in the street, his landlady's daughter, and went with her for a walk. Then her brother, a rich miller, took him hunting. They started asking him to lunch. The pies the mother had baked! Every evening Tsveta asked him to take her walking along the main street, her brother often accompanying them, until one day he said to him: "The whole town is talking about you two. What are you going to do about it?" Pa-laveyev got confused. He wanted to defend himself, to tell them about Elena, but her brother slapped him on the shoulder and laughed, "Come on, there's nothing to be afraid of!" And he was

married. At the wedding party her brother's friends got drunk and
fired their guns all night long, while Palaveyev kept smiling stupidly
and despising himself. The second week he realized that he did not
love his wife. They had a child, then there came the revolution, and
Palaveyev became rooted in the town. The years slipped by unnoticed. There was only one consolation in his life—his son.

"But you won't keep us apart." He recalled the girl's words.
"Why hadn't Elena used such words at the time? Instead, when she
learned the news, she wrote him a sad letter and forgave him magnanimously. Had she loved him? Yes, she did, but she was unlike this
girl . . . apparently girls weren't like that then."

Later on, when he was leaving, just in front of the door, Palaveyev ran into a short, rather plump girl, who was carrying a new
briefcase under her arm. On seeing him the girl recoiled and looked
at him with fright.

Palaveyev knit his brows, ready, as always, to be rude, but
with surprise he found himself asking her in a soft and unfamiliar
voice: "Are you looking for me?"

The girl became confused: "I'm the new attorney . . . I
wanted . . . I was coming to meet you, but if you're off . . . in
fact, it's rather late . . . "

And from her timorous voice, the undisguised alarm in
her eyes, the way in which she had drawn to the wall, Palaveyev
could tell that her colleagues had already managed to prejudice her
against him. Instead of getting angry he sensed that he was sorry
about something. He looked attentively at the young lawyer, and
suddenly it seemed to him that at the bottom of her eyes, behind the
timidity, there was a spark of hope, as if she had not believed everything they had told her about him. Perhaps there had been such a
spark in every glance, but he had simply not noticed it.

And with an awkward cough, Palaveyev opened the door
wide and said in a low voice: "Come in, please! . . . It's not too
late."

Translated by ANDREI DANCHEV

Lyuben Dilov

(1927–   )

Lyuben Dilov was born on December 25, 1927 in the town of Cherven Bryag. He spent his childhood in Sofia and as an adolescent during World War II he was in Germany with his parents. He finished secondary school in Loukovit and majored in Bulgarian language and literature at Sofia University. Now he is working as Fiction Department Editor of the *Septemvri* magazine. Besides his short stories, novelettes, and novels for adults, he has written many tales, stories, and science fiction for children.

He has published the following books: *Doves over Berlin,* a novelette for adolescents (1953); *The Atomic Man,* science fiction (1958); *On a Last Day,* short stories (1960); *Koko and Kiki,* a book for youngsters (1961); *Boyan Darev's Holiday,* short stories (1962); *The Goblin Well,* a novel for adolescents (1963); *A Memorable Spring,* a novel (1964); *The Stranger,* short stories (1964).

His novel *The Many Names of Fear* and the novelette *A Sketch of Oneself* are to be published soon.

The Stranger

According to some people, life had arranged itself amazingly well for Peter Lechev. Those who appreciated his genial disposition and his modest devotion to his work were glad of this; others envied him and, behind his back, they repeated the tale of the meek lamb he once had been. But Peter Lechev was no more aware of those who envied him than of those who wished him well. Absorbed by his books and his public duty, he noticed few things which had any bearing on his private life. He had stopped being concerned with himself as early as his adolescence when he had begun to be elected regularly to take charge of cultural affairs in the organizations of which he was a member; he seemed to be born for this post, and nobody ever thought of offering him another.

He had been extremely poor as a student and then, all of a sudden, his pockets began to fill with money, which he generously gave away in loans that were never repaid. He was granted a special scholarship simply because it had to be granted to someone who deserved it for high grades and for active and selfless participation in organizational life. Lechev had already been a member of the Faculty Bureau. He graduated with honors and was appointed assistant professor while still a postgraduate student. Just as quietly and unobtrusively, though through brilliant defense of his dissertation, he took his degree, and he was immediately invited to give a series of lectures on philosophy at one of the colleges. He also began contributing articles to newspapers and scientific journals. His first book came out—his former research adviser saw to that—and it got favorable reviews despite the fact that it contained no startlingly new ideas. But how could a young man say anything startlingly new in modern philosophy? More important were the indomitable fervor and the solid erudition with which he fought his ideological adversaries. It surprised him to have his lectures praised at Faculty Council meetings or to be pointed out as a highly conscientious lecturer since he regarded lecturing as his foremost duty to the teachings of the great thinkers he had chosen to serve.

His former professor, who had meanwhile become an important personage at the Academy of Sciences, also took care of Lechev's marriage. He often asked Lechev to his house, constantly and in different ways expressing his benevolence and his ambition to leave a worthy successor behind. Guided by his pedagogical approach, he strongly suggested to Peter Lechev that he was not getting any younger and that bachelorhood was no longer compatible with his social status. Furthermore, it probably hampered his research. Peter had not been aware of this. However, he could not but agree with this idea, because the innate optimism of his philosophy demanded that he perpetuate the human species. He agreed and most probably he would have remained a bachelor; he was unconscious of the girls among his undergraduates and postgraduate students who were ready to offer him their youth and beauty in spite of his thick glasses. His figure, exuding an ascetic, romantic aura, and his profound seriousness, not to mention his good name and the still better future predicted for him, testified that he could be the solid pillar of a happy family. But the academician did not leave him in peace.

Himself childless, with a pertinacity touching and a trifle ridiculous for one of his rank, he kept looking high and low for a wife for his spiritual heir until he finally settled on Zaharina.

"She's one of us!" he said. "She comes of a good family. Her father and I were in jail together for some time before September ninth. He was a wonderful man! But they beat him so badly during the questioning that the poor man fell ill. He died a few years ago . . ."

Zaharina had long since grown accustomed to the idea that she was "one of us" and that she must not marry the first man who came her way. But she also felt that she had long since reached marriageable age, and she had nothing against meeting Peter Lechev, about whom she had heard only the best of things.

Peter liked her ready smile and her eyes, big and beautiful like most shortsighted eyes, and above all, her patience in listening to his discourses on American microsociology, Neothomism—a new decadent trend in philosophical idealism—and other such problems and subjects which occupied him outside of his teaching and public activities. He did not know women; alien even to the most harmless vanity, he couldn't, for instance, puzzle out why Zaharina refused to wear her eyeglasses, but put them on only at the movies or the theater, and then only after the lights were out, preferring, the rest of the time, to squint at people in a rather endearing and intriguing way. Peter was already in love, and this act inordinately excited him until he realized that by squinting she was only trying to see a bit better. He also failed to understand why she would introduce herself as Inna, when, in fact, her name was Zaharina. But how was he to know about women? Schopenhauer was the only philosopher who had dwelt on women, and one could not trust him implicitly because he had died single.

He was carried away by his fervor in explaining the inconsistencies of Neothomism, and he kept failing to make any other kind of declaration until one day Inna interrupted him bluntly: "Now listen to me, Comrade Lechev, have you forgotten that they want us to get married?"

Both Neothomism and American microsociology had been completely clarified to her, and she squinted her pretty eyes, smiling boldly and merrily into his face.

Peter adjusted his glasses in confusion and asked the way only a real philosopher can ask: "Who wants us to?"

"Who? Your academician does and his wife and so does my mother."

"Hm . . ." said Peter and lapsed into silence.

"But you don't seem to want to," she said after a sufficiently long pause, a certain note of embarrassment beginning to creep into her jocular smile.

"Yes," he stammered, "that is, no! What I meant to say was . . ." and his voice trailed off because sometimes "yes" stood for "no" and vice versa. Then unexpectedly he asked the most stupid question possible under the circumstances.

"Do you want to?"

Inna blushed but answered without changing her voice. "I do."

Her flush had smoothed out the coarse-grained skin of her face. Peter looked at her with admiration, thinking: "This is the new kind of woman! Frank and forthright!" and he was so overwhelmed by his discovery that he quite forgot the woman standing in front of him.

"You're impossible, really!" Inna laughed. "You either go your way or . . ."

It took him a few more minutes to do what he had been wanting to do for a long time. His embrace was so clumsy and his kiss so timid that Inna fell even more deeply in love with him.

"You are wonderful!" she said. "But for the life of me I can't figure out what kind of a husband you'll make!"

"I'll make a good husband, you'll see!" he assured her warmly. "I have a very serious attitude to the problems of matrimony."

Her laugh was gayer than ever, and she put her arms around him and kissed him as if she wanted to show him how one should kiss one's beloved.

They celebrated the wedding in high style in the apartment left to Inna by her mother after the death of her highly praised father, and the envious ones were convinced once again that Peter Lechev certainly knew how to feather his nest. At one stroke he had acquired a good wife, an influential mother-in-law, and an apartment. They immediately set about partitioning the spacious living room so that he could have a study of his own.

The wedding guests were all eminent personalities: professors, generals, and public figures, invited according to a long and carefully drawn-up list. There was even a deputy minister who had no doubt only recently been appointed, since he was aglow with the honors accorded him. The feast was superb; the guests were pleased with the food and drinks, and they enjoyed the fact that the the two young people were in love and were perfectly suited to each other.

Peter moved about like a sleepwalker amid the glittering and convivial bustle around him. He finally managed to tear the deputy minister away from the fine wine, pressed him into a corner, and set out to prove to him that microsociology was a teaching only such ignoramuses in philosophy as the Americans could have devised. Just imagine their practical inferences: they preached that society should be reorganized and regrouped only according to profession, family relationships, and personal likes. The deputy minister listened vaguely, nodding condescendingly throughout, with a smile on his face that seemed to whisper happily: "How wonderful it is to be a deputy minister, but microsociology is all stuff and nonsense!"

Lechev lived through their so-called honeymoon in the same strange sleepwalking state which had overcome him on his wedding day. He felt more than he thought, and though he tried to define why, he failed time and again. He had the sensation of having been plunged into a warm river whose waters pleasantly carried him lightly along somewhere . . . but where? His cozy study was replete with carpets and rugs, armchairs and little tables, with books, bric-a-brac and paintings, all of which tempted him to caress them with his eyes; he took pleasure in just looking at them, yet he still found it hard to write his lectures in the study. But why? Inna's figure filled out, becoming more supple and more beautiful, and she somehow changed abruptly into a woman who infused him and the air around him with a thick, languid sweetness which stuck to his consciousness like a sugary syrup. Something mysterious and powerful lurked in her metamorphosis and called for submission. But what was this something, and where did it come from?

Peter had stated to his wife that he had "a very serious attitude to the problems of matrimony," but it turned out that he had no attitude at all; the "problems" were to him as hazy as the category of beauty which had always been the Achilles' heel of his knowledge. Just as in the universally accepted definition of beauty there was something which disconcerted him, so in all that was pleasant and pretty around him there was something which deeply disturbed him. What was it?

Once he shared his doubts with Inna. He was so touchingly helpless and endearing that, after she gazed at him with her squinting eyes, she found nothing to worry about. Inna was bursting with knowledge—she was an art specialist—with business-like vigor and with a purely feminine spiritual vitality and the self-confidence of the happy wife.

She stroked his unshaven cheek with maternal kindness, smiling as she said: "This is all new to men; they're savages, they must get used to things, learn and be tamed . . . while we women are born with it. Dear philosopher, do you want me to confuse you still further? I hear that on his deathbed Rodin said something like this: 'I believe we'll never be able to find out exactly why a certain thing is beautiful.' What do you say to that?"

"A pure example of idealism!" Peter Lechev was indignant. "Man must know in order to . . ."

"But if he unravels all the secrets of beauty, will it seem beautiful to him any more?"

She did not deliver this as an argument in a dispute but as a flirtatious, good-naturedly ironic piece of moralizing. In addition, she threw her arms around him and spread the dizzying softness of her body all over his chest so that the divine wrath of the scientist against such a fatalistic reconciliation with the secrets of life did not explode in his heart. His heart beat faster in a different fashion, and Lechev again admired his lovely wife, her practical cast of mind, and her wonderful natural knowledge of everyday life, knowledge which had always evaded him or which had cost him hours of intense and contradictory cerebral activity, fruitless more often than not. And he gave in. After all, the problems of love and marriage were not his province; there were other, real enemies he had to combat on the barricades of philosophy. What was more, the two women took loving care of him; they protected him, parrying all blows that might surprise him from whatever direction.

Deprived of a man's presence in the house for so long, they took him to the tailor's and other shops, but soon gave it up because he annoyed them with his soft-spoken preachings: You shouldn't patronize private tailors even if they are better. Or: Superfluous objects tend to imprison man by burdening his consciousness and leading him astray from the mainsprings of life!

"All right, don't go astray!" Inna laughed happily and dressed and fixed him up as she had probably dressed her dolls in her childhood. Peter felt ill at ease in the fashionable suits, in the expensive shirts and underwear which felt cold to his skin, in the pinching foreign-made shoes, but . . . his social position required it . . . and then, man must be trained to appreciate beauty."

Inna was riding on the crest of the passions and ambitions of the young bride, and her husband could not resist her. Sometimes she herself would come up with a start: "I wish all this ado were over! I've completely neglected my work!" meaning the scientific paper she was about to begin work on. But only a sweet weariness and not a hint of regret sounded in her complaint.

"This won't do!" said her mother, who began to rebel against her son-in-law's awkwardness in family affairs. "You're ruining your career. I'm busy, too. He must also give us a helping hand."

But Inna defended him. "His work is more important, he's fighting on the ideological front."

"Some fighter!" her mother wrinkled her forehead, wrinkled as it was. "Let him fight, but who's to repair the hot plate?"

More and more frequently she began using her favorite expression, "This won't do!" She barked it out rapidly and sharply like a military command. She was small but extremely agile and militant and spent her days shuttling back and forth between the offices of the prominent friends of her late husband to set right all kinds of injustices with her "This won't do!" She was always boiling over with indignation about something, and even when she was about to intercede for someone she would begin with: "This won't do! He's one of us—a very capable fellow!—His father . . ."

She was really busy. In the evening she sat on all kinds of committees and public commissions until late at night; the rare times she was at home she was always hopping around the phone, gesturing wildly and shouting to somebody: "This won't do! Just imagine! They've fired him under the worst paragraph in the labor code!"

At odd times, mostly on Sundays, she would unexpectedly utter her battle cry and rush around the house cleaning and arranging things in such a way if something was lost it could never be found until it popped up of its own accord weeks later.

Bent over his manuscripts in his study, Peter would stop his ears because her "This won't do!" pierced his brains mercilessly, shredding to bits the formulations he had pieced together with such difficulty. Nonetheless, he did not find it unpleasant to have someone do things for him in the next room. It sometimes occurred to him that his mother-in-law might talk less on the telephone or at least in a lower tone, but he never mustered enough courage to tell her so. He would stop working, take a handkerchief—usually the newest and the best one—and start dusting his books, so that Inna would give a helpless cry. At such times he usually managed to knock over some of the numerous bric-a-brac arranged along the shelves of his bookcase, and if anything broke, he would be more frightened than if all the idealists and vulgar materialists in the world had leaped at him in one bound.

Then Inna would be sure to say: "You're awful! You've no sense of beauty! That's why you're no good at esthetics."

Her mother would bark out her comment "This won't do!"

like an infuriated sergeant before his platoon. "We must look for domestic help!" and she would rush to the phone to unburden herself to one of her innumerable co-activists. However, this sort of thing happened rarely because the carpets in the study were soft and they kept the objects from breaking.

Peter Lechev's life seemed to be cushioned with the same kind of soft, thick carpet; he could step on it softly, with pleasure; the pages of his book attacking microsociology began piling up, and his file filled out like Inna's rose-colored cheeks. She was invariably charming in spite of her plumpness and just as incomprehensibly and endearingly took offense if he happened to call her "Zaharina." Peter felt very comfortable in his new home, and perhaps it was for this reason that his mother-in-law's decision to hire a domestic scared him beyond words. A stranger in the house would disrupt the idyllic hours of solitude and the intimate dinner-table talk. Inna, at least, ought to have been aware of this, but neither she nor her mother would listen to him. As a matter of fact, they had long since ceased asking his opinion and met all his arguments with a condescending smile. But he did not dare voice his timid conviction that two healthy women could cope with the day's meals and a three-room apartment.

"Inna's not going to be your slave!" the mother-in-law announced in a voice that precluded all objections. "When is she going to be able to write her 'Humanism' or something?"

The rebuke was as unfair as could be, because Peter had insisted on making his own bed, ironing his shirts, and shining his shoes —something he had done ever since he could remember—but which Inna had taken over from him. Just the same, just the same, to his strange mind it was more appropriate for Inna to do those things than some total stranger whom he visualized as a mumbling and moaning old lady. He secretly gloated over the fact that it was so difficult to get a maid these days.

But he had not adequately estimated the determination of his energetic mother-in-law, and this was to cause him a shattering surprise. One evening when he came home from a department meeting, he found the living room crowded with women. Or so it seemed to him in the semidarkness caused by the thick shade of the floor lamp in the corner. Peter did not appreciate the comfort of such lamps, which only made him strain his eyes. And so, as was his habit, he switched on the large chandelier, which had the spread of a spider. Amid the blinding waterfall of light which suddenly gushed forth from the ceiling, his mother rose and Peter hugged her with affection.

"When did you come? What finally made you come and see us?"

Mother Raina, a good-natured and talkative old lady, rattled off: "Well, here I am. I have to straighten you out, too, don't I? You're still only children, after all, only children!"

"Why didn't you send a wire?" Peter failed to notice the secret smiles of his wife and mother-in-law.

"You scientists just haven't time for anything! You haven't thought of writing me a letter in ages. But I'm not staying long this time. The old man hasn't a grain of sense left in his head. He'll let the chickens die off. But I've brought along a girl to help you in the house."

It was only then that Peter saw the girl who sat unnaturally erect, as if petrified, on the edge of the sofa. Her bare feet, sun-tanned and slender, stuck out in a pair of unbelievably large sneakers which had long since lost their original color. Peter blinked behind his glasses in confusion, frowned, and held out his hand.

"Her name's Tsonka. She's from Rossen, you know her family. Tsonka, come on and kiss his hand! Come on!"

"Mother!" Peter was hot with indignation. "Am I a holy man or something?" and he snatched his hand away from under the nose of the bending girl. As a matter of fact, another thought, another rather crazy comparison had flashed through his mind. Unable to shake it away, he turned about-face and entered his study without a word.

"He'll get over it!" Inna laughed. Mother Raina, already informed on everything, began to bustle about the place.

"Now let's fix up the girl for the night, because I'll be off first thing in the morning." And she dragged all her bundles and baskets toward the kitchen.

Peter had opened a book, but it took him some time to realize it was an English dictionary of idiomatic phrases; he spent an hour or two brushing up on the language every evening. He tried hard to concentrate, but the commotion in the living room irritated him and besides, they gave him no peace. His mother-in-law called on him (not noticing his anger) to help her bring down the sewing machine from the neighbors upstairs. She was an aggressive, fearless little woman who had gone through a lot, but she was mortally afraid of infection. For this reason the first thing she did was push the girl into the bathroom and heap her scanty clothes in a closet. Then, together with Raina, they set to fixing her up with two or three of Inna's dresses.

They grunted and groaned taking the machine down, and

Peter bruised his fingers against the banisters. But this time Inna did not utter her little shriek—now she had something else on her mind —and he himself had to put some iodine on the cut. He went into his study again and sat down at the desk, but his fingers hurt and when he looked at the big iodine stains on them and remembered that the girl had been about to kiss his hand, something snapped inside him. He was hungry; the cigarettes he lit one after another increased his hunger instead of killing it, but the sewing machine in the next room whirred like a machine gun aimed at his head. It occurred to no one that it was already past dinnertime.

They called him only after he had begun to outline his lecture for the following morning, and he left his study with a still deeper frown on his face. The couch in the kitchen had been converted into a bed, and the girl sat by the table looking even more helpless and pathetic with her wet hair streaming down. She was a tall girl, very thin, with a pallid face, and eyes set so far apart that Levchev had the feeling he was being watched by two persons at once.

"What made you decide to be a maid?" he asked the eyes, but they looked down quickly and made no answer. "Why don't you choose something better to do? Aren't there any jobs to be had on the farm? Why?"

"This won't do!" his mother-in-law tried to cut him short, but his mother was quicker.

"What?! The co-operative farm! The girl is not to waste her life away in the wilderness the way we did! She'll meet all kinds of people here, make something of herself, get a better husband for herself. Tsonka, don't you listen to him, dear! They're all the same, these scientist fellows, always telling you what to do. But he's a good man, is Peter, you'll see!"

Inna's eyes squinted angrily and her mother's forehead had ominous wrinkles in it, so he grew silent. He was no longer hungry, and his fingers were still numb. Peter had two or three mouthfuls and left the table.

Inna went in to him shortly afterward. She stroked his hair and asked: "Are you going to work?"

"I must!" he replied.

"Don't be cross! The girl seems nice. She'll get used to us and will be like a member of the family."

"The ideological work in the countryside must be very poor. Go and build socialism with such people! A young girl and yet . . ."

Inna again stroked his head and smiled.

"Don't get upset over nothing! You've got more important work to do!" She kissed him.

Around midnight, having finished his lecture, he stood up, squared his stiffened shoulders, and realized that his throat was completely dry from too much smoking. He needed a drink of water and started toward the kitchen. But in the foyer he suddenly recalled that the kitchen was no longer empty, that a stranger was sleeping there. She would surely be embarrassed if they went in and out like that after she had gone to bed. She was a grown girl. But his throat contracted, his old pharyngitis was flaming up, and Peter swore under his breath, "What the devil! If she wants to be a maid she'll have to get used to it."

He had cautiously reached for the doorknob when all of a sudden he heard soft, subdued sobbing. Nothing could be seen through the small frosted pane at the top of the door, but Peter stood glued to the spot with his heart pounding until the weeping, which sounded more like a mournful whine, had come to an abrupt stop. The girl had probably become aware of his presence; he went back to the living room. He lit another cigarette and nervously puffed it as he walked about among the numerous easy chairs. Then he entered the bedroom. One of the bedside lamps was on, but Inna was sleeping her sound and probably happy sleep; she always dreamed of beautiful things because she was an art specialist. Peter stood watching her—she had blossomed out into relaxed rosy plumpness like the beauties in the pictures that were once sold at country fairs—and he hastened to put out the light.

He undressed in the dark and went to bed but was unable to fall asleep. Tortured by his thirst and his thoughts, he had forgotten that he could have gotten a drink of water in the bathroom. His last thought was "This won't do!" and he would have been angry with himself for using his mother-in-law's phrase had he not already sunk into the heavy intoxication of uneasy slumber.

In the morning, drunk with sleep and just as upset, he left the house much earlier than necessary. He wanted to ask some of his colleagues for advice, but he was ashamed to admit that he had suddenly become the master of a stranger, an employer—an exploiter. Yes, according to all the laws of logic, formal logic at least, this very much resembled exploitation, and he had to face up to it because it did not suit his profession to be such a person. He could have asked for advice from his old mentor, the academician, who had had a housemaid for years, but there the situation was entirely different. The academician even had a private secretary, he was a man of nationwide importance, and most of all, he was an elderly person. His wife could not take proper care of him or their home as befitted his rank. No, he had to settle this matter all by himself and the sooner the better!

However, it was no easy job despite the fact that the premises and syllogisms fell into place quickly in his head; he truly envied his wife and her mother who were visibly able to deal with the problems of life so efficiently. The two of them danced about the girl, vehemently issuing their instructions to her. "Tsonka, this is how you should do this, this is where you should put that! Tsonka, Tsonka . . ." Her name was constantly on their lips but the two women said it almost in caressing tones, and even the mother-in-law's favorite expression "This won't do!" sounded soft and without malice. They bought a new electric range as if for Tsonka's sake, and then took the girl to the hairdresser's, so that, with her hair neatly done and dressed in one of Inna's pretty frocks, she no longer looked so homely. Since Inna was a little shorter, Tsonka's small knees, slightly pointed and somewhat moving, were always peeping out from under her skirt. When he became aware of his eyes lingering on them—he frequently and involuntarily let his eyes wander over to Tsonka's disfigured rubber sneakers which seemed to trample on his heart—Peter was horrified at himself. He was all the more horrified when Freud's name, one of his fierce ideological opponents, flashed through his mind.

"How much were those shoes?" he once asked his wife, pointing to her shoes.

"Thirty-five . . ." she answered somewhat abashed, since she was not used to his showing an interest in such matters. "Made to order."

"Here, take this money! Let the girl buy herself a pair of shoes."

Inna narrowed her eyes as though some sand had been thrown into her face. "What's come over you? If you don't need the money, you can give it to me!"

"But she's got no shoes! Those tattered . . ."

"Now look here! Tsonka gets her wages and she'll buy whatever she pleases. I'd have let her have some of my older pairs, but they don't fit her peasant feet."

"How much is she paid?"

"Twenty leva."

"Twenty?" Peter was stupefied. "How is it possible?"

"What about her food and lodgings? We'll raise her wages later. This is how it's done."

"But then . . . she can't buy shoes like these!"

"You're such a darling little fool! Why should she have exactly the same kind of shoes! There are cheaper ones. Come on, you have no idea about these things!"

Peter said no more, but he did not give in. The shoes became an obsession with him, and he felt that his equilibrium would be restored only if the girl got the same kind of shoes. He knew this feeling was stupid, that there was something spurious about it, but nevertheless he could not get rid of it. He felt a little better only after he had managed to give Tsonka money for new shoes.

She looked at him with fear in her wide-apart eyes because she had probably never had so much money in her life. He hastened to turn his back on her and avoided her eyes, which caused him some sort of ill-defined yet powerful feeling of guilt and shame.

On the following day Tsonka said to Inna: "The master told me to get a pair of shoes. Could you come and pick them out for me?" Her face was alight with pleasure.

"Have you got the money?"

"He gave it to me."

The color fled Inna's cheeks, but she quickly regained her self-possession. "Oh, yes. You see, the money was advanced to you against your wages, but we're not going to have you pay it back all at once. We'll do it little by little and you'll never feel it."

Inna had good taste and bought a pair of good shoes, though considerably cheaper than hers, but she did not say a word about this to her husband.

"Are those what you bought with so much money?" Peter frowned as he once found Tsonka cleaning up his study wearing a pair of fluffy yellow slippers on her feet.

"Oh, no!" the girl answered happily. "I wear these around the house. The others are for going out."

She ran out to fetch the shoes, and her dress again bared her little knees. Peter looked the shoes over with approval, but he turned his glance away because the two creatures in Tsonka's eyes were observing him with tender devotion.

"I'll take just a minute, Master!" Tsonka said, calling him "Master" like this for the first time since she had begun dusting his desk.

"What is this about being her master?" Peter Lechev was thinking furiously. "Isn't this the way the human conscience is bought? Isn't this the way the slave mentality is formed? Was mine an act of justice or an act of bribery? Was it a well-deserved reward or a tip?"

He didn't know that Inna had taken care of justice in her own way and secretly he continued to watch the girl, his mother-in-law, his wife, and himself with his earlier sharpened sensitivity because Tsonka's new shoes had not brought him the peace of mind he had unconsciously and naïvely hoped for.

Tsonka was begining to fit very well into the family routine. She turned out to be a simplehearted and unpretentious but intelligent and deft girl, and she followed instructions to the letter. She developed an attachment to her employers, and when Peter's penetrating glance happened to meet hers, he only detected the earlier fear in her eyes from time to time. The two women gradually let her do all the chores; the mother-in-law was again swallowed up by her committee work, but whenever she was at home she shouted even louder into the phone, as if finally able to concentrate all her energy into her favorite phrase "This won't do!" However, Inna had not yet begun her writing project "Humanism and Democracy in Bulgarian Art During the Revival Period," which was long overdue. She had continued to grow plumper and prettier (the roughness of her skin had vanished completely), but Peter—who knows why—began to discover more and unpleasant features in her.

One day the two women dragged in a giant TV set with the aid of technicians, planted it in the living room, bustled around it all day long, and finally sat down in front of it in the evening. Lechev stood around for a few minutes, frowned, and then went to his study to work on his English. His project was not going well either. In contrast to his wife, the file on microsociology had stopped growing fatter, and he had begun to repeat his lectures mechanically with no trace of his former zest. Now, more frequently than ever before, Tsonka's sobbing would be in his ear, the mournful whine which had shaken him so that first night she spent in their house. He was convinced she still cried when she went to bed, and once he went so far as to check on it. Inna had gone to bed, her mother had dashed off to some meeting or other, and he tiptoed to the kitchen door. At first he even heaved a sigh of relief, a profound sense of satisfaction spread through his being—it couldn't be otherwise, she was crying, tortured and humiliated by her position—and the blow was all the harder when the hallucination of autosuggestion crumbled to pieces as the sounds of a soft, playful tune reached his ears. Tsonka was singing. Shaken to the marrow, he peered through the glass, almost touching the window with his glasses. He saw the girl's young silhouette on the pane of the window opposite. Tsonka was undressing as she prepared for bed and . . . singing. Her thin little shoulders had lost their sharpness in the milky half-light of the kitchen, and they gave off a soft sheen which grew in intensity around the small breasts visible under her slip. Her body swayed like a rich grapevine, and Peter could not take his eyes off the unexpected sight.

A voice within him exclaimed: "But she's already a woman!" and in this exclamation there was a strange burning tremor, born out of the collision of something pleasant and unpleasant, out of the sweetness of curiosity and the bitterness of disappointment. Was it really too late, was he really a pathetic and laughable Don Quixote who himself did not know what he wanted or why he wanted it? He was ashamed of himself and, like a night prowler tiptoeing back to his room and his marital bed, he felt like a man on the verge of committing a loathsome crime. His quickened breathing and nervous movements woke Inna.

"Is that you? What took you so long?"

"Go back to sleep!" he whispered, recalling her promise to sit up for him.

"Some luck being married to a philosopher!" Inna murmured angrily as she turned her broad back to him, rosy and luxuriant like the lace of her nightgown.

Lechev instinctively stretched out his body, trying to banish the tension from his muscles. Failing, he switched off the bedside lamp without taking off his glasses. He couldn't think without his glasses; if he chanced to take them off in the daytime, he immediately felt like a lost lamb, unable to find the way out of a dark, beast-ridden forest. Actually he did not feel like thinking now, he'd rather have run away from everything, but he knew it was impossible for him to act dishonestly, even to himself, that he couldn't rest until he had grappled at least with one problem, though not necessarily the most important problem. But which one?

"This is what philosophy is like!" Peter Lechev was thinking, but his thoughts were unusually feverish and heretical. There had never been such thoughts in his once sober and well-balanced mind. "Yes, all philosophy is contained in one single person who sings when she ought to be crying, and you're facing her the way a calf would face a very tall wall, not knowing what's on the other side— grass or weeds. It is contained in the lace of Inna's nightgown, and in my mother-in-law's wrinkling forehead, but you never had the right glasses for it. It is in you, too, but you're facing it like a naked child studying his own reflection in the mirror for the first time, realizing with horror and amazement and shame that there's more to him than he ever dreamed and that some things have different functions from the ones he knows. Peter, Peter, you wretched spiritual leader, you don't even know which way to go in this minor upset of life!"

Peter Lechev came to these bitter conclusions that night, but in the morning he woke up with an unexpected inner calm; it filled him with a determination to do something, but he had no idea what. It stemmed entirely from his conviction that he had no right to compromise with his feelings or with the inner resistance of things. He wished he could stay in the warm bed a little longer and clarify his strangely gay mood, but something very powerful was pulling him to the kitchen. He took a shower, and in his impatience he cut his face several times while shaving. He dressed quickly and though there were a few tiny red nicks on his cheek, he remained exuberant and cheerful.

Breakfast had been served, the coffee was steaming in the cups, and the three women were waiting for him. Inna observed a strict ritual at mealtimes: the entire family had to assemble at the table. Tsonka had to sit with them, although she was constantly kept on the run to the kitchen and back.

Peter sat down and unfolded his napkin on his knees. He noticed the wrinkles on his mother-in-law's forehead, the angrily questioning squint in Inna's eyes—Inna had evidently not yet fully wakened—and then he turned his eyeglasses to Tsonka. In the gray light of the fall morning she was the same plain, underdeveloped, and helpless child. But the vision of the previous night kept playing in Lechev's mind, and the feeling that something pleasant was going to happen fluttered in his heart. "Stop getting up all the time!" he ordered, lowering his head as he sensed fear in Tsonka's eyes and puzzlement in the other two women. He took a sip of his coffee and to his surprise found himself asking:

"How old are you?"

"Seventeen," the girl whispered.

Peter was surprised—he had thought her older—but the next question was already on his lips: "Have you a boyfriend?"

The girl flushed, and—who knows why—the pleasant sensation in his chest grew stronger.

"Peter, this won't do!" his mother-in-law said stridently. "What kind of talk is this, anyway?"

But he would not let them divert him. "Why not? She's a grown girl. She should have a boyfriend. In a word, she should go out more often to the movies, to the theater, to dances . . ."

"We bought a TV set, didn't we?" the mother-in-law objected.

"You're the ones looking at it, while she's washing dishes. Listen, Tsonka, you're a modern girl. Are you planning to be a maid all your life?" Now he raised his eyeglasses more boldly, even defiantly; their glint, strengthening his inner calm, seemed to suffuse his gaunt face. "Communism does not require maids, but strong, free women; it requires harmoniously developed persons. You must go in for sports; read and learn!" Lechev raised his voice, carried away by his sudden thought. "We'll have you enrolled in a night school, then the university, in a word . . ."

Inna's cup shook noisily in the saucer.

"Tsonka, clear the table!" the mother-in-law commanded. "Whoever's finished has finished." And she dashed off after her daughter.

Peter looked around in confusion. Had he said anything wrong? "Listen, Tsonka!"

"Master, I have to clear the things away!" The two creatures in the girl's eyes were about to burst into tears.

"Listen to me, I tell you! Sit down and listen! Do you know what communism is all about?"

He waved his hands, his eyeglasses glittering as though he were in a large auditorium packed with adversaries. Tsonka sat there trembling because she hadn't the foggiest notion as to what was wanted of her. Then she sobbed aloud as she caught sight of the shadow of her older formidable mistress across the glass door.

"Peter, Inna's calling you," his mother-in-law said in almost sweet tones through the half-open door as she rapidly disappeared into the next room.

Lechev frowned with annoyance, but he threw down his napkin. As a matter of fact, he had said what he had to say. He smiled at Tsonka and asked: "Is everything clear to you now?" And, patting her on the shoulder, he felt her pointed shoulder blades quiver like a pair of wings. Then he made for the bedroom in high spirits. But Inna wasn't there: she was waiting in his study, and she attacked before he had had time to cross the threshold.

"You . . . you . . . Are you an idiot or what?" she gasped for breath and Peter, who had never seen her in such a state, wilted like a broken branch.

"Inna . . ."

"What the devil are you about? We could hardly find the girl! How many times have I told you not to interfere in things that aren't any of your business!"

"Inna!" Lechev groaned. "But after all we're . . ."

"That's enough!" she screamed savagely. "I'm sick and tired of your philosophizing! Fool that you are!"

She squinted her eyes and clenched her plump little fists looking as if she might jump at him any minute. Smitten by a sudden unbearable pain, Peter pulled himself together and left the room in silence. He seized his raincoat off the rack, stumbled down the stairs, bumping into some woman who said "Hello" and smiled after him. It was only when he reached the outer entrance that he realized he couldn't see a thing. He took off his glasses and wiped them carefully with his handkerchief which trembled and shook in his hands. At the university he remembered he had forgotten his lecture notes.

What had he planned to speak to his students about? He did not always use his notes and was considered a good speaker, but now he knew he could not utter a word. And he wanted so much to talk, talk: about how you can love a person, feel close to her, think her the closest of them all, believe in her as you believe in yourself, and then, all of a sudden, you discover that there is another person dwelling in her who does not understand you, who can call you an idiot and a fool precisely when you think you're acting most wisely and honorably. It wasn't so much the insult inflicted by those words that gnawed at his heart, although he had never before heard such offending words applied to himself. He was a softspoken and self-disciplined man, and it had never occurred to anyone, not even in the army, to hurt him in this way. A precipice had suddenly gaped open between him and the woman in whose love he had trusted, and now he stood on the edge of the chasm, painfully asking himself whether it had always been there or whether it had suddenly opened now for reasons he could not as yet fathom. And, what was more important, he could not see a bridge spanning it or a track leading back.

He had never before quarreled with Inna, and somewhere in his mind he wished to believe that their scene was one of those squabbles he had heard were inevitable between husband and wife, which were the product of that deepseated and insurmountable difference between the sexes, irrespective of feeling. However, this was merely one way to judge the matter and offered him neither the hope nor the consolation he craved for.

A young man overtook him under the chestnut trees in front of the university, but Lechev was unable to grasp the young man's question, and then instead of answering he blurted out:

"Would you please do me a favor? Would you take a taxi and go to my house?"

The young man was one of his good students; he liked him

because of his fearless and uncompromising statements in class, and now he felt he had no right to cancel his lecture. Inna handed the student the manuscript through a half-opened door—she wanted to hide her swollen eyes. She had managed to get rid of her mother who had fallen upon her the minute Peter was out of the house: "Inna, darling, he's fallen in love with her! We made a big mistake in bringing such a young girl into the house!"

"Don't be ridiculous!" said Inna indignantly, but her mother was already ablaze with her perpetual faultfinding.

"You don't know men, dear! They're all scoundrels as far as that goes. I've got eyes in my head if you haven't. He keeps looking at her, and she just stands there gaping at him. I've been thinking for a long time now: This won't do!"

"Mother, please, Peter is not that kind of a man."

"They're all scoundrels, Inna dear, believe me, they're all good-for-nothings."

"Get out! Do you hear? Get out!" Inna had screamed, all of a sudden having remembered the shoe incident, her husband's glowing face that morning, and the fact that he had taken to staying up all hours in his study, too late for her to sit up for him.

Peter Lechev had no idea about the monstrous accusations gathering over his head. When lunchtime came he wanted to go home, but the corrosive pain was still eating at him, and he accepted his bright student's invitation to lunch and a walk afterward.

It was one of those fine fall afternoons when the sun, having driven away the morning mists, suddenly poured down its warm gold all over the world and everything around shone bright with the short-lived intoxication of the earth's last prewinter urge to life. The park was as tranquil as a fairyland cave strewn with rubies and emeralds; only the dry grass rustled under foot, as if in protest at being disturbed in its eternal sleep. The stillness and languor of the warmed forest was not conducive to conversation, and perhaps it was for this reason that the young man invited his teacher, who was sunk in thought, to his room. He wanted to read him something.

Peter let himself be led as if he had no will of his own. He was in no listening mood, but he felt so unnerved that he offered no resistance. His student lived nearby in a rented room stuffed with books; he paid an exorbitant rent because the apartment contained a Viennese sofa of the last century. He brought out a bottle of homemade brandy and a closely written manuscript, but he hadn't even read the title because, while he was still washing the brandy glasses, his roommate came home with two girls. The young man was in the same class and after he got over his initial confusion, he exclaimed with hearty pleasure, though with the slight affectation of the young: "This is a red-letter day—a lecturer visiting his students! It calls for a celebration! Musicians, strike up the band for Comrade Lechev!"

The girls were equally free and gay, and one of them immediately produced a transistor radio which only gave them the Daichovo station despite vigorous shifting of the dial.

"Let's not be scared by symbols!" the student cried out. "We're neither at Heidelberg nor at Oxford."

"We were supposed to read something . . ." Lechev fidgeted about but they shouted him down.

"No reading! Haven't you had enough of our silly talk in class? We'll get the gang together in a jiffy and we'll have a real philosophic party! These are orders!" The young men had recently come back from their summer military training camps. "Deployment of forces: Mimi, you go to the phone! In half an hour the tape recorder must be brought into position! Jana, you're the vanguard patrol next to Comrade Lechev's right knee. You're to engage the enemy in slight patrol skirmishes and make him expose his flanks. Boris, the wine jug is your department. Later someone will run over to the cafeteria and sell our meal tickets!"

"We'll have a reading session some other time, Comrade Lechev," said Boris, also reconciled. "You ought to come to see us, the young generation, more often, you shouldn't stay away from us . . . we need you, not only in the classroom."

He introduced Lechev to the girls as their most cultured, their most intelligent, in a word, their best lecturer, and Jana exclaimed: "We have no such handsome associate professor!" She plumped down on the rickety Viennese sofa, and the blue garters of her stockings were visible for a moment.

Peter, whose eyes were beginning to burn with the brandy, remembered with sorrow that not a single young girl had ever entered his room when he was a student, and he wanted so much to say something fine and edifying to these good young people. But the radio continued to blare out its accordion dances, with Jana playfully beating time with her bare knees opposite him, and someone now and then offered him a glass full of brandy. He could only grin because he had never developed the knack of joining in this type of jocular conversation.

"So this is what a finished philosopher looks like!" the girl was splitting her sides with laughter. "Boys, aren't you to be pitied!"

"Are you a Jesuit, by any chance?" Mimi, who had just come back from the telephone, joined in the fun.

Peter engaged in self-criticism and began to expound his ideas about the harmoniously developed personality, to make references to his own youth, but more students trooped in and a tape recorder wiped out the good old accordion. A girl asked him to dance, and for the second time since his wedding Lechev tried to tango. But his feet refused to obey him this time, too. Later he tried to slip in a word about microsociology, but the boys all fell upon him: it would be much better if our philosophers finally explored the problems of dogmatism and the cult period. They showered him with such bold ideas that he was downright frightened. He glanced at his watch—how did it get to be so late! They must be terribly worried at home. He hadn't called all day! He left them, in spite of the persuasive words of Jana and Mimi, who finally escorted him all the way to the front door.

He came to on the street and laughed out with embarrassment when he suddenly realized that his knees were buckling and felt as soft as rubber. In his chest a good, all-forgiving being was laughing, prodding him on to hurry and tell Inna about these splendid kids who were so intelligent and so daring and . . . right because they had grown up free in a time of justice. He would apologize to her . . . it was only one day he hadn't seen her, but it seemed to him that this unsuspected longing in his heart had been accumulating there for years. Inna would understand. She couldn't but understand that their very love for each other obliged them to help that poor, blind creature also become as free and daring as his students. The girl was entitled to it just as anybody else was, and Inna . . .

But Inna turned her back on him; she sat next to her mother in the living room which was full of a spectral luminescent semi-darkness, watching TV which seemed to patch up all quarrels. She did not answer his timid greeting but said over her shoulder: "Your dinner's in the study."

Lechev rummaged in vain through his pockets for his cigarettes—he had left them in his student's room—and he felt he was growing cold and sober; a throbbing, chilly hatred for these two women welled up in him. They sat, perched like two owls in the darkened room, fiercely watching the TV screen, while Tsonka . . .

Almost involuntarily he went to the kitchen, and the girl jumped up in fright from her couch. Her pale little face was wet with tears.

"Why are you crying?" Peter asked sharply.

"The mistress . . . has told me . . . to pack up and go."
Tsonka burst into sobs. "Tomorrow . . ."

Lechev froze for an instant, then he rushed into the living room and, horrified, he shouted from the threshold: "Inna, what have you done?"

"It's none of your business! Go ahead and eat!"

A powerful determination pulled his slouching figure upright. Lechev buttoned up his raincoat, which he had not had time to take off, and ordered Tsonka: "Get dressed—we're going!"

The trembling girl stood looking at him with terrified eyes.

"Get dressed, I tell you!" Peter shouted as he threw her worn-out coat over her shoulders, seizing her by the hand.

Inna stopped them on the landing. She had screwed up her eyes so tightly that only her pupils flashed like two slender piercing rays. "Where are you going?"

"We'll go and look for a night school!"

"Scoundrel!" Inna yelled. "Filthy woman-chaser!" And she banged the door after them.

Outside, the evening fog had descended from the Vitosha Mountain, and the street lamps swam in it like egg yolks. Peter could make out only the street lamps, dragging the girl along in their reddish yellow glare without knowing where he was taking her. He heard the girl's hoarse breathing, her stifled sobbing, and he clutched her hand more firmly. Her fingers were small like a child's, cold and trembling, and they filled him with tenderness and determination, but he had no time to think about them.

He was thinking about his wife and the new insult she had hurled at him, and he wondered where on earth she could have got wind of the party and the girls. He asked himself if there was anything wrong with that—they were his own students, his children, so to speak! Was it possible for her to suspect him of such duplicity? How could one live with a person if he had no trust in him? Yes, how could one go in living like this?

But where was that damned school?

They walked on and on and still found no school. As a matter of fact, he did not know where it was because he had noticed it only at night, and each time he was surprised to see the windows all lit up until someone had told him it was a night school. He asked a man who had swum, specter-like, out of the depths of the fog.

"It must be somewhere around here," he said, "but in this fog . . ."

"It should be in sight," Peter said irritably, peering in the direction the man had indicated.

"It's too late. That's why the lights are all out," the man said as he walked away.

Peter reeled like one stunned. The hands of his wrist watch could barely be distinguished as they pointed to 11:15. Something cried out in him: "Oh, no! Was it really that late! It couldn't be so late! It mustn't be so late!"

The girl stood huddled in her shrunken coat, and his whole bristling being knew she expected him, the intelligent, strong, and older man to lead her, to tell her what to do and how to live. He stood perplexed before the hands of his watch, unable to see anything but the orange glitter of the street lamps which snickered viciously overhead, and he did not know what to do or where to turn.

"Master, let's go home!" Tsonka moaned, but he snapped: "No, no!" and again he seized her by the hand and dragged her after him.

The fog became denser and more acrid as they neared the city center. His eyes itched and smarted, but Peter walked as fast as if somebody were at his heels, imagining how he would have this frightened child put up in a luxury hotel, the kind he had seen only in movies, how tomorrow . . .

What about tomorrow? What about now? What if there was no hotel available? Hadn't they told him that the most difficult thing to get in Sofia was a hotel room?

He stopped in his tracks again, thinking that he and the girl must resemble two frozen stray cats. But he knew he just could not go back to that house which had always been full of the same acrid fog. All this time he had been fighting a remote, a very remote enemy, whereas a vicious and treacherous foe had lain in wait in his own house, ready to grab him by the throat, strangle him and cast him out into the fog outside. And he had never seen him, nor could he see him now, nor he could he call him by name; but he had to flee from that enemy, flee . . . somewhere into the light, back to other people, to his own kind, perhaps to those daring, merry young people. In a flash he saw them waving their hands in the small room, somebody asking him in a joke: "Are you a Jesuit?" and he felt like laughing or coughing or weeping because the old pharyngitis was clawing at his throat.

Peter Lechev again clutched Tsonka's ice-cold hand.

Somewhere in the fog a siren screamed—a fire engine or an ambulance. It shrieked like a madman in mortal fear and sped where somebody was waiting for help, where something needed saving.

Translated by GREGOR PAVLOV

Nikolai Kirilov

(1922–   )

Nikolai Kirilov was born on May 24, 1922 in the village of Yakimovo near the town of Lom on the Danube. He comes of old peasant stock who lived in the village for many generations. He spent his childhood in his native village and his adolescence in the towns of Lom and Vidin, where he finished secondary school. During the summer he worked in the fields.

Kirilov began his higher education in 1942 in Zagreb, Yugoslavia, where he studied medicine. On his return to Bulgaria in 1943 he was imprisoned and deprived of civic and political rights for his participation in the underground struggle.

After the Bulgarian revolution of 1944 Kirilov enrolled at the Medical Faculty in Sofia to continue his education but was called up by the army in 1947 for cultural and educational work. For several years he worked on various newspapers and magazines, making his first attempts at writing in 1956.

His first book, *Spring Rain* (short stories), was published in 1960; his second, *Dustless Sky*, in 1965.

Radiant Skies

"So you're getting ready for a celebration, are you, Uncle Kotsi? Fine!" Evlogi said turning to his chief, TV cameraman Kotsi, with whom for a week now they had been shooting pictures of a leading pig-breeder, running in the elections for the people's council of the provincial town.

"Ugh! I'm sick and tired of all this mud," Kotsi answered, "so I thought we might just as well throw a party tonight."

Evlogi looked toward the window through which he could see a large yard, surrounded by low brick buildings, resounding

414

with the voices of the loaders and the thunder of the trucks which every now and then got stuck in the puddles.

"I might go and have something to drink tonight! You'll probably bring along some woman, so . . . !" said Evlogi in a low voice.

Kotsi was startled by his words. "He's itching to be back in Sofia," he said to himself. It wasn't that their assignment to the provincial town had been too long. But every time this handsome, silent fellow touched the knot of his necktie, which his wife had bought him as a present, his face grew paler, longer, and his thoughtful eyes darkened with muffled irony. Maybe he was longing for Rodi, his wife, though who knows whether she was so particular about her fidelity in Sofia, where there were so many people, such crowds that one got lost among them.

"Human nature, that's it!" Kotsi thought and took a small blue notebook out of the inside pocket of his coat. "Women are like the earth, merciful. Well, man is like a dog! A woman meets death with greater self-composure, whereas a man is frightened, being more alienated from nature! Well, they'd be celebrating, all right! But a celebration without wine, without songs, and without a woman was nothing! That was human nature!"

Kotsi looked at Evlogi's back once again and then proceeded to put his accounts in order. By force of habit, every evening he recorded his daily income and expenses. They were going to get a pretty good fee out of their present assignment, because Tsibranski, their chief, hailed from these parts. He had been active here as an underground member of the Resistance, and Mourgin, the secretary of the co-operative farm, complied with his every last wish; to humor him he had ordered the guard room cleared for the cameramen and free meals for them.

There was a rap at the windowpane, a cap was seen moving, and the next moment Istas, president of the people's council of one of the villages in the united co-operative farm, came stomping into the guard room with his boots. He was dressed in a military jacket, without shoulderboards, familiarly negligent, with the abrupt bearing of a benefactor. He stood with legs apart and informed them in an even voice that the men from Sofia, "the movie men," were to go in his jeep to the first-class restaurant on the Danube bank, where Mourgin and Tsibranski were waiting for them.

"When the restaurant closes down, we'll go on to my village, at the far end of which there is a villa!" Istas concluded, taking Kotsi's topcoat from the rack and holding it with hands spread out for Kotsi who was winding a yellow, checkered muffler around his neck and tilting his French beret so as to cover his bald head with the half circle of thin hair left on it.

Impatient, Istas went out, hopping from stone to stone under the eaves of the guard room to avoid muddying his boots, wading across the water in front of the gate, and energetically stamping his feet as he waited beside the jeep. As soon as the cameramen had seated themselves in the jeep, Istas looked around and remarked that the Danube wind might cause the mud to harden during the night and that it might even bring snow from Rumania. On the way he was silent, livening up only after they had walked across the length of the restaurant where, in front of the orchestra, a tipsy, sweat-covered chain dancer in a white flannel gymsuit and with a flower tucked behind his ear, was hopping about and grinning at the waiters. Istas chose a table in the adjacent alcove, separated from the big room by a drawn red curtain. Two tables away, near the huge India-rubber plant which covered one half of the large window looking out on the river, Mourgin and Tsibranski sat talking.

"Istas," Mourgin turned with a reproachful smile to the small table, "aren't you ashamed of yourself? We've been waiting for you for two hours, and you're breaking away from us!"

The two looked at each other as men who kept no secrets the one from the other. Istas explained that he had not wanted to disturb their conversation, knowing them to be old friends.

After they went over and sat at their table, Evlogi began cautiously to examine Mourgin, asking himself what it was that he liked about him. What they all knew about Mourgin was that he had voluntarily relinquished his high post in the capital to come and wade in the mud of the co-operative farm. "But had they not got rid of him under the pretext of sending him to a more challenging job?" Evlogi was asking himself.

Somewhat in his cups, Mourgin patted Evlogi's shoulder patronizingly: "You're always silent, always weighing us in the balance! It's not to one's advantage to be friends with you. Look at him, Tsibranski," Mourgin said turning to his companion who was leaning over the table in order to hear what Tsibranski was saying, who as a matter of fact was jokingly explaining that he had had just that in mind in recommending Evlogi for his TV job.

Mourgin asked the waiter with a wink to find something special for them, then told Istas to check once more whether they had caught any fish, this being a stretch of the Danube where both Rumanian and Bulgarian rivers flowed into it, and to let him know at once.

As Istas left the table and made for somewhere, Mourgin called out emphatically after him: "Fresh fish, mind!" Then, slightly relaxed, he bent his head low and touched his chin: it was good that he had shaved twice against the beard. He hoped that would bring him good luck.

Then, as if suddenly remembering something, he said forcefully: "Let me come back to what I was saying. Try the beefsteak, you'll be sorry if you don't. As to myself, Tsibré, I despise all feelings, because they are an obstacle! Well, it's all right for women to have them. I prefer to take advantage of them, and the women's weakness makes me strong and powerful. Don't think that I'm drunk. We, Tsibré, did not fight with smiles, but with cement. Let me make myself clear: supposing I had a powerful weapon which, when it exploded would spare only the buildings, factories, and machines of the enemy. These days I've been strolling in the park along the riverside with my son. You see trees and flowers, you know, you see the sunset reflected in the Danube, couples in love on the benches in the dark—beautiful, you know. Now, what I'm asking you is, if the enemy has no such weapon as yet, and it depends entirely on you to use it or not, would you use it against him or would you wait until the enemy outwits you and discovers it, too? You'll tell me that there are gardens, feelings, children, and beauty there, too! What sort of revolutionary are you, my dear, when mere feelings paralyze your hand and prevent it from inflicting, if necessary, even the most terrible, most unheard-of blow against the enemy? Ha-ha! Go ahead and try the beefsteak. Why did you suddenly give me such a surprised look?"

Mourgin laughed out triumphantly, feeling that he had produced a crushing argument against his silent interlocutor.

"You can achieve a lot with the bayonet, you can rule the people, but can you show me one man who sits on a bayonet?" Tsibranski asked jokingly.

"I'm speaking about things that are of significance to the whole world, and not about your pig-breeder whose pictures you've been taking. If it weren't for me, he'd never be running for people's councilor. Titmice have yellow around their beaks. At least you, Tsibré, know that I'm not a suckling."

"Of course, you're no titmouse, but if I called you a vulture, you'd choke it down and rightly, too! Please, wait a bit! I could

never imagine socialism being a hearse and you its driver. But you're
surely joking. I'm no fledgling either," Evlogi said, parrying Mourgin's long, bristling look.

"Lower your eyes, young fellow! What are you saying?
Don't you know that Mourgin was never a slam-bang go-getter?"
Mourgin said, attempting a smile. "A lot indeed you seem to have
learned. A vulture!"

"You're taking his words at their face value, but what he
means is something else, and he's right!" Tsibranski ventured to put
in timidly.

"To your health, young fellow! What did your father do for
a living in the past?" Mourgin asked. "I'm giving you a mark of
'excellent' for your words!"

"Oh, he was a bookseller, or a peddler, rather! I've read all
kinds of books and I've quarreled with all kinds of authors so as not
to allow them to get the better of me. That's where I learned to
suffer and hold my tongue, yet no one ever gave me an excellent
mark for it." Evlogi answered, trying to ease the atmosphere by
lightly fending off the attack of Mourgin's fiery eyes.

"I don't like, I don't like people who corner you so that you
can make no reply!"

Mourgin lowered his eyes, then turned to Evlogi in a pardon-
ing and good-natured way, gave him a friendly nudge and then, with
a silent smile, raised his glass to Evlogi. At that moment Istas ran up,
and they all turned to him, surprised at his noisy and enthusiastic
arrival.

"What are you looking so flushed about, Mourgin? Keep
your gunpowder for afterward!" Istas remarked in a familiar tone.
"Everything has turned out all right. She caught at the bait. We and
the cameramen are leaving; you, she and Tsibranski will follow suit.
Floro will meet us: to be specific—the celebration will be at the
villa."

Kotsi took advantage of the short lull and rose to his feet,
because a heated argument might easily ruin the celebration and, on
the other hand, the last one at the table might be asked to foot the
bill.

"Get up, Evlogi," he said to his assistant, "because in footing
the bill you may not only get a failing mark, but a round zero!"

"Don't bother about money!" Mourgin said, smiling.

"We've known each other for a long time, Mourgin, haven't
we? I threw the bait to Tamara. They were going to set up an orchestra. I told her, so why should she go on playing the piano in the

tavern, I asked, and not in the theater? She became thoughtful. I thought it out well, didn't I? Then I attacked: Was she going to turn down the request of a group of responsible men to play for them in the villa? Her husband's case might be brought up in the conversation, and that might quite unexpectedly lead to his release from prison. Then I opened the door of your car, and now she's waiting in it downstairs. No one ever caught a fish like that in his net. A real goldfish, I tell you!"

"You're a real bragger! Don't let's expose ourselves, don't let any rumors start going around, because you know the line they follow on these things at the top. O, Lord!" Mourgin remarked hesitatingly and then asked: "Did you make doubly sure about everything?"

"No one'll ever know she's there!"

Mourgin waved to the others to start, and when he remained at the table alone with Tsibranski he said with a frown: "In a word, that's a sweet little peach coming with us. Some years ago she was married by the bishop, and there was a whole train of carriages, you know, and officers—you can't possibly imagine what a fine procession it was! I was the one who fitted her wedding dress for her. What a figure, what lines, my God! I'm a sinner, though I don't know how you stand in this respect! I'm ready to give you priority in this case. Let's go!"

Tsibranski smiled meaningfully. Mourgin paid the bill, took him under the arm, and with resolute steps pulled him toward the exit where the car was parked in a small side street.

Snow had piled up outside: the trees alongside the river were white; snowflakes floated in the dispersed light of the street lamp and covered the roof tiles and the muddy asphalt in the white darkness. A white, sobbing silence began to spread in Tsibranski's soul, and he took a deep breath, but as soon as he opened the car door he saw that the unknown woman was waiting inside. For a moment the car was lighted up when Mourgin turned on the ignition, and in this flash of light Tsibranski got a look at the woman. She was young, dressed with good taste (who knows who paid for it), well cared for, with a smooth, pure skin. She was truly photogenic! Tsibranski had the feeling that he had met this woman somewhere once, or a woman like her.

"I'm asking myself," Tsibranski said, pulling himself together, "whether I once met you in the company of Mrs. Bratoeva, or maybe I'm wrong. Don't think me forward. It's just an idea, maybe mere tactless curiosity."

"Oh, not at all, sir. You're quite right. The Bratoevas and we lived in the same courtyard, but I can't tell you exactly when they left our town. Are you related to them, if I may ask? The husband was a lawyer, wasn't he?"

"What did I tell you!" Tsibranski answered, the beautiful woman's voice still ringing in his ears. "So I wasn't wrong, then. I have to be thankful to you for a great service you did me then, for which I hadn't even asked you. But you obviously don't remember anything about it, do you?"

Tamara turned down the collar of her fur-lined coat and withdrew to the corner in puzzled curiosity.

"I'm not joking. You hesitated a little. At that time I was exempted from all oral school-leaving exams, and the president of the school asked me to bring him a certificate from the police authorities proving my trustworthiness. Otherwise my mark in deportment in my school-leaving certificate would have remained unsatisfactory, because it would have indicated the profession of leftist ideas. How could I possibly get up the courage and go to police headquarters of my own accord? It would have been too naïve to suppose that I'd be the one they'd be willing to render a service. Well, then I dropped in to say goodbye to my guardian, the lawyer, and in the yard I came upon you and his wife. After I told you the case, you looked surprised and asked: 'Is that so? Why should one have to ask the opinion of idiots about a good student? Mr. Tserovski, my husband, will surely be able to put in a good word for you with the police. He's an Army officer.' Then the lawyer came up and laughed a little, remarking that a student with an unsatisfactory mark in deportment was always a worth-while citizen. And he advised me to get a note from the parish priest saying that I went to church regularly, so that he might thus somehow put the police off. But that, too, proved a vain hope. Do you remember, now?"

Mourgin turned round slackening the speed of the car.

"You've forgotten all about it! Imagine!" Tsibranski said in conclusion. "Oh, the devil take it! Yesterday I got out a certified copy of my school-leaving certificate, and there, in the registrar's office do you know what I found? Next to the data collected by the police was a grayish piece of paper, held in place by a rusty pin. A former officer, your husband, guaranteed, without ever having seen me, that I was a trustworthy young man, loyal to the Balkans. That's exactly how it was put, 'to the Balkans' while at the same time, my dear Mourgin, I got arrested as a man without a country. A really strange situation! Imagine, if that letter had been found some ten years ago, how hard it might have been for me to explain my relations with . . ."

Tsibranski felt a little awkward after his own last words, because he became aware of Tamara's caustic, suppressed grin in the darkness.

"What man would refuse to comply with a whim of Tamara's?" Mourgin remarked. "Well, did you like him then, Tamara? It does Tserovski credit. But you know, don't you, that some other people also intervened for certain comrades and allegedly supported them—the way a rope supports a hanged man. And we didn't know anything about it. I find it all very interesting."

Tamara suppressed her amazement, and Mourgin, noticing that her face was composed, concluded: "You can control yourself, and you aren't an easy game bird, Tamara dear, but neither was I born yesterday! . . . We'll take this up again, but not with everybody around! Here we are! The lights are on the upper floor. Let's see now what this much talked-about celebration will be like," Mourgin said, quickly climbing out of the car and stamping in the snow to get warm.

A man was coming down the wooden staircase of the two-storied villa, one hand leaning on the railing and the other raising a smoke-covered lantern above his head. The light of the lantern danced in the snow, forming a circle with a dark spot in the center. "This way, this way!" the man called, peering into the falling snow. "Step carefully, because it's dilapidated and slippery to boot. It has served lots of people for many long years!"

Mourgin gently steered Tamara and Tsibranski in front of himself, informing them that in the past the villa had been owned by a high official at the king's court, but that now it was at the disposal of the young Pioneers for summer vacations. The upper floor of the villa shook under their steps, and the floor in the corridor was unsteady. The first door on the right-hand side of the corridor, which had an iron hook on it, opened. Mourgin looked in and a merry shout went up. Inside the room, a few men sitting around a table with a roughly nicked surface were drinking and passionately discussing something. Evlogi fixed his eyes on the door: Tamara was entering. As the delicate woman slowly raised her hands to shake the snow from her dark, moist hair, she brought with her the scent of the sea. Two blue drops emerged and disappeared intermittently in her eyes. Her neck, as white as meerschaum, and Tamara's whole figure seemed to whisper intoxicatingly to Evlogi: "You were suspicious, you thought who knows what about her, yet she is a human being—a boundless expanse—she has brought you snow and shores. Don't you hear a distant splash of waves?"

Tamara reacted with concealed timidity and looked around: in the corner a stove was burning with a black cauldron on it; the water was boiling and hot steam was coming out. In front of the stove on a box full of logs lay a few chickens. Istas passed a filled earthen mug to his friends, and Floro, the man with the lantern, kept coming and going, carrying wood in his arms and throwing it on the floor with a crash. The practical jokes, related with clumsy sincerity, and the disdainful vivacity in Evlogi's eyes raised Tamara's spirits and she, crossing her hands on her chest, refused to drink. Slightly closing her eyes and putting away Evlogi's hand, she said "Count me out, Sofia friend!"

"Floro, does Mourgin still scare you the way you keep dropping wood to the floor?" Istas asked jokingly, and Floro, obviously flattered, started babbling quite unexpectedly:

"Oh, come, it was a revolver and no joke, after all!" he said and, putting a chicken into the boiling water, moved uneasily from one foot to another. "They were bigshots, quarreling who was to bow to whom, and poor me between them. Mourgin came to the pub. He and Istas had criticized each other and were watching each other's moves like hawks. The council, as you know, is five paces from the pub. 'Go,' says Mourgin, 'and tell Istas to come over here at once!' Istas, however, says: 'Tell him either to come here to the council himself, or to leave the village!' I go back to the pub, which is full of as many people as there are grains of sand on the seashore, all listening to the man come from town who was then the first man in the whole town. Mourgin asks me from afar: 'Is he coming?' And I, who knew him for a bigshot, how could I tell him in the presence of all those people to leave the village? I said: 'He told me, Comrade Mourgin, to ask you to go to the municipality!' Mourgin then flew into a rage and made me go back again! So poor me went back and forth like a shuttle!"

"I seem to recall there was something of the kind!" Mourgin remarked.

"Well, I came back to Istas and he rushed up to me as if to beat me up!"

"Oh, to beat you up, indeed; don't talk nonsense!" Istas said.

"Well, he didn't exactly rush up to me to beat me up, but he was furious and he cursed me. 'Who pays you, isn't it me? Didn't I appoint you to your job?' 'Yes!' 'Get your gun then and go and arrest him! What is he strutting about like that for? As if he wasn't the one who sewed my grandfather's peasant breeches!' "

"Ha, ha, ha!" Kotsi suddenly started shaking with laughter. "And did you arrest him? He isn't an easy one to deal with."

"That's what I was ordered to do!" Floro answered. "But how did I dare arrest him when he could stand up against the whole village? Mourgin jumped up, and I felt the earth burning under my feet. I gathered all my courage and muttered: 'Istas told me to arrest you!' 'Me?' Mourgin asked startled, and there was a hush in the room. 'Me? I'll send him to kingdom come, the rascal!' And he took out his pistol, a Browning."

Istas wiped his lips with the back of his hand, passed the mug to Kotsi and raised an admonishing palm, saying: "That's enough now, Floro! Look after your cauldron there! Mourgin darted into my room, a man full of fire and fury. Everyone trembled before him, yet I, a village mayor, kept sitting quietly in my chair when he rushed in. I was writing something and pretended not to see him. Then I laughed and said: 'Great God, you have to thank me for not having chased you out of the village! You set out from town to come and see me, and the municipality is here and not in the pub. Come, give me that pistol; I've got a brand new Walther here for you!' He got over his anger, because I was tactful enough to make him come and present himself to me personally. And it was also for the first time that he found his match! Well now I'm the one who goes to him."

"That's the way the wheel of fortune turns. You can't be up if you aren't down first," Floro said, but no one paid any attention to him.

Mourgin shook his head warningly and smiled a forced smile, but it was obvious that he liked Istas and that people who were as close friends as they were could afford to scold each other in the presence of others.

"Oh, the devil take you! You're all great guys. With such men I'd go anywhere!" Kotsi the cameraman called out.

When the mug had made several rounds among the merry company, Mourgin turned politely to Evlogi: "Ask the lady to help herself to the wine. This here's a Christian house! Tell her so, so she won't refuse. Let's hope she won't turn down your wooing this time."

Evlogi moved over to Tamara and invited her to take a sip of the wine. She hesitated silently for a while, weighing the question in her mind, and after she asked him whether he really insisted, she took the mug. Evlogi asked her why she was here, alone among so many men at midnight. She peered at his swarthy face and, realizing that deep in his heart he despised her, she said simply: "Why shouldn't I be able to afford to do what you men do?"

"That was a good answer!" Evlogi replied, dropping his eyes.

"That's what I've been taught. I haven't said anything that's particularly wise."

"Was it people who liked you that taught you that?"

"Oh, I'm fed up with compliments. Tell me something else . . . do you often go to concerts? As for me, I . . ."

Suddenly she became talkative and spoke about Richter, his wife, his wonderful playing, adding as if speaking to herself: "Is he a normal man? Such a talent. Oh, yes!"

Evlogi noticed that Tamara was transfigured: her smile was no longer a war cry or a warning, but something different. "The devil take it, I can't define it," he thought. Her eyes were looking for a dreaming expanse, far away from restaurants, far away from these chickens, from that mug, but suddenly a quiver ran across her brightening face and, crossing her legs, she asked for a cigarette, waved the smoke away with her hand and, with a sharp and provocative glance, tried to see what impression she was producing as a woman. He noticed this imperceptible change and examined her round knee with annoyance.

"It's quite plain that you're having a good time," she said jokingly.

"Do you believe that your power lies hidden in your knee, the way you display it?" he asked.

Tamara's face grew cold for a minute, but that same moment her nostrils expanded willfully, for she liked his sincerity and she again fixed her eyes on Evlogi's forehead.

"You shouldn't speak that way to a woman," she said softly, giving him a good-natured, reprimanding look. "I wonder why you're always looking for what's bad in people? Why is it?"

"Because of love!"

"Love! But isn't there a little meanness in it, too?"

"Maybe, maybe! Pardon me, but you shouldn't drink any more," Evlogi said, moving away from her, because Mourgin was angrily eyeing him with a look that was saying: "Don't you try to compare your strength with mine. A Bulgarian woman doesn't attach too much importance to a man's good looks, she isn't like other European women; she doesn't care about chatting with men, she is after a job and her interests! And I'm the one who gives out jobs, not you!"

No one noticed when and why Mourgin was called to go out: they were all carried away in their arguments, interrupting each other, not listening to what each other said. Floro was pulling out the boiled chickens, breaking them apart, and putting them on the table. He bent over Tamara and told her in a low voice:

"Mourgin wants you to go to him and tell him about your husband. He is waiting for you at the far end of the passageway in a room to your left. The piano's there, too."

Tamara gave him a tense, inquisitive look and as she met with sympathy and encouragement, she dropped her eyelids and said: "Thank you." Tamara looked at Evlogi, as if wishing to ask him whether to go or not, but he was absorbed in conversation with Istas and did not notice her leaving with Floro. Although the drunken shouts were heard in the passageway, Floro, to satisfy his rustic curiosity, stood listening at the door of the room Tamara entered. Soon he made out Mourgin's low voice:

"As I said, some of us have been thinking of late to set right a certain wrong attitude with respect to your husband. How long has he been in prison? Now, an influential person like Tsibranski will be very useful with the facts he could bring forward."

"If being of service to my husband won't do you any harm! He's a former officer, and you . . ."

"Why harm? Oh, let's talk about something good, about happy things. While one's alive one's always learning, that's how it is with Tserovski, and me and you, too, no? Let's talk about cheerful things, eh?"

"Words!" Tamara said, with a wave of indistinct incredulity in her voice.

After a short silence the man's voice was heard, quivering and panting: "Tamara, you know, I . . . I was the one who fitted you for your wedding gown, and ever since I . . ."

"Please, don't touch me! Are you going to let me out of here or not? Oh, you've locked the door!"

Rapid steps were heard. A man's rapid steps overtook the woman's steps with a lustful laugh. "Oh, stop your joking! I know that you're a man and won't insult me! Shall I believe you? How? But please, let me go, do you hear?"

Floro was listening with bated breath, leaning against the wall, then suddenly he held his breath: there was a tussle; frequent quiet pleas were heard, whispered exhortations interrupted by weeping and moaning. Suddenly a resounding slap was heard, and the peasant held his breath, not daring to breathe. Then he heard cloth ripping, and a moment later a short but terrible wail reached him.

"No, no! Don't touch me! Oh, mother, mother dear, where are you? Oh, oh!"

Floro withdrew on tiptoe and paused for a few minutes: the weeping turned into a moan. Suddenly Mourgin carefully opened the door, stood in front of Floro and, shaking a warning finger, whispered to him: "You're a loyal old horse! I'll not forget you! Now do what I tell you. Call out: 'Did you fix the carburetor, Comrade Mourgin?'"

Trembling, in Mourgin's eyes Floro saw not eyes but two wounds, a cheeky smile quivering around his chin, and Mourgin, before opening the door of the room where the men were carousing, scolded Floro magnanimously: "Oh, man, what are you shouting like that for? Haven't you got a broom to let me clean the snow off my boots? Never mind, don't bother!" Then he stamped his feet and entered the room with a feeling of infinite pride in his heart, resolute, tough, and sinister.

"Istas," Mourgin said jokingly, "where's our lady guest? Oh, she must be examining the piano in the room; she sold hers, didn't she, when she was left without her husband and jobless. Had to scrape up a living, somehow. Tsibranski, I think we ought to put an end to our dogmatic attitude toward Tamara. Please write down what I heard you say in the car."

As Istas was watching him with obedient admiration, running steps were heard in the passageway. That same moment Floro's wife burst into the room, frightened. She was young but looked old from overwork and from childbearing. Barefoot and dressed in a nightshirt, she ran over to her husband and, trembling, clung to his arm.

"Floro, who was calling for her mother? The children woke up and started screaming! Has a crime been committed? Has someone been killed, or did a bomb fall, eh? Floro!"

Istas stood up in front of her, grinning, and while he told her that there were some circus actors among them, one of whom had done his act, he gave her some wine to sip to regain her composure. The peasant woman covered her chest and shook her head in sinister silence, clicking her tongue: "Is there no justice here? This is the wine that belongs to the farmers, and yet you're drinking it free of charge! Which one of you has ever wielded a hoe?"

Floro looked pleadingly at his wife and said: "Krotka, dear Krotka, be careful!"

"Floro," the peasant woman asked with surprise, "were all these dead chicks again killed by foxes? A woman was screaming here, the children jumped up from their sleep with fright, and children don't lie! Shame on you, Floro. Come, come on, man, let's get out of here! It's dawning!" she said, pulling her husband by the elbow. Mourgin peered through the window. On the pane the snow-flakes had begun to melt, the drops running down and gathering at the wooden frame.

He ordered Istas to gather up everything and "not a word to anybody!" Tsibranski, who was in no hurry and who had seen and heard nothing, asked, puzzled: "What's this rush all of a sudden? Has the dawn frightened you?"

Somebody picked up a demijohn, another wrapped up a boiled chicken in a greasy newspaper, and then everybody made for the car. Having heard the noise, Tamara, sick at heart, dragged herself down the stairs, but soon pulled herself together, and with drooping eyes turned up her coat collar. She stood by the car, waiting to be invited to get in, but the car started without her, and she ran to overtake it, covering her eyes with her hand. A laugh lashed her in the face. The car stopped, the door opened, a hand got hold of her, and she dropped down in the back seat, next to Evlogi and his chief. The Volga swept across the snow-covered plain. Kotsi was complaining of being cramped for space, looking at Tamara with dissatisfaction, then he started joking. Tamara held her throat when Kotsi remarked that women were merciful, concluding finally that every woman was just a woman and nothing else. Then, satisfied with his own words, he started humming a song, which he knew was to the liking of his chief, Tsibranski:

How much suffering you have seen,
How many secrets you are guarding,
Oh, native Balkan Mountains!

Tsibranski was affected by the song. His eyes grew soft and kind, and he began singing the melody in his full, bass voice. In the end, he shared his admiration of the song with Mourgin: "A wonderful song, isn't it? Touches your very heart! Well done, Kotsi! La . . . la . . . la . . . la . . . . I seem to've forgotten the words somewhat!"

"Oh, it doesn't matter! You fought for the Balkan Mountains. Let those remember them who are strutting around today!"

Evlogi cut him short: "You fought, you say! God knows how you fought! Why do you have to get the Balkan Mountains mixed into it? We mustn't forget the past, if we don't want to see it recur as a horrible future, but I, too, would give my life for the Balkan Mountains! You, Tamara, what are you gnawing at your lips for? Richter, eh? You're afraid of bursting into tears, for fear of looking ridiculous. Go ahead, cry a little. Do you know that I compared you to a boundless vastness . . . in spring . . ."

"That's interesting. And against whom would you be ready to fight?" Mourgin asked unperturbed.

"Against the hearse! But why don't you mind your own business? Against the one who lives only with his memories and who sees nothing around him now. Against the one who has yellow around the eyes, yellow . . ."

"So that's it! But why?" Mourgin asked with condescending curiosity, like a mature man who appreciates the enthusiasm of young people.

"Well?" Evlogi replied and paused, and then spoke in a low voice as if to himself: "Because Wrong and Right ate together and drank together and did not pay, and when the barefooted woman got scared by a cry of 'Mother!' and asked: 'Where are you, Right?' Right replied: 'I'm here, in the car, I've forgotten the song about the Balkan Mountains somewhat, but I too ate, and I too drank with Wrong.' There you are, there you are!"

"Ach, Evlogi! He can't drink more than one glass, it goes straight to his head, but he's tops at making jokes! Yes, he's tops at it!" Kotsi said, trying to give the conversation another turn. Then he started singing again.

In the white plain they saw alternating rows of blue willows and other trees, and all of a sudden the sunrise burst forth like an explosion, and all the landscape was set on fire, the trees covered with hoarfrost burning like candles, and the snow melting. Yellowish mud was being sprayed on both sides of the road by the moving car, the slanting sunrays coldly sparkling in these drops which from a distance looked like golden embroidery on a white silk shirt. The snow thawing in the wake of the car was tinted in countless hues.

At every splash, Tamara would gather her hair with her wet palms, bite her lips, and sob out in an unexpectedly hollow and muffled voice. Kotsi was humming a song; somebody was accompanying him; and Evlogi, bewitched by the sunrise, whispered: "But how can you make even the mud in the snow look beautiful? And you keep splashing, splashing!"

Tamara was frightened by his whisper and raised a hand to

fend off these entreaties, but then suddenly covered her face with her hands: she had seen large tears welling up in Evlogi's eyes, running down his swarthy face, and as his eyes smiled with infinite purity at the sunrise, the tears fell at their feet. The car flew on at breakneck speed; at every bend of the road Tamara would sob, yellowish mud was being sprayed on the soft snow; and in front and far to the sides—everywhere—the pure landscape was burning in the hoarfrost and in its austere white blanket.

Translated by ZDRAVKO STANKOV

Boundless Time

That morning, as usual, Boudinsky opened all the letters in the evening mail. A circular threateningly ordered him to sow ninety crops in 1956: various sainfoins, soybeans, mint, and so forth. Another circular instructed him to "develop stockbreeding and to secure skimmed milk for a thousand sows."

"If I fulfil the first circular, not one-tenth of a hectare will be left for grain and green forage," Boudinsky reasoned. "And how can you milk hungry cows? Where, then, am I going to get them the skimmed milk? Skim!"

The telephone rang, interrupting his thoughts. He was told to get ready to meet a minister from a neutral country. The interests of the state dictated that the "cream" of the Gold Mine Co-operative should be shown to the minister.

"Ha, ha, ha!" Boudinsky laughed. "You know our 'flourishing' condition, don't you? There are good co-operatives to be shown around, but not ours. Give me three more years and we'll be able to meet God Almighty himself."

Impatient, intemperate visitors invaded the room—team leaders, clerks, craftsmen, crop-raisers.

"Stop this dodging!" the telephone rang coolly. "Hello! No one's to blame for your condition. If the minister wishes to visit a co-operative farm, you'll have to show him your positive experience— or else."

The noise in the corridor was growing: "Hello, Vikenti, you've again girded a cartridge belt around your waist like a harnessed stallion; you must be getting ready to chase foxes, eh?"

"Comrade Chairman," another one called out, "come on down—two women are fighting about a cock!"

The bricklayer, a weak man with a protruding Adam's apple, pushed the visitors aside and, seeing that the receiver was trembling in Boudinsky's hand, turned to the visitors: "Oh, shut up all of you! Can't you see that he's dancing on a hot griddle?"

"I see what you mean!" Boudinsky said into the phone. "You want me to let you have a program on his visit! I see! Hello . . . hello!"

After he hung up, Boudinsky raised his head to the people milling around, and it was only now that the noise subsided.

"Where am I to find them? You want those fifteen bags of cement," Boudinsky said, turning to the bricklayer. "Is the runway ready for the agricultural plane? Not yet? They promised to give me cement. Drop in in three days! Next?"

"I want you to let me have some money on account!" Vikenti, the team leader, said, elbowing his way through the crowd.

"There's no money," answered the woman accountant, who was standing quietly beside Boudinsky's desk with a folder in her hand.

"I don't care! Find some!" Vikenti shouted. "Do you know, my dear, that the sick child of Lavri, the brickmaker, has come back from the children's sanatorium? And the doctors say he is not to sleep in the old house since it's all wet and moldy? Do you know that the child must have a sunny room?—'There's no money!'—Haven't you got any other answer?"

"Get it from the Social Security Fund!" Boudinsky ordered the accountant.

"That's empty, too," the accountant said with an even voice. "The bank, Comrade Boudinsky, ordered us to transfer 34 per cent of our income for taxes and insurance. That's what our expenses amount to. They needed money, they said, for the nitrogen fertilizer plant. I made out the form, and now we haven't got a penny."

"Not a penny? How can you talk like that?" an aged man remarked, trying to make them listen to reason. "Kouncho!" he added, turning to Boudinsky, "fill out a ration slip for one liter of milk. My grandchildren have arrived from Sofia, and they're used to it there, whereas here you have only set aside twenty liters for the whole village. I was told you gave skimmed milk to the sows."

"I'll try to fix up everything tomorrow!" Boudinsky said. "You heard, didn't you, that we'll be meeting a foreign minister? They want me to show him the 'cream.' Where am I to get it? If we had finished the construction projects by now, it would have been different. Where are the plans?"

The office boy had turned on the radio in the next room, and the words crashed out: "On this day five years ago Nikos Beloyanis was shot. In the capital today on Levski Street a fashion show will be held. Men's fashions for the year, slightly wider trousers with cuffs. Return to the Charleston. Fashionable colors: beige and Turkish blue. Pleats . . ."

Boudinsky went out to turn off the radio; when he came back, he found his office empty. The rigid trees in front of the windows of the floor below were awakened by the wind which suddenly attacked them. Their dense branches shrank into a ball, and at that same moment were scattered, sobbing like churned-up drops breaking on a craggy shore. The emerald cold which had descended from the vault of the sky was swallowed by restless clouds, the shining reflections of which glided over the desk, now pure, now turbid. The wind would suddenly shudder and sweep up the dust from the pavement, raising it in a whirling spiral in the air, but whenever the sun broke through the clouds and the room flared up in a dense, yellow light, the pavement was again covered with dust and garbage. "If the wind didn't clean the pavement," Boudinsky thought, "it would be much cleaner than when it blows the dust over it again."

The cypress tree, rising amid chestnuts and trimmed mulberries, and beaten from all sides, was cracking, but the wind, sheltering it from its own strength, seemed to draw it out and make it stand up still more proudly.

Boudinsky opened the folder with the designs and stopped to examine plans of future construction projects. To the left of the runway for the agricultural plane was the forage shop for fodder cakes and mixtures. A long pipe through which the fodder was to flow led from the shop to three spacious cowsheds containing modern milking equipment. "This is the gold vein, *the cream!*" Boudinsky thought. "Instead of helping me, they make me show what I haven't got yet!"

Boudinsky felt an awkward, oppressive sadness, and not for himself, because what is it that a man needs, after all? A cheap suit and a job. But why was it that after the triumph of socialism had been solemnly proclaimed, that gold vein had still not been found? How long would an obscure lack of order and "skimmed milk" be drowning it? And was it so only here? How long would this go on?

"Until we look things squarely in the face, openly and courageously," Boudinsky thought with a start. "But who's covering things up? Don't you remember that last year a comrade holding a responsible post came here, and after getting all the people together, he promised them solemnly that not a hair on their heads would be harmed if they explained why the farm couldn't make a go of it? Don't you remember no one said a word for a whole hour until at last a gypsy woman took the courage to speak up: 'Why does a lemonade cost more than a kilo of wheat?'—although she was a beggar and a sorceress and had never worked in the fields? Why did those who were being asked only for their own sakes say nothing? Why didn't the man from Sofia answer when they asked him: 'The county leaders were courageous revolutionaries, weren't they? Then why didn't they find the courage to tell you the truth—that things are in a terrible mess? Have they become fearful now that we're in power, or have they become liars now that the comrade has come here personally to see how the people live with his own eyes?' Why didn't that one say anything—the one who has promised no one would come to harm for talking?"

Boudinsky rubbed his temples. He did not want to think; he was afraid his thoughts were slanderous, in fact, criminal, because, well, was it with such thoughts that he was going to meet a foreign visitor who had come to find out something good?—just as Boudinsky in the past had trembled over the communiqués, expecting with fantastic devotion that moment for which he was ready to bid good-bye to his twenty years, provided he would live long enough to see the horsemen with the Soviet caps led by the first marshal watering their horses at the Danube.

The wind was pouncing upon the branches, the cypress was trembling as before, the sky was azure blue in the distance, clouds were creeping somewhere there above the mountains enveloping the lowlands, and those lowlands looked amazing to Boudinsky, because it was thanks to them that the proud peaks were outlined against the sky.

Through the warped door connecting Boudinsky's office with the accounting department, where adding machines had been clicking until awhile ago, he heard two women chatting. Boudinsky realized that he had to find a way to regain his self-composure and that is why he listened to the women. He discerned, along with the well-known voice of the accountant, another, altogether unfamiliar, mezzo-soprano voice.

"If you're going to meet a foreigner, you have to get ready for it, naturally," the unknown girl was saying. "Hair swept up in a knot is no longer the fashion, or platinum hair! I've got a good hair-dresser, but he's a bit expensive."

"How did you manage to lose so much weight?"

The chat ended because somebody entered the room: the firm, slow steps of a man were heard. The girls kissed each other with a loud smack, and then women's high heels were heard provoc-atively tapping along the passageway. Boudinsky recognized Viken-ti's voice, trying to persuade the accountant to let him have some money on account, while she, exasperatingly silent, forced him to repeat his request. Since she was torturing the man, ignoring his own order to let him have the money, Boudinsky got angry and entered the accountant's room.

Slyly frowning, Vikenti, who had made himself comfortable on a battered chair, was peeping into the barrel of his gun and check-ing the trigger.

"Isn't it enough for a woman to be beautiful? You also let her hold the purse, eh, Boudinsky?"

Boudinsky handed the folder containing the designs to the accountant and noticed that, on the wall above Vikenti's head, some-body had pinned up a picture of Sophia Loren in pants; it had been cut out of some illustrated magazine.

"It's not these folders, Boudinsky, that'll help us out of our troubles, but three plants as big as the one in Pernik—only listen—not for steel but for fodder, for fodder cakes."

"Please, sign this," the accountant asked Boudinsky. "Just your initials here! Thank you!" She counted out 28 leva for the team leader.

Vikenti checked the money three times, then rubbed the notes against his chin and, putting the bank notes into an envelope, said: "Good luck to all of you!" But he was not able to complete his thanks because Boris, the accountant's husband, a young man dressed in a white turtle-neck sweater with black stripes across the chest, darted into the room. He was excited and dazzled in the presence of his wife and seemed to be still running. He had probably come to see whether the night before they had looked over his application for the position of planner at the co-operative farm.

"It's good you hurried to come," Vikenti said, straightening in his chair. "But why were you in such a hurry to marry?"

With reserved modesty the accountant held a ballpoint pen in her white hand, at rest on the table. Moral uprightness was reflected in her alternately pouting and smiling face. Her deep, serene eyes looked still more brilliant against the beige band tied around her neck.

"I mean," Vikenti tried to explain his words, "that if you had put it off for awhile, we could have invited the minister coming to visit now to act as your best man. But maybe it still isn't too late, eh?"

Still somewhat confused, Boris did not understand what Vikenti was saying, because he was looking at his wife's low neckline. It was only when Vikenti asked him whether a month before he had had a wedding or had just signed a civil marriage contract in his wife's village that Boris assumed a livelier air: "A wedding?"

"I'm asking you, do you take pride in your village, or is it all the same to you whether it's shown up or not?" Vikenti asked impatiently. "The foreigner isn't coming to look at our humdrum daily drudgery—they've got plenty of it at home. We needn't show him our loam, no, or our tiles, they've got plenty of those there, too, so what then? He's come to see our best side, our human side. If you invite him to be your best man, everybody will be happy, and for a happy man all women are beautiful."

The young wife stood up, as if incarnated all in white, exactly like the color of the wall.

"Who wouldn't like to have a wedding party that will be remembered, but we aren't ready yet," she said.

"The farm will help you, if only Boudinsky gives his consent," Vikenti said, taking up his gun. "I've shown you your best man, now you use your head, as the saying goes. Where has a minister been welcomed with a wedding? Nowhere! That's my idea, but it's up to you to act as you see fit!"

Boudinsky was somewhat reserved in his calculations: to ask a man to get married to his wife so that you can hide the flaws of a whole co-operative farm, wasn't that disrespect for one's own self, a scandal? Vikenti stood at the window and laughed. Boudinsky looked that way and saw that among the crowd on the highway two women were now advancing toward each other, now withdrawing shaking their fists in the air.

"They can't divide a cock," Vikenti explained. "Each one claims that it's hers, but can a cock talk? The yards of the two are divided by the highway, but does a fowl know what a boundary is? Imagine the foreign minister riding up in his car and seeing them! All our talk of peace and understanding will go overboard! Go and try to fix things up afterward, ha, ha, ha. Come, let's get them to calm down!"

Throwing his chest out, Vikenti took Boris by the arm and dragged him toward the door, but as soon as he made a step down the stairs he stopped dead, because some wild chestnuts rained over them from the chestnut tree in front of the building. A swarthy man with stooping shoulders jumped down from the branches of the tree; it was Lavri, the brickmaker. He gathered the chestnuts into his cap and stood up before Vikenti with an inquisitive smile.

"They say that if you put some chestnuts in your pants, they'll cure your rheumatism. They're curative. I'll give them to the child. They're a remedy that costs nothing, after all."

"Let's hope they are!" Vikenti remarked. "Take this envelope. We have to thank Boudinsky for signing. You're a special worker, Lavri, on every holiday they carry your portrait in the parade. Why don't you draw some more money from your mutual-aid fund? Because I can't see what you'll be able to do with the money I gave you."

"I have debts! Good morning, Comrade Boudinsky," Lavri said with a bow.

"Ahem, is that so? Then let someone else draw the loan in his name, and give you the money."

"That never occurred to me. Can that be done? If it weren't for the people, how should I have finished with the brickwork? But now, by hook or by crook, in a week or so, Uncle Vikenti, I'll have to get a room ready; otherwise, I hate to think about it!"

"I know, I know! At the worst, I have a room at home, but it has a northern exposure, too. If you got a snake to live in your old house that would freeze, too, not to speak of a sick child. I'll ask Boudinsky to help you!"

Boudinsky stood between the two women who kept pulling him now to one side, now to the other, while he, confused and stupefied, did not know whom to believe. The crowd grew noisy. A boy in a student's jacket and with a cigarette between his fingers, crowed out like a cock. The older woman, realizing that Boudinsky was unable to settle their dispute, pounced on Vikenti. He threw his chest out, listened to her in an affected manner, and then went over to the younger woman, letting her whisper her secret into his ear. His face brightened up in a wily, ironical expression. Vikenti picked up the cock and resolutely chased the people away from the highway. They stood hushed and waiting, lined up in two rows across the highway, craning their necks. Vikenti bent the cock's neck, thrust its head under its wing, then took the bird with both hands and started swinging it to this side and that, in a concentrated and serious manner.

"Vikenti is like the crowd, and that is why they listen to him," Boudinsky thought. "A sage would not enjoy the respect Vikenti has with this crowd."

From the swinging, the bird's liveliness disappeared. Vikenti put it down on the road and stood up triumphant. The cock was asleep. He fixed his ironical eye first on the one and then on the other woman, gave a conspiratorial wink to the crowd, and then quite unexpectedly stamped his feet. The cock jumped up, fluttered its wings, and darted crowing toward the yard of the older woman.

"It has spoken and said whose it is!" Vikenti said with a shrug and a wave of the hand.

The boy with the cigarette looked at him with admiring eyes. He shouted to the others enthusiastically and got angry because he couldn't make himself heard. He finally managed to outshout them all, saying that Vikenti was great.

The losing woman threatened to sue the other one because as an official it was the chairman's responsibility to discover the thief and not hide him, washing his hands of the matter by leaving it to Vikenti.

"The bird cannot lie," Vikenti said, "because it does not know laws, and has wings to boot! That's why we'll kill it for the wedding! Shall I tell them, Comrade Boudinsky, to be getting ready for a chain dance?"

"You're not against it, are you?" an old, dark-faced man said, standing next to Boudinsky. He claimed himself to be first to have planted the Golden Parmena apple variety in the village and wanted to have his picture hung up in the Library Club. "If a guest is expected to come, a minister moreover, the proper thing to do would be for us, the founders, who are still being cursed and slandered, to meet him with wine flasks!"

"Yes, but with a flask coated with gold leaf, so as to shine, to shine!" Vikenti said.

Boudinsky looked around awkwardly. He cast a cold glance at Boris' silent face. "Why don't you speak up?" he asked. "It's your wedding party! The people want to make merry, and I don't want to stand in their way. You're going to invite him to act as your best man, aren't you? Go ahead, decide!"

The bridegroom's stubborn face roused Boudinsky's anger, and he wondered how to break his stubborn resistance. "If you're afraid of somebody saying that you are getting married for a second time, don't worry. They say my wife wears the pants in the family. If you listen to everybody you'll finally have to go and shoot yourself. Your wife is working at the farm."

Boris grunted and looked distrustfully at Boudinsky.

"Why don't you say something?" Vikenti asked. "Or do you want me also to keep my mouth shut when we discuss your application for the planner's job? If you want to get something you have to be ready to give something!"

"Well, all right, all right! And what about the money?"

"Don't worry about that," Boudinsky answered, flushing with shame. "Go and inform your parents. And your wife!" But he was still deeply impressed by the way Vikenti had advised the brickmaker to ask somebody else to draw money from the mutual-aid fund at the brickyard and how he had put the cock to sleep.

Boudinsky somewhat disconnectedly told Boris to ask his wife to tell the directors of the brickyard and the Len Co-operative to come to his office at once on important official business. The readiness with which the bridegroom set out to warn his parents and his sudden consent surprised him, because he had hoped secretly that Boris would refuse. For how long was he going to demand of the people, and through them, the most sacred thing— their intimacy— to subordinate it and display it as an attained social ideal? Only the weak acted under duress, but wasn't the bridegroom's stubbornness up to this moment only a sly maneuver, of which both of them were fully aware? Didn't Boris first of all wash his hands of the matter by being allegedly forced to accept it for the sake of the farm? But then power is not judged by the coercion it resorts to, but by its historic mission. "This mission will free men's minds from all those superfluous, humiliating, insulting dregs. It comes out that this coercion is a dictatorship of joy, of the love for man. And who would dare condemn me for that?" Boudinsky thought indignantly with clenched teeth.

"What are you standing speechless like that for, as if you were a young bride in a freshly washed nightshirt?" Vikenti asked, pulling him by the sleeve. "Don't worry! Everything will go off in accordance with our ideology! We're all going to help you."

"Ideology! Yet we all waited for the gypsy woman to speak up!" Boudinsky thought, hurrying toward his office, hardly able to hold himself in check. On entering the room he thought with bitterness about himself: "You let yourself be carried away again, and again you're using high-sounding words: mission, dictatorship; wait a bit! The matter is quite simple. You put the cock to sleep, and then pronounce a judgment!" Boudinsky cranked the telephone, put himself through to town and informed them that the farm was going to have a wedding and was inviting the foreign guest to act as best man. They asked him whether he had thought out all the details and, congratulating him on the original "measure," reminded him to call them up again if he ran into any difficulty. This conversation barely finished, the two directors entered his study. Boudinsky nervously sprang to his feet (which meant that he had no time for long discussions or objections).

"Glad to see the young people!" he said, extending a hand to the director of the brickyard, a man with an aquiline nose and narrow lips hidden behind a thick mustache. The director hesitantly touched the tip of the extended hand, and Boudinsky felt his cold scorn. The director of the Len Co-operative left his white hand in Boudinsky's grip as an experienced but frightened man, accustomed even when it was unnecessary, to offer his services to the more influential.

"I have been ordered," Boudinsky said with emphasis, "to meet a prominent statesman from a neutral country. For this meeting I need money!"

"Why didn't you tell us you were getting us over here for money?" the director of the brickyard asked. "But maybe the comrades from the Len Co-operative are ready to open their purse!"

"If you lend me the money, I'm ready to be of service to him!" the director of the Len replied, spreading out his hands.

"If you've got no money, that's nothing to worry about. There's the telephone: ring up the district committee and tell them. Or shall I ring them up?" Boudinsky said, reaching for the telephone.

"It isn't that we haven't any," the director of the Len hastened to answer officiously. "We have money, but there won't be any regular way to justify the expenditure. You'll need at least three hundred to four hundred leva!"

Malicious anger and disgust were reflected on Boudinsky's countenance, and his gray eyes twisted in a caustic smile: "You played into my hands, helping me raise the price, to put your colleagues in a tight spot and render me a service."

"But that isn't anything to worry about either," the director of the Len said, turning to his colleague. "For you it's easier. You've got such a well-known shockworker, like Lavri. Just issue an order giving him an award, and send the money here! That's it!"

"What's that? Nonsense! Don't try to pass the buck," the director of the brickyard burst out angrily.

"It's all quite simple," the other one replied rubbing his hands. "Do I have to tell you that the curved tiles you make weigh on the house, but also cover it?"

"Was it one hundred and fifty leva?" the director of the brickyard pretended not to have heard the sum. "Or was it four hundred? All right, I'll send it over!"

The door behind them creaked; the hinges had to be greased. Boudinsky propped his chin on his fist without knowing that precisely at that moment something in his face revealed his devastating self-hate, which foreboded that he would be merciless toward the faults of all others. But he knew that some obscure cashier would come running in any minute, and when a pregnant woman followed by the cashier of the Len Co-operative stood before him he began to study them carefully. He hated them, not because they spat on their fingers while counting the bank notes, but because, affected by the fever of men through whose hands millions passed, they hated every man who, though having no knowledge of financial operations, was getting much more than they.

Boudinsky motioned them to leave. He instructed the driver what presents he was to buy in town, and the rest of the money went to the newlyweds. In the hallway, the office boy was sweeping up while whistling and then singing hoarsely: "A monk is winking at me, the flirt, and lifting my skirt."

The words cheered him up: "Wasn't this grotesque nihilism bringing to naught the 'cream,' the 'gold vein' of life?" He felt his chin: he needed a shave, and the most pleasant minutes were those when he was busy with his own person in front of the mirror. "How do you know," he asked his reflection in the mirror, "that you and I are one and the same thing? You are an image, and I am alive! The image is a shadow."

As he was shaving, he heard the beating of a drum and turned to the window. Down at the square a small drum was heard and the thin tunes of a violin. At the turn of the street a brass band made its appearance, led by Vikenti. He was marching with his hunting gun, tapping at his boots with a thin willow twig, and cutting the air with his hand above his head like a conductor. Men dressed in their Sunday best, wearing heavy caps and white flannels, marched after the hunched drummer. They were offering wine flasks to other men's wives, all of whom looked around suspiciously to see which man was secretly watching what woman. A number of children dressed in white blouses with red neckties raced up the highway, disappeared at the turn, and came back out of breath a minute later to tell Vikenti that no car was yet in sight. The drummer, a once-famous oboe player of "horsey" and "rumba negra," who had given up playing because his teeth had fallen out, was deftly wielding the drumsticks on the extended skin with the inscription "27th recruitment" and was judiciously whispering with a lisp to the oboe player: "One doesn't play with force, but with one's soul." At the end of the wedding crowd Boudinski saw Lavri the brickmaker, bareheaded, holding a pale child in his arms. The child was dressed in a sailor's blouse with ribbons which had the inscription "Bulgarian Black Sea Fleet." The child had thrown one arm about his father's neck and was leaning against his chest, while with the other arm he was trying to free himself and run about like all healthy children. "He isn't going to let go of the child," Boudinsky smiled.

The telephone rang.

"Yes, I hear," he said, seizing the receiver. "What do you mean, the visit is canceled? He has an appointment to attend a meeting in town? That's a fine kettle of fish. Everybody here is expecting him with a band!"

At this moment Vikenti appeared at the door, listening with a frown. He took the receiver from Boudinsky's hand, and said: "Hello, sir. Oh, come, you can't play us such a dirty trick! Don't tell us cock-and-bull stories now. Who am I? Vikenti, my dear, Vikenti! I'll make him stop all right!"

"What do you think about it all?" Boudinsky asked.

"What I think is this. He'll be traveling by car, won't he, and there's only one road—there's no other road he could take. I'll lead the chain dance across the highway, and if he has the guts, let him run over the people! Listen, we're men, too, after all, although poor and simple. All right, all right, I know what we'll have to do. You'll say you didn't know anything about it, and you can't be held responsible. That's it. I'll forget all about telling you that I was going to stop him. That's the way we'll do it."

Vikenti spread out his hands, adjusting the gun on his back.

"You're a strange fellow, you are! Do you remember, when they arrested you and while you were being marched in chains along the main street in town, the lawyer who had spoken to you all at the meeting drove by in a Phaeton. After that meeting you were almost beaten to death, but he was setting out on his honeymoon trip with his wife."

"Of course, I remember. The horses were scared by my chains, which went clang, clang, clang!"

"Ahem! The orator told you at the meeting: 'You, poor peasants,' and the rich ones looked at each other and shouted hurrah along with the poor. You were the one who shouted the loudest, and that's why you got arrested. My father said to him: 'Why do you cheat these people, don't you see that there are rich men among them?' His reply was: 'Let them not be so simple as to believe me; they pay me and I speak.' When he met you, the lawyer did not shout 'Hurrah' at your chains, did he? And you were breathing with difficulty and barely managing to drag yourself along after the way they beat you."

"I didn't mind the beating. I was thankful for those kind words."

"Look now what a wedding we've put up! Fine!" Vikenti said and set out for the chain dance. In a loud voice he ordered the people where to dance the chain dance, and he instructed the musicians they were to start and to stop playing when he gave them the sign.

Boudinsky stood by Lavri the brickmaker. The child looked at him with a confident, winning smile. The color of the boy's eyes was a mixture of the father's, pitch black, and the mother's, bright blue, and was therefore somewhat gray and somewhat green. Boudinsky realized that father and son were linked by a fine and delicate feeling which he was encountering for the first time in his life. He felt like caressing the soft, golden hair of the child, but on noticing its waxen hands something pricked his heart, because he realized that a sinister and inevitable fatality was creeping toward those thin wrists that showed from the black sleeves, and was emaciating the child's face. The worker lifted the child to enable him to see everything.

"What a strapping young fellow he'll grow up to be, as straight as a candle and as strong as a lion! He'll be able to see everything around, and the girls will be making eyes at him."

The brickmaker became thoughtful, his head drooped, and Boudinsky thought that he cast an appealing glance at him.

"What's your name? Let's hear your voice!" Boudinsky said, caressing the child's hair.

"He's a little bashful; who he takes after, I don't know," Lavri replied. "His name is Kouncho!"

"Kouncho?" Boudinsky exclaimed with a start. "My name is Kouncho, too!"

"They had him twice at the antirheumatic sanatorium in Bankya for a treatment," Lavri explained. "I'm very thankful to them! But now I'm afraid of that cursed mold in the old house. What shall I do if it attacks his heart for a third time? 'Lavri,' the doctor said, 'Kouncho shouldn't stay a minute longer in that ice box.' That's why I've been running around borrowing money, though it may be shameful. I'd run any risk! I've brought him here to let him see the wedding and have a good time like the other children."

"How has the mold eaten away my heart, father? Is the heart an apple?" the child asked, trying to get down from his father's arms.

"Come to my office tomorrow," said Boudinsky, "we'll try to find some way out! Don't worry, the state is taking care of everything now!"

"I'll come, of course," Lavri said hopefully. "This uncle will catch the mold and kill it with a revolver! Kiss his hand, Kouncho. Now see how that car's flying. To-o-ot! Don't move about like that, be patient!"

The sound of a horn cut the air. Frightened by the car's breakneck speed, the peasants withdrew from the highway, and the next moment the car raced past them. Vikenti started shouting at them for running like rabbits and ran about to collect them, because this was the first car. It was only clearing the road, he said; a second one, carrying the minister, was sure to pass. Vikenti took the bride by the hand and began dancing on the road like a rich landowner, without jumping and hopping, but with his fist propped against his hip, with very measured steps. Then he bowed his head, raised it and jumped up, and started swinging his legs and clicking his heels without moving from his place, getting ready to plunge forward and then suddenly straightening up and dancing on swimmingly, flexibly, full of ceremony and dignity.

A black car with a waving flag crept up to the chain-dancer.

The back door opened, and a man with graying hair stepped out. With his palm he smoothed the hair above his ears and respectfully opened the front door of the car, from where a middle-aged gentleman, careful and reserved, white so that even his eyes looked white, and dressed in a gray flannel suit with a slit in back, stepped out on the road. Vikenti nudged Boudinsky to move forward, and Boudinsky, flanked by two aged peasants, came up and stood before the stranger.

One of the two peasants took off his cap and said: "Bonjour! Je vais vous dire ce que je me rappelle tout le temps!" Then he continued speaking timidly in Bulgarian: "The wedding has happily coincided with your passing through our village. We invite you to act as best man at our co-operative wedding!"

The foreign visitor, to whom the translator explained that according to Slav custom the word of the best man is law for all, made a reserved bow and asked to meet the newlyweds. At that moment the bride put a fur cap on his head and flung several presents over his shoulder: an embroidered shirt, socks, a flannelette nightshirt. Then she cast a timid glance at him and, folding her hands on her full breasts, made a low bow. Many hands were extended toward the minister; everybody was offering him his wine flask. The crowd surged forward. Vikenti signaled by pulling his ear, and the band at once struck up a chain dance, so that the wedding guests might line up for it and ease the press around the minister's person.

"Invite him to lead the chain dance!" Vikenti whispered to the bride and, on hearing that she did not know how to do it, got slightly angry: "You are a woman, and you ought to know how to invite a man to a dance."

The bride offered the minister a small wedding banner with an apple stuck on it. When he took it, she thrust her hand into his bent elbow and told him with a charming smile that he was expected to lead the chain dance. The guest watched for a minute or two until he caught the rhythm of the steps, and finally led the chain dance along the highway. Vikenti stepped forward and shot into the air. Several unknown people darted forward to take away his gun, but he managed to slip past them. He smiled and with the gun propped on his shoulder danced alone in front of the dumbfounded minister. Not to be left out of it, the oboe player moved to the minister's side, continuing to play at his ear, and then started squatting and alternately thrusting a leg forward as he played on. The visitor wiped the sweat from his forehead and applauded Vikenti's dancing.

"Well done, comrade chairman!" the translator said gratefully. "This is the first time the minister has been in such high spirits.
He is perspiring from the chain dance!"

Then a man with a camera came up to the minister and whispered something into his ear, which suddenly caused the minister to
smile. He waved a hand to Vikenti, inviting him to have a joint snap-
shot taken of the two of them, while he examined him carefully
from head to toe. The translator asked Vikenti whether it was true
that he could put cocks to sleep, and the minister was exclaiming
with surprise: "Yo! Yo!"

But this time Vikenti failed to understand what this "Yo!"
meant. The translator took down the address of the newlyweds. The
minister stretched his hands forward to bid goodbye to the people,
but before he made for the car an aged woman came up to him and,
rising on tiptoe, put a string of onions around his neck, a symbol of
good health. A young woman appeared behind, her skirt swaying
and a tray in her hands covered with a napkin. On removing the
napkin, the minister saw the initials of his name on the crust of the
bread, surrounded by sunrays. Other girls tied wedding kerchiefs
and beads to the headlights of his car. Vikenti ran up to give the
minister his gun as a present. A skinny woman with a turned-up
apron in which something was moving gave him a shabby cock with
its feet bound. The foreign visitor caught sight of Lavri's child and
beckoned to it with his hand. The child brought his fingers to his
mouth and then stretched them out in the direction of the minister.

"Au revoir!" the old peasant said, taking off his cap and standing at attention. The crowd surged after the car, and the band struck
up a march. The white kerchiefs unfurled, and they waved in the
dry breeze for a long time like doves' wings.

As soon as the cars disappeared, Boudinsky thought that there
was nothing for him to do but go home, because during the night he
had seen where he would be able to find skimmed milk for the sows
and to prepare his notes for the general meeting of the peasants
where he would have to persuade the people that they still had to set
aside something from their scanty means for the new construction
projects, because without them it was impossible to "get hold of the
gold vein of life." But the bride begged him to visit them at their
house. Amid much loud talk and noise Boudinsky found himself at
the home of the newly married couple. The mother of the bridegroom did not take her eyes off him and kept urging him: "Come,
my son, help yourself to everything! It's to you that we owe it all—
the radios, and the blankets, and the people's esteem!"

Tipsy men with caps pulled over their eyes lined up for a chain dance. Opposite them buxom women marched with mincing steps, shaking their arms and humming a melody. Somebody, intentionally tripped up, would fall sprawling on the floor, the chain dance would be broken because everybody would run over to help the man rise and beat the dust off his clothes, while the man would eagerly insist on joining the dance, looking for an opportune moment to give it back to the one who had laughed at him the most. A small woman was complaining that not enough food had been served to the wedding guests at the end tables.

"I tell them that's what they have allotted from the Bonus Fund, but they answer: 'The ones at the main tables have already forgotten that they've eaten; there, they're dancing a chain dance! How long are we supposed to wait?' Unreasonable people I call them!"

The bride was surrounded by a number of women timidly touching her tight dress and asking her about face powders, about her seamstress, about the face creams and lipsticks.

A little befuddled, Vikenti looked at the bride's tight-fitting dress, then went to Boudinsky and dropped into a chair. He was speaking thickly, but Boudinsky understood the trend of his thoughts. It was good, he said, that three hundred people were making merry at the fact that two would be making love tonight.

"Did you see? We did quite well! We met the man in accordance with our ideology! Yet, you were afraid! Lavri, come over here, man! Sit down, don't wait for an invitation."

Somewhere to the side, with only his head in the lamplight, the brickmaker stood dumbfounded, as if in another world. On hearing his friend's voice he livened up, but as soon as his eyes fell on Boudinsky, he at once turned around, as if suddenly lashed from behind, and instantly disappeared in the dark. "He is preoccupied with his child," Boudinsky thought, "tomorrow I'll help him." Vikenti began to talk again; all those construction projects for fodder-cake plants and so on were for the future, but did Boudinsky ever stop to consider that the future isn't far off but today, because it is today that children come to life, it is today that they are growing. You will say: we have given freedom to the coming generations—is that little? Let them guard it, and let us live well today. No, it is we that shall build the plants for "skimmed milk," for the people's health.

Vikenti did not finish his thought, because from somewhere the office boy ran up to Boudinsky with a telegram. Boudinsky read that he was to go to the capital the following morning to attend a qualification course, which meant that he had to leave without any delay.

"They've judged you correctly!" Vikenti said. "There's the beginning of a run of good luck for you!"

At the gate, the bride offered him her white hand: "It was very kind of you, Comrade Boudinsky! Best wishes to your wife! I'll cross my fingers for your success in the course! All the best!"

"Good luck to you. We shall be waiting for you! It seems that my application will have to wait till you come back?" the bride-groom said with a bow.

After a sleepless night and with a feeling of bitterness in his heart on the following day, and after having convinced the county committee that he should be released from the course, two weeks later he arrived in the village and stood in front of the scaffoldings at the fodder mixture plant construction site. While the man mixing the concrete complained that the cement was all gone, the woman cashier of the brickyard stood silently in front of him. She asked him to sign a receipt for four hundred leva, which he, in the common interest, had spent for the wedding. He brought the receipt closer to see his signature and handed it over to the cashier, smiling.

"If Lavri had got this money, as it stands written in the order about his award, he would have fixed up that room and his child would have been running and laughing by now. Even if you give a million now, it's too late. The doctors are drawing water from the child. One does not need much money, Comrade Boudinsky, but one needs it in good time."

"In good time?" Boudinsky asked, his forehead burning. "What has happened?"

"Oh, it's terrible. It's wasted away, the poor thing. The child kept asking if the mold can eat—was his heart an apple that it ate away—Lavri couldn't watch the scene any longer, so he ran away."

"He ran away? Where? Go and tell him to come here!"

"A truck took his baggage away—there are so many con-struction sites in Bulgaria. They took the child away on a stretcher —the face was pinched and wasted. Such a clever, bright child, with such intelligent eyes! Oh, don't let's talk!"

Boudinsky's eyes swung around. The cashier was scrambling over the scattered bricks. Boudinsky sat heavily down on a pile of bricks. Drops of sweat appeared on his forehead. But had they not all celebrated and been happy; had not the higher interests of the state induced him to act as he had done; had they not ordered him to show the "cream" to the foreign visitor; had they not congratulated him on his idea about the wedding? Wasn't this what the dictatorship of joy and love had expected him to do? Had the doctors succeeded in saving the child? Or was it too late? Wasn't it the director and not he who had issued the fictitious order about Lavri's award? And was the child still alive? But how was he to learn when no one knew where Lavri had gone? If he asked, wouldn't they think that he was conscience-stricken? Is that why Lavri ran away from him that night?

The pulleys of the scaffoldings were squeaking—two buckets were exchanging positions. As soon as he spied the curved tiles scattered around, Boudinsky put himself through to the director of the brickyard.

"Excuse me," he said. "But why are you sending us curved tiles? We're building a whole plant here, and you wouldn't build a single room for Lavri! Where is he? I'd promised to help his child! Is the boy alive?"

"A child?" the reply came, rude and bitter over the telephone. "Are you going to get me involved in some mess again? Or is the tongue touching the aching tooth? Listen, I'll look into the matter, but don't you dare rake up further trouble. Keep it quiet!"

Boudinsky dropped the receiver. And instead of that hidden little human being which was always asking him: "How long is it going to be this way?" the image of another child with a captivating smile, a boy with soft, golden hair, remained sealed in his heart.

And he could never forget it.

Translated by ZDRAVKO STANKOV

Georgi Mishev

(1935–   )

Georgi Mishev was born in 1935 in the village of Yoglav, Lovech district, which is on the Ossum River. His father was a cooper. He finished elementary school in his native village, and afterward attended a veterinary school in Lovech. In 1953 he enrolled as a student of journalism at the Sofia University. Since 1958 he has worked as correspondent of the children's paper *Septemvriiche* and has lived in Lovech. Georgi Mishev is a member of the Bulgarian Writers' Union.

He has written the following books. For children: *The Blue-Eyed Fisherman*, short stories (1958); *Two Boys and Olympi*, a novelette (1961); *The Little Boy*, short stories (1964). For adults: *Ossum Stories* (1963); *Adamites*, short stories (1966); two books now in print are *Well-Dressed Men*, short stories, and *Matriarchy*, a novelette.

The Rabbit Census

"The state wants to know everything," the man from the statistics department said. "All it has to do is say the word and we'll count the grass blades in this meadow."

They were walking over the meadow and the soft green grass, which had grown since the mowing, obediently went flat under their feet. Wherever they passed the fall dew came showering down, leaving dark traces behind. The moccasins of the peasants softened up with the damp—they were made of pigskin—while the statistician turned up his trouser legs, revealing his red-and-yellow-checkered nylon socks.

"Game is our national wealth," he went on, because he sensed that the peasants were listening. "A newspaper wrote that it is the living gold of the fatherland. And the state wants to know what this wealth amounts to."

He was speaking in his pleasant, deep voice, with the timbre of a real public speaker, and this could not fail to impress his audience. They had never heard real orators before—all those others who came to talk to them either mumbled or read their written speeches in bored voices. But this tall man with the severe face and an equally severe dark suit of expensive cloth, even though slightly ridiculous with his upturned trouser legs, awed them, and they walked close by him, carrying the rolled-up hemp nets on their shoulders.

The severe man had arrived by bus the night before and had immediately summoned the members of the hunting club and the more prominent villagers. He had talked to them for a long time before setting up the committee; then he went to have supper at the house of the hunting-club president, where he also spent the night.

The next morning, when he appeared before the local council building, the members of the committee were already waiting. They had brought the nets, which were wrapped around poles and resembled huge spindles, while a young man, apparently still a new hunter, was equipped as if for hunting—with a new double-barreled gun on his shoulder and a black-brown dog, which dozed on its leash up against the right seam of his breeches.

"Are we ready?" the statistician asked in a high and determined voice.

"All present," the young hunter said, "with the exception of those absent." Everything about him showed that he was just back from army service and could still not forget the jokes of the barracks.

"Who's absent?" the statistician asked.

"Tsvetan," said the chairman of the club, "the vet."

The statistician asked whether the veterinary station was nearby, they answered that it was one street away, and the committee moved off in that direction.

The vet was standing next to a tethered horse in front of the station. A large wound showed black on the horse's left foreleg; the blood had trickled down and coagulated, like drops of resin oozing through the bark of a tree that has been slit. In his hand the vet held a ribbed bottle containing a blue liquid, with which he soaked a tampon and dabbed the wound. At every touch the horse gave a shudder, the skin of its leg wrinkled, and the chain rattled.

"I say, Tsvetan!" the man from the statistics department said.

"What were we talking about last night, and what are you doing now?"

Tsvetan went on dabbing the wound.

"That won't do, young man," the statistician said. "You're one of us, a state employee; you've got to carry out the orders you're given."

"Can't you see I'm busy?" the state employee said, as he straightened up. "Am I to drop my work and rush off on a wild goose chase?"

"If you don't come it will be reported," the man said, and this seemed to impress the vet. He carried the bottle into the station and returned, having taken off his apron; in his hand there clanged a bunch of keys. He glanced at the horse as he passed it by and started off.

The primary-school teacher walked behind the committee. "It can't be helped, brother," he told the vet in a low voice, taking hold of his arm above the elbow. "I left two classes behind—they'll wreck the school—but I had to come along."

"They'll bring in some sick animal," the vet said. "And when they don't find me they'll go about complaining. It always happens like that, the moment I stay away for a while."

The man from the statistics department had a keen ear and, looking at the two whispering men, said that no matter what anybody said, it was always more difficult to get our working intelligentsia to co-operate.

"I've counted mulberry trees, vines, and cherry trees," said the primary-school teacher. "I've been on about a dozen committees so far."

"The state wants to know everything," the man from the statistics department said, and then elaborated on his idea about the grass in the meadow.

They walked on this grass, which had faded in the summer sun, carrying the spindles with the nets on their shoulders. The man from the statistics department strode in front of the rest, and the handle of his leather briefcase creaked just the least bit.

It was the end of September, the time of the first hoarfrosts. The countryside had begun to turn all colors; frost-bitten by the night colds, the withered cornstalks were yellow, the sumac burned a cyclamen red, and the country roads were lined on both sides with black elder bushes intertwining with wild vines. The poplar trees were the first to take leave of their foliage—the stems were long and their sap was the first to go back down into the earth.

Amid the soft fall triumph of yellow, light green, and auburn, there was a single spot in the field, where the unique, bright sheet-iron color of the cabbage field loomed blue.

The committee came to a halt at the cabbage field balk. "That's the place you're most likely to come across rabbits," the club chairman announced. "If we're lucky we'll catch something."

"Good luck," the young hunter said.

The peasants were thinking of other things. "Look at the cabbage, the way it's grown," they kept saying. "To think we sowed it only two months ago, when we reaped the barley."

"It's the water makes everything grow," they concluded, while unfurling the nets. So as not to stay idle the man from the statistics department opened his briefcase and inspected the documents, the seals, and the pencils—the point of one was broken, and he sharpened it carefully. Everything was in order now; they could begin.

"We should have called in the newsreel men," the primary-school teacher said. "I once saw a film on a rabbit hunt somewhere in the Bourgas district. It was very interesting."

"Damned nonsense," the vet said, thinking of what might be going on at the station. By now the foreman had probably taken away the lame horse, but what if they brought in another animal? Once he had been called to a conference in the town in a similar manner, and while he was away they brought a buffalo cow, which had overfed on beet leaves. It had been grazing all night long and was bloated like a balloon, even a professor would have been no use, but when it died it was him they held responsible and they sued him for one-third of its worth.

"Do I unleash the dog?" the young hunter asked. He had taken off his windbreaker, revealing the big laughing teeth of a new cartridge belt.

"Unleash it," the statistician said, and the dog shook itself the moment it felt the thong releasing its neck, whereupon it started off between the cabbage beds, almost dragging its muzzle on the ground. It ran quickly and they soon saw it at the other end, but it was still not barking.

"It doesn't seem to have scented anything, does it?" the statistician said. He expected the hunter to encourage him, but the latter replied that tracking rabbits wasn't as easy as some people seemed to think. One could get dog tired with roaming the fields all day long and yet not so much as catch sight of a single one. Although still a novice, the hunter was not overoptimistic.

"Ye-es," the statistician said at his words, and fell to musing. For the first time this morning his mood began to falter. While still in the village, everything had seemed quite simple and easy: one stretched out the nets, and the living gold of the fatherland would jump quite by itself into their folds. But that was the way things looked back in the village, where each little street could be barred easily and even a sparrow could be captured. Whereas here, in the middle of the fields, crisscrossed by roads and canals, with shrubs and crops everywhere, things had taken on another complexion.

These doubts flitted through his mind, but he hastened to dispel them, because it was his principle never to doubt anything, and he prided himself on that.

"Do we start?" he asked, when the peasants finished stretching the nets and connected them. "We'll first surround the farther end; we'll make a 'sack.' "

"Wait," one of the peasants spoke up. "The farther end lies low. The net must be on the high end, because a rabbit always runs uphill. It never runs downhill, for its hind legs are long and it would roll over." They stretched the nets across the slope, and two of the peasants were left behind to hold them while the rest fanned out and entered the cabbage field.

"Look under the larger leaves!" the chairman shouted. "Some rabbit might be hiding in there."

They walked between the beds, clapping their hands, yelling and whistling, while the man from the statistics department kept tapping on his briefcase. His briefcase was of doghide—smooth and shining—and it gave out a dull sound, like the barking of a sick old dog. The peasants stooped down, picked up clods of earth, and hurled them forward. The clods scattered into small bits, and the bits spattered down on the cabbage leaves like rain; the peasants resembled sowers, except that they carried no bags.

When they reached the next balk the hunter decided to try out his weapon. He slid a cartridge into the barrel and shot into the sky. The blast did not cause the slightest stir in the vast openness of the plain.

"Don't waste your powder," Tsvetan, the vet, told him. He alone walked with his hands in his pockets, neither yelling nor hurling clods of earth.

"I'm calling the dog back," the hunter said, as if in justification for the shot. "The animal has gone astray, it's nowhere to be heard."

After awhile the dog turned up indeed, whining guiltily, its muzzle covered with dust from seeking rabbit trails.

They moved the nets farther afield, by the corn block. This time the statistician stayed behind under the pretext that two were not enough to attend to the nets. But the others realized that he had stayed behind because of his suit.

"He's dressed himself up like a lord," Tsvetan swore, when they were far enough not to be overheard. "He's come out here to the country in an expensive suit, the son-of-a-bitch."

"Maybe he hasn't got an older one," the teacher said. "You know what those white-collar people get paid?"

"Two hundred!" the vet replied. "No less than two hundred a month."

"You don't say so!" said the peasant, who was walking alongside them. "But what, in new money?"

"Bah! old money!" Tsvetan said derisively. "He isn't one of you."

They strode through the cornfield, whistling and kicking the earth lumps, then they grew tired of whistling and only kept kicking until the end of the field showed and they reached the net. The net was empty and motionless. A slight wind was blowing, but the net did not stir, because the holes were so large that the wind blowed through it so that it remained undisturbed.

"Damned nonsense!" Tsvetan said again. "We'll get nothing done this way. We'd better go home."

"Whatever we do, that's it," one of the peasants spoke up. "We're getting paid for it."

"But that's wasting money," the teacher said.

"I didn't ask them to call me," the peasant said, and his face became malicious. "If they call me they have to pay."

"You'll get paid, of course," the statistician said as he joined them. "I guess two work days is a decent enough wage. Do you fellows earn more otherwise?"

"That's why our co-operative farm can't get on its feet," the teacher said. "The bottom of its till is like a sieve—everything flows out."

"Did you say you were an accountant?" the statistician inquired.

"I'm a primary-school teacher."

"You'll learn a lot more before you come to be a high-school teacher," the vet said.

"You talk like people who doubt our big advances," the statistician said. "And doubts are our enemy number one."

"One must doubt everything," Tsvetan retorted. "That hasn't been thought out by me."

The peasants snickered, enjoying the conversation. They had listened to arguments between the vet and visitors from the town on other occasions as well. He was very good at that sort of thing, because he was not afraid of anybody. He was the only vet in the whole district, and if they fired him there would be nobody else to take care of the animals. On the other hand, the teacher was more restrained, because there was a pedagogical institute in the district town and the villages had plenty of primary-school teachers.

"Come on, let's drop this," the chairman said. "We'd better find some shade and see what our wives have put into the lunchbags."

Half of the day was over, indeed—far to the south the sun had reached its zenith—and the hour for lunchbags had struck. They sat down under a pear tree and laid out the food, drinking brandy from lemonade bottles, roasting cheese, lying sideways, and nobody felt like walking over the fields, shouting and hurling clods of earth into the shrubs.

Even the man from the statistics department, giddy from the brandy, did not talk about his mission any more; the others kept silent as well; and everybody knew that this census was going to peter out, too, the way so many other storms had raged and abated over their village.

Only the memory of a dewy fall morning would remain, of the cyclamen fires of the sumac and the azure color of the cabbage beds, of the shouts over the deserted fields, and of those long sagging hemp nets, in which they had set out to catch rabbits for a census.

Translated by ANDREI DANCHEV

Nikolai Haitov

(1919–   )

Nikolai Haitov was born on September 15, 1919, in the village of Yavorovo, Plovdiv district, and graduated in forest engineering in 1944. From 1946 to 1954 he worked on various forest farms in the Rila Mountain and the Rhodopes. His first short stories were written in 1955, and his first book, *Rivals*, a collection of stories and essays, was published in 1957.

He has since published several collections of prose works: *Sparks from the Fireplace*, short stories; *Letters from the Wilderness*, travel notes; *Rhodope Unveiled*, travel notes; *Hornbeam Leaves*, stories and essays. He has also written two plays: *Round the World* and *Locked Spring*, and several books on historical subjects, including *Haidouks*, *Lords of the Rhodopes*, and *Father Matei*.

Paths

Someone knocked at the door and opened it gently. Into the office came a man on the tall side, with graying dark hair. He took off his cap and bowed clumsily.

"Good morning, I'm Vlasho."

The Highways Department Head put the newspaper aside and carefully looked over his early visitor.

"So you're the one who's laying footpaths near the town for nothing," he said, peering at the man.

"That's me," Vlasho said, attempting a smile.

"Are you from this town?" the Department Head asked, pulling at his white cuffs and leaning back in the chair which groaned under the weight of his sturdy body.

455

"Yes, I am!"

"I haven't seen you before," said the Department Head.

"It is a big town. I rarely go in. I have no business there," Vlasho explained.

"Don't you work in the town?"

"I work at home. I'm a shoemaker. I mean—a cobbler."

"How's that? You're a cobbler and you make pathways at the same time?" The Department Head shrugged his shoulders.

"Why not? Is there a law against it?" Vlasho shifted his cap from one hand to the other and smiled shyly.

"Well, I'm not saying that . . ."

"Because the roadman who brought me said: 'I've got an order from the Highways Department Head,' said he, 'to bring you to him,' so I thought . . ."

"I never told him to 'bring' you, but to ask you to come to me," the boss said emphatically. "I wanted to see you and talk to you. We must pay you what we owe you. I'm in charge of the roads in these parts. So, how much is it?" the Department Head took off his glasses and began cleaning them assiduously.

"I don't lay paths for money."

"But the state won't have it! You've worked and you'll be paid. Yes, you will be paid . . ."

"Well, all right. Let them pay."

"How much do you want?"

"I never signed on. Whatever they pay."

"How long have you worked on the job?"

"I haven't counted the days. I work only afternoons."

"What do you do in the morning?"

"I mend shoes," Vlasho smiled, revealing a row of worn false teeth.

"Do you make a lot mending shoes?" the Department Head asked after a short pause.

"One lev. One-sixty. Sometimes two leva. It depends. The wife helps, too. She washes the laundry at the restaurant. Gets her food there. The boys are grown up. They've all left home. All married."

The Head put down his glasses. "That's interesting! You don't seem to be that old."

"Of course not! I'm only about sixty."

"And you make pathways every day?"

"Every afternoon!" Vlasho corrected him.

"And you've never taken money for this kind of work?"

"Where would I get it from? Who'd give it to me? I love making paths so I just do it. Nobody makes me do it. Only once the pensioners asked me to build a walk in their little park and promised to give me two leva, but they forgot all about it when the walk was finished."

"I see. Now, let's come to the point," the Head said. He put on his glasses and looked Vlasho straight in the eyes. "Can you lay a small walk for us as well?"

"Sure. Why not? But first let me finish the path to Lipnitsa, and then I can do it!"

"Do you want to be paid by the day, or . . . ?"

"Whatever you say."

"How much do you want?"

"Whatever you give me."

"Tools? Have you got tools?"

"Yes."

"And explosives?"

"What do I need them for? I never use explosives."

"Why not?"

"It frightens the wood. The birds fly away."

"Oh, I see, the wood." The Head became thoughtful.

"Yes, the wood."

"How, then, do you manage the boulders that block your way?" The Head started drumming on the desk with his fat fingers, looking with growing interest at the man who had become animated.

"I go round them! Or I use the pickax. When it's possible— just a pickax. If it's not possible I go round them. I know which of the boulders has roots and which hasn't. Can I sit down?" Vlasho asked, nodding in the direction of a chair.

"By all means, please sit down!" the Head said. He took out a pack of cigarettes and offered him one: "Do you smoke?"

"No, I don't. So we were talking about boulders; some of them don't budge an inch. They've got no veins. Men and stones without veins are no good. They won't open up. No pick or spade can help. You go round and round it but it doesn't budge. It doesn't give a hang about the pathway you are making. That's why my shirts don't last more than a month. The sweat rots them, and that's the end of them."

"Don't work so hard, then! I hear you cut all your pathways through steep and inaccessible places." The Head leaned back in his chair, blew a smoke ring toward the ceiling and then sent a second one in pursuit.

"Well, yes, but then, what do you need a pathway over level ground for? I've never touched level ground with my pickax. There is a way of getting across level ground even if there is no path. But up there in the mountains—the mountains are beautiful!—Steep but fine!"

"All right, but who goes along your steep paths?" The Head blew another smoke ring, this time in the direction of Vlasho.

"There are people for every path. Lovers, for one. People go to pick cornel cherries . . . people use them—pensioners more than any one else." Vlasho lifted himself from the chair and pointed toward the mountain peaks covered with lush verdure. "Many get off as early as daybreak. They go to air themselves: some because of their heads; others because of their nerves. All the nerves you want these days! Some are quiet, others laugh . . . still others quarrel with me."

"Why do they quarrel with you?"

"You know, everyone's got his own problems. The other day someone got angry with me because I hadn't made a path to the top of the mountain and his pants were all torn. I said: 'Why do you have to go all the way to the top of the mountain? Can't you wait until there is a path to it?' 'I'm a dying man, my friend,' he said, 'I've got no time to wait. I want to look at things from high up there as long as I can, because when I go into that black earth there's no coming out.' 'Well,' I said, 'I'll make a path for you to the top!' So that's what I'm doing now."

Vlasho waved his cap to drive away the smoke and continued: "Some time ago Harachev, you must know Harachev—he goes out walking because of his blood pressure, for he's fat and paunchy—he got angry with me, too: 'What kind of paths are yours, all so steep? Why all this drudgery? Yours are not paths for people, but for eagles! Better make them level,' he said, 'because if I get at you . . .' Harachev—that's him."

"And what did you do?"

"What could I do? I made a level path for him and that's all. Dr. Shoumkov took to it, too. He goes out every morning. The path is level and leads to a water spring. I put a spout on it, and there is water now. You get thirsty, you have a drink of water, and back you go. Those are my kind of customers—hard to please. Ah, well, there are the hikers, too. Hikers are grateful." Vlasho raised his hand and placed it on his chest. "They are grateful. The other day they gave me a whole shopping bag full of tomatoes. One of them—he was from Sofia—told me: 'I'll get you a medal!' he said. He must have been a Party member, because he said: 'You're one of ours, but you are going too far with your enthusiasm!'"

"Is that so?" the Head stared at him and touched his eye-glasses as if to take them off, but left them on. "So there is that sort, too?"

"Yes, there is. They were a gay lot. They laughed a lot, nearly burst their sides laughing. They hung around for about an hour watching me and laughing. When another one saw my small broom he asked me what it was for. 'I sweep the small stones off the path,' I said. 'Why do you sweep them off?' he asked. 'Some people walk barefoot, and can hurt their feet.' 'Are there any barefooted people?' he asked. 'Have you seen any people going barefoot in Bulgaria today? Do you mean to say that Bulgarians walk barefoot? Look here,' he said, 'give me your identity card!' 'Here it is,' I said to him. 'Vlasho. Look it up if you want. I'll still be Vlasho!' 'Smile!' he said. 'I want to see your teeth, because you look different in the photo.' I smiled—he saw them, my teeth." Vlasho pointed to his teeth. " 'Why have you got false teeth?' he asked. 'Mine fell out,' I said. 'But you've got your own teeth on this,' he said tapping the passport picture. 'They were my own,' I said, 'the identity card is from 1953. A lot of water has flowed under the bridge since then.' He left off talking about my teeth and started about my paths. 'Who pays you for them?' 'Nobody!' 'So, just for nothing?' 'Just for nothing,' I said. 'Come along with me to the Town Council. We must find out what kind of benefactor you are!'"

"Did he take you to the Council?"

"No, he left me alone. But I was told he hid and watched me. Well, I've been talking too long. You probably have work to do," Vlasho said. "May I go now?"

"Go on, go on, I'm quite interested. Tell me more. I'll call the accountant to tell him to prepare work clothes for you," the Head said and reached forward for the telephone.

"The accountant won't agree," Vlasho interjected.

"Why not? Do you know the accountant?"

"Not this one, no, but I had something to do with the accountant of the forestry. The forester stuck me with a job. It was in the summer when it's hard to find workers. 'Come and fix the road for money or for nothing,' he begged. 'The water has washed parts of it away and this may cause trouble.' I started work and next day the forester told me to go away. 'Why?' I asked. 'I'll tell you,' he said, 'but let it be just between you and me: the accountant says he doesn't want to have anything to do with madmen. . . . He says there might be an accident and they would hold him responsible.' I could continue work only if I produced a medical certificate."

"Is that so?" There was surprise in the voice of the Head. "So there are people like that, too?"

"Yes, there are!" Vlasho became agitated. " 'I don't need people like him,' the accountant had said. 'Send him away.' And he sent me away."

"I still can't understand why you work for nothing, when you could work for money."

"Everybody asks me that question. The road builders the other day, they asked me, too: 'Why, you blockhead,' they said, 'do you work for nothing? You undercut our prices. We all do it for money and you—for nothing! Why?' A fierce one among them shouted: 'Let's throw the fool into the river. One fool less won't bring the world to an end!' They would have done it too, if the woodcutters hadn't come just then. 'Your place is in the madhouse, you skunk!' "

"And what did you say?"

"What? Oh, I told them that that's what I like to do—make paths—so I do it. First, there's nothing but shrubs, weeds, stones, and then, all of a sudden, a pathway winding along! At first nothing, just a wilderness, and then you see a man walking . . . listening . . . a couple passing. Life is there! It's not the same when you do it for money. There is no pleasure in it then. The other day a young fellow and a girl passed by. They saw I was lopping off branches to widen the path and they said: 'Carry on, comrade, but don't go too far, because some pensioners like to watch.' They meant they wanted to be alone," Vlasho smiled shyly. "A place where they wouldn't be seen. Everyone has got his own likes and dislikes. And then, the woodcutters need the paths, too. They saved me from the road builders, from the ones who build state roads for wages. Sometimes they give me kindling and dry wood. And when I was down with pneumonia they picked herbs in the woods and made poultices for me until I was up and about. 'We need you,' they said, 'we don't want you dying, not before we say—never . . .' That's what the woodcutters are, jolly people, kind people."

"Wasn't there anyone at home to take care of you?" the Head asked.

"I told you, the wife works in a restaurant. She gets eighty leva and her food there. The sons don't know anything about poultices. They're interested in other things."

"What things?"

"In houses . . . things for the house . . . every one according to his desires and his bent."

"And your bent is making paths, is that so?" the Head laughed, showing two rows of strong white teeth.

"Oh, and what paths there are!" Vlasho slapped his cap on one of his knees.

"Tell me," the Head asked with interest.

"It's not up to me to tell you about such things. You're the one who is Highways and Pathways Department Head."

"Still, what do you mean exactly? What kind of paths—straight, winding—bad, good—short, long?"

"No, you're wrong, Comrade Head of Department. There are no bad paths. If it's a path, then it leads somewhere and that's good. Where a path leads to is quite another matter. One of them, for instance, goes to the Kele—the peak up there. It goes up and up until it reaches the highest point where it tells you: 'Look now! See the whole plain, the town! Where else can you take in the whole plain at one glance?' Another one goes on and on and then suddenly there is a spring before you. 'Stop and have a drink of cold water!' it tells you. 'Take your breath, what's the hurry? It doesn't matter whether you hurry or not, you'll get there just the same!' Last year I made a path just because of a lime tree—it's up there below Ravdin. An old lime tree, old and big, all covered with flowers. You sit under it and the scent makes your head swim. There! No path—no lime tree! That's why I called it the 'lime-tree path.' The name stuck—it's 'the lime-tree path' now. Sometimes when I see someone coming down from the mountain I ask him: 'Where have you been?' And he says: 'I went for a walk along the lime-tree path!' I often ask the question on purpose. I play this trick because it makes me happy to hear the answer! Yes, everyone follows his desires and his bent. I also have a path leading to the peonies."

"What peonies?"

"The red ones. Flowers. The only trouble is that people pick too many of them and pull them up with the roots." Vlasho's face darkened. "I'll block that path up because the way they're picking them there won't be any flowers left."

"That's interesting!" the Head said encouragingly.

"The most interesting are the old paths, the blocked ones. There was a village once—it's disappeared but the path to it is still there. You get on one of those paths, you walk and wonder: 'Where does this one lead to? In what direction does it go?' You walk and walk and you come to an open space: there used to be a field there.

The rains have washed it away, carried the soil away, but the path shows there was a field there once. If you look around carefully you'll even find a threshing floor. Yes, there are such paths. Another one will lead you to a place where there are holes in the ground. That shows that people had dug for ores there. A third will wind and twist until it takes you to some old walls. A stronghold!"

"Well, what do you do with such paths? Do you restore them?"

"It depends, there are paths which . . . there are things dead and gone. For instance, what do you need a dead field for? What good is a fallen stronghold? Ruined . . . if it could be of any use that would be another matter. If there is, say, water or a shady spot, or dry branches to gather, something nice to look at—well, then, yes! You open it up! Next year I'll move to the other side of the river. There are lots of blind paths for opening up there."

"Blind paths?"

"Well, yes!"

"I see, there are all sorts of paths!" the Head agreed and lifted the telephone receiver. "Hullo, Didov, come over here . . . come here and see . . . something."

"Was that the accountant? Will he give me clothes?" Vlasho asked and his face lit up.

"He'll give you clothes and like it!" the Head said and crushed out his cigarette with such energy that the ashtray screeched on the glass top of the desk.

The next minute the door opened and a man came in. His graying hair was carefully combed, and he was wearing armbands.

"Didov," the Head said, "you must give some clothes to this man who makes paths for nothing in our area. That's him," he nodded in the direction of Vlasho. "His name is Vlasho. Are there any fur-lined jackets?"

"Fur-lined?" Vlasho sat up, astonished.

"Well, yes! It's autumn now," the Head said, also sitting up straight. "The damp is unpleasant. You had pneumonia. Is that right, Didov?" the Head asked.

"It is so, Comrade Head of the Department," Didov agreed.

"Fur is no good!" Vlasho remarked. "You sweat. Blue dungarees . . . working clothes would be better."

"That's what I mean: you sweat and then you need something warm. Right, Didov?"

"You are absolutely right," Didov answered.

"Oh, please, don't, Comrade," Vlasho flushed. He put on his

cap and then took it off again. "That's too much trouble . . . for nothing!"

"What do you mean 'for nothing!' Are you nothing? You have become well known throughout the town. How can I leave you without suitable clothes? You might catch a cold some day, you might, so to speak, die. Is that so, Didov?"

"That is so. He is a valuable man. We must take care of him."

"Well, if that's so, thank you, thank you very much!" Vlasho said and bowed clumsily.

"Nothing to thank us for. It's our duty. We'll even try to get you a pension. . . . What would you say to that, comrade accountant?" the Head addressed Didov.

"He deserves it," Didov said and nodded. "People like him deserve it."

"A pension?" Vlasho looked at the accountant and then at the Department Head and started laughing. At first his laughter was sharp and short; then, suddenly, it burst out and filled the room.

"Why are you laughing? Don't you believe me?" the Head asked quietly and folded his arms behind his back.

"Of course I believe you, Comrade. Why shouldn't I believe you. I must believe you," Vlasho continued laughing, "only . . ."

"What? Don't you want a pension?"

"Why not? Who doesn't want a pension, only . . ."

"Ah, so you do want a pension, do you?" the Head asked and then added quietly but clearly: "you rascal!" Then he shouted at the top of his voice: "Rascal! Why not! So he has nothing against getting a pension. The money-hating saint, who works out of generosity! The public benefactor! It's because of him I got into trouble, they wanted me to explain why the paths in the mountains are being built by lunatics. Said the Department was asleep, didn't know anything about it! Out of my sight! And you are not allowed to set foot up there again! Out, I tell you! If we catch you in the mountains I'll fine you! I'll sue you! Out! Out!"

Overwhelmed by this unexpected and terrible turn, Vlasho tried to say something, he opened his mouth, but the torrent of words dazed him, he took a step back, his mouth still open, his eyes growing wider and wider.

Then he turned his back and ran out, the shouts of the Head following after him: " 'Why not?' the rascal. 'Why not?' Did you hear him, Didov? 'Why not?' "

Translated by VLADIMIR FILIPOV

Vassil Tsonev

(1925–)

I was born on April 25, 1925, in Sofia.

After five years of military service I realized I would not make a pilot. I enrolled to study architecture. This time I needed ten years to understand that I would never become an architect, either. Then I rolled up my sleeves and began writing. After twenty years' hard work on my part, every schoolchild will tell you that there is some little difference between me and Shakespeare. Unfortunately, it is too late for me to look for a new career.

God knows that I am committing this crime to earn my living. Once, for the sake of a loaf of bread, Jean Valjean spent I don't know how many years in convict prison. I firmly believe that the readers will be more charitable than Javert and will forgive me.

VASSIL TSONEV

Let's Go Vacationing

I

On Vacation with My Wife and My Daughter

It all started the moment I was instructed by my wife to go and find four big suitcases and three smaller ones right away; then I was ordered to wait out in the yard and stay out of the way. Half an hour went by, and my wife appeared at the window.

"Bring up Auntie's big collapsible trunk!"

I brought the collapsible trunk (there was a popular joke among the relatives, that during the war my uncle had transported the bedroom furniture in it) and was ordered outside again. Presently I heard a moan.

"What is it?" I asked timidly from outside.

"You keep hanging around outside, and you ask!" my wife shouted. "You have always been a parasite."

"Hey," I said. "You're the one who told me to get out, weren't you?"

"Don't you try to pick a row, but come here!"

I went in and saw my wife struggling to cram the night table into the collapsible trunk. The seven suitcases were locked and ready in the middle of the room, bursting at the seams. To this day it is still beyond me what was inside them. Throughout our vacation we opened only the small overnight bag my wife had remembered to take at the last moment; she had stuffed pyjamas, two dresses, two of my shirts, and a frock for the child inside.

We started for the station. My wife was marching ahead, a strained expression on her face, and the child was skipping at her side waving a flag. I was tagging behind with the overnight bag. Seven porters and a cart with the collapsible trunk came last. Every other day over the next three months I had to appear before the Accommodations Board and explain that I had not moved out, but had only been on vacation.

In the train, all of a sudden my wife decided that there was a draft: "There is a draft," she said.

I made a complete investigation of the sleeping compartment, but did not detect even a tiny crack.

"I am telling you there is a draft," my wife declared, when I had resumed my seat.

This time my investigation was even more thorough. No draft at all.

"And I say that there is," she insisted.

"I don't feel any draft."

"You don't, but the child does."

I gave up and went to sleep. A frightful shriek woke me up at about five in the morning: "There is a draft!" It was my wife. I sat up and felt that there indeed was a draft. The porter had opened the door to ask if we needed anything. When the porter left, my wife shut her eyes and went to sleep, happy she had finally convinced me that she was right.

We arrived at the resort town together with a huge cloud, which poured a terrific rain down on us. My wife looked at me with distaste. I shrugged.

"Stop playing dumb."

I answered I was not doing anything of the sort.

"Don't you see it is raining?"

"I do."

"So."

"Nothing."

"Nothing!"

I stared.

"And it is all the same to you?" my wife asked me.

"Why all the same? On the contrary, I am sorry."

"Couldn't we have come in another season?"

"When? It rained in July, too."

"And in June?"

"Ha, June! Who goes on vacation in June? Then how could I possibly know it would be raining in July and August?"

"Stop inventing arguments," my wife shouted. "I am sick of them."

Luckily it stopped raining. Half an hour later the clouds were swept away and the sun shone.

"Phuy, what a heat!" my wife scowled. "An illness in the making."

The room I found, after five hours of wandering all over town, turned out to be the worst possible, according to my wife. There were traces of damp, and most probably mice; the child of the landlady did not look quite right; the walnut tree in the yard was throwing too thick a shade—an illness in the making; the heat coming in through the south window—we had not come to be fried alive. I put on my bathing trunks and started for the beach.

"Where?" my wife looked at me horrified.

"To the beach."

"Alone?"

"Come along."

"But I don't want to."

"What should I do, then?"

"So you are leaving us alone?"

"Come along."

"I told you I don't want to, didn't I?"

I threw up my hands and fled.

Just as I was up to my knees in the water and intended to plunge into the clear waves of the sea, I heard my wife's voice: "Come here!"

I went back.

"The child wants some boiled corn."

"So what," I said. "Buy some for her."

"Who, me? Do I have to?"

"Who else?"

"Where shall I find it?"

"And where shall I find it?"

"How? You are her father, aren't you?"

I felt ill and splashed into the water in two jumps.

Back again I found my wife weeping and pressing the child to herself. "What happened?" I asked, scared.

"Go away!" my wife shrieked. "I don't want to see you again."

"Is something the matter with the child?"

"Yes, with the child indeed. It sneezed."

"Ha, for heaven's sake! Are you crying because of that?"

"Crying, that is it, crying! And he, our fine gentleman goes swimming for hours out into the sea. You might drown and I'd be left alone with the child, just when she might be taken ill. A heartless father. Go away!"

I started.

"Stay here!"

I stopped in my tracks.

"Now you're trying to escape, to desert us here alone."

"But it was you! You said: 'Go away!'"

"Shut up! I have had enough of your rows!"

The next day the child had a mild diarrhea. The good, loving mother had let it eat an entire melon. In order to keep my temper, I took my trunks and started for the beach.

My wife blocked the way with her body. "Where?" she asked me, terrified.

"To the beach."

"Now! When the child is ill?"

"Ha!" I laughed. "It is only a slight diarrhea, give her some cocoa and she'll be all right."

"You're laughing? My God, the child is ill and he laughs!"

"Would it get better if I started crying?"

"Heartless man. I wonder how there can be such coldhearted people! Go away!"

I started.

"Stop!"

I stopped.

"Go away!"

I started.

"Stop!"

Thus I spent my vacation three years ago. I came back shaking, with my nerves all shot, after I had taken a horrible oath in front of the foamy waves of the endless sea never again to set my foot there.

But three years went by, and I started for the seashore again.

II

On Vacation with My Daughter

Before starting I was charged with forgetting I was a father, that such a treasure like my daughter withered and wasted for lack of paternal caresses, because, being preoccupied with work, meetings, and conferences, I had failed to notice what a wonderful creature—what an angel out of this world—had been sleeping under my roof. And I was moved. Tears gushed out of my beautiful eyes. I gave myself up to harsh self-criticism and self-disgust. Taken up by office and social duties I had neglected the family hearth; I had deprived it of my warmth and caresses, and left it to smolder. Then I took two suitcases, and my daughter and I went on vacation.

I traveled by streetcar, train, bus, ship, and horse cart, and finally, exhausted and staggering, I reached the resort. I was badly in need of sleep; I was sleepy as hell. I was so sleepy, I felt like whining and weeping out of exhaustion, but my daughter felt like having a lark. She had thought that we should travel at least ten days and see what happened! Trying to soothe her I promised that next time we would spend our vacation at the North Pole and was asleep a moment later. Suddenly I felt something pinch my nose. I sprang up and switched on the lamp. I expected to see a centipede, a scorpion, or at least a beetle, but there was only my daughter, who had climbed out of her bed and was standing at my head.

"Daddy, do crocodiles have seven feet?" she asked.

"Rubbish!" I waved the suggestion away. "Only four. And now go to sleep!"

"Why did Pesho say they had seven, then?"

"Who is this Pesho?"

"In our nursery."

"And you found him here?"

"Oh, no, Daddy, he told me that before."

"When was that?"

"In the winter."

When I had got over that answer I said in a conciliatory tone: "Fine. Everything is clear now, isn't it? Go straight to bed and be kind enough not to wake me up to ask whether elephants have a dozen pair of trunks."

"And how many pairs do they have?"

"Not even a pair. One trunk only, one! This is an 'odd number' not a 'pair.' "

"What does 'odd number' mean?"

" 'Odd number' means . . ." I started by force of habit, but suddenly realized that if I took up an explanation of the meaning of "odd number," there would be another question cropping up next, then a third, and I was so sleepy that my eyelids were glued together. So I cut my explanation short and yelled:

" 'Odd number' means that if you ask me anything else you are going to get such a spanking that it will look like an 'even number' to you. Get into bed this instant!"

My daughter opened her eyes wide, jumped into bed, and pulled the blanket over her head. I switched off the lamp and also shut my eyes, but remorse started gnawing at me.

"See what a boor I am!" I thought. "It is only a day I've been alone with my daughter and I'm already threatening her with spankings. God only knows how long the thought of crocodiles with seven legs has been tormenting the child, and instead of explaining it properly as I should have done, I started with 'odd' and 'even' numbers. Most probably the poor child won't be able to sleep all night thinking what 'odd' and 'even' numbers mean." My sense of guilt was so bad that I sat up and said:

"Since you want to know so much about what 'odd number' means, it is the opposite of 'even number,' that is, with an uneven number of things we have the concept of 'odd number' and the other way about would be correspondingly 'even number.' Is it clear now?"

My daughter was silent. She was sleeping as quietly and gently as an angel. I shook my head and closed my eyes, but sleep would not come. Everybody has had such an experience: you are dying for sleep, but none comes. I kept pressing my eyelids together, jerking, throwing myself about, turning over, but all in vain. Only when day was dawning I felt my lids go heavy and I dozed off. Suddenly someone shook me.

"What is it?" I sprang up. "Is it time to get up for work?"

"Daddy, what does 'correspondingly' mean?" my daughter asked.

I was ready to bellow out, but checked myself in time, remembering not to repeat last night's mistake and said easily: "It is all very simple. 'Correspondingly' means the same as 'respectively.' So, for instance, if I say that the cat has a left foot, it would mean that it has a right foot correspondingly, because, you see, whatever is 'corresponding,' or let's say 'respective' . . ."

By that time I was so mixed up that I stopped. And much as I tried to extract something out of my sleepy head, I could not come up with anything at all.

Then my daughter rescued me with another question: "And are the feet of the rabbit corresponding?"

I opened my mouth to explain, but then decided it would be best to give in. "Of course," I said. "Of course, you are dead right, but please be so kind and keep quiet, because I am awfully tired and sleepy."

"Why don't you sleep, then?" my daughter asked.

For heaven's sake! I shut my eyes and dozed off. And just as the gray clouds were whirling around me, the pillow was snatched from under my head and thrown on the floor. I sprang up and roared: "Are you making fun of your own father?"

"No," my daughter answered.

"Then why did you pull my pillow away?"

"I am looking for my doll."

"And how would the doll find its way under my pillow?"

"Where is it then?"

Snarling and gnashing my teeth I sprang up, poked about here and there, and found the doll under my daughter's pillow.

"Just see where it was!" she exclaimed. "And see where I looked for it!"

"Silence now!" I whined. "I have to sleep."

"Shall I sing you to sleep?" my daughter asked.

"No," I shouted. "And shut up, or I'll knock your head off!"

I buried my head in the pillow and pressed my eyelids together, sobbing. The same moment there was a terrific crash, and I heard my daughter's voice: "Oof, that doll!"

"What do you want?" I screamed.

"Why, the doll wanted to look out of the window, and the chair went over."

"Enough!" I sobbed. "I want to sleep!"

"But, Daddy, I am not sleepy at all and the children are playing outside."

"Put your clothes on and get out!"

I waited deliberately until she had dressed herself and gone out. At last I relaxed and closed my eyes. A bang. The door crashed against the wall and my daughter marched solemnly into the room.

"Outside!" I shrieked. "Outside!"

"But Daddy!" my daughter whined. "One of the girls said I hadn't any cream-colored dress."

"Tell her you have and scram!"

"But she does not believe me."

"So what, perhaps I should give you a note saying that you own a cream-colored dress?"

"Oh, but no, Daddy, I want to get the dress itself."

"Where is it?"

"In the suitcase."

And she had to step on my head to get something out of the suitcase.

I opened the suitcase, snatched up the cream-colored dress, and shot it out the door. "If you come in here once more I'll beat you to a pulp!" I screamed. "I'll eat you up! Leave me alone so I can sleep!"

My daughter went out and I shut my eyes once again. I was shaking all over, clenching my teeth, sobbing, gnawing at the pillow. Then I gradually relaxed and dozed off. Limes in bloom were swaying gently above me, the sky dissolved, and nightingales were singing the songs of May. Just at that moment I sensed someone breathing in my face. I opened my eyes and recoiled—there were a dozen kids bending over me, studying me with curiosity.

My daughter threw out her chest, pointed her finger at me and declared: "This is my father!"

Translated by TSVETAN PETKOV

Vassil Popov

(1930–   )

Vassil Popov was born on July 29, 1930 in Mindya, Veliko Turnovo district. He is the author of the following books: *Short Stories* (1959); *Stale Bread*, short stories for children (1960); *The Small Mine*, a novelette (1962); *Man and the Earth*, short stories (1962); *The Roots*, short stories (1967). And the plays: *A Legend*, a tragedy in four acts (1966) and *He Is Alive Still*, a film script on the life of Hristo Botev, after which a wide-screen feature movie in color is being filmed.

Translations of Vassil Popov's short stories have appeared abroad in anthologies and literary publications in English, Russian, German, Italian, Spanish, Swedish, Czech, Polish, Hungarian, and other languages.

This Beautiful Mankind

When they turned off the lamp the mirror fell asleep too. The streetlight tried to find it, but the little curtains were in the way. Lucia lay in the bed—on Saturday nights they used to take her home and leave her in the living room. She was trembling with emotion. "No, no, it won't find it," she repeated to herself. "Sleep, mirror, sleep, SLEEP!"

Whenever she came home the mirror was the first to meet her, enormous and open. It swallowed her up like an eye and then it returned her—UGLY, skinny, with thin legs and arms, with one eye lost at birth and a taut face, white and frightened. That was the way, too, that the large, wide eyes of the woman supervisor received her at the retarded children's home. The eyes swallowed Lucia up like a mirror and then returned her UGLY. Lucia made this trip every week, between the mirror and the supervisor's two eyes. Now the mirror was asleep, and the supervisor was THERE.

Now Lucia was alone in the large hall. Her single eye was open and refracted the weary lights of the day along the winged silver paths to sleep, and watched her. Oh, how this eye of hers watched her! If she closed it, it would look at her still more intently, and would speak up at last.

"You're ugly," the eye would say.

"I'm not," Lucia would say.

"You're an ugly little monster," the eye would insist. "Just remember the way the supervisor put it once—'oh, my ugly little monster!' "

"I remember. I know I'm a monster. I know, I know, I KNOW. Shut up now, eye. Shut up, shut up, SHUT UP! I want to sleep."

"You sleep," the eye would say, "and I'll watch."

That is what the eye would tell her if she closed it. "No, I'm not going to close it, let it watch NOW," Lucia whispered to herself and smiled. Her eye smiled at her, too, as it closed halfway and stretched out slightly. Her body also smiled at her and stretched slightly in the cool, crisp sheets. Lucia knew that she was BEAUTIFUL now, that she was always beautiful when she smiled, but the others did not know that and she was not going to tell them for anything in the world. Neither her father and mother, nor her two brothers, nor the supervisor, knew. They could not understand—they were always beautiful, especially the supervisor, that red-haired woman with close-set eyes and a somewhat staring look. Her lips were full-blooded, and the open nostrils of her thin nose quivered like the wings of a little bird which was about to take off.

That was THERE. The supervisor received Lucia's parents and brothers, and the skin of her face and arms grew still redder against her white apron, and her red hair shone above the face. She smiled, but was not so beautiful. Lucia stood among her beautiful parents and brothers and the beautiful supervisor, blinking her single eye and swallowing them with it, but they were not aware of that and stayed in their places. They did not know that she was swallowing their beauty and not them. They did not know that she was also swallowing their shame, and the pity, and the pain, and the misery, and all the feelings and thoughts, which flitted among them, INVISIBLE at that moment. They didn't know anything.

While her parents spoke with the supervisor, Lucia was with her two brothers, who were chewing gum. Both sported ties and were awfully conceited. They chewed and were conceited. Their eyes were conceited, too; they were so conceited that they didn't see anything.

"You still drawing?" the elder brother asked.

"Still," Lucia replied.

"You're not drawing," the younger one said. "This is no drawing."

"Then WHAT is it?" Lucia asked.

"It's scrawling," the younger brother said. "Father showed your pictures to an artist and he said they were SCRAWLS."

"That's what he said," the elder brother confirmed. And both kept chewing with their beautiful mouths.

"They're not SCRAWLS," Lucia said stubbornly. "He doesn't know. And you don't know either, you don't know, YOU DON'T KNOW."

"You think you're the only one who knows," the elder boy said. "At school we draw, too. The teacher puts an apple on the stand, he explains everything, and makes us measure the distance and squint with ONE EYE. Then he inspects the drawings—on all the sheets the apple is the same, looks alive, like a real apple."

"This is no apple," Lucia said.

"Then what is it?"

"Nothing, nothing, NOTHING."

Her two brothers exchanged glances. "DO THEY SEE EACH OTHER?" Lucia asked herself. Then they laughed with their beautiful eyes and went on chewing.

"Let's not quarrel," the elder one said and hugged her. The WAY he hugged her. "You're too little, you don't understand yet."

"I'm not too little," Lucia said, tight-lipped. "I'm not, I'm not, I'M NOT."

Then her parents would come up and kiss her before leaving. The WAY they kissed her. They would go away, the door and the street swallowing them up like a mirror, but not returning them. They would grow small, and the beautiful car would grow small, too, and disappear down the street, in the town, as if it had never drawn up before the retarded children's home, as if her parents and her brothers had never come. Then Lucia would go back to her room and start drawing them, so as to restore them to their places. When she ran out of paper she continued drawing them on the sand in the alley, then on the water in the small pool, and finally in the air. NOBODY could see how they were hanging in the air, with their eyes wide open, how her brothers chewed gum and smiled, how they hung in the air and smiled.

Now they were sleeping—all of them—her parents and her brothers. The WAY they were sleeping. Lucia had seen how they slept, how their faces relaxed and became more beautiful when their eyes were closed. The walls, the air in the rooms, and the eye of the television set were sleeping, too. The utensils in the kitchen, the icebox, the electric plates on the range, and the faucet were also sleeping; everything was relaxed and hushed, everything was breathing slowly and calmly at regular intervals, and Lucia, with her little fist under her chin, listened to the sleep of beauty.

"Come on," the eye spoke up. "The window's expecting us."

"All right," Lucia said.

Late at night on Saturday the window would wait for everybody to fall asleep and then call them. It was tall, reaching from floor to ceiling, and when it wanted to call them it swayed a light transparent curtain. It was stirring the curtain now, too.

Lucia threw back the blanket and crept barefoot to the window. The cool night wind crept under her nightdress and caressed her. The curtain caressed her, too; it touched her leg—it simply rose a little and touched her leg.

"Look," the eye told Lucia, "the town is asleep."

"I see," Lucia answered. "How beautiful it is."

Outside, the big houses, the big trees, and the big streets were asleep. The sky had descended low over the roofs, the foliage, and the pavement, together with the night dew. One could not make out exactly what there was outside, sky or air. The night air was dark, as dark as the sky.

Lucia stretched out her hand and drew the night. The houses entered into one another, flat and light; transparent trees clung to them like silent shadows; the water drops and traces of laughter and sighs sprang to life from under the slim white finger, stretched forth in the darkness; then people appeared—BEAUTIFUL people—walking or standing on the corners, sitting on the benches in the garden or reading papers; some seemed to have stopped suddenly. The street filled with people.

Lucia smiled contentedly. She sketched the big night houses, cutting them into apartments and rooms, and then people and beds took shape in the drawn and in the real night rooms. They emerged quite easily from under her pointed white finger, stretching out in the beds, lying still on the pillows, hugging each other or lying alone, with their eyes closed, sleeping in the BEAUTY. Now the beauty was simultaneously night and sky and air. It was in the houses, in the people, in the silent relaxation of things. It flowed from Lucia's little finger, and the little girl felt the lines flowing out of her, turning about, revolving on their axes, fencing in the very last nooks of the night, and peopling it with objects and persons.

When she felt tired and lowered her hand, Lucia asked her eye: "Are you sleeping?"

"No," the eye replied.

"Sleep, sleep, SLEEP," Lucia said. "Look, you sleep now, and I'll sleep a little later, do you hear?"

"I hear," the eye said. "But why don't you draw a picture of me, too?"

"I don't want to," Lucia retorted. "I want to draw the other one."

"Which other one?"

"THAT ONE."

"It was lost," the eye said.

"It wasn't," Lucia said. "It's here, here, HERE."

The eye sighed. She heard how it sighed and how the sigh floated out the window like a falling leaf, swaying and rising, in order to dart down with a fresh spring, to stop as if hesitating, and then again down, down, DOWN.

Lucia laughed. The eye did not know that the sigh was going to turn up shortly. Lucia raised her hand, and the finger picked up the sigh from the wet pavement; then it picked up another one, too, and all over the picture of the live night a crowd of dancing and swaying sighs appeared, which neither fell nor rose.

Her mother's warm hand touched Lucia's shoulder, and the girl gave a start. "What are you doing?" her mother asked with concern. Her beautiful white face, covered with night cream, was worried, the tears ready to gush forth from her big moist eyes. Lucia knew that.

"Nothing," she replied. Her smile vanished, along with the sighs and the two sleeping nights—the deserted one and the drawn one.

"Why aren't you sleeping?" her mother asked and hugged her thin shoulders, the WAY she hugged her. Her warm breast touched the little girl's scraggy neck, and she pressed her cold cheek against it. The breast was throbbing like a heart. Lucia closed her eye.

"Why aren't you sleeping?" her mother repeated, and a tear dropped onto Lucia's cheek. It smelled of night cream.

"I don't want to," Lucia said and opened her eye, pulling back. She started for her bed. Her mother's breast followed her, leading along the hand and the nightdress, and her mother's crying eyes, too. Lucia slipped into bed. Her mother sat beside her, the WAY she sat.

"My sweet little girl," her mother whispered. "I had to take sleeping pills again, and I can't sleep."

"Go away," Lucia said from under the blanket.

"Why?"

"Go away, go away, GO AWAY!" Lucia repeated. "I'll sleep."

"You're not deceiving me?" the mother groaned.

"No."

"But why did you get up? Tell me!" . . . (Why, why, WHY?)

"Were you drawing again?"

"Yes, AGAIN."

"What did you draw, do tell me please, what did you draw?"

"Everything," Lucia said and shut her eye yet tighter, so as not to see her. "When people sleep they're beautiful, I want to sleep, mummy!"

"You're beautiful," her mother groaned. The WAY she groaned! "You're so beautiful and tender."

"I'm sleeping, I'm sleeping, I'M SLEEPING," Lucia said, without opening her eye.

"All right," her mother said with a sigh and got up. Lucia heard her footsteps going toward her room, the nightdress and the breast moving off in the same direction, together with the fragrance of the perfume and the night cream; she felt them pulling her after them, OPEN, as if they wanted to swallow and return her again. Lucia threw back the blanket uneasily and opened her eye, which had begun to smart. Her mother had disappeared.

Instead of her, the face of the supervisor loomed red. "Don't bend your head that way," the supervisor said, and the little bird on her nose fluttered its wings. The WAY it fluttered them.

"All right," Lucia said.

"All right, but you've almost crept into that sheet of paper!"

"It's the sheet that's creeping into me," Lucia said. The sheet gave her a friendly nod.

"What?" the supervisor arched her red eyebrows.

Lucia did not answer. She leaned her cheek against the white sheet. Her eye followed the pencil from so close a distance that she could see the little pieces of chalk dust on the black graphite. The pointed end scratched lightly and cut the white sheet with a deep line, which flowed out of Lucia's hand. The supervisor bent down and noticed the female figure on the sheet, the crossed legs, covered with thin unruly hairs, the heels of the shoes, the two enormous eyes. The line had got hold of the fold on the belly, the curve of the back, and went on cutting into the sheet seeking out the buttons of the dress and the shape of the breasts, all in one stroke.

"My goodness, the monsters you draw!" the supervisor said. "What's that, Lucia?"

"A woman," Lucia said. "A woman, a woman, A WOMAN."

"Who's this woman?"

"It's you," Lucia said. "You, you, YOU."

The red hand snatched the sheet up together with a shout, and the bits fell to the floor. The fragments of the woman, the WAY they fell. Lucia did not raise her head from the table, and the pencil did not lift its end, poised on the board, on which there were numerous thin crevices and dents. The wood had remembered the line without retaining it on its surface; the woman was STILL there.

"You're rude," the supervisor said.

"I'm not rude," Lucia replied.

"How can you make fun of me?" The supervisor's voice rose, and the little bird on her nose spread its wings a little more. "This is not me, not me, do you hear?"

"It's you," Lucia said placidly and raised her head. The pencil lay down on the board to rest. "It's you."

"You're abnormal," the supervisor said. "You draw all kinds of monsters."

"They aren't monsters," Lucia said. "They're people. People are not monsters."

"If they're not, then why have you drawn me in such a way?"

"Because that's how I see you," Lucia said.

"That's enough," the supervisor said.

She was not given any more sheets after that. Outside, the other school children sang halfheartedly in various pitches, while Lucia stayed in her room and kept drawing on the blanket of her bed. The blanket had a pattern of different trees and leaves on it, but they seemed to be dead and did not resent Lucia's drawing. From time to time she stopped to kiss her fingertip. It kissed her, too.

"I can also draw," the finger would say. "You need not sharpen me—the others don't see what comes out of me anyway."

"They'll see," Lucia told him. "They CAN'T HELP SEEING."

"Then let them see," the pencil acquiesced. "And what are we going to draw now?"

"Mankind," Lucia said. The supervisor had spoken to them about mankind and peace. The WAY she had spoken to them. "We're going to draw it. Do you want to?"

"I do," the finger said.

"How are we going to draw it," the eye spoke up, "since we've never seen it?"

"You shut up," Lucia snapped at the eye. "Shut up, shut up, SHUT UP! The others will see it."

"Shut up," the finger threw in, too. "If you can't see, then you can at least keep quiet and not interfere with our drawing of mankind."

"All right," the eye said in a conciliatory manner. "I'll keep quiet if you want me to, but tell me, how are we going to draw it?"

"The whole of it," Lucia said. "We shall draw the whole of progressive mankind."

"I'm ready," the finger said and rose.

And they began. They drew town after town, nation after nation, country after country. They drew enormous surfaces of earth and water, strewn over with people and animals, with houses and machines. They drew the birds of peace, and without tiring, the finger went on to draw its uninterrupted line on the bedsheets and blankets, in the air, on the water in the pools, on the bottom of the empty plates, on the leaves of the plants and on the tree trunks, on the warm macadam and on the cement playground. It had a checkered pattern drawn on it by the children, who played hopscotch there. When the children hopped with the small bit of tile, trying to hop into the squares and not on the lines, they did not know that they were stepping and hopping on plants and people, on rivers and mountains, on towns and oceans, on the birds of peace. And the cars which drove in the streets, and the people who walked on the pavements did not know that they were treading on themselves—on mankind. And the planes which flew in the air, and the birds which flew before or after them did not know that they were flying through themselves—high above mankind and within it.

"Sleep now," the eye told Lucia and her little white finger, which had been drawing for such a long time.

"All right," Lucia said.

The finger rose a little, but the eye said: "You sleep, too, now, take a rest. I'll draw now . . ."

"All right," the finger said, "you draw better at night."

"Come on, keep quiet," Lucia spoke up. "Let's sleep, let's sleep, LET'S SLEEP!"

She curled up and hugged her knees with her arms, and the finger curled up in her hand, too. The eye smiled and closed. Lucia knew that when her eye closed she would be SLEEPING, she would turn into SOMEBODY ELSE. And now, when she was falling asleep on this Saturday night, she experienced anew the terrible pain of the transition, when she became different, BEAUTIFUL in the realm of sleep, when her eye went on drawing mankind, town after town, nation after nation, country after country. The pain sprinkled Lucia's forehead with drops of pearly sweat, which resounded in the silence of the night.

Translated by ANDREI DANCHEV

Date Due

PRINTED IN U.S.A.   CAT. NO. 23 231

68725

891.8
K58i

Kirilov, Nikolai
Introduction to modern Bulgarian
literature...

LIBRARY
OHIO DOMINICAN COLLEGE
COLUMBUS, OHIO 43219